The King's Garden

The KING'S GARDEN

FANNY DESCHAMPS

HARMONY BOOKS
NEW YORK

Cautionary Notice: The herbs, spices, and remedies listed throughout the book are for historical interest only and *not* for contempo-
rary use in the form given.

Copyright © 1982 by Editions Albin Michel
English language translation copyright © 1985 by Crown Publishers,
Inc. *Book One • Jeanne,* translated by Frances Frenaye. *Book
Two • Love's Progress,* translated by Patricia Wolf.

Published by Harmony Books, a division of Crown Publishers,
Inc., One Park Avenue, New York, New York 10016, and
simultaneously in Canada by General Publishing Company Limited

Originally published in France in 1982 by Albin Michel, S.A.
under the title LA BOUGAINVILLE.

HARMONY and colophon are trademarks of Crown Publishers,
Inc.

Manufactured in the United States of America

Library of Congress Cataloging in Publication Data

Deschamps, Fanny.
  The king's garden.

  Translation of: La bougainvillée.
  I. Title.
PQ2664.E756B6813   1984   843'.914   84-3804
ISBN 0-517-55085-7

10 9 8 7 6 5 4 3 2 1
Designed by Claudia Carlson
First American Edition

for Albert,
without whom this novel
could not have taken place

TABLE OF CONTENTS

The King's Garden

BOOK ONE
Jeanne

PART

I

A Château
in Dombes

CHAPTER 1

he fire had died down. It was sinking slowly into the ashes, and Jeanne, wrapped in its fragrant warmth, felt as if she were in the hollow of a cradle. She was at peace, save for her fervent wish to be in the arms of Philibert.

Philibert. . . . She closed her eyes to savor his image more completely. *Already two years—seven hundred and thirty days—without him. Impossible, but all too real.*

She was sitting on the rug, with her arms around her legs and one cheek leaning on her knees. She was only fifteen, but life seemed to bear down on her with the weight of a thousand years. With a sigh she picked up the book she had let fall beside her. Nothing captures so well the longing for days gone by as a rondeau of Charles d'Orléans:

> *Ye who would heal your pains of love,*
> *Pluck memory's flower, so strong to move,*
> *Take juices from a columbine.*
> *Withal that you must weep and pine*
> *Your sorrow is the final proof.*

The double tap of Mme. de Bouhey's cane pounding the floor of her room roused Jeanne from indulgence in her melancholy. She leaped to her feet. *That's it!* she thought angrily to herself. *She's sick. I could have wagered on it.*

That morning, April 1, 1762, in order to celebrate the fifteenth birthday of her ward, Jeanne, Baroness Marie-Françoise de Bouhey had selected an assortment of delicacies that filled up seven small pots, four big round pans, three tureens, and three chicken spits. At her regular noontime Sunday meal, she had sampled six dishes, indulging herself with three more in the evening not counting the desserts! As soon as she had gone upstairs and lain down, the canopy of the bed seemed to dance before her, and sweat broke out on her forehead.

"My God, I'm dying! This time I'm going to die," she groaned between two hiccoughs. "Jeannette, deeeaaar, save me from dying!"

Her nightcap had slipped to one side and she lay on her back, across the pillows, with her hands limp, her nostrils pinched, and a dying expression on her face. Pompon, the chambermaid, dipped a cloth in a bowl of water and vinegar and bathed her forehead. Jeanne had run up the stairs and behind her had already gathered a half-dozen figures in white undershirts, who had come, candles in hand, to find the source of the commotion. Delphine de Bouhey, the baroness's daughter-in-law, had gone to look for her medicine chest.

"Shouldn't someone go to Neuville and fetch Father Jérôme?" Pompon asked the company.

"It's done," said Mlle. Sergent, the housekeeper. "Thomas has just gone off to Neuville."

No one really thought that the baroness needed the last rites, but Father Jérôme, chaplain of the Abbey of Neuville, was something of a healer. When the sick woman heard his name she was seized by panic and called for her lawyer. She suddenly had a wish to fiddle with her will. They had to wake up Longchamp, her son and daughter-in-law's manservant, to go with a light cart to Châtillon, since Thomas had taken the carriage to fetch the priest.

For the last fortnight a persistent rain had fallen on the Dombes region, turning sky and earth into a kingdom of water. When Maître Etienne-Marie Aubriot, the notary and lawyer, arrived at the Château of Charmont he shook himself and announced his presence so noisily that for a long minute Jeanne did not see Philibert behind his father, dripping all over as he waved his hat and smiled at her.

"My son happened to be at my house," old Aubriot explained. "And I thought you could use a doctor as well as a lawyer, so I brought him along. Now, Mademoiselle Jeanne, what's going on?"

Philibert stepped forward. "With your permission, Father, the doctor will go first. . . ."

Jeanne, petrified, saw the object of all her daydreams approaching. Speech deserted her, and everything around her seemed to stand still. But she saw the lips of her dream lover move, and she held out her hand, which was tickled by Philibert's ruffled cuff, and she knew he was very real. Her blood rose to her cheeks and her hearing was restored.

"Shall we go upstairs?" asked Philibert.

How did she manage to lead him to Mme. de Bouhey's room? Did they speak to each other on the way? She was to remember only the carnal joy that flooded her whole being as she walked at his side, her body floating on thin air.

* * * *

Ever since he had opened up his office at Belley, in an area known for gluttony, Dr. Philibert Aubriot had prescribed a simple cure for the effects of overeating: a good dose of emetic ipecac, followed by a period of fasting, broken only by numerous cups of wild chicory tea. To these things he added a lecture on the nouvelle cuisine.

In Paris, where there were enough literary gourmets to consume ideas rather than roast capons, this new philosophical cuisine, based on broths and juices, on vegetables and milk, was the rage among the aristocracy. Alas, Dr. Aubriot's provincial patients continued to stuff themselves with fats, and to be stricken with indigestion, gout, kidney stones, and apoplexy. The doctor, who was a brilliant talker, went on preaching the delicate delights of buttermilk and *taraxacum dens leonis*, more commonly known as dandelions, which the gluttons, behind his back, made into a salad, seasoned with bits of bacon. To Mme. de Bouhey, as to the others, he extolled greens and whey. But he had few illusions; a stomach ache is quickly forgotten, while a good meal sticks to the ribs and lingers in the memory.

"In every dining room," the doctor would say caustically, "I'd like to see painted on a banner a pile of golden-brown roast chickens and, under it, the motto '*Vulnerant omnes, ultima necat*'—'All wound, the last one kills.' "

Now, at the bedside, he carefully observed the sick woman's face, whose grimaces reflected the last spasms of her stomach. The emetic had done its bit, and splotches of pink had returned to her cheeks. She smiled faintly at the doctor and motioned at him to stay awhile longer.

Dr. Aubriot had little faith in medicines, but he believed in the role of the doctor who can benefit his patients by his presence. So he held her hand in a friendly fashion, which did much to comfort her.

* * * *

In the newly painted ground-floor drawing room, with its lemon-yellow woodwork set off by lilac wallpaper, Jeanne had ordered refreshments: chicken, cream cheese, and a carafe of Mâcon. Philibert was not given to staying up late, but he had to wait for his father.

Mme. de Bouhey had somewhat recovered, but she would most certainly prolong the notary's visit. Making and unmaking her will was a pastime of which she never tired. It allowed her to list her worldly goods.

Except for the coachman, Thomas, and Pompon, whom Jeanne heard moving to and fro in the old lady's room, everyone had gone to bed. Father Jérôme had felt reassured and gone back to his abbey, and the elder Aubriot was patiently listening to what his client had to say. Jeanne would have Philibert all to herself. *Very soon, any minute now* . . . she would hear the click of his heels on the stone stairs. . . . Her inner trembling grew more acute. For the tenth time in a quarter of an hour she got up to look at herself in the mirror over the fireplace.

She had bathed her face, straightened her hair, and dabbed perfume behind her ears. Jeanne was becoming a lovely young woman, yet she was still like the wild little girl with whom Philibert had walked in the Dombes countryside. She wanted passionately to believe that Philibert had shaped her, quite egotistically, for himself. That from him, and for him, she had drawn her liveliness . . . her agile, tireless body, her boundless curiosity about the life of trees, plants, and flowers, her ecstasy before the beauties of nature and the patience with which she sorted medical herbs and laid them out to dry. Philibert Aubriot, the passionate botanist, had infected her with "green fever." He had confessed to her that sharing his passion with others was his favorite pastime. He was one of the king's botanists, had a medical degree from the University of Montpellier, and an excellent reputation as a doctor.

Jeanne was ten years old when she caught the green fever. Her mother had died giving birth to her, and her father, a slater from Saint-Jéan-de-Losne, had been killed when he slipped and fell off a roof at Charmont when she was eight. Madame de Bouhey, hearing that Jeanne was left an orphan, took her in. She quickly became attached to the little girl and had her educated in the château, with her two grandsons, Charles, the older by one year, and Jean-François, the younger. Jeanne had a sharp mind with a natural curiosity, and she seemed to get more out of the Abbé Rollin's lessons than did the boys.

The first time she saw Dr. Philibert Aubriot was at the wedding of the late Baron de Bouhey's half-sister—a festive occasion at Charmont. It was a hot June day, and the guests were strolling about the garden in search of fresh air. Seated on a terrace, among a bevy of female admirers, the doctor was describing various sources of perfume. He might just as well have been talking about the bone structure of Mediterranean fish.

Her recollection was like a scene from a fairy tale. Clad in bright silk hoopskirts, the ladies clustered about the speaker in his dark garb, who seemed to be at the center of a crown of colored petals, iridescent in the light of the setting sun. Little Jeanne, quite dazzled, advanced to the edge of the giant flower. It was there that her heart was captured. She was bewitched by the passionate, resonant voice of the speaker and by his jet-black eyes, which outshone the splendor around him.

It is quite possible to fall in love at the age of ten. And so it was that Jeanne fell in love with Philibert Aubriot. Totally in love, every inch of her, from head to foot. She was overwhelmed by a burning desire to draw the unknown beloved's gleaming eyes to her small person. Taking advantage of a moment when he was talking to Father Jérôme, she said in her most appealing voice:

"Sir, I heard you talk about the perfumes distilled from flowers. How well you described them! Abbé Rollin doesn't know about any such things."

Like the simplest man, Philibert Aubriot was charmed by the pleasure of having one of his pet subjects brought up for discussion. He launched into the history of the geranium and then that of the tulip. Taking the pretty little blond girl by the hand, the two of them, forgetting the marriage party, went off to the vegetable garden, which the gardener had bordered with aromatic herbs.

When Mme. de Bouhey was asked how it had come about that her ward was the botanist's herb-hunting companion, the old lady laughingly replied, "Why, it's perfectly simple, he loves to talk and she loves to listen."

Seasons passed. Jeanne's slender shadow gradually lengthened, without either of them noticing. They continued to walk, with their noses almost to the ground. He was the teacher who thought out loud; she was the donkey trotting at his heels and carrying the boxes of herbs. On the flat country paths of Dombes, with its gentle faded coloring, Philibert taught Jeanne natural history. Watery meadows, forests rich in game, and ponds abounding in birds produced colorful, musical, and lively learning material. Was there ever such an idyllic school as this one?

But even the most wonderful childhood must eventually come to an end. When Jeanne was almost thirteen years old, she suddenly thought of Monsieur Philibert as a man, and one she might well lose.

Mlle. Marthe, the dressmaker from Bourg-en-Bresse, was fitting Jeanne's first fine gown, an apple-green silk with white stripes. In the shepherdess style, it was the latest word from Paris. The long bodice, fitted to an elasticized foundation, was fastened, in front, by a ladder of knots. The narrow sleeves widened at the elbow into a funnel trimmed with three pleated linen flounces. In order to fill out the skirt, which was short enough to expose a pair of round-toed white leather shoes, Jeanne was to wear a half-hoop of quilted cotton with a horsehair lining. Because a young woman had to be reconciled to the good sense of her guardian, Mlle. Marthe had placated Jeanne by assuring her that "in Paris full crinolines are going out of fashion." Actually, Jeanne didn't need to be mollified. She was delighted with the gown and with the reflection of herself in the mirror. She saw herself transformed from a clumsy child into a graceful young woman.

Until now Jeanne had never been pleased with herself. Delphine de Bouhey, and even the ebullient Pompon, were always telling her that she was too tall, too skinny, too tanned, that her mouth was too large and her shoulders imperfectly rounded, that she had the hands and feet of a peasant girl who messed about in the vegetable garden and ran barefoot through the grass. As for her sense of fashion, they refrained from comment. The silly girl dressed for comfort, to keep herself warm or cool; that was all there was to it. Actually, Jeanne was happiest in boy's clothes. She would borrow a shirt and breeches from Denis Gaillon, the bailiff's son. Denis was two years older and so devoted to his Jeannette that he couldn't refuse her his finest red breeches.

Jeanne's thoughts had never strayed to seduction. But now her image in the mirror gave her troubling desires. *When Monsieur Philibert sees me like this. . . .* She saw a blush rise to her cheeks. On her girlish, fashionably bare neck she imagined Monsieur Philibert's burning gaze. Good God, what delight! She had fallen in love one afternoon when she was ten years old. Since then, she had watched her body grow beautiful, saying to herself that it was all to provide pleasure for the eyes and hands of Monsieur Philibert.

Jeanne had keen eyes and ears and a sharp mind. At thirteen years of age she was no silly little girl. She knew that a pretty girl could interest a botanist with things other than the ability to distinguish *Rosa eglanteria* (sweetbrier) from *Rosa canina* (dog brier). Although he was frugal at table, the doctor was reputed to be anything but frugal in bed. Not all the flowers he gathered in the fields were dried and classified. As a naturalist he loved nature in all its forms. Yesterday he had picked a Lisette, a Françoise, a Madeleine; today he was busy culling a Marianne, a Margot; tomorrow he might add Jeannette to his collection.

As the slater's orphan daughter, Jeanne did not aspire to being anything more than the doctor's mistress. Philibert Aubriot was the scion of an upper-middle-class family whose coat of arms displayed a gold stripe on a blue background, a silver star and a crescent. But Jeanne was not discouraged by this limitation.

The century was neither bigoted nor prudish. Mme. de Pompadour, the royal mistress, had set the tone for the rest of the nation at Versailles. Provincial drawing rooms, at Charmont and elsewhere, abounded in libertine rather than romantic conversation. Jeanne felt sure that Mme. de Bouhey would congratulate her for aspiring to the brilliant doctor. *Surely it would be better than marrying Denis. What a thrilling prospect! To coarsen and grow ugly, to give birth and wash diapers. What a bore.*

Everything she knew about the life of Philibert Aubriot reinforced her idea that she who shared his love of knowledge was meant for him. Philibert was thoroughly devoted to the classification of herbs; medicine and women were only sidelines . . . distractions. Rest and relaxation were not in the picture. Jeanne could not imagine a wife interrupting this sanctified scene, producing noisy brats who would trample the precious grains of Chinese lilac. Such a catastrophe was unthinkable, and the adolescent Jeanne looked forward confidently to the day when the handsome doctor would return her love.

The announcement, in 1760, of his marriage to a woman from Bugey was a bolt from the blue. Two or three months earlier, when he came back from a botanical expedition, she had heard him mention a girl whom he had met at his cousin's house in Belley. But he certainly hadn't sounded like a man in love. He had described her as "the sister of Abbé Maupin, the priest at Pugieu, a mature young woman versed in literature and philosophy, who had some looks and wit and, incidentally, an inheritance of sixty thousand francs."

So that was it! The traitor! Like a middle-class penny-pincher he had married money.

Philibert had set up his office at Belley, and Jeanne was left brokenhearted, angrily clenching her fists in the direction of Marguerite Maupin. *A moneybags, that's all she was. The female philosopher of Bugey! And she'd never have caught Philibert, even with her sixty thousand francs, if she hadn't taken to herb-hunting, that hypocrite. Somehow, she'd persuaded him that she would accept a lifetime of ankles chilled by the icy winter morning dew, knees stained with grass, fingernails caked with dirt, and an aching back. The liar! By pretending to share his mania, she had gotten what she'd wanted. Besides, without his magnifying glass, he was blind. A scholar can be a simpleton in affairs of the heart. Obviously he hadn't noticed that his Marguerite wore an old-fashioned iron-ribbed corset, a barbarous garment against which he had always fought tooth and nail. A twenty-eight-year-old "mature" woman had every right to disguise her bulges. But how many herbs could she pick with that vise around her waist? Philibert would soon see!*

And so Jeanne nourished the false hope that, within a week, Philibert would tire of his aged bride. She revised this figure to three weeks and then to two months. But many more months went by. Belley seemed more and more remote and the absence of her loved one, the death of her joy, ate deeper and deeper into her heart. With his ghost beside her, she walked the familiar paths in every season.

Philibert had told her fables of the woods and the streams, of the fox and the crow, of the weasel and the rabbit. He had leaned on her shoulder, teasingly pulled her hair ribbon, and bit into her slice of buttered bread. Drunk on these memories, she lifted her hair with one hand and, with the other, stroked her neck remembering the moment when he had stanched the bleeding caused by a bramble. She threw her arms around a tree and laid her cheek against the trunk. If she did not press too hard, the bark reminded her of the way his rough wool jacket felt against her skin.

She, who was once so lively, now felt the grief and knew the despair of a widow. Company bored her; people seemed either frivolous or dull. Never one to shun gossip, she pricked up her ears only when there was news about the Aubriots of Belley.

The couple seemed to be happy. The wild Philibert was tame:

working by day and sleeping by night, eating two hot meals, playing chess with his brother-in-law the priest, going to church on Sunday and, after vespers, walking with his wife on the mall. The female philosopher of Belley had captured an eagle and reduced him to a sparrow.

Jeanne's malaise reached its lowest point when she heard that Marguerite was expecting a child. *Philibert a father, what a waste!* All night long she sobbed with anger and sorrow. For Philibert to get his wife with child was the supreme betrayal. She couldn't and wouldn't bear it.

* * * *

Nervous as a kitten, Jeanne looked into the mirror. She hadn't changed her silk-and-wool birthday dress, knowing its honey color harmonized with both her dark complexion and her wheat-blond hair. At fifteen years of age Jeanne was a captivating beauty. She knew how to use her large brown eyes which, when wet with emotion, became pools of burnished gold. During the absence of her beloved, the "beanstalk," as they dubbed her, had done well in spite of herself.

On the floor above there was a rumble of chairs. Excitedly, Jeanne practiced her smile and the expression of her eyes, wetting her finger-tips and using them to curl her long lashes.

When Aubriot came into the room she was on her feet, leaning against the back of a chair. The dazzling gleam in her eyes was a reflection of love. He looked at her in silence. She had often seen him look, just as intensely, on his return from an expedition, at a cutting planted before his departure. Now his scrutiny turned into smiling approval.

"Very good," he said at last. "I see that in two years my sensitive plant has flowered." And, going over to the round table set out in front of the fireplace, he added, "I'm going to enjoy the rich fare that I have just forbidden Madame de Bouhey to partake of. Will my former pupil keep me company?"

Jeanne noticed that he hesitated between a formal and an informal manner. But he still called her his sensitive plant. His slightest touch was enough to make her tremble like the leaf of a mimosa.

She sat down on a stool across from her idol, her forearms crossed on the tablecloth and her eyes fixed blissfully upon his face. Between bursts of conversation, he munched a chicken breast. His deep voice, flooding her senses, was unforgettable. But, what was he talking about?

For once she was listening not to the words but to the voice alone. How handsome he was!

Philibert was wearing a superb coat. Jeanne thought it out of keeping with the man she had known—its beige color, easily stained, was so impractical. Once he would wear nothing but a worn, shabby jacket; now he looked like a model from Pernon, the fashionable tailor of Lyon. *Marriage can change a man, especially if the bride brings him a dowry of sixty thousand francs.* She dug her nails into her arms in order not to cry out with jealousy. *Her* Philibert had never dressed so expensively. Torn between adoration and disapproval, she scrutinized the coat's rich braiding and chiseled silver buttons, the fine muslin of the shirt, the freshly pleated jabot and the white-powdered wig. She imagined that his wealthy wife had picked out the fine clothes herself.

". . . but if Mademoiselle Pompon can't find *Papaver rhoeas*, field poppy, at the local pharmacy she can surely get it from Jassans, the hospital apothecary."

"What for?" Jeanne answered distractedly, having caught only the reference to field poppies.

"Come, come," the doctor exclaimed in surprise. "For the poultices to be placed on her inflamed eyelids. You must keep track of the treatment, because she's in no condition to remember. The dried petals are to be soaked for ten minutes in a cup of boiling water. As for *Petroselinum sativum*, parsley, you'll have all you want of that in the summer, the curly variety with crinkled leaves. Make a brew by boiling leaves and roots together and give her two cupfuls a day for her rheumatism. . . . And now that I've discharged my medical duties, do you want to hear about the book that I'm writing on the trees and shrubs of our Dombes region?"

"Oh!" Jeanne exclaimed. "Have you actually begun it?"

"Yes. And I don't want it to be dull. I hope that my style will make the landscape come alive, with the simple charm . . ."

He left the sentence unfinished, put down his knife, pushed back his chair and drew closer to Jeanne by leaning his elbows on the table. His eyes lingered on her face.

"You, Jeanne, know better than anyone else what I hope to achieve. . . ."

"Jeanne," he had called her, she said to herself, trembling all over. Not "Jeannot," as when she tagged after him in boyish breeches. And not "Jeannette," as she was commonly known. No, for the first time he had unveiled the name of "Jeanne," and the long monosyllable lay, with a heavy sweetness, between them. Almost a bedroom secret, she thought, dizzy with joy. Once more they were alone together, enclosed in an intimate circle of tremulous candlelight. As in earlier days, in a forest glade, before the hateful Marguerite had existed. Now, as if he, too, was taken by the charm of the moment, he went on in a more deliberate voice:

"What I hope to get into my natural history, if my talent allows it, is the white mist of a wintry sky, clinging to birch branches; the juicy flavor of June grass; the presentiment that pulls you up short when you are hiding among the reeds at the edge of a pond before a flock of wild ducks descends upon it; the heavy gallop of an approaching roebuck . . ."

In Philibert's strangely deliberate tone of voice, Jeanne heard the heavy gallop descending upon her as the animal's fugitive shadow passed among the tree trunks speckled by rays of sun. She had to tell him that she understood, that she understood everything he meant to write, without any need for further explanation. In a low voice she whispered, "In short, Monsieur Philibert, you are going to write our memoirs."

CHAPTER 2

e's bored with his wife! That old woman's a bore, I'm sure of it!
A single hour of being close to Philibert had revived Jeanne's hopes. He would come back, he needed her to listen to him as he wrote his book. He would come back, and with definite intentions. He would put his arms around her and hold her tight. And his lips would . . . no, there was no verb to describe what his lips would do. *Dear God, give me a kiss from Philibert tomorrow; give me . . .*

"Jeannette!"

From the depths of her wing chair Baroness Marie-Françoise de Bouhey detected the smell of something burning.

"Jeannette, I asked you to toast us some bread, not to burn it."

"Jeannette never has her mind on what she's doing," Delphine put in sharply. "You can't expect her to notice that the toast is smoking right under her nose. She has smoke in her eyes and hot air in her head. Thank God Abbé Rollin did better in educating my boys. They, at least, have their feet on the ground."

"All too true," the baroness retorted; "your sons are pure-blood Bouheys. And they keep their feet in their boots even in bed."

Delphine bit her lip and got up. "I'll go find out what's delaying the tea."

Jeanne laughed, put the plate of burned toast down on the table, and went to sit on the rug at the baroness's feet.

"You're always teasing Madame Delphine," she observed. "What do you have against her?"

"She's given me two grandsons who are cut from the same cloth as my son. As if it weren't enough for him to be just like *his* father. Of course, no woman can do the impossible, but the fact is, no good can come from a Baron de Bouhey. The Bouheys are nothing but troopers, from generation to generation."

"But handsome troopers! Your portrait gallery is filled with handsome men."

"And fine horses. There's nothing like a succession of handsome men on fine horses to ruin a family fortune. A gallery of equestrian portraits goes with a rotting roof and an empty silver chest. When I got married the Bouheys didn't have a single spoon."

"What did that matter? You loved that handsome colonel of yours and you could buy silverware with the money you inherited from a long line of drapers."

"I loved him, yes, but like a silly girl. When you marry a colonel you marry a regiment. With the price of uniforms . . . and in the cavalry every man has to be supplied with a horse. I wanted my son François to break with the family tradition and buy into a regiment of infantry. But not so. When a Bouhey isn't astride a horse he feels as if part of his backside is missing."

"Oh, madame, must you?" protested Delphine, coming back to the drawing room followed by Pompon, who was carrying a tray loaded with cups and saucers of Japanese porcelain.

"Delphine, don't be a prude. You know I can't bear it."

"It hurts me to hear you speak ill of our officers. My husband . . . and your son are fighting for the king, and . . ."

"My son is fighting because it's the only thing he knows how to do. War is his pastime, just as it was his father's, grandfather's, and all the Bouheys' before them."

"A pastime? His letters are very sad."

"Of course! They write sad letters because making us cry is part of their little game. But they don't cry over the lockets we hung around their necks. The truth of the matter is that war is fun. Marshal de Saxe put on theater, and the king invited ladies to supper parties in the trenches. While we tremble for them, our officers are gambling and tumbling peasants' daughters in the hay."

"Madame, I beg of you!" the outraged Delphine protested again.

Marie-Françoise de Bouhey shot her a gentle smile and tranquilly concluded, "Believe me, Delphine, all today's warrior needs to make him happy is a remedy for the pox."

This time Delphine could not resist taking her revenge.

"How can a woman who lost her husband at the Battle of Fontenoy speak of the joys of soldiering?"

There was an angry gleam in the baroness's eyes. "You believe in the glory of military widowhood, but what do you know of its pains? I know that, among the nobility, it's quite the thing to have lost a man at Fontenoy and to display the loss as if it were a decoration from the king. But my draper forebears held that it was stupid to spend money courting death when one could stay alive at home at no expense. But we've talked too much about this matter."

She fingered her pockets nervously and added, "Jeannette, look for my snuffbox, will you? I've mislaid it again. Do you think I'm allowed currant jelly on my biscuit? Your friend Aubriot purged me with so much extract of chicory that I'm empty enough to hold a whole leg of lamb."

Father Jérôme, coming into the room just in time to overhear these last words, burst into laughter.

"I came to see if you'd recovered, and now I have the answer. But as for a leg of lamb . . . didn't Dr. Aubriot put you on a special diet?"

"Aubriot's a fanatic. If I were to listen to him I'd flagellate my rheumatism with sheafs of nettles and graze on grass, like a cow. By the way, Jeannette, what did he tell you last night, after he'd made me empty the contents of my stomach?"

Carriage wheels on the pavement of the courtyard saved Jeanne from answering. Looking out the window she announced, "It's Madame de Saint-Girod and her sister."

"Speak of a wolf and you'll see lambs," the baroness said mockingly.

It was common knowledge that both Genevieve de Saint-Girod and Stephanie de Rupert had had Dr. Aubriot for a lover.

Countess de Saint-Girod, pretty and vivacious in spite of her thirty-five years, lost no time in proclaiming the object of her visit.

"You don't seem a bit ill," she exclaimed, kissing Mme. de Bouhey. "But I was told you were so stricken last night that you had to send for Dr. Aubriot. Is he staying with his father? Did he say that you'd soon be well again? Will he be staying for a day or two at Châtillon? Did you find him looking any older?"

"Come, come!" said the baroness. "Which question am I to answer first? Do you want news of the patient or of her doctor?"

"Well," said Mme. de Saint-Girod, "frankly, the patient is in such good shape that I'm no longer worried about her."

"Very good," said the baroness. "For news of the doctor, you'd do better to question Jeannette, who had more time to look him over."

"Is that so?" asked Mme. de Saint-Girod, casting a piercing look at the young girl. Jeanne stared back defiantly.

Although no one else present knew it, they had a memory in common, an encounter, over two years before, in the Aubriot garden at Châtillon.

Genevieve de Saint-Girod had frequent consultations with the doctor for her . . . vapors. One afternoon, when she emerged from his office with her wig askew, she passed in front of Jeanne setting out some herbs on a drying board. In a moment of acute jealousy, Jeanne had looked daggers at the older woman. Genevieve had paused and, cupping Jeanne's chin in one hand, had said provocatively, "Little Jeannette, don't waste your hatred on me. Your time will come. I predict that one day you'll be laid amid your mentor's herbs. You'll be catalogued as a splendid blond species, *Nympha fidelis*, the faithful nymph."

Now Genevieve lowered her eyes and strove to find a wounding remark. "Well, Jeannette, did Aubriot tell you about the prize that he wants to award to some deserving young thing in honor of his virtuous wife?"

"A prize for virtue?" Jeanne repeated incredulously.

"That's what they say. When a man goes to bed with a priest's sister he inevitably turns into a hypocrite."

"I must go," said Father Jérôme, raising himself only halfway out of his chair.

"Stay where you are, Father!" the baroness commanded. "We're going to have a very special cake. And you know quite well that God has changed considerably since the death of Louis XIV and is no longer so easily offended."

"It will be amusing to see Philibert Aubriot rewarding a young girl for having preserved her virtue," said Stephanie de Rupert. "So far he's gone in for cuckolding rather than encouraging virginity."

"A vocation for chastity usually blooms late," the baroness put in.

"Personally," said Jeanne, "I'm sure that this story of a prize for virtue is only malicious gossip."

"Child," said Father Jérôme, "you're defending Dr. Aubriot as vehemently as if he were accused of setting up a prize for pickpockets."

Mme. de Bouhey cast a sidelong glance at her ward before inhaling a pinch of snuff. The cake was brought in and with it a jug of barley syrup. Stephanie de Rupert took a large slice. It was consoling to know that Philibert had taken to moralizing at the same time she was putting on weight. She wasn't the only one to have left the age of cavorting behind.

"Shall we see the captain this evening?" Genevieve de Saint-Girod asked abruptly.

Adultery was the impetuous countess's favorite pastime. She had not yet snagged Captain François de Bouhey, a full-blooded male and a daring rider who was very much to her liking. Ever since he had taken up winter quarters in his mother's château she had openly flirted with him.

"My husband isn't here," said Delphine, happy to disappoint her. "He's gone to round up some recruits. There are vacancies in his company."

"Does he have to do the recruiting himself?" Genevieve asked in astonishment.

"My dear, our peasants have come to know a thing or two," replied the baroness. "You can no longer rope them in by beating the drum, getting them drunk, and promising them wine, women, and song in the army. They've caught on to the fact that these things are for the officers and that their lot is more likely to consist of fleas and flogging.

And so you catch them pissing on the recruiting posters. But if a fine captain comes in person to harangue them about good pay and glory, well, gilt épaulettes still make an impression."

"Bah!" interposed Stephanie. "If his company ranks are thin, he can put in some dummies to be passed in review. It's done all the time these days."

Recruiting was, indeed, difficult. And because the army wanted men of a certain height, many impoverished tall fellows rented themselves out to regimental and company commanders for parades and then went home. If, after the first battle of a given campaign, they were listed as dead or missing, the officer's count of his men came out correctly, and the royal bureaucracy was satisfied.

"I'm not against padding the ranks," the baroness observed. "If dead men rise and fight again, then everyone should be happy."

Delphine was visibly annoyed by the turn the conversation had taken. Her embroidery hoop trembled between her fingers and finally she pricked herself with a needle.

"A Baron de Bouhey will never use dummies," she announced. "François has a keen sense of honor, and he would never deceive his king."

"Too bad," the baroness insisted. "Because our peasants are tired of being killed in earnest. We've been warring with England and Prussia for six years, and that's too long. When the king demands too much of his subjects they're justified in cheating."

"God forgive me!" interposed Father Jérôme. "Isn't this republican talk?"

"Oh, well," said Genevieve lightly, "in this day and age a lot of things are being said that ought to be punished, by the king and later by God. But God has become easygoing, and the king lets things ride."

"Yes, they do say the king's very indulgent," said the abbé.

"That's better than calling him lazy, isn't it?" the baroness asked ironically. "The Marquise de la Pommeraie, who's very close to Choiseul, says reform bills are stalled because the minister has to trick the king or wear him out before he can wrest a signature from him. But, after all, he's been king for forty-seven years and reigned for forty. Small wonder he's so tired. He doesn't really rule; he simply endures."

"The reforms of the Duke de Choiseul may not be altogether acceptable," said Delphine. "François says there's a question of doubling the forces of the artillery and letting several regiments of infantry go."

"Well, many of them won't be the worse for it," the baroness retorted. "A gentleman officer has to spend more than his pay on his uniform and equipment. Careers in the infantry and the cavalry are things of the past," she concluded. "The future is on the sea, when it comes to making money. Officers of the Royal Navy have a right to go in for trade."

"A fine career for a gentleman," exclaimed Delphine scornfully. "Buying and selling! I call it demeaning."

" 'Demeaning'?" the baroness repeated. "That's a hopelessly old-fashioned word. An army man can sack a city, burn, kill, rob, and rape without demeaning himself, while a navy officer loses face because he goes in for trade! The Knights of Malta are not ashamed to make their pile aboard the king's ships or those of their Order. I know some of them who do a bit of pirating on the side."

The blue eyes of Countess de Saint-Girod lit up.

"Are you, by chance, referring to the Chevalier Vincent, madame?"

Stephanie broke into a laugh as melodious and sensual as the cooing of a dove. "The Chevalier Vincent has all of a corsair's charm. The odors of wind and wave are truly intoxicating."

"Mmmmm," Genevieve lustfully chimed in.

Jeanne, who had kept silent because she found the conversation boring, was attracted by the mention of the sea. "How does it happen that I've never seen this noble corsair whom all the rest of you seem to know?"

"You were only a little girl when he last came to hunt at Charmont," the baroness told her. "But you'll see him at the end of the month. I heard that he was coming down from Paris to Marseille and I invited him to my party."

At once Genevieve stormed her with questions.

"Really? Did he accept? Do you expect me, as usual, to put up two or three of your guests? Will he be among them?"

"I, too, should be happy to provide a bed for the Chevalier Vincent," put in Stephanie.

Every year, at the beginning of spring, before her son went off to his summer encampment, the dowager Baroness de Bouhey held festivities of several days' duration, with hunting, a late-evening formal supper, and a ball. Because she could not lodge all of her many guests she distributed them among her neighbors.

"I'll give you your choice," she said maliciously to the two sisters, "but I can't promise you the Chevalier Vincent. He makes his own arrangements, at Vaux, with his lovely Pauline."

"Is that still going on?" Genevieve asked disappointedly. "His affair with Madame de Vaux-Jailloux has come to be a common-law marriage. How many years have they been together?"

"Six," said Stephanie as promptly as if she had added them up regularly.

"Six years!" Genevieve exclaimed. "That's not fidelity, it's inertia!"

Jeanne couldn't help protesting. "And why shouldn't two people love each other and be faithful their whole life long?"

All three ladies smiled at her ingenuousness, and Genevieve tapped Jeanne's cheek affectionately. "Jeannette, we'll see how you feel about it in twenty years."

"You know," the baroness said, "that those charmers, Pauline and Vincent, are separated two years out of every three. This may be why their affair is so long-lasting. The chevalier hasn't set foot ashore since the end of 1759. The Order lent him to the king for service in the Indian Ocean."

"Well, your handsome corsair didn't save the day," said Jeanne knowingly. "Since the governor, Monsieur de Lally-Tollendal, was forced to surrender in Pondicherry, Abbé Rollin says that the peace treaty will give the Indies to the English."

Mme. de Bouhey looked over at her with surprise and amusement.

"I never thought, Jeannette, that you took an interest in our Indian affairs."

"I'm interested in all the colonies," Jeanne answered seriously. "France needs them."

"Nonsense!" exclaimed Genevieve. "All intelligent people are against colonialism—the king, his ministers, and even the philosophers. You must know of Voltaire's letter to Choiseul begging him not to waste our soldiers in defense of the snowy wastes of Canada."

"It's all very well for Voltaire to scorn Canada," remarked Jeanne coldly, "since the English have already taken it from us. I only hope they'll be kind enough to leave us our sugar islands and those in the Indian Ocean."

Mme. de Bouhey was still scrutinizing Jeanne. "Are you, by chance, planning to hunt herbs on the islands, Jeannette dear?"

"Of course, of course!" put in Delphine disdainfully. "Why not? I know how this notion got into Jeannette's head. Abbé Rollin has been smitten with island fever. Although, among us, he enjoys comfortable lodgings, good food, and agreeable company, he thinks enviously of the gallows' birds and prostitutes deported to the islands' sugar plantations."

"Madame, you lack imagination," Jeanne retorted, her nostrils quivering. "The abbé thinks of the islands as blessed lands where God has made all men equal. And what I dream of is the beauty of their flowers."

"Come, come," the baroness interrupted. "I suggest that we talk more about the islands with the Chevalier Vincent, who's acquainted with them. Meanwhile, let's have some of this quince jelly, which Charlotte brought me from Neuville. I think you'll find it even better than that from the Abbey of Notre-Dame."

Father Jérôme had dozed off, but the odor of the jelly aroused him.

"There's no one like the lady canonesses to make delicacies out of fruit," he sighed.

"They're unequaled in many things," said the baroness. "Their cooking seems to draw on the secrets of alchemy."

"The good ladies have a taste for good food." The priest nodded. "And our prior's peas are famous. In summer, when the bishop comes for a game of piquet with the prior, the stakes are a peck of peas in exchange for a bound copy of the episcopal edicts of the year gone by."

The ladies laughed heartily.

* * * *

As Jeanne stood at the window her thoughts were far from the vegetable garden of the ladies of Neuville. Her eyes traveled through the sloping gardens down to the Irance River, bordered on both sides by tall poplars. The trees were still bare, but soon they would be clothes in green leaves, and the wind would rustle through them. Jeanne didn't know why, but ever since childhood the quivering of wind-swept leaves had given her a feeling of mingled pleasure and anxiety. The music of the storm produced a state of expectation. Closing her eyes and letting herself go, she felt as if she were floating away. She seemed to become a sail, embarked on a long voyage between the blues of sky and sea to a sun-drenched horizon.

The islands . . . lands of refuge, where shepherdesses married their princes. *I wonder whether this Chevalier Vincent knows something of the flora and fauna of the islands. Can a sailor have an eye for anything but ports and prostitutes?*

CHAPTER 3

he baroness paused, as she often did, before the portrait of Colonel Jean-Charles de Bouhey. A sumptuous image in blue, red, and gold, this was all that was left of a man who had taken part in the victory of Fontenoy. The bodily remains—a couple of pieces of bloody meat extricated by his attendant from a tangle of corpses of men and horses—had been hastily buried in the church graveyard.

A candle, borne by Jeanne, lit up the portrait with a gentle, compassionate glow. In the flickering light the colonel smiled down on them benevolently.

"Jeannette," said the baroness, at the threshold of her room, "don't believe me when I speak ill of my Jean-Charles. He deserved the dowry I brought him. You must never give heed to the complaints of an old woman. She is only mourning the loss of her youth. Brrr . . . April's not exactly springlike this year. Throw a log on the fire, will you, and put the stool under my feet. There, thank you. And the shawl over my legs. Now you've only to look again for my snuffbox."

Jeanne squeezed the bellows over the smoking fresh log. A short blue flame emerged, and then a red tongue shot up devouring the smoke.

"Aren't you going to take off your shoes?" the baroness asked.

Jeanne loved to walk in her stockinged feet, voluptuously sinking them into the rare Gobelin rug, as thick and soft as a well-groomed lawn. It had been seven years since Jeanne had first entered this dazzling room. And it never ceased to entrance her, so different from a peasant's hut with mud floors.

The chamber was enlarged by a spectacular view of the surrounding landscape, which was so grand as to enter the room through three tall windows. The middle window opened onto a graceful, semicircular stone terrace beyond which one could see the poplars along the Irance and the woods of Romans.

The Polish-style bed with cherry-red draperies, the blue-framed Persian panels with bird motifs, the gilt frames on the pictures and armchairs, the Venetian chandelier with its many-colored flowers, all these created a joyful and stimulating atmosphere more conducive to reading or talking than to relaxing. Nothing was more pleasant than this moment each night when the baroness and Jeanne talked freely to each other before going to bed. They spoke of things both important and trivial or else remained quiet together as a dense calm fell over the château.

Two days after her brief upset, the baroness came back to something that had given her food for thought. "Tell me," she said, "do you really want to go to the Indies?"

"I dream about them, that's all. I have considerable curiosity and I'm given to daydreaming, you know that. You were talking about the sea and a certain corsair. That made me think of the islands. There's a connection. I'm thrilled by the idea of meeting a corsair. Do you think he'll dance with me?"

"Watch out for your heart, Jeannette! Vincent is a heartbreaker!"

"I can resist him, never fear," said the fifteen-year-old indignantly.

"Very good!" the baroness said, laughing. "But watch out, just the same. A young girl may overestimate her powers of resistance. The corsair may be handsomer than she imagines."

"Is the chevalier so handsome?"

"You'll tell me after you've seen him. He's thought to be very attractive."

"Tell me some more about him."

"I don't know him so very well. He's been at sea since the age of fifteen, sailing, selling, fighting. My old friend Pazevin, the shipbuilder from Marseille, says that he consumes everything new in the fields of navigation, science, and business as relentlessly as a shark. He was born poor, but he's made a fortune."

"Really?" Jeanne asked, pouting. "So this model knight is fundamentally searching for gold. Has he no ideals whatsoever?"

"Ideals? What do you mean? The words that trickle down from a sedentary philosopher's pen, or the lands discovered by a sailor standing on the forecastle? For my part, I think there's a bit of everything, including ideals, in a corsair."

Jeanne looked at her with surprise. "How did you gain your knowledge of the corsair's soul?"

"I knew a few corsairs once upon a time, when I still spent the winter in Paris. But don't make eyes at me, Jeannette! I've no romantic tales to tell."

Then, relaxing into a faraway smile, she added, "Some fifteen years ago there was a corsair from the Falklands that I might have loved. Even late in life we're not safe from a passing folly. But this was very late, and then, an autumnal love for a younger man."

"Such things happen."

"So they do. But I didn't give way. I examined the matter from every possible angle and before all my mirrors I weighed the pros and cons. Yes, horrors! I had become a reasonable woman. It's a sad day, Jeannette, when we realize that never again will the heart prevail over the head."

Jeanne took her protector's rheumatic hand and stroked it with the tips of her fingers. The baroness laughed and recovered her self-control, annoyed with herself for having lost it, even for a moment.

"But why should you be involved with my grandmotherly nostalgia? That chicory tea did me no good whatsoever. Would you have the courage to go down to the cellar at this hour?"

"No, I wouldn't."

"Listen, my dear, let's be reasonable. A few drops of Condrieu wine would do me a world of good. I feel it in my bones."

"No," Jeanne repeated. "Do *you* have the courage to drink Condrieu at eleven o'clock at night?"

"That I do!"

"Forgive me, but you can't have it. Monsieur Philibert gave me your diet, and I shall stick by it."

"Devil take your Aubriot and his punitive prescriptions! Because of him my best wine will spoil. Condrieu has to be drunk young."

"Others will drink it, have no fear."

"You mean that I should pass around my Condrieu? A wine so rare, so precious that you have to pray for it!"

"Then it would make a good sacramental wine, and you can give it to the priest at Châtillon."

The baroness frowned. More than once she had been on the brink of posing a certain question, but she had drawn back at the last moment. Now, since Jeanne was refusing to indulge her a small satisfaction, she would have her revenge.

"You have a keen wit, my pretty one. Enough to make sport of me, but not enough to make sport of yourself."

And, when Jeanne looked up, puzzled, the baroness continued. "Come sit on my stool, so that I can see you when you lie to me. Now, look here, Jeannette, you're young and pretty and anything but stupid. Why do you waste your time pining for a married man, living miles away, who doesn't love you?"

The question struck Jeanne like a cannonball, but she did not flinch and she did not lie.

"I love Monsieur Philibert, that's true. How long have you known?"

"The mere sound of his name makes you glow. But what can you expect to obtain from pursuing this whim? How long will you make love in your imagination with a man fifty miles away?"

"He'll come back. His wife bores him."

"So soon? Did he tell you so himself?"

"I understood it. I'm sure that he'll come back to Châtillon."

"Even so . . . he'll come with his wife and child."

With a shrug of her shoulders Jeanne dismissed Philibert's family.

"So," said the baroness. "You're a pretty intelligent fifteen-year-old girl and you're ready to be satisfied with a quarter of an hour of love between one doorway and another?"

"I love him."

" 'I love him. I love him.' Those are words to go into a silly novel. Today you love a man who's absent, tomorrow a man who's distracted. And the distracted one makes for much more sorrow. You have to fall in with *his* hours, to take and leave him at *his* pleasure. Look here, can't you find someone easier to love than Dr. Aubriot?"

Jeanne leaped to her feet, her face aflame, her fists clenched.

"I've loved him since the day I first laid eyes on him. And I'll love him to the end of my life!"

"Let's hope that it's to the end of *his* life," the baroness amended gently. "He's twenty years older than you. Come now, sit down. Let's talk frankly, woman to woman. I don't want to prevent you from going to bed with Aubriot, Jeannette, I only want to save you from pain."

Jeanne was taken aback by the frankness of the baroness's speech. She had never minced words, but tonight she was more direct than ever.

"Don't start to blush so soon," the baroness said authoritatively. "We've just begun to get into the subject. I was trying to tell you that a love affair can charm and amuse, even if it causes tears. That is, as long as we don't suffer."

"If I were to be the mistress of Monsieur Philibert I'd suffer neither regret nor remorse," said Jeanne passionately.

"Remorse? Who said anything about remorse? Remorse for the wrong you would do to Madame Aubriot? Believe me, the unhappy look on the face of a lover's wife is like the polluted air of Paris. You get used to it very quickly and even enjoy it. No, regret and remorse don't kill a scholar's mistress. She dies of the same ailment as the other women in his life . . . sheer boredom."

"Boredom? How could I ever be bored in the company of Philibert Aubriot?"

Mme. de Bouhey smiled. "A girl your age has illusions about the word *lover*. A busy lover is as forgetful as a busy husband. Your Aubriot lives the life of the mind, among his herbs and grasses and magnifying lenses. An occasional five minutes with one woman is more than sufficient. A man of learning never makes a good lover, believe me. Do you know who is the most pleasant and obliging lover? An ordinary priest, a womanizing priest, of course, but there are plenty of them. When I lived in Paris I saw them in boudoirs all over the city. For everyday use there's nothing like them. They are masters of good manners, letters, gossip, games, and music. They are deliciously hypocritical and sometimes they know enough Latin to read erotic masterpieces. And, best of all, they can give you plenty of their time, since the works of God demand so little of them. So, Jeannette, what do you say?"

"Forgive me for not laughing," said Jeanne somberly. "You're making light of a subject that involves my deepest feelings."

The baroness leaned over and raised Jeanne's face in her two hands. "You love him so much, do you?" she questioned sadly.

Jeanne made no reply, but tears gleamed in her eyes.

The baroness took another tack. "In that case, Jeannette, let me make a plan for your benefit. Let me arrange a marriage for you."

Jeanne could not believe her ears.

"Just listen," the baroness went on. "I can offer you a good match. You haven't noticed him, because your head is so full of your botanist. But I know that Duthillet, the surrogate, doesn't come twice a week to Charmont just to make a third at our game of ombre. He devours you with his eyes, in fact that's why he invariably loses. Louis-Antoine Duthillet is from a good bourgeois family. He lives in one of the finest houses in Châtillon and has his own carriage. His family is well established, in Trévoux, Dijon, and Lyon. And his office must yield him at least thirty thousand francs a year. You'd go to supper and theater parties in those towns and to the governor's ball on the feast day of Saint Louis. So, tell me, quite frankly, what do you think of Monsieur Duthillet?"

Jeanne had listened, openmouthed, to the baroness's suggestion, without taking it seriously. Her answer to the final question was to laugh uncontrollably.

"Good!" said the baroness. "One can talk reasonably of a man only if one can laugh about him."

"Gooood Lord! Surrogate Duthillet!" gasped Jeanne between gales of laughter. "The man always dresses in black with a solemn bobwig!"

"If he didn't wear black he'd be most ungrateful. After all, he owes his income to the dead and those that mourn them. One-third of the inheritances that the adjudicates goes into his coffers. His black garb is made of either silk or the finest English wool, and cut by Pernon of Lyon, and his handkerchiefs are of pure cambric."

For sheer fun Jeanne pretended to embark on a serious discussion. "Isn't this man-in-black a bit old for me?" she queried.

"My dear, a husband is always too old when a woman is dreaming about a lover. And, in this case, the husband is thirty-four years old and the lover thirty-five."

Jeanne bit her lip.

"What's more," Mme. de Bouhey went on, "a surrogate's wife always has young men around her. Her husband employs five or six twenty-year-old clerks. All of them will be in love with you, blush when you pass by, leave flowers on your windowsill and, if they're very daring, touch your foot under the table. All the lawyers of the town will dance attendance upon you and shower you with New Year presents, in the hope that you will influence your husband to allot them a case. I can promise you'd enjoy being the wife of the surrogate of Châtillon."

"To live with any man other than Monsieur Philibert could never be enjoyable," said Jeanne vehemently.

"It's a question not of living with another man but of living with a husband," was the baroness's patient reply. "It's easy to live with a husband, because there are so many other things to do. Believe me, my dear, a husband can be treated lightly, but a marriage is something substantial. To run a fine house is a pleasure. And you seem to have forgotten that Duthillet's house is only a few doors away from that of Aubriot. If Aubriot comes back you'd have him practically at the foot of your bed."

Mme. de Bouhey was talking in profanely realistic terms about Jeanne's great love secretly nurtured for so long. The girl's romantic spirit was outraged.

"Madame, you must be joking, trying to make me laugh."

"Yes. I want to see you laugh rather than cry. In the house of a rich husband there's room for laughter, even amid the pains of love. You may have an aching heart, but you also have fine dresses, good dinners, and a carriage in which to go to a lover's meeting without muddying your shoes."

Jeanne choked with anger and crossed her arms defensively over her breast.

"And there's a husband to come home to bed with," she said, in words almost as realistic as those of her interlocutor.

"There you are!" protested the baroness. "You read too much. Modern novels turn a girl's head."

"I'll belong to Monsieur Philibert or to no one!" Jeanne announced.

"Be quiet!" the baroness commanded. "To hear an intelligent girl say such stupid things makes me lose my temper. You know very well that the world is what it is. A woman has to devote herself to either a husband or God. Life in a nunnery is tolerable only for the well-born. Others are slaves."

"I know. That's why I never thought to shut myself up in a convent. I'd rather earn my living. Haven't I some abilities?"

"You're not a poor but worthy young *man*, Jeannette, my dear. You're a poor but worthy young *girl*, and that's a harder lot. If I don't marry you off before I die, what's to become of you? Will you read aloud to another old lady and sit on another footstool? Don't turn down the chance to occupy an armchair in your own house."

"I know that I depend entirely on your kindness," Jeanne admitted in a humble manner. "But is that a reason for selling myself to the surrogate? If I'm unlucky enough to lose you . . . Oh, pray don't talk to me as if I were already a woman. I want to remain a little girl a while longer. . . ."

She buried her head in the baroness's skirt and the latter stroked her hair.

"Calm yourself," she said affectionately. "You are a little girl, to be sure. But, alas, my time is running out. I'm sorry that I tried to rush you into something prematurely. Actually, I am the one in a hurry. I'm becoming impatient to make those I love happy."

Jeanne raised her teary eyes. "I can be happy only with Monsieur Philibert. Don't you think I can compete with his old wife after I've ripened just a little?"

"Stupid, again! A woman should understand that her beauty isn't given her for the pleasure of just one man, but in order that she may please herself with as many men as she desires."

* * * *

Jeanne wanted above all to sleep, to sink into a slumber where Philibert awaited her. But her nerves were on edge and her feet frozen. She got up, lit a candle, slipped on a sweater and skirt and, taking care to avoid the creaking planks of the hallway floor, went downstairs to the kitchen. Her intention was to boil some water, fill the "English monk" and take it back up to bed. But Pompon had already taken it. This new invention, imported from London, had been a gift to the baroness. But she could not be persuaded to give up the hot bricks which she used to warm her bed. Somewhere the chambermaid had heard that the new hot-water bottle cost all of twenty-four francs, and the idea of putting so expensive an object against the soles of her feet satisfied her craving for luxury.

Jeanne toyed with the idea of snatching it from Pompon's bed, but finally she shrugged her shoulders and took refuge beside the dying fire. She needed to "get up her courage." When her father woke up feeling tired he would stretch himself and say, with a smile, "I'm not in good form this morning, my girl, I'll have to get up my courage." And he would slowly eat a slice of bread soaked in a mixture of wine and water. When, instead, his daughter had seemed unable to cope with sweeping the house or peeling vegetables for their dinner, he gave her the same remedy, with the addition of a pinch of sugar.

Now the fifteen-year-old Jeanne looked back with emotion at the child she had once been. She cast her eyes about for the carafe of claret. Every evening Delphine ordered some to be drawn from the cask so that her younger son might dip his breakfast bread in it the next morning. The claret was on the kitchen table, beside the broth and the two eggs that Jean-François was to eat, washed down with his portion of mulled wine. Jeanne took a loaf of bread out of the breadbox, cut a slice, made the two eggs into an omelette, and poked up the fire. Then she sat down again with the plate on her knees and the claret at her feet.

The act of eating seemed to get up her courage. She poured herself another glass of wine. Before this evening's talk with her guardian, Jeanne had never given much thought to the faraway day when she might have to leave Charmont. Tomorrow in her mind was totally occupied by the image of Philibert. Tomorrow Philibert would return to Châtillon. Tomorrow she would resume her little-girl life but with the addition of his caresses. But just now she had learned that, in order to have a future, she must find something other than an improved version of the past.

For two years she had played at being the Sleeping Beauty, waiting for her prince's return. Now she had awakened to reality and found herself in a darkened kitchen. Her Prince Charming was happily begetting children at Bugey, fifty miles away. She shook her head angrily to dispel the tears that flooded her eyes, and downed another glass of claret. *No! I won't let my fate be decided by others.*

Jeanne realized that if she didn't fight to make a place for herself in the world, she would be relegated to the lower class, from which she had been temporarily rescued. When she was grown and on her own, the doors of society would be closed to her. The baroness was right. If she didn't play her last trumps, she would risk sinking to the status of "reader to a dowager," only a degree and a floor above the kitchen staff.

As she was buttering a second slice of bread a familiar thought came to mind. *Why not disguise myself as a young man?* This notion always put her into a good mood. She imagined herself at ease in Denis' red breeches, her hair gathered into a braid at the back of her neck, and over her shoulder a stick with a bundle of clothes at the end of it. She would walk jauntily down to the docks in Marseille, board a ship, and sail across the blue waters. There, in the islands, she would plant acres of sugarcane, coffee, cotton, pepper, cloves, and other spices. Cargoes that would earn her thousands of gold louis. *Monsieur Philibert would be sorry to have sold himself for a mere sixty thousand francs.*

She had drunk most of the claret; blood coursed through her veins and she felt quite lightheaded. The future rolled out like a red carpet. There was nothing so very hard about winning the man she loved. When Jeanne's friends Emilie and Marie spoke of love, it was to tell triumphantly how the men they wanted were brought to their knees. *Woman calls the tune. Everyone knows, if she goes at it without shame or fear and . . . supplied with money. Yes, money.* When Emilie plotted the strategy for catching a lover she spent money like water for gowns, wigs, perfume, and extravagant suppers where champagne flowed freely and elaborate dishes were powdered with expensive aphrodisiacs.

Jeanne wondered whether a surrogate's wife, like a marquise or an opera singer, would serve champagne at her suppers? *Yes, it would take a rich man.* And she could throw dust in a rich husband's eyes while flirting with the man of her choice. M. Duthillet certainly had enough money in his coffers to provide sumptuously for his wife's guests. Jeanne poured what was left of the claret into her glass and lapped it up with her tongue. She let herself sink into a state of cozy adultery. The dear baroness was right . . . marrying Duthillet presented definite advantages.

CHAPTER 4

 n spring, the residents of Charmont awoke around six o'clock in the morning. The grinding sound of a winch in the paved courtyard was Bouchoux, the factotum, drawing water from the well. As Nanette was lighting the kitchen fire, Bellotte came down from her attic.

Tatan, who had reigned for twenty years over the pots and pans, did not show her face before eight o'clock, but her arrival was made noisily. Yawning behind her came Mlle. Pingault, Delphine's chambermaid, and Pompon, for the baroness. They staked out a warm spot near the stove, engaging in their usual small talk while they sipped their café au lait. Promptly at nine appeared the imposingly buxom figure of Mlle. Sergent, the housekeeper. Fifty years old, mustachioed, and fiercely devoted to the Bouheys and their house where she had been born, Mlle. Sergent held absolute sway over the domestic staff. And Charmont was maintained beautifully.

The estate was prosperous. Marie-Françoise de Bouhey knew how to run her affairs, in spite of her husband who had been in a hurry to bankrupt himself with horses and entertainment. When her parents died she did not take over the inheritance but left the money in the two serge factories at Amiens and Abbeville, which her only brother, Mathieu Delafaye, ran for their common benefit. When Mathieu's two sons were grown, the baroness set them up in Lyon in the silk business, which thrived, for silk was increasingly popular at court. The baroness reinvested her profits in a nearly bankrupt cloth factory in Languedoc which she miraculously revived. Finally, in the last ten years, she began to receive interest from the shipbuilding enterprise of her friend Pazevin in Marseille.

The baroness also dabbled in real estate, fulfilling a long-standing promise to buy back three farms sold by her father-in-law. This was not easy, because the peasants had begun to join forces to combat the takeover of their lands by their masters. The baroness managed, somehow, to make her repurchases without incurring ill-will.

Mme. de Bouhey had not been born into the aristocracy, did not share its prejudices, and cared little for the observance of her rights as a landowner. Her bailiff had orders to shut his eyes when the peasants failed to make the "just due" payments of five hens, three ducks, or a lamb or when the harvesters held back part of their due of grain. Because the baroness was yielding, her peasants seemed to love her.

All her dependents had free access to her. She received them in her own room, which she did not leave until two o'clock in the afternoon, having spent the morning dictating letters to Abbé Rollin and discussing the sums she owed to Gaillon, the bailiff.

In any case, after almost fifty years of Louis XV's reign, there was little rebellion against the local nobility. The real protest was directed at a more distant enemy: the royal revenue service and its host of tax collectors.

M. Pipon, her business counselor from Lyon, came twice a week, very early. He happened to be there this morning, when a loud noise and shouts and footsteps were heard suddenly from the kitchen. The baroness had to ring the bell four times before Pompon, pink-cheeked and excited, came to give her an explanation.

"It was Tatan, madame. She was running after Nanette with a poker. The greedy girl ate up the eggs and drank the claret laid out last night for our little gentleman."

"That's a lot of noise for a couple of eggs and some low-grade wine," said the baroness. "Doesn't the girl get enough to eat at the kitchen table?"

"She eats like a pig. And she lays hands on anything else she can find outside of mealtimes. It's a sort of sickness. But this is the first time she dared to . . ."

At this moment Jeanne pushed open the door and interrupted the story. "Pompon, before Tatan kills Nanette, tell her that I'm the one who made a midnight supper of the eggs and claret."

"Well, well!" the baroness exclaimed.

Even unsmiling, Jeanne was charming to look at, with her white cotton robe and her smooth blond hair falling down over her back. Mme. de Bouhey scrutinized her attentively.

"Monsieur Pipon," she said, "will you be so good as to step into my boudoir? And you, Pompon, run along and deliver your message.

"So," the baroness said to Jeanne as soon as they were alone, "you turn down Condrieu at eleven o'clock and you drink claret at twelve. Don't you know that poor quality wine is only good for getting drunk?"

"I had to get up my courage. I came, now, to tell you . . ." She stopped short.

To make things easier, Mme. de Bouhey sat down before her mirror, giving Jeanne her back.

In the mirror's cloudy reflection Jeanne caught the keen eyes which her guardian was fixing upon her. She went on, more firmly, "I came to say that if you can, as you say, secure Monsieur Duthillet, I'll accept him."

* * * *

Five days later Jeanne and the surrogate were betrothed. Mme. de Bouhey had thought of everything.

M. Duthillet was as obliging and as generous as a well-heeled thirty-four-year-old bachelor who had fallen in love with a young girl should be. According to the marriage contract, he conferred upon the bride a sum of thirty-five thousand francs, which would be drawn from his liquid holdings. And in case of his death he left her the use of his house and furniture, plus an income of a thousand francs a year. On her side, Mme. de Bouhey pledged a complete trousseau, some small gold jewels, a toilet case in silver and tortoiseshell, and a purse containing fifteen hundred francs. To this respectable dowry Captain François de Bouhey added Jeanne's favorite mount, the mare Blanchette.

The marriage was scheduled for mid-September. As soon as the betrothal was official, lengths of muslin, batiste, linen and cambric, laces and ribbons, fine cloth from Abbeville, drugget and silk were ordered from Paris and Lyon. But it was agreed that a dressmaker and seamstresses, hired on an hourly basis, would not be engaged until May, when the château's annual festivities were over. Laurent Delafaye, the baroness's great-nephew, lost no time in bringing a royal gift: two pieces of silk, one a shimmering blond faille with traces of iridescent rose, the other a heavy white brocade ornamented with bouquets of red flowers. Gowns made of these silks promised to make the surrogate's wife the center of attention at the balls given for the feast of Saint Louis.

Pompon gave yelps of joy and buried her face in the fine fabrics. She was enjoying the wedding vicariously, humming with joy and telling Jeanne, a dozen times a day, that she had been born with a silver spoon in her mouth.

Jeanne had an odd feeling. Although she was titillated by the joy of Pompon, reassured by the courtesy and reserve of Louis-Antoine Duthillet, warmed by widespread smiles, questioned, envied, congratulated, hugged, and kissed, she felt as if she were living on the surface of her true self. At this peripheral level life was highly agreeable. But the pleasure was a frail one.

When Pompon draped her in the brocade with the red bouquets, she realized what a splendid figure she would cut. Yet the idea of shining forth on the arm of Louis-Antoine brought tears to her eyes. Jeanne thought of her fiancé as a well-dressed and well-mannered man in black, who conversed and played cards without ever raising his voice. He was a distinguished judge by day and, in the evening, an agreeable host or guest. Perhaps he might be a more than passable husband and, after all, a discreet and reliable friend.

He had given her a charming first present—a *bonbonnière* of Sèvres porcelain, filled with pralines. The box was shaped like a heart with a group of chubby cupids painted in gold relief. Jeanne was so pleased that she held out her hand to Louis-Antoine and did not object to the light kiss which he planted upon it. He asked her to go with him to Trévoux, where he had business with the law court, and the baroness gave her permission.

* * * *

Pompon, radiant in her Sunday best, was a distracted chaperone. Jeanne had a foretaste of the privileges of a surrogate's wife as the carriage rolled down the street, and passersby stared at her, first with curiosity and then with admiration. While Louis-Antoine attended to his business, the two women went window shopping and then boldly ventured into the Armenian's café, where they regaled themselves with mocha and rose jam. Provincial cafés were beginning to be decorated like those of Paris. The small establishment of the Armenian had pale blue and gold wall panels, interspersed with mirrors, a hanging candelabrum, and small marble-topped tables.

Pompon, her mouth full of jam, chatted joyfully. "Didn't I tell you, mademoiselle, that you were born with a silver spoon in your mouth? A good man, and one that knows how to live. You'll be able to afford all the gowns you want, theaters, coffee and chocolate shops, journeys in a post chaise, pots of the best rouge, lobster dinners. . . . Mademoiselle, take me with you to Châtillon! You'll be needing a chambermaid."

"I was right to think that you wanted to be a third party to my marriage," answered Jeanne, laughing.

"Well, mademoiselle, there's nothing like a generous man's money to make a woman happy."

The excursion to Trévoux was a happy one. When Louis-Antoine came to fetch the two women he found them in a notions shop, babbling away over the purchase of a length of ribbon. He took advantage of the situation to buy Jeanne an object which she admired, a little brown taffeta umbrella with a silver handle, which could be folded in two and carried in a pocket. The shopkeeper called it a "broken" umbrella and touted it as the latest thing from the Royal Parasol of Paris. The spontaneity with which the surrogate made Jeanne this expensive present reawakened Pompon's bubbling joy.

"Mademoiselle," she whispered, while the surrogate went over to pay the shopkeeper, "here you have not only a good husband but a lover as well. He must be wild about you to put his hand in his pocket so easily. It's a good sign, I tell you!"

Jeanne started. The word *lover* burst her chaste daydream of eternal friendship. When they were back in the carriage she studied the profile of her intended. Duthillet was neither handsome nor ugly. His air of serene—perhaps too softhearted—kindliness made a pleasant impression. A touch of shortsightedness gave a gentle expression to his pale blue eyes. His black garb created an aura of seriousness which he probably thought was consonant with his judicial duties. But Jeanne saw at a glance that his coat was cut from a high quality, mixed silk-and-wool cloth, with piping all around and costly jade buttons. The jabot, lace sleeves, and powdered wig were a striking contrast and set off the black with touches of white.

Jeanne found the wig heavy and old-fashioned, resolving to make him wear one more becoming. She smiled to herself when she realized that she was taking an interest in her fiancé's appearance. Suddenly she wished she could dine with him, tête-à-tête, at a local inn. First, because she had never dined in such a place. And second, because it would give her a chance to see how he would take care of her. Would he see to it that she was well wined and dined and given her choice of the ripest fruit and the most succulent desserts . . . ? Of course she didn't love him. But that was no reason for not testing *his* love. Instead, she had to go to a family dinner at the house of Jean-Jaques Duthillet, Louis-Antoine's brother.

Jean-Jaques was also a jurist, counsel to the court of Trévoux. Tonight he upset Louis-Antoine by offering his future sister-in-law too simple a meal, consisting of soup, mutton chops, artichokes, rabbit stewed with prunes, a salad, custard, jam, and sugared almonds.

When they left this inadequate table Louis-Antoine murmured to Jeanne apologetically, "My poor brother has a wife who imposes her thriftiness on their guests. He can do nothing about it. What man of today, I ask you, can do anything about what goes on in his own house? The law assures him that he is the master, but the best he can do is to shut himself up in his office with this assurance."

Jeanne laughed. "With this in mind, monsieur, aren't you afraid to put your future into my hands?"

"No, my dear. I think that you'll keep a good table. I can see from your face that you enjoy eating. Did you notice, she's all sharp lines—

her nose, chin, shoulders, elbows, even her voice—and she is thin-lipped to an extreme?"

"Whereas mademoiselle has full lips and rounded shoulders," said Pompon, intruding upon the conversation.

Louis-Antoine reddened like a young boy. The chambermaid's words called up the confidence he had in his betrothed's potential sensuality, which he judged by her generous lips, shining eyes, frequent blushes, the way she stroked furs and silks, the delight she took in dancing, and the way she yielded herself to the wind when she galloped on her mare.

Pompon did not fail to notice his embarrassment, and she gave Jeanne a sidelong look that seemed to say, "Didn't I say that he was wild about you?"

Before leaving for Châtillon Jeanne wanted to visit the law court and was amused to read the list of fines posted in one of the corridors.

> For a counselor wearing a knotted wig: One dinner.
> For bringing a dog into the great hall: One dinner.
> For sleeping during an audience: One dinner.

There was a long list of such misdemeanors, each one punished by the fine of a dinner. Having decided upon this penalty, judges and lawyers dined well all year long.

"That's how my brother has managed to survive the diet his wife imposes upon him," remarked Louis-Antoine. "He makes up for it with dinners at the inn fifty times a year."

The day at Trévoux had been so pleasant that on the way home Jeanne, warming up to Louis-Antoine, decided to share her two passions—botany and geography. Louis-Antoine listened politely but, even while he looked at her with attentive eyes, she felt that his mind was wandering, perhaps planning the menu of the dinner that he had to give as a fine for having written the word *bordello* instead of brothel in an official report. As she tried to reveal the beauties of *Viola cornuta*, the horned violet, and the delights of l'Ile de France, his eyes were glazing over. He masked his indifference under a grave mien. Barely hiding her disappointment, Jeanne changed the subject to the great hunt at Charmont, which was to take place the day after the morrow.

* * * *

The three-day festivities at Charmont took place every year at the end of April, before Captain de Bouhey went off to join his regiment. They cost the dowager baroness a pretty penny, plus considerable commotion. There were sixty guests at supper the first evening, and at least thirty were still there for the evening of the third and last day.

Starting the week before, peasant women streamed in to offer their services and were set to work opening up, sweeping, waxing, beating mattresses, and making beds in rooms unused during the rest of the year. The château was cleansed of mice, spiders, and accumulated dust. The laundryman from Bourg came to rent faultlessly starched table linen. And, after him, came Florimond, the master chef, descending upon the premises with his assistants and his cooking utensils.

They took over the kitchen and pantry, ignoring the housekeeper, catapulting Tatan out of their path, terrorizing Bellotte and Nanette, recruiting Bouchoux, Longchamp, and Thomas to do their errands, enlisting peasant women to kill and pluck poultry, to wash and dry dishes. They ransacked cupboards and bins, jeered at the paucity of pots and pans and shouted out, at intervals: "Onto the stove!" or "Into the sink!" In short, they invaded the château as if it were enemy ground, starved out the regular staff until the eve of the festivities, rejected their laments and, like temperamental artists, threatened to leave them in the lurch if anything was put in their way.

Finally, when everything was in motion, the great Florimond complained that he was "short of everything" in spite of the fact that he had been furnished with six sheep, one calf, sixty pounds of beef, fifty chickens and ducks, a pile of pigeons, eight hams, a tank of shrimp, eels, pike, and carp, a wheel of Gruyère cheese, butter, lard, cream, sugar, flour, eggs, the vinegar and wine for making a court bouillon, liqueurs, extracts, spices, raisins, green walnuts, Italian almonds, and everything else a cook could desire.

Still, Florimond was not "satisfied," he insisted on chocolate from Arnaud in Lyon, who got it from Oufroy of Paris. And Oufroy's chocolate was the only one "suitable" for special desserts. So Thomas *must be* dispatched to Lyon, twenty-five miles away; otherwise Florimond would wash his hands of the whole thing!

Mme. de Bouhey displayed her annual fit of bad temper, after which, humiliated, she sent Thomas to Lyon and shut herself up in her bedroom with a rosemary poultice. After all, she couldn't afford to antagonize the chef on the eve of a supper to which sixty guests had been invited.

"*Tout pour la tripe*, everything for the belly," she sighed ironically, not for the first time.

When she removed the poultice she saw Jeanne and her grandson, Jean-François, running across the terrace and laughing. It was reassuring but, at the same time, these days, surprising to see Jeanne laugh so wholeheartedly.

The baroness had not been overwhelmingly happy when Jeanne had announced her decision to marry Duthillet. Yes, Jeanne had made a reasonable choice. But what use would reason be when she found herself naked in the conjugal bed? True, Marie-Françoise had proposed the match with Duthillet. But on this early morning, she remembered when she was a seventeen-year-old bride. . . . Across the intervening years she could still feel her handsome colonel's masculine chest crushing her bridal cross into her right breast. She admitted to herself that, on Jeanne's wedding day, she would be glad to see the ceiling of the chapel crumble and Aubriot fall at the bride's feet and cry out: "Me first! My beloved, there'll be time later for your husband."

"I deserve to have a headache," she said to herself. "My imaginings are as wild as those of a fifteen-year-old girl."

CHAPTER 5

eanne ran down the wide path to sit on a bench assuring herself a magnificent view of the start of the hunt.

The Château of Charmont was neither very large nor very old. Colonel Jean-Charles de Bouhey's grandfather had built it in 1680 as an improvement on the dungeonlike edifice he had inherited from his ancestors. As Jeanne saw it, the house was a fine but simple dwelling with seven windows on each of the two floors, square balustraded towers at each of the four corners and, over all, a mansard roof.

Seven years earlier, just before his death, Jeanne's father had replaced the original slate with green and yellow varnished tiles laid down in a herringbone pattern. This Burgundian style had given the château a gay air, especially when the regilded weathervanes turned, catching the rays of the sun.

The morning sun had not yet reached the weathervanes. It was no more than seven o'clock, but to the left, over the stables, Jeanne detected a radiant pink mist. The hunters were to have a fine day. Fifteen or more guests had begun to assemble in the drawing room, but Captain François de Bouhey never gave the signal for departure until eight o'clock.

Above the grassy slopes leading down to the plane trees, the pack was ready. It was made up of sixty big dogs from the region of Poitou, black-haired with tan-and-white spots. The dogs, silent but quivering, were held on leashes by their trainers. They stood at the ready, behind the buglers, colorfully clothed in royal blue. In the background were the ladies' and gentlemen's horses—twenty-four of them, led by twelve grooms.

At this point Baron de Bouhey appeared, flanked by his two sons, all of them in splendid blue coats trimmed with silver braid, tan cashmere vests, and bucket-top boots, holding their tricorne hats under their arms and, with a simultaneous gesture, clapping them on their heads. Then Charles and Jean-François moved aside so their father could offer his arm to the Marquise de la Pommeraie, who stepped forward to join him. Behind this couple the hunters filed across the terrace, twenty-one of them according to Jeanne's count: eighteen men in brown or tan coats and three ladies in dark skirts and brightly colored, fur-edged jackets.

Alongside the group from the château there were five neighbors, among them the pretty Countess de Saint-Girod, wearing a purple jacket trimmed with marten. The priest from Chapaize went to join her. Soon all the ladies had mounted, while the gentlemen waited in close formation, their boots rubbing one another. The picture was a feast to the eyes, and Jeanne drank it in with sensual enjoyment.

Departure seemed imminent, and Jeanne wondered why, this year, Pauline de Vaux-Jailloux had not joined the hunting party. Her cart was conspicuously absent. Pauline de Vaux-Jailloux always followed the hunt in a light pleasure cart drawn by two beribboned white horses and driven by a pale, handsome twenty-year-old youth, who was the subject of much gossip.

As though on cue, the cart rounded the corner of the château and made a graceful turn in the courtyard. The lady Pauline leaned out of the door and shook her handkerchief in response to the doffed hats which greeted her arrival.

At the same moment, Jeanne was distracted by the sound of a galloping horse coming down the road from Neuville. The rider was heading for Charmont. He rode straight through the circle of plane trees, without any regard for Jeanne, who was sitting among them. As he approached the baron, he slowed his bay horse and fell into line, just in front of Pauline, who leaned out again from her cart to favor him with a lovely smile.

Jeanne had never seen this casually elegant rider before. His pearl-gray coat was a model of its kind. He had such a perfect seat he seemed more like a centaur than a man on horseback. Only steel-sprung knees could have enabled him to rein in his galloping mount so suddenly and keep him under total control.

Who was this man? Pauline's lover? Jeanne's reverie was suddenly interrupted. Baron de Bouhey had given a signal to Baudouin, the hunt master. The horns sounded a fanfare, and the procession got under way.

From her balcony Mme. de Bouhey, enveloped in a shawl, waved a lace handkerchief. At the second-floor windows ladies still in their nightcaps motioned with their hands, while on the terrace the servants devoured the spectacle with smiling eyes.

Jeanne went back up the path between the trees, feeling somewhat sad as the retreating sound of the music finally faded away. Philibert and she had admired the beauty of the deer drinking from the pond at dawn. With her passion for riding in all weathers she would have pursued a deer without frightening him. But the others, as she knew, must have their deer dead. Jeannette could not bring herself to participate in this grim game. But she nevertheless felt left out when she witnessed the departure of the hunters. Now, when she saw that no one was left on the terrace, she quickened her pace.

* * * *

Jeanne's long, thick, wheat-blond hair, with its gold and chestnut strands, would have shown to advantage simply hanging down her back, tied with a ribbon, or gathered into a net. But fashion willed otherwise. And so on festive occasions she felt obliged to submit to the torture inflicted by Le Niçois, an artist-hairdresser who had won both fame and fortune. He had arrived at eight o'clock, but by nine he had the desperate air of a man who would never have enough time to give his attention to all the heads that needed his deft touch. At the moment, he was flitting around the baroness, making her head reel with his fussy gestures and gossipy chatter.

Le Niçois' specialty, after curling and frosting, was passing along the latest gossip from Paris. He himself was the first to be amused—telling scandalous stories in a whisper, with frequent omissions, mumbling names with hypocritical discretion, repeating pungent phrases with suspenseful punch lines, laughing joyfully all along.

"They say, madame—but of course I wasn't present with a lighted candle—that Grandval has had the Duchess of Msssuust. This lady invited him to her house under the pretext of showing him her portrait gallery, ha, ha, ha! When she felt herself giving way she sighed, with one eye on the portraits: 'What would my ancestors say if they saw me in your arms?' And the great actor of the Comédie Française answered: 'Madame, they'd say you were a trol—!' Ha, ha, ha! . . . Now, if madame were to be so kind as to turn her head. Mademoiselle Pompon, is there a hand mirror with which to show the baroness the back of her head?"

Even before he had put down the mirror the hairdresser laughed again and launched upon another story.

"What just happened to Maisonneuve is excruciatingly funny. While she was playing La Gouvernante, the young lady, all afire with her role, fell down and exposed her . . . The public was delighted and cheered the actress's . . . And, to the joy of the makers of fine underwear, there's going to be a decree making it obligatory to wear panties on the stage. Can't you just see a police commissioner sending his men to the theater to verify? Hee, hee! . . . Now, here's a pretty little head all ready to be powdered. What does madame say?"

Marie-Françoise, sitting before her flounced dressing table, submitted good-humoredly to the hairdresser's comb, curling iron, and flood of gossip. The result of her martyrdom gave her satisfaction. He knew how to create an array of curls like those of Mme. Pompadour, which was most becoming to her.

"What do you say, Pompon?" she asked.

At that moment the hairdresser came out with a succession of despairing cries. "Lord help us, mademoiselle, your *hair!*"

The words were addressed to Jeanne, who had just entered the room.

"So beautiful, mademoiselle, and yet how you neglect it! But we'll fix that, won't we?"

"Yes," Jeanne sighed. "We'll pull it, burn it, grease it, and then plaster it down."

"Oh, mademoiselle!" the hairdresser exclaimed reproachfully.

"Madame's head is a thing of beauty," Jeanne said to console him.

Pompon picked up a spray, filled it with orange-blossom toilet water and sprinkled her mistress's head. A delicious, sweet fragrance filled the room, and the baroness fanned herself in order to spread the wonderful smell. Then she applied rouge to her cheeks and one beauty spot on her forehead. For festive occasions, she liked her hair to be "frosted."

"Wouldn't you like to do Mademoiselle Jeanne's hair next, and then powder us both together afterward?" she asked the hairdresser.

"That would be my pleasure, madame."

"Very good," said Jeanne, "I'm ready, but I insist—no tight curls. I want you to make me long curls that will fall over my neck, in the English fashion."

"I see that mademoiselle has followed the beauty advice in the *Mercure.* She wants tomorrow's style today," cooed the hairdresser delightedly.

Three hours later he had four heads ready to be sprinkled, those of the baroness, Jeanne, and two lady guests, Mme. Rocher de Chazot and Viscountess de Chanas. The four of them, swathed in long dressing gowns, made their way in single file toward the stairs. Behind them came the hairdresser, carrying a big powder puff, followed by his assistant with a bucket of flour. Since, on this particular day, Marie-Françoise was inclined to be wasteful and knew that there were plenty of servants to clean up the floor, she installed her little group on the ground level, at the foot of the stairwell, where they covered their faces with cardboard cones. From the head of the stairs Le Niçois looked down solemnly at his victims.

"Are the ladies ready?" he called out in stentorian tones.

He plunged his arms into the flour and, with the gestures of an orchestra conductor, scattered it from the puff onto the heads below. The powder descended gently on the still sticky curls, which grew steadily whiter and whiter.

"You see," said the hairdresser, his eyes teary from the white dust, "there's no other system. There's a waste of flour, to be sure, but the frost effect can be produced no other way. If you throw the flour up at the low ceiling of a small room it doesn't fall from a great enough height or have sufficient space in which to scatter. True frost must fall from . . . shall we say, the heavens. Ladies, it's nearly done. If you'll raise your heads toward me, ever so slightly . . . There we are! The result is exquisite. Exquisitely natural!"

He himself was covered with flour like a fish ready to be tossed into the frying pan, and the ladies' four heads were like meringues. The effect was supremely becoming to the baroness and to the faded face of Mme. Rocher de Chazot. But the Viscountess, with her round, pink cheeks, looked like a Dresden doll. As for Jeanne, the frosting did her no harm; her natural beauty could withstand the most extravagant fashion.

When the flour was no longer falling, Mlle. Sergent sent two maids to clean up the mess at the foot of the stairs.

"A shame, I call it," said one of them to the other, "to waste flour that should have gone into breadmaking. There must be three pounds of it here on the floor, without counting what went on the ladies' heads and what stuck to the hairdresser. Bellotte could have made it into three loaves, at least."

"Today you have to be really down and out not to be frosted at least on Sunday," said Le Niçois, who was dancing around his artistic creations. "On Sunday, in Paris, you don't see a single hair that's kept its natural color, not even on the head of a porter. In Paris white's in style. They've even whitewashed Notre Dame. Hee, hee! The cathedral gets the same treatment as a lady!"

"We're an extravagant people," said the baroness. "We're willing to exchange buckets of money for hairdressers' buckets of flour."

Old Count Pazevin, arriving upon the scene, declared: "Don't let's be hard on our hairdressers. Without them Europe wouldn't be French. The regiment from Limousin got itself beaten in Prussia, but the men of Provence, who came after, armed with razors and powder puffs, caused every head to bow before them. All the way to the depths of Russia, France rules, not by merit of its generals, but by that of its cooks and hairdressers. The two professions are matched equally in fame, power, and tyranny.

"And now, professor," he added, turning to Le Niçois, "have the ladies left you enough time to freshen up my wig?"

CHAPTER 6

he hunters returned at dusk, muddied, weary, and happy, having galloped their fill through woods and marshes, jumped hedges and ditches, splattered themselves with the heavy soil of the fields, torn their habits on woodland brambles and worn their horses to a frazzle, all for the unspeakable pleasure of two kills. In a Bernardine priory, between the boar and the deer courses, they ate a stand-up lunch of tender mutton chops and a wine from Vougeot. The priest of Chapaize and the Marquise de la Pommeraie, both connoisseurs, were still talking about the wine in the interval before supper.

"God help us," Jeanne said to herself, "when are we ever going to dance?" She excused herself and went to greet her friend Marie de Rupert, who had just arrived with her mother.

Marie was graceful rather than pretty. She was a quiet and cultivated girl who had acquired from Jeanne an interest in botany. They collected herbs together and exchanged ideas, both of them happy to have found a confidante of her own age.

"Too bad that your fiancé can't see you this evening," Marie said to Jeanne as soon as they met.

The surrogate had been detained at Lyon by the settlement of a complicated will. Jeanne preened herself.

"Do you think I look so very well?"

"Prettier than ever, and it's not surprising. A fiancé does wonders for a girl's looks, even when he's not here. That is," she added, with a touch of melancholy, "when you don't have to wait too long for him."

Jeanne squeezed her hand. Marie had been promised to a distant cousin, Philippe Chabaud de Jasseron. She was genuinely in love. The dashing twenty-year-old lieutenant was waiting in Paris for the chance to acquire a captaincy. Marie's mother, Madame de Rupert, would not let them wed until Philippe's rank was secured. Unfortunately, the demand was greater than the supply, and Marie spoke of the end of war as "the threat of peace." "Well," said Jeanne consolingly, "tonight there'll be two of us unescorted. Let's see who's available."

Of her two silk gowns, Jeanne had chosen the one whose red and white stripes harmonized with her frosted hair. The artificiality of her hair was not displeasing because its whiteness was set off by the tiny red arrows on her dress. Her tight bodice outlined a discernible soft curve. She saw herself so much a woman that she had plucked a beauty spot from the baroness's dressing table and playfully stuck it on her dimpled cheek. Then she had drawn a blue pencil over two veins in her forehead. The effect was one of blue blood coursing under a delicate skin.

Amid a rustle of silks the company moved forward to the supper table. Suddenly a man detached himself from a group of dawdlers and walked across the room, joining the other guests. Jeanne started with recognition. This morning she had had only a glimpse of the man on horseback. Now he was in full view. To satisfy her curiosity, she eavesdropped on Count Pazevin and the handsome stranger, discovering that he was the notorious Chevalier Vincent. The count detained him under the light of a candelabrum.

The Knight of Malta had broad shoulders and a powerful chest. The most attractive things about him were the ease of his walk and manner, the contrast between his white teeth and his wind-tanned face, and his dark red lips that seemed to be of Moorish origin. There was a soft gleam in his coffee-brown eyes.

They haven't the fire of Philibert's. But perhaps they're more tender. Suddenly she blushed with shame for having made such a comparison. She transferred her interest from the newcomer's looks to his dress.

Again, as in the morning, his coat was gray. The cut, new to the provinces, was like that of an English frock coat. It was unpleated and very tight, sculpting his back and waist, while opening wide over a pair of equally clinging gray breeches, which revealed a flat stomach and long, hard thighs. This new Parisian style of breeches with a flap front left nothing to the imagination. Under his coat he wore a short, embroidered canary yellow vest with the gold chains of two fob watches draped over it. Jeanne had never seen such handsome and original shoe buckles, very large and seemingly of yellow jasper framed by filigree silver. To emphasize certain gestures he made use of a tassled handkerchief. Such elegance, refined and at the same time almost flashy, was overshadowed by the fact that he was a corsair.

A corsair! Jeanne was intoxicated by this word, which called up the indigo blue of the sea and the island of Malta which excited her imagination as well. She conjured up images of an enchanted isle with an African climate: an Ali Baba's cave filled with spices and jewels, silks and rugs, many-colored calicoes and exotic fruits, flavored by the sun. The port of Valletta was the nearest Oriental bazaar to France. Jeanne imagined that anyone coming from there was impregnated with the fragrance of the East.

She was startled out of her dream by the pressure of Marie's hand on her arm.

"Aren't you coming to supper? I thought you were just behind me, but I see now what kept you. He certainly is handsome. Luckily he still dances. He's thirty years old, but he doesn't give a hoot for conventions. His is a libertine spirit."

"You seem to know him," said Jeanne.

"I know everything about the Chevalier Vincent," answered Marie, smiling. "You know that he and Madame de Vaux-Jailloux . . . Well, she and my mother are friends, and I listen. Pauline spends most of her time alone. The chevalier is seldom in Europe in the spring, but this year it seems that he has business at Versailles with Monsieur de Choiseul."

"But he doesn't belong to the Royal Navy, does he?"

"Yes. From time to time the Order lends him to the king. It seems that the Duke de Choiseul wanted to keep him. But he wasn't willing. The minister needs privateers now that his fleet has been decimated by the English."

"By the way," asked Jeanne, "what's his full name? I've never heard it."

Marie laughed, in the same cooing fashion as her mother. "Vincent de Cotignac. He was born in the village of that name, just north of Toulon."

"I know that village. Gerard, a botanist friend of Monsieur Philibert, lives there. But I didn't know there was a lord of Cotignac."

"Vincent is not the lord of Cotignac but his adopted son."

She cast an eye toward the door and squeezed Jeanne's arm. "Let's go to supper. It's already too late to find the places we want. The story of the Chevalier Vincent is a long one. . . ."

The great room hummed with anticipatory pleasure. A gay, slightly out-of-tune melody from a comic opera by Philidor floated in from the yellow-and-lilac drawing room where the baroness had installed the musicians.

For major receptions a large room on the ground floor, usually closed off, was put into service as a dining room. The decoration went back to the time of the original builder. The walls were covered with light brown Cordova leather. The vaulted ceiling was green, with muted gold trimmings. Three tables were set with twenty places each. A flaming fire in the pink stone fireplace, a glittering candelabrum, and a profusion of carved torches made for a gala atmosphere. Four voluminous bouquets, pink and white carnations from the greenhouse, branches of pussywillow and sweetbrier, tulips of every color, narcissus, primroses, clusters of lilacs, and flaming broom, arranged by Jeanne, brought springtime to the corners of the room. As the guests entered, they drew in their breath and then exclaimed with enjoyment.

Since the seating was unassigned, Jeanne and Marie made their way toward a group of young people, pausing to observe the customary commotion around the chair of Pauline de Vaux-Jailloux.

She had been born in San Domingo to a French officer and a Caribbean maiden. Her Creole beauty was as attractive to men as honey to a bee. Her gown was designed to reveal three-quarters of her breasts. Jeanne noticed, with a certain irritation, that the Chevalier Vincent had seated himself directly across from her, thus adding esthetic and sensual enjoyment to that of his supper.

"Apparently," Jeanne said to Marie, "six years have not dulled the chevalier's passion. It's true that she provides him with a very pleasant pied-à-terre. The Château de Vaux is a comfortable house with a newly furnished drawing room, two baths, and a first-class cook. Very attractive indeed to a man when he returns from traveling the seven seas!"

"You're a bit malicious, aren't you?" exclaimed Marie. "You make it sound as if, where Pauline is concerned, the chevalier had purely utilitarian designs."

"Well, how old is she? Older than he, I warrant."

"She's thirty-six. But I predict that Pauline will never grow old, unless in the manner of Ninon de Lenclos, surrounded by faithful admirers. Her attraction never fails."

"I suppose not," said Jeanne out of the corner of her mouth. "There *are* men, I suppose, who like slightly worn goods."

Marie looked hard at her friend. "Why, are you jealous? You speak as poorly of Vincent's Pauline as you have of Philibert's Marguerite."

"Oh, I like to tease. You know that. Don't hold it against me. You promised to tell me more about the chevalier. . . ."

Soups and ragouts were being served, and the hungry young hunters went for casseroles of chicken, eggs, and vegetables. The two girls took a creamy shrimp stew. Marie leaned over to talk to Jeanne.

"I told you that Vincent was born at Cotignac. But his birth took place very discreetly in a room of the Abbey of Notre-Dame-des-Grâces. His father's identity has remained unknown. His mother is rumored to come from a noble family. No name has been given her, but people have said . . ."

"People have said . . . ?"

"The most romantic things! Certain peasants engaged in picking olives claim to have seen a dark-skinned young woman nursing her baby and covering him with kisses and tears in the abbey garden. One of them has sworn he knew her and that she was a descendant of the famous Misson. If that's true it's no wonder Vincent has so much success as a corsair. He came by it rightfully."

"And who was Misson?"

"The great pirate of Provence in the days of Louis XIV. Of noble birth, a bastard himself, he fathered an illegitimate son before leaving Marseille. This child was Vincent's maternal grandfather. If the legend has it right, Misson was an exceptional pirate, famous for the size of his treasure and also for his gallant and humane spirit. He flew a white flag with 'liberty' inscribed on it instead of a black flag with a skull-and-crossbones. In short he was a pirate philosopher."

Jeanne smiled ironically. "He laid hands on other men's ships, however. The pirate may have been a philosopher, but the philosopher was a pirate as well."

"He knew his business," said Marie. "But he conducted it honestly."

" 'Honestly'! There's a fine word for a pirate!"

"That's exact. He took cargoes and let ships go."

"And gave the ladies back their jewels?"

"That I don't know," admitted Marie. "But I do know, at least Pauline says, that he freed some slaves who were aboard one of his captured vessels. Vincent got into trouble with the grand master of his Order for doing something similar, freeing some Negro slaves. Perhaps he was inspired by his ancestor."

"Does he really believe that he's a descendant?"

Marie shrugged her shoulders. "Pauline says that Vincent's secretive on this point. He's very sensitive about his mother. She disappeared. When he was three months old he was handed over, together with a bundle of money, to the priest at Cotignac, who consented to bring him up. At eight years of age he was taken in by the Knights of Malta, perhaps through the offices of some secret protector. He was a brilliant student of the humanities, and also of mathematics, astronomy, and drawing. When he was fifteen he set sail on a ship of the king's navy. He won immediate recognition. He was a born sailor, one of those who have a 'sixth sense' for the sea."

"But since he was in the Royal Navy, why did he go over to the corsairs?"

"He's ambitious. And, as a corsair, he soon attained command of a ship and great wealth."

"I still don't see how he entered the Order of the Knights of Malta. How could he prove noble birth without a father or mother? Did his father reappear?"

"No. At least not openly. Vincent is a knight not by right but by special concession. The Order takes in a certain number of common-ers who are judged to possess uncommon merits. Vincent's taste is for money, not great sea battles."

Jeanne raised her eyebrows in astonishment. But Marie could not continue, for the servants were bringing on the main dishes. Soups and grilled salmon gave way to creamed turbot, eels in a tartar sauce, chicken breasts with mushrooms, a ragout of duck, and candied squab stuffed with chocolate.

The company was now highly animated. The sound of the violins could barely be heard above the chatter. Once again Baroness de Bouhey had entertained with success, offering succulent fare amid tasteful surroundings. Her guests, in return, testified to their enjoyment, with their *gourmandise*, their elegance and wit. Silks and velvets, lace and embroidery, gold and silver trimmings, the sparkle of diamonds and other precious stones produced an array of luxury, to which the frosted heads of the ladies added an extra note of refinement.

Jeanne wanted to slip the baroness a congratulatory smile, but could not catch her eye. Seated at the far end of the room, she was talking to her neighbor, Marquis Caracciolo of Naples. At the hostess's table were Vincent and Pauline. Flanked on one side by Pazevin the shipbuilder, and on the other by the prosecutor-general, Basset de la Marelle, it seemed as if these two gentlemen had gallantly prearranged to wear black and green velvet in order to bring out the luster of Pauline's peach-blossom satin bodice. She drew glances from all the men just as Vincent drew them from the women. The two lovers shared their popularity in equal measure.

"They annoy me," Jeanne said to herself for the second time, and for the second time with no good reason. She forced herself to transfer her attention to Marie, who was devouring an eel.

"Keep your appetite for the roast," she said sternly. "When you eat you can't talk. And I want to know why flight from battle is a good quality in a corsair. Perhaps this Vincent is a coward."

"I didn't speak of flight, but of prudence," said Marie, regretfully leaving her eel. "From what Pauline tells me, it's a corsair's job to take over a cargo without destroying the ship. The Knights of Malta are interested less in glory than in merchandise. So, logically enough, they prefer prudence to indiscriminate gunning."

"So the handsome Vincent is a seafaring grocer, is he?"

"You might call him that," said Marie. "He's a rich man, that's certain. He's just built himself a frigate of the finest wood, with the finest sailcloth and the finest cordage. A dream boat, they say, and he's madly in love with it."

"Can a Knight of Malta have a ship of his own?"

"They say that there's no limits to the knights' rights, as long as the grand master of the Order gets ten percent of all their gains on land and sea. The grand master has heavy expenses, and needs money to meet them. The Order does good works and, at the same time, the members have a taste for magnificence. That's obvious, isn't it? Isn't the knight we have with us a model of elegance?"

"I love it!" Jeanne exclaimed so forthrightly that Marie burst into laughter. Because her cooing laugh was contagious, Jeanne joined in it and so did their table companions, without asking why. By this time everyone had drunk a good deal of wine.

A great roast was set down at the center of the table. Around it were patties containing bone marrow, sweetbreads, and a ham mousse. Roast meats were not yet customarily served in this fashion, and the guests quickly abandoned the braised carp and fried gudgeon at both ends of the table to fix their attention on chef Florimond's new masterpiece. Jeanne bit distractedly into a patty.

Thank the Lord, the longest supper winds up with dessert. Jeanne called for Spanish wine to go with the floating island. As the banquet drew to a close, three or four of the waiters were staggering, after finishing off the wine left in half-empty glasses. One of them, young, dark-haired, with almost girlish good looks, wore a bemused, beatific smile. Jeanne found him interesting and asked Marie if she knew him.

"That's Mario," her friend informed her, "Vincent's valet. If his master spots him in this condition he'll get a whipping. Mario was an orphan at Cotignac. Vincent took him aboard his first ship as a deck boy. But the boy got seasick and dizzy and couldn't climb up in the rigging. So Vincent made him into his personal servant. Mario is his master's shadow and never lets him out of his sight. Pauline is jealous. She claims that he bathes and dresses the chevalier with a lover's hands."

"Perhaps Mario is a girl dressed as a boy," Jeanne suggested. "I'd be glad to disguise myself that way for the sake of going to sea."

"Jeanne, you've always let the sea run away with your imagination. The life of a woman on a corsair's ship . . ."

The music, a gavotte rhythm, was coming from the ballroom while, in the supper room, many women were still seated freshening their makeup. Rouge boxes and beauty spots were laid out on the table before them. Countess de Saint-Girod reached out to tug at Jeanne's arm.

"You'll be seeing Dr. Aubriot before I do, because I'm off to Italy. Would you give him this sheet of paper which he dropped at my house?"

Out of a pocket she pulled a folded sheet which she handed to Jeanne, adding with a confidential air, "I asked him to come see me, to take care of my vapors. There's no hurry about the paper. It's only a personal reminder, and he has no lack of memory."

And, just as Jeanne started off, she put in a parting shot. "You must have heard that his wife has given birth to a little boy. Our Philibert must be in seventh heaven."

* * * *

Jeanne waited until she was in her own room to unfold the paper. It was a list of masculine and feminine first names, of which one, Michel-Anne, was underlined. She had a stabbing intuition that this name would be given to the baby just born at Belley. This had been the way a great scientist had spent his time as he watched his wife's belly grow.

He had jotted down possible names for his child on a piece of note-book paper, just like any villager proud of his fatherhood.

Her eyes burned as she stared at Philibert's untidy writing, studded with capital letters that were indistinct because of a scratchy pen. Her eyes were not teary but abnormally dry. Her sorrow was a hard knot in her throat. Jeanne had thought of the child as Marguerite's, not Philibert's. She now realized that Philibert had wanted and waited for a baby who would have the name of Michel-Anne. A baby who would grow into a little man and be led by his father over hill and dale, learning the names of flowers and plants along the way. She remembered how, only five years ago, Philibert had wrapped his big, warm hand around her childish one and had led her to the château's kitchen garden. Was it possible that, in the near future, he would give Michel-Anne what she no longer had?

With a brusque gesture she threw open the window, devoured by jealousy. She breathed in the night air and drank a glass of cold water. She must go downstairs. The baroness and Marie must be looking for her and Genevieve de Saint-Girod would be overjoyed at the harm she had done. To think that Philibert had held this treacherous female in his arms, had kissed her. . . .

CHAPTER 7

s Jeanne was about to pass through the door of the drawing room, she was stopped short by the sound of a man's voice. She knew at once that it belonged to the Chevalier Vincent. The mellow tone was produced by a developed larynx, no doubt of that. Gay, stimulating, harmonious, and in the medium range, it carried an invitation to places far away. Jeanne imagined him trumpeting orders into a storm.

Instead of hurrying on to the dance, impulsively she sat down behind a Japanese screen. The speakers had not noticed her and went on talking shop. Pazevin, with his splendid laurel green coat and heavily rouged cheeks, was questioning the corsair.

"Will you be sailing your *Belle Vincente* this summer?"

"I hope to take her out for a run. She's a bride, and I mean to get to know her by slow degrees. How do you like her?"

"She's a beauty. But, my dear sir, she's not a bride, she's a mistress."

"There's something to what you say, since she's my ruin. I'm left with nothing but debts."

"Bah! In this country debts signify nobility."

"In that case, I should be a duke. I've mounted twenty-four cannons, and not one of them has been paid for."

"Twenty-four cannons on a three-hundred-ton three-master? You could have mounted more."

"That's quite enough. On the high seas God isn't with the big guns. He's with the wind."

"Don't be so modest. I consider the captain of the *Belle Vincente* a good investment, regardless of the power of his artillery. If you need capital, I can find you all the investors you could need. The sea is very much in fashion."

"True," said Vincent. "Today's upper-middle class dreams of the sea, but the dreams are two hundred years behind the times. They can't forget that they lost the race against the galleons of Spain. No rich man talks with me for more than five minutes without mentioning his dream of a cargo of gold. And I avoid making an answer. I don't want to disappoint him by confessing that I gallantly let cargoes of gold and silver, with their armed naval escort, go by. I wait for a lone merchant ship and gallantly request the commander to hand over his shoes, sheets, chinaware, and plain nails."

"If you don't want businessmen associates I'd like to suggest a woman."

"Young and pretty?"

"Chevalier, I'm speaking of a business partner."

"So you say. But, in my experience, a woman who wants to speculate on a corsair's ship is half-shopkeeper, half-poet. The shopkeeper wants to make money, and the poet wants the corsair."

"Ha, ha! You've defined your profession!" said Count Pazevin, pointing his chin toward the approaching Canoness Charlotte de Bouhey, sister-in-law to the baroness.

The lively rhythm of a jig rang in Jeanne's ears, but she had no wish to budge from her hiding place. Up to now she had thought of the sea as a vast blue expanse which she would cross in her flight to some flowery botanical paradise. But Vincent's succinct words made her see

* 56 *

it as a place to live. Standing a few feet away was a man from another world, who was as at home at sea as she was on land.

"Well, Chevalier," said Dame Charlotte, "has the count told you of my ambitions? I'm tired of calculating my income on the basis of cords of wood and bushels of rye, tired of being involved in lawsuits with priests and landowners over a field or vineyard the size of a handkerchief."

"Ah, madame, who isn't involved in lawsuits? Our century is given to contention. That's why men of law eat so well."

"I can't bear the quibbling and pettifoggery over the right to the crop of wheat from a field that's been disputed ever since 1556. The fact is, there are too many people on land. Isn't it sensible to look to the sea?"

Vincent flicked his handkerchief with an air of amusement.

"Madame, you may not see it from Neuville, but the sea, too, is overpopulated."

"Come, now," said Dame Charlotte, lowering her voice, "haven't you French sailors secret routes, unknown to other navigators?"

Vincent's eyes sparkled, and he gave the canoness the benefit of his dazzling smile.

"I may surprise you, madame, but I've never watched for a trade wind that would enable me to get out of the doldrums around the equator, without seeing an English, Dutch, or Spanish ship that was sharing my watch. We Frenchmen don't realize it, but others, too, have compasses, and pilots who know how to use them. I can tell you this . . . you can find as much bad company in the Caribbean as in the Tuileries at the hour of the promenade."

Dame Charlotte would not give in. "Bad company or not, Chevalier, you go where you will. Our corsairs are the best in the world, everyone knows that."

She spoke with as much assurance as if she were writing for *La Gazette de France*. Vincent smiled drolly.

"If the English felt the same way as you do about it we shouldn't be losing our colonies," he said.

"Are we really going to lose all our business in the East Indies?" asked Basset de la Marelle, joining the trio.

A little circle formed around the shipbuilder and the corsair.

"The East Indies can't be saved," said Vincent. "It's too late."

"Our army's not to blame for the defeat," the Marquis de la Pommeraie declared trenchantly. "Lally had already lost the Indies by the weakness of his government. First he was incompetent and then he was a coward; it's as simple as that."

Vincent looked so antagonistically at the marquis that Pazevin broke in to prevent him from making a stinging reply.

"I think, my dear Marquis," he said, "that it's difficult to judge Lally's behavior unless one's been on the spot."

"He was locked in by the siege, without men or munitions or supplies," Vincent put in, "forgotten by king and country. At home there may have been no cowardice, but there was certainly neglect."

"And could the navy do nothing to raise the siege?" Viscountess de Chanas asked imprudently.

With a flick of his handkerchief Vincent removed a rose petal from his sleeve. "To what navy do you refer, madame? The English navy successfully dislodged Lally from Pondicherry. A beautiful squadron, I can tell you; fourteen ships of the line crossing and crisscrossing in the harbor. A magnificent show!"

"What's that, Chevalier?" exclaimed Mme. de Chanas. "Were you there?"

"No, but close by, madame. I saw it through field glasses."

The air was heavy with silence. Except for the ignorant and fatuous Mme. de Chanas, everyone in the little group knew that Vincent had recently come back from the Indies and had avoided questioning him about how he had escaped unharmed. But, for the moment, the corsair seemed not the least embarrassed.

"But, Chevalier," Mme. de Chanas asked in a loud voice, "how could we lose a battle in which you were involved?"

Vincent made a deep bow, as if he were enchanted by the compliment. "You see, madame," he explained patiently, as if to a child, "the result of a naval battle depends heavily on the number of ships and guns on both sides."

"I understand, Chevalier," said Mme. de Chanas, trying to look serious. "Did the French have fewer guns than the English?"

"I had sixteen," Vincent answered.

The listeners showed surprise, and Basset de la Marelle asked, "Do you mean, Chevalier, that you were alone against the English ships?"

"Solitude is a corsair's protection," said Vincent. "Often it brings him good luck, but not in the face of an enemy squadron."

"Dear Lord!" cooed Mme. de Chanas. "How does a ship's captain feel in so tragic a situation? What can be done, I ask you?"

"A madman goes to the bottom, a wise man runs away," answered Vincent, still smiling.

Useless heroism was so fashionable among the military aristocracy of Louis XV that all eyes turned away from the captain who admitted that he had no use for it. Pauline de Vaux-Jailloux saved the situation.

"Isn't it inconsiderate," she asked nonchalantly, "to talk at such length about colonial politics in the salon of Madame de Bouhey?"

"You're quite right," said Dame Charlotte. "And it's all my fault for having expressed a desire to do business with overseas France."

Marquis Caracciolo took over. "There'll never be an overseas France, madame, because there'll never be French society overseas. Why would people of a certain class bury themselves over there when their own country is the best place in the world to live?"

"There are beautiful places elsewhere," said Vincent.

"But the most beautiful place of all is the Place Vendôme!" Caracciolo exclaimed with honest enthusiasm. "Paris, sir, Paris! Can anyone who's had a taste of Paris ever leave it? It was a miserable trick on the part of nature that caused me to be born in Naples."

"Agreed," said the Abbé Galiani, Caracciolo's secretary. "Just listen to the clamor raised by the Jesuits, whom your minister is trying to expel. How well I understand them! Monsieur de Choiseul would be less cruel to hang them than to send them away. Better dead in France than alive anywhere else!"

These last remarks set off a round of gossip, accusing the Jesuits of highly irregular behavior in the dormitories of their boys' schools.

Vincent leaned over to whisper mockingly into Pauline's ear, "How very French! At opposite sides of the globe we're losing the most important war of the century, distractedly handing over a worldwide empire to the English. Yet what really interests us is a record of priestly confessions. Come, my dear, let's dance."

* * * *

Charmont's great night was ending with young people dancing chaperoned by a few ladies.

"Where have you been?" Marie asked Jeanne. "Everyone was looking for you."

Just then, the two friends were swept apart by a swirling group of young men in bright velvet breeches and satin coats. They gathered around Jeanne. By sheer chance she gave the first dance to Hector de

Chanas. As she slipped her hand into his, she shot a glance at Vincent who had just chosen to dance with Emilie de la Pommeraie.

"Even at the age of fourteen a canoness shouldn't dance," Jeanne said to herself spitefully.

She wanted Vincent. From her gold-flecked brown eyes to her soft lips, from her lips to her breasts, from her breasts to her narrow waist . . . she wanted to feel his gaze upon her. *I want him to notice me.* She nervously pressed Hector de Chanas' fingers, who could not believe his good fortune.

After Emilie, Vincent invited Marie. He seemed to be deliberately teasing Jeanne. He looked at her over her friend's head, unhurriedly, with shameless satisfaction, as if he could see through her clothes. Jeanne was outraged to feel her silk gown falling away like a piece of burned skin. *Could this handsome grocer of the sea read her mind?*

Even Denis annoyed her tonight, as he pretended to ignore her. He was the one to dance, now, with Emilie, the little comic-opera nun, and his face wore an ecstatic expression. Jeanne herself had inspired the same expression often enough to recognize it. Did this silly son of a bailiff think he had anything to offer a lady of Neuville, armed with sixteen-quarters of nobility?

In her distraction she fell out of step with the minuet, and to his surprise Charles de Bouhey had to pull Jeanne back into rhythm.

Minutes later, as the musicians began another tune and Jeanne stood listlessly facing her partner, she felt herself suddenly surrounded by two strong arms which spun her swiftly around and off into a spirited dance.

"Are you vexed because I danced with your friends before I asked you?" Vincent inquired as the rhythm slowed.

"Oh, did you? I hadn't noticed."

"Too bad," said Vincent mockingly, "that your tongue is not as honest as your eyes."

Jeanne forced herself to laugh, but without conviction.

Vincent was grinning and she responded as if he had playfully bitten her. In a flash she passed herself in review, hair, powder, rouge, beauty spot, gown, wondering if everything was still in order.

Since she did not speak, Vincent went on, "Where did you go after supper? I was looking for you, mademoiselle."

"I couldn't know that, Chevalier."

"I always seek out the most beautiful woman . . . but I can't always get to her right away. On land there are all sorts of polite hurdles before you can taste a dish at the far end of the table or touch the hand of a lovely girl. Life at sea is much simpler. If a pretty frigate passes under my nose I have only to fire a warning gun and, if she doesn't want to be hurt, she signals me to come aboard."

"The frigate is a weak sister. In her place I'd resist."

"You mean you'd sail off, leaving me the pleasure of overtaking you? The idea of overtaking *you*, mademoiselle, fills me with joy."

"You don't seem to realize, Chevalier, that I might get away."

"You might, or you might not."

As he paced and wheeled her around in time to the music, he was slowly and intensely scrutinizing her, pausing, without embarrassment, over the points that particularly pleased him. Under his searching eyes Jeanne experienced an agreeable tickling sensation all over.

"Well, then?" she asked flirtatiously.

"Hmm," he said. "I shouldn't be too sure of my triumph. Long slender ships are often capricious. Their speed depends on a number of factors, some of them unknown. But it's hard to predict which of these will come into play during the first hour of the chase. And now, mademoiselle, shall we continue this trifling, or wouldn't it make more sense to go flirt behind a screen?"

"Oh!"

"Don't assume a shocked air. You must have hoped that, as a corsair, I'd be audacious. Ready yourself to forgive my audacity. I intend to court you—and they've told me that my approach is very direct."

"Who has told you that?"

"Pretty hypocrites, of course."

She laughed gaily.

"I'm going to adore making you laugh. You laugh with gusto and you dance with gusto. Unfortunately I had my back turned to you at the table. Do you eat with gusto as well?"

"When there's something I care for. Speaking of food, take me to look for a sherbet. Florimond made one flavored with blackcurrants."

Vincent chose one with mint.

"Now let's chat," said Jeanne, when they had cooled their throats. "I want to go to my favorite place to hear you talk about the sea."

Vincent followed her to the library, a large room, severe and welcoming at the same time. The walls were lined with bookcases of dark oak with grille doors. On this unusually lively night two corners were lit up and occupied by card players. But the corner picked out by Jeanne remained in the shadows and lent itself to confidences.

"This is my favorite place for dreaming," said Jeanne, pointing to the heavy Regency sofa.

She was accustomed to lingering there for hours with a pile of books beside her, dipping into one after another, leaning her head against the back of the sofa to savor a sentence which stimulated her imagination, breathing in the odor of leather from the four thousand bindings, the odor that spoke of an immense store of dreams.

"Tell me about the great world," she said abruptly. "Tell me of lands beyond the seas."

"You embarrass me," he answered with a mock-humble air. "Young girls have turned into bluestockings. They question me about the points of the compass, the astrolabe, the tides, the thirty-three-pounder cannon, the latitude of l'Ile de Bourbon, the average speed of a three-master, and Lord knows what else. One day they'll be knocking at the doors of the Ecole Militaire and the Academy of Science."

"Of course. Why not? Science is much more amusing than embroidery."

"Frankly, my dear, looking so beautiful in your ball gown, it is unreasonable to ask me for a geography lesson. Wouldn't both of us prefer that I speak of your golden eyes? Besides, I'm not the one to ask about distant lands. I'm a homebody."

Jeanne stifled a laugh in her handkerchief so as not to disturb the card players.

"Yes, believe me," said Vincent. "The only country a sailor really knows is the sea. I go from port to port, and between stops there is nothing but sea. My nest is there. Shall I tell you about the captain's cabin? It's so small that I know every inch of it by heart."

"But you've just got yourself a new ship."

"Yes, I think the luxurious *Belle Vincente* would appeal to you. And since a clever, pretty girl is always welcome in the captain's cabin, I invite you to come see it. The *Belle Vincente* is moored at Marseille, which isn't far. Come soon, and I'll take you with me. You'll see the world with your own eyes."

"Madness!" exclaimed Jeanne, with a smile.

"Why so? When you dream of far countries don't you see yourself embarking on the ship that will take you there?"

"Oh, Chevalier, if you knew how often I've had just such a dream!"

Jeanne

Her response was so passionate that he looked at her long and hard. A tête-à-tête flirtation is a succession of moments. With a look, a smile, a gesture, a word, there suddenly comes a time when the participants cease playing. Vincent knew all the games. He also knew when to seize the moment, passing into something deeper and more concrete. He lowered his voice.

"Jeanne," he asked, "have you ever *seen* the sea?"

She shivered when he called her by her first name. He had totally disarmed her. Still a little girl, she longed to tell her dreams to this passing stranger who was suddenly so close.

"The sea . . ." she began slowly. "I've seen the sea only in paintings. But my head is full of it. I don't know how it's happened, but the sea is, for me, a novel without end."

"The sea *is* a novel without end. A sailor is always starting out and never arriving."

"But I do arrive! In the Indian Ocean. That's where the sea usually carries me."

Vincent shook his head. "The sea carries you nowhere. You have to force its hand. If it's the road most fascinating to man, it's also the most difficult."

"Is that why you love it?"

"That's one of the reasons. Nothing can prevail against love of the sea. To me it's like opium. The farther I am from my ship the greater my need to return to it. I dance as impatiently on land as the waves dance in the port."

Vincent fell silent. Looking into the moonless night outside the library door, he smiled to himself. The silence continued, but it was so much a part of their conversation that when Vincent spoke again it was in a very low voice.

"You see, Jeanne, there are three sorts of men, the living, the dead, and those that go to sea. The Greek who said that must have lived long at sea. He had learned how you can change your entire being without having to die."

"Change your entire being . . ."

Vincent's phrase struck a familiar chord. "Change your entire being . . ." she repeated. "To land in a new country, to be renewed. I've dreamed often of that, too, Chevalier. Is it possible, after all?"

"It is, I promise! And I'm ready to keep my word. Come away with me, and I'll sail you to the Southern Hemisphere. There, night after

* 63 *

night, you can see the pole star sinking gently into the horizon and your body will acquire a new soul. The Jeanne that you know so well will be swallowed up in the sea. At sea there's neither past nor future. Landsmen divide time into a past and a future. They linger over their regrets or escape into their dreams. At sea you have to live in the present, trimming your sails according to the wind."

"And does a perpetual present make you happy?"

"Yes, it frees you."

"Frees you from what?"

"From yesterday and from tomorrow. The sea brings you up against realities. Propitious or unpropitious, they're concrete. I like the concrete. I'm an epicurean."

"Yes, I dream too much," Jeanne admitted. "I know it. My dreams drag me down, strangle and stifle me and don't give me the pleasure they once did. Here, on this sofa, I lived a life of fantasy with which I was entirely satisfied. Now I'm bored. Suddenly this corner, this refuge, seems to be a prison. I have pins and needles in my legs and a feeling of constriction in my chest. I'm here, daydreaming, instead of going somewhere where there's real life, where the joy of living isn't just fantasy, where . . ."

Her raised hands, with the palms turned upward, groped at the air as if to catch it with her fingers. With a touch of humor she finished her sentence, ". . . where happiness is a shining fish, to be caught and greedily eaten."

Then, looking at Vincent, she added, "You're laughing at me, of course, and you're quite right to do so. What I've been saying is ridiculous."

"I'm not laughing. I'm smiling. There's quite a difference."

"I know that I shouldn't have allowed myself to say such silly things. If Madame de Saint-Girod had heard me she'd say that Rousseau should be burned at the stake for having written *La Nouvelle Héloïse*, where young girls find encouragement for their silly talk. But this time the fault is yours . . . yes, yours. Do you realize how you talk about the sea? You make it sound like a place where happiness is at one's fingertips. Listening to you I wanted to reach out and touch happiness, like a cat, a peach, a rose. *You* are responsible."

Vincent looked at her with an expression of mingled irony and tenderness. Jeanne was silent, breathing a trifle heavily and staring at the points of her red satin shoes.

He leaned over, took her hand, and carried it to his lips, moving them gently over her wrist and the length of her arm to the vein beating in the soft, warm crook of her elbow. Jeanne let her arm lie limp, numbed by the tingling sensation which rose to her head. Behind the sofa's high back, the card players' conversation buzzed on.

She sighed with well-being, while Vincent's barely opened lips lingered damply on her skin. Jeanne's eyes were on his bent, bewigged head. She had an impulse to tear off his wig and run her fingers through his hair.

The thought of Pauline brought Jeanne down to earth. Brusquely she drew back her arm.

"Madame de Vaux-Jailloux wouldn't have liked to see that," she said in a voice she hoped sounded icy.

"Madame de Vaux-Jailloux never sees anything she oughtn't to see," Vincent answered calmly. "She has a perfect heart."

"And you, Chevalier?"

"My heart has, I hope, some merits."

"If you're speaking of its size, I grant you a point. It can hold a number of feelings at one time."

"Dear girl, are you paying me the honor of a jealous scene?"

"Chevalier, now you're the one that's dreaming. We can be jealous only of someone we want to possess. I don't want to possess you. Besides, I belong to another man."

"Oh!" exclaimed Vincent, raising an eyebrow. "And where might he be?"

"Traveling on business. We're engaged, and our marriage will take place in September."

"Oh, I see!"

"That's why," she went on, playing her part, "I must ask you to stop your little game . . ."

"Oh!" he exclaimed for the third time.

" 'Oh! Oh! Oh! Oh!' Is that all you have to say?"

"Yes."

Again he concentrated the whole weight of his scrutiny upon her, and again she felt herself give way.

"Jeanne, how old are you?" he asked.

"Fifteen," she said, unable to refrain from making a reply.

"I'd have said you were twelve. You don't understand men's ways, or else you'd know that I wasn't playing a game. You'd know to take my kiss seriously. You'd know, too, that the only thing I want is to kiss you again. Can't you see, darling, that I want to so badly that I'm capable of acting like a savage?"

The unexpected "darling" sent a strange shiver through Jeanne's whole body. Momentarily she was struck deaf, and picked up what Vincent was saying only in the middle of his next sentence.

". . . and that I'm more and more serious about my offer to take you away. Look here, I'll give you two days to pack your things. It's far too much wasted time, but I can postpone leaving until the day after tomorrow. Although, really . . ."

He slipped a firm hand under her chin. "There's no reason you can't be ready tomorrow. At dawn, which is coming on fast."

Jeanne freed her head and tried with difficulty to gather her scattered wits.

"Chevalier," she said weakly, "why must you mock me? Plainly, you can't be serious about running off with another man's fiancée? You've known me for scarcely more than an hour."

"How long do you think it takes me to appreciate a pretty girl and to know that I want her? As for your belonging to another man, every catch I make is the property of someone else. That doesn't bother me in the least."

"You're mad, Chevalier," said Jeanne, trying to rise.

He had no trouble holding her back. "Mad, if you like," he admitted, "but not bad, believe me."

He leaned her comfortably against the back of the sofa, imprisoned her in his arms and lowered his smiling face to hers. She shut her eyes. When she reopened them they had a tawny glint. Vincent crushed her against the back of the sofa and pressed his lips to hers. Their teeth clashed, but almost immediately she yielded. Vincent could have drawn the kiss out to the end of time before Jeanne would have dared stir. When he finally pulled back he could not prevent her pretty, powdered head from burying itself against his shoulder.

Twelve years old, that's what I call her. Vincent felt touched and amused rather than annoyed. Obviously her fiancé had not taught her how to make love with a powdered headdress. *I don't know why preachers are always raving against cosmetics. The fashion for fancy headdress is a girl's best weapon against a big bad wolf.* He laughed softly to himself.

His flirtation had rumpled his coat. But he was proud to have made a young girl enjoy her first kiss, as proud as if she were the first virgin to be his prey. His only worry was that his valet might not be in the hall to brush off his gray silk coat. The last time he had seen Mario the fellow had looked decidedly unfit for duty.

CHAPTER 8

sn't it a shame to spoil such a lovely piece of handiwork," Bellotte grumbled as she rinsed Jeanne's hair.

"Wash everything out, my Bellotte, rinse away, and top it off with a solution of vinegar."

Tatan viewed the scene disapprovingly. "Madame won't be exactly happy to see you with your hair in this state at midday dinner. There are still guests, and you look as if you had just got out of bed. And your fiancé will be here for supper tonight. Had you thought of that? What will he say, when he's always neat as a pin?"

"The other ladies powdered yesterday by Le Niçois wisely sat up in bed all night with a muslin scarf tied around their heads," said Pompon, yawning as she drank her early morning coffee. "You're the only one, mademoiselle, to come downstairs in a dressing gown. It's a wild thing from the woods you are."

"And just look at my floor!" Tatan exclaimed. "There's no place for such a mess in my kitchen. Why didn't you clean yourself up in the bathroom?"

"I'm glad you agree with me, Tatan, that flour is messy," said Jeanne gaily. "The baths are overrun. And here I have Nanette's good fire. Come, Tatan, don't scold me any more. Give me a cup of coffee while I dry off. I know you like my natural look."

Jeanne needed to know that she was in good form. She had a secret appointment with Vincent, at noon, in an abandoned hunting lodge in the woods of Neuville. How delicious it was to share a secret with a man! The night before, when they had rejoined the company, she had been aware, in the crowded room, that a secret bond attached her to

Vincent. Pauline had run her eyes over them before saying that she was terribly sleepy. Vincent had thrown a big Indian shawl around her shoulders and taken her home.

Did he kiss her on the way? And later, at Vaux, did he take her into his arms? Going to bed at three o'clock in the morning with these questions on her mind, Jeanne had an uneasy sleep. Up at six, she saw herself unwashed and ugly, with her aristocratic coiffure askew, transformed into a fallen meringue, crusty and peeling. Now, sitting on a wooden bench in front of the fire, sipping a cup of hot coffee, she was resuscitated.

Jeanne had decided to wear Denis' red coat and riding breeches to her rendezvous rather than a skirt. Bouchoux had carefully waxed her tan leather boots and copiously spat upon them. Even the heels were shiny. With the back of her hand Jeanne puffed her jabot and looked for the last time into the mirror. She was excited by the idea of showing herself in this guise, with no makeup and with her hair casually tied at the back of her neck with a black ribbon.

I couldn't be much bolder if I were to go without a blouse, bare-breasted. Women are brought up in a really stupid manner.

The morning air was shot through with white light, but icy cold. Jeanne walked rapidly across the paved courtyard, meeting only a few servants on her way to the stable. A groom helped her to saddle Blanchette. The mare, as usual, was ready to gallop, but her mistress held her to a slow trot in order not to be the first to arrive at the appointed place. The joy of riding toward her secret was so intense that she sought to prolong it.

She took the usual paths leading to the woods of Neuville. But a young girl's route to her first lovers' meeting is never an ordinary one. Under Blanchette's hooves the grass was unusually green and Jeanne could hear, without straining her ears, the whisper of the sap in early budding trees. The vital juices rose in her veins as well. She was in love with everything that came within sight. She felt a rush of gratitude toward a clump of blossoming broom, a rush of tenderness for a squirrel climbing a tree. She smiled at the song of an invisible wren and stopped her horse from stepping on a toad, in the middle of the path. The flight of an oriole traced a yellow stripe across the patch of blue sky between two elms, a blackbird trilled over her head.

Entering the half-light of a thicket she slowed Blanchette down to a walk. The silence crackled and rustled, and there was an odor of wet moss. There were clusters of pale violets on both sides of the path, outshone by yellow primroses which had flowered in spots of sunlight. She breathed deeply of the keen air, which was redolent of wild mushrooms.

She was lighthearted and fearless, for her head was perfectly clear. What had happened the night before was the fault of the Spanish wine, the violins, the rhythm of the dance, the relaxed and yet overstimulating atmosphere of a supper party. Of Pauline, who annoyed her; of Philibert, who had forgotten her. Of Louis-Antoine, who wasn't there, she felt little.

Waiting for her at the end of the road was a sparkling hour, nothing more. The handsome chevalier was a great flirt, and a bit of flirtation was exactly what she needed. If she had not used her reason when the chevalier had started to seduce her, it was because she was so new at the game. But now that she had gained experience she'd no longer be taken by surprise. What the devil! Whatever daring words the corsair might utter, she had only to make a sharp reply, narrow her lips in a mocking smile, and extend nothing more than her hand.

Now she was only a mile from the lodge. This former hunting lodge had served once as a storehouse for the ladies of Neuville, but they had abandoned it. It was a large, two-story structure with mud walls. A disorderly collection of broken, rotted, worm-eaten furniture, enveloped in cobwebs, cluttered the ground level. The entrance hall was filled with firewood, which had to be bypassed to reach the stairs leading to the one livable room on the second floor.

When he was fifteen years old Charles de Bouhey, without asking permission of anyone, had fixed it up as a place to take pretty peasant girls during his school holidays. Now it served his younger brother, Jean-François. But neither boy came there when there was the prospect of a hunt. Jeanne smiled to herself when she thought of how she would surprise Vincent with a lunch improvised from the gingerbread, jams, and Condrieu wine which Charles got out of his grandmother and brought here to feed his easy conquests.

Vincent was striding up and down, striking his boots with a whip, patiently. He was singing the war song of the galleys of Malta, which came out of his mouth in a ribbon of steam:

"From Valletta to Rabatto,
From Bayda to Sirocco,

Pass the reef, boys, heave her to!
A lighthouse and six channels to go . . .
Pass the reef, boys, heave her to!"

Jeanne dismounted from her mare directly into his arms. Immediately she felt less sure of her ability to play the game.

"I'm cold," she lied. "Shall we go for a gallop?"

"You aren't cold at all," Vincent retorted calmly.

He seemed to be fascinated by her hair, and she by his. His head was covered, most unconventionally, with thick, short black curls. Jeanne could not take her eyes off them.

"You may not have the courage to ask me why I go around like a newly escaped convict, who hasn't had time to let his hair grow. It's so that, aboard ship, I don't have to wear either a wig or a cap, which would catch my head in the rigging."

He pulled at the ribbon that tied her hair. Then he picked up the soft blond mass in both hands and carried a lock to his lips. Jeanne had perfumed herself with a mixture of iris, lily, and chamomile flowers, and Vincent wished his nose were made of clay so as to absorb and retain the odor. When he spoke again it was with a muffled voice.

"My dear, you make a very attractive page. *Belle Vincente* would be happy to take you on as a ship's boy."

"Come, Chevalier," she said, trying to break the spell that held them standing face to face with hands yearning to meet, "surely you won't start to mock me again."

"And aren't you mocking me?"

He strode over to the door of the lodge and pushed it so hard that it opened, creaking with rust.

"A regular pirates' den!" he exclaimed. "Isn't it a bad joke to use it for a lovers' tryst?"

Jeanne smiled, preceding him into the lodge and showing him how to bypass the stacks of wood. The upstairs room was swept clean, sufficiently furnished, warmed by heavy curtains and provided with a fireplace. The fire was ready to be lit, there was extra wood in a woodbox, and a supply of candles and wine and clean sheets on the bed. Vincent immediately realized that the preparations had been made by a loyal valet who was charged with equipping a love nest.

"By Jove, mademoiselle," he said coldly, "I never expected to see you set up like this just a few miles from Charmont."

Jeanne was taken aback by his tone of voice, without completely understanding the reason for it. "This place is not mine—it's been set up by Charles de Bouhey. It has a certain charm, doesn't it? Charles brought everything over from Charmont, with the help of his valet, of course. No one must know, not even Madame de Vaux-Jailloux. Charles comes here to conduct certain experiments in the field of alchemy, which his mother won't allow him to make at home."

"I see that quite clearly," said Vincent, pointing to two carafes and two wineglasses. "These vessels are obviously used for scientific purposes."

Both of them burst out laughing.

He sat Jeanne down on the couch upholstered in tattered crêpe, pulled the quilt over her knees, then went to light the fire and open a bottle of Condrieu wine. Before filling the glasses, he tapped them to ascertain the quality of the crystal.

"If Bouhey's girlfriends match the quality of his wine and wineglasses, there's a lot to be said for him."

"Madame de Bouhey can't tolerate ordinary glassware. She spends a fortune buying the very best. These glasses are among the first crystals to have been cut in France. The wine, too, is more or less stolen. Doesn't that bother you?"

"I don't give a rap for stealing, I told you that last night. We're all born thieves. We have to make an effort not to steal, and my profession is robbery on the high seas."

"You've acquired a taste for it, then?"

"Yes, I love to steal, especially when I can keep the booty for myself. I steal on behalf of the king, the grand master, and my investors. In other words, the product of my stealing is stolen from me, and I resent it. Well, let's drink. To your health, Jeannette!"

She was pleased by his calling her Jeannette, like everyone else. The way he said it was entirely different and uniquely intimate.

"Well," he said, "aren't you drinking? Drink up, my dear! Wine changes mere pleasure into joy."

"Yes, I'll drink. But first I must speak to you."

"Yes?" said Vincent, taking back her glass and putting it on the table. "Why speak? Do you know how we love in the world of corsairs? It's the only wise way. The man says to the woman, 'Whoever you are, I take you. I ask no questions about your past, just pledge me your future.' "

"And what does the woman reply?"

"Nothing, absolutely nothing. A woman doesn't need to speak. If she's there it means that she wants to be taken."

"Give me back my glass," said Jeanne brusquely.

He gave it to her and, at the same time, put a hand under her chin. "You have to say something, do you? Just because you have a tongue? On l'Ile de Bourbon, winter and summer, even on the lava slopes of the volcanoes, there are short-leaved ferns that the natives call 'women's tongues,' because nothing can stop them."

"You're really unbearable! All you can do is tease. But after what's gone on between us, there is something I must say."

"Nothing has gone on between us. At least not yet."

"Exactly. I came to tell you that there can be nothing. Nothing is possible, Chevalier. I've pledged myself to another man."

"Come sail with me. You'll be his later. Your fiancé is a patient man, and he'll wait."

"What makes you think he's so patient?"

"I've guessed it, that's all."

Jeanne looked at him indecisively. With his tasseled handkerchief he flicked some wood chips off his sleeve. The orange-blossom scent of his toilet water stung her nose. It was obvious that he was treating her like a little country goose.

"Chevalier, it's not the thought of my fiancé that holds me back," she threw at him abruptly.

"I never thought it was," he answered mockingly.

"There's still another man, whom I really love," she said with a defiant air.

"That's good news. A woman who deceives one man can just as easily deceive two. Let me be the third. It seems as if you could love me without too many pangs of conscience."

Jeanne flushed with anger. "You're daydreaming, Chevalier. What presumption! I met you only yesterday and already you expect me to be in love with you!"

"Jeanne, falling in love isn't conducted by a timetable."

"You're wrong," she protested, with emotion. "I know you take me for a little goose, fit to offer you some amusement. But for years my heart has been full . . ."

She bit her lip and concluded dryly, "I owe you no confidences. . . . Shall we try the plum preserve or the raspberry jelly?"

Standing in front of the fire, Vincent rubbed his hands in its warmth and then wheeled around to face her.

"Now that my hands are no longer frozen, give me yours in all friendship. Come look at yourself. The mirror's not good, but you'll improve it. Look at your smooth skin, your bright eyes, your expectant lips, your quivering nose and breast. You have a body that's very much alive, and you shouldn't give up substance for shadow. If you hold back you'll betray your true nature."

"Substance for shadow?" she asked of Vincent's reflection in the mirror.

"Forget your formal manners and touch my jacket. It's not made of 'Provençal English' cloth, but of genuine Scottish tweed. Feel my shirt cuffs, pure muslin from the Indies. Now give me your hand again."

"Will you kindly explain this little game?"

"I'm teaching you to recognize substance, Jeanne. Will you let me go, when I'm so substantial, so accessible, and go on pursuing the shadow of Dr. Aubriot?"

She stared at him, speechless, her eyes dilated, her mouth half open. "I don't want to hear that name pronounced here," she said hoarsely. "And then, who . . . ?"

"Who told me, do you mean? Madame de Vaux-Jailloux."

"So!" she hissed through clenched teeth. "Madame de Vaux-Jailloux is in the plot, is she? Shall we be three on the voyage?"

"I adore you when you're jealous," he answered, laughing. "Pauline, my darling, is very subtle. She asked me for the truth and I gave it to her. You see, Pauline and I have promised each other nothing but friendship and pleasure."

"Madame de Vaux-Jailloux had no grounds on which to speak. She knows nothing."

"But her friend, Madame de Rupert, knows, through her sister, Madame de Saint-Girod, that you had a childhood passion for Dr. Aubriot. He taught you botany. You had a crush on him and, because you're fifteen years old, you think you're in love. It's all quite simple."

"This whole province is a gossip factory!"

"The whole of France is that. The times demand it. We gossip about everything. But why do you care about the spread of your little-girl secret? You're no longer that little girl."

"But I do care, yes, I do. You can't know what Dr. Aubriot means to me. He taught me all I know and made me what I am. You seem to like the way I am."

"No, no," he said, taking her hand.

"Yes! Dr. Aubriot has the sacred fire of genius. You can't imagine the joy of our early morning walks. He made me hear the grass grow and guess at the hiding place of a trout beneath the water. There's no perception as sharp as his. And his passion for discovery is aroused the minute he steps out the door. Can't you understand the joy of living beside a scientist who falls in love with everything he sees, and tells you about it in such a way that the smallest and most familiar objects astound you? Take a bed for watercress, for instance . . ."

Jeanne's voice vibrated through the small room, charged with devotion, and shone in her gold-flecked eyes. Vincent's heart was chilled. She seemed a mystic, speaking of God, and he foresaw that it would be more difficult than he had thought to uproot her idol without giving her pain. But he refused to eat watercress seasoned by Dr. Aubriot. Brusquely he leaned over and planted a quick kiss on her lips.

"Oh!" she exclaimed.

"Forgive me," he said. "It was just to get myself back into the conversation."

Vincent continued, "You talk like one of Racine's heroines about an offstage lover. Quiet, there, sailor! Aubriot had time to sell you his green, now let me sell you my blue.

"I, too, have some nature to offer—an immense blue field with whole countries for backdrops. Listen to my itinerary. I leave Marseille for Malta, pausing in Corsica, Sardinia, Sicily, and Naples. A cruise for business and pleasure—I'm not looking for trouble, so that I'll have time to make love to you. And, in between, I'll give you a scare by sailing you within range of the guns of Corsican bandits, take you to buy Sardinian embroidery, to bathe, naked, in the bay of Gaeta, and to pick wild parsley at the base of a Greek temple. What do you say to my menu?"

"That you've left out Malta," she answered with an involuntary smile.

"Malta's the dessert. I have a house there. It has a tiny, terraced vegetable garden overlooking the sea."

Now, Jeanne's eyes held the same wet, golden gleam as when she had spoken of Dr. Aubriot's watercress a few minutes before.

Vincent was happy to the point of feeling silly. But that was how he wanted to feel. And he continued to describe the delights of an ingenuous lover.

"Soon the king will have to make peace with England and I can sail you, without risk, through the Straits of Gibraltar and into the Atlantic. I'll take you around the Cape of Good Hope to your beloved East Indies."

And he added, with almost aggressive malice, "I don't say that the beautiful impressions you've had of our Dombes region are to be belittled. But I'll give you pictures of all the world that can be seen from a sailing ship. You'll see that they're not too bad, either."

Jeanne sighed with well-being, shook her hair, and gazed silently into the distance at the dream he had spun out.

"What grows in your Maltese garden, Chevalier?"

"You'll tell me the Latin names," he said, holding back his laughter. "Just now I'd prefer to explain my plan for carrying you off tomorrow. Or else I'd like to kiss you."

"Explain the plan," she said, quickly drawing back.

He had prepared a quite definite plan, to be carried out beginning at dawn of the next day. He wanted her to dress, as this morning, like a young man, with a minimum of luggage. Mario would meet her at whatever door of the château she said was most suitable. At the edge of the garden there would be horses waiting to take them to the post chaise which he had already hired for going away.

He had seen to every detail, including the way he would later effect a reconciliation with Mme. de Bouhey. Jeanne listened like a child to a fairy tale, half credulous, half incredulous, thinking she might wake up any moment to find herself reading a book on the couch in the library.

"I wonder if you've heard me?" Vincent asked. "What's your answer?"

Answer? She couldn't possibly. You can't answer a proposal of abduction with a yes or a no. She wondered which monosyllable pleased her more. In order to gain time, she timidly touched the eight-pointed cross which she saw in his buttonhole.

"What does the grand master say when a Knight of the Order brings a mistress back to Malta?"

Vincent saw the lively old man in his Arabian Nights garden wearing the look of an inquisitor.

"As a man our grand master, Pinto de Fonseca, is as gay as any

Portuguese. For security's sake he builds his paradise here. Since he is as much of a wit as he is a libertine, he is indulgent."

"You have an answer to everything, Chevalier. And no doubt you know from experience how the grand master receives your mistresses. Lighthearted love is your specialty, I imagine, your favorite pastime."

"Lord help us, Jeanne, what else do you think love can be? A painful task? I want to rid you of that idea here and now."

He took her into his arms. Because she was taken less by surprise than the time before, it took him longer to penetrate the barrier of her clenched teeth. But after he had awkwardly made a breakthrough, she made sporadic attempts to respond.

He unbuttoned her red coat. Realizing that she had nothing on under her chemise, he began depositing chaste kisses on the fine cotton. The tips of her small, round breasts hardened. She stiffened and trembled all over. He waited until she yielded, melted into his arms, to push aside the chemise and imprison a bare breast in his hand. He held her, a willing captive, while he let his tongue play inventively in her mouth. She showed so plainly that this was her first contact with a man, revealing her newborn sensuality so confidently, that he felt a wave of tenderness as well as of desire. Vincent momentarily let her go, leaned her gently against the back of the couch and drew the two edges of her blouse together.

Jeanne neither moved nor spoke. She made no attempt to protect her breasts. Smiling to herself, with half-closed eyes, she surrendered herself to the caress of Vincent's eyes like a docile kitten responding to a gentle, coaxing master. Vincent prolonged his contemplation, thinking of the hundred ways in which he might sacrifice his virgin and regretting that he must choose only one among them. Waiting was an exquisite pleasure.

A sudden sound of galloping horses brought Jeanne, scarlet-faced, to her feet, fumbling with the buttons of her blouse. The sound subsided as the horses apparently turned to the left, but the magic moment was irrevocably lost. Vincent tried to help her trembling hands find the buttonholes, but she pushed him back, saying curtly, "I wonder who those riders could be and whether they saw my mare."

She picked up her riding whip from the table and ran down the stairs. Vincent took a shovel and beat out the fire, calling himself all the names synonymous with idiot that he could muster.

Dejectedly, Vincent came out of the lodge and was astounded to see that Jeanne was standing there, scratching Blanchette between the ears. Seeing her again, Vincent felt a surge of happiness that he wished could last forever.

The sun, emerging through the mist, brought out the golden glint of her hair. Jeanne came toward him smiling and holding out her long tresses.

"I couldn't run away, since you have my ribbon in your pocket."

He came around behind her and gathered her golden locks into the taffeta ribbon, just as he might have done after lovemaking. His hands trembled awkwardly. When the knot was tied he said, in a manner graver than the words he spoke, "If you don't come tomorrow morning, at least send me your ribbon."

"I think I'll come, Chevalier," she said, looking him straight in the eyes.

He took hold of her and pressed her to him.

"Chevalier," she said seriously, pulling herself away, "I don't want to tell a lie. I don't love you. I want to escape from a melancholy marriage, that's all."

"You're quite right to do that. To have eloped at the age of fifteen will console you at fifty. And I promise you an elopement that you'll remember. Now tell me when and where you can arrange to meet Mario."

"In the courtyard, at six o'clock, while the rest of the household is busy over morning tea."

With hands crossed under one of her feet he gave her a lift into the saddle. She felt a wave of complete confidence in this almost total stranger. At this moment, he seemed closer to her than anyone else she knew, and running away with him the next morning, the most natural thing in the world.

"Aren't you going to kiss me goodbye?" she asked boldly.

This time her mouth opened at once, like a ripe fruit.

"Luckily," he said a few minutes later, "my kisses are not in the category of the things you don't love."

"I love your hair, too," she answered, trying to imitate his casual manner.

With a sweeping gesture he took off his cocked tricorne hat and made a deep bow.

"I shall make a list of your kind words," he said. "I hope you'll tell me, along the way, what else you find lovable about me. When we disembark at Valletta, I hope to have won a niche for myself in your heart. Malta's a place where one can't live without love."

* * * *

Only twenty people, close friends, attended the second evening's supper. Everyone planned to go to bed early. The time went by in frivolous chatter. Jeanne's memory seemed to be storing up the last words of Marie, Delphine, and Abbé Rollin. The trifles, which the next morning's dawn would swallow up when she left them behind, imprinted themselves on Jeanne's mind.

"If you want to hunt woodcock, go to the priest of Chapaize. His choirboys are famous beaters. And the sacristan a first-class whip." The voice was that of Captain de Bouhey.

"Aunt, I promised the Marquis Christophe d'Angrières a piece of buckskin. Buckskin for officers' breeches is hard to find anywhere except in Lyon, and I thought . . ." The speaker was Anne-Aimée Delafaye.

"I shan't ask to be released from my vows unless it's for a true love match. I'll have no husband that isn't a lover," said the little canoness Emilie.

"My Rossoli liqueur? Why, madame, I make it in the usual fashion, with fennel, anise, coriander, caraway, chamomile, and sugar, soaked of course in brandy." This last from Mme. de Bouhey.

Jeanne held back a sob. Within a few hours, this dear voice would be dead to her as well. How long would it take a letter to travel from Malta to Charmont and from Charmont to Malta? And would the baroness even write to the ungrateful girl who had fled without farewells, throwing herself into the arms of a passing Don Juan?

"My dear Jeanne, I always wonder how you manage to be more beautiful every time I see you," said her fiancé, who was back from Lyon. "This evening you've outdone yourself. You're all aglow."

Jeanne had to make an effort to acknowledge the compliment. She felt so removed from this comedy of manners; every demand made her more restless. After a few words to her fiancé she relapsed into silence.

Mme. de Bouhey leaned over to whisper to her, "You don't seem to have your two feet on the ground tonight, my Jeannette, but on a flying carpet. Can't you come back to earth?"

Jeanne had an impulse to break down and tell her everything. If only she could look back as she went away and see her guardian on the balcony, waving a handkerchief, smiling and blowing her a kiss. If only she could be pardoned in advance, sure of keeping the old affections intact. Even when you're chafing to leave your childhood behind, it's good to know that someone has kept a warm spot for you.

She lightly stroked the baroness's hand, and tried to be more attentive to the conversation. Mme. de Saint-Girod was, as usual, blasting the young girls of the time.

"It's worse than ever! They're romantic to a degree. . . . I can see why Rousseau couldn't be burned at the stake, but his tearful Héloïse, at least, could be consigned to the flames. A good fire would dry her out."

"My dear madame," said Father Jérôme, "it's the works of Abbé Prévost that ought to be burned. Ever since they've read *Manon Lescaut* our good girls are ready to let themselves be carried away. It's all the fashion, even in convents."

"To be abducted is a good way of telling your father something he hasn't wanted to hear," said Emilie.

"Engagements drag on and on, interminably," sighed Marie.

"And many parents are as fearful that their daughters may marry beneath them as they were in the days of Louis XIV," put in Anne-Aimée.

"Where there's boredom, escapades will follow," said Emilie.

"Just listen to them!" exclaimed Mme. de Saint-Girod. "Didn't I tell you that all the girls of today take themselves for heroines of a novel? Soon they'll be apologizing for the fact that they haven't run away in a post chaise."

"Well," said Emilie impertinently, "I haven't yet said my last word. My cousin Eléonore de Saint-Clair de la Tour got herself carried off by a young ensign whom her father refused to let her marry. It seems that their adventure was a great success. Of course, when she came home, they had to let her have her ensign, with the blessing of the priest of Saint Roch. Meanwhile, she'd had a fabulous journey. The police chief showed her all sorts of kindnesses, and the ladies of the town brought her wine and delicacies in return for her romantic story. It's not only in the novels of Abbé Prévost that well-brought-up girls come to a bad end. . . . If you're traveling in a post chaise, it's best to go in the spring; in the summer you sweat and in winter you freeze."

"Such talk would be shocking in the mouth of any young girl," Father Jérôme grumbled. "But in the mouth of a young girl of Neuville, I call it the wrath of God."

"My dear Jeanne," said Louis-Antoine Duthillet facetiously, "forgive me for not having abducted you yet."

He got up to go, and Jeanne accompanied him to the hall.

"Must you go so soon?" she asked politely.

"Unfortunately, yes, my dear. I must get back to Châtillon. I've promised my carriage to the Aubriots. Madame Aubriot and her daughter want to leave at midnight for Bugey. I didn't mention it for fear of spoiling a pleasant evening. But the doctor's wife had an attack of childbed fever and died only yesterday."

CHAPTER 9

eanne threw herself onto the bed without taking off her clothes, and broke into sobs. With throbbing temples and swollen red cheeks, she buried her face in the pillows and cried her eyes out.

The news of Marguerite's death changed all of her plans. The man whom she had adored since childhood would be once more within her reach! Images and memories of Philibert stole back into her mind. For two days she had forgotten Philibert. For two days a lusty sea wind had blown the love of a lifetime away. She saw herself in Vincent's arms, and blanched at her betrayal.

What was she to do with Vincent now? She plunged her face into cold water, then, shivering, she wrapped herself in a shawl and sat down at her desk. The words she needed to bid Vincent goodbye would not come. The image of his dark good looks, the memory of his kisses, caresses, and promises filled her thoughts. Jeanne tore up three letters and started a fourth. It was strange that, having miraculously regained her hopes of Philibert, she could still see Vincent's laughing brown eyes and hear his mocking voice. His presence kept intruding. She could feel his hand lifting her chin and his lips brushing lightly over her hair, eyelids, neck, and mouth. Jeanne threw her pen down in frustration and crushed her fourth letter into a little ball.

At last, on the tenth sheet, she coldheartedly wrote, "Go without me!" and she picked up a stick of sealing wax to close it. Suddenly she opened her letter and slipped into it her black taffeta hair ribbon. When Vincent's valet, Mario, came to fetch her, he found only a damp envelope smelling of chamomile and lilies.

Jeanne had completely forgotten her fiancé, poor little Louis-Antoine. She didn't think of him until midmorning and then only to wonder how she could persuade the baroness that she must break off her engagement. One thing was certain, she simply couldn't marry the surrogate.

The idea of keeping herself available for Philibert was not the only reason. The memory of Vincent's embraces filled her with apprehension. If Louis-Antoine tried to embrace her the same way she couldn't bear it. Vincent had shattered her innocence. She could no longer resign herself to marrying a "suitable" husband. She must find an excuse to give Mme. de Bouhey.

The baroness guessed at once, of course, that Dr. Aubriot's sadly won freedom was the true reason for breaking the engagement. She mustered a dozen fits of anger, a trickle of tenderness, and a flood of common sense in defense of Duthillet. As usual, she did not mince words. If the surrogate had heard her he might not have appreciated the points she made in his favor—that he was the ideal cuckold, and the one nearest to Aubriot's house.

Everyone in and around Charmont worked to persuade Jeanne that it would be irreparably foolish to give up the position and prosperity of M. Duthillet. The stubborn girl had everything against her, the scorn of Delphine, the sermons of Abbé Rollin, and the shrill voice of Pompon. Even Mlle. Sergent emerged unexpectedly from her customary reserve to extol the poetry of housekeeping, of jangling a chain full of keys, of ruling over a linen closet and presiding over days dedicated to putting up preserves and supervising the laundry. All to no avail.

"My dear Marie-Françoise, your project's gone up in smoke," Dame Charlotte said to her sister-in-law one day. "We're living with the young women of 1762, and with a host of women writers who pound it into their heads that they have the same rights to love as men do."

"Come, come!" the baroness exclaimed. "Is that such a great discovery? And does proclamation of women's right to love increase the number of lovers? We've always had to divide them up behind their wives' backs. Getting married was just the conventional way of breaking into the game. But today young girls demand freedom to dispose of their bodies."

"Ever since Monsieur Maille invented his astringent vinegar the most rough-trodden virginity can be patched up for the wedding night. Maille has made a mint of money," said Dame Charlotte.

"He'd better rake it in while he can," the baroness grumbled. "Soon girls won't want husbands at all, either before or after. You heard little Emilie the other night, didn't you? They want a lover or, if such a rare bird is to be found, a lover-husband."

"Well, after all, Aubriot is a widower," said the canoness.

The baroness started. "Are you serious, Charlotte? The Aubriots are proud of their coat of arms and their bourgeois status."

"Duthillet belongs to the same class, and yet . . ."

"True. But the fact remains that Aubriot isn't the kind of Prince Charming that marries a pauper. I can swear to that. Besides, he's said to be quite inconsolable."

* * * *

As a boy he had chased skirts. As a young man he had enjoyed adventures. But now Philibert was a different person. The same rumors repeatedly reached Jeanne's ears. "Dr. Aubriot is not recovering from his loss. He is brokenhearted. His poor state of mind is injuring his health." All of his friends were urging him to seek distraction in Paris.

One of his best friends, Jérôme de Lalande, had already gone there and was pressing him to follow. Bernard de Jussieu, the famous naturalist of the Jardin du Roi, the King's Garden, was equally insistent. The invitations were flattering, and Aubriot only hesitated when he looked at his son, little Michel-Anne Aubriot, smiling from his cradle.

The baby's uncle, Abbé Maupin of Pugieu, offered to take care of him, but Michel-Anne was part and parcel of his dead mother, for whom Philibert had cared deeply. Philibert blamed himself, both as a man and as a doctor, for having been the unwitting cause of her death and for having been unable to prevent it. He remained in his office and went back and forth between Belley and Châtillon.

Jeanne wandered about Châtillon, but never caught him there. She went up to her room and, leaning her forehead against the windowpane, stared at the calm horizon. She shut herself up again to wait for Philibert, but not with the same patience as before. She was no longer a little girl satisfied with dreams of love.

Vincent's kisses had awakened her appetite. Love had been in her hand like a ripe fruit, ready to be eaten. Now she longed for Philibert to take her into his arms, to reward her for her fidelity. To hear that he was inconsolable only exasperated her. With the cruelty of a fifteen-year-old, she blanked out Marguerite and Philibert's love for her. *Why didn't he come back to Châtillon and resume the life of a doctor and botanist?*

Mme. de Saint-Girod was the first to run across him in Châtillon and gave the news to Mme. de Bouhey.

"Did you know that our good Dr. Aubriot is worn to a frazzle? All because he tries to forget his sorrow by overworking."

She looked over at Jeanne, who was playing chess with Father Jérôme in the corner, and went on, "He's gone back to running about all day and sitting up through the night, as if he were still twenty. In spite of a persistent cough and rheumatic pains, he goes to collect herbs in the rain. Mother Nature, he says, is good to him. He has no use for medicine, an attitude that harms both his personal health and his reputation as a doctor. I hope he'll find a flower of the fields pretty enough to console him for the loss of Marguerite. His friend Bernard, the pharmacist, insists that he will live on only the memory of his beloved wife. But I don't share his confidence. A man who has loved once is bound to love again."

Mme. de Saint-Girod had spoken without pausing to catch her breath for fear the baroness would interrupt her. She didn't wish to turn her former lover over to Jeanne. But if the girl could save a thirty-five-year-old scholar from languishing away by sacrificing her virginity, it would be for a good cause. And Jeanne readily agreed. *But how could she say to him: "Monsieur Philibert, take me and cure both your trouble and mine?"*

The baroness considered Jeanne a moment and then said to her friend, "Couldn't we ask Aubriot to a quiet dinner, to assure him of our sympathy and friendship? I'll invite him for one evening next week."

Jeanne waited impatiently for the hour when she would be alone with the baroness in her bedroom.

Four hours later, when the baroness was settled in her armchair, Jeanne seized her hand and rubbed her cheek against it.

"It's very good of you to ask him," she murmured.

"It's not good of me at all. I have no time to waste," the baroness replied gruffly. "I'd like to see you catch your Aubriot like chicken pox. At your age one is easily cured and never suffers from it again."

* * * *

Dr. Aubriot's reply was that he simply couldn't bear to go out. Jeanne's hopes were dashed.

Baron François had gone off to the army, and Charles and Jean-François were sent off to their respective academies. As autumn began, Jeanne was left with only the baroness and Delphine. As for Denis, he no longer lived at the château. At his school in Trévoux, the bailiff's son had sharpened his mind and had been trained as a chemist. Having turned seventeen, he found employment with Jassans, the apothecary of the hospital in Châtillon. In her boredom Jeanne tried to take an interest in Denis' work, but he discouraged her attentions. And so she found herself on the library couch, daydreaming.

At dinner, even when neighbors came to dine, conversation was as dull as the steady September drizzle. The war, having now dragged on for seven years, threatened to end badly. The people of France had lost interest in the remote and overly long war. From the front, Baron François was sending alarming letters. The list of the dead and wounded grew longer every day. The Royal French Fleet, or what remained of it, was scattered across the seas. Plainly Duke de Choiseul would have to sign an unfavorable peace treaty.

At Charmont the mood was so heavy that the baroness decided to send Jeanne to spend a week at Lyon with her Delafaye nephews.

* * * *

The Delafaye household was a cheerful one. When Mme. de Bouhey had set up her two nephews, Joseph and Henri, in Lyon she had married them off to two amiable sisters, daughters of a prosperous silk merchant. The two families had five children between them and they lived together in a large new building in the Bellecour section of the city. The children, all of them around the same age, were a joyful lot. Their families left them unsupervised, being busy with their weaving plants, their big shop on the Rue Mercière, and their export business.

When Jeanne arrived at the Place Bellecour, Joseph's son, Laurent, was readying himself to work for Pazevin, the shipbuilder of Marseille. At twenty years of age, he had been given the great responsibility of signing contracts for the firm. Full of himself, he had demanded a complete new wardrobe so that he might cut a dashing figure in

Marseille society. Since he was the only son in the two families, the four girls considered it a great lark to assist him.

Laurent entered the shop of the tailor Pernon surrounded by a group of chattering women, each one desiring to dress him according to her own taste. His sisters, Elisabeth and Margot, were all for the classic French style, suitable, they said, to a serious man of business. His cousins, Anne-Aimée and Marie-Louise, on the other hand, clamored for the red, blue, and black velvets worn by the flamboyant "men of fashion" who frequented the coffeehouses of Paris. Jeanne favored muted tones of grays and breeches with a flap front, like the ones Chevalier Vincent had worn at Charmont. Rolls of fine materials were laid out on the counter at the rear for their inspection. But Jeanne's attention was drawn to a scene in the center of the room, where M. Pernon was fitting a bright vermilion jacket on a gentleman who looked about thirty-five years old.

The man was tall, broad-shouldered, and slender-waisted, with a swarthy complexion and very red lips. His aquiline nose and slightly protruding black eyes gave him the air of a bird of prey. When he saw the young people, he displayed a set of fine teeth in a broad smile and stared at Jeanne with obvious appreciation. As he fingered some satiny cloth for breeches he cast caressing glances at Jeanne and wet his lips as if anticipating a tasty morsel. His French was perfect, but with a slight singsong intonation. There could be no doubt that he came from Italy. With apparent impatience, he terminated his fitting and went behind a screen to put on his own clothes.

When he emerged, the young people could not restrain a gasp of amazement. He was wildly, excessively elegant. He wore a pearl-gray, gold-embroidered coat, over which he threw a black silk cape. And the pièce de resistance, tucked under his arm, was a big, old-fashioned three-cornered hat, ornamented with Spanish stitching and white feathers! Trinkets of gold, enamel, and precious stones hung from the chains of his vest-pocket watches, and there were rings on every finger of his slender dark hands. In Lyon, where wealth was soberly displayed, his extravagant outfit could hardly escape notice.

Mme. Pernon stepped forward and, in a simpering manner, introduced the Chevalier Casanova de Seingalt to the Delafayes. After a low bow to the girls, Casanova turned to Laurent, as if to offer him moral support.

"I see that you're in good company, too good, perhaps. Of course we men enjoy fulfilling the whims of the fair sex. But when so many whims are indulged during our visit to the tailor, we risk coming out clothed as birds of a very strange feather."

Laurent found it so comical having this ridiculous fellow cautioning him about fashion that he burst into laughter, echoed by the others.

While the apprentice showed Laurent materials, Casanova gave his unsolicited opinion, trying all the while to stay close to Jeanne, who moved around the little group, like a rabbit unwilling to be caught.

Outside, a drizzling rain turned into hail, which beat against the shop windows.

"Now we're in a fix!" exclaimed Margot. "We came all the way from Bellecour on foot, for the sake of a walk. There's little chance of finding a cab and we'll reach home spattered with mud."

"Certainly not, mademoiselle," said Casanova. "I've rented a carriage for the length of my stay in Lyon. It's waiting for me outside, and my coachman can drive you home in two installments. As it happens I, too, am going to the Place Bellecour, as a guest of Madame d'Urfé."

"I thought that the Marquise d'Urfé had gone to her house in Bresse," put in Laurent, who mistrusted this gilt-edged nobleman and his glib tongue.

"True," said Casanova. "She had already gone when I arrived at her townhouse. There I found a note asking me to join her at her country house or at a manor in Vaux, which belongs to one of her friends. I meant to go there tomorrow, but . . ."

He cast a lingering look at Jeanne, who announced, "I live near Vaux, at the Château of Charmont."

"Then it's my good fortune to have met the most amiable of guides. It is very easy to get lost in a province with which one is unfamiliar."

The Venetian's facile speech and gesticulation irritated Laurent, the sober citizen of Lyon.

"Sir," he interrupted, "have no fear of getting lost in the region of Bresse. Your driver will find the way. The drivers of Lyon know all the highways and byways."

"But I have to go through the marshes of Dombes. In Geneva I was given a parcel to be delivered to a scientist at Châtillon."

"Really?" asked Jeanne. "And what is this scientist's name?"

"Dr. Aubriot," he answered. "When I was dining at Ferney with my friend Voltaire, I met a Swiss botanist, Dr. de Haller, who gave me two bundles of Alpine plants for two colleagues. One for a Monsieur Poivre, who lives here in Lyon, and the other for Dr. Aubriot. I'm in a hurry to deliver them because they contain some cuttings that should be replanted as soon as possible."

"God help us!" Jeanne exclaimed. "I hope they were wrapped in wet cloths and that you've taken them out of the wrappings from time to time to give them fresh air and water! Couldn't you put them in my care? Monsieur Phili—I mean Monsieur Aubriot will be most unhappy if the cuttings aren't in condition to be planted."

She spoke with such excitement that the little group fell silent. She blushed violently and added, "You see, Chevalier, I'm a bit of a botanist myself, in fact, a pupil of Dr. Aubriot."

"Mademoiselle," said Casanova, delighted with the turn of events, "I can't deprive the plants the pleasure of passing through your hands. If you'll go with me to Madame d'Urfé's, where I left them . . ."

Laurent interrupted brusquely. "Monsieur, we'll all go there together, shortly."

But Jeanne was quivering with impatience. "Come, Laurent, I know that to you botany is a bore. Finish making your purchases with your sisters and cousins. I'll go to Bellecour with the chevalier in order to assure the cuttings the care they need as fast as possible. As soon as I reach the Place Bellecour I'll send the carriage back for you."

Laurent did not insist. After all, Jeanne wasn't his sister, cousin, or fiancée.

No sooner was Casanova seated in the carriage than he justified Laurent's mistrust by casting velvety glances in Jeanne's direction. She smiled in return. How could she be angry with a man who furnished her with an excuse for seeing Philibert?

"I see, Chevalier," she said quietly, "that you're quick to flirt."

"Flirt?" said Casanova in a sorrowful voice. "Do you take my compliments so lightly? Don't you realize that your beauty won my heart, at first sight?"

"Your heart?" Jeanne replied maliciously. "It's very frail, then. To be sure, it's made of lace." And she fixed her eyes on his voluminous jabot, trimmed with more Valenciennes lace than she had ever seen on a man's chest.

"Go ahead and laugh at me, mademoiselle," he retorted. "When you laugh you enchant me all the more. Your teeth are pearls."

"Come, come, monsieur! Are Venetian girls satisfied with such trite compliments?"

"In your presence I lose my wits," said Casanova. "My fear of displeasing you makes me stupid. I can hold back no longer. You are the most divine girl I've met since arriving in France."

With this he fell to his knees and passionately kissed her skirt.

Astonished, Jeanne replied, "Go to it, monsieur. You must work fast since we haven't far to go. But lay a handkerchief under your knees, I beg of you. The velvet of your breeches is of such a delicate color . . ."

Her teasing took Casanova to the brink of despair. Throwing himself back on the seat cushions, he began a fiery speech so loaded with long words, gestures, supplicating looks, and even tears (he could cry at will) that Jeanne felt as if she were in a theater, listening to a tragedy of passion. She had never seen a gallant move to the attack with so little restraint. But then, she did not know that Casanova was the greatest womanizer in all Italy.

Alas for the pride of the triumphant seducer, Jeanne found his goings-on more ridiculous than romantic, and she burst out laughing. Casanova paled beneath the pink powder on his cheeks.

"Don't make fun of me," he begged her in a muffled voice. "You can't know how much I desire to take you into my arms. But no, my angel, you have nothing to fear. I'd rather die of thwarted desire than subject you to force."

And he handed her three little gold scissors which were hanging from one of his watch chains.

"At least give me a lock of your hair . . . enough to weave a rope, if you'll have none of *me*."

Jeanne laughed again. "You seem to be prepared at all times to cut enough of a lady's hair to hang yourself. But I prefer to keep my hair, thank you.

"No, no, please!" she exclaimed as he made a sudden frontal attack. Jeanne pushed him away abruptly so that he fell to the floor, where he seized the unexpected opportunity to raise the hem of her skirt and kiss her ankle.

"That's enough, Chevalier," she said firmly, drawing back her foot.

"What?" he cried out. "Won't you accept a kiss that touches nothing but your shoe? Will you grant me nothing?"

"But of course, Chevalier, I grant you hope," she said holding out her hand.

He kissed it with such transport that, for a moment, she was frightened. Plainly, this man from Venice knew nothing of the French code of flirtation; he was a total savage.

* * * *

The next morning Jeanne called a cab to take her to the Rue des Quatre-Chapeaux. She had both bundles of Swiss plants from Casanova. One would allow her to meet the famous M. Poivre. The other would give her the perfect opportunity to visit Philibert at Châtillon.

Pierre Poivre was only forty-three years old, but in his native city he was already a legend. His passion for botany had precipitated an unusual adventure in trade. The idea of planting a great spice garden on l'Ile de France, an island off the coast of Africa, would enable France to break the Dutch spice monopoly. With the blessing of the French government, he went to sea. He moved from a frigate to a corvette, from a brigantine to a freighter, slipping among pirates and patrols, crawling under fences and successfully fleeing battles, for he had to steal a few of the clove and nutmeg trees jealously guarded by the Dutch.

After nine years of frenzy, he returned to Port Louis on l'Ile de France with a cluster of clove and nutmeg seedlings clutched under a shirt, still soaking from the last storm. These he planted at Monplaisir, in the garden set up by Mahé de la Bourdonnais, the governor.

But, behind his back, a jealous fellow-botanist sprinkled the seedlings with a solution of mercury and caused them to die. Poivre, maddened by rage, set out for Paris, where his grievances were heard by George-Louis Buffon and Jussieu at the King's Garden. They were sufficiently moved by his story to take him to the king.

Louis XV had a fancy for gardens. He personally planted tulip bulbs in the flower boxes on the terrace at Versailles. He visited the vegetable plots, talked to the gardeners, and ordered bouquets for Mme. de Pompadour, who put them all around the *petits appartements*, her private quarters.

Poivre easily touched the king's heart. And, much to Poivre's delight, the king promised to buy back l'Ile de France from the Indies Company, making him the superintendent of the garden. To ensure his success, he gave him a well-armed frigate, plus a storage ship with which he could plunder the clove and nutmeg trees of the Molucca Islands— right under the Dutchmen's noses!

Poivre left the court thinking that his dream of a lifetime was well on its way to becoming a reality. But Louis XV did not always follow up his promises, and Lyon was far from Paris. And now, at the end of 1762, Poivre was still waiting for the frigate and all that went with it. To alleviate his impatience, he began to plant a large garden on the hill of Saint-Romain-au-Mont-d'Or near Lyon, which contained an exotic collection of herbs and spices.

This was the romantic character whom Jeanne was going to see with two bundles of Swiss herbs. Her heart was aflutter with curiosity.

Poivre lived in the heart of old Lyon, the area around the Church of Saint-Nizier and the Holy Apostles, on the Rue des Quatre-Chapeaux. Nothing had changed since the Middle Ages in the tangle of streets, alleys, and houses next to the grain market.

Pierre Poivre was no longer the young daredevil with the steel muscles, of whom she had heard so much. As a true Lyonnais, that is, a hearty eater, Poivre had put on weight. Dressed in a well-cut tan coat, set off by fine linen, and wearing a powdered three-roll wig, he was a bourgeois of distinction.

He served her a cassis accompanied by candied fruit, after which she asked him to speak of his travels in the Far East. They sat down on a bench with a view, and Poivre talked of China, Java, Manila, the Moluccas, and l'Ile de France.

"Have you no nostalgia for those marvelous lands? Those fragrant flowers under a tropical sun that you know so well?"

"I long for other lands, other flowers and fragrances, other suns, those I've not yet seen. And I dream of planting, here and now, an exotic garden, filled with frail tropical trees and plants." Poivre gazed at the far horizon. "To make a garden into a whole universe . . . can you imagine a more subtle pleasure? It will bring me peace in my old age. There's so much to be enjoyed that we must keep a good appetite to the end of the road."

Poivre's single hand had settled on the fragment of a sculpted female torso lying on the ground near the bench. He warmed the bare stone shoulder, letting his hand travel up to the neck or down toward the rounded beginning of a lost breast.

He's like Vincent. Jeanne was struck by the blissful expression on Poivre's face. *He's a happy animal. An accident has crippled him, but his instinct for happiness has overcome his disability. And so it will always be.* This idea evoked a wave of melancholy. *Why didn't Philibert have the same ability to capture a fleeting joy? Why did he linger over a happiness that was dead and buried? Why hadn't he kissed her when they had supped together while Mme. de Bouhey lay stricken upstairs?* She felt, suddenly, that if Poivre had been in Philibert's shoes, he would have reached out to touch her. . . .

As they walked slowly back toward the city he asked her, "Mademoiselle Jeanne, will you come to see me again?"

Jeanne was overcome by joy. The famous Pierre Poivre had offered her his friendship.

"Do you mean it?" she stammered. "It wouldn't be a bore?"

"You must never ask that question of a man," he said, with a kindly look. "At least not when you are young." And smiling, he kissed her hand in farewell. She had succeeded so well with Poivre. How would she fare with Philibert?

CHAPTER 10

eanne stood motionless for several long minutes in front of the Aubriot house. Mustering her resolve, she knocked tentatively at the door.

Philibert's youngest sister, Clémence, answered, appearing surprised and pleased to see her.

"He's just gone to the hospital. The chaplain has called him. But if you want to wait in the sitting room you'll find good company. There's a certain Chevalier Casanova whom Philibert left in my care. A handsome man, and divinely dressed, covered with lace and jewels. A prince traveling incognito is my guess."

Jeanne made an impatient gesture. The Don Juan of Venice was hard to shake off.

"If you fancy him so much, Clémence, I'll leave him to you. I'll look for Monsieur Philibert at the hospital."

Before leaving, she went upstairs with Clémence to wash her hands and tidy her clothes. Jeanne's heart pounded wildly. She saw herself at home in Philibert's house, wandering about in her petticoat, with bare arms and bosom. What a wonderful feeling! Wonderful enough to make her kiss her image in the mirror. It was just as if . . . She put on an almond-green jacket and skirt which set off her complexion, and a diadem-shaped bonnet of pleated white muslin, ornamented with a rose of the same material, a flattering new fashion called "sweet tease." *Should I spread rouge on my cheeks? No, they're sufficiently colored by emotion.* She sprinkled toilet water on her neckline, glanced in the mirror and proclaimed out loud, "I look wonderful!"

For the first time in weeks, Jeanne felt self-confident. She tried out some provocative gestures—moving her hips, throwing out her breasts, moistening her lips and holding them half open.

It was time to throw herself into the arms of the absent minded botanist of Châtillon.

* * * *

The town, in the bright sun, shone as if decorated for a holy day. Jeanne wondered whether in all of France there was another town with so many flowers. Autumn colors exploded from every lawn, balcony, and window box. Wildflowers lined the riverbanks of the Durdevant River. Boatloads of them floated on the Chalaronne, and garlands of them, brightened by nasturtiums, trailed from the covered bridges that spanned both streams. The water below was thick with watercress.

When the season was done, thousands of seeds were carried by the wind and scattered all about the ruins of the medieval castle, the ramparts of the old town, the tower and belfrey of Saint-André, and the grass of the Pré de la Foire. The whole town sprouted flowers.

Jeanne wondered how Philibert could have left Châtillon for Bugey, a sober town surrounded by thick, dark woods. She reached the hospital, a fine classical structure. The gateman told Jeanne that she would find Dr. Aubriot with M. Jassans, the hospital apothecary. The wood-paneled walls of the small room were lined with shelves holding big-bellied earthenware pots filled with mysterious contents. The doctor and the apothecary seemed to be exchanging recipes for some alchemic mixture. They stood near a pan of scales resting on a counter covered with tin measuring cups and pestles.

"Jeannette!" Philibert exclaimed. "I trust no one's ill at Charmont."

"No, everyone is well." She could barely pronounce the words. "I've brought you the cuttings which Monsieur Casanova entrusted to me."

Aubriot ended his conversation with Jassans brusquely. Taking

Jeanne's elbow, he led her out into the sunny courtyard. Her head reeled as the warmth of his hand came through her fine wool sleeve. All the confidence she had felt in her good looks vanished.

She had planned a strategy worthy of a courtesan. *One: gaze into his eyes. Two: show my teeth in a bewitching smile. Three: twist my ankle and cling to his arm. Four: cry Ouch and start to limp . . . so that he must hold me up.*

They walked through the hospital gate and into the cloister of the Ursuline nuns.

"Let me see your face," said Philibert, coming to a halt. "Look at me! . . . Well, I'm pleased with your complexion. It's very healthy. And I'm glad to see you, Jeannot," he added with a smile, "with or without the cuttings."

This last sentence moved Jeanne deeply. This was the moment, dear God, to cry out, *I'm not glad, Monsieur Philibert, I'm ecstatic, bursting with happiness, because I love you!* She was vexed by her dumbness, her inability to get out a word. It made no sense to be so in love with a man. Respect for Philibert overcame her and she began to tremble.

"You've never been a chatterbox, Jeannette," he said, giving her a quick glance. "Do you now talk less than ever?"

Jeanne made an effort to say something. "I find you pale," she said painfully. "I'm sure you work too hard and don't sleep enough."

"That's because you no longer watch over me," he said good-humoredly. "I'll write out a prescription for myself saying that you should visit me twice a week whenever I'm at Châtillon. By the way, did you know that I've just come back from an expedition in Auvergne? My mountain plants are in a state of disorder. What would you say to helping me classify them?"

Jeanne tried to check the tears that welled up in her eyes. Leaning over the bridge, she tried unsuccessfully to wipe her face.

The doctor looked at her in silence and then asked gently, "Why are you crying, Jeannette? What's the sorrow you came to confide? Can't you put it into words?"

"No, no," she stammered, dabbing at her cheeks with her soaked handkerchief. "I've no sorrow, on the contrary . . . it's something new. . . . I cry when I'm happy. Father Jérôme says it often happens to girls my age. He advises cold baths."

"Cold baths?"

"Yes, have you anything better to prescribe, monsieur?"

"It could be."

The shadow of a smile brought out the strong line of his jaws and the thinness of his face.

"I have a prescription for this evening, in any case," he went on, "and that's that you have some fun. Do you know Chevalier Marlieux?"

"Of course," said Jeanne. "He comes, from time to time, to Charmont. Last summer he 'electrified' us, something he does to perfection."

"Well, you shall have supper with Marlieux this evening. I'm going to his house to meet Jassans and Abbé Rozier. I've given him a taste for botany to add to his interest in physics. Chevalier Casanova will also be there. He's waiting for me now. I owe him at least an evening's entertainment for having brought me a parcel all the way from Geneva. They say he's amusing, with his talk of alchemy and all sorts of magical nonsense. But, of course, you've already seen him. Did you find him interesting?"

"He's a terrible talker. And a lady killer."

"Aha! Did he flirt with you, Jeannette?"

"Yes, he did," she said with a touch of coquetry.

"And did his flirting please or displease you?"

Pretending to straighten her bonnet she replied impetuously, "I like to be flirted with, yes."

"Is this, too, something new?"

"Yes," she said, not daring to look him in the eyes.

He scrutinized her and asked, not without malice, "And what does Father Jérôme advise for that? Prayer?"

"I actually do pray, Monsieur Philibert," said Jeanne and then, emboldened by the joking nature of their exchange, "I pray that someone will pay court or, at least, flirt with me."

He burst into a quick but hearty laugh, like that of days gone by. What a long time since she had heard it. Yes, there are moments of paradise on earth!

* * * *

"Have no doubts," said Casanova, "Madame d'Urfé knows all the lore of the philosophers' stone. At her house in Paris, on the Quai des Théatins, I've seen the treasures of her library."

"Knowing the marquise as I do," put in Jassans, "I see that she hasn't been able to make *aurum potabile*, the liquid gold, that restores youth and beauty."

"Oh, the marquise is still a beauty," said the gallant Casanova. "A beauty of the time of the Regency, of course."

"It's forgivable to have a Regency face," remarked Aubriot. "But not to have a Regency mind in the forty-eighth year of the reign of Louis XV."

"Madame d'Urfé's no fool," Casanova maintained, with a vexed expression. "She is particularly well read in the field of medicine. Do you realize that she knows Paracelsus by heart?"

"I fear this knowledge isn't very useful to the ailing," said the doctor sarcastically.

"And are ignorant barbers any better?" Casanova retorted.

"Bleeding's better than an enema," replied Jassans.

"No, I prefer an enema," said Aubriot. "At least the patient survives it."

"The latest is removing stones from the bladder, an operation that can cost as much as six hundred francs," said Jassans.

"Has the technique of such an operation been perfected here in France?" asked Casanova.

"Certainly, Chevalier. The operation is miraculous. The proof is that you only hear about it from the patients who've been cured. The others have nothing to say."

The apothecary laughed.

Mme. Marlieux, who had been trying to regain control of the conversation, managed to interrupt.

"Isn't it time for a game of electricity? Is your Leyden jar ready?"

The Chevalier Marlieux stood up. "Of course, my dear Rose, that goes without saying. If you all agree . . .

"My dear Aubriot, I predict that some day electricity will furnish you with a magic curative agent."

Jeanne waited impatiently for the signal to begin the "game" and form a circle. She anticipated the moment when she could slip her hand into Philibert's. During the meal she glowed with happiness. Sitting at his left, she purred silently. They were breathing the same air, eating the same food, drinking the same wine.

Philibert took her hand when the circle was formed and squeezed it as he leaned over to ask, "Are you afraid?"

"No. I've had an electric shock on two occasions already."

The current passed around the little circle so quickly that the three ladies present gave three little cries and Casanova fell back on his chair.

A silly game, Aubriot thought, as he took the Venetian's pulse. *We should know more about the phenomenon before we trifle with it*. But the others, including Casanova, were happy to have been properly shocked. They chattered excitedly, eagerly exclaiming over their sensations.

It was decided that Casanova and Abbé Rozier would spend the night at the manor house and that Jeanne would be taken back to Charmont in the old hospital carriage. But, at the last moment, Casanova offered her the greater comfort of his hired carriage. Aubriot frowned and Jeanne tried to refuse the unwelcome invitation.

Madame Marlieux came to the rescue. "I think that Jeanne would enjoy my husband's cabriolet even more. She admired it last summer when we drove over to call on the Baroness de Bouhey."

"Oh, yes, Chevalier!" Jeanne responded. "If your coachman hasn't gone to bed, do send me home in the cabriolet!"

In Paris pedestrians were run down by cabriolets every day. But at Châtillon they were quite new, and pedestrians stared after them in admiration.

"No need for the coachman," Marlieux said gaily. "I'll drive you myself."

"Look here," Aubriot broke in. "Why don't I drive? I've been wanting a chance to try out your superb rig. Why not this evening? A man must feel young again when he drives a cabriolet."

A servant loaded Jeanne's luggage behind the box as Philibert climbed nimbly onto the driver's seat. At a slow trot they entered the silent Boulevard du Bourg.

Once they had passed through the town gate the horse's hooves began to clatter. The peaceful grassy countryside enveloped them. The full moon's luminous glow transformed everything. On such a night elves might be dancing in the fields. Jeanne let herself succumb to the poetry of the moment. Their destination was only five miles away, but in five miles anything could happen.

"Are you cold, Jeannette? You seem to be shivering."

"Oh, no," she said in a low voice, mechanically pulling her shawl around her shoulders.

"Wrap the blanket around your legs. I don't need it. We've gone about many times together, but never by moonlight. Isn't that true?"

"Tonight everything is unreal."

"Traveling at night takes you out of reality. Now that science is so rapidly encroaching on the supernatural I'm not sorry to see that moonlight still has its mystery."

"I feel the same way. I always feel the way you do."

He laughed lightly. "That's because I taught you my ways of seeing and hearing. Perhaps in doing that I stifled your own natural reactions, which might be superior to mine."

"Oh, no! I'm happy to know that I resemble you in any way. I'd like to think that you fashioned me with your own hands."

During the rest of the drive she wondered whether she had been too familiar, for he said nothing more. But she chose to interpret his silence as a sweetness without words, a foretaste of greater sweetness to come. When they came to the giant elm at the crossroads, where they branched off toward Charmont, Philibert pulled in the reins, slowed the horse down to a walk, and said gaily, "I'm glad that you want to be like me, Jeannette, but for heaven's sake, don't emulate my looks. Yours are much better."

She quivered and summoned her courage to ask, "Do you like my looks, Monsieur Philibert? Am I turning into an attractive woman?"

"You're easy on the eyes," he said, laughing.

He stopped on the narrow, mossy road that led up to the courtyard, so that the grinding of the wheels wouldn't wake anyone asleep in the château. After he had leaped to the ground he went around to the other side of the cabriolet and held out his arms.

"Jump down!" he ordered.

In just this way, when she was a little girl, he had made her jump from an embankment to the bottom of a ditch.

"I'll go in by the kitchen," she said in a low voice. "The back door is never locked."

He put her bag down at the threshold. Before going in she turned around to bid him farewell. The moon had emerged from the mist and made it possible for them to see each other. In the fraction of a second, Jeanne thought, the magic hour would be over. Why couldn't an act of will prolong it? So sharp was her fear of losing him again that she leaned forward until she nearly touched him, her head thrown back and her lips obviously inviting a kiss. Philibert laid his hands tenderly on her thin shoulders and kissed her on both cheeks.

"I'm glad to have seen you, Jeannette. Don't forget to look in on your old teacher from time to time."

How could I forget to love you? Jeanne said to herself, so intensely that later on she wasn't sure whether or not she had said it out loud.

"Go on in," Philibert said, in the authoritative voice of a doctor. "Hurry up! You know that a moonstroke isn't good for you. If you don't hurry, you'll have a chill."

And he climbed up into the driver's seat without a backward glance.

CHAPTER 11

 eanne used all her self-control to restrain herself from visiting Châtillon the next day. She waited until the day after and, early in the morning, set out. On arrival, she was disappointed to find that Philibert had gone to Belley to close his office there and settle his affairs. But Clémence put Jeanne to work right away, classifying the herbs and plants from Auvergne, and she did so, singing. Obviously, Philibert was putting the past behind him and their romance would soon be in full flower.

But Philibert did not come back! Not that day, or that week!

After a month of anxious waiting for some word, a letter arrived at Châtillon saying that he was going to Orange and then by ship to Majorca, where he planned to study the tropical flora. He had to hurry, he said, in order to get there while this island was still a French possession.

Jeanne was totally devastated by this turn of events. The meaning of it escaped her. Was the enchanted drive in the cabriolet only a dream? She felt sure that Philibert had guessed her love, especially at the moment of farewell. She held her dream in the hollow of her hand.

All the way back to Charmont she sobbed into Blanchette's mane. When she came to the giant elm she held back the mare who automatically turned toward home. Instead she spurred her on toward Rupert, where she could weep on the shoulder of her friend Marie.

Marie advised seeking the counsel of Emilie. And so they both set out for the abbey.

Although she was only fourteen years old, Dame Emilie de la Pommeraie, the young canoness of Neuville, was more than willing to give advice in affairs of the heart. She was gay, witty, mischievous, and mature beyond her years. Knowledgeable in the discussion of friendship, passion, marriage, adultery, and all sexual matters, her wisdom had been acquired from her unusual powers of observation, the reading of novels, and the secret but copious correspondence she carried on with friends. Her personal diary was a long meditation on the state of being in love.

Her parents, the Pommeraies, lived beyond their means on the ancient glories of their illustrious family. They had had six children but three had died, leaving two boys and a girl. They did everything for the boys, and put Emilie into a convent. Fortunately her noble origin made it possible for her to become a canoness rather than a simple nun.

Jeanne would never forget the chill that struck her heart when she saw her friend standing before the altar, like a bride without a groom, in a ceremony that effectively made her a widow. Jeanne had gazed with horror at the cap, a narrow band of white muslin with a black stripe, which the new little canoness called her "husband."

But Jeanne soon learned from Emilie that the estate of a canoness was an enviable one. It seemed that few canonesses took advantage of their right to be relieved of their vows. A canoness automatically received the title of countess, ample pocket money, and a comfortable lodging. She could leave the abbey at any time and was free to receive relatives and friends. The only limitation was the regulation that male visitors must leave the abbey before vespers. The flexibility of this monastic rule actually brought out the virtues of the lady canonesses of Neuville, who led a dignified half-cloistered, half-worldly existence. Their devotions, although intermittent, were sincere, and their faith was widely admired. It was an esthetic pleasure to see them at high mass, clad in long black silk robes and graceful bonnets, marching in solemn procession, to the choir stalls of the Church of Sainte-Cathérine, followed by pageboys who held up their ermine-bordered trains.

The severe but beautiful black silk robe was only for religious ceremonies. In their own quarters or in the outside world the canonesses wore whatever colors they chose except for pink, which was associated with dancing. Emilie dressed in green, white, and violet, the colors which she thought best matched her curly red hair, freckled skin, and gray-green eyes. Now Jeanne and Marie found her in a white negligée, with her head bent over an account book.

"Do you know how lucky we are to be living in this province of Bresse?" she said to her visitors. "This morning we bought chickens for fifteen sous the pair, butter at six sous the pound, and eggs at three sous a dozen, while in Paris eggs have gone up to ten sous and butter to thirteen. And guess how much it costs to have a fish stew in a café on the Champs-Elysées? Six francs per person! People go bankrupt buying good food there! Are you dining with me? Three days ago I was brought some gray snails, and they ought to be ready to eat."

"Yes, yes!" exclaimed Marie. "Do give us a snail dinner!"

"Good. I'll ask for white Mâcon wine and some cheesecakes for our dessert."

"I'm not really hungry," Jeanne sighed.

Emilie's gray-green eyes shot her a sly glance. "I know why, Jeannette. Monsieur Aubriot is still stupidly playing the widower."

"I can't force him to return my love," said Jeanne in a dying voice.

"That's to be discussed," said Emilie. "But first I must give my orders."

When she returned she had changed into a pale green muslin gown and wore a cross of gold and white enamel with a representation of Saint Catherine around her neck.

The three friends sat down to dine in a little drawing room which Emilie had decorated in white with green trim and furnished with soft sofas upholstered in white damask. The inlaid floor, in the style of Versailles, was a marvel, and so was the rococo fireplace, of green Florentine marble. The rule did not allow a canoness younger than twenty-five years old to live alone, but Emilie had a perfect chaperone in old Dame Donatienne. She was rheumatic, half blind, and totally deaf.

Emilie drank a swallow of wine and took a second helping of snails. "Let's speak of the condition of Jeannette's heart. I agree that your Philibert has turned tail and run away. But you've not been sufficiently bold. In spite of your keen mind and strong character, you have behaved like a little donkey. You cater to his whims with a respect that no one, nowadays, has for their father!"

"Well," put in Marie, laughing, "she can't very well abduct him. That's not yet in style. She has to wait for him to run away with her."

"No," said Emilie firmly. "She has to push him into it. All the cases I know have been engineered that way. In matters of love a man is likely, at the last minute, to get cold feet."

"No wonder," said Marie. "If something goes awry the abductor pays with his head, whereas the girl is let off with a few months of detention in a nunnery. Do you remember the abduction of Anne-Marie de Moras? If Count de Courbon didn't literally lose his head it was only because he'd taken her over the Alps by the time the court condemned him."

"That's a story of twenty years ago, which our parents held up as a dreadful example. In any case, when it comes to Jeannette and Dr. Aubriot, I don't see what judges . . ."

She stopped herself in embarrassment, and Jeanne said with a half-smile, "Speak up, Emilie! One time in a thousand there's some advantage in common birth. What judges, indeed, would bother their heads if a girl called Beauchamps were to run away with a bourgeois from Châtillon? The trouble is that the bourgeois doctor doesn't want to run off with Jeanne Beauchamps. Philibert likes me, it's true, but he doesn't love me."

Emilie shook her red curls furiously. "I don't believe it. A pretty young girl always attracts a man, at least long enough for her to get what she wants out of him. A man may have a dead heart or a distracted one, but he'll still enjoy all the affairs that come his way."

"It's true," said Marie, "according to the conversations I hear between my mother and Madame de Vaux-Jailloux, men are quite different from us in matters of sex. Love doesn't necessarily come into it."

"But I want to be loved!" cried Jeanne, who was not in the least consoled by the turn the conversation was taking.

"Of course," said Emilie. "Every woman should aspire to love. To be loved by the man you love, to live out a mutual devotion and fidelity, that is a woman's fulfillment. I'm sure of it. But I know, too, that this miracle doesn't happen very often. The best of men adore us and at the same time are unfaithful. That's a matter of common knowledge."

"There are exceptions, though, aren't there?" asked Marie, her mind on the faraway Philippe. "Doesn't a fickle fiancé fall under the spell of his bride once they are married?"

"It happens, I admit," said Emilie. "Thank God, possession has its effects."

And, addressing herself to Jeanne, she added emphatically, "To be frank, my friends, I think you can get a better hold on a man when you have him in your bed than when he's wandering on the highways and byways."

Jeanne turned crimson. "Thank you for the advice! You're telling me to go for Monsieur Aubriot like a . . . strumpet, and a low-class one, at that. I'll wager that even a dancer at the opera waits for a man to take the initiative."

Emilie raised her hand as if to say that she wouldn't take up the wager, and rang for the servant to bring in a second helping of snails and salad. There was a happy odor of hot garlic butter, which Marie breathed in deeply. Of the three loveless girls she was the one who best knew how to make up for the absence of a lover with the pleasures of the palate. After the servant had withdrawn, Emilie returned to the discussion of her favorite topic.

"There's a lot to study about the unwritten laws that govern the relationship between men and women. It seems that certain very young shepherdesses make passable lovers out of boys twelve years old and less. It's only later that the girls simper and the boys pursue them. And why? Because they've taken to imitating the ways of the gentry."

"And are we to imitate the ways of the peasants?" asked Marie, laughing, while Jeanne looked away with an offended air.

"I don't say that, Marie. But it's plain that young men may be timid. Only old men press their suit, and since they're not our concern, we must encourage the others.

"My dear," continued Emilie, "we women mustn't start living too late. Look at the fun people make of an old woman who falls in love at the age of forty. Twenty! I say that's the limit, we must arrange to enjoy ourselves no later than that."

"Don't discourage me completely," cried out Jeanne who, although she was not yet sixteen, saw herself fast approaching the year when it would be too late. "After all," she added, "isn't it living just to be hopelessly in love?"

"That's what I thought when I was twelve," said Emilie ironically. "It's been some time, now, since I was attracted by the role of a virtuous heroine in a novel, who pines away, with a listless air and tears in her eyes, unable to eat or utter a word. . . ."

"That role wouldn't become you, that's true," said Marie.

"You don't think it would become me, either, do you?" Jeanne asked. "Well," she continued, "I'm not going to weep while I wait. His leaving was no rejection. Monsieur Philibert really has weak lungs, and the climate of the south will be beneficial. He hasn't forbidden me to hope."

"That's a bit of hypocrisy with which you might very well reproach him," Emilie insisted. "If he understood your feelings, but couldn't respond to them, it would have been kinder to say so."

And, before Jeanne could object, she went on. "No, don't tell me that it was kind to let you hope. No man behaves that delicately. There's calculation in his kindness. He took you for a drive in the moonlight but didn't kiss you. He urged you to come see him while, all the time, he was making ready to go away. If he didn't dampen your hopes before leaving I say it was simply because he didn't want you to find consolation during his absence. I imagine him saying to himself, as he rides to the south, that somebody he has left behind loves him. She looks out of her tower, so to speak, every morning, at the road from Orange, to see if the hooves of his horse are kicking up the dust that will announce his return. If I were you, my dear, I'd resent being put in storage to wait upon his convenience."

"There's some logic to what you say," said Marie, eying the largest of the cheesecakes.

Jeanne had caught some of the fire of Emilie's speech.

"And so," she said, half inspired, half dreamy, "you agree with me, Emilie, that Monsieur Philibert is pleased that I love him even though he has put off telling me so."

The canoness tossed her red curls. "Jeannette, you make me ashamed to be a woman. You interpret what I told you as encouragement to wait until Aubriot sees fit to make use of you. And you haven't the courage to write to reproach him for his selfishness. You're throwing your youth away, believe me!"

* * * *

The winter dragged on in harmony with her lassitude, gray with rain and heavy with mud. Spring arrived but the soft air seemed to deepen her feelings of nostalgia. It brought back violets and buttercups, sunshine sparkling through the morning dew, the fragrance of hawthorn in the hedges, all the beauties of Charmont, but not the return of Philibert to Châtillon.

Jeanne turned sixteen joylessly. The nightingale of the woods of Neuville, the bird that sings only to make his listener weep for a lost love, sang its song for her.

In May, she received a long letter. Jeanne read and reread the letter over a dozen times. But she found that after her initial joy had worn off, the letter appeared less propitious than she had originally fancied. Philibert spoke only of himself and his petty pleasures. He seemed to have thought of her only at the end, and then just to give her orders. He had sent a box containing two hundred dried specimens expecting Jeanne to start making the plates for a Provençal herbal. The affectionate greetings were purely conventional and did not make up for his abrupt departure or her broken heart.

Emilie, she felt sure, would tear the letter apart, and so she did not show it to her. But she did show Emilie and Marie the presents she discovered at the bottom of the box of herbs: a bottle of lavender water in an olive-wood case, candied orange and lemon peel, and a roll of Provençal songs.

"Monsieur Aubriot is obviously distracted," opined Emilie. "He has sent you superfluous things before getting down to essentials."

"Bite your malicious tongue!" said Marie, whose fiancé had never sent her so much as a pin. "I find these offerings delightful and a sign of good things to come."

Several weeks later, a second letter arrived, posted from Roquesteron, a village in the southern Alps.

Ordinarily Philibert wrote in a plain style, except for the encumbrance of Latin names and phrases. But here, in order to describe the episcopal reds and violets of the fuchsias, the vanilla smell of heliotrope, the natural beauties of his excursions, the length of the Estéron and the coast of Var, his style waxed positively lyrical.

A whole page was dedicated to the announcement of a second box, containing frail, fresh plants. Jeanne thought this letter worthy of being communicated to her friends. She read its finest phrases aloud in her most melodious voice.

"What a gift for reading!" said Emilie complacently. "Too bad the profession of actress isn't respectable. You'd be a stunning success. I wonder whether, if I could win Dame Charlotte over to my side, the prioress would allow me to set up a theater in one of our large houses. We might . . ."

"But the letter!" Jeanne interrupted impatiently. "What do you say about Monsieur Philibert's letter?"

"I felt myself transported to the banks of the Estéron," said Marie. "I'm inebriated by sounds and smells. Some parts are so poetical. I was happy to let myself go. . . ."

"*You* might get sucked in," Emilie warned her mockingly. "But the man's prose lulls *me* to sleep."

Jeanne shot her a furious glance and did not speak to her again for a whole month.

The second shipment arrived from Hyères. It had been delayed on the way, and the cuttings were in a sad state when they reached Châtillon. At least a third of them had dried up and could not be revived. Jeanne decided to take the most endangered of the survivors to the botanical garden in Lyon, where there was a well-equipped hothouse.

Mme. de Bouhey, who was watching distractedly from her window, suddenly called out to Jeanne, "Jeannette, if you're going to Lyon you may as well stay longer than two days. Take some clothes, and stay for a fortnight with the Delafayes. Lyon is a happy place."

And when she saw Jeanne hesitate, one foot on the running board, she added, "Don't be a silly girl, Jeannette. You can play Penelope just as well there as here, only the time will pass much faster."

CHAPTER 12

n 1763, Lyon was flourishing. The Seven Years' War was over, at last. With expanding industry and trade, a brilliant coterie of intellectuals, the social life was animated and elegant. The city reflected the prosperity and optimism of the entire kingdom. Although France had been forced to give up Canada, the protectorates of the Indies and Minorca, as well as Louisiana, no one attached importance to the papers signed by princes. These were the king's affair. His subjects were busy making money. As long as the king held on to the plantations of the Antilles, there was sugar for everybody, and all was well. As for the Canadian, American, and African daydreams, goodbye and good riddance. A million men had died in the war, but they were not there to complain, and the survivors were well enough off to forget them. There was no unemployment and for the enterprising Frenchmen life was good.

The Delafayes' life was colored with silver and gold. And so Jeanne wrote to ask Mme. de Bouhey for permission to stay until winter. The business world had begun to interest her almost as much as the botanical world. She went to the Merchants' Exchange to observe the transactions of the Delafayes' broker. Amid the feverish faces, shouts, and gesticulations of the crowd involved in buying and selling, Jeanne felt as if she were at the pulsing heart of the city, the source of its growing wealth and power.

It was impossible to mingle with the society of Lyon without hearing about Andrinople red, the fashionable color for cotton thread, the competition sponsored by the academy for the best process for degumming silk, and the news of English manufacturing techniques reported by French industrial spies. There was talk, also, of how the Indians dyed their calico, how the Dutch printed their chintz, the cinnamon used to flavor fruit jellies and jams, the extract of amaranth with which cabinetmakers ornamented chests of drawers, and the "poc-poc," which apothecaries were selling to "relax the stomach."

The stream of new discoveries and inventions seemed endless. The lectures given at the Académie des Sciences, des Arts et des Belles-Lettres had audiences as large as those of concert halls and theaters. Women were present in large numbers and took a passionate interest in the diseases of blackberry bushes and the cross-pollinating of wheat.

Pierre Poivre was the city's most eloquent lecturer and its most eligible bachelor. While waiting for Philibert, Jeanne would have liked Poivre to fall in love with her. Alas he displayed the same charm to all the women.

The absence of Philibert no longer made her forlorn. It only got on her nerves and prevented her from going to sleep at night. In her dreams she relived their ride in the cabriolet, jumped down into his arms, and imagined the kiss he had not given her, which paradoxically tasted like Vincent's. Thousands of needles pierced her flesh, a painful hollow opened up in her body, and she ended up by beating her fists angrily against the pillow.

In the afternoons, Jeanne went with Marie-Louise and Margot to the Delafayes' big shop, Le Cocon Enchanté, on the Rue Mercière. She either worked on the ground floor handling retail sales or worked upstairs with Marie-Louise.

Marie-Louise, now eighteen years old, had been put in charge of foreign transactions, under the instruction of Edmond Chapelain, a clever thirty-year-old lawyer, to whom she had become engaged. At first Jeanne had thought that she would be bored in the company of two business people. But very soon she found they shared a fascination in common: the sea. Marie-Louise and Edmond talked about it constantly.

Jeanne would not have imagined the oceans of the world could be a pervading presence in an office over a shop on the Rue Mercière in Lyon. Yet it seemed to be just outside the door. As seen from Le Cocon Enchanté, the sea was a broad blue road on which caravans traveled to the East loaded with goods, and came back loaded with gold. Leafing through the export book, Jeanne felt sails growing out of her shoulder blades, swelling with wind and pushing her on toward adventure. On an order from Marie-Louise, ships were filled with treasures and sails were run up their masts like great white birds. Gliding over the Mediterranean, their fleet distributed taffetas, ribbons, braid, lace, top hats stacked like hot cakes, well-made shoes in Moroccan leather, fine linen handkerchiefs, crystal chandeliers, belts, gloves, pins, silk and cotton stockings, reels of embroidery thread and, finally, in two cases out of three, "good red wine."

"Marie-Louise, the records of your sea trade read like novels," Jeanne said one day, closing the export book.

"The sea is a novel," said Giulio Pazevin.

This sentence echoed words Jeanne had heard before.

"Yes, a sailor said that to me once," she murmured, raising her eyes to look at the speaker.

Giulio was of medium height, with the elegance and grace of a dancer. Count Pazevin had never married but had gladly legitimated Giulio, his bastard son.

Giulio was thirty-two years old. He could sing, dance, strum the guitar, play the harpsichord, and sell almost anything . . . especially clever with women customers. Giulio came frequently to Lyon, to buy merchandise or to sell shares in his father's shipbuilding enterprise. And Margot had fallen in love with him.

But he was in no hurry to choose among the many who adored him. He drew closer to Jeanne and sat down casually on the corner of her desk.

"Do you dream of the sea?" he asked with a smile.

"Yes, but without ever having seen it. You, no doubt, are a regular seadog."

"That I am," said Giulio complacently. "I know all the Mediterranean islands, the Barbary shores, Greece, Constantinople . . ."

"And l'Ile de France?"

"Not yet. I'm waiting for a captain I know to take me there. But he's lying low until the island is ceded to the king."

"When will that be?" put in Edmond Chapelain. "Does anyone know?"

Giulio shrugged his shoulders. "When the king and the Indies Company reach an agreement on the price of the Mascarene Islands. The company wants ten million francs and the king offers only six or seven. Eventually they'll compromise."

"The sooner the better, as far as businessmen are concerned," said Edmond. "When the company no longer has a monopoly, we'll be able to sell more freely."

"That is, if the colonists have the money to pay for your goods," Giulio observed ironically. "For the moment what they need is money. Chevalier Vincent told me that Port Louis is almost in ruins. The colonists haven't the money to rebuild it. They're waiting for the king to buy up their island. I'd like to set up an office for slave trading there. When a country is beginning to develop, the niggers . . ."

The mention of Vincent's name made Jeanne dreamy. Although she had lost him forever and, probably, he didn't even remember her, the casual mention of his name made her ears and heart hum.

". . . if the cultivation of cotton and sugarcane continues to grow, more and more slaves will be needed. Good black flesh is going to be increasingly rare and sought after."

There was a moment of silence. For moral reasons, the Delafaye brothers had never wanted to invest in the slave trade. They argued with young Laurent who wanted to buy into it.

"I'm not keen on slave trade," said M. Henri. "It's too speculative, either you make money or else you go bankrupt."

"That's because it's carried on inefficiently," Giulio insisted. "Chevalier Vincent told me that few traders protect their merchandise with any intelligence. They're satisfied to deliver no more than half of them alive, in a condition more or less salable. You need specially equipped ships and captains who are kind or at least have some human feelings. Believe me, that would be financially advantageous as well as moral."

Jeanne felt suppressed anger rising within her as she listened to the future slave trader's admonitions. She tried to keep her feelings under control as she asked, pointedly, "And is your friend, Chevalier Vincent, a captain capable of treating the black animal as kindly as if it had a white soul?"

The involuntary emotion in her voice drew all eyes to her. Giulio smiled ironically and countered, "No doubt, mademoiselle, you are among the enthusiastic readers of Baron de Montesquieu."

"Yes, monsieur," she said, returning his ironic smile. "I'm not ashamed to say that I'm against slavery. Let's drop the subject, monsieur. We shall never agree. I only wanted an answer to my question. Is Chevalier Vincent going into the slave trade?"

"Do you know him, then? Is that why you ask?" said Giulio with astonishment.

"I know him very well. And I know that he won the disapproval of the grand master of his Order because he freed some slaves rather than transport them to Malta. Have you persuaded him to change his philosophy?"

"Mademoiselle, if you are interested in my friend Vincent's frame of mind, you need have no fear. He's not likely to embrace the slave trade. He refuses to believe that niggers are happier as slaves than in their own land. But, believe me, mademoiselle, we do them a favor by rescuing them from their savage state. . . ."

"Everyone has heard of the philanthropic ideas of slave traders," Jeanne interrupted. "But, let's change the subject. I'm curious to hear about the *Belle Vincente*. No doubt you've seen her."

"Yes, and I'm still dazzled. A truly splendid frigate, the most elegant lines I've ever seen in the harbor of Marseille. And below decks, total luxury. The captain's cabin is a boudoir, the mess a drawing room, and the officers' quarters fit for ladies. Even the cabins of the pilot and surgeon have creature comforts. Since you are so fascinated by the sea, why don't you come to see the *Belle Vincente* with your own eyes? She's tied up at the dock. Come with me to Marseille and I'll take you aboard."

"In that case, monsieur, you must take me, too," said Margot, smitten with jealousy. "I'm dying to have a look at the sea."

"Your brother Laurent has promised you a trip to Marseille for your sixteenth birthday, this coming spring," said Margot's Uncle Henri. "It's no fun to be on the road in winter."

"Besides, you'd have to make it in a single stage, without even stopping to take off your boots if you wanted to be sure of seeing the *Belle Vincente*," said Marie-Louise. "A letter I've had from Marseille says she'll raise anchor on the seventeenth of December, and it's already the eleventh."

"No," said Giulio, "she's not leaving before the nineteenth or twentieth. She's waiting for some gold and silver cloth and three cases of vermeil dishes which won't be ready before."

Now that she knew that Vincent was in Marseille, Jeanne fell silent. She was taken aback by the troubled feeling which this news had aroused in her, and by an almost uncontrollable trembling.

She put on a disdainful air and said, "Modern times are far from romantic. To think that a corsair should have to submit to the will of clothiers and jewelers as patiently as any captain of a merchant ship!"

"If you were to voyage through the eastern Mediterranean, you'd see that doing business there is as adventurous as any pirate could desire," Giulio told her. "Pirates are all over the map, and only a corsair ship can safely carry precious goods to be sold in the Near East."

"I see," said Jeanne. "But I had a different idea of the life of a corsair."

"By the way," asked M. Henri, "why haven't we seen Vincent in Lyon?"

"That I don't know," said Giulio. "But we haven't seen much of him in Marseille, either. He's been on the move, without saying where."

* * * *

He's at Vaux, I'm sure of it. Jeanne was mechanically folding her petticoats. She had decided to return to Charmont. There was a knock at the door and when she opened it, she saw the round, pink, and slightly alarmed face of Appoline, the Delafayes' little maid-of-all-work.

"There's a man downstairs asking for Mademoiselle Jeanne Beauchamps. He made the request in a very formal manner, without giving his name, but . . ." She paused and then went on, with a mysterious air, "I recognized him, mademoiselle. He's Monsieur de Beaulieu, the chief of police."

"The chief of police? Are you quite sure?"

"Oh, yes, mademoiselle. If you want to get away you can go down the back stairs and leave from the rear of the house," said Appoline in a lowered voice.

"Don't be silly! Go tell Monsieur de Beaulieu that I'll come down at once."

At Jeanne's bidding the chief of police sat down. He was tall and impressive with a certain air of distinction. There was nothing sinister about him.

Jeanne stared at him in silence, with her hands trembling slightly in her lap.

"Have no fear, mademoiselle," he said, smiling. "I'm not here to bring any accusation against you. But you may be able to help me settle a serious matter. I'm told that you're a friend of Denis Gaillon, son of the bailiff of Baroness de Bouhey."

Jeanne nodded, feeling more and more surprised.

"Well, then, did he tell you that he was planning to go away? No? Well, the fact is that young Gaillon has disappeared. He's been gone from Châtillon for two days."

Jeanne opened her eyes wide, and M. de Beaulieu reflected that they had the most moving expression he had ever seen.

He went on, in a fatherly voice. "When a nineteen-year-old man leaves home to see the world, it is of no interest to the police, even if his father knows nothing about it. But if on the same day Dame Emilie de la Pommeraie also disappears from the Abbey of Neuville, it becomes a matter of great interest."

"Oh, no!"

As she exclaimed, Jeanne rose from her chair and stood, pale-faced, with her heart pounding. The police chief motioned to her to sit down.

"Your reaction shows me that you were not in on the secret. And that is a very good thing. Complicity in an abduction can be severely punished, with the brand of a fleur-de-lis, a whipping, and banishment. That is, when it doesn't lead to hanging."

Jeanne summoned up the courage to question her interlocutor. "And what makes you think, monsieur, that the two flights are linked? Did either fugitive leave a letter?"

He looked at her with almost disconcerting approval, drew up his chair and said, lowering his voice, "It's not a bad idea, mademoiselle, to look at the two events separately. If you were absolutely sure of your theory I'd be greatly relieved, unless someone brought me proof of the contrary."

Jeanne looked hard at him, trying to follow his reasoning.

"I don't like to see a love story come to a tragic end," he said. "But is there really a love story? To my knowledge neither party left a letter. You see, the police of the entire kingdom will be looking for the daughter of the Marquis de la Pommeraie, and eventually they'll find her. And it would be better for her if she's found alone, even if she parted company from her possible traveling companion only an hour before. She'd be quietly returned to her abbey, that's all. But if a pharmacist's assistant is caught with her . . ."

"Denis is more than a simple pharmacist; he's a chemist . . ."

M. de Beaulieu cut her short. "From the towers of the Château de la Pommeraie, a chemist has no more status than an apprentice pharmacist. In any case, if they're caught together he'll be thrown into prison and hanged, that is, if he's lucky. More likely he'll be broken on the wheel."

"The wheel!" Jeanne cried out, tears in her eyes.

"There, there!" said the chief of police gently. "They haven't yet been caught."

"And perhaps they won't be?"

"I fear they will. The police have become quite efficient. It's a cat-and-mouse story. And where will the mice run? To the nearest port, hoping to leave the country by ship? My colleague in Marseille is an expert at nabbing loving couples at loose on the docks, purse in hand, on the lookout for a greedy captain and unaware that such a one will sell and betray them. Besides, there are police informers in all the harbor taverns."

Jeanne listened, but her thoughts were aroused by the mention of Marseille. Perhaps Emilie and Denis had learned from Mme. de Vaux-Jailloux that the *Belle Vincente* was anchored there. And had they, for this very reason, set off two days before in the knowledge that this ship would offer them passage?

The chief of police, surprised by her sudden smile, paused in the middle of a sentence and asked, "Have you had a new idea, and one that makes you happy? What can it be?"

"No, monsieur. I've nothing in mind that can be helpful to you."

The chief of police got up, and bowed. "If you hear of anything . . ." And from the doorway, he turned around to add, deliberately, "I haven't given orders to make a search in Marseille. My clerks are overburdened with work and may not get around to it until the day after tomorrow. I can close my eyes temporarily but not indefinitely. The matter is urgent because it concerns a canoness of Neuville."

"Thank you, monsieur," said Jeanne. "You've been very kind."

"Not really. I'm trying to be just, and justice contains a measure of cruelty." Looking into the distance he added, "I once saw a twenty-year-old mason broken on the wheel after having tried to rape a nun while he was working on her convent's chapel. The punishment seemed to me to exceed the crime, because the nun had recovered."

CHAPTER 13

What's going on?" asked Jeanne, opening her eyes wide at the chaotic scene that greeted her return to Charmont.

Bouchoux dragged the wicker trunk into the entrance hall of Charmont. Cadiche and Lison, the two chambermaids from the Château de Rupert, followed, carrying toilet cases. Last came Pompon, her arms extended straight out like a scarecrow, a shawl draped over them and a muslin bonnet in either hand. Mlle. Sergent stood in front of the door to the drawing room, surveying the operation unsmilingly.

"Mademoiselle Jeannette! Mademoiselle Jeannette is here at last!" shouted Pompon in the direction of the drawing room. Mlle. Sergent opened the door.

"So here you are!" exclaimed Mme. de Bouhey. "How did you get here so fast?"

"I . . . I left Lyon early in the morning," said Jeanne, somewhat disconcerted.

"Early in the morning?" the baroness repeated. "You came on your own initiative, then?"

"Yes. Why do you ask?"

"Because, early this morning, I sent Thomas to fetch you and bring you back as quickly as possible. Didn't you meet him on the way?"

"No, I didn't."

"Never mind. He'll be back. But why did you decide to come?"

"Emilie and Denis . . ." said Jeanne quite simply.

"How did you hear about them?"

"The chief of police at Lyon came to see me."

"Oh, Monsieur de Beaulieu?" the baroness asked with evident anxiety. "Then the search got off to a quick start. Denis is mad. He'll be hanged for sure. His poor father can't stop weeping. If I had Emilie in my hands, I'd give her a sound whipping. Drawing a good boy into an adventure that may cost him his life, just for her own amusement. . . ."

" 'Amusement'?" Jeanne queried timidly.

"Don't you try to defend Emilie! Of course, it's the arrogance, the insolence, the devil-may-care attitude of the Pommeraies, everything for their amusement, for their pleasure, whoever may have to pay."

"I noticed that Denis . . ." Jeanne began again.

"Not a word!" the baroness scolded. "However they feel about each other, Emilie was the one to instigate this affair, I'd swear to it. When you're a Pommeraie, you should look for a partner in your own class. You don't impose the risk of being killed in bed, or in a duel, on a man who doesn't have your advantages. Now, tell me, how did you answer Beaulieu's questions?"

"Carefully, but quite honestly. After all, I knew nothing."

The baroness cupped Jeanne's chin with both hands and looked her in the eye. "You knew nothing, really? You weren't in on the secret?"

"No. I give you my word."

"Good. At least I'm relieved of the fear that you were involved in a bad piece of business." She kissed Jeanne on both cheeks and released her.

"If the lovers send you a call for help, let me know. And don't go to Neuville, where everything's topsy-turvy. The bishop is there passing every single soul on the premises through confession. Things are chaotic enough here. Jeannette, your friend Marie and her mother are coming to stay with us. During last Monday's storm, lightning struck the old elm on the west side of the Château de Rupert, and it toppled over onto their roof, causing considerable damage. Carpenters and tilers are at work repairing, but they make an infernal noise, which increased Stephanie's headaches. I invited them here and they'll arrive before supper."

"What's bad news for Rupert is good for Charmont," said Jeanne, who was glad to have the company of Marie.

"I quite agree. They'll help us prepare for the wedding."

Jeanne looked questioningly at the baroness, whose face wore an almost mischievous smile.

"Marie's wedding, you mean? Has Madame de Rupert consented?"

"It's nothing to do with Marie. I'm marrying off my grandson Charles in January."

"Charles? Did you get him engaged?"

"I didn't get him engaged. I'm getting him married. A little more time and we'd be dealing with a baptism. Yes, my lovely. On every side they're playing *La Surprise de l'amour*. Some run away, others go to bed. No one can call today's young people dull. They keep us on our toes."

"And who is Charles' intended?"

"Little Adrienne de Saint-Vérand."

"The chubby little dark-haired girl, the good dancer?"

"Yes, she is fresh, healthy, and intelligent, besides. I'm delighted. Delphine is still reluctant to give her elder son to a girl from a family of country squires. But I'm perfectly pleased. They'll dance, sing, ride, hunt, tumble between the sheets to produce children and, without benefit of books or ideas, they'll enjoy life."

"Well then, this accident makes you happy."

"I'm happy because it may make our family of cavalrymen into one of horse breeders. Adrienne loves horses. The Saint-Vérands own a big stock farm five miles north of Pont-d'Ain, and Adrienne is their only daughter. What do you say, Jeannette? You, too, love horses."

"I say that you've given me a lot of unexpected news," said Jeanne. "Have you nothing else up your sleeve?"

"Yes, I do. A second marriage. Madeleine de Charvieu de Briey arrived from Lorraine yesterday evening, to ask for the hand of my great-nephew, Laurent."

"And how long has she been in love with Laurent?"

"Since she got the idea of investing a considerable capital in cloth manufacture. She's inherited her father's glass factory and a large amount of cash. In order to diversify her investments she's been looking into textiles and metals, and finally . . ."

"She's decided to make money in silk rather than in iron?"

"Don't let malice run away with you! She finds Laurent handsomer and more agreeable than the heirs to the ironworks."

"And do you think, madame, that she'll have her Laurent?" Jeanne exclaimed, laughing.

"I believe he's quite capable of a passion for fresh capital and for the manufacture of crystal." Her laughter rolled through the drawing room. "As for Charles, I am planning a fine wedding. Delphine wanted to shame the bride and groom and have no more than a midnight blessing. But I want the whole family to be at my grandson's marriage. A seventeen-year-old girl is sufficiently punished for her sins by the precocious burden in her belly, without having to endure a mournful wedding."

Jeanne threw her arms around the baroness's neck and kissed her.

"I love your gracious ways," she said, resting her head for a moment on her guardian's shoulder. "By the way, will you invite Madame de Vaux-Jailloux? Have you had news of her lately?"

"Why should I leave out Pauline?" the baroness asked with surprise. "I didn't know that you were so friendly with her."

"There's no secret," said Jeanne casually. "I like to hear her talk about the islands, that's all."

"Always your dreams of a sea voyage," the baroness sighed. "And I'd like to keep you in France."

Since the baroness had given no news of Pauline, Jeanne felt she must find out for herself. There was plenty of time to ride over to Vaux before the arrival of the Ruperts . . . but under what pretext? After racking her brain she ran to the hothouse to pot two of her precious double pinks. Frail, and hardly an inch above ground, she had grown them from seeds given her by Pierre Poivre.

The botanist had received them from the son of the head gardener of the King's Garden. Young Thouin had found a way of doubling a highly fragrant pink by increasing the number of its petals. Jeanne knew if she came with two transplants of the miraculous pinks, she would be warmly welcomed by the lady of Vaux.

Jeanne

* * * *

Although the manor of Vaux was built in the classically solemn style of Louis XIV, its Creole mistress had given it an informal cachet of her own. The new trend of domestic comfort had trickled down from Paris to the provinces and Pauline had called an architect, a painter, a decorator, and a cabinetmaker to bring her house up to date.

With false ceilings covered in stucco, painted woodwork, alcoves in rock work, pier glasses, door panels decorated in the style of Boucher, with angels and pastoral scenes, walls and chairs draped with bright brocades, mirrors everywhere, and a few good paintings in which nymphs and shepherds disported themselves among poetical Roman ruins, she had decorated away the forbidding chill of the preceding years.

The exotic and lovely Creole appreciated the delights of both body and mind, and a considerable fortune enabled her to afford and enjoy them. Pauline had inherited her mother's sugar plantation and mill on San Domingo, which were now run by a comparatively honest uncle. Moreover, she had managed to become, at the age of twenty, the widow of a rich man of sixty. Wishing to see the land and other property which he had left her in France, she traveled to Europe with an officer of the Royal Navy. In France she was so fêted and flattered, sought out by friends and lovers, that she never returned to her native island. After becoming a close friend of Stephanie Rupert, she bought the manor house of Vaux, next door. Calling herself Mme. de Vaux-Jailloux, she set out to live as pleasantly as possible on her sizable income.

It was in a moment of peace and quiet that Jeanne found her. Cocotte, Pauline's favorite black maid, led her into an intimate cream-and-honey room, filled with tropical plants. Jeanne immediately noticed a new black lacquer screen with a golden landscape painted upon it.

The latest present from Vincent. The décor was a testament to the passage of a corsair who had spread out the contents of his trunks upon returning from a long voyage. Blue-and-white chinoiseries and translucent porcelains from Japan lined her shelves and Oriental rugs were strewn over the floor.

Well, he has to pay something for his pied-à-terre. But Jeanne couldn't help running a sensuous hand over a red Chinese vase on top of a highboy, even if it was the detestable gift of an attentive lover. A sudden panic made her want to run away. *What if Vincent were at Vaux and suddenly came into the room?*

"I have newer things than that to display for your admiration," said the caressing voice of the Creole from behind her. "I've just been given a dozen exquisitely designed ruby-red plates. They're still in this drawer. Come and look at them while I order tea. Or would you rather drink punch?"

Cocotte moved to and fro, wearing a striped skirt and tinkling bracelets, but the tea tray was brought in by Cupidon, a princely looking black man whom Vincent had bought at Port Louis on l'Ile de France, saving him from a cruel master. He served the tea with slow, harmonious gestures. Its fragrant steam wafted out of the filled cups. There was magic in the air. Jeanne felt as if she were living a moment out of time. When Cupidon grated some sugarloaf into the tea, he seemed to be sweetening it with the soul of his country.

"Madame," said Jeanne, "in your house one can nurse one's nostalgia for the islands. Do you never miss their flowers, their birds, their skies?"

"I pine less for my island than you in your imagination," Pauline said with a smile. "Longing for the unknown is greater than nostalgia for the familiar."

"How do you know that I dream of going to the islands?" Jeanne asked, with sudden irritation.

"If I were Cocotte I'd answer that a little bird told me. By living among black people we become open to all the dreams that float around us. Blacks are bundles of dreams."

Jeanne let her eyes wander through the glass panes of the double door to the front hall beyond. Cocotte was pacing indolently up and down, her arms crossed, humming a plaintive, languorous tune.

"Is your servant unhappy?" Jeanne asked.

"Sentimentality and self-pity are blacks' favorite occupations. They indulge in them here as much as in the country where they were born."

"Where they were born slaves," Jeanne corrected her.

Pauline's smile broadened, but she did not raise her voice. "This is a pleasant moment. Don't let's spoil it by talking philosophy. I've owned slaves, and you haven't. I might tell you that I was a good mistress to them, but you wouldn't believe it. It's by choice, however, that Cocotte and Cupidon stay with me. They were married in my house and have already given me two little ones to feed. They have no wish to be freed and returned to San Domingo. Life in France is so much more agreeable, even if Frenchmen don't always know it as well as foreigners."

"Perhaps they're afraid to return to a land where they were once captives. A traveler returning from the islands told me that blacks' eyes are prisoners' eyes."

Pauline laughed lightly, picked up her fan and opened it with a graceful turn of the wrist. "Tell your traveler that when he next goes to the islands he should look into the eyes of colonists and Creoles as well. All islanders have prisoners' eyes. On San Domingo everyone I knew dreamed of getting away. The colonists who had made their fortune, the Creoles who wanted to see Paris, the unlucky blacks who sought escape from their poverty, and everybody else who simply desired to set foot on real land. An island isn't land. It's a raft that everyone aboard wants to get off."

Then, looking at her caller's incredulous expression, she added, "But, my dear girl, I don't want to color your dream with my experience. Besides, if one day you land on the shores of your island you'll bring with you a cargo of hopes which will enrich your surroundings and give you happiness."

The Creole gently swept the air with her fan. The gesture was becoming to her. And she knew it. The empty-handed girl sitting across from her was annoyed, as Pauline had intended her to be.

How had this pretty little goose resisted Vincent? Virgins are tempting but, thank God, they're stupid as well. The minute they fall in love, they fancy they've chosen the most wonderful man on earth and they let other better would-be lovers go by. Actually Pauline was more vexed with Jeanne for having disappointed Vincent than for having attracted him. It was eighteen months since his unsuccessful attempt to abduct Jeanne and Vincent still seemed to have some feeling for her.

When last he came to Vaux, at the beginning of December, he talked of women more cynically than was his custom. The following evening he casually questioned Pauline about Charmont. And when, in passing, Pauline mentioned Jeanne's name, he abruptly turned his back to her, pretending to be absorbed in pouring himself a cup of coffee.

Pauline's prolonged silence bothered Jeanne and she made an effort to revive the conversation. "I brought you two pots of double pinks," she said. "Your Cocotte took them in. Did she show them to you?"

Pauline stood up, with a contented air. "Double pinks? What a miracle! Why didn't you mention them before? Let's go look at them."

The afternoon passed pleasantly enough. The two women engaged in superficial patter as they exchanged notes on exotic plants and the like. Jeanne's visit was drawing to a close. Unspoken questions burned her tongue as she uttered the conventional phrases of leave-taking.

She came to question me about Vincent, but she didn't dare. Pauline watched Jeanne prepare to go. *Well, I may as well relent. I believe I'm as curious to hear her speak of Vincent as she is to hear me.*

Aloud she said, "Before you go, wouldn't you like to see a bathroom that I've just redecorated? It is part of the quarters where Chevalier Vincent stays when he pays me a friendly visit. By accident it was flooded so I had it redone."

Jeanne followed Pauline with a pounding heart. Vincent's bathroom was tastefully luxurious. There were two copper tubs, one for soaping, the other for rinsing. Sculpted dolphins decorated the paneled woodwork. And painted on the inside of the doors and shutters were bathing scenes. The men and women had rosy bodies and touched each other with obviously amorous intentions.

"Beautiful!" Jeanne exclaimed. "Worthy of a prince, a prince and a libertine!"

"Quite right, my dear. It's a copy, as exact as possible, of the bathroom of Louis XV. I'm afraid, though, that my paintings are by an artist less renowned, and of a character more ribald. Just look at those pink bottoms, they're like strawberry sherbet."

The dressing table, made for a man, was of layered mahogany. Reflected in the central mirror was a set of engraved vermeil brushes, combs, scissors, a curling iron, and half a dozen flasks made of Vincennes porcelain. Jeanne couldn't resist slipping onto the stool in front of the table and lifting the corks to sniff.

"Aromatic vinegar . . ."

"For after shaving," said Pauline.

"Orange blossom from Malta . . ."

"For the handkerchief."

"Eau de Cologne . . ."

"From Jean-Antoine Farina, the best. For rubbing into the skin."

"Essence of lavender . . ."

"He dabs drops of it behind his ears, to ward off germs."

The two women's eyes, sharp and defiant, tawny gold and deep black, met in the mirror.

"Mmm," murmured Jeanne, raising her nose from a glass bottle. "This scent has an entrancing freshness, but I can't identify it."

"Really?" said Pauline, seizing the bottle and hiding the label with her hand. "Haven't you smelled it before?"

Her voice lingered teasingly over the words. Jeanne obediently took another sniff.

"No, I can't guess," she admitted.

" 'Treasure of the mouth'," announced Pauline deliberately. "The celebrated mouthwash made by Sieur Pierre Bocquillon of Paris. It's said to perfume the breath in a way that makes for the most delectable kisses."

Jeanne turned crimson with anger at having been trapped that way. In the mirror she saw the Creole's lips part in a malicious smile. She imagined Pauline's mouth yielding to Vincent's. At the same time, she relived the memory of his lips on her own. Present and past melded into something persistent and sensuous.

Pauline's eyes played perversely over the girl. She visualized Vincent's hands as they must have worked to arouse her. Because she had come on horseback, Jeanne had gathered her hair up in a scarf. Now Pauline slipped her fingers between the silken scarf and silky skin, freeing the blond locks. They tumbled down to cascade over Jeanne's shoulders.

"Oh!" Jeanne objected feebly. But she did not move when Pauline picked up a brush and ran it over her hair. "Give me some orange blossom," she murmured softly.

Pauline reversed the flask several times and then applied the dampened cork to Jeanne's hair. The penetrating scent went to Jeanne's head. She quivered and shut her eyes, remembering how, with a flick of his handkerchief, Vincent had banished a particle of dust from his sleeve. She was so absorbed in this memory, she did not even notice when Pauline undid her muslin cravat and the top buttons of her blouse in order to slide the cork over her neck and let droplets of orange blossom trickle down between her breasts.

"My dear child, if you want it to go all the way to your navel you'll have to help me undress you," Pauline's voice suggested softly.

Jeanne gave a deep sigh, opened her eyes, and tried to adopt a bantering tone.

"The chevalier has nothing left to desire," she said, waving her arm toward the dressing table. "He has all the equipment of a true gallant."

"The equipment of a courtesan, if you like! In any case, my dear, Mario uses everything you see there for preparing him to go out. And it seems that, at sea, he gives him all the same attentions!"

"It seems that Mario is a most devoted servant."

" 'Devoted'? The word is too weak. Mario idolizes Vincent. I'm almost sorry for the poor devil because he has him for a master and not for a mistress!"

Jeanne blushed and began to rearrange her hair. Pauline lent her a hand, for the pleasure of fingering the silky tresses.

"Jeannette," she said, for the first time calling her by name, "before you go, tell me the real purpose of your visit. No one gives away two double pinks without good reason."

"That's true, madame," said Jeanne, looking her in the eye. "I wanted to know if the chevalier had been recently at Vaux. Now I've seen his traces. I wanted to ask you, also, whether he had promised my friends Emilie and Denis to take them aboard his ship."

"I don't really know," said Pauline, shaking her head. "A captain has no right to take on fugitives from justice. If he does, it's such a serious matter that he's not likely to talk about it. He left Vaux on the eighth of the month for Marseille. He had a great deal to do before sailing. Your friends disappeared on the ninth, I believe. You see, I know no more than you do."

"What was the chevalier's destination?"

"Smyrna. His precious cargo is going to palaces in that city."

"Would Smyrna provide a good refuge for runaway lovers?"

"The best recourse for runaways is gold," said Pauline.

"They've not much of that, I fear."

"If they're with Vincent they'll have Vincent's gold. He's a very generous man. And it happens that he loves abductions. Did you know, my dear Jeannette, that there are times when he runs away with a young girl as boldly as any musketeer?"

"Oh, really?" said Jeanne, looking with a candid air into the Creole's sparkling eyes.

CHAPTER 14

he wedding of Charles and Adrienne went off without a hitch. Everyone admired the bride. She was chubby, with dark, curly, unpowdered hair. Her pink cheeks spoke more of happiness than of makeup. Three months pregnant, she looked like a Madonna in a stained-glass window. And any priest would have given her communion without a preliminary confession.

The dancing did not end until two o'clock in the morning when a supper of cold meat, salads, and sweets was served. Mme. de Bouhey had arranged a separate table in the library for the young people. In the familiar room, redolent of old leather, but elaborately lit for the occasion, Jeanne felt at home. The candle flames caused a flickering light to pass over the old bindings, and the books seemed to be smiling down at her. She knew their places so well that often, at night, she came down and took one from its shelf in the dark.

She sighed, feeling alone. This evening, even Marie had her fiancé Philippe with her. Their happiness made them oblivious to the rest of the world. They fed each other choice morsels of cold chicken, raising their glasses and drinking to each other's health.

Jeanne sipped a glass of Spanish wine as she listened to Laurent and Madeleine, who were across from her at the table. As Mme. de Bouhey had foreseen, the silk scion of Lyon and the daughter of the gentleman-glassmaker of Lorraine had quickly come together. Already lawyers were drawing up papers. The marriage was to take place in the spring, and the couple were exchanging business proposals.

Dame Charlotte de Bouhey, Emilie's godmother, came into the library to see how things were going. She sat down beside Jeanne and leaned over, whispering in her ear, "Jeannette, how can you bear to listen to such a boring couple? Their love duet is too modern for me. And their children, most likely, will be like the little peasants who toss pebbles from one hand to another and sing, 'Choose, choose; how many pennies have I in my shoes?' "

Jeanne smiled. "If Emilie were here she'd regale us with barbed comments on love during the industrial age. Obviously not all young girls have softened their brains by reading novels."

"Let's go sit somewhere else," Dame Charlotte proposed. "I was never very wild, but too much practicality doesn't agree with me."

The two adjourned to the yellow-and-lilac drawing room, seating themselves behind a screen. At once Dame Charlotte asked, "Jeannette, where do you think she is?"

"At sea," said Jeanne firmly. "They must be at sea, safe from the officers of the law. Of course you miss Emilie, don't you?"

"I do, indeed," Dame Charlotte said mournfully. "Neuville has lost its firefly."

"I'm surprised that she didn't send a letter, even to you. She loves you very much. And she enjoys putting her thoughts on paper."

"But she did leave me a letter. I've shown it to no one but my sister-in-law. She asked specifically for me to share it with you." Out of her skirt pocket the canoness took a letter many times folded and refolded. She held it out and Jeanne read:

Madame, and dear Godmother,
   You'll be angry, of course . . . then you'll forgive me. Life among the ladies of Neuville is like a sweet slumber. In spite of the love that is impelling me elsewhere, it will take a lot of courage for me to tear myself away from the cloister tomorrow. But I was afraid that I wouldn't wake up until the day of my death, when it would be too late to stick my nose outside. During this year I've thought of changing my life. I've had ample time to reflect on what I'm leaving and what awaits me. I'm leaving a privileged life. It is mad, certainly. And perhaps silly. But I want to find out what I am worth for myself alone.
   I don't feel as if I belong to my family. Nor do I fear that my actions tomorrow will cause them any sorrow. They were dry-eyed when they packed me off at the age of nine. Besides, a good hunting party is enough to wipe out any of their chagrin. For you it will not be the same, dear godmother. So I promise to send you news as soon as I can

do so without endangering our future. I don't ask you to pass this on to my father and mother. But please inform my friends Jeanne and Marie, for whom I shall always have faithful and tender feelings. I embrace you, with all my affection—

Your Emilie, who asks for your prayers

Jeanne wiped the tears from her eyes, and Dame Charlotte blew her nose.

"The sad thing is," she said, "that in reading and rereading this letter I wonder if I've really lived. I go to the abbey library and spin the globe, imagining a tiny Emilie trotting across it. She crosses green and brown landmasses, ventures into the white spaces of the unknown, strides over blue seas, while I tread in my own footsteps, day after day. Tell me the truth, Jeannette. Do you know where Denis planned to take Emilie?"

"No, madame, but I fancy Emilie will be the one to decide."

"Jassans, the pharmacist, told me that Denis had become a first-rate chemist, corresponding with others, especially a certain Lavoisier. Do you know whether Denis was making any plans with him?"

"No, madame. Probably his passion for science drove him to ask questions about his profession."

"Well, if you get news before I do, will you pass it on? You see, if I were ever to learn that Emilie had settled down in some beautiful, faraway place . . ." And she leaned over to whisper into Jeanne's ear, "I might go take a look myself!"

* * * *

It's unpardonable! He's gone too far. Jeanne's patience was exhausted. He had promised to come back to Châtillon no later than the beginning of 1764. And now it was mid-February. She would never have believed it! Almost seventeen years old and still not kissed by Philibert. She bit her fist with anger.

When her frustration was too much for her, she jumped on Blanchette and galloped through the cutting winter air until her body was numb with cold.

Jeanne often rode home by way of Vaux, where Pauline laughingly restored her natural warmth. She poked up the fire, tossed on some slow-burning paper impregnated with incense, strewed cushions over the heated floor for the two of them to sit on, got Jeanne slightly drunk with a hot rum-and-vanilla punch, ruffled her hair, and played with her like a cat with a kitten. Pauline dressed Jeanne up in her own clothes, winding striped scarves around her head like those the black women wore on her native isle. She doused her with perfume, planting tickling kisses on her neck and singing her Creole lullabies. Jeanne was hypnotized. She did not report these afternoons at the manor with Pauline in the confessional.

One evening she stayed later than usual and came home after dusk. Mme. de Bouhey greeted her in scolding tones.

"So here you are at last! Blanchette may fall dead between your legs one of these fine days."

"I stopped at Vaux to play backgammon with Madame de Vaux-Jailloux."

The baroness's eyes were dancing. "Well, you picked the wrong day. You had a caller. He waited for over an hour. Yes, my lovely! I'll never again believe what they say about lovers' intuition."

Jeanne sank into a chair, her face so white that the baroness rang for some concentrate of melissa.

"And, oh, some brandy, too," she called after Pompon. "Jeanne, my dear, you're too emotional," she said. "I don't dare tell you any more."

"Please, I beg of you . . . I'm better now. I was worn out by my long ride, that's all."

"Well, then, your Aubriot has come back from Switzerland wanting to talk with you. He has a proposal to make. I don't approve, but I told him he could make it."

"You mean I won't know what it is until tomorrow? Can't Thomas drive me to Châtillon right away?"

"It would serve no purpose. Aubriot went off, without pause, to visit his son in Bugey. But I said I'd convey his message to you. So listen, and don't interrupt until I've finished." She added, in a harder tone of voice, "He wants to stay with the little boy until summer. After that he's going to Paris. He's convinced that his degree from Montpellier is outdated. He needs to brush up on the latest advances. He wants to attend the botany lessons given at the King's Garden. And, in Paris, he will need a secretary, a housekeeper, a-goodness-knows-exactly-what-else. He was so confused and flustered that I think he hasn't thought it all out clearly yet. But he asked me if he could take you along for this purpose."

Jeanne drew herself up, her eyes sparkling. "You mean he proposes to take me . . . to take me to Paris?"

"Yes, at a salary of a hundred and eighty francs a year. Plus, of course, board and lodging," said the baroness curtly.

"You mean he'd pay me to go with him?" Jeanne stammered. "Pay me money?"

She looked so horrified, trembled so hard, and spoke with such difficulty that Mme. de Bouhey's heart went out to her. Affectionately she warmed Jeanne's cold hands with her own and spoke to her soothingly.

"The words he used are unimportant," she said. "I'm not sure that he himself knows what he has in mind. You may know better than he does. The fact is he wants you to leave me toward the end of the summer and follow him to Paris."

Jeanne burst into tears. "I'd like to go with him, but without leaving you!"

"I can understand that, Jeannette. But you'll have to choose. You have a few months to think about it."

"I've waited so long . . ." said Jeanne, still choked with tears.

"Are you sure you're not confusing a child's love with a young girl's?"

"I'm sure, yes! I love him more and more every day."

"Well," the baroness sighed, "you can't say no to him and then spend the rest of your life waiting for him to return."

"So you advise me to say yes?"

"God forbid!" exclaimed the baroness angrily. "Did I ever advise you to fall in love with the man? I'm allowing you to decide for yourself, that's all."

"Madame, I'll go, I know it."

Marie-Françoise laid her hands on Jeanne's blond hair. "Don't say it yet, my dear. Give me a little time to doubt you're leaving me."

There was a long moment of silence, which Jeanne broke with a touch of melancholy. "A hundred and eighty francs, plus board and lodging." Then almost violently, "What right has he to set my value at a hundred and eighty francs . . . to calculate my worth in money? How can I tolerate his paying me to go away with him . . . to love him? If I give him my life . . . I'll take nothing in exchange but love, love . . ."

Jeanne could not speak for sobbing. She slipped down onto the rug and buried her face in the baroness's skirt.

"Don't be distressed for such a trifle, Jeannette," said the baroness as she smoothed Jeanne's ruffled hair. "When a man realizes that a woman loves him, he no longer offers to pay her. I'll wager that Aubriot won't pay you even your first year's wages."

CHAPTER 15

Jeanne and Philibert set out for Paris on the sixth of September, 1764.

The countryside was dried up and crackling. After two months of drought, the dust had stripped the trees of their foliage. Every shrunken stretch of water mirrored the hot sun, dazzling their eyes. Taking advantage of the cool dawn, they left at four o'clock in the morning. But by nine the travelers were sleepy from the heat. The postilions called a halt every two hours, preferably in a shady spot. The passengers got down, loosening their clothes, exposing their red faces and perspiring necks to the refreshing shade and drinking the tepid water they had brought with them. After a ten-minute rest, they climbed back into the coach and resigned themselves to two more hours of hellish travel.

Aubriot tried to read, but the bumps and jolts made this nearly impossible. On the second day, after they had left Roanne, he closed his book with a bang.

"The base of the spine isn't the only part of the anatomy to suffer from travel," he said with a sigh. "My eyes are hurting me as well."

"You can't rightly complain of the roads, monsieur," said a man from Lorraine, who was sitting across from him. "France has the best roads in Europe, and the one from Lyon to Paris is the queen of them all."

A bright-eyed woman, whom Jeanne had mentally baptized the Blue Lady, for the color of her dress, commented, "So, monsieur, in your country travel is no longer an adventure, is it?"

"On the contrary, madame, adventure is still the right word for it. You can quite easily be stuck through with a kitchen knife or murdered by the poor food."

This statement started the Blue Lady off on a tirade of sordid, petty misfortunes encountered in inns where, without intending to kill their guests, the landlords had poisoned them.

Now they'll all want to recount their stomachaches. Jeanne was already sickened by the prospect. *When they've finished with the stewed cat passed off as rabbit, the salads truffled with flies and the vomiting that followed, they'll move on to the other side of the coin. Menus that were gastronomic triumphs, composed of pâtés, princely roasts, and the choice of half a dozen "divine" desserts.* She yawned discreetly, behind her hand, and turned to look out the window.

"You're too hot, my poor Jeannot," Aubriot said, leaning toward her.

He called her Jeannot because she had asked permission, for comfort's sake, to travel in boy's clothes. The disguise was eminently successful. She was tall, slender, with broad shoulders, narrow hips, high buttocks, small breasts, easily effaced by a tight band, and features fine but not frail. With her hair tucked up under a cap, she could pass for a young man. Strangers, among them the Blue Lady, took her for a boy with a skin too smooth, speech too soft, and slightly precious gestures. Certain young men do, after all, have something girlish about them. In the torrid heat this disguise had only one drawback, she could not loosen her clothes and suffered, stoically.

"Won't you drink some lemonade?" Aubriot asked her. "It may be refreshing."

Jeanne would even have drunk hot water for the joy of accepting the flask from his hand. Philibert was looking after her. As she drank, she cast a triumphant look at the Blue Lady who wore the mocking smile she had displayed ever since their departure.

What times these are! Nothing is hidden, not even the unnatural. But this thought did not stop the Blue Lady from flirting with the doctor. A taste for pretty boys doesn't necessarily exclude a taste for beautiful women. Young, shapely, with peaches-and-cream skin and lightly powdered blond hair, she thought herself appetizing enough to replace a handsome boy in a man's bed.

Partly as a diversion and partly to take revenge for the 180 francs offered for her companionship, Jeanne made a point, at every rest stop, to play the part of the devoted valet. But she wasn't going to carry devotion to her master so far as to let him flirt, right under her nose, with a loose woman. Rebelliously, she took advantage of the next jolt to roll her head onto Philibert's shoulder.

Philibert, taken aback by this surprise, looked at Jeanne, who was looking, mockingly, at the Blue Lady. He understood the game and smiled faintly. To be a bone of contention between two women was highly agreeable. Ever since he had started out for Paris, with Jeanne beside him, he felt that he had been living too long encased in ice. Now he was breaking out, and his heart was melting.

At thirty-seven years of age Aubriot was still in good form. He was well built, of medium height, with athletic shoulders, muscular legs, and not an ounce of fat. He dressed soberly but elegantly and was definitely attractive to women. He spoke convincingly and his face, with its strong jawline, was lit by the magnetism of his intelligent eyes. His approach to life, although tempered by maturity, was still charged with enthusiasm. He was as outspoken as a youth and no less quick to mock stupidity. Yet he had suffered a loss of health. His legs were rheumatic and, although he'd always had a cough, it had become more severe over the last three or four years. The stay in the south had done him a world of good. But he found no ready cure for his disabilities and so adapted a stoic motto: "Let your spirit gain strength as rapidly as your body declines, and you'll strike a balance."

At times, however, he was saddened to feel that his body was declining faster than his mind. He knew that he would not live long enough to finish the cataloguing which he had undertaken, even if he attained the age of three-score years and ten. He ate frugally, got plenty of fresh air, and spent his time working. His life had become so austere that, when he met Jeanne in Lyon, he had a moment of panic and remorse. *Would she interfere with his working habits? How would she stand up under the conditions he meant to impose upon her?* But it was too late for second thoughts. He couldn't very well leave her there, on the Quai des Célestins. *She's far too eager to go with me.*

Philibert was anything but unscrupulous. When he seated Jeanne beside him in the coach he knew that she loved him. But he persuaded himself that hers was not a carnal love. It was a love born out of an admiration which Paris, with all its marvels, would cure. Since he expected to frequent scientific circles, she would be plunged into an atmosphere of intellectual stimulation. She would meet exciting new acquaintances. If, at home, she had centered her dreams upon him it was because the men she met in provincial society bored her.

At this point in his reasoning he became aware that the idea of Jeanne's transferring her interest to others was not entirely agreeable to him. But, at least, it satisfied his conscience. He was taking her away to a world where she could find happiness. She might well marry a young botanist from the King's Garden. His imagination went further. . . . He would offer lodgings to the young couple. . . . Two households together can live more cheaply than one. And he would have two assistants at his disposal.

As the coach swung along its way, Philibert accustomed himself to his chaste role of adopted father. In carrying off the little Jeanne, he was doing a good deed. His fears at the moment of departure had been unfounded. For one thing, she was no encumbrance. She hardly opened her mouth, drew no attention to herself, and simply sat at his left side like a snuggling kitten.

At Tarare, where they changed horses and ate their first dinner, everyone crowded around the table in the hope of sitting near Aubriot. Jeanne took an instant dislike to the Blue Lady, whom Philibert politely seated at his right. Jeannot, the valet, was relegated to the foot of the table.

French inns had a poor reputation. They were apt to be sloppily kept and never had enough beds. Travelers counted themselves lucky when the accommodations offered half of a bed with doubtfully clean sheets. Dr. Aubriot's "valet" was assigned one of the mattresses in the attic. Two rough fellows who had ridden behind the diligence were already pulling Jeanne after them when Dr. Aubriot peremptorily ordered her to come with him. Without regard for propriety, Jeanne found herself sharing Aubriot's quarters.

His bed afforded her little rest. To stretch out beside him for the night, even in a shirt and trousers, was . . . well, it almost seemed that she had to stay awake to believe it. Curled up on the edge of the bed, taking care not to slide into the middle, she lay there. Awake. So self-conscious that she began to tremble.

"You can't sleep, Jeannot?" Philibert queried in a low voice. "It's the heat, and the moonlight streaming in through the curtains. Our innkeeper must be really poor, to judge from the furniture of his rooms. I'm going to give you a sleeping draught. I always carry something of the sort with me when I travel."

She took two spoonfuls of bitter valerian syrup and was able to relax, calmed more by the doctor's attentions than by his prescription, for Philibert had propped himself up on the bolster and was gazing down at her.

Jeanne was lying on her back, with her arms hanging limply at her sides. Streaks of moonlight lit her loose hair. She was lost in a dream, which lent a tranquil beauty to her expression.

Philibert was overcome by a mixture of tenderness and desire. She had kept the sweet odor of her childhood. Poppies, wild cherries, and apples stolen from the Ursulines' garden jogged his memories of the little girl at Châtillon. But now she was a lovely and available woman.

As he leaned over Jeanne, he realized, for the first time, that he had accepted the idea of taking her. He gently wiped the beads of perspiration from her forehead with his handkerchief, freed strands of damp hair from her neck, opened her shirt, and rolled the sleeves up above the crook of her elbow, so that the veins near the surface were exposed to the air. Then, noticing that she had kept on her stockings, he carefully pulled them off. He watched her tenderly as she slept. A little later, he saw her chest rise and fall too rapidly, so he took her pulse. Jeanne's heart was beating in his hand. Touching her in the guise of a doctor, the man in him smiled gently. Unconsciously he was taking possession of her. The process continued until his body gave him clear indications that his tenderness was not entirely chaste. Indeed, far from it. He leaped out of bed and went to get a breath of air in the courtyard below.

Pacing up and down in the moonlight, he gathered his thoughts together. Hadn't he always balanced his natural appetites with an ideal of sobriety? When he was young, his fellow-students had dubbed him "Passionflower." But since those lusty days, he had matured. Between his body, hungry for women, and his mind hungry for knowledge, he had given greater attention to the latter. Lovemaking was his favorite pastime, far above chess. But an amorous escapade with Jeanne . . . no!

The next morning he tried to regain his self-control and the care-free mood of the journey's first day. But he soon found that dawn had not delivered him from the new feelings born overnight. His innocent, fatherly role was repeatedly at war with a sensual desire he had no heart to chase away. Jeanne had taken over his imagination. Indeed, he knew that he was waiting, with more curiosity than fear, for the next test—the night to be spent at Moulins.

* * * *

"Thank God," said the Blue Lady, "we'll be laying over at Bessay rather than Moulins. Those of you who aren't acquainted with the Hotel de La Belle Image at Moulins don't know how lucky you are to miss it. Once, sixteen of us were charged forty-five sous per person for only a few platefuls of inedible stew and two small bowls of salad. As for the rooms, they're papered with cobwebs and furnished with bedbugs!"

"Is it true that the cuisine of Bessay makes it worthwhile to go slightly out of the way?" asked the man from Lorraine, pricking up his ears.

"Monsieur, it's the feature of the journey," the Blue Lady assured him. She proceeded, enthusiastically, to enumerate the quail, partridges, crayfish in white sauce, guinea hens with raspberries, flanks of beef with tomatoes, tripe with crabapple juice, the tarts and creams and, finally, the wines from under the counter in minute, stomach-turning detail.

"However," pronounced Aubriot, "on my word as a doctor, in France good food kills more people than bad."

"Oh, Doctor!" the Blue Lady exclaimed. "Good food is so . . . good! I hope you won't persuade us to give it up."

Aubriot gave a dry laugh and looked, not unfavorably, at the shapely, blond creature with the dimpled, pink cheeks.

"I can assure you, madame," he answered, slightly inclining his head, "that I shall undertake no such difficult task. This is the country where Frederick II, attacking the Prince de Soubise, ran up against a regiment of cooks and scullions, armed with pots and pans. Our king himself is the prime example, priding himself on his ability to cook. Everywhere I look, I see that my countrymen live to eat, even if they die doing it."

"Lord help us, Doctor, isn't the joy of living in joy, rather than in life?" She leaned forward to show her breasts and cast him a languorous look.

Jeanne wondered how long she could resist scratching the Blue Lady's pink cheeks. A loose woman, beyond a doubt! Philibert had gazed so complacently at her bosom that, in order to distract his attention, she broke into the conversation.

"I only hope that the beds at Bessay are good as the roasts. To me the joy of living lies as much in a good bed as in a good table."

If she had hoped to produce an effect, she succeeded. The ingenuous and at the same time ambiguous remark of the beardless boy made everyone smile. The Blue Lady choked with laughter.

Aubriot shot his Jeannot a mocking glance. But in her tawny eyes he read a rebuke. His look softened and Jeanne smiled back, feeling reassured. There was a moment of silent tenderness between them. Meanwhile the man from Lorraine replied to the question.

"There are good beds at Bessay, young man, and plenty of comfortable rooms. Even the servants' quarters are neat and clean."

"That's good news for delicate boys," said the Blue Lady sarcastically. "And better yet for their masters, who won't have to share a bed in order to protect them from prickly straw mattresses and fleas."

The sun had sunk behind the horizon when they finally arrived at Bessay-sur-Allier. Only four post chaises stood in the courtyard and out of the twenty rooms sixteen were free.

Jeanne was ecstatic in the high-ceilinged room reserved for guests of special distinction. She exclaimed with relief at the sight of a bathroom. The Blue Lady claimed the first bath. Aubriot followed. The others spruced up and changed their clothes in their rooms in their hurry to go down to supper.

Custom demanded that, before they sat down to the innkeeper's masterpieces, they take a look at the kitchen.

Fanfan Lafleur knew how to strike a pose for his appreciative audience. Like many of his peers he had come out of the army. He had acquired his skill during the Austrian War of Succession, when he was a prisoner at Ulm. Happy days in Moravia! There were tears in his eyes when he spoke of the goose liver of Krems, accompanied by a dry, fruity white wine. And mention of the freshwater crayfish of Carinthia still made his mouth water.

"Once I had rolled under my tongue a morsel of this pale, crisp fish, fragrant with fresh water . . . well, gentlemen, that is when Lafleur became aware of his true vocation. I got it into my head to invent divine sauces to set off its flavor."

His jovial face, rounded out by the consumption of butter, was vainglorious. In a lowered voice, he drew his flamboyant conclusion. "Ladies and gentlemen, on the day when my regiment surrendered to the Austrians, France lost a battle but won a chef. A past master of sauces, who will give her long-lasting glory!"

Jeanne listened with amusement. But soon she left the scene and went to stretch her legs while Philibert relaxed with the rest of the passengers in the sitting room.

The courtyard was teaming with activity; the clatter and chatter of the cooks in the kitchen could be heard through wide-open windows. Straining her eyes to pierce the growing darkness Jeanne wished upon a star. *Let him love me, God, let him love me!*

After the long, dusty road and its traffic, the infinite, empty silence of the sky was balm to body and soul. Those of the travelers who had stepped out for a breath of air were going back inside, but Jeanne lingered in the cool evening air. As she was about to turn back, a young man emerged from behind a carriage and approached her. He was one of the valets who rode behind the diligence—the rougher and louder of the two. Jeanne paused. But as he drew closer, something aggressive in his manner caused her to turn around and quicken her pace in the direction of the kitchen.

"Hold on there, good-looking!" he called out laughingly. "I've made a wager with my companion here, and I want to win. There's a bottle of wine at stake."

Just then the second valet emerged from the shadows and barred her way. Jeanne looked desperately toward the inn, across a now dark and empty courtyard.

"Very well," she said, trying to gain time by entering into the game. "What is the wager? Out with it, because I'm in a hurry."

"It's quickly explained," said the first fellow. "After seeing your master give you an inside seat, offer you his flask and bed you down beside him, I'm wagering you're a girl in boy's clothes. My friend here says you're a boy that your master uses for a girl. Just tell *me* I'm right."

"No," said Jeanne sharply. "Your friend's the winner. I'm a boy."

And she tried to go her way.

"That's a lie," said the first valet, catching her by the waist. "A lie, I tell you. And I'm going to look under your shirt to prove it."

In spite of Jeanne's efforts to free herself, the husky valet managed to touch her breasts and shouted triumphantly.

"So help me God! If this isn't girl-stuff, my beauty, I'm ready to be hanged at dawn!"

"Or be booted from here to eternity!" an angry voice broke in.

Jeanne saw the fellow catapulted by a powerful kick in the buttocks, landing headfirst against a carriage wheel. A firm hand took her arm, preventing her from falling with him. The other valet disappeared as if by magic.

Aubriot leaned over his victim, who lay there in a daze. Plunging his hand into the fellow's thick hair, he carefully examined his cranium.

"You're getting off with a bump," he pronounced. "It's a cheap price to pay. Put a cloth soaked in cold water on your head. And, now, away with you!"

The fellow staggered off, and Aubriot turned to Jeanne, who stood there trembling with shame.

"Get yourself inside," he said curtly. "I don't want to pick fights with servants on your account. I'm too old for that sort of thing, and it's not my way."

Hot tears rose in Jeanne's eyes. "It's not my fault," she stammered. "I'm sorry about what happened. I didn't call for help because I didn't want to disturb you and yet, in spite of that . . ."

"Good for you, mademoiselle! You're very brave," he interrupted ironically. "Next time something of the sort occurs, let yourself be raped in order not to disturb me. Well, let's go to dinner. And please walk faster. I trust this adventure hasn't harmed either your legs or your appetite."

Jeanne stifled her tears and they went back, in silence, to the inn.

In the dining room there was a long table, but the diners could sit in small groups if they wished. Aubriot did not want to be seen tête-à-tête with his attractive companion. Anyway, he was of a mind to punish Jeanne for having put him in an ill-humor.

He dispatched her to the end of the long table, taking a certain satisfaction in her discomfort, purposely sitting down beside the Blue Lady, who had kept a place for him and welcomed him warmly. He began to chat, with feigned gaiety, but underneath he boiled with anger every time he looked at Jeanne. He was furious because someone had laid his hands on her, furious at his violent reaction to the assault, and doubly furious for still being angry a quarter of an hour later.

The provocation had not really been so great. But emotion was stronger than reason. The picture in his mind, of the valet's dirty hands feeling Jeanne's breasts, made his fists clench in rage.

The gross young idiot! He might have been killed. If his head had struck the carriage wheel just a bit harder . . . Jeanne . . . the silly girl, was she going to complicate his life? He gazed at her severely. *The poor child.* Her downcast eyes staring at an empty plate seemed so unhappy that he longed to take her into his arms, gently open her shirt and lay his lips where the young oaf had touched her.

He was dreaming of how he would efface the outrage when his neighbor's cooing voice broke in. "Aren't you having some moorhen?" she asked. "It's delicious. But you've no appetite. Do you always eat so little?"

He was eating, as usual, soberly—meat, salad, fruit, and a little red wine. Jeanne usually took whatever he did, but now she couldn't even swallow. She suffered not only from having displeased Philibert but also from her bitter resentment of the Blue Lady.

The Blue Lady had changed into other clothes, still blue—a vulgar, glaring shade of it. The low cut of her cotton gown was positively indecent. It revealed most of two creamy white globes which drew the eyes of all the male diners. *Satyrs, all of them!* Philibert's eyes seemed to take in the view no less greedily than the others. Jeanne thought angrily that if she were dressed like a woman, she would display breasts *far* more delicate.

"Give me something to drink," she said suddenly to a passing maid.

She gulped down half a glass of wine and felt better. She resolved to wait until later, when she went up to her master's bedroom, and take Philibert to task for his shocking behavior.

Just then three officers came in and sat at the common table in the empty places near Jeanne. They were infantry lieutenants who downed two bottles of wine before starting to eat and deafened their neighbors with loud, stupid conversation, loaded with barrack-room obscenities.

Aubriot, watching Jeanne out of the corner of his eye, was disgusted at what was being said in her presence. He caught snatches of it over the Blue Lady's provocative cooing and the nostalgic ramblings of the inebriated gentleman on his left. *Was the girl going, for the second time, to put him in an embarrassing situation?*

Abruptly he called to her. And, when she stood behind his chair, he said commandingly, "Jeannot, go upstairs and take a box of digestive powder out of my bag. Dissolve a pinch of it in a glass of water and put it beside the bed. Then wait for me there."

Knowing Philibert's good digestion, Jeanne was about to exclaim in astonishment. But, on second thought, it occurred to her that he was sending her away in order to flirt with the lady in blue. Full of indignation, she summoned up the courage to say, "Very good, sir. I'll prepare the medicine. But kindly allow me to come back down. There's a cake I haven't yet had a chance to taste."

It was the first time she had ever opposed him. With surprise and amusement he said in a purposefully cold voice, "Jeannot, I've given you an order. Don't ask me to change it. Just do what I say."

The Blue Lady giggled. Jeanne shot her a fiery look, turned on her heel and went toward the stairs.

"Your fine boy deserves a whipping. Can't you see that he's jealous and wants to keep an eye on you?"

"Madame," said Aubriot gallantly, "it's obvious that the mere sight of you shows him how easily I might lose my head."

* * * *

The room at Bessay was large and the walls were covered in cotton *toile de Jouy*, decorated with pastoral scenes. Jeanne was touched that Philibert had chosen this room with her taste in mind. She exclaimed with pleasure at the sight of all the pink sheep guarded by their pink shepherds sitting under the pink trees. She immediately identified the trees as examples of *salix fragilis*, brittle willow, mistakenly bearing the leaves of *salix viminalis*, basket willow.

Of course, if Philibert had chosen the room only to sleep with a shameless woman elsewhere, she would feel differently. *If he doesn't come soon to take the digestive potion, I'll take it down to him.* If she was just a valet he cared so little about, it couldn't matter if she ate her cake while he was flirting. *I'll have my cake, whether he likes it or not. Does he expect me to wait, in fear and trembling, for his forgiveness? No, no, no!* She certainly wasn't going to cry. That would give him too much satisfaction. Was it her fault that she had been set upon by a brute?

She paced, with long steps, fueling her anger and checking the tears that welled up inside her.

All at once the door opened, and Philibert came in. She stopped short between the two beds. Was he going to force a sleeping draught upon her and go off to his vile pleasures?

Philibert raised his eyebrows. "What are you doing in the middle of the room, like a statue of justice with dangling arms? Can't you choose a bed? They're quite alike. Make your choice, or else we'll draw lots."

"I prepared your medicine," she stammered. "There . . . I put it there."

"Thank you. But the medicine was just an excuse to get you away from those soldiers. I didn't want to see you in more bad company."

She was too upset to understand, but his voice was kindly and so she murmured, "Thank you, sir."

"Well, go to bed. Aren't you tired from the journey? Tonight, luckily, you can be comfortable."

With a gesture he pointed to the bathroom, charmingly decorated in pink with gray stripes. The washbasin, in white ceramic, was decorated with bouquets of flowers, the commode filled with water. And a pitcher of warm water stood on the floor.

In a trancelike condition Jeanne undressed, poured water into the basin and splashed herself all over. She slowly brushed her hair and perfumed it with a rustic toilet water, made from Easter lilies which grew around an old pear tree in the garden of Charmont. When she stepped back to examine her hairdress she realized that she was stark naked. Never before had she brushed her hair without any clothes on. Had the misadventure in the courtyard and Philibert's anger caused her to lose her mind?

With a sigh, she slipped on the long, schoolgirl nightdress, with ribbons at the collar and cuffs, that Mme. de Bouhey had told her to pack for the journey. It was no use wearing flounced, fine linen nightgowns if she was to be alone.

She stood in the bathroom for some minutes, gathering the courage to emerge. No sound came from the other room. Had Philibert gone to sleep? Could she tiptoe across the room and slip into bed without his seeing her in her nightdress? The idea of letting the night go by without knowing if he was still angry was unbearable.

She half opened the door and called out, in a stifled voice, the name which she had given him as a little girl, "Monsieur Philibert!"

"Yes, Jeannot."

The voice seemed to come from so far away that she ventured into the room. Philibert was sitting in front of the window, with his back to her, jotting down something in a notebook. He had taken off his jacket, neckband, and wig. His chestnut hair was loosely tied in the back by a black ribbon.

"Yes, Jeannot," he repeated, still writing.

"Monsieur Philibert, this evening . . . in the courtyard . . . the valet . . . it wasn't my fault, really."

"I know, Jeannot," he said, without turning around. "I was tired and nervous, and I let myself be carried away. Let's forget the whole thing."

But how could he? She had just brought the whole affair up again. The obscene picture of the valet's hands on Jeanne's breasts took hold of him, followed by the desire to claim her for himself. He threw down his pen and rubbed his face with both hands, as if to rid his head of a criminal idea.

Dear God, You won't let me do it, will You? I won't do it, I can't. For a second he thought of going to assuage his desire in the arms of the Blue Lady. He gave a nervous laugh, which made Jeanne shudder. She took four noiseless steps into the room.

"Monsieur Philibert," she called again. Suddenly, she felt lost in an unknown climate and didn't know what to do next.

As she spoke, he realized that she had come out of the bathroom. He rose from the writing table and turned around. She stood, straight and white, in her virginal nightdress. Her blond hair hung softly at both sides of her face. Her lips were half open in an expectant smile, and there was a glint of gold in her eyes.

In a weak voice she repeated, "Monsieur Philibert . . ."

Stilled by emotion and hardly daring to breathe, he let her come toward him with hesitant steps, like a doe.

When she came to a halt before him, he opened his arms and closed them around her, as if by magic she had opened and closed them for him.

* * * *

The clamor in the courtyard of the coach being readied for departure woke her up. She was alone in the bed. A feeling of abandonment came over her, and she gave a loud cry.

The curtains parted. And there stood Philibert, with a smile on his face, fully dressed and booted, wearing his powdered wig. Memory turned her cheeks scarlet and she was about to retreat under the sheet, when there was a knock at the door. A moment later, the odor of hot coffee and fresh bread filled the room.

"Come have some breakfast, Jeannot," said Philibert.

She realized then that she was naked. How could she ask for something to put on? Almost immediately, thank God, she found her undershirt, which had fallen between the bed and the wall. Awkwardly she hid herself in it.

"Well, Jeannette? Are you coming?"

Philibert was busy spreading butter on the bread, as if nothing had happened between them.

"Well, sit down."

Pouring milk into the coffee he repeated, "Sit down, Jeannette. This is a day, you see, when masters wait on their valets."

The noise in the courtyard was louder, as the coachman berated the footmen for their clumsiness. Jeanne looked toward the window.

"But, Monsieur Philibert, they're going to leave without us."

"So they are. But haven't you had enough of that hotbox full of tedious people? Economy be damned! I've ordered a chaise, and we'll proceed as we choose."

She understood at once that he was offering her a honeymoon. Her reserve crumbled and she melted with happiness.

She threw herself into his arms and buried her face in his jacket, murmuring over and over, "I love you! I love you!"

To overcome his own emotion Philibert finally raised her head and put a piece of bread in her mouth. But when she took it out, explaining she was too happy to swallow, he picked her up and laid her on the bed.

They drank their coffee that had grown cold.

* * * *

That incredible journey, a tour of Venus' island of Cythera! It was like a ribbon of delight. They had suffered from the heat, swallowed pecks of dust, been jolted almost out of their skins, overturned at the marketplace of Pouilly because of a half-drunk driver, encountered bedbugs at the Grand Monarque of Briare and a mattress on the floor at the Magdeleine of Montargis. At the Etoile of Fontainebleau they were robbed and at the Ecu of Essonnes the roast mutton stank of goat. But oh, the incredible journey!

Every change of horses allowed them caresses; every stage a night of love. A bottle of Spanish wine made a thrown-together meal into a fine supper. They looked so hungrily at each other that they were oblivious of any ugliness in the decoration. Night after night Philibert's hands and lips invented new sensations, which left Jeanne, in the morning, with a stunned body, an idolatrous heart, and a delicious good humor.

One day at Nemours her feelings ran so high that she asked him, "What can I do to let you know that I love you as much as I do?"

In reply he lightly kissed her neck, chin, mouth, eyelids, and hair, answering, "You don't need to do anything, Jeannot. I know it." He spoke as if he really did.

* * * *

But once they were in Paris, work retook possession of his daytime hours. And oftentimes he did not return home until midnight. There is never enough time for a scientist bent over his microscope. And a provincial botanist, camping out on the steps of the Academy of Science, hoping to wedge a foot in the door, is busy even during his leisure hours.

Jeanne took the change very hard and felt neglected. This was not so. Philibert took her to the garden, used her help in his work, encouraged her to study, and entrusted her with the housekeeping. She was anything but forgotten. But he no longer had time to rave about her tawny eyes at three o'clock in the afternoon.

Jeanne had not had her full share of devotion. Can a woman in love ever be sated? Men are what they are. The most faithful nymph may wonder if she doesn't need a number of men to pay her due tribute.

PART

II

The King's Garden

CHAPTER 16

lle. Basseporte, the official painter of the King's
Garden, had taken Jeanne under her wing as soon as
she had arrived, three months before. She remem-
bered the difficulties of her own beginnings well enough to lend a
hand to a young woman capable of finding a small place in the
garden. Of course, Jeanne had come in the wake of Dr. Aubriot, who
had been welcomed with open arms by the Jussieus, natives of Lyon,
and with whom he had long corresponded. Mlle. Basseporte had introduced her to George-Louis Buffon, the keeper of the garden, and the
other important men of the place. By this time Jeanne felt completely
at home and took pride in being recognized by scholars whose lectures
enjoyed a wide popularity.

"Monsieur Buffon is always so agreeable," she said, entering Mlle.
Basseporte's room. "Indeed, everyone's most kind."

"You're a pretty girl," said Mlle. Basseporte, with a smile.

Jeanne looked silently at the older woman. Her faded face still wore
traces of her beauty as a young woman.

"Tell me," Jeanne said, with unconscious cruelty, "did your good
looks help your career?"

"They didn't hurt. With a woman a pound of beauty weighs more
than a pound of enthusiasms. So, if the two are combined . . ."

After a moment of hesitation Jeanne inquired, "How did it happen
that a woman with your charms, set down in a world of men, never
married?"

"Thank God, my men friends married other women."

The painter laid down her brush. "Jeanne, don't judge my heart by
yours. Yours craves love; mine was distracted by ambition. I always
wanted to create flowers rather than children."

"But you've spoken of your love for Monsieur Linnaeus."

"We loved each other. And we still do . . . in letters. Occasionally, I
send him one of my flowers. But his dear Sarah-Elizabeth has given

him five children. While she was risking her life in childbirth he wrote me that, if he was widowed, he wanted me to be his second wife. Don't you think a mistress has more satisfaction than a wife?"

"So you don't regret not having married him?"

"No. Believe me, in the long run one can put up with a man only if he's often away. Are you sorry not to be Dr. Aubriot's wife?"

"No. But a man is more apt to leave a mistress. I wonder if he'll always want me. And that makes me afraid."

"And will you always want him?"

After a moment of surprise, Jeanne shot back, "Yes, always!"

"My dear child," said Mlle. Basseporte, "you may not know it, but you've the heart of a nun. In this case the best thing is to marry either God or a . . . gardener. Only these two can live on love without losing their paradise. Better marry Thouin. He's in love with you, and you'd make a delicious companion to the king's gardener."

* * * *

Thouin and Jeanne had struck up a friendship at first sight. Jeanne soon realized that he loved her. But his love was so timid and unobtrusive that she enjoyed it without feeling guilty for encouraging it. At eighteen years of age, round-cheeked and slender, André Thouin still had something childlike about him. A year ago he had been offered the prestigious title of head gardener in the King's Garden, a successor to his father, Jean-André, who had died prematurely. The post was so sought after that Louis XV was startled when, on one of his rare visits to Versailles, M. Buffon suggested an adolescent.

"Monsieur, you can't mean it!" the king had exclaimed. "Even if I were to choose this boy, he couldn't last. The older and more experienced men to whom I should have given precedence would destroy him."

But Buffon was adamant. "Sire," he insisted, "no one will protest. No candidate can match the abilities of the Thouin boy." And so the king consented.

André Thouin lived in his garden and produced beautiful flowers. His green thumb transformed a simple, pale corolla into a brilliant work of art. Fine ladies flocked to admire his creations and to ask for seeds and cuttings. Young Thouin had learned from direct observation of nature, trotting in his father's footsteps.

Now, simply clad in rough breeches, a shirt, and an apron furnished with ample pockets, he possessed not only an inexhaustible wealth of practical ideas but also such erudition that many a visitor to the garden sought him out. Jeanne was delighted with their friendship.

"The king's gardener . . . tell me, André, can there be any more splendid title?"

"No. And I aspire to no other. I can live the life I want without budging so much as an inch."

"But do you never want to budge?"

"But, Jeannette, I *can't* budge! You can't leave a garden alone."

"Even to travel in search of new flowers?"

"New flowers are brought to me."

All the year round, indeed, sailors, missionaries, and explorers brought in plants, bushes, and young trees which they had gathered in the course of their journeys. Thouin received them with silent joy, mended, bandaged, and acclimatized them.

"I'm a gardener, Jeanne, not a conqueror. I sow, plant, and water because I want to see my flowers grow. Last year I sent out fifty thousand seed packets."

"Yes, to think that your double-pink seeds came all the way to Charmont, through Monsieur Poivre! That way we became friends even before we met."

How strange it was to be in love! André had ingenuously pledged to take no interest in girls, so as to devote himself entirely to flowers. He thought that no girl could be as beautiful as a flower, without cosmetics, elaborate dress, or affected manners. Then came Jeanne, with her freckled skin, her unrouged cheeks and unpowdered hair, her casually worn breeches, her nimble hands, tireless legs, and the relaxing silence she maintained while at work. This was a girl like no other. Little by little he began to compare her to a flower. Love's blindness prevented him from seeing that she was the shadow of the new botanist attached to Jussieu.

The early December morning was exceptionally mild. Autumn, it seemed, would not die. There were clumps of russet leaves on the trees, chrysanthemums blooming, and even a few butterflies.

Jeanne and André went in the direction of Les Coupeaux, which overlooked a rustic site studded with windmills. Below the garden there were vegetable patches of the Clos Patouillet, on both sides of the Bièvre River. Jeanne gazed at the landscape laid out before them.

"What is most surprising to a country girl new to Paris," she remarked, "is the great number of gardens. The monks of Saint-Victor allow me occasionally to dig up a cabbage from their patch. Those are the sounds of Paris I hear while I'm scraping a cabbage root just the way I used to do at Charmont."

"That's because, even in Paris, you've chosen to live in the country," said Thouin, smiling. "For me Paris is one vast garden."

"And yet I'd like to know the real life of Paris," Jeanne said impatiently.

"The real life of Paris? But, Jeannette, the hub of Paris is here. I assure you," he said, "if you sit on the bench in front of my door you'll eventually see everyone that counts for anything in the kingdom. And isn't life in the garden happy?"

"Very happy," Jeanne admitted. "The atmosphere's crackling with scholarly good humor. Wonderful! Yet I'd like to escape sometimes, in order to do silly little things. Such as eating crayfish down there . . ." And she raised her chin in the direction of a tavern, built somewhat askew, on the bank of the Bièvre.

Thouin shook his head. "Whoever told you about the crayfish of the Bièvre must have been an old man. They say they were the best in the country, but that's long past. The crystal-clear Bièvre is a dumping place for the refuse of the tanners, leather dressers, and skinners of the vicinity. The foul water has long since put the crayfish to flight."

"What a shame!" exclaimed Jeanne. "I was born too late."

"I can find you some survivors, in the convent garden of the Grey Sisters, upstream from the Gobelins."

"How good of you, André, to offer me such a treat! The truth is, I want to do all kinds of things. To go to the Opéra, the Comédie Française, Versailles, to the fair at Saint-Germain, the shops on the Rue Saint-Denis, to a hairdresser on the Rue Saint-Honoré, to drink a glass of white wine at La Courtille, to eat beignets on the Pont Neuf, to dance at the Moulin de Javel, everything and anything that will allow me to say, 'I live in Paris and I've become a true Parisian.' "

Jeanne's desires worried Thouin. He raised his eyes and took up her last words.

"The beignets on the Pont Neuf are said to be greasy. And the Moulin de Javel is a mill like any other, on the outskirts, except that it's been fixed up for drinking and dancing. But that's a place for . . . loose women."

"I know, I know," said Jeanne, changing the subject.

The Moulin de Javel was a private matter between Philibert and herself. One evening Philibert had gone there and wouldn't take her along. Of course not, if he was going for the women. No, Jeanne wasn't going to condone Philibert's visit to the Moulin de Javel, at least not until she, too, could go to kick up her heels and drink wine outside the city limits.

The escapade had been promoted by Jussieu's nephew, Antoine-Laurent, to celebrate his admission to medical school. Philibert had consented to play, for an evening, the role of a country doctor corrupted by his city cousins. As if it were the most natural thing in the world, he had left Jeanne at home, come back at three o'clock in the morning, and offered not a single word of apology over the breakfast table. He downed his coffee and bread and butter, tucked his hat under his arm, waved goodbye, and went off to the garden.

Jeanne cried long and hard until her sadness turned into blazing anger. She decided to sulk, to sleep alone, for at least a month. This resolve held for no more than a quarter of an hour.

"Are you ill? Where does it hurt? Let me take your pulse. Stick out your tongue! Have you been coughing? Do you feel it if I press here, and here, and there?" Philibert was an odd sort of doctor, who poked his hands into everything. He fingered her chest and sides and belly until . . . until she had to admit to lying, and to being ticklish, as well as jealous and angry.

He laughed, and swore that they'd go dancing on a Sunday, in some other dancing establishment in La Courtille, just like a working-class couple. But a scientist knows no Sunday. And so far Jeanne remained ignorant of the gay and inebriating Paris life which she desired so dearly.

CHAPTER 17

 step echoed in the vestibule of the flat. Jeanne peered into the mirror above the fireplace in order to smooth her bodice. The white muslin sat as lightly as if it were meant to be parted by the hands of a lover bent on sampling the hidden pink sweetmeats below.

Jeanne sighed, like an idle courtesan. When Philibert came home, his head was churning with ideas. He was researching the mysterious green pigment which colors a vegetable skin. Compared to this, of what interest were Jeanne's rosy nipples?

Every night, however, she had to admit, Philibert was very much there. Even when he came home late and she had already fallen asleep, he never failed to wake her up with a greedy kiss.

Philibert had built up their relationship in a practical manner, benignly tyrannical on his side and happily acquiescent on hers. He found the mixture of her timidity and sensuality altogether enchanting. She quivered, moaned, and purred at his touch, but never initiated a caress. He might have encouraged her to do so, but he preferred her passivity. He had had his fill of sophisticated and aggressive women.

With a sort of perverse paternalism he treated Jeanne as if she were still the little girl of the woods. He alone invented their sensual responses, and his own were tinged with a complex, almost incestuous tenderness. Since Jeanne seemed happy to be his nighttime plaything, they were a perfect couple. He would have been surprised had she confessed to moments of impatience and melancholy, or complained of neglect.

Indeed, even when she felt vaguely dissatisfied, Jeanne wondered what exactly she did want. She was young and beautiful, she had Philibert, she had Paris and, besides these, she had a new bonnet.

The thought of the new bonnet restored her smile. She took it down from the shelf, put it on, and came back with a hand mirror, looking at herself from the side and the rear. Stunning! There was no other word for it. Only Mlle. Lacaille on the Rue Saint-Honoré, whose name she had heard on the lips of Pauline de Vaux-Jailloux, could create something so inspired. The price was extravagant, to be sure, but once Jeanne had stepped into the shop she had not been able to resist temptation.

And yet Philibert was blind to fashion and would probably not even notice. When he came home he saw at once that the dwarf Mexican cactus had lost a thorn from the second branch on the left side, but not that Jeanne had on a new bonnet.

Jeanne picked up a book and sat down, glancing at the cold supper she had set out on a round table. Even the slices of roast veal didn't seem happy to be waiting for Philibert in so stark a room. The two-room bachelor quarters cut out of Dr. Vacher's spacious flat—an improvised kitchen, a large toilet, and dressing room, were not exactly gay. But Philibert had found it convenient.

Philibert was not rich and he was prudent. Descended from a long line of notaries, he had inherited the habit of keeping his accounts in order and tailoring his expenses to his income. The rooms were dark, coldly decorated, and encumbered with heavy old furniture. But the Rue du Mail was only a few steps from the grassy lawn of the monastery of the Petits-Pères, the Little Fathers, the Place des Victoires, and the Palais-Royal.

In reality, Jeanne's studies at the garden, her clerical services to Philibert, and her housework did not leave her much time for idle strolling. But she managed, once a day, to walk through the Palais-Royal, preferably just before dusk, when this happy enclosure was truly the crossroads of the capital.

On her walks, she saw fashionable people, clad in silks, with powdered hair, and she wished to meet someone important and well known. Jeanne had identified only one celebrity so far and that was Diderot.

Every day, at five o'clock, Diderot sat on a bench in front of the Hôtel d'Argenson. The other strollers, even the newsmongers, so respected the philosopher's reverie that not one of them usurped his seat. Jeanne wondered if she could ever work up her courage to sit there, just to see what would happen. And one evening that is what she did.

She perched at the very edge of the bench, and Diderot, in astonishment, turned his head, ready to scowl. *Hmmm. . . . The presumptuous creature is very pretty.* The great man curled his lip in a half-smile. Jeanne gave him a full, dazzling one in return. At first he was startled. Was this an available girl of a superior kind? Or a naïve young woman of the middle class? His first words were as commonplace as those of an everyday skirt chaser.

"This year December hasn't put an end to our Indian summer, has it, mademoiselle? It's a real gift of the gods."

She nodded assent. Then, biting her lips, she ventured, "May I ask you a question, monsieur? Monsieur Diderot, if I'm not mistaken."

He nodded. A man is never indifferent to recognition by an intelligent woman. And this woman was intelligent. In a melodious voice she launched into discriminating praise of the *Encyclopédie*.

"Never mind my articles in the *Encyclopédie*," he said, after a few minutes. "On that subject we agree. I think highly of them myself. Tell me about your own work. You are a writer, I presume."

"No, I'm not, really."

"I can't believe it. In our day and age an intelligent woman without a pen in hand is inconceivable."

"But I am just such a one, although I do write summaries of lectures on science. It's a service I perform for"—she hesitated and blushed— ". . . my master. I'm secretary to a great botanist, Dr. Aubriot."

"Dr. Aubriot? I know the man. I met him when he was very young and had come to study in the King's Garden. After that he went back to the provinces. Is he here again now?"

"He's been here since September."

"Since September? And I haven't yet run into him at the house of Baron d'Holbach. How does that happen?"

"Why should you expect to meet him there?"

"Because on Sundays and Thursdays the baron feeds all the philosophers and scientists of Paris, and no one wants to deprive him of this pleasure. He'll be vexed to hear that Dr. Aubriot hasn't turned up. I must remedy the damage at once. Please tell your master to ask for me at the baron's on one of the appointed days. At dinnertime I'm always there."

As Jeanne walked away she thought to herself, somewhat irritatedly, that Diderot would take Philibert to Baron d'Holbach, just as Lalande had taken him to Madame Geoffrin . . . without her. In the great salons of Paris they made a point of receiving only the most exceptional women. But she was cheered at the realization that the great Diderot had spoken to her! She had relished the expression on the faces of passersby as they stared at the young woman speaking with the father of the *Encyclopédie*. Suddenly the girl from the provinces had become an habituée of the Palais-Royal.

Night was falling when she came to the Rue des Petits-Pères and slipped into the monastery. As she had hoped, Father Joachim was still in the library, leaning over an unrolled map.

"You've come at just the right moment, my dear child. Father Eustache has just brought me the latest map of the harbor of Port Louis."

He knew that Jeanne was interested in the faraway Ile de France. The chubby old man had the soft voice of a dreamy child. As curator of the monastery's collection of marine cartography, he had long since abandoned real life to live in a fantasy world of faraway oceans and unexplored continents. Jeanne had taken an immediate fancy to this Augustinian monk.

Now he unrolled a second map and led her, mile by mile, over a distant coast, with a description so detailed that she felt the rolling and pitching of the ship as his wonderful voice carried her along.

"Here is Coromandel," he said, "and here is Malabar. You can see all the possible anchorages, even the most precarious. In bringing them up to date, we relied on the observations of Captain Vincent and the pilot serving Captain de Beauregard." The name of Vincent caused Jeanne to start. It summoned up her cherished memory of the hunt ball at Charmont.

"You're miles away," interposed the soft voice of Father Joachim. "On l'Ile de France or in the Indies?"

"Neither one," said Jeanne. "I was thinking of Monsieur Diderot. Do you know, Father, I just had a long talk with him!"

"Well, you don't expect me to congratulate you, do you? Diderot's freethinking crowd can only put wrong notions into your head."

"Are they so very terrible, then?"

"They're headed for damnation. The baron's house is the Vatican of unbelievers."

"Oh! But they say that it's frequented by the very best people."

"Quite likely. They tear down God over a gourmet's table. Their evil minds are coupled with good stomachs."

"Have no fear, Father, Monsieur Diderot didn't invite me to lose my soul at one of the baron's dinners. They're reserved for men. But Monsieur Lalande speaks ill of God and yet you like him."

"If Lalande discovers God at the end of his telescope he'll shout it out from the housetops. And one day he'll surely find Him. Contemplation of the miracles of the skies is bound to lead a man to God."

In the silence that followed Jeanne relived the excitement she had felt when, through the lens of his telescope, Lalande had brought her closer to the stars. The astronomer had installed a small observatory on the roof of his house on the Place du Palais-Royal and when he invited friends to supper he gave them constellations for dessert. Jeanne appreciated the dessert all the more because, among Philibert's friends, he was the only one to invite her to his house and to welcome her as warmly as if she were Mme. Aubriot.

The monastery bell rang, calling the monks to their early supper. Jeanne remained alone. She was looking out at the vegetable garden when she saw Lalande and Philibert enter the cloister. Their discussion seemed to be lively.

"I'll leave them to their chatter," Jeanne said to herself, picking up a book. But her ears should have burned since she was the subject of their conversation.

"Don't laugh," Aubriot grumbled. "I don't like what you're telling me. So, they make fun of me in the garden, do they?"

"You should be glad!" exclaimed Lalande. "By inspiring mock verses, your lovely hermaphrodite draws attention to you as well."

"I know your ways of making yourself popular, and I don't approve of them. I came to Paris to display my merits, not my mistress."

"How provincial! Take my advice, and don't scorn notoriety. Merits are slow to win recognition."

Aubriot faced Lalande with his legs spread wide apart, his arms crossed over his chest, and a hard look in his eyes.

"Very well. Advise me further. Should I send Jeannette to ask the minister for the audience which he is so slow in granting me?"

"There's something in that, I'd say. She could obtain it more quickly. I know Choiseul. He may not have a single minute to spare, but he always has time for a pretty woman. In his arms a clever girl would soon produce an academician."

"Watch out, Lalande! I was born with a hot temper. Don't provoke me!"

The astronomer threw back his head and laughed. "At last you're admitting the truth. For three months, I've waited to hear you say you're in love."

"Such a lofty feeling is not for my age," said Aubriot dryly.

"But your little girl has restored you to the age of twenty-seven. Thirty-seven plus seventeen makes fifty-four. Divide fifty-four by two and you have twenty-seven."

"All well and good. Let's leave this childish subject. I . . . ."

"No!" Lalande interrupted. "I want to hear you say that you love Jeannette."

Aubriot shook his head. "I have no right to. I made a vow over the grave of my poor Marguerite."

Lalande refrained from making a sharp reply. "You'd make me laugh if I didn't care for you so much. Instead you make me angry." Then, giving way to his natural liveliness, he added, "Look here, Aubriot! At Bugey you were infected by virtue. Morality is about as becoming to you as modesty would be to me. What sin were you expiating with your vow?"

"The death of Marguerite."

Silence fell, like a knife, between them. Finally Lalande resumed calmly, "Many women die in childbirth. Are men guilty?"

"They're not innocent . . . especially when they're doctors."

Lalande took his friend affectionately by the arm. "Aubriot, the only thing we could do for our dead would be to awaken them. But even a thousand years of weeping can't achieve that. And the dead understand. You can't imagine that they expect something from the living. Just observe any dying man; he pays us no attention."

"Marguerite isn't entirely dead. She left me a son. And he needs all my love."

"More Rousseau!" exclaimed Lalande. "There's time before he'll need a father. For the moment all he needs is a nurse." And, without waiting for an answer, he went on, "I'm afraid that your reluctance to love comes less from fidelity than from selfishness. I know this to be true of myself. The private happiness we find in our research leaves little room for a woman who loves us. And that we should love her in return seems to be asking too much altogether."

Aubriot reflected before replying. "I gave up my freedom and much of my ambition when I married Marguerite, and I wasn't sorry. But I'll never marry again."

"A vow not to remarry and a vow not to love don't necessarily go together. Selfishness is enough to keep us from loving. But to avoid marriage demands a scarcer and more capricious quality—clear-headedness. If God existed I'd pray to Him to protect my bachelorhood. I can't see myself wasting my evenings with a family. I have enough trouble fitting mistresses into my schedule."

"From what I hear, you don't fit them in—you let them perch on the edges!"

Lalande exploded with laughter. "I haven't met my Jeannette, that's all." There was a note of tenderness in his voice as he added, "Don't let me steal yours, Aubriot. I could be so madly in love with her that I'd waste no end of time."

"You'll not steal Jeannette, Lalande," said Aubriot calmly. "Nobody will steal her from me."

Lalande narrowed his eyes. "Do you take her for an ivy branch wrapped around you?"

"Exactly," said Aubriot.

"Hmmm . . . and if you finally obtain what you want, a botanical expedition to some faraway place, what will become of her?"

"She'll wait for me."

"Men are incorrigible dreamers. You call yourself an inconsolable widower, and here you are, expecting a Penelope."

"At the moment, Choiseul isn't giving a franc to the Jussieus to finance the voyage of a Ulysses."

"He may very well do it, though. He wants great, unforgettable things to happen under his ministry. The discovery of an unknown land would put him on the map."

"But even if Choiseul releases the money for a scientific expedition I can't be sure of being included. There are other naturalists who'd like to travel: Adanson, Poivre, Commerson, Valmont de Bomare. They have an equal chance. And my closest rival is still Dom Pernety. He does remarkable drawings, and Colonel de Bougainville praised him to the skies when he came back from the Falklands."

"Some personal connection, that's what will count. You must cultivate and pay court to the right people."

"You mean to the king?"

"Don't be naïve. Even to go to bed with him requires going through his personal valet."

"Well, I'm close to the Jussieus, as you know, and on good terms with Buffon."

"What about Le Monnier? Do you follow his anatomy lessons?"

"I see no point. He's commonplace."

Lalande sighed. "Ever since we were in school together, Aubriot, you've had the gift of making enemies with a few well-chosen words. Have you forgotten that Le Monnier is first physician ordinary to the king? He has the Ear, my boy, the Ear! So don't dismiss him as commonplace. Acquire him for a patient. Or, better still, let him take care of you. Have you no little growth that needs cutting out?"

"Botanomania, that's my only trouble!" said Aubriot, laughing. "But I'm afraid it's in my blood."

"Well," said Lalande, "from what I know about his bleeding treatment, he'll get it out of you." Once more he laughed so hard that his wig nearly fell off. "Don't think so much about going away," he added. "It took me years to tear you away from the provinces. Now let yourself enjoy Paris. You have great learning, you're highly attractive, and botany is the rage. All the women go for it. Spread yourself around the salons and the bedrooms, and in six months you'll be the talk of town. The academy has an eye on you, believe me."

"Then I hope it soon gives me a sign."

Behind them the two men heard a contralto voice. "Who, sir, is to give you a sign?"

Aubriot turned around and smiled at Jeanne. "Good fortune," he answered.

"Then invent some miraculous remedy. Parisians love to buy quack cure-alls, promoted in astrological jargon. If you concoct a powder and Monsieur Lalande provides the astrology, I'll sell it on the Pont Neuf and all three of us will make a fortune."

"Jeannette finds my scholarly life so tedious that she's looking for an excuse to get into the hurly-burly of Paris."

"Her idea is sound," said Lalande. "Astrology is worth its weight in gold. If I could permit myself to sell horoscopes . . . but now we must think of dinner. Come to supper at my house. A parcel arrived this morning from Picardy. At Montdidier I have a woman admirer who spoils me with a pâté made from suckling pigs."

"Good," said Aubriot. "But first let's go to my place to pick up a bottle of aged Burgundy, sent to me by a lady from Dijon, because I contributed some herbs to her collection. Our fathers were quite right, Lalande, when they said that, with your stars and my flowers, we'd live on bread and water."

CHAPTER 18

inter went by and spring returned. Dressed like a boy, Jeanne walked through the streets of Paris on her own.

Oh, the streets of Paris! She never wearied of them. By seven o'clock the milk carts had already gone by and the day's business had begun. Shopkeepers opened their shutters, craftsmen in leather aprons went to call on their customers or stayed in their workshops, spitting into their hands before they picked up their tools.

Jeanne had come to realize that the Parisians made a point of buying from the loudest hawkers, who were encouraged to outshout one another. The Pont Neuf was full of life early in the morning. But the peak of excitement occurred after ten o'clock. The mixture of people of all classes and conditions lent charm to the area. Noblemen, bourgeois, workers, artists, and flea-ridden outcasts rubbed shoulders. This was one of the rare places where one could hope to gratify a taste for the unexpected, the desire to meet somebody new.

Jeanne leaned her elbows on the wall overlooking the Seine. The river glided by, teeming with boat traffic. Suddenly she became aware that someone was staring at her, and she turned around.

The man seemed no more than twenty-five years old. He was wearing a green velvet coat which seemed secondhand rather than cut to measure. He had a hat on his head, like a peasant. His face was a full moon, with chubby cheeks, a large nose, and a dimple on the chin, crowned by a mass of curly reddish hair, barely dusted with powder. His chestnut eyes and small but fleshy mouth were smiling. It was obvious that he wanted to talk.

"A newcomer to Paris?" he asked, raising his voice above the surrounding noise.

"What makes you think so?" asked Jeanne, vexed at being taken for a new arrival.

"A Parisian your age wouldn't waste time looking at the river," he said, placing his hand familiarly on her shoulder.

"You don't look all that old yourself," she answered.

"I'm not your regular Parisian. I live by loafing. In short, I'm a writer."

"I thought that writers were tied to their desks and had no time to roam the streets."

"I'm not your regular type of writer. I don't write about what I've read but about what I've seen."

And he laughed at his own witticism.

A cacophony of bells tumbled out of La Samaritaine.

"Will they never tune those bells?" she asked.

"La Samaritaine brings in six thousand francs a year for its owner, and with that it accomplishes its purpose. Only a libertine spirit, like yours, could demand harmonious bells."

"Isn't that revolutionary talk?"

"Indeed it is! This country needs to be turned upside down. La Samaritaine should be destroyed because it obstructs the view of Paris. The academicians should be dismissed because they're ruining the language. The Comédie Française should be closed because it corrupts the public taste with the ridiculous tragedies of Racine and Corneille instead of staging the far superior plays of Mercier."

"Who is this Mercier of whom you think so highly?"

"A topnotch playwright, put down by the critics," said the stranger gravely. "He is standing before you."

At which they laughed together.

"From what I see, you take your bad luck philosophically," Jeanne remarked.

"I feel I'm about to be rescued. Monsieur de Crébillon the Younger, our censor, has read my last tragedy in verse."

"And will he stage it?"

"No, but he advised me to write in prose, and in prose I'm a master."

"What sort of material are you looking for on the Pont Neuf?" she asked.

"Words!" exclaimed Mercier. "Pungent, juicy, well-rounded words! Here on the bridge you have the people. And their language hasn't been emasculated by the academy. It's simple and spicy and just what I want to put into my books."

"No doubt you've a good ear, monsieur, but there's not much real French to be picked up around here."

"But why should the language of Paris dominate the rest?" said Mercier. "That's another idea of the academy. I want nothing to do with those pedants. I want the people, in all their vulgar diversity." He threw out his arms and declaimed loudly:

"*City of dung, now let us see*
The truth of what they say,
And whether it's the enemy
Whose tongue will hold you in its sway."

He's a bit mad. Jeanne watched Mercier. Inebriated by the sound of his own words and by the public's attention, he continued as a group of curiosity seekers gathered around them.

> *"As we stroll along the Seine,*
> *'Good-morrow, La Samaritaine!'* "

Yes, he was mad. A gentle madman of the Paris streets, bold with a light touch, talkative, a spectator of himself as well as of others.

Eventually the group drifted away, two or three of them putting the coin back into their pockets, which the performer had apparently not wanted to collect. A man of better class, in a long coat, took off his hat to Mercier.

"Monsieur," he said, "your verses are in old-fashioned style but nonetheless enjoyable." He spoke fluent French but with an English accent.

"Monsieur," said Mercier, doffing his hat in return, "the verses aren't mine. Their author went up in smoke. Our late king had him burned at the stake."

"Oh! What crime had he committed?"

"He was happy-go-lucky, monsieur, and put his poverty into verse. In the days of our Jesuit-ridden Louis XIV this poem was blasphemy and called for burning."

The Englishman opened his mouth to reply, but he was interrupted by the drumbeats announcing Grand-Thomas, the dentist. Grand-Thomas was pulling out a molar tooth, and his assistant beat the drum in order to drown out the patient's lamentation. The amateur dentist, riding in a great wagon, conspicuously decorated with green and gold paint, was perhaps the bridge's most celebrated character.

The flower seller passed in front of them, her hands filled with bunches of pale wild daffodils. Jeanne stared mechanically at the yellow flowers and then started, as if coming out of a dream.

"My God!" she exclaimed. "I should have been back at the garden long ago. Isn't it very late?"

"Nearly eleven," said Mercier, looking at his watch. "What garden are you going to?"

"The King's Garden."

"Are you studying botany or anatomy?"

"Botany, and a bit of zoology."

"I'll go with you part of the way. I have business to do on the Rue des Bernardins, with a writer friend."

"Well . . ." said Jeanne hesitantly.

"You mean 'yes,' " said Mercier, taking her by the arm. "Now that we're friends, perhaps you'll tell me your name."

"Jeannot Beauchamps," Jeanne replied with a broad smile, and they walked on together.

This young Beauchamps was devilishly good company. Mercier had been able to set forth, without interruption, the project of his imminent masterpiece, "The Year 2440." Jeanne had listened with rapt attention to his Utopian reverie. He foretold the future—from the destruction of the absolute monarch to the invention of an infernal powder strong enough to reduce everything to ashes.

Mercier sighed deeply, then rose out of his "ashes" to say, "Let's meet again on Sunday. You're free that day, I presume. Come at three o'clock to Landel's on the Rue de Buci, where there is good wine and fresh oysters. I dine there every other Sunday in the company of other scribblers. More famous than myself, but they are equally good fun. Over dessert we break into song. Come along, and you'll breathe in some Paris air. Is it agreed?"

Jeanne wanted nothing better. But how could she get Philibert to go to Landel's? Mercier was surprised by her reticence.

"Well, what about it?" he asked.

"I can't come," she said discouragedly. "This spring, every Sunday, my master, Monsieur Aubriot, gives a lesson in herb collection in the woodlands of Boulogne. And I have to go with him."

"But that's early in the morning, and we dine at three o'clock."

Because she still seemed undecided, he threw a brotherly arm around her shoulders. "I know what it is to be young and penniless," he said. "I'll pay your share. I have a sermon in pure Gothic style, ready for the market on my desk. It will bring a good price."

Jeanne bit her lip before saying, tentatively, "I don't know. Tell me . . . are ladies invited to your dinners at Landel's?"

Mercier smiled indulgently. "So that's the rub. It's not your master, but some girl that keeps you on the grass after the lesson. Bring her along, my friend! We like to love just as much as to laugh, drink, and sing. Listen to this song . . ."

She couldn't prevent him from raising his voice right in front of the entrance to the garden, and—Lord help us!—at the very moment when M. Jussieu was coming out.

> *"To see a pretty girl*
> *Respond to instant call,*
> *La, la Landel!*
> *La, la Landel!"*

* * * *

How would she convince Philibert to dine at Landel's on Sunday? As the week wore on, she became obsessed. Convinced she could never explain the events of her afternoon with Mercier, she kept putting off speaking to him. Jeanne had to admit to herself that she was too subservient to Philibert. It was an instinct she could not overcome. When she was by herself, she thought in terms of her own aspirations, even when they ran contrary to his. But in Philibert's arms her self-respect dissolved.

After Friday night's lovemaking she tried to rebel. Her head lay on Philibert's bare chest. She turned it, laid her half-open mouth on a nipple, and bit it. Philibert opened his eyes, raised himself slightly on the pillow, and looked at her, curious as to what would follow this sudden audacity. Her face was hidden from him. All he saw was a mass of blond, silky hair spread over his chest, shimmering in the light of the bedside candle. Jeanne's mouth alternately bit, kissed, nibbled, bit harder, and then licked away the hurt, only to bite again. The play of an amorous kitten. He hugged her tight and stroked her hair. She was momentarily appeased, then went back to the game and covered him with pecking kisses until, weary at last, she gave up.

But, just as he was about to sink into sleep, she said abruptly, "I was thinking of Sunday. The Bois de Boulogne is very pleasant. But it's always the same."

"Well, this Sunday we're not going to Boulogne. One of our students is ill and I've canceled the lecture entirely. So I'm free for you. There are just the two of us. I'll take you to Vincennes. This time of year the trees and shrubs give off an invigorating odor of balsam. The weather will be fair and we shall enjoy the day. I'll pick dandelions for next week's salads. We'll find violets, primroses, perhaps the first buttercups, and surely watercress and wild chervil."

She lay upon him, motionless, as heavy as if she were dead.

"Are you asleep?" he asked.

The movement of her hair told him that she wasn't.

"A little above Vincennes there are wild hills with thousands and thousands of rabbits. We'll take a picnic lunch, and . . ."

He paused abruptly. His chest felt wet. With both hands he took hold of Jeanne's hair and raised her face.

"Why are you crying, Jeannot? Have I reminded you of Charmont? Are you homesick?"

"Noooo."

"Then why?"

"Because I love you, because I—I—I love you too much," she sobbed.

He blew out the candle, laid his hand on her hair, and let her cry. There was nothing else he could do.

* * * *

Aubriot was surprised when, late in the morning, Lalande came to the garden and proposed going to dine, on Sunday, at Landel's.

"You promised us a fine Sunday, and now you want us to spend it in a cellar?"

"Landel's cellar is no ordinary tavern. An invitation to dine there is a particular Parisian treat. Jeannette will enjoy it."

Aubriot was even more surprised. "Jeannette? You wouldn't take Jeannette to Landel's, would you? It's a cabaret famous, isn't it, for its . . ."

"Aubriot, babies are no longer brought by storks," Lalande interrupted. "The singing at Landel's is licentious, but there's no license. Crébillon presides over the Sunday dinners, and that's a guarantee of propriety. Everybody knows that Crébillon's vices are confined to his novels."

Aubriot carefully took a specimen of *Melianthus*, honey bush, from under a microscope and laid it on a sheet of white paper. He sat down on one corner of his desk, folded his arms, and looked hard at his friend.

"Please tell me, Lalande, how you who, like myself, refuse to waste time, can recommend frequenting Landel's."

"Aubriot, I'm fond of you, and I'd hate to see you cuckolded. But that's what happens to scientists, with no taste for frivolity, who bore their mistresses."

Aubriot answered with a short, hard laugh.

"Yes, I know, I know," said Lalande. "When one's a great lover one can't imagine playing the cuckold. But even the sun can be eclipsed."

CHAPTER 19

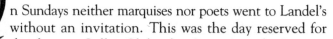

n Sundays neither marquises nor poets went to Landel's without an invitation. This was the day reserved for the famous Cellar Club, the *Compagnie du Caveau.* The president, Crébillon, was known for his courtesy. But also for his bluntness. He was quite capable of swiftly dispatching a ticket of "no-return" to an unsuitable guest. A shrewd host, Crébillon never turned down an unexpected visitor like Lalande, a fashionable scientist with a provocative wit. This Sunday the astronomer was doubly well received because he had brought with him two worthy friends, one of them a beauty.

Delighted smiles welcomed Jeanne, who was in an emerald-green dress so shockingly décolleté that Philibert had insisted that she add a scarf (which she had put aside as soon as she sat down). Crébillon had put her at his right, and she had the supreme happiness of being praised in spicy verse by some of the most celebrated wits of Paris.

Present were the habitués. Crébillon, the poet Gentil-Bernard, Panard, and Collé, writers of the most numerous and most famous comic texts in the kingdom, and Piron who, as he said, was "nobody, not even an academician," but so bristling with epigrams and witticisms that, at the age of seventy-six, he was received in the best drawing rooms of Paris. These pillars of the company were joined by five persons highly regarded in the city: Carlo Goldini, the celebrated Venetian dramatist imported by Louis XV, Simon Favart, the famous author of light operas, and his wife Justine, the brilliant Philidor, favorite of operagoers, and the sprightly Abbé de Voisenon, nicknamed "Fancy-Man," who was always hanging about the skirts of Mme. Favart. And, finally, Louis-Sebastién Mercier, who was staring at "Beauchamps" ecstatically.

Jeanne was in seventh heaven. She leaned over to take an oyster from the great plate in the middle of the table, laughing and inadvertently offering a view of her two round, amber breasts below the décolleté of her green bodice. Charles Collé, his cheeks already flushed, raised a glass to toast his neighbor:

> *"I seek to calculate your charms,*
> *Discovering more and more,*
> *And those I see a mere foretaste*
> *Of hidden ones in store."*

"Monsieur Collé," said Crébillon, with mock severity, "don't turn to gallantry too soon; we're only at the third basket."

"But at the seventh bottle!" Collé retorted.

"There are a lot of dry throats among us," said old Panard. "Mine, for instance. If I had to sing, my vocal cords would crumble into dust."

"Landel, furnish Papa Panard with some lubrication," said Crébillon. "This young lady"—inclining his handsome head in Jeanne's direction—"must hear some of his verse."

The old man, author of innumerable songs, washed his throat with a gulp of wine and rendered four lines of thanks:

> *"My body's grown, of late, so slow,*
> *So fearful and so subject to distraction,*
> *It takes a double dose of wine*
> *To goad it from its torpor into action!"*

The high-pitched laughter of Mme. Favart rang out above the rest. For the last twenty years she had played, danced, and sung the parts of lady, nymph, and shepherdess at the Théâtre des Italiens. After it had subsided, Panard raised his feeble voice. "Doctor, don't you think that a penny-roll dissolves in a pint of white wine as well as two baskets of oysters in a bowl of milk and costs far less money? I'd go bankrupt if all week long I ate oysters and the good, fresh milk of Monceau."

Jeanne smiled, like the others, at the touching figure of the old man. With his round, kindly face, his large rolled wig in the style of Louis XIV, he was reminiscent of a portrait of La Fontaine. Indeed Paris dubbed him "La Fontaine de la Chanson," the fountain of song. He shared the distractions of La Fontaine, the wit contrasting with a simple air, the productiveness, the carelessness with money. After writing the librettos of eighty light operas, he had to rely, for a good dinner, on the generosity of his friends.

Among all those who feasted their eyes on Jeanne between two mouthfuls of oysters, Mercier was certainly the most astounded; his eyes were as big as saucers. He was thrilled to exchange the companionable boy of the Pont Neuf for the alluring girl of Landel's. But, on second thought, he wondered how far he could go with her. This Dr. Aubriot was barely middle-aged and not at all sedate in appearance. It was certain Jeanne performed her services as a secretary by day and by night.

In order to improve his own chances, he drank more than usual, never taking his eyes off Jeanne. In the dim light of the low-ceilinged room, his green coat shone like a symbol of spring. He hummed "Green, green, green, are all my summer dresses" in a pointedly languorous manner. Old Piron, sitting at his left, leaned toward him.

"Yes, from what I can see out of my dimmed eyes, there's a pretty green tree over there; any bird would like to nest in it. But sometimes, my boy, a tree doesn't want to harbor two robins."

Mercier looked at him resentfully. "They say, monsieur, that, in order to win back the favor of the court you've given up writing obscenities."

"Of course, my boy, of course! But you'll see how it goes. You give up something at forty and go back to it at seventy."

A rich odor of country sausages, sizzling in their grease, wafted over the table. Landel himself carried in the platter, as solemnly as if it were the holy sacrament. The sausages were still smoking on a bed of charred vine shoots.

They were into their second helping when a gust of air came through the door and, with it, Abbé de l'Atteignant and two friends. The old Canon of Reims no longer had the strength to say his mass in that city, but he managed to recite his songs all over Paris. He always had one in his pocket and was happy to submit it to the assembly at Landel's.

Several hands reached out to take the sheet. In one corner of the room there was a harpsichord, which was now pushed over toward the table. Favart sat down before it, and Philidor took out his flute. After a moment of tuning there was complete silence. Crébillon woke up Panard and then the canon, in a quavering but true voice, sang this gay hymn to tobacco:

"I've good tobacco in my tobacco pouch,
I've good tobacco, but not for you, you slouch;
I've coarse tobacco, and fine tobacco, too . . ."

The good abbé's song won unanimous acceptance.

"It's simple and well turned," pronounced Crébillon, "and it should make its way. Monsieur l'Abbé, it calls for a libation!"

"I really shouldn't drink any more," Jeanne said to herself; "my head is reeling." But she carried her goblet to her lips. A hand suddenly closed on hers. It was Mercier's. He had slipped quietly into a place beside her. Jeanne freed herself and looked guiltily over at Philibert.

But Philibert was not pining. Squeezed between Alexis Piron and Justine Favart, he was laughing heartily with one and cooing charmingly in the direction of the other. Cabaret life seemed to suit him. From time to time, he leaned over and spoke to Lalande, who was sitting on the other side of Mme. Favart. Philibert's powdered wig was brushing against her half-exposed breast, and she was not drawing back. Quite the contrary. Tinkling laughter fell from her mouth straight into Philibert's waiting ear. No one could hear what she was whispering to him. But it certainly wasn't a botanical question. Jeanne was jealous and looked to see how M. Favart was taking it. He didn't seem to notice.

The flirtation between Justine Favart and Aubriot did not escape the sharp-eyed and malicious Abbé de Voisenon. He viewed Justine with the indulgence of a light-opera husband, having long been the third in a ménage à trois with the Favarts. At almost sixty years of age he was as restless as a bag of fleas. At the moment he was sitting at the elbow of Piron.

"Tell me, Piron," he whispered, pointing to Justine and Philibert, "will he or won't he?"

"He'd be well advised to seize the occasion. There's no quicker way for a provincial doctor to break into society."

"Well, a connection with a doctor would be good for me," said the abbé. "My asthma comes back every spring. Dr. Pomme has become expensive. Bouvart and Tronchin are already steep. I could use a little free medical care."

The banquet was well into the singing phase. Any diner who addressed another had to do so in verse or else pay the penalty of polishing off a whole goblet of wine. Jeanne was dizzy with wine, songs, and madrigals. Her head was beginning to pound like a drum. Suddenly Goldoni announced, "Your turn, mademoiselle."

"My turn?" she echoed, failing to understand.

The diners all turned to look at her.

"Don't you know some songs from your province?" Goldoni suggested.

"Yes, a country song, that's a good idea," said Philidor, who seated himself at the harpsichord and ran his fingers over the keys, producing a simple, sprightly overture.

"My dear Philidor, you enchant us!" exclaimed Simon Favart.

"In my native Normandy you can pick up ravishing little masterpieces," said Philidor, casually. "Normandy is surely the most tuneful of our provinces. I think it produces as many songs as it does apples."

"And in your province, mademoiselle," asked Goldoni insistently, taking Jeanne by the hand and leading her over to the harpsichord, "don't they sing of sowing and harvesting and treading the grapes?"

Jeanne panicked and flushed deeply. "Monsieur," she said, trying to wriggle out of this trial, "I'm from Burgundy, and there we sing mostly at Christmas, to celebrate the abundance of food. Every one of our Christmas carols is full of larded veal, forcemeat, young turkeys . . . and nobody here can possibly be hungry."

"Hear, hear!" interposed Lalande. "I'm a local patriot if ever there was one, and I shan't let you paint Burgundians as a people of heartless stomachs. Our Christmas carols are indigestible, I agree. But spring comes, as it does everywhere, and I insist that you sing us a May song."

Jeanne was unnerved and furious with Lalande for having betrayed her. She said to him coldly, "You know, monsieur, that our May songs are duets. If I play the girl, will you play the gallant?"

"I'd like nothing better!" said the astronomer, rising to his feet.

Then something very surprising happened. Aubriot stood up and grasped Lalande by the arm.

"You've already sung your fill," he said. "I haven't yet paid my due, so cede the May song to me."

Jeanne was pleased and surprised by Philibert's gallantry. She felt as though she had just downed a glass of powerful liquor. Her voice rose ecstatically as Philibert moved to stand behind her.

> "I had a rosebud all my own;
> Gallant, you stole it from me,
> Gallant, you stole it from me . . ."

His hands encompassed her waist and his sweet, strong voice stirred her curls and tickled her neck as he sang:

> "*Dry your tears,*
> *My beauty,*
> *You'll have it back some day . . ."*

She waited for the kiss that came in the second refrain . . . and he planted a loud one at the base of her neck.

I love him! Her song was borne aloft by her passion, rising sweetly as she sang the last verse.

CHAPTER 20

Patiently and in her best handwriting Jeanne set to work penning the virtues of *Pervinca vulgaris* or periwinkle, an astringent and remedy for fever. She was at work in the library at the monastery. Jeanne smiled when she came to *Melissa officinalis*. Lemon balm was something for which Philibert had a special weakness. He would crush the fresh leaves and make a poultice, which eased the pain of insect bites. The flowers, soaked in brandy and sugar, formed the base of a medicinal liquor which aided digestion and tasted so agreeable that many households in the region of Bresse used it only for its flavor.

She lay down her pen and began daydreaming about Charmont. She was running over sunny slopes ahead of Monsieur Philibert, discovering the clumps of blue flowers before he did. She remembered that he had put a fistful of crumpled leaves into her hands and said, "Smell them! Smell them hard!" Later he had let her taste the liquor. She wiped her moist eyes, overpowered by nostalgia.

Father Joachim's frail, childlike voice startled her back to the present. "Your work has slowed down. I think you need to take a few minutes off for a chat. Come with me to the kitchen. I just caught a glimpse of the baker's boy. We'll steal some fresh canary bread from Brother Amédée."

They sat down in front of two glasses of barley syrup.

"Did you ever taste such good canary bread?" Father Joachim asked.

"No. The crust is crisp and the inside contains a cloud of white cream that melts in your mouth. Where does it come from?"

"From the Rue de la Verrerie. Nowhere else do they taste as wonderful. When Favart sold his bakery he sold the recipe with it."

"Is this Favart related to the one who sings light opera?"

"He's the singer himself. He started out as a baker. His father perfected canary bread, and the son made it fashionable."

"Only yesterday Monsieur de Lalande introduced me to Monsieur Favart," said Jeanne, taking care not to mention the name of Landel's, fearing the father's censure.

"That's not surprising. Our astronomer enjoys the company of theater people."

"I met Madame Favart, as well, and Monsieur Philidor. And . . ."

In an excited voice she named all her new celebrity acquaintances.

"I gather that you had an exceedingly happy Sunday," the monk said with a smile.

She looked at him in a suddenly serious manner. "I'm perpetually in need of change, of something new. I'd like to have something new happen to me every day! Why do you think I'm this way, Father, always wanting more?"

"Because you're eighteen years old."

"Eighteen, yes. Isn't that too old to always dream about tomorrow?"

"Daughter, I'm seventy-eight, and I still haven't the courage to look at things as they are."

"But, Father, I'm happy. I ought to be satisfied with what I have."

The monk shook his head. "Happiness that never cloys is called beatitude. And that doesn't exist here on earth."

"Oh, yes, it does!"

The words came out in a rush, unintentionally, and it was too late to take them back. Jeanne blushed at the images of beatitude which were in her mind. But Father Joachim was too intelligent not to have guessed at the real relationship between herself and Philibert. Still she was not prepared for the frankness of his next remark.

"What you take for beatitude, my child, is only passion. Your feeling of boredom with your copy work may be due to the fact that you have less passion for botany than for the botanist."

Passion. Father Joachim's remark distracted Jeanne for the rest of the day. As her pen traveled across fields of facts, through the aromatic odor of juniper, the myriad secrets of huckleberries, the digestive, diuretic, expectorant, and emmenagoguic virtues of wild thyme, all she could concentrate on was passion. She stopped short, pen in air, seized by panic. She had never had this sensation of yearning. Philibert, so long the forbidden fruit, had let himself be plucked. She suddenly realized that this marvelous fruit no longer fully satisfied her hunger. *I must be mad or very tired.* Anxiously, she wondered why she wasn't happy, but she wasn't, she really wasn't. There was an emptiness in her soul.

The truth is that I was born an incurable dreamer. I need dreams the way I need food and drink. She needed to find herself a new dream. Something to lend a touch of excitement and uncertainty to her present. Jeanne craved the dazzling color of a new conquest.

The idea came to her while she was listing the merits of sage tea, recommended for all sorts of ailments, including intermittent or chronic psychic fatigue. Psychic fatigue, was that her trouble? The more she thought about it, the more she was convinced that she suffered from the "intermittent" form.

What if I were to open a herb-tea shop? She saw herself behind the waxed wooden counter of a little shop on the Rue Saint-Denis, teaching the use of her herbs to an elegant and attentive clientele.

Jeanne's hands began to flutter in the air, and her thoughts were so agreeable that she smiled to herself.

From the desk opposite her Father Joachim caught the smile. "Are you passing through the gates of paradise, mademoiselle?"

"I'm thinking of something I must ask the Father Apothecary," she said, brusquely rising to her feet and leaving both her work and the astonished Father Joachim behind her.

Quite an undertaking, to open a shop of one's own. As she envisioned transforming her dream into reality she became increasingly aware of the obstacles in her way. She thought of moving it from the Rue Saint-Denis to the Rue Saint-Honoré, then decided against it. If possible, she could set it up near La Rose Picarde, the largest and most flourishing draper's establishment, owned by old Mathieu Delafaye. Her thoughts raced and then she had a rude awakening. The guild of apothecaries and dry-grocers might well conspire to keep her out of such a choice location.

Bah! I'll go to the area around the Temple. And there I'll do much better. Everyone knew that neither guildsmen nor royal tax-enforcement officers could go beyond the boundaries of the Temple. Parisians flocked there because they believed they could buy contraband goods at rock-bottom prices. This place of asylum, where creditors and process servers were not admitted, had only one fault. The area was too small. A sliver was rented at a premium.

Within a fortnight Jeanne had confided in Mercier her project of opening a shop in the area of the Temple.

Life is lunatic. It drags along for months, moderato, then suddenly accelerates into allegro and sets you to dancing. Up to the happy Sunday at Landel's, Jeanne's Paris days were all cut from the same pattern, until one day, on the Pont Neuf, the wild man Mercier fell, like a stone into a quiet pond, making waves.

Mercier was intelligent enough to court Jeanne only from a distance, waiting for a propitious occasion, when she would be bored—if only at intervals—by her middle-aged lover. *I'll be a friend to Jeannot and make her laugh. And then we'll see.* Every other day he called for her at the King's Garden and they walked together, laughing, to the Palais-Royal. Mercier cultivated his extravagance and treated every subject in a vein of absurdity, but with a strain of common sense. Because he went everywhere on foot, he knew his Paris inside out. He was enthusiastic about her plan.

"Your idea is pure gold! Three or four years ago a bankrupt grocer recovered his fortune at the Temple, with a purgative tea. He sold as many as twelve hundred pints a day. Parisians are tired of doctors and apothecaries. Give them a healer's recipe and they'll flock to your door. I promise to promote a song about you at Landel's. Four lines of verse are the most effective. And then Dr. Aubriot can send patients to you with a prescription."

"He isn't practicing just now," Jeanne told him. "Although perhaps he'll have to if he doesn't get a fixed post at the garden. But I'm upset to hear that Parisians are forsaking their doctors."

"They make fun of them. But doctors still make money. A good many keep a carriage."

"But how can a doctor become famous in such a big city?"

"By having a specialty and getting himself talked about, taking care of a definite ailment, or prescribing an expensive cure, or sporting a conspicuous peculiarity. Take Tronchin, for instance. He enters the sickroom, calling out, 'Air! Air! Fresh air! Monsieur's (or Madame's) lungs are choked up for want of air!' He sets the servants to opening windows, taking down curtains, rolling up rugs, and throwing juniper on the fires. In short, he makes himself noticeable. Arnaud has his cardiac patients jog in order to strengthen their hearts. The treatment is new, and the cardiac patients that don't die swear by it. Bouvart is sought after for the malice of his witticisms and Pomme for his prescriptions of Vichy water. Dr. Aubriot could make a specialty of prescribing a herb tea dispensed by you alone. By the way, when he's called to a patient, how many stairs does he climb?"

"What?" Jeanne queried with surprise. "Why, he climbs to the floor where the patient lives."

"Really? That's true dedication. It's obvious that he's just arrived from the provinces. Here no reputable doctor climbs more than one flight of stairs. Monsieur Aubriot could specialize in third floors. Second-floor patients are pretty much spoken for already and on the fourth floor they're too poor."

Jeanne laughed and laughed. When she regained her composure she said, "Let's talk about my project. Do you think there might be a place near the Temple where the rent isn't too high?"

"Before talking money you have to find the place. It so happens that a fellow from Venice has just been evicted. His main building has been rented. But he also had a small annex down the street, which would serve your purpose admirably. It's in good shape and attractively decorated, because he used it for private sessions with the prettiest of his female workers."

"He came from Venice, you say?"

"Exactly! It was plain for all to see. He went about in carnival colors, under a black cape, with trinkets pinned all over him and a plumed hat, like that of Louis XIV."

"And his name?" asked Jeanne, putting two and two together.

"Casanova de Seingalt, Chevalier Casanova de Seingalt, he claimed."

Jeanne smiled broadly. "Mercier, that's just the place for me. It will bring me good luck. To rediscover the Chevalier Casanova at the Temple is such an amazing coincidence that it must be a favorable sign. You *must* help me, Mercier."

"Well, it seems quite possible. The new tenant of the larger building wants to sublet the annex. She's a shopkeeper with credit at court, and the favor of Prince de Conti, Prior of the Temple. And she's indebted to me because I wrote some verses to glorify her merchandise and her personal charm. She plans to deal in fine clothes smuggled into the country from England and the East. The location is good. Passing Knights of Malta always stay at the Temple. And every Maltese that goes to sea deals in contraband. Amelie Sorel is close to a certain Chevalier Vincent. If you want a hat made in London or a Turkish dressing gown, Sorel's is the place to find it."

"Mercier," said Jeanne insistently, "I want that place above any other. I want it so much that I simply have to have it!"

The name of Vincent had further excited her. She walked as if there were wings on her heels. Although Mercier would have preferred to dawdle, he was powerless to hold her back. When they came to the middle of the Pont Neuf she leaned against the wall and gave him a partial explanation of her excitement.

"There are signs, portents, in what you said. And I believe in signs. There are other reasons, as well. I wonder if I couldn't profit by dealing in contraband? Exotic teas, for instance. Don't you think they'd find a market?"

"A brilliant idea!" Mercier exclaimed. "Pure gold, Jeannot! If you package the aphrodisiac brew that the grand pasha takes in order to honor his harem, there'll be a crowd at your door. Prince de Conti will be the first in line to buy your aphrodisiac by the pound. In the bordellos, it's well known that nothing much comes out of Prince de Conti but hot air."

"Mercier," Jeanne protested, "you've a spiteful tongue!"

"A journalist's tongue, that's all. It's better to pick a man's words than his pockets. One day, I said exactly that to the Chevalier Vincent. And he had to admit that I was right. He came to box my ears and went away pacified. We became friends. I can recommend you to his good offices."

Jeanne managed not to blush and asked in a detached manner, "What did you do to arouse his anger?"

"Oh, all my troubles come from my pen. I have to supply my gazette with so many lines every day. One evening when I had no better subject, I wrote something about the love affair between the chevalier and the dancer Robbe."

"And Chevalier Vincent rose up to defend the honor of a dancer?" asked Jeanne angrily.

"That wasn't the point. Robbe was the mistress of Count Lauraguais. He didn't know that she had cuckolded him until he read the news."

"And then?"

"Well, Vincent and Lauraguais met on the dueling ground."

"On account of a dancer? They dueled over a dancer?"

"No, they dueled because Lauraguais called Vincent a pirate. No corsair can accept that!"

"And so, what happened?" said Jeanne impatiently. "The way you break off, it's too exasperating."

"What happened? Nothing much. To avenge the insult, Vincent drew a drop of blood from Lauraguais' hand. Lauraguais, for his part, didn't demand satisfaction for the infidelity of the dancer. They embraced and went away, hand in hand, to eat oysters and to make up a schedule for Mademoiselle Robbe."

"Shocking!" Jeanne exclaimed, her eyes sparkling.

"What, does that disturb you?"

"It doesn't matter to me," she said angrily. "Why should I care how two rakes spend their time? But a woman can't help being angry when she hears another example of men's casual behavior. Here are two of them who join together to share their mistress without so much as inviting her to share their oysters and taste the champagne they drink to her health. That's going too far. Sometimes I think we women are silly to cry over such beasts. We should love them the way they love us, just for laughs."

Jeanne walked through the cloister of the Petits-Pères collecting her thoughts before going home to cook her modest dinner. Why should she care about Vincent going to bed with a dancer? Or a dozen dancers, or the whole corps de ballet? A sailor on shore leave is known to have vulgar tastes. Poor Pauline!

Suddenly she felt sorry for Mme. de Vaux-Jailloux, whose lover deceived her with a little opera mouse. What use was it to decorate and redecorate his pied-à-terre in Dombes? What use to copy Louis XIV's bath for his pleasure, to keep his China-silk dressing gowns, his brushes, combs, and curlers, his thirty-six flasks and bottles of toiletries in perfect order? And then to be forgotten between the legs of a paid dancing girl? Jeanne came close to crying over the misfortunes of Pauline.

* * * *

Mlle. Sorel rented Jeanne the small space for 280 francs a year, of which half was payable in advance. These were usurer's terms, but within the vicinity of the Temple there was not a single honest landlord.

And the site was ideal. Whatever his destination, a visitor to the area had to pass her shop.

"And you're on the way to Nadine's, too," said Mercier. "She is a great attraction for foreigners."

"Does she sell jewels?" Jeanne asked him.

She knew that Temple jewelry, fake, but well made and often very expensive, attracted souvenir buyers. But Mercier laughed loudly.

"Yes, Nadine lodges half a dozen girls who sell their 'jewels.' If you carry scent, you'll have them for customers."

"And if I keep English greatcoats I'll have *their* most prudent customers for mine," Jeanne countered.

"My word! You're taking on a free-and-easy speech for a shopkeeper who serves duchesses!"

"You're my mentor, Mercier, and your speech is always at the peak of fashion."

Jeanne felt light as a spring swallow and in a mood for banter. If the work on her shop went ahead as rapidly as it had begun, it should open by the first of July. Every day, when she left the garden, she went to inspect the carpenter's progress, and she had already commissioned a Temple craftsman to make her sign. The emblem was a large white teapot decorated with a spray of thorny butcher's broom with its red berries. Above this the name, La Tisanière, The Herb-Tea Shop, in round gold letters, encased in a bottle-green frame.

As Mercier had told her, the space was in good condition. For his amorous purposes Casanova had furnished it like a boudoir and sealed off the windows facing the street. These Jeanne immediately reopened. For the paneling and shelves the carpenter had proposed brown cherrywood with purple reflections, which she would wax rather than paint. For the chimney piece, Mlle. Basseporte recommended an apprentice of the fashionable decorator Clermont. And for eight francs and fifteen sous, this sixteen-year-old artisan painted a cluster of field flowers strewn on a table beside a broad-brimmed, beribboned gardener's hat. It was fresh and cheerful. Even Philibert said that the painted flowers were reproduced accurately.

For Philibert, at last, was in on the secret. Jeanne had been so afraid of upsetting him that she had told all her friends first. Mlle. Basseporte and Father Joachim approved. The ever-generous Lalande offered to lend her money. Thouin voiced a word of caution. Jeanne seemed to him very young to go into business. But soon he promised to help purchase the classical medicinal plants which were grown in many monastery and convent gardens. Finally there came responses to the letters which Jeanne had written to Mme. de Bouhey and to Marie, both of them enthusiastic. Marie offered what she could—herbs from her garden, black currants and borage, a herb abundant all summer long at Autun, in the stony surroundings of the Porte Saint-André. As for Mme. de Bouhey, she wrote as follows:

> Succeed, that is the gist of what I have to say! If you make a fortune with your shop I shall be happy. It was with a heavy heart that I saw you go off with Aubriot. But if, thanks to your stubbornness, you achieve independence, I shall find consolation. I'll no longer pray that you may stop loving the man before it's too late. I like the idea of your dealing in medicinal plants so much that I want to help you make a start. For money or advice, go to my brother Mathieu, at La Rose Picarde. And tell me what plants you need, so that I can pass the word along to my gardener. What's more, for eight sous a day, I can engage a girl to pick wild herbs. . . . You seem hesitant about letting Aubriot in on your plan. Do you really think he'll mind your making enough money to pay for your gowns and your hairdresser? Who gave you such a mistaken idea? Most men don't insist that a mistress be entirely dependent upon them. On the contrary, they're glad to have a mistress who costs them nothing.

Actually, at first Aubriot was surprised and piqued to learn that Jeanne had conceived an idea all her own and pursued it without consulting him. But he was quickly calmed and implied, without explicitly saying so, that her idea was not a bad one. He went to see the shop and later sat down at his desk to write out recipes for different teas and a list of purchases to be made before the opening.

Jeanne overflowed with happiness. She got up at dawn, worked like a slave, and never went to bed before midnight. And, in spite of her hard work, she had never felt as well.

"I only wish I knew my first customer!" she said over and over, making it a game to guess who he or she might be.

"In your place, Jeannette," Mercier advised her, "I'd try for Madame Favart. Her career as an actress is over, but don't forget that she's the 'niece' of the Abbé de Voisenon and the 'widow' of Marshal de Saxe. These two connections have brought her a host of worldly friends. If she says a word at the Théâtre des Italiens, the whole company will beat a path to your door, followed by lovers and mistresses, most of whom are from good society."

"But I haven't seen Madame Favart since the Sunday at Landel's."

"Oh, you'll see her one of these days," prophesied Mercier. "She's bound to discover some ailment requiring treatment by Dr. Aubriot."

"What do you mean by that?" asked Jeanne, frowning.

"I mean that she asked me about him only yesterday. And I told her he could be seen, on Tuesday evenings, at the Café de la Régence."

* * * *

Everybody who was anybody wanted to be seen at La Régence. And by dropping in there, one could be sure of eying "the two hundred" who made up the intellectual society of the day. This café, on the Place du Palais-Royal, had become popular since Parisians had acquired a passion for chess. Chess players of various degree went there frequently. Men of letters, journalists, retired officers, old bachelors, and foreign visitors were always to be seen. Toward the end of the afternoon, a few ladies came to gossip and eat Bavarian creams. And their presence added to the charm of the place.

Philidor, the composer and champion chess player, made Tuesdays especially lively. He arrived at exactly six o'clock, the hour when the games were being organized.

Jeanne watched the players take their seats while waiters put two candlesticks and two cups of coffee beside the chessboards. She withdrew to a corner where Lucien, her very own waiter, smilingly brought her a Bavarian cream flavored with island rum and a copy of the daily *Gazette*.

She was seldom able to read for ten minutes. For, invariably, two or three people would come to engage her in low-voiced conversation. At La Régence one was accepted as a habitué from the start, or never at all. Jeanne became one immediately. Her beauty, charm, and intelligence guaranteed her popularity. She had her own circle of devotees, including the chatterbox Mercier and the Marquis Condorcet. A somber, silent young man, Condorcet's distracted appearance proved that his thoughts were still on the latest geometry problem. This Tuesday he was accompanied by M. Lavoisier, a botanist.

The marquis explained, "He has a mass of plants which he picked on Mont Valerien during an expedition. I told him that you would help him to classify them. He won't be a burden, I can promise."

The name of Lavoisier gave Jeanne a start. Wasn't that the chemist with whom Denis Gaillon had been in correspondence before he ran off with Emilie? The young scientist was so open and cordial that, as soon as they had exchanged the conventional greetings, she said, "A childhood friend of mine, in the provinces, Denis Gaillon, spoke often of his admiration for you."

"Do you mean that you come from Châtillon-en-Dombes?" he asked with interest.

"From very close by."

"I was surprised to read, in a letter from Malta, that Gaillon is there. I was expecting him to come study with Monsieur Rouelle, at the King's Garden."

Jeanne was overjoyed. Her instinct had not betrayed her. Emilie and Denis were safe, in Malta. Only Vincent could have taken them there. A question from Lavoisier interrupted her train of thought.

"Why did Denis leave France?" he asked her.

"An affair of the heart . . ." she said after a moment of silence.

"Oh! Too bad. I think that here in Paris he'd have advanced his career."

"Perhaps love means more to him than chemistry," Jeanne ventured.

"Perhaps, mademoiselle, perhaps," said Lavoisier in a manner that belied his words.

Jeanne laughed nervously. "Your tone of voice tells me that you wouldn't leave your vials and vessels to sail across the seas with a woman you love."

"I don't believe I would, no, mademoiselle. And why would a woman I love want to part me from my vials and vessels? A chemist can be quite amusing, I promise you. Come to the amphitheater of the garden some day when I'm working with Rouelle, and I'll show you some of my tricks."

"I know that chemists and physicists are great conjurers. But to learn secrets, I choose sailors and . . . astronomers."

She shot a conspiratorial look at Lalande.

"You're backing the wrong horse, mademoiselle. Just listen to me, and I'll let you in on fantastic secrets. For instance, I can tell you how you breathe."

"That's no secret! I know very well how I breathe."

"Then teach me. To tell the truth, I don't know the secret of breathing."

"A great pity!" broke in the well-modulated voice of Aubriot. Lavoisier had not seen Aubriot approach them. Now Aubriot said to the chemist, "When you know more about breathing, I'll be better able to treat lung diseases. And I have urgent need of this ability."

These last words were so portentous that Jeanne looked at him anxiously. She knew he had spit blood on two or three occasions when they first arrived in Paris. She thought it was the change of climate. Had he started suffering from attacks again without her knowing it? He continued. "Future doctors will have to be chemists *and* physicists. That is, unless they want to go on being utterly ineffectual."

The two men had met at a course given by Rouelle. They started to talk about chemistry and Jeanne left them to join her other friends.

By Parisian law, cafés had to close at ten o'clock. But in the case of one as well known as La Régence, the watchmen pretended not to notice that the lights were still on. The police chief's informers lingered among the other patrons, cocking their ears to catch some seditious remark directed at their master or some piece of gossip to be reported to the king. Marmontel and d'Alembert led them on by holding a revolutionary conversation in code language.

"The 'shanty,' what do they mean by that?" Jeanne asked Lalande innocently.

"Why, the government, of course!"

"And 'Leroux' stands for Choiseul?"

"Yes, because of his red hair."

"And 'the viscountess'?"

"Prince de Conti," said Lalande, with a gleam in his eyes. And, in answer to the questioning look in hers, "The prince has a countess for his mistress."

He laughed unrestrainedly and just managed to catch his wig before it slid off his head.

A chorus of angry "Sshhs!" rose up around the two jokers. Lalande and Jeanne tiptoed away and ended up standing with Mercier behind an Englishman who was making sketches. Suddenly Jeanne heard the rustle of silk.

Mme. Favart was making a theatrical entrance. With her chest thrust forward, her head held high, and an ultrared smile painted on her lips, she advanced toward Jeanne with outstretched hands as if they were the closest of friends.

Jeanne wondered how Justine Favart had ever managed to become the darling of Paris. Her face outrageously colored in red and white, her hair plastered flat against her head like a mud pie, her hollow cheeks, pointed chin, and the gaudy red-and-yellow stripes of her skirt made it difficult to believe she had once been a celebrated singer. Jeanne was embarrassed as the lady pressed her, literally trapping her against her bosom.

"My dear girl, I came especially to see you," said Justine, accompanying the words with an exaggerated number of kisses.

"To see *me?*" asked Jeanne incredulously.

"Everyone who knows me will tell you that I live on enthusiasm. I make friends or enemies on first sight, and I took a liking to you the minute I saw you at Landel's. You're as pleasant to hear as you are to see. That's why I'd like to have you sing a romance at the little gathering I'm holding in Belleville for Saint Claude's Day."

"Saint Claude's?" Jeanne echoed.

"Claude is the first name of my good uncle, Abbé de Voisenon. Didn't you know that? The Duchess de Choiseul is about to take him off with her to the spa of Barèges. She's afraid of being bored so she's surrounded by her usual group of entertainers. She's leaving in mid-June. And before the abbé goes away, I want to give him a surprise party. My garden will be filled with cherry trees and roses. I'll station musicians under the arbor. And we'll sing, dance, and laugh to our hearts' content. Just let me know what you might sing."

The woman's mad. "But, madame, I shouldn't dare sing for your guests. I'm flattered, of course, that you should think of me, but . . ."

Before she could protest further, Mme. Favart interrupted her. "June will be a good month for collecting herbs in the outskirts of the city, I know. Dr. Aubriot doesn't want to disappoint his students. And he needs your assistance. He told me as much when I sent him two invitations, one through Philidor and the other through Crébillon. But I'm very stubborn. So I've come to deliver my third invitation in person. I'm addressing myself to you, because we women must league together when men try to prevent us from having fun. So, you'll come, won't you, and bring your scholar with you?"

As Mme. Favart rattled on Jeanne grew increasingly angry. Philibert hadn't told her about the invitation from Mme. Favart. Of course, when she was a child, he had led his own life. But the little girl had grown up. And it was time he took notice.

"You're right, madame," Jeanne answered with a fiery look, "women must help one another to enjoy life. I'm happy to accept your invitation. And I'll do my best to bring Monsieur Aubriot along, although it's not easy to make him change his mind. My unimportant person has little value except in the shadow of his. But I hope you won't mind if I come alone to your gathering."

Mme. Favart assured Jeanne that she'd be welcome, alone or accompanied, in Paris or in Belleville. As she reflected on the girl's heated words, she guessed at a certain tension between the lovers. She must maintain contact with Jeanne in order to be informed.

"Come to see me, on the Rue Mauconseil, one of these mornings, and we'll rehearse your song. You know the street, don't you? Near the Théâtre des Italiens . . . anyone can point out my house. I go to bed late and get up late, so you can be sure to find me reading in bed up until noon. These days I stay in bed even later." And, raising her voice in the hope that it might reach Dr. Aubriot, she added, "Doctor's orders!"

"Are you unwell, madame?" Jeanne asked politely.

Justine had been waiting for just this question in order to let fly in a loud voice a catalogue of her complaints—dizzy spells, suffocation, throat spasms. And to conclude, still more loudly, she announced her need to find a doctor who would take her symptoms seriously.

Jeanne was amused by the futility of her effort to catch Philibert's attention. He was talking to Rouelle about the new substance, extracted from urine, which the gentlemen of the garden handed around as if it were ambrosia. In order to distract him from such a passionate subject, Mme. Favart would've had to give a loud cry and swoon at his feet. Meanwhile Jeanne asked maliciously, "Have you thought, madame, of leaving off your corset?"

"Impossible!" Justine protested. "Disastrous to the figure to be left unsupported! Of course, that's Dr. Tronchin's prescription. Don't tell me that Dr. Aubriot believes in the same cure!"

"Oh, he does, he does. But there are different ways to persuade a woman to give up her corset. And Dr. Aubriot knows how. You can't imagine how many women have stripped themselves of their armor in order to give him satisfaction!"

Justine read the mockery in Jeanne's eyes and answered as best she could. "It's true that the whalebones are reputed to raise lumps on the breasts, but . . ."

"If you're worried about lumps, you can show your breasts to Dr. Aubriot," Jeanne went on, perversely. "He makes very accurate diagnoses, if he can touch the sore spots with his hands."

Justine quivered with anticipation and asked impulsively, "Is it true, then, that he has the ways of a veterinary?"

"To some extent it's true. But I've noticed that certain women with a strong animal cast to their nature are quite at ease under his ministrations."

The two women exchanged dagger glances. Then Justine murmured a sweet goodbye and took her leave. As soon as Jeanne was alone Lalande came up to her.

"Weren't you afraid she'd bite?" he asked.

"Lalande, tell me, does Madame Favart attract you?"

The astronomer's narrow eyes gleamed with malice. "Let's put it this way. I'd never play you false with her."

"I adore you! You always say exactly what I want to hear."

Lalande's sly black eyes became slits. "Dear girl, why does it surprise you when a genius has fits of inspiration?"

CHAPTER 21

When Jeanne told Philibert of her decision to go to Mme. Favart's surprise party for the abbé, he responded by putting on the air of a confessor outraged by a gross sin. "Very well, mademoiselle. Indulge in this folly, if vulgar country parties amuse you. But don't be surprised when I treat you like a child."

What did he think? She was not going to brood in silence over his reproaches. She was not going to give up the party or ask him to take her, as usual, to Boulogne for more serious and "intelligent" purposes. She was not going to beg his forgiveness. No, no! She was much too eager for a day of fun.

The next day Jeanne came home early from the garden. She took off her boy's clothing, opened her chest, and considered the problem of what to wear. She had promised Philibert that she would never wear a corset or use cosmetics. But she often cheated. Going bareskinned into a world of women who were always made up, even when they were buried, was too much to ask. As she patted on the "Blond Shepherdess-Pink" powder, she thought—with perverse pleasure—of Philibert's disapproval.

Jeanne had arranged for Mercier to accompany her. She was thrilled when he told her that the Marquise de Mauconseil would be there. The marquise was a lady great enough to have been received by the king. The king! Jeanne was overwhelmed by her good fortune.

But what to wear? The small apartment was strewn with brightly colored garments over the bed and chairs. There were red and green highlights even atop the pile of books which Philibert kept on the marble washbasin. Two pairs of truly regal dancing slippers trampled on literature with their high heels covered in red silk. It was a dazzling display. It wasn't a secretary's salary that afforded Jeanne this finery. The clothes were hers due to the generosity of Mme. de Bouhey and the ability of Mlle. Marthe, the dressmaker of Bourg-en-Bresse. At long last, one of these treasures, shut up for so many months, would see the light of day. Jeanne's patience was truly admirable.

Since her arrival in Paris, she'd had no occasion to wear anything fashionable. Her way of life required that she appear as a coquettish, but fundamentally virtuous, middle-class woman. Aubriot was often asked out alone, and the unexpected invitation from Mme. Favart gave her the inebriating chance to dress up. She had an idea that eventually she would decide upon the guise of a shepherdess, wearing the summer dress of Alsatian cloth painted with bouquets of flowers. But she didn't want to hasten her choice. She was in front of the mirror, trying on a delightful flat straw hat, when Philibert walked in.

"Dear God!" he exclaimed, opening the door. "Do I live, without being aware, in a fashion shop?"

Jeanne bit her lip, chagrined to be taken by surprise.

"So," said Philibert ironically, "is this the shepherdess's hat that's so eager to go to Madame Favart's?"

"Dr. Vacher takes out his dog every day, doesn't he? Is it any more foolish to take out a hat on Sunday?"

Philibert smiled. "Don't take it amiss," he said. "The hat is most becoming. And so I'm sure is the dress. Tell me, is your gentleman escort, Mercier, going as a shepherd?"

"He'll wear what he pleases," she said, gathering up the clothes. "It's no matter to me." She didn't want to give him the satisfaction of seeing her disappointment. But it came out in spite of her. "In any case, I'll cut less of a figure on his arm than on yours."

With two long steps Philibert was in front of her. He caught her by the chin and looked into her eyes.

"Really? I didn't know that you considered me an adjunct to your finery. But from a coquette, that may be a compliment."

"Oh, come with me . . . come along!" she pleaded cajolingly.

"Very well, then, I'll come. I'll come for the sake of your dress."

"Really and truly?" she asked, opening her eyes wide, incredulously. "You'll come? I love you, I love you, I love you!"

"'Ring the bell, ring the bell; if I lie I'll go to hell.' "

She spun, like a top, around the room. Her arms filled with clothes, addressing the plants lined up in one corner, she sang out to the dwarf cactus, "I love him, I do!"

* * * *

The sky was softly aglow with the light of an invisible sun. This first Sunday of June might not be bright, but it promised to be warm, a good day for swimming in the Seine. The unaccustomed warmth had spurred the opening of the women's baths, situated on both sides of the Pont Marie. Every year jests and laughter greeted the appearance of the sign PUBLIC AND PRIVATE BATHS FOR LADIES. By eleven o'clock in the morning a throng made up of old men and young gallants crowded the bridge, ogling the women as they frolicked in the water below.

Food and drink vendors were having a heyday, as the population streamed through the streets like schools of fish. Cabs and carriages struggled to make their way, and the air was filled with cursing and shouting.

The cabby who was driving Philibert and Jeanne to Belleville seemed to seek out crowded streets in order to exercise his lungs. As they left the city behind them, the landscape became a medley of greens: rolling meadows, orchards in bloom, damp woodlands, and fields of wildflowers. Small villages dotted the countryside with their fragrant kitchen gardens. Modest cafés lined narrow streets. A light breeze swept the sky clear of clouds and set the weathervanes a-spinning.

The cab set them down at the bottom of the Butte Chaumont. Cab horses were notoriously short-winded and the steep road that led to the house was too much for them. Many guests of the Favarts were proceeding on foot to the house on the heights. Aubriot and Jeanne soon overtook Crébillon, old Piron, being held up by Mercier, young Caillot, an actor from the Théâtre des Italiens, Abbé Cosson, a master of arts at the University of Paris, Goldoni and his wife Nicoletta. The air was fragrant as the breeze blew hawthorn petals into the climbers' faces. Jeanne threw back her head and breathed in their subtle perfume.

The house, with its large garden, was situated above the cafés of La Courtille on the main street of La Villette. The view was both restful and gay.

Jeanne's contemplation was interrupted by the voice of the smiling Simon Favart, his pipe in hand. "Do you think you'll like Belleville, mademoiselle?"

"Well, I love your garden, I know that," she answered pertly. "It's a bit of heaven."

"Then you must come often and make it all the more heavenly."

Jeanne pointed a white gloved hand at a narrow, dusty road running between the arbors.

"Isn't that where I should look for the cabaret of the famous Ramponeau?"

"No. Le Tambour Royal is nearer to us. The cabarets you're pointing at are on the Chemin des Couronnes. But they do share the bad reputation of La Courtille and Les Porcherons, and the nobility love to go slumming in them."

As Favart escorted Jeanne toward the wooden gate which led to the front door, the carriage of the Duke and Marshal de Richelieu, drawn by six splendid light-bay horses, pom-pomed in the duke's colors, stopped in front of the house.

The ceremonious bows of welcome were just beginning to turn into noisy chatter as Mme. Favart hurriedly ushered everyone into the house.

"Sshh!" she said, with a finger to her lips. All thirty of her guests were herded into the small drawing room.

"Silence, I beg of you! Our good Uncle Claude suspects nothing. We must try to maintain this wonderful surprise. It's very nearly one o'clock, and he'll turn up any time now."

The guests were instantly cooperative and quiet as mice. Minutes later, they could hear the gravel crunch as the abbé walked unsuspectingly up the path. An outburst of happy cheers greeted Mme. Favart's little lover as soon as he appeared at the door.

Nothing was too good for the hero of Saint Claude's Day. Justine, with a bunch of roses in her arms, handed them one by one to the abbé, accompanying each with a couplet. His face shone with childish joy.

Jeanne had to pinch herself to believe it. *Ridiculous and in bad taste.* The scene played by the lovers, one of them a scandalous sixty-year-old priest and the other a faded singer, dressed up as a gardener, with a bonnet that looked like a handkerchief laid out on a bush to dry, really astonished her. The elegant company invited to witness this vulgar display seemed to enjoy it thoroughly.

How could a Goldoni, a Crébillon, a Philidor, a Vanloo, a Greuze listen, patient and smiling, to Mme. Favart's infantile song? Even Vanloo's wife, Christina Somis, whose ample voice and exquisite looks had enchanted all Europe, seemed to be won over. And the cynical Mercier looked delighted. *They must be acting.* Philibert, thank God, had sufficient taste to take no interest in the comedy. But alas, he seemed absorbed in the still beautiful Christina Somis.

Jeanne had also attracted an admirer. And the intensity of his gaze caused her to turn her head, involuntarily, confronting the piercing, greedy eyes of Marshal de Richelieu.

Ever since Mme. Favart had introduced them, the marshal had not taken his eyes off her. This tireless seducer, even at sixty-nine years of age, knew how to undress a beautiful woman from a distance. It did not surprise him that the lovely shepherdess was troubled by his stare. Jeanne turned away. But she couldn't help casting rapid, furtive looks in his direction. She was repulsed and attracted to him at the same time.

Yes, he was sure he would get her into his bed. Who could turn down Louis-François-Armand de Vignerod, Duke de Richelieu, great-great-nephew of the famous cardinal? He was governor of Guyenne and Gascony, marshal and peer of France, first gentleman of the king's bedchamber and the most amusing member of the academy. Seen from the outside, he might appear a bit decrepit, but how beautifully wrapped! Besides, money is always twenty years old. Yes, he would have this girl, no doubt about it. Voluptuously he inhaled a pinch of snuff as a foretaste of pleasures to come.

"Dinner, dinner! Pray sit down!" cried Mme. Favart. "I'm told that if the capons are left another minute on the spit they'll be charred."

Under beribboned arbors covered with pink and yellow roses, a long table had been set up, surrounded by smaller ones, at the edge of the garden. Golden juice dripped from the capons. Spicy stews were set out on silver chafing dishes. Large rounded pâtés, spinach pies, and prune tarts made patches of brown, green, and purple on the white tablecloth.

The aging hero of the festivities tickled to his right and pinched to his left.

Marshal de Richelieu sank his teeth into a capon leg, with his eyes still on Jeanne. She had been carried off by the painter Vanloo and seemed enchanted by their conversation.

With a hand barely wiped on the tablecloth, he reached out for the hostess as she passed by and, winking in the direction of the shepherdess, said ingratiatingly, "Dear Favart, is that pretty child a friend of yours?"

"I hope so, monseigneur."

"I hope so, too. She interests me. Has she a family?"

"That I don't know." And she added, with a trace of bitterness, "No family will block your way. She has come, just recently, from a distant province."

"Where does she live?"

"On the Rue du Mail, with Dr. Aubriot, sitting over there. He's a botanist said to enjoy a good name at the King's Garden."

"Her lover?"

"Not publicly. She passes for his pupil and secretary. She, too, is skilled in botany."

"Oh, a bluestocking!" the marshal exclaimed disgustedly. "With her looks that's a waste."

"Come, monseigneur, can't a woman have a mind?"

"Very well, very well," Richelieu mumbled. "Don't let's argue the point. Believe me, madame, only pederasts go for intelligent women. Of course, this one seems like an exception . . ."

He got up and pulled Justine into a corner. "Can you arrange for me to see Mademoiselle . . . What did you say was her name?"

"I've always heard her called Jeanne. Mercier calls her Jeannot."

"Jeannot, then. Can I count on you for an appointment? And soon, because I must go back to my government at Bordeaux in ten days. If you make the appointment, I'll see to it that Mademoiselle Frédéric, your rival, loses all her upcoming roles in the Théâtre des Italiens."

The first gentlemen of the king's bedchamber had jurisdiction over the acting profession.

"Monseigneur," said Justine, feverishly, "I ask nothing . . . only to serve you."

"No, no," said Richelieu. "Nothing is too dear. I'll give your Frédéric for Jeannot."

Mlle. Frédéric was a promising young actress who was reaping applause at the aging Mme. Favart's expense. Justine's dearest dream was to get the better of her.

She curtsied deeply to the duke and said, "Monseigneur, I shall try my best."

"Trying won't do."

"But, monseigneur, what if, in spite of my efforts, she'll have none of you?"

The duke made the gesture of polishing the agate knob of his cane against his silk sleeve.

"Dear Justine," he said, smiling, "doesn't every woman want a marshal's baton? You had yours with Marshal de Saxe. I don't see why Mademoiselle Jeannot should refuse the use of mine."

The rustic feasting went on for another hour. Finally the diners trooped back to the drawing room. The entertainment began. First a dance by members of the Théâtre des Italiens, and then it was Jeanne's turn to sing. She was blushing and afraid, but a glass of white wine restored her self-confidence. She sang deliciously. Her light contralto voice followed the melody. She sang without effort or striving for effects. At the end, there was prolonged applause. Christina Somis got up to embrace her, followed by Richelieu, who opened up a pair of arms swathed in ivory silk.

"A kiss for me, too, beautiful nightingale!"

Jeanne felt as if she were drowning in musk. But she endured it stoically. This was the embrace of a marshal and a peer of France.

"This child is a treasure," said Richelieu, sitting down beside Madame de Mauconseil. "Her skin is pure satin. . . . She melts in the mouth." And sighing, "She has a natural fragrance.

"Regrettable, I call it," he went on, "that there's no lovemaking after dinner. It's an item distinctly lacking from the menu. A plague on middle-class houses!"

The marquise laughed, leaning toward him. "Perhaps another time you can be better provided for."

Instantly Richelieu thought that she might be a more effective ally than Justine Favart. What's more, he knew that she was ruined financially and on the lookout for the least bit of money.

"I offer a five hundred franc reward," he said crudely.

"Make it a thousand," the marquise shot back. "She's worth it."

"Very well, then, a thousand francs, if you act quickly. My appetite is impatient. But after all, perhaps I have only to speak up. You say the girl's intelligent. In that case, she can't refuse."

"Don't make a head-on military attack," the marquise warned him. "You can see by her face the kind of a girl she is, fresh from the provinces and with provincial values."

Richelieu shrugged his shoulders. "I'll give you two or three days."

"Leave it to me, my friend," said the marquise, "and don't interfere. Have I ever failed you?"

"That you haven't," he admitted gallantly. "I recognize you as one of the subtlest go-betweens in Paris."

"That, from you, is no small compliment," she answered. "For you, my dear Richelieu, are one of the most active clients."

"Because I'm two clients in one," he said with an air of complicity. And, following his own train of thought, "This nightingale is fit for a king."

Madame de Mauconseil scrutinized him closely. "Are you really playing for two?" she queried.

"I've done it before, with far less promising material."

Silence fell between them, punctuated only by a harpsichord rendition of a two-step. Then Richelieu spoke in a more serious vein. "There are too many goings and comings in Louis' bed, on a vulgar level. His valet exercises too much influence, especially when I'm away in Bordeaux. Choiseul is trying hard to place a creature of his own choosing as successor to Madame de Pompadour. If I don't beat him to it, I'll have an enemy in the royal bedchamber. Frankly, I'd like to position a creature of my own there."

Richelieu's words raised the Marquise de Mauconseil's hopes to dizzying heights, recapturing the times when she was young and rich. She pictured herself filling the empty rooms of her villa at La Bagatelle with a gay and gallant company. She could definitely expect a reward from the king. Louis XV was aged, melancholy, and prone to vulgar adventures.

Actually this would not be the first time Mme. de Mauconseil had supplied the king with lovers. Her role as a go-between was not a new one. But dealing with Versailles required a façade of luxury and wealth. Unfortunately the marquise had spent more than she had made. For now, she had fallen on hard times.

If only she could renew her services to the king and see noblemen flock again to afternoon love games behind the screens and alcoves in her country house. Yes, the unsuspecting Jeanne would serve her purposes well. Her hopes soared to the sky.

But the marquise had formidable rivals and time was of the essence. Mme. de Pompadour had been dead for a year, yet her private rooms at Versailles were still empty. The king was distrustful. According to the latest gossip, he was bored with the treacherous offers of duchesses and countesses. He had gone back to the lower-class girls provided by Mme. Bertrand, proprietress of the Parc-aux-Cerfs, his private bordello. These women reassured him of his virility yet did not intrigue on behalf of their relatives for posts in the army, church, or administration.

The factions at court were biding their time. But the unexpected could always happen. Mme. de Mauconseil knew that Richelieu would not rest until he had found Louis a plaything, and one intelligent enough to help him contrive the downfall of Choiseul, his arch rival. For years Richelieu had wanted to run the shop. Now, he saw his chance to place an ally in the household of his cousin, the king, and collect his due.

* * * *

The Marquise de Mauconseil lost no time in pouncing like an ogress. The day after the surprise party for the abbé, Jeanne received a note from the marquise, inviting her to the Wednesday performance of *Les Trois Sultanes*, The Three Sultans, by Favart and Marmontel at the Théâtre des Italiens.

"Everyone that mattered would be present," she said. And Jeanne's refusal would throw her into despair.

Jeanne was somewhat, but not entirely, surprised to receive this letter. She wisely suspected that the figure of Richelieu was lurking in the background. This flattered and amused her. She felt quite capable of defending herself against the libertine marshal. And she wouldn't for all the world miss a chance to go, at last, to the theater.

If Philibert objected she was ready with an excuse: to meet as many people as possible in order to spread the news of her shop, which was to open in mid-July. Besides, Philibert could hardly complain since he was now in the habit of coming home late every night himself. Theater performances ended early and she was certain to return to the Rue du Mail before him, anyway.

Happily she penned an acceptance letter to Mme. de Mauconseil.

CHAPTER 22

intin, the fashionable hairdresser on the Rue Saint-Honoré, had combed Jeanne's hair into long English-style curls, gathered at the nape of her neck by a creamy-white ribbon bearing a single pale yellow rose.

Her brocaded gown was magnificent. Bunches of pink roses, tied with green knots, gleamed against a background of cream-colored silk. The sleeves were elbow length and layers of lace spilled down the sides. Her tightly fitting jacket opened in front over a low-cut bodice. A narrow neckband of entwined muslin rosebuds and a pair of pink satin slippers with gilt buckles completed the outfit.

The hoopskirt was so voluminous that Jeanne could rest her hands on both sides of it. It was the first time she had worn anything so elaborate. And she looked forward to the attention she would draw by the sheer amount of space she occupied.

She wondered if Mme. de Mauconseil would offer her a sherbet after the theater, perhaps at La Régence.

As Jeanne waited for the marquise's duenna, Chaulieu, to fetch her she thought lovingly, gratefully, of dear Mme. de Bouhey who had given her this sumptuous gown.

* * * *

"Dear Lord!" Jeanne exclaimed when she saw the number of men gathered in front of the theater. "Can't we get down from the coach a little farther on?"

The big black woman sent to accompany her shook her head.

"Hide your face behind your fan," she suggested.

"But I wasn't thinking of my face," Jeanne retorted.

It was impossible for a woman wearing a hoopskirt to get down decently from a carriage.

"Come along!" said the duenna. "It's the same for everyone. What do you think the gentlemen are doing? They're hoop-watching. Go to it. You're proud of your legs, aren't you?"

Chaulieu cleared a pathway through the crowd, brandishing a cane. Jeanne followed, with a rustle and swishing of silk. She hid her face with her fan, while a storm of exclamations broke out.

"Marquis, have you ever seen such ankles?"

"Never, Chevalier, but the bosom is their equal. And what a queenly walk!"

"Baron, have you any idea who she may be?"

"Come," said the duenna, "let's get inside."

It was not wise to linger outside. Valets jostled the crowd in order to make way for their owners. And roughnecks took advantage of the disorder to snatch purses, watches, or to feel a breast. Inside, the passageways leading to the seats were kept free by guards, and the gate in front of each box seat was locked.

"Open up here," the duenna ordered, taking a key from under her skirt and handing it to a guard in dress uniform.

"Lovely!" Jeanne exclaimed, looking at the sumptuous interior of the box. "Let's look down below."

She stepped forward to open the gilded wooden grille separating the box from the theater, but the duenna halted her.

"I'm not sure, mademoiselle, that Madame would want you to open it. When the lights go up you'll be able to see."

Jeanne did not dare insist, although she was sorry not to show off her fine gown from the front of the box.

The Théâtre des Italiens, with its predominance of white and gold, was itself a spectacle both lavish and gay. There were white columns and the ceiling was decorated with lyres, rosettes, and laurel crowns.

As Jeanne looked down, wide-eyed, on the gathering crowd, she discovered the princely privilege and pleasure of seeing without being seen.

The box was like a gilded cage. There were small-scale furnishings in modern style, of mahogany with bronze trimmings. Out of curiosity, she opened the drawer of a dressing table and found it filled with pots of makeup cream and pillboxes.

"If you like sweets, here's something better," said the duenna, handing Jeanne a box of Sèvres porcelain, containing sweetmeats.

"Thank you," said Jeanne. "I'll take one later. Marquise de Mauconseil's opera box is a jewel, a treasure."

The duenna made no reply. She had been instructed not to tell the young lady that this box belonged to Marshal de Richelieu and not the marquise. He called it his "musical love box." But Jeanne felt a nagging suspicion come over her again. She had heard that boxes of this type cost a fortune to rent. And she knew that the marquise was penniless.

A sudden clamor caught her attention. The pit gate had been lifted and a flood of people rushed in. The open boxes, their walls hung with yellow damask, were filled with powdered heads and gleaming silks. Fans fluttered and precious stones glittered. The sight was one of luxury and magic. Jeanne recognized Marmontel and Crébillon sitting beside a young woman in a pink dress.

"Won't you point out some of the celebrities, madame?" she asked the duenna.

As an expert at the game, the duenna named the cream of Paris and Versailles for the benefit of her dazzled companion. Madame de Mauconseil had been right when she told Jeanne that everyone of any importance would come to applaud Justine Favart in *Le Trois Sultanes*. Even Prince de Conti.

The Prior of the Temple stood in the center of his box, clothed in gleaming yellow satin and diamonds. Jeanne found him stunning. Since her herb shop was at the corner of the Rue Meslay, the prior was, in a way, her landlord. The lady sitting in front of him was Madame de Boufflers, Prince de Conti's reigning mistress.

Jeanne had recently learned from her landlady, Mlle. Sorel, that when the Chevalier Vincent came to Paris, he lodged at Mme. de Boufflers' house on the Rue Notre-Dame-de-Nazareth. It was quite natural that, like most Maltese, he should stay within the confines of the Temple. Conti was the protector of the Knights of Malta. But, as she examined Countess de Boufflers through her lorgnette, she realized that there was another reason why Vincent stayed on the Rue Notre-Dame-de-Nazareth. Vincent obviously had a weakness for mature women of means and amiability.

Like Pauline de Vaux-Jailloux, Marie-Charlotte de Boufflers must have been close to forty years old. But her face was still fresh and rounded under a wreath of lightly powdered blond curls, crowned with pink silk roses and strands of pearls. Her low-cut bodice revealed half of her milky-white breasts. *The Chevalier must like big-breasted women.* But, no matter how much she wanted to, she could not honestly say that Mme. de Boufflers was either ugly or vulgar. Her mien was not that of a courtesan but of a great lady. There was something gentle about her.

The duenna's voice interrupted her reflections. "It must be an important evening," she said. "Here comes the Duke de Choiseul."

The duke had just made his appearance. On his arm was a distinguished-looking little old lady. Following him was another woman not particularly beautiful, but wearing conspicuous jewels and holding her head high. Two other couples, with princely airs, took their seats behind Choiseul as he smiled, responding to the audience's greetings.

"I didn't know he was so small," murmured Jeanne.

Because he was always spoken of as a great man, Choiseul's modest size surprised her. He was richly turned out in a shimmering lavender-and-blue silk coat with blue embroidery. The minister had a youthful, robust air. Although Jeanne found him almost ugly, he made up for it by the cordiality of his demeanor.

"Well," said Jeanne, lowering her lorgnette, "our government has my approval."

Above the hum of conversation, crude jokes, and catcalls rose the words "Be-gin, be-gin, be-gin!" The armed guards all around stiffened, as if to make eventual troublemakers aware of their presence.

Almost immediately the three ritual beats sounded. A rough man's voice shouted, "Off with hats!" To which another retorted, "Off with your big nose! That's what blocks the view." The candles around the proscenium flared up. And the red, gold-embroidered curtain rose on the first act.

The petulant Roxalane, played by Mme. Favart, had just begun to tickle the appetite of the Pasha Suleiman II when the Marquise de Mauconseil entered the box.

"Chaulieu," she said to her servant, "light the candelabra so that I can see my guest."

The sprightly shepherdess the marquise remembered from the afternoon at Belleville was, to be sure, a pretty girl. But she was not prepared for the beauty that she now saw before her. The girl's grace and distinction were breathtaking. The marshal had been right. She was a morsel fit for a king. An old hand at the game, Mme. de Mauconseil now had no doubts that the girl had only to be placed in the king's path for the plan to work. Louis was very easily inflamed.

Jeanne submitted impatiently to her hostess's scrutiny.

When Jeanne returned to her seat behind the grille she said with demure malice, "If the Duke de Richelieu is much later he'll miss the whole first act." She had barely finished speaking when he arrived.

It was impossible to be unaware of the duke's arrival. With the scent of musk assailing her nostrils, Jeanne started to rise and curtsy, but Richelieu's hands pinned her to the chair.

"A truce to good manners, Mademoiselle Nightingale! Stay where you are!"

The old man's breath on her neck made Jeanne feel ill at ease. But she relaxed as he removed his hands. Richelieu was accustomed, at Versailles, to slipping his hand under a hoopskirt. Tonight, however, he was on his best behavior.

In the palace there were open doors and gentlemen had to take advantage of a passing moment for a tête-à-tête. But Richelieu had promised the marquise not to endanger their project by scaring the bird away. Of course he wouldn't have been afraid to give the girl an initial shock had he been sure she wouldn't protest. But the accommodating marquise was right, she wasn't a victim to be snared without due preparation.

And so he sat, motionless, behind her, his lips only inches away from her satiny shoulders, and his fingers restless but discreet. At the intermission he grew agitated and said to his accomplice, "Aren't you curious, Marquise, about what's going on in the other boxes with closed grilles?"

Excusing herself, the marquise quickly left the box. A moment later, Richelieu sent the duenna to buy some rose-flavored sherbet.

Then he furtively bolted the door. In the candlelight Jeanne's blond hair, tawny eyes, and silken gown were glowing.

"Nightingale, a virtuous girl has no right to be so beautiful," he said, genuinely dazzled. "But are you virtuous? May I offer you a glass of Cyprus wine and some sweetmeats?"

"Yes, monseigneur," she answered with a smile. "And that is yes to both questions, about my virtue and about the wine."

"I applaud one answer and deplore the other," he said good-humoredly.

He opened the secretary and took out two glasses and a crystal flask, engraved in gold. After serving her, he tried for a minute to follow her intelligent remarks about Favart's opera music. But his mind was so distracted that he made a stupid reply. She looked at him with astonishment, and he decided to be frank.

"You, Nightingale, are responsible for my stupidity. Don't you know that frustrated desire makes the most intelligent man into a fool? Pray, don't make me foolish or I'll have little capacity to please you. And to please you is what I want most. Be kind, my lovely, and give me the kiss that will revive my mind. You were so engrossed with the stage when I came in that you didn't wish me good evening."

"I'll do so when I leave, monseigneur."

"That's not enough, my lovely. I'm known to be a glutton for kisses. I want good-morning kisses, good-evening kisses, and more still."

Jeanne laughed heartily. "Monseigneur, I am always amazed by Parisian gentlemen. They wouldn't dream of stealing a handkerchief, but they shamelessly try to steal a kiss."

"What gentleman can help having a taste for rose petals?" Richelieu exclaimed, coming threateningly close.

A loud noise from the pit gave Jeanne an excuse to look through the grille to see what was happening.

"Just the usual thing," said Richelieu, after a quick glance. "Young fellows raising a rumpus."

The audience had gone out for the intermission. And below, in the empty pit, young fops were playing with swords.

"Good Lord!" Jeanne exclaimed. "This seems more like a den of rowdies than a fashionable theater."

Her worst fears were realized when Richelieu's hands clutched her breasts and his mouth fastened itself onto her bare back like a leech. She clenched her teeth and fought to free herself. Breaking away, she wheeled around and struck the duke's face with the end of her fan. The old man was indulgent toward women, but he didn't accept the rebuff with good grace. The rejection wounded him more deeply than the blow.

"Mademoiselle," he said haughtily, "you forget who I am and who you are."

She looked into his eyes without either fear or anger. "Monseigneur, you are not a sultan, and I am not a slave in your harem."

The reference to the evening's opera caught the duke's fancy.

"Very good," he said, "you're exonerated. But I must have a kiss."

Graciously she picked up the two glasses of wine. "I drink to your benevolence, monseigneur."

"And I to your beauty, Nightingale. But, mind, I'm not benevolent every day. Let me tell you a story. Once upon a time a marshal of France fell in love with a lovely girl. A girl foolish enough to turn down a marshal of France. And what do you think happened? They wasted quite a lot of time when they might have been happy. He chafing under his desire and she regretting her disdain . . . in a convent."

"Is that all, monseigneur? How does it end?"

"Naughty children locked in the closet always beg the pardon of the grownups whom they've offended."

"Some children are stubborn, monseigneur."

"I know that. I've been shut up three times in the Bastille. But it was tedious, I can tell you."

Jeanne wet her lips in the heavy wine. "Monseigneur, I beg you to send me to the convent of the Ursulines at Châtillon-en-Dombes. I have friends in the neighborhood, so it would be less tedious. And the nuns make delicious anise-flavored wafers. I'll send you some."

When Mme. de Mauconseil returned for the beginning of the second act, she opened her eyes wide in astonishment. Jeanne was sitting alone, in silken splendor, on the sofa. Richelieu was seated on a chair, with his hat on his head, one leg crossed over the other, and his right hand on the knob of his cane. Talking and laughing, he seemed the happiest man in the world.

"Ah! Here's Chaulieu with our sherbets," he said when he saw the duenna behind her mistress.

"My Nightingale, you can cool your palate. But no doubt you want to hear more of the opera. Go ahead, turn your back on me. I'm going to stretch my legs for a moment." He took the marquise's arm and led her into the passageway.

"The girl is a treasure, a pink pearl! She's driving me mad. Yes, mad, and making me enjoy it! I feel as if I were only twenty!"

"You mean that you've made the deal?" asked the marquise worriedly.

" 'Made the deal'! Madame, why must you speak in such crass terms?

That will be for tomorrow. Tonight let me indulge my heart. My heart has a new life. I tell you it's a miracle! You see, I'm in love."

"In love? You?"

"Yes, none other. It's never too late to enjoy something new. The girl is ravishing, I tell you! And so clever and witty. She has the ability to speak her mind with amazing boldness. She's full of surprises. I've never met anyone quite like her."

"My dear Duke, you come from the court, where nothing shocks or surprises you. You have become equally hardened to the familiar joys of the bordello. No wonder this fresh and innocent girl seems to offer something new! You are jaded, sir. But, tell me, does your falling in love affect our little plan?"

"Marquise, I want Jeanne more than ever. But I don't want to push her too hard. Keep track of her and soften her up. Meanwhile, take this . . ."

There was a greedy look in the marquise's eyes as she took the purse.

"Spend the money freely," Richelieu continued. "Every woman has her price. Find out what she wants. Perhaps she has a brother who needs a situation. I've noticed that sisters will do anything for their brothers."

"All this will take time," the marquise told him. "You're off to Bordeaux next week and won't be back for a year."

"True! I must have her before I go, or else I'll have to carry her off in my luggage."

"No! No abduction, I beg of you! It's 1765, Marshal, 1765! A duke doesn't carry off a shepherdess without arousing the big bad wolf. You'd have the philosophers against you, and the press and Parliament, not to mention the church . . ."

"Well, do the best you can," Richelieu said. "And, as soon as she consents, chalk up her expenses to me without waiting for my return. You could settle her in my little house at Les Porcherons, and . . ."

"Not there! The king would get wind of it. When you're serving him a delicacy, it's not a good idea to let him know that you tasted it before him."

"Oh, the king . . . he can wait."

"What? Are you so in love that you are discarding our plan?"

"Who knows? Louis isn't young, after all. Such a beautiful and guileless child might be embarrassing to him. There are times when he can't make it."

Mme. de Mauconseil listened with admiration to this man, nearly seventy years old, taking pity on the impotence of a fifty-five-year-old king.

"To lose the capacity . . ." Richelieu said sadly. "What a shame. It's as bad as cowardice in battle. The penis and the sword, these two make the man. All the rest is illusion."

CHAPTER 23

ichelieu was not a man who could ignore the object of his desires, no matter how patient he had decided to be. And he knew enough about women to know how to impress them.

Jeanne had been wild with joy when Chaulieu brought her an invitation to the Opéra ball.

The prospect seemed all the more romantic when the duenna added, "Dress simply, and not too voluminously. You'll find a domino and a mask in the carriage. There will be a little supper afterward, an intimate affair."

She understood, and her fear of the aggressive old marshal only fed her feeling of intoxication. It was exciting to be courted by a duke and peer of the realm, especially when the greatest ladies said that he was a milestone in any ambitious woman's career. She hadn't the slightest desire for Richelieu. But she wouldn't object if he lavished attention on *the other* Jeanne, the unknown young woman whose enigmatic and seductive white velvet mask she now saw reflected in the mirror.

The mask, with its fringe of lace, Venetian style, covered her face. Under its protection she was a stranger to herself, living a borrowed life. In spite of her coolheadedness, she was in a mood receptive to folly. After all, it was the carnival season.

From Richelieu's box at the Opéra, with his other guests, Mme. Favart and Mme. de Mauconseil, Jeanne looked down at the many-colored throng, studded with black dominoes, which was swirling around the dancers. Figures dressed like milkmaids cavorted happily with centaurs and bears. Lace petticoats and velvet waistcoats pranced with gypsylike abandon below her. She was living out her dream in a great emerald green and gold cage.

Richelieu's large box at the Opéra was a veritable thoroughfare. Although he was wearing a mask of gold cloth and a wig which his twenty-nine mistresses at Bordeaux had stitched with gold thread in his honor, his friends recognized him. They came to greet him, lingering a moment while they tried casually to brush up against the mysterious young blond domino.

The mystery was all the more provoking because the marshal took part in the game, interposing his cane between her and any gallant who came too close. Jeanne played along by throwing the hood of her cloak over her head and turning away. News of the Marshal's latest infatuation must have traveled throughout the Opéra House, for the box was filled with a steady stream of curiosity-seekers.

One gentleman pushed his way into Richelieu's box.

"Victor of the Battle of Minorca," he said, with a low bow, "forgive me for trespassing. But I wanted to pay my respects."

These words, pronounced in a resonant voice, reminded Richelieu of a glorious moment in his past. He smiled, radiantly, took off his mask, and opened his arms to the newcomer.

"My deck boy, how well I remember you! I'd be vexed if you hadn't come. Step up, now, and let me embrace you and look at you more closely."

The visitor was worthy of notice. He was tall, handsome, and elegantly dressed in a mottled black coat, embroidered in gold, over a gold-cloth waistcoat. The stitched tricorne hat held under his arm, the ruby pin on his jabot, and the two bejeweled watches hanging on chains from his pockets completed his ensemble. He held a narrow black mask, which he had removed when he entered the box.

"So, here you are ashore," Richelieu went on.

"There has to be some time for lovemaking, monseigneur."

"If you're not in too much of a hurry for that, have supper with us after the performance. I'm offering simple fare. But if, afterward, you're still hungry, you can have a second round at Conti's. Let me introduce you to the ladies, who, no doubt, will be glad of another man when we attack our chicken."

"Come, come, Duke!" broke in Mme. de Mauconseil. "No introduction is necessary. Chevalier Vincent used to dance at La Bagatelle."

Vincent bowed to the old marquise, to the singer, and then fastened a curious gaze on the white mask of the young blond girl.

How can I still be alive? Why haven't I fainted away? Hearing the sound of Vincent's voice, Jeanne felt as if she were floating over the room, disembodied. *Only my cloak is holding me up. If I take it off, I'll fall to the ground.* The hand she held out to Vincent was numb. At the touch of his lips, it came to life. But she feared that its trembling might betray her emotion and give her away.

Vincent held her hand, questioningly. He was staring at her mask so intensely that she thought it would burn away.

Richelieu must have detected something amiss, for he took hold of Vincent and pulled him away.

"Easy there, my fine fellow. Don't linger too long. You realize, of course, that I'm offering to share only my roast chicken."

"I was afraid so," Vincent murmured. "But can't you tell me at least the name of the 'chick' that you're keeping for yourself alone?"

"Giving out names is risky, and I've become cautious. I've made too many cuckolds in my time."

Then, in a louder voice, smiling at his three women guests, "Have these ladies had their fill of the ball? Are they ready to favor me with their company at supper?"

"Dear me, yes, I say that we go," sighed Mme. de Mauconseil. "These balls used to be pleasant enough, but they've become a bore."

Richelieu gave Jeanne his arm. "Come, my Nightingale. Will you forgive me for not inviting you to dance? I am feeling the old wound in my leg, the very evening when I'd like to kick up my heels."

"Marshal," said Vincent, "may I perform this duty in your place?"

Jeanne felt she must say something. In the attempt to disguise her voice she came out with a whisper, "Thank you, Chevalier. But let's go to supper. I'm perishing of hunger."

Actually she was wondering if she would be able to swallow.

The corridors were filled with swishing skirts. Vincent walked on the other side of Jeanne, taking advantage of the confusion to come very close and inhale her fragrance. She cursed her habit of mixing various recognizable scents into a pungent blend. She had sewn sachets into her petticoats and, with every movement, they gave out an odor of orange blossom, chamomile, iris, and white lilies. And she remembered how, at Charmont, Vincent had complimented her on this bouquet. He had sniffed her skin and buried his face in her loosened hair.

Could it be that, having possessed so many women in the meantime, he would still remember the scent connected with a passing fancy? She both feared and hoped that he would. But she didn't want him to recognize her on the arm of the most famous rake of the kingdom. How could she explain, to such a mocking spirit as his, the innocence of her flirtation with Marshal de Richelieu? At the moment, she almost felt guilty.

While the duke and the marquise were lagging behind greeting their friends, Jeanne, Justine Favart, and Vincent went into the garden of the Tuileries. As they stopped in the darkness, waiting for the others, Jeanne stumbled on a stone and groped for Vincent's silk sleeve. His hand moved to imprison hers. Once more she shook all over, wondering what Vincent made of her hand's trembling. All three of them fell silent. Jeanne and Vincent, because this was no time to talk. And Justine, because she had glimpsed Vincent's gesture, felt herself to be an intruder.

Indeed, at this moment, Jeanne wished that the earth would open up and swallow Justine. She wanted desperately to go off with Vincent to the ends of the world. For all eternity. *I love him.* The realization rushed to her head, filling her with joy. Impulsively she leaned her head on Vincent's shoulder.

Justine cleared her throat violently. Vincent released Jeanne's hand, stepped away, and walked back to the Opéra House.

"The carriage of Monseigneur the Duke de Richelieu!" announced the doorman.

"Dear deck boy, how did you come here?" Richelieu asked Vincent.

"In a run-down cab that's waiting for me down the street. The old nag should last long enough to take me to your house. It isn't far."

"The carriage of Madame the Marquise de Mauconseil!"

Jeanne moved, with Justine, toward the marquise's carriage. Richelieu let Justine by, but held Jeanne back.

"Do me the honor of driving with me, mademoiselle. . . . As things have turned out, there will be nine of us to eat the chicken. I'm asking you not to a supper, but to a famine!"

* * * *

The magnificent house on the Chaussée d'Antin, which Richelieu had owned for the last eight years, provided a sumptuous background for his receptions. The sculpted woodwork, the paintings, the draperies— everything had been chosen to delight the most fastidious eye. Every piece of furniture was a masterpiece of cabinetmaking, every object a marvel of bronze, porcelain, or gold. A rich collection of old china, great screens displaying landscapes outlined in gold, paintings by Titian, Holbein, Van Dyck, Oudry, and Boucher, and bouquets of artistically arranged flowers contributed to the luxury of the whole. The floors were covered with rugs from the Near East or La Savonnerie, and the marquetry was in the style of Versailles.

A dazzled Jeanne walked through several antechambers before reaching the brightly lit drawing room. The night was clear and Jeanne saw a group sculpture by Michelangelo under a rose-covered arbor in the garden.

A valet opened the double door leading to a small round room where the supper was laid out. It was clear, immediately, that the famine predicted by the marshal would be easily endurable. True, there were only two fat chickens, stuffed with truffles and smothered in cream, but they were surrounded by platters of cold meat and elaborate desserts. Silverware, plates of vermeil, porcelain, and Bohemian glass were laid out on a circular table in the center of the room. Around them, artfully arranged for buffet dining, were mahogany trays.

"I thought we'd enjoy serving ourselves," said the marshal.

With a wave of the hand, he dismissed the servants. Then, holding out one hand to the marquise and the other to Jeanne, he led them to the table.

"Load your trays, and sit down where you will. I claim the right to serve you the tea! Tell me, Marquise, will you start with white or red?"

Richelieu's cellar in Bordeaux was famous. He had won over all of fashionable Paris to the wine of his province. Society called it "Richelieu's tea."

Jeanne asked him to choose on her behalf, and he selected a honey-colored Graves de Vayres.

Vincent served her some smoked sturgeon and she found herself, once more, between him and the marshal.

Richelieu raised his glass. "To our mysterious beauties."

Around the table there were three young masked women. Jeanne had been relieved when, in the courtyard, she had seen two other female masqueraders. One of them was with Count de Lauraguais, the other with the Marquis and Marshal de Contades. Their escorts were obviously reluctant to reveal the identity of their latest conquests, and it was agreed that the masks need not be removed.

Vincent, the only unaccompanied man, was the first to answer Richelieu's toast. "Gentlemen, to your forbidden fruits!"

"It's a long time since I've had supper with masked ladies," said Contades. "We chase after crude realities and ignore the pleasures of imagination."

"Imagination can play tricks, however," said Richelieu with a grimace. "After a night I spent with a masked woman in Genoa I swore never again! What a rude surprise I had when I discovered her face beside me the next morning!"

"For once you did a good deed," said Mme. de Mauconseil. "Don't regret it, for you won't have many to present on Judgment Day."

"Only a young man can be willing to oblige an ugly woman," said the marshal. "The rest of us have no less drive, but our taste is more demanding."

"Speaking of masks," said Contades, "do you recall, Duke, the 'undress ball' you gave one evening in Hanover?"

"Do tell us about it," said Lauraguais. "I presume that masks were the only dress!"

"Good God, Count!" Mme. Favart exclaimed. "Now you've launched our marshals on their war stories! They'll go on into the night."

Indeed, Richelieu and Contades, their cheeks red with excitement, were fighting the Prussian campaign. Nothing gave them more pleasure than to relive their battle exploits.

Vincent leaned over toward Jeanne. "A drop of wine? Our tea grower has forgotten us, and he may be absent in spirit for some time."

"I'd like to look at the sweets," said Jeanne, leaving her seat to go with him.

She no longer trembled or disguised her voice. Now she was determined to make the best of the situation. It no longer distressed her. The heady presence of the man who had taken her into his arms, covered her with kisses, and desired her to the point of carrying her away made her feel unbelievably alive.

Tonight, in this drawing room, if he would grasp her hand, draw her to him and say, "Let us be off!" she would follow him without a word.

"Which wine will you have?"

"Oh, choose one for me . . . "

She took a swallow, thinking, *Here's to my madness!* And, with the second swallow, *I want to be mad!*

One of the masked figures, bored with war stories, came over to the buffet and started to stuff herself with sweets. The boniness of her chin, shoulders, elbows, and wrists showed that she was still an adolescent, perhaps no more than fourteen years old. The Marquis de Contades had a passion for very young girls. Between two mouthfuls of nougat, she plunged her nose into a big bunch of pale roses arranged in a silver bowl.

"How good they smell! Pretty, too, aren't they? They're the color of rose-petal jam."

"They actually make good jam," Jeanne told her. "Puteaux roses, that's what they are. They can be made into tea and syrup, as well."

"I don't care for teas," said the girl, making a childish face, "but I adore rose-petal jam. I like it when they give it to me with my breakfast coffee. That's elegant, because it's really expensive, everyone knows."

Jeanne shot an embarrassed glance at Vincent, who had moved a short distance away. The way the poor girl talked, showed all too clearly that she came from the stable of either Gourdan or Brisset. And the girl treated her, Jeanne, in a familiar manner which made it seem that they were of the same ilk.

"Do you like my dress?" the girl asked.

The dress was pretty and tasteful, made of white silk, ornamented with many-colored flowers.

"Very pretty," murmured Jeanne.

"I've never worn anything quite so fine before," said the girl contentedly. "It's all because I'm with the Marquis de Contades, who's a very generous gentleman. Of course, Marshal de Richelieu is richer. I suppose he may be even more generous. That almond-green color of your gown goes well with your hair and complexion, and you have enough of a figure to set it off. Tell me, does he give you jewels, too?"

Jeanne, very tense, managed to shake the girl off and returned to Vincent.

"You seem to know flowers," he said casually, picking up a prune and pointing to the roses.

Jeanne looked at him, defiantly. "Yes, I do."

Painstakingly, he made up a plateful of sweets and took it to Mme. Favart, then a second for the Marquise de Mauconseil, and a third for the figure dressed in buttercup yellow sitting with Count de Lauraguais.

"I thought of studying botany at one time," he said, returning to her side at last. "A young woman botanist was to sail with me on my *Belle Vincent*. But at the last minute, she changed her mind."

"Were you sorry?"

"For a while, yes. She was charming and intelligent."

Jeanne's voice was soft and almost imploring as she asked, "So you don't miss her any more?"

His response was sharp as a whip. "No, not at all. By now she's old."

"Old?" Jeanne muttered, barely managing to go back to the table before her legs gave way and tears came to her eyes. *Was Emilie right, after all? That, for a woman, so soon it was too late?*

Fortunately the atmosphere was by now so heated with the food, drink, and licentious conversation that no one noticed Jeanne's melancholy. The two marshals, carried away by their memories, their heads ringing with gunfire and the music of fighting and drinking songs, were calling for a rendition of "La Fanchon."

" 'La Fanchon,' madame, 'La Fanchon'!" they called out, raising their glasses to Justine Favart.

"Madame," said Richelieu, turned suddenly sentimental, "as long as you're here to sing 'La Fanchon,' France can still respond to the glory of Fontenoy. Do you remember the officer in a torn uniform covered with black gunpowder who sat on a drum in front of Saxe's tent scribbling a song in honor of the victory?"

Justine started as if under the dig of a spur, pulled up her petticoats, climbed onto a chair, and bellowed the famous refrain that had spread from Fontenoy all over the country.

> *"Sweet is her converse, sweet and true,*
> *Merit and glory are her due;*
> *She likes to laugh, she likes to drink,*
> *She likes to sing the way we do."*

Everyone except Jeanne joined in. Vincent had sat down at the harpsichord and hammered out the tune. Fifes and drums were lacking, but there was an echo of the joyful noise raised by carousing soldiers and camp followers.

Richelieu, with a shrill voice, tried shamelessly to drown out the others. Standing straight as a ramrod, he took Jeanne's hand in his and beat out the rhythm. Suddenly, inspired by a lusty line, he dropped the hand, threw his arm around her waist, and planted a kiss on her neck. Luckily, Vincent could not see.

Jeanne angrily wrenched herself free and hissed into his ear, "Marshal, you're behaving like a common soldier!"

Richelieu's eyes blazed with fury, but he chose to turn the offense into banter.

"Impertinence has its charm, Nightingale, when it comes out of such a pretty mouth," he said in an intimate manner, slipping his hand under the muslin ruffle and tickling her arm.

"Monseigneur," Jeanne answered in the same bantering tone, "your indulgence is reassuring, and I shall take advantage of it this very minute by asking you to remove your hand."

"La Fanchon" set off the conventional dessert songs, to which everyone contributed, willy-nilly. Such was the ironclad custom at the end of a festive meal, whether the participants were noblemen, scholars, or members of a country wedding party. To get into the mood required producing at least one vulgar example, and most people knew several by heart. The young girl corrupted by the Marquis de Contades could offer nothing but a village song. Her faint, high-pitched voice intoned the ingenuous and cruel lament for a new bride:

> "Her petals will fall
> Like a rose's that day;
> She will be devoured
> Like a plum from the tree.
> The poor hapless girl
> Will soon fade away . . ."

Jeanne was stricken with pity for the child courtesan and hatred for her procurers. Suddenly she sensed a malevolent stare fixed upon her. Raising her eyes, she encountered Vincent's. Their hard gleam intensified her unhappiness. She wished only that this evening of torture might come to an end. She wanted to run home and weep into her pillow. Not daring to leave, she stayed on and despised herself for it.

Soon she had an additional source of worry. The evening promised to turn into an orgy. Contades had installed the young girl on his knees and was feeding her frangipane. Lauraguais' buxom buttercup Venus was clucking like a happy hen as he lavished her with attention.

Jeanne was protected, to some extent, from these goings-on because she was between Richelieu and Vincent. The marshal was talking over her head about the Battle of Minorca. The former deck boy could not escape from the rocks of Port Mahon unless he bodily removed himself from the scene. And this he did not choose to do. He listened attentively, with a courteous smile on his lips, as if he were ready to stick it out until dawn. His gaze swept, at intervals, over the silent young woman on his left side, whose hand, beside a plate of un-touched candied fruit, trembled unconsciously.

Finally Jeanne sighed and leaned toward Richelieu. "Forgive me, monseigneur," she said, "but I have a terrible headache, perhaps be-cause of the wine. Will you allow me to take my leave? If Madame de Mauconseil will lend me her carriage, I'll send it straight back when I reach home."

Vincent broke into the stir raised by this declaration.

"Marshal," he said, "I am going, as you know, to the house of Prince de Conti. I can leave Mademoiselle off on my way."

"No, no!" exclaimed Richelieu. "That would be most unwise. Made-moiselle must not go out in the night air until she is feeling better."

And, turning to Jeanne, he said with genuine concern, "I'll give you a glass of my opium brew and you can lie down and rest. And when your headache has subsided I'll have you driven home."

Jeanne had a hard time living down her lie, escaping the marshal's solicitude and the ministrations of a hastily summoned chambermaid, who appeared in a petticoat and nightcap.

She spoke in a strong voice, as if she had made a miraculous recovery. "A thousand thanks, monseigneur. I'm touched by your kindness, but I do really prefer to go. I have, at home, a drug to which my headaches always respond. I'm sorry to have disturbed the supper party. I'd feel better if you were to go back to it and worry no more. Since the chevalier has offered to escort me . . ."

Richelieu had little desire to send Jeanne home with the corsair, who had been a budding rival in Minorca, years before. He made a gesture of alarm to Mme. de Mauconseil.

"My dear child, I simply can't let you go alone in this condition. I'll have no rest until I've seen you safely home," said the marquise soothingly.

While a servant went to rouse the marquise's coachman, Vincent asked his host's permission to scribble a note on the writing table in the foyer.

"A love letter to slip into a fair one's bodice later in the evening," he said with a smile.

Vincent wrote only a few lines.

The marshal could not prevent him from taking Jeanne's cloak from a lackey and throwing it around her shoulders. She quivered with pleasure when he deftly slipped the note between her breasts.

Richelieu put the two ladies into the carriage, leaving Vincent in the foyer, where Lauraguais joined him.

"Since the duke's nightingale has escaped you, Chevalier, I trust you won't go away."

"Ah, but I must go."

"Zounds!" the count exclaimed. "It's beginning to get boring, isn't it? Stay just long enough to be polite. Then we'll leave together and go wherever you like—some place more amusing. To my house, if you will. My Roseline is a treat to the eyes, even without a mask, and there's plenty of her. . . ."

"Thank you, but no. I wouldn't be much fun. I'm in a bad humor."

"Perhaps we can cure your humor with champagne."

"Another time, if you'll ask me."

"Of course, but I don't like to see you go like this. Whatever you pay you'll never get anyone as good as Roseline. Too bad the duke's little bird has escaped you. I'd have given anything to unmask her."

"It shouldn't be too difficult. Just root around at the house of Mauconseil, and I wager you'll turn her up. They seem to be hand in glove."

"I had the same idea. But I don't want to poach on your preserve. Are you willing to cede her?"

"My dear count, let her go to the highest bidder," said Vincent icily.

* * * *

Jeanne tiptoed into the room. A lighted candle was waiting for her on the commode. She was anxious to read the note. But she heard footsteps in the next room and hastily pushed it back into her bodice.

Philibert appeared, looking cross. "Do you know how late it is?" he shot at her.

"Yes, I do. But how could I leave the Opéra ball before three? Anyway, you knew very well who I was with. You should have gone tranquilly to bed." Her voice was impatient.

"You must let me do as I choose, Jeannette."

He sat down on the edge of the couch and went on, "I don't like your growing intimacy with the Favart circle."

"And I don't like to be left alone every evening while you pay court to Buffon at the Jussieus' or attend the freemasons' secret meetings with Helvétius," she said defiantly.

"Don't be childish, Jeannette. You know why I force myself to go to these evening gatherings. A scientist needs to be stimulated by the talk of his colleagues. I must think of my career. After all, I have arrived late on the scene. I'm thirty-eight years old, Jeanne. I've no more time to waste."

"Do I represent a waste of time, then?" she asked angrily.

He sighed and smiled. "I can't discuss time with you. You don't seem to feel the hours go by, while I feel every minute passing. I'm devoured by curiosity, yet my knowledge grows too slowly. I despair, at times, when I imagine the discoveries I won't live to see."

Jeanne was taken aback. Philibert had never said anything like this before and she didn't know how to react.

"You know so much already. And you have a long life ahead of you in which to learn more. Are you weeping in advance for all the flowers you won't have gathered?"

"Do you know, Jeannette, that I even weep for those that are within my reach. I find myself thinking how soon these splendors will be lost to me. Beyond death is there anything but sterile blue fields?"

Jeanne observed Philibert closely. She had never seen this melancholy side of him. When he spoke it was always about concrete things—a book, a bone, a feather. . . .

"Is it that . . . are you not feeling well?" she asked fearfully and threw herself down beside him on the couch. "If you were to be ill, Philibert . . . oh, I'd take care of you and cure you. . . . You'll not die soon! I simply won't let you!"

"No, no," he said, smiling and shaking his head. "What can you mean? I feel perfectly well. I don't know why I said so many silly things. I only meant to scold you for coming home so late."

She slipped off the couch and knelt down with her arms around her lover's knees. Between her breasts Vincent's letter burned like a mortal sin. How could she have imagined that she loved another man? Sheer madness . . . carnival madness! The man of her life was here, before her. She leaned adoringly against his legs, feeling like a bird that has returned safely to the nest after a storm.

Philibert laid his hand on her elaborately coiffed hair and began to remove the artificial green and white flowers.

"Monsieur Philibert, let's go away!" Jeanne said in a muffled, passionate voice. "Let's go to the ends of the world together."

"Where are those ends?" he asked teasingly.

"No matter, somewhere far away."

"You're tired of Paris? That's something new! I thought you were happy at the garden, enthusiastic about opening your shop and amusing yourself with your new friends."

"Oh, I'm happy, yes. I'm excited about the shop, and I've been having fun, yes. But . . ." There was something like anguish in her voice as she added, "In the long run, the happiness I've found in Paris seems so superficial."

"Bah! What a strange idea!"

"Oh, the city is distracting and so full of amusing people. But too many people come between us. Even on Sundays, when we go to gather herbs, we're not alone. Don't you miss our expeditions in Dombes? In the woodlands of Boulogne we're followed by a crowd of chattering people, scaring off the birds and shouting for you when they find the smallest plant."

"So you want to get me out of Paris because you think I'm becoming too popular, is that it? Do you imagine that I might forget you?"

"No."

He raised her head and looked deeply into her eyes. "Are you afraid that *you'll* forget *me*?"

"No, no!"

There was a tense silence between them. Then Jeanne went on, "Here we can't live as a couple. People and things are always coming between us. Philibert, I know what makes you happiest . . . putting on your oldest jacket, your oldest cap, and running over hill and dale with me at your heels!"

"That's quite a strange tack you're taking, preaching a return to nature when, more and more frequently, I find you in a ball gown!"

"Do you want to know the truth?" she asked. "I'm not so sure that running around the town is what I really want. And you, do you so deeply hanker after a seat in the academy and the Cordon of Saint Michael?"

"No. But I'm only a man. If I could get along without things I don't really care for I'd be a philosopher."

* * * *

Jeanne had decided not to read Vincent's letter, at least not right away. One day, perhaps, out of curiosity, when she'd come to her senses and Vincent was only a memory. Late in the night, lying across Philibert's chest, listening to his heartbeat, she decided to burn the letter unread.

But the next morning, her thoughts were once more filled with Vincent, and she eagerly opened the letter. Her pleasure suddenly turned to shock and despair. There before her was the ribbon she had given him three years before. For a few moments she could do nothing but stare at the faded band. Why had he sent it back to her? What message did it convey? At last she pushed the ribbon aside and read these terrible words:

> Take back this memento. Coming from the heroine of an
> innocent escapade, I cherished it. But belonging to a
> high-class slut, it has become abhorrent to me.

In vain she bit her lip until it bled and clenched her fists. Her sobs persisted and she threw herself on the bed, flooding it with her tears. Humiliation and anger mingled together.

At last she rose up from the pillows. She had suddenly had a comforting thought. *After all, he kept my ribbon for three years. Where had he kept it? On a watch chain? In his waistcoat pocket? Near his heart? Attached to his Cross of Malta? If he kept my token for three years, didn't that mean that he cared for me? If he bothered to send it back, didn't that mean he still cared for me?*

She feverishly walked up and down, her eyes aflame, twisting her handkerchief. She would make him sorry for the way he had treated her, for his base thoughts and horrible accusations.

On his knees! I'll make him beg me to forgive him! And even then, I might never forgive him at all!

CHAPTER 24

Jeanne's shop, La Tisanière, had great charm. The highly polished cherrywood shelves and drawers gleamed like silk. On the shelves, she had placed some stout blue-and-yellow earthenware pots creating an effect that Mercier never tired of admiring.

"How do you like the placement of the pots? Have I successfully harmonized the colors?" she asked Mlle. Basseporte.

The garden's official painter moved back to the door to gain a better perspective. "Perfect," she declared.

She had just finished hanging the watercolors which were her gift to Jeanne: a brilliant poppy, a branch of juniper with big violet berries, a bouquet of sunny dandelions, and a cluster of bluebells. These four paintings, and the fresco of flowers decorating the chimney piece, created a charmingly cheerful effect.

"I owe you two kisses on each cheek," said Jeanne to her elderly friend. "You've given me real works of art. It looks as if all I have to do now is sit down and wait for my customers."

She went to perch on a high stool behind the counter, smiling at her friends who had come to add the finishing touches to the shop.

"May I light the chandelier, mademoiselle," Lucette the clerk asked, "to test its effect?"

"Yes," said Jeanne, "and the wall candelabra as well."

Just then, the booming voice of Aubriot cheerily announced, "This is Versailles! No luxury is lacking—six candles on the ceiling and eight on the walls. . . . Jeanne, are you sure that your profits will pay for all of this wax?"

"I shan't need lighting until winter. I'll have made my fortune by then, for sure," said Jeanne.

"That's so, I'll vouch for it," said Mercier. "Look around you, Doctor. You'll see that we have something to suit every taste."

"True," chimed in Father Firmin. "I've never seen an herb shop so well stocked."

Indeed, the variety of herbs at La Tisanière was all that Jeanne could have hoped for. There was an array of classical plants grown in far-off convent and monastery gardens, a generous sampling of fragrant herbs from Provence, especially the cure-all rosemary, pounds of thyme, laurel, bramble leaves, and beech bark, stems of angelica and rhubarb and other products of the garden at Charmont, an ample assortment of flowers from the whole Dombes region and blackcurrant leaves, climbing ivy, and rose petals.

"Absinthe . . . blueberry . . . maidenhair . . . mullein . . . nasturtium . . . tarragon . . ."

Aubriot read the labels out loud. "A superb collection! But I don't see any cherry stems."

"Oh, my cherry stems!" Jeanne exclaimed. "They're still with the monks of Saint-Victor. I forgot to call for them."

"Don't worry, mademoiselle," said Lucette. "I'll send my little brother, Banban, to fetch them, early tomorrow morning. Because the doctor is right. You'll lose customers if you don't have cherry tails on opening day. The way men are concerned about pissing, it's incredible! They leap out of bed and make for the chamber pot. The more they fill it, the happier they feel. You'd think it was the best part of lovemaking."

Jeanne cast a worried look in Lucette's direction. She had already been warned about using vulgar language. The clerk, who had recently worked in a brothel, had won Jeanne's confidence because of her good nature and genuine desire to reform. Jeanne hoped she hadn't made a mistake.

While Mercier, Thouin, Mlle. Basseporte, and Father Firmin were listening to Aubriot talk about the way to use certain herb concoctions, Lucette approached Jeanne and said in a low voice, "It's true that your gentleman doctor knows how to talk. And he seems to know all about when to boil, to steep, to infuse, and such like."

"Monsieur is a great scientist," said Jeanne proudly.

"In that case, perhaps he could do something for women. Because if there's one thing we need it's a brew to reduce swelling bellies. A secret formula. If your doctor can give you that, we could put it up in envelopes, and the shop would be the most successful in all of Paris, I can tell you."

"Come, come, Lucette," said Jeanne with some embarrassment. "You know such drugs are strictly forbidden."

"We're at the Temple, mademoiselle," said Lucette. "And at the Temple there's a bit of everything. It's the perfect place. Women will have confidence in it because they know it's against the law."

"But I'm looking for a fashionable clientele," said Jeanne, "and I don't believe ladies would come to a respectable shop and ask for . . ."

"Maybe not your bourgeois ladies, but between noblewomen and common sluts, you'll find plenty! Nadine, for instance, sells something of the sort, but I'm in a position to know that it's no good. But your good doctor, who's a scientist, can do better than the madam of a house or a charlatan on the Pont Neuf."

Jeannette, however, found herself more and more embarrassed. "Lucette," she said, "don't ever bring up this subject again!"

"Very well," sighed Lucette. "I mentioned it because the sale of such a drug would fill your cashbox and be very useful besides. But if you won't hear of it, so much the worse. You're in charge. . . ."

Jeanne was greatly troubled by Lucette's words. She imagined herself questioning Philibert. It was unthinkable; only loose women like Lucette would think of talking about such things to a man.

But, seeing that Lucette looked hurt, Jeanne smiled at her and said, "I shan't turn down all your ideas. Feel free to tell me others. I'd really like to know where to get exotic plants. I know that many Maltese sailors stay at the Temple when they come to Paris, and I'm told they deal with tradesmen."

"Yes, the Knights of Malta lodge here, mademoiselle. Go to the Café de Malte and you'll find all the Maltese you want. The knights do business on a grand scale. But not with individuals. Oftentimes, though, a few of them are hard up and might do business with you."

"I've heard of a certain Chevalier Vincent," said Jeanne, lowering her voice. "He's even willing to do business with Amelie Sorel, the clothes dealer."

"But Mademoiselle Sorel isn't small potatoes. The corsair brings her luxury items from the East and dresses and hats from London. Gorgeous things, in the latest style."

"So you don't think my herbs would interest this Vincent."

Lucette looked her up and down with twinkling blue eyes.

"I don't know about your herbs. Your looks are a different matter. Chevalier Vincent has an eye for the ladies."

"So you know him personally, do you?"

"Everyone around here knows him."

"But you better than most, perhaps."

"Chevalier Vincent doesn't go for the girls at Nadine's. When he's here, he stays with the idol, and so . . ."

"The idol?"

"Countess de Boufflers. She rules over the prior's house and she's called the idol of the Temple."

"Is the chevalier staying there now?"

"He was awhile ago. But he returned to London to fetch another consignment of fine clothes. He also travels on behalf of Prince de Conti."

"Is the prince in business, too?"

"Well, all sorts of things go on in his house. Travelers are always arriving from abroad and they spend hours visiting with the prince. I've seen him ordering his carriage, going off to Versailles with a big portfolio under his arm. State secrets, the servants say. But nobody knows, not even the countess, who resents being kept in the dark."

"Do you mean that the prince is a spy master, and Chevalier Vincent is a spy?"

"Sshh, mademoiselle! I said nothing of the sort. You mustn't talk about it," said Lucette, suddenly frightened. "I heard tell of a man who tried to steal the prince's portfolio. They said he was working for the Duke de Choiseul. But the would-be thief never had time to plead guilty or not guilty. He was strangled in his prison cell."

"I've no interest in the prince's state secrets," said Jeanne. "I only want to know when this Chevalier Vincent is expected to return."

"I'll ask Banban," Lucette told her.

The twelve-year-old Banban ran errands for both the prince and the countess and knew a good deal of what went on behind their doors.

"Good!" said Jeanne as she saw her friends get ready to take their leave.

* * * *

From the very first day, La Tisanière was a spectacular success. Fashionable Parisians flocked to Jeanne's door. M. de Buffon was one of the first visitors. In his loud voice, he proclaimed the high quality of the herbs and the merits of the plants Jeanne carried.

Very early one morning, Countess de Boufflers appeared wearing a pink satin dressing gown. She came to inquire after a remedy for "sudden hoarseness." Jeanne prescribed a decoction of elderberries and honey, used as a gargle. The countess was charmed by Jeanne and quickly cured by the brew. With this timely stroke of good fortune, La Tisanière became the idol's official supplier. The Temple's many tenants made valued customers.

Toward the end of August, even Prince de Conti came in, looking for something better than the blueberry lotion he used to relieve his tired eyes.

Jeanne was duly intimidated as she rose from a deep curtsy. But she gave the prince her advice in an assured manner. "If your Royal Highness will take my word for it, he will continue to use the blueberry lotion. I know of nothing better. Our peasants call it 'eyeglass-breaker.' Perhaps His Highness's lotion is stale. It should be very fresh with a pinch of forget-me-not."

Banban was ordered to take the prior a vial of freshly prepared blueberry lotion every morning. A week later, the great man was swearing by Mlle. Beauchamps, calling her the best herb doctor in the kingdom.

Because the doctor was as pretty as she was learned, and the prince admired beauty as much as learning, he proposed to subsidize her shop to the tune of six hundred francs a year in order to keep it within the confines of the Temple.

At this news Lucette remarked, "Mademoiselle, you were born with a silver spoon in your mouth. We're off to a flying start. The prior is a good man. Some people say he's out to make money. And he certainly does go after it. But he spends what he makes and more. He's wealthy and at the same time full of debts. That's a very good sign. A real prince is supposed to die penniless."

"There's a philosophy for you," Jeanne said, laughing.

"Mademoiselle, a prince is either good or bad. If he's good, the only way he can show it is by giving away his shirt and sometimes the skin with it. And skirt chasing, for a prince, is only a venial sin. Our prince is said to have two thousand sins to his credit. And he hasn't finished yet."

Jeanne was amazed at the number. "Two thousand?" she exclaimed incredulously. "You mean the prince boasts of having had two thousand mistresses?"

"That's how Banban tells it. He says the prince has a box of rings, one for every one of his lady loves. Banban was there one evening when the prince got his chaplain to count them."

"And do you believe it?"

"I believe the story of the rings, yes, mademoiselle. One of them is mine."

"Yours?"

"I was fifteen years old and a virgin, mademoiselle."

"And you gave a ring to a prince of royal blood?" Jeanne asked, trying not to be too sarcastic.

"When it's a ring for the prince, all the jewelers around the Temple give you credit and take a rake-off for themselves. They sell you a one-hundred-and-fifty-franc ring for double the price. And when you bring it to the prince he's gentleman enough to pay you five hundred. That way everybody's happy."

"I see," said Jeanne coldly. "Shall we speak of something else? I don't like it, Lucette, when you fall back into that coarse talk."

"Well, mademoiselle, I have to tell you what's what. Probably one day the prince will call you to the Temple to question you about your herb teas. If you don't want to add to the rings in his box, you'd better look sharp. The prince has charm. If you knew the number of rings bearing the coat of arms of a duchess or a marquise . . ."

"Really?" said Jeanne, with genuine amazement.

"And the prince has a reputation for being considerate. He follows the code of a gentleman, in bed as well as out. And that's rare, I can tell you. He always has a handkerchief in hand to catch that which might turn into a baby, even if . . ."

"Lucette!"

"Even if du Breuille says that he does it only to conceal the fact that all that comes out of him is hot air."

"Lucette, you're impossible! I can't have you babbling about our customers' private affairs."

"Mademoiselle, by your good grace, I can't help laughing. When I see in our notebook that Banban is to deliver remedies for Monsieur d'Alembert's piles, the Marquis de Contades' colic, the pain in the younger Countess d'Egmont's bladder, the fibrous condition of the prostate of Monsieur Jelyotte, the leucorrhea of Madame Bagarotty. . . . Soon we'll be so well informed that police informers and gossip writers will be at the door."

She began to count some fennel seeds. Suddenly she raised her head. "By the way, you must double the price of the blueberry lotion you supply to the prince."

"Why so?"

"One of his officers has asked for the same thing, to treat his red eyes. You can't make him the same price as his master. That would be dishonest."

Ever since the opening of La Tisanière, Jeanne had not had a minute to herself. Mornings she still went to the botany course at the garden. From there, she hurried to the shop and stayed late into the evening.

The Temple area afforded her considerable enjoyment. It was a great marketplace, crawling with life. A large number of its four thousand inhabitants were shopkeepers and craftsmen, who attracted a constant flow of customers and sightseers. At certain hours the streets were filled with a mixture of middle-class women, fine ladies, prostitutes and servant girls, messenger boys, pages, and foreigners. All these fingered the merchandise outside, entered shops, or sat down in a café to chat over a cup of coffee. Indeed, the smell of coffee was so strong that it submerged the smell of urine. For any part of Paris this was no small attraction.

Because her time was taken up by work, Jeanne had almost forgotten her vendetta against Vincent. She still brooded when she thought about him. There was time to concentrate on her revenge when he came back from England and was within her reach. What form her revenge would take, she did not know. But a woman shouldn't have difficulty in finding a weapon against a man so sensitive that, for three years, he had kept her hair ribbon. For the moment she was preoccupied with the ill-humor of a man closer to her.

Plainly Aubriot was pleased with Jeanne's success. Especially since, as Mme. de Bouhey had predicted, he no longer paid for her dresses, bonnets, and coiffures. But he had lost his secretary, Jeannot. Jeanne tried to keep his herb collections in order. Because she had no time to copy papers and write letters, he had to hire someone else. He also had to increase the wages of Dr. Vacher's housekeeper who now had to prepare supper since Jeanne came back to the Rue du Mail only in time "to slip her feet under the table."

As they ate their soup and beef salad she listened as religiously as ever to Aubriot's account of his day. Now he noticed that there were moments of distraction, when her eyes wandered. She'd bite her lip or frown, doubtless thinking of her own affairs. He said nothing, but harbored a bitterness akin to that of a god betrayed by a little nun who has cast off her habit.

The new Jeanne, for her part, was aware of Philibert's sulking. When he "forgot" to rub her back caressingly after lovemaking, she did not complain, but laid her head as usual on his chest. The next morning she realized, with surprise, that she had slept soundly, despite her lover's humor. He no longer had the power to keep her awake, troubled because she had displeased him, waiting for the morning in the hope he would look at her more kindly. She felt vaguely uneasy about what she felt was a lack of sensitivity. But the business of daily life so involved her that she soon forgot both Philibert's mood and her self-reproach. She knew she loved him as much as ever. But she had ceased to live only for and through her lover.

Aubriot was not the only one to notice that it was no longer so easy to lead Jeanne by the nose. The Marquise de Mauconseil found her influence on the wane. She could not tear Jeanne away from the shop or persuade her to go out in society.

* * * *

Five days after the masked supper party, when Richelieu left for Bordeaux, he gave the marquise instructions for completing the conquest of the "nightingale." And he repeated them, at frequent intervals, by letter. "Accustom her to the luxuries money alone can give and I'll do the rest." This was the strategy that had succeeded so well in the past with courtesans of high and low degree. He even told the astonished marquise that he would lodge Jeanne in his house on the Chaussée d'Antin, thereby fully recognizing her as his mistress, instead of his smaller place at Les Porcherons. The old rake had fallen genuinely in love with this girl who had, so far, rejected him.

But Jeanne seemed to be less and less disposed to go along with the marshal's plans. Mme. de Mauconseil succeeded only two or three times in taking her to the fashionable promenade on the Cours la

Reine or for a lemonade under the trees along the Champs-Elysées.
Jeanne would go, occasionally, to the Comédie Française or the Opéra.
But she refused to attend any after-theater suppers. And, in the same
polite but firm manner, she turned down the gift of a bonnet, a fan, a
snuffbox, or a lacy handkerchief which the marquise offered her on
the marshal's behalf.

The marquise, however, believed that the refusal of these trifles was
calculated on the expectation of greater gifts. She spent the money
that Richelieu had left, for her own purposes. She was waiting for him
to return and put a house, a carriage, and an abundance of jewels at
Jeanne's disposal. In order to justify her expenditures, she sent him
glowing accounts of her friendship with Jeanne, when actually she saw
her very seldom.

Mme. Favart, for her part, came often to La Tisanière, where she
had established a small financial connection by taking a ten percent
commission on everything sold to the young singers of the Théâtre des
Italiens. Jeanne soon realized that she would make three times as
much money in beauty products as in medicine. She dug up formulas
for creams and lotions to whiten the skin, banish pimples and wrinkles,
tighten pores, firm up the chin and the bosom, soften the hair, and
shrink ankles. Finally, she made up an ointment from cucumber seeds,
to be applied at night, and a bottle of astringent lotion to wash it off
in the morning.

In less than a week, the "magic mask" arrived in the dressing rooms
of the Opéra House and on the dressing table of the Duchess de
Choiseul. Orders poured in, until Jeanne and Lucette were overwhelmed.
Jeanne had to engage a second helper, Magdeleine Thouin, a young
cousin of André. The girl was only sixteen, but well acquainted with
medicinal herbs. She took over their preparation, affording Jeanne a
modicum of freedom.

Jeanne had every reason to be proud of her rapid success. The shop
opened in mid-July, and by November it was in full swing. Young
Banban had been engaged, for six sous a day, as a messenger and
delivery boy. The name of Mlle. Beauchamps, "at the Temple, you
know," was beginning to be as well known as those of Tintin, the
hairdresser on the Rue Saint-Honoré; Mlle. Sorel, the dealer in exotic
dress; and Sieur Bernard, the shoemaker of the Rue Mauconseil. Men,
especially those of gentle birth, were wont to call her "La Belle
Tisanière," the Beauty of the Herb Shop.

Jeanne

CHAPTER 25

hilibert Aubriot had never asked himself whether he loved Jeanne. He had taken her with emotion as well as pleasure and a large measure of tenderness.

His was an early eighteenth-century soul, devoted to pure reason and content with dry, matter-of-fact feelings. Philibert had a superior mind whose constant activity left him little time to listen to his heart. His thirst for knowledge led him, early on, to study nature. But he did not gape, dreamily, at his marvels. Curiosity prevailed over sensibility; never did the tireless herb collector write an ode to the rose. Why then, had this meditative man, so at ease alone, encumbered himself with Jeanne when he went to make his fortune in Paris?

He did not like to dig too deeply for an answer. On this subject his thoughts were muddy, and he insisted on clear thinking. He had looked on her as a child. The little girl of Charmont, even before he had a child of his own, had awakened his fatherly feelings. The tawny-eyed little girl was obviously fascinated with him. Docile, imitative, she had always been ready to gather the manna that fell from his lips. In short, the ideal heir.

Little Michel-Anne had not had time to disappoint his father, or to satisfy him, either. When Philibert left Bugey his son was a mere baby. Jeanne was still his ideal child. At bottom it was with "Jeannot," the model son, that "Monsieur Philibert" wanted to live—the alert, laughing, obedient Jeannot. Yes, it was Jeannot that he had included in his luggage. That Jeannot had turned into Jeanne was all very well, indeed extremely agreeable. But that Jeanne should take on more importance than Jeannot . . . And, worse still, acquire independence to a point that was really excessive . . .

Aubriot started when, one spring evening at La Régence, the Marquis de Condorcet, as tactless as he was awkward, introduced him to a friend by saying, "It's to this gentleman that we owe the presence in Paris of the fair lady of the herb-tea shop!" Even in a rare moment of insecurity, Aubriot couldn't imagine himself merely the consort of a celebrated shopkeeper.

Back on the Rue du Mail, he icily turned down Jeanne's suggestion that she ask the Duchess de Choiseul to call the minister's attention to the merits of Dr. Aubriot. No matter how long it took, he wanted to reach Choiseul through Jussieu or Buffon. Certainly he wouldn't accept a girl's intercession.

Jeanne's friendship with Michel Adanson, a botanist she had met through Mlle. Basseporte, increased Aubriot's feelings of uneasiness. Adanson was the man he most admired, who had answers to all his questions. He had spent four years in Africa studying exotic plants, was an expert on cross-breeding, and a member of the academy. Suddenly, Jeanne began to rave about him and to extol his knowledge and his discoveries. He esteemed the man's mind too highly to dampen Jeanne's enthusiasm. Since there was no question of confessing his jealousy, even to himself, he took refuge in silence. He was annoyed with his own bitterness because it revealed one of his weak spots to Jeanne. He was at this point of ill-humor when he found, quite accidentally, the best way for a man to restore his self-confidence: the conquest of a prestigious woman.

Aubriot had been one of the first supporters of vaccination, which, in France, was slow to win recognition since both the Academy of Medicine and the church were against it. Count de Lauraguais, a staunch believer in progress, decided to try. "Gentlemen," he said one morning, in the garden, "there's a craze for everything English. If we present vaccination as coming from England, it will spread like wildfire." And so he organized a fashionable tea party, at which, between a sip of tea and a bite of scone, the famous Dr. Tronchin of Geneva vaccinated the entire company. Soon vaccination parties multiplied.

Aubriot was not practicing medicine. But he was flattered by Lauraguais' invitation to officiate at one of the count's vaccination parties. A mark of confidence from one of the most talked-about noblemen of the day won him instant notice. And a marquise for a mistress.

The Marquise Adelaide de Couranges was the prize of the party. She had long, well-proportioned legs and slender ankles, full breasts and, even at the age of thirty, a pretty face with an amiable expression. Added to these charms were sparkling diamond jewels and an obvious liking for men. She made it clear, in a tasteful manner, that she was available. The marquise was not only vaccinated by Aubriot, but also immediately attracted to him. During the night, she had an attack of vapors and the next day she sent her carriage to call for him. She received him, since she was ailing, in bed.

That evening, after feasting on the marquise, Philibert felt somewhat uneasy as he caressed Jeanne's golden hair spread over his chest. But man is quick to take up a new habit and he got used, very soon, to living between two mistresses. One was still reticent and blushing, the other sophisticated and audacious—a perfect combination. Soon, too, Philibert found an excuse for his lack of remorse. Mme. de Couranges had had many highly placed lovers and could ask favors of them. Choiseul received Aubriot because he was a protégé of the marquise and wrote her a gallant note in which he said that he would remember what he owed her "when there was a possibility of a post for her botanist."

A week later, Aubriot was named "supernumerary royal censor," a title that carried no duty other than collecting a four-hundred-franc salary. When he told this to Jeanne she clapped her hands with such joy that Philibert felt entirely justified in having gone to bed with the marquise.

"You know," he said, after she had calmed down, "this first mark of esteem gives me great hopes. In spite of the competition, I may obtain a post in the garden sooner than I dared imagine."

"No post will be free until somebody dies," Jeanne reminded him.

"While waiting for a death, I might be granted a right to the succession. But it's more likely that I shall be entrusted with a mission in the colonies. The duke seems to me anxious to investigate their riches."

"He talks about it, I know," said Jeanne. "But if you were sent to one of the colonies you'd have to go without me, wouldn't you?"

"I suppose . . . perhaps not," he said hesitantly.

"I suppose *so*," she said, biting her lips in order not to add, "*Only a wife has that privilege.*"

"Oh, well, an exploratory mission never lasts more than a couple of years. If an overseas mission is proposed to me I shouldn't have the courage to turn it down. I haven't a thousand years ahead of me in which to get to know the world. And so, you understand, I . . . "

"Have no fears for me," she interrupted. "I care as much about your career as you do. If you were to stay away too long I'd find a ship to take me to you."

He smiled with the amusement reserved for a child's idle boasting. But suddenly the air tasted better to his lungs and he drank it in deeply.

Jeanne didn't really think he'd go away. *We'll see. If Philibert goes, I'll go after him. As things stand I can always earn the necessary money.*

She looked proudly around the shop. This was the empty time of day, when she was the most relaxed. Her customers were at dinner and their servants on duty. Only a few housewives came looking for herbal remedies. When she came back at two o'clock from the garden, she sent Banban to eat and laugh with the scullery boys of Mme. de Boufflers, and Lucette to have a bite at the cook shop at the end of the street.

She was writing a letter to her friend Marie when someone knocked at the shop door and she ran downstairs.

"Damned if I thought I'd meet the owner of the shop that's the talk of the town!" said a resonant, mocking voice.

The figure she saw before her coincided so closely with her thoughts that Jeanne stared incredulously, wondering if it were not a product of her imagination. The speaker had time for more mockery.

"Does Monsieur de Richelieu give you so little pocket money that you have to sell spices?"

"You may think what you please, Chevalier Vincent," she said with great effort, "but not in my house. Kindly go away."

"Not before I've bought what I came for. They say you know everything about herbal teas."

"Very good, but be quick. What's your ailment? Stupidity or grossness?"

He burst into loud laughter, but his hard stare never left her face. She realized that he was seeing her for the first time in four years. In June, at the Opéra, she had been masked. In spite of her anger she was glad to be wearing turquoise blue and a bonnet from Mlle. Lacaille's.

She let him take it all in before answering icily, "I'm very busy, monsieur. I'd like to be done with you as soon as possible. What will you have?"

He came closer, with a wolfish grin. "The shopkeeper! How much? For one hour."

"Out! Out with you!" she exploded.

"La, la! What a temper! Take some lime-blossom tea. Or, better still, bathe in it. They say it's soothing to the nerves. I came to ask you for an hour of . . . consultation. I hear that you call on your customers who can afford to pay for your words of wisdom as well as your herbs. I'll be generous. You won't have far to go, since I'm lodged nearby."

Jeanne's eyes were darting flames, but she kept her self-control. "Your information is correct," she said. "But I don't go into the city before four o'clock. If you wish to make an appointment . . . "

He came closer. "Forgive me, mademoiselle, I was only joking. No one could want to pass after the Marshal de Richelieu. No one who cares for his health."

At first she failed to understand, but when she did her cheeks turned crimson and she struck him across the face. He took the blow without flinching and continued to stare at her. Then he seized her, brutally, by the wrists and spat out his disdain.

"How could you sell yourself to that rotten swine? Why didn't you faint with disgust when the old satyr pawed you? How can you not die of shame when you remember his putrid flesh in contact with yours?"

His words were too wounding. In spite of her urge to strike back she could only sob, "Do you really believe that of me, Vincent?"

He stared for a moment longer, then dropped her wrists and turned away. She had fallen into despair. All she wanted was to go off by herself and cry. Vincent was calm now, but perplexed. Could he have been wrong?

At last he said, "My dear, the world goes by appearances. And, since you weren't there for business, what *were* you doing at that supper party for masked sluts?"

She had to take hold of herself. Drawing herself up she threw back, "And you, monsieur, what were *you* doing there?"

"I was enjoying myself, that's all."

"I was amusing myself, also. In this country women are allowed to amuse themselves with their friends."

"I didn't know, Mademoiselle Beauchamps, that the Duke de Richelieu was one of your friends," Vincent retorted.

"Monsieur, you travel too much. You're turning into a barbarian. Parisians of all classes mingle nowadays, in order to please the Encyclopédistes."

There was a moment of silence. Vincent strode up and down with studied nonchalance, pretending to read the labels on bottles. Finally he remarked, "Well, if you want to act like a slut without actually being one, it's up to you, I suppose."

"Once more, monsieur, let me remind you that you're just off the ship. Democracy is the fashion. You don't have to be a great lady or one of Madame Gourdan's fillies in order to look like a slut if you want to."

This answer brought a smile to Vincent's lips.

"Time's going by," she said. "If there's nothing you want . . . "

"I want peace," he said. "Let's make peace, Jeanne."

"Peace has to be earned, Chevalier."

"I forgave you for breaking your word. You were only a child, and I was a fool," he said. "So we can make peace."

She continued to look at him, without speaking.

"I really mean it," he added. "Just state your terms. I've brought back from England a magnificent cargo of summer dresses and straw hats. They'll take your breath away. Come, take everything. Plunder and ruin me. Leave me without a rag to my name . . . "

"On your knees," she said abruptly.

"How's that? What did you say?"

"On your knees," she repeated.

"On my knees? On the floor?"

"Or on the ceiling, if you want to make it harder."

He laughed again. But this time heartily and without malice, made a deep bow, and lowered one knee to the floor.

"Forgive me," he said, "for having wanted to strangle you."

"Why didn't you do it?"

"Because then I'd have had to kill an old swine of a marshal, and I'm rather fond of him. Have I won my forgiveness?"

"I swore to myself that you'd wait for it a thousand years, on your knees."

She held out her hand, and he kissed it so passionately that she drew it back, trembling all over.

"May I get up?"

As he rose to his feet, he pulled out an embroidered handkerchief and flicked it over his knees, filling the air with the fragrance of orange blossoms.

"And now," he said, coming so close that she blushed like a Puteaux rose, "my offer of dresses and hats still holds. Come, to make your choice before Mademoiselle Sorel lays her hands on them."

"I won't say no. But I shall only look."

"As you like."

"Is everything at Madame de Boufflers'?"

"No, only a small part. The rest is at Vaugirard in my house."

"You have a house at Vaugirard?"

"Yes, a small one."

"Oh! What they call a 'folly'?"

"Just a small house with lilacs all around. That is, when they bloom, in May. Unfortunately, I'm never there to see them."

"Prince de Conti has a house at Vaugirard, too, doesn't he?"

"Yes, not far from mine."

"A high-class brothel, I'm told. The most luxurious . . ."

"I'm not his age, and I haven't his money. His tastes are not mine. But now, shall we go? Haven't you an assistant to keep the shop?"

"I've two," said Jeanne. "But that's not the question. You can't hope to take me off, just like that, to your house at Vaugirard."

"I find you quite charming, you know. Blue is becoming to you, not as becoming as green, but good enough. At Vaugirard you can change as often as you want, and there's a color for every taste."

"You . . . you . . . you're always . . ."

She did not finish the sentence, but leaned over, nervously, to straighten out a bag of herbal tea. Finally she said, "I'll look at what you have at Madame de Boufflers'. Why are you laughing?"

"Because you go to Richelieu's house and not to mine. You're afraid of the wrong man."

"I'm not afraid of anyone," she said dryly. "I haven't time to go to Vaugirard, that's all."

"Then come drink a cup of coffee with me at the Turk's on the Rue du Vertbois. He has the best mocha to be found here at the Temple."

"But I . . . well, yes, tomorrow. We'll go to the Turk's tomorrow. I'll arrange for Lucette to be on duty early."

"No," said Vincent firmly. "No, Jeannette, that won't do. Never again will I let you make an appointment to see me the next day. I don't make a fool of myself twice for the same reason. Call your Lucette. She can't be all that far off."

"Chevalier, don't change from a fool to an imbecile. I'm no longer fifteen years old."

"True; you're no longer fifteen . . ."

There was such melancholy and even tenderness in the unfinished sentence that Jeanne's eyes glinted with emotion. Vincent's glowing brown eyes looked penetratingly into hers. The silence between them was dense with avowals that words couldn't convey, with the awareness of time gone by, and time now miraculously regained. The drumbeat of their hearts was as intense as if they had never been separated. Jeanne took care not to break the enchantment as she murmured, almost inaudibly, "That night in the Tuileries, when I turned my ankle and you took my hand, had you recognized me?"

"I was afraid it was you."

"On account of my perfume?"

"My hunting instinct!" he said, returning to a joking tone. "A hunter always recognizes the prey that escaped him."

She lowered her eyes, seemed to reflect, then asked, with a smile, "Do you still want to take a cup of coffee at the Turk's?"

"My dear, that was a last resort. If you've the kindness to suggest something better . . ."

"I do feel . . . kind. Let's say, then, that tomorrow . . ."

"Tut, tut! No 'tomorrows'! You'll not trick me again."

"Very well, then, this evening. That counts as today, doesn't it? Half-past eight at the entrance to the Opéra House café. I'm to meet Madame Favart, and we're to sup afterward, but I'll excuse myself from that."

"I'll be there. Will you sup with me?"

"If I'm hungry."

His eyes were sparkling and she waited for his sparkling words.

"Does your adopted father, Dr. Aubriot, give you permission to run about the city at night in dubious company?"

"No, he recommends good company, and usually I obey him," she said with a smile.

They went on talking of sweet nothings in order to put off the moment of parting. Lucette came in carrying a basket and, out of the corner of her eye, recognized the handsome customer with whom her mistress was talking. She curtsied, went discreetly to the other end of the shop and began to pot some plants. Just as Vincent was about to leave, Jeanne held him back.

"Chevalier, I can't wait until tonight to ask you about my friends Emilie and Denis Gaillon. Are they safe and happy?"

"How should I know?"

"Chevalier, I can keep a secret."

"I, too, Jeanne."

"Please, I beg of you. I love them dearly."

"Then forget about them." And he added, in a low voice, "The police of the entire kingdom are still looking for the young Countess de la Pommeraie. Her father insists that any accomplices to the abduction have their heads cut off."

"Oh!" said Jeanne. "Then I withdraw my question. I'll continue to hope for the best."

"I believe Dame Emilie's strong willed and charming enough to persuade a sensitive sea captain to take two clandestine lovers aboard," said Vincent lightly. "So sleep easy."

"Thank you, Chevalier. Until this evening . . ."

"Until this evening. But, first, give me your bonnet."

"My bonnet?"

"So that you won't send it this evening in your place."

She shot him a luminous look, took off her bonnet, and handed it to him.

"A pledge," she said simply.

Lucette watched him pocket the bonnet and her eyes opened wide.

CHAPTER 26

eanne got rid of Mme. Favart as fast as she could. Then she went for a stroll in the shop-lined great hall. It was nearly half-past eight. But no one had left yet, except a pit guard, who had laid his weapon at his feet and was idly chatting. A gust of cold air swept down the hall. In order to protect herself from it, Jeanne covered her head with the hood of her long black velvet cape. Suddenly Vincent stood before her, smiling.

He was more splendid than ever in a tightly fitted silk-and-wool coat with gold stitching and buttons. His English-style white wig stood out slightly over his forehead and his hair hung down, gathered together by a black ribbon, over the back of his neck. Jeanne ran her hand caressingly over the cream-colored satin of her favorite gown.

The elegance of her dress blended perfectly with that of Vincent's, and her hair, like his, was done in the English style, with loose curls massed at the back of her head.

They went down into the Tuileries gardens. *I love him.* She was giving in completely this time to her feelings.

"What now, my dear?" asked Vincent.

"Have you a carriage?" Jeanne inquired.

Before he had time to answer, a livery carriage drew up before them. A handsome young footman opened the door, giving Jeanne a broad smile. It was Mario, the corsair's faithful valet, who had waited for her in vain one long-ago April morning.

"I feel as if I am being abducted after a delay of four years," she murmured.

"That's it exactly," retorted Vincent.

"But this time it's just a lark . . . and I can laugh about it."

"There's surely no reason to cry."

I'm quite mad. I really shouldn't trust him. She sat down in the carriage, gathering her silk skirt under her.

"So, what would you like to do now?" Vincent repeated.

"Is it up to me to say?"

"I thought that was how you wanted it. Do you prefer to have me take charge?"

"No, no," she said emphatically. "Shall we have a Bavarian cream at La Régence?"

"At this hour we'd run into a line of ladies ordering from their carriages on their way home from the theater."

"But, Chevalier, that's exactly what I want. I want to fall into line with the ladies. I've never had my favorite cream brought to my carriage."

"Very good!" he said, laughing. "I'm lucky, because you're still fifteen years old."

Only half a dozen carriages were pulled up in front of La Régence. Two boys shuttled back and forth, carrying silver trays loaded with refreshments. Jeanne savored, very slowly, her cream flavored with rum from the islands.

"And now?" asked Vincent when she had finished.

"Weren't you to take me to supper?"

"What do you say to L'Escharpe?"

Jeanne frowned. "Are you proposing one of the private dining rooms?"

"Since you're in such dubious company, that would be the better part of discretion."

"I didn't spend a fortune having my hair done by Tintin to hide my head in a private room. Let's go with the crowd to the Rue des Poulies."

* * * *

For some months it had been the fashion to go to Boulanger's on the Rue des Poulies, whose proprietor had just acquired the new title of restaurateur. Tavern keepers had always had the right to serve wine with a "plate-meal." That is, at a table, accompanied by a simple dish. Boulanger had launched a new fashion. He invented and served "restoring" soups, called "restaurants," recommended by doctors for delicate stomachs. He won immediate success. A sharp businessman who knew his Paris, he underlined the country origin and nutritive value of his soups. He served them on marble-top tables, without a tablecloth, and at an exorbitant price. To eat in rustic style, in unembellished surroundings, was the height of chic. Dukes and lords came back over and over again. So did readers of Jean-Jacques Rousseau, dieting patients of Dr. Tronchin, and women of a certain class, available for supper-and-bed, at six hundred francs an evening.

The restaurateur, decked out like a gentleman, with a curled and powdered wig, a sword knocking against the calf of his right leg, and a tricorne hat under his arm, was walking up and down in front of his tavern. He greeted newcomers as if they were princes, with a calculated mixture of obsequiousness and jovial familiarity.

He welcomed Jeanne and Vincent when they stepped out of their carriage and led them to the door. Once inside, they were taken in tow by the beautiful Mme. Boulanger, whose charm was of great consideration to her husband's success. She settled them at a small table and went back to her cashbox throne.

At Boulanger's there was no such thing as an intimate supper. The proprietor aimed at a democratic promiscuity among his guests. The tables were all close together. Fashion demanded sharing your soup with your neighbor. Every soup had its history, from the watercress and vermicelli, invented by Dr. Pomme, to the consommé Napoli whose recipe was a gift from the Marquis Caracciolo.

Jeanne and Vincent found themselves between the table of Count de Guibert and Abbé Morellet and that of a famous habitué, Marmontel. He sat with Diderot and d'Alembert. Men of letters, no matter how slender their means, could enjoy Boulanger's. Even if they ordered nothing more than soup and a boiled egg they could pass for dieters rather than paupers.

D'Alembert's wandering eyes ran over Jeanne and Vincent with frank curiosity. Marmontel, too, stared shamelessly at the handsome couple. When there was cuckoldry in the air, Marmontel's long nose quivered and stretched out like an elephant's trunk, all the better to suck in the latest bedroom gossip. Diderot cast more discreet glances. All three spoke at once with advice to the newcomers about what to choose on the menu. They agreed upon "The Genuine Divine Restaurant the Way Grandmother Used to Make It." It had chopped white chicken meat cooked in veal broth, with hulled barley, rose petals, and raisins from Damascus.

"And the 'Restaurant à la Clarion,' how's that?" asked Jeanne.

The actress's name aroused general laughter.

"What do you expect?" said Vincent. "With a name like that it must be all skin and bones."

This witticism set off a string of anecdotes about the Comédie Française. Jeanne listened distractedly, looking at the room and its purposefully crude decoration. At a time when other hotel and café proprietors were ruining themselves with Saint-Gobain mirrors, crystal chandeliers, paintings, and fine china, Boulanger had gone back to whitewashed walls, straw-seated chairs, white earthenware plates, and tin goblets.

Suddenly, the hum of voices abated and there was a moment of silent anticipation. The Marquis d'Egreville had come in, bringing with him a young thing with a beguiling face and dress.

"Aha!" murmured Count de Guibert. "Egreville has been keeping something from us. Where do you suppose he got this exquisite child?"

"From Gourdan's, if you must know," said Marmontel. "But she was of too good stuff to stay there. Verceuil, that's her name. At sixteen she was budding and, two years later, I see that she's bloomed. The marquis has taken her on and installed her in a little house in Montmartre. He's waiting only to marry off his son before he produces her in public."

"It sounds as if you discovered her before he did," said Guibert ironically.

"In my capacity of fortune-teller, that's all," said Marmontel. "I've a pretty good nose for the success of a girl's career."

Jeanne resented the way in which, with these last words, he rested his insinuating gaze on her. *What do I care what people think? Let them think what they like. It's all the same to me. And there may be a grain of truth in it. Tonight I couldn't vouch for my own morality.*

"Well, have you chosen?" Vincent asked her.

"I'll take whatever you choose for me."

"You don't seem to be hungry," murmured Vincent a little later.

"I'm tired," she said. "Do you want to stay longer?"

"This evening I want only to obey your wishes. Wasn't that agreed between us?" He took her arm and they rose to leave.

* * * *

"And what directions should I give the driver?" Vincent asked, when they were seated in the carriage.

"We're going dancing."

"Dancing?" exclaimed Vincent. "Where is there dancing tonight?"

"At Ramponeau's," said Jeanne, laughing. "Isn't this the first Saturday of spring?"

"Hurrah!" cried out Mario. "Hurrah for mademoiselle! Let's gallop to Ramponeau's!"

After they were under way Vincent said to Jeanne, "The air's still sharp. Won't you be cold up at La Courtille?"

"I'm never cold when I can do as I please. And I've been dying to go to La Courtille. This will be the first time."

"This first night of spring is the 'first' for a number of other things," teased Vincent. "The first time you've ordered a Bavarian cream from a carriage, your first supper on the Rue des Poulies, your first quadrille at La Courtille. . . . Tell me, love, have you ever before deceived your adopted father?"

"Oh!" exclaimed Jeanne furiously, striking him with her fan. "Must you make fun of everything? Turn back, Chevalier. Take me home. I simply can't bear your sarcasm, on this night. Let's turn around, I beg of you, before you ruin everything."

Vincent responded to the genuine emotion in her voice.

"Forgive me again, Jeannette!" he said, taking her hand. "I want you to stay as happy as you were before. I'm a fool. Shall I get down on my knees?"

"Oh, no," she said, smiling. "Your breeches are so fine."

The village street was still muddy from a rainstorm the previous day. Vincent lifted Jeanne down from the carriage in his arms and deposited her in front of the tavern. Ramponeau came to welcome them, his round face beaming.

"Monsieur," he said in his jolly voice, "I don't know in what sea you caught this treasure. But a treasure she is. I must remind you that treasures often attract thieves. And I allow no swords to be drawn. But with your fists you may defend her as much as you are able."

"Thank you, my friend. I haven't forgotten the customs of your establishment. Give us a table in the quietest corner, send us a bottle of wine, and tell your fiddler not to afflict our ears. Mademoiselle wants to dance."

"And does mademoiselle want a bouquet?" said a little girl carrying a basket full of violets. "And a gingerbread manikin with her name on him?"

"The name is Jeanne," said Vincent, giving the vendor a franc.

"And what shall I write on monsieur's gingerbread pig?"

"Vincent," said Jeanne, blushing.

"You see, mademoiselle," the vendor explained, "it's against the law to sell gingerbread in these shapes. You can sell gingerbread hearts, but pigs and manikins will land you in jail. They're afraid someone will name the big pigs of Versailles. But at Ramponeau's, everything that is forbidden elsewhere is permitted here. The best things of life *are* forbidden, aren't they?" And she winked at Vincent.

"What makes you think he's my lover and not my husband?" Jeanne asked boldly.

"Well, unfortunately, husbands are never so handsome. And they never buy gingerbread."

Vincent took a firm hold of Jeanne's hand and steered her through the crowd.

She was justifiably afraid. She lived in the fine section of the city. And her shop at the edge of the Temple was frequented by people of quality. Here she was entering the rough, chaotic world outside the city gates.

People came to Ramponeau's from all over Paris, to guzzle meat and drink, pinch the girls, and dance the jig to the sound of a cheap fiddle. The pleasures of Le Tambour Royal were frankly gross: smelly sausages, meat-stuffed pastries, pots of tripe and of beef stew. Drinkers drank pint after pint of a sour, bluish wine, which got them drunk for a pittance. Dancers jumped, glided, and somersaulted, bellowing the songs loudly, drowning out the screeching violin. Lovers slipped their hands between girls' breasts or legs.

The tavern was crowded with simple people seeking to shake off the gloom of winter, young toughs ready for a fight, curious foreigners, and a few gentlemen of vulgar tastes.

"Well, Jeannette, here you are at Ramponeau's, like a slumming princess," said Vincent. "Does it live up to your expectations?"

"I didn't dream it was so picturesque."

The enormous room, with its mud floor, was a cross between a barn and a cellar. The high windows had lead-framed bottle butts for panes, and the whitewashed walls were decorated with paintings, good and bad, by artist patrons. The rough wooden tables and chairs were squeezed along the walls, allowing space in the middle for dancing. A patron of Ramponeau's had to accept crowding. But the proprietor knew who was who and separated the wheat from the chaff when it was opportune to do so. He placed Jeanne and Vincent in a corner. He, himself, brought them their first jug of wine and two glasses.

"Here, monsieur, is wine to drink to mademoiselle's beauty. But it would take a whole barrel to celebrate her perfections. Meanwhile, aren't you going to dance? I've just told the fiddler to play a quadrille."

"Come," said Vincent, holding out his hand to Jeanne.

When they drew near to each other, he inhaled deeply as if she were a flower, his nostrils wide open, his eyes closed, and his lips seeking her hair.

"Chevalier, you still haven't told me whether you care for my looks the way you did before," she said coaxingly. "Does that mean the answer's no?"

He stood back to scrutinize her. She was ravishing in her close-fitting satin gown, with a fluid skirt, tight sleeves, and a daring low-cut neck, whose indecency was emphasized by a spiderweb muslin fichu. The dramatic English style was enhanced by the creamy color, laced with rose, which harmonized with her slightly darker curls, clear skin, and the tawny eyes that Vincent had never forgotten. As beautiful as when she was fifteen? Far *more* beautiful. First, because she really *was*. Second, because he had thought of her so long and so longingly that his dreams had endowed her with even more. She was more tempting than before. The softer lines of her ripened body and the shining, liquid sensuality in the depth of her eyes filled him with jealousy and desire.

"God help us, Chevalier. How long must you examine me before pronouncing a decision? You make me tremble! Have I so lost my looks that embarrassment makes you dumb?"

"Have no fear! You're a thousand times more dangerous now than then."

" 'Dangerous'? Is that a compliment?"

"Yes, and you know it. Every beautiful woman wants to ensnare men. That's what makes her dangerous."

"Let's sit down again," said Jeanne coquettishly. "I want to taste the wine of La Courtille."

"You'll not like it, I can tell you."

She took a sip of the bluish liquid and made a face. "Good God! How can they drink it?"

"Because it costs only three and a half sous a pint."

"That's not enough of a reason."

"Ah, yes, Jeanne. When you're of the people, from time to time you have to forget it. The people cherish the name of Ramponeau above that of Voltaire, because he's a far more practical philosopher. Voltaire pens hopes for the benefit of those who can't read. Ramponeau sells them forgetfulness at a price they can pay. And the king needs wine most of all."

"The king?"

"Exactly! Saturday nights and Sundays his little people of Paris come here to drown the woes of the week gone by. When Monday comes they're more easily ruled. Did you know that Choiseul comes often to La Courtille? He finds it reassuring. Back in his offices he can dismiss the warnings of those who say that unless he taxes the rich and helps the poor there'll be riots and revolution. Here he sees people enjoying themselves—singing, dancing, laughing, and drinking. He goes away persuaded that the 'philanthropists' are lying, simply in order to advance their own ideas."

Jeanne looked at the joyful tumult around her. "Do these people really look angry to you? Don't they seem content with their lot?"

"They find it simpler to enjoy themselves than to rebel in the hope of something better. They prefer peace and quiet to struggling with ideas. But if they're pushed too far a tavern will no longer console them. Only yesterday, on the Place Louis XIV, the king's head was crowned with a dustbin."

Jeanne listened attentively. Never before had he spoken to her of anything but love and frivolities.

"How does it happen, Chevalier, that so elegant a man as yourself sees into the minds of the poor?"

He gave a faraway smile. "I spend my life with the poor, Jeanne. A sailor possesses nothing but what fits into his cap. What does he do when he's in port? He spends his pay on wine and women. Yes, sailors are poor men par excellence. Whatever money they put aside goes for . . . oblivion. The poor that we see around us here spend their money at secondhand clothes and wig dealers to cut a good figure on the dance floor. Beside my sailors they're millionaires."

"I'll wager that your sailors are the best off of any in the kingdom!"

"Let's say that I give them as much money to burn as I can afford. But that doesn't prevent them from remaining beggars. Poverty is a vice that won't let you go. And a share of the captain's booty is no salvation."

"You really love your men, don't you?"

"My men? I try to be just. They're not easy to love. And they're not angels, I can tell you."

"But they love you, don't they?"

"I don't know. I'm the captain. There's no statue of me on deck for them to crown with a laurel wreath or a dustbin in the dead of the night. But what the devil are you getting me into on this beautiful spring evening? Do you really want to hear my ship captain's philosophy? Let's talk about my philosophy of love. On that score I've a lot more to say."

Jeanne laid her hand on his sleeve. "I've dreamed that you'd talk to me just this way, saying what you mean, as if I were not a little girl but a woman."

He looked at her long fingers, fastened caressingly on his arm, as eloquent as a declaration of love. Covering them with his tanned hand he said, smilingly, "You've chosen the wrong place for a heart-to-heart talk."

"Then let's go."

"So soon? Tell me, why the devil did you decide against running away with me before? It seems like your sort of adventure. And if, now, we were to go . . ."

He was interrupted by the appearance of a laughing gypsy, who picked up the bunch of violets lying on the table and roughly thrust it down Jeanne's bosom.

"Princess," she said, "you don't know the rules. A bouquet of flowers is the mark of a lover. It has to be worn next to the heart."

Vincent seized the gypsy's wrist and twisted it. She cried out and opened her fist, releasing Jeanne's expensive, embroidered handkerchief.

"Oh!" Jeanne exclaimed in astonishment. "This is a trick I didn't know."

The gypsy tried vainly to free her wrists from Vincent's grasp, shrilly imploring, "Pity, monseigneur, have pity on me! You've got back the handkerchief. Don't call the officer. Have pity, and God will bless you."

"I never call a police officer to settle my affairs. Tonight is quite special, and I'll pass on my good fortune to you."

And he tossed her a gold louis, which she caught in the air.

"God will bless you," she said gravely. "But, meanwhile, I can give you something for your money."

She seized his hand, kissed and held it, in a way that gave Jeanne a sudden stab of jealousy. The girl was young and pretty, with blazing black eyes and flashing white teeth.

"Are you the new fortune-teller?" Vincent asked her. "The one that was here before was as wrinkled as a baked apple, but she told convincing lies."

"That was my grandmother. She's dead now, but she left me her ability to see into the future."

Jeanne's eyebrows were raised in surprise. "Chevalier, do you really believe these Egyptian witches?"

"Princess, you don't know your man," answered the gypsy. "Only landlubbers are unbelievers. Sailors have faith in me."

"The sea fosters superstition," said Vincent. "But, let me warn you, woman of Egypt, you musn't tell me anything that isn't pleasant to hear."

"You smell of the sea," the gypsy began. "There are drops of salt spray on your skin, and before they dry you'll be off again."

"You're earning your money too easily," said Vincent, laughing. "Let's start with the present. Tell me what you see for tomorrow . . . for tonight."

"No, that I can't do."

"Why not? Are you farsighted, like old people? If you can't find anything good for tomorrow, look at the day after."

"You've a long blue road to travel before you find happiness," said the gypsy. "It's a flat land, with low houses. . . . The soil is black and the sky is blue, and filled with birds of all colors. I see rivers, too, rivers overflowing with fish. And horses. A multitude of horses . . . and cows . . . yes, and people, as well, white and black. The men are wearing great white hats, so large that they seem to have wings, and the women have white cloths on their heads. The blacks are dancing, very fast, and singing. They wear long striped shirts whose tails flap around their bodies. And then . . . Wait a minute," she said, dropping Vincent's hand. "I'm tired. Wait, and don't speak."

Jeanne shot Vincent a questioning look, but he only raised a finger to his lips. The girl picked up his hand, held it to her breast, closed her eyes, and resumed her monologue.

"I see a garden. There are trees so heavy with fruit that the branches are breaking. . . . Now I see a river, a broad river, bordered by flowering plants. . . . That, monseigneur, is where happiness awaits you. You take it in your arms and carry it off to sea. But quickly! There are flashing fires around you, but you're not burning. After that . . . it's too far. I see only the blue of the sea."

She brought her gaze back from a distance to rest on Vincent, who asked, "What sort of happiness awaits me in the garden of Montevideo?"

"You could recognize the place, then? That's more than I do."

"I think so. But you haven't answered my question."

"I shan't answer," she said, shaking her head. "I don't want to spoil your surprise. When you enjoy a pleasure in advance, then the real thing is disappointing. It's enough to know that happiness is waiting for you in a place with a familiar name."

"Very well," Vincent sighed. "We can't force words out of divinely inspired seers. But you must take payment proportionate to the joy you've given me."

He tossed her a purse and she weighed it in her hand.

"I'm taking the whole thing," she exclaimed. "In Montevideo you'll be sorry for anything you held back."

And she ran off, laughing, with the purse in her hand.

"Chevalier, you're quite mad," said Jeanne. "Tell me, do you believe her?"

"No, I can't."

"Why not?"

"The happiness I'm waiting for can't be at Montevideo. Unless you've a twin sister there!"

Jeanne blushed, and answered with a question. "If you don't believe her, why did you listen so carefully and give her so much money?"

"I was actually paying for the fortune her grandmother told four years ago. She told me that I'd find a girl with long blond hair in a country château, that she'd escape me, but later return."

"Chevalier, you're lying," said Jeanne indulgently. "But I love the way you do it."

Again she laid her hand lovingly on Vincent's silk sleeve. He lifted her arm and ran his closed lips over it. She succumbed completely to the disconcerting pleasure of his caresses, which traveled from her skin to deep down within her. She forgot all about the surrounding crowd and its noise until a drunken fellow, hoisted by his companions onto a nearby table, began to shout the refrain of "La Mére Gaudichon," which the others took up in chorus. And, a moment later, the greasy smell of a string of sausages assailed her nostrils. "I think I've had enough of the atmosphere of La Courtille. Didn't you suggest showing me the latest English fashions, those you keep at your country place, at Vaugirard?"

* * * *

Vaugirard was at the opposite end of Paris. A long journey, and in the dead of night. Before leaving, Vincent made sure that his pistols, carried by Mario, were loaded.

With four fresh horses it took them no more than an hour to gallop through the sleeping city. Jeanne showered Vincent with questions about London and the Far East, in order to fill silences which, otherwise, might have been filled with kisses.

Ever since they had left Le Tambour Royal she was feverishly excited, breaking into a flood of incomplete sentences, which only augmented her fever. The idea that she was galloping of her own free will into the wolf's mouth gave her a pain at the pit of her stomach, which she wouldn't have exchanged, at any price, for the peace and quiet of an ordinary day. At moments, in order to heighten the feeling of adventure, she imagined brigands emerging from the night, their pistols directed against her. Her fear lasted until she leaned her cheek against the shoulder of the corsair, her savior and hero, her invincible knight. . . .

Jeanne's behavior left Vincent perplexed. While he answered her nervous questions he tried to fathom what she expected from him and what he hoped from her. Just now, when she had asked to be taken to Vaugirard, her confidence had aroused gentle and chaste feelings. Then he fell prey, again, to suspicion. *Surely she was no longer such a child as to try on dresses, late at night, in a man's country house, with no thought of what might follow. And how did she manage to dedicate her nights to passing whims? Last June the Opéra ball and supper with Richelieu, now an evening spent running from one public place to another without fear of recognition? What was the honorable Dr. Aubriot doing? Why was he so patient? What did he say when his child-mistress-secretary came home at three or even six o'clock in the morning?*

Vincent had learned from Pauline de Vaux-Jailloux all that had happened to Jeanne since she had broken the famous appointment of four years before. His resentment of her refusal had been so deep that he would never have tried to see her again had she not crossed his path in Richelieu's box at the Opéra. To find her there, dancing to the old rake's tune, and then at his house for supper, along with the conniving Marquise de Mauconseil, a third-rate singer, and two masked prostitutes, had wounded him so deeply that he couldn't help insulting her. In the following days he had tried in vain to wipe this degrading image of her from his mind. To imagine her with Aubriot caused him no such pain. After this, a secret mission for the king had detained him across the Channel and dimmed his anger. But when he came back to discover Jeanne as La Belle Tisanière of the Temple, his wound reopened and he wanted to crush her in his two hands in order to take away her power to enrage him. Then she had displayed teary eyes, a choked voice, trembling hands, blushing cheeks, and a sweet smile. She had made denials and something like a promise, and he had believed her again. At the age of fifteen she hadn't been ready, now she was. In her face he had read *I love you.*

Now, suddenly, he was once more skeptical, fearful of having been tricked by a woman so artful that she could pass for an entrancing silly girl, while making fools of three men: Aubriot, Richelieu, and Vincent; perhaps others as well.

"This street," she said, interrupting his train of thought, "is it the main artery of your village?"

Vincent, whose mind had been elsewhere, looked out the window. "Yes," he said, "we're home."

A crescent moon, peering out from the clouds, and the lanterns of the coach relay lit up the length of the Grand-Rue de Vaugirard. The carriage made a right-angle turn, coming to a halt before a garden gate. Vincent's house was the last one on a short country alley, at the edge of a vineyard and under a hill covered with windmills. Across the way were the hunting preserves of the king and the Prince de Conti.

"Oh, oh, oh! How beautiful!" Jeanne exclaimed, clapping her hands like a child in a toy shop when they entered.

The drawing room was no larger than an outsize boudoir, but its decoration was both carefully studied and spontaneously gay. The walls were covered in ribbed, buttercup-yellow silk with embroidered bouquets of flowers in old silver and framed in pearl-gray woodwork. The small armchairs were upholstered in the same material as that of the walls, and so was a graceful, cozy loveseat.

"So you like my little place, do you?" asked Vincent.

"Do I like it? I do, I do!" she sang out, letting her cloak fall onto the floor. "Oh! And the rug!"

She kicked off her gold satin slippers and dug her feet into the deep pile of the flowered, yellow Aubusson rug. How good it felt! It seemed a century since she had walked in stockinged feet on the thick wool rug in the room of her beloved baroness at Charmont. The sudden memory of those happy days very nearly made her cry. She closed her eyes, dreamily, and when she opened them she saw that Vincent was looking at her in a strange and distant manner.

"Chevalier, why are you suddenly so cold?"

"Am I cold?"

"So it seems to me."

"You made me promise to spend the evening as you wanted. I'm only obedient to your desires."

She moved closer to him, then paused and said provocatively, "Chevalier, you're *too* obedient."

Vincent was more and more perplexed. He kept his distance in a way that dissatisfied her. Suddenly Mario appeared at the door, carrying a bundle of kindling wood which he used to quickly build a fire. The flames leaped upward, roaring as if in a forge.

"Mademoiselle, in five minutes you'll feel as if it's midsummer," Mario said gaily. "I'm going to heat the upstairs as well."

Vincent greeted this blunder with an angry look, but Jeanne exclaimed playfully, "Yes, of course I want to see the upstairs. Let's go have a look. I'm dying of curiosity."

She would have run up the hall stairway had not Vincent grasped her arm. He was more than ever puzzled. Was she a late-blooming young girl or a wily courtesan, stupid or shameless, slightly mad or an outright hussy?

"You haven't seen all the ground floor. The dining room, for instance . . ."

"Speaking of dining," put in Mario, "our good housekeeper will bring you a pot of pâté de foie gras, goat cheese, and a bottle of old Bordeaux."

But when Jeanne saw the housekeeper, clad in black, she blushed like a convent girl caught in a musketeer's bed by the mother superior. Instinctively, she drew closer to Vincent and stood there, silent, with her cheeks flaming.

"Since you have company, monsieur, I'll bring you some biscuits and a bottle of champagne."

"Champagne, that's a good idea," said Vincent. "Jeanne, will you have some?"

"Yes, please," she answered weakly.

Her self-assurance seemed to disappear, leaving her with a lump in her throat and a slight tremble. The housekeeper went off to bed, and Mario was about to follow. He picked up Jeanne's slippers and cloak from the floor and laid them on an armchair, smiling at Vincent as if to say, "Some of her defenses are already down." He attended to the fire and finally went out of the room, closing the door behind him.

"What next?" Vincent asked Jeanne.

"Well . . . weren't you going to show me some English fashions? That was my reason for coming."

"If you're quite sure . . ."

"Of course."

"Good. They're upstairs. I'll bring an armful of dresses to my room, since Mario has lit the fire there. Unfortunately, I've no lady's maid to help you try them on, but if you'll accept my services . . . I'm quite good at it, you know." He looked her in the eyes before adding, "Well, will you come?"

Jeanne bit her lip and did not move. Finally she said, "Chevalier, let's stay down here. It's so very agreeable, and it doesn't seem quite proper to try on dresses in your bedroom."

He gave a long, mocking laugh. " 'Proper'?" he queried ironically.

"You have a way of coming out with the most inappropriate words. You were dying to see my room. Let's go have a look at it."

"No, absolutely not. This hour of the night is no time for trying on dresses."

"Well, I won't quibble over such a common-sense statement. It's too late or too early for dressing. But for *undressing*, the time is exactly right."

In a deceptively calm manner, he slipped behind her, deftly pulled off her scarf and started to unhook her bodice.

She wheeled angrily around, snatched the scarf, and said firmly, "After cold courtesy, vulgar roughness! Is this the way a corsair treats a guest?"

"You, my dear, are no easy guest," he sighed nonchalantly. "Obedience isn't to your taste. And disobedience shocks you. If you don't want me to yawn with boredom until we leave in pursuit of some other whim, tell me frankly what you expected from the visit to my house? I'm still at your orders, as I promised."

Her only response was to look at him like a lost doe. He grasped her two hands and looked deeply into her eyes.

"Tell me, Jeanne, why did you come here and put yourself at my mercy?"

"Well, I thought that . . . it was so noisy at Ramponeau's, not nearly such fun as I'd expected. We could barely hear each other. . . . So where could we go? It was too early to say goodbye. I hoped we could talk, like good friends, in some quiet and pleasant place. And perhaps I wanted to see your house. I love the countryside in the spring, outside the city gates, where there are fields, vineyards, mills, meadows filled with daisies, woodlands with rabbits and birds. . . . It's quite simple, really. . . . We had to stay together a little longer, just the two of us . . . because we have things to talk about, don't we?"

She stammered on, without looking at him, ever more feverishly, pacing between the loveseat and the fireplace and twisting her fichu in her hands. Vincent looked on in silence. Never had he seen or even imagined her this way, talkative, excitable, and out of control, like a ship whose masts have been swept away. He didn't try to follow her fragmentary sentences, but their rapid and chaotic flow told him what he wanted to know. He awaited the moment when she would break down in a flood of tears and he would take her into his arms to console her.

The fire saved Jeanne's nerves from giving way. Suddenly a charred log fell out of the fireplace, showering sparks. Some of them struck Vincent and he tore off his coat and threw it on a chair before pushing the log back into the fireplace. Then he knelt down, cursing, and piled some fresh logs on the fire.

Jeanne's monologue was cut short. She gazed, with amazement, at Vincent's arms. He was wearing an unusual sleeveless waistcoat and his arm muscles stood out through the sleeves of his fine cotton shirt. Jeanne's mouth was dry with the desire to touch his skin. She moved toward him like a sleepwalker. He wheeled about on one knee and raised his face. She laid her hands on his wig.

"You took my fichu," she said, trembling and tender, "let me take this in exchange. I'll treat it carefully."

"Here you are!" he said, pulling off the wig and throwing it across the room.

She plunged her hands into the shiny black curls, lifted, stroked and separated them, then rolled them around her fingers, while a flow of words poured from her lips.

"My curly-haired love . . . my silky lamb . . . my angel . . . my knight with the locks of a Greek shepherd . . ."

Slowly he rose to his feet and took her into his arms, biting off the words as they came out of her mouth before opening her lips with his. Their kiss ended only with exhaustion, and they stood, welded together.

"Come!" Vincent said at last.

Jeanne perceived a whirl of green, red, and gold, sinking into a soft linen sheet, fragrant with orange blossoms, whose lacy edge tickled her shoulders and saw, leaning over her, the smiling face of Vincent.

"Give me back my hands."

She realized that she was still holding his hands and held them even tighter.

"Wait," she said in a low voice. "You haven't said you love me."

"I love you!"

"Again!"

"I love you! I love you! I love you! I love you! And if you want to make sure of it before the end of the first night of spring, let go of my hands. Dawn is not far away."

"No, the sun will never rise again!" she said vehemently, releasing his hands in order to throw her arms around his neck and press him passionately to her. "This night must never end, never! Love me, my chevalier, so hard that the world comes to a stop. Love me for a hundred years of nights. Love me to death, so that I shan't have to face tomorrow!"

He lowered her onto the pillows and gazed at her head with its frame of silken hair. She turned from one cheek to the other, as if to escape from desires beyond her control.

"Love me to death before tomorrow," she repeated, beseechingly.

Tenderly he called her name. "Jeanne! Look at me, Jeanne. Tell me, are you afraid that tomorrow Aubriot will want to fight a duel?"

"Fight a duel?"

She raised herself onto her elbows, with a bewildered expression. "You mean fight a duel with you? About me?"

"Well," said Vincent, "in Dombes I never heard that Dr. Aubriot was an easygoing man, much less a coward. But since he's also said to be intelligent, perhaps we can strike an agreement elsewhere than on the dueling ground. After all, he robbed you from me; I'm only taking back my own."

Jeanne looked at him wide-eyed, with a mixture of astonishment and incredulity. "But, Chevalier, you're not going to tell him? . . . Monsieur Aubriot mustn't know, not ever!"

Vincent could not believe his ears. He rose up with clenched fists and said harshly, "So you, my dear, meant to go from my arms to his?"

"I . . . I meant nothing at all, I swear it; I wasn't even thinking. I was happy, that's all. What is it? Why have you pulled away as if you no longer loved me? You do love me, don't you? Come back, my love; take me into your arms, I'm cold. Come, Vincent, my love!"

There were frozen tears in her eyes, but a smile on her lips. Vincent was famous among his men for his self-control, but it took more of that than usual to stop him from throwing himself upon her and venting his frustrated desire. Instead, he took a chair, sat down beside the bed, caught the hands that were feverishly groping for him and said firmly, "Calm yourself, Jeanne! I insist that you listen to me. I love you, but I'll never be your plaything."

"But I love you, too, Vincent. I'll always love you!"

"Even in Aubriot's bed, no doubt," he said, raising his voice above hers. "It's hard for me to believe, but you've suggested it yourself. I refuse to share you. I won't do it. If I take you I keep you, and I carry you away. I don't want to be loved in secrecy and shame. I demand that you make a choice, now or never. Either I take you and you follow me, or else you go back to Aubriot."

She twisted her hands in his. "Why, Vincent? How can you be so cruel? What have I done to deserve it? You see how much I love you. Why do you demand that I hate Philibert? That I can't do. And why should you want it?"

"I don't ask you to hate him, I ask you to leave him. One day, without hating me, you left me for him, do you remember? I took that harder than I knew. And, more recently, you've made me doubt you, to the point that, this very evening, I didn't quite know what to think. But I'll stick to the corsair pledge of love: 'Whoever you are, I take you. I ask no questions about your past, just pledge me your future.' Do you remember those words?"

"Yes."

"When I said them to you, in a woodland hunting lodge, you were touched, but the next day you played me false."

"I was a very young girl."

"Well, now that you're a woman, will you give yourself to me, now and forever?"

She lowered her head reflectively, then said quietly, "May I have a glass of water?"

When he brought it he found her up and sitting on a chair.

"Chevalier, give me a turn to speak. Come closer . . . "

He took a stool and sat at her feet.

"I love you as best I can. At this moment I'm more in love than any woman in the kingdom. I found out that I love you too late. I'm sorry, but it's not my fault. Now that I see things more clearly, I realize that I fell in love with you at first sight. But I was blind. My childhood passion for Aubriot was in the way. I must tell you that it still endures, that it will never die. It's engraved on my flesh and has grown with me. It's infinitely sweet and I'm not in the least ashamed of it. If I had to tear it away I'd be permanently mutilated."

Vincent made an attempt to speak, but she held a finger to his lips and went on, more rapidly.

"But my love for Aubriot takes nothing from you, and vice versa. I love him and I love you. You can't hold it against me that we have only one verb to express two such different feelings. You can't be so cruel as to ask that I stop loving someone I've loved since my childhood just because I've discovered that I love you more than life itself and want to belong to you more than I've ever wanted anything."

He leaped angrily to his feet, strode up and down the room, then approached her and pulled her to a vertical position, digging his nails into her arm.

"Are you aware of what you're saying? Forget those schoolgirl ideas of heart and soul and such nonsense and think of your body!"

He seized and tugged at her silk bodice.

"No!" she cried out as the bodice gave way, revealing the chemise underneath, whose top he tore off with equal ease.

"I'll take the left one," he said, closing his hand around one breast, "and leave the right to Aubriot. Only, my dear, not all your charms come in pairs, and when it comes to the one and only I refuse to share it. Get that into your stubborn head. I'll never share! Oh, I forgot to tell you what follows the pledge of fidelity made by the corsair's bride. The husband passes his pistol below her nose and says, 'Don't you forget it!' "

Jeanne choked back her sobs as she tried to put her bodice back in place. Vincent went away and came back with a magnificent cashmere shawl, which he threw around her shoulders. He couldn't resist taking her into his arms.

"Don't worry about your dress. I'll replace it with half a dozen."

"The dress doesn't matter. I'm crying because you're so hard . . . because you refuse to understand."

"Beloved, I've understood for some time," he said, stroking her hair. "I understand, but I don't accept. Perhaps I didn't put it clearly. I don't want to prevent you from loving your adopted father, the teacher you've revered since you were ten years old. I just want to stop you from going to bed with him. Many little girls are tempted to marry their fathers, but there comes a time when childish games must have an end. You can't go on sleeping with Papa after you've taken a lover."

"You say the most abominable things!" she exclaimed, with a look of horror.

"I mince no words about things I understand better than you. Besides, you must make a choice between land and sea. Aubriot and I live in two different worlds. I'm leaving in six days. Jeanne, will you go with me?"

"Six days? . . . But you'll be back soon, won't you?"

"If you don't go with me I'll never come back for you, never!"

"Chevalier, don't throw me into despair. I want to be yours, I swear it. But without hurting Aubriot. I want to break the news to him gently. And how can I do that in so few days?"

"Good God! Won't Aubriot demand an explanation when you return, now, from a whole night beneath the stars?"

"He's gone, for two days, with Daubenton, to Alfort. To study some diseases common to sheep and men. Lucky for us!"

So that's it! he said to himself, with a sudden return of rage. *She was ready to give me her night because she knew she could do it without any penalty. She had a night off and a corsair can help pass the time very pleasantly and disappear in the morning. The little tramp! Well, they're all the same, as at home among lies as sirens in the sea. And yet this one, with her honey hair and honey skin and voice! I could have loved her. . . .*

"I'll bring you an armful of my English dresses," he said aloud, coldly, going toward the door. "It's time for you to choose among them. Daylight is breaking. What can I order for you, tea, coffee, chocolate?"

"I want nothing, Chevalier," she said with infinite sadness. "I want only to die before awaking from my dream to discover that you don't love me."

"My God!" he exploded. "You're the one to turn me down."

"Turn you down? I ask nothing better than to be yours, this very minute."

He clenched his fists and closed his eyes, then said with hard-won self-control, "Jeanne, there are two ideas I have to knock out of your head. The idea of giving yourself to me. And the idea of going back, afterward, to Aubriot. In that sequence they are not possible. First you must straighten things out with Aubriot and then you must pack your trunk and come back to me. At that point I won't deny you."

She reddened. He was pleased and resumed his mocking tone. "My idea is the simple and perhaps stupid one of a man in love: I don't want to be a cuckold."

She started with joy. " 'A man in love,' did you say?"

"I did. You have six days, Jeanne, to make your choice."

She moved closer to him, rose to the tips of her toes, deposited a chaste kiss on his lips and said gravely, looking at him out of moist eyes, "Whatever the cost, my mind is made up. I love you too much, so much that I can give you only a stupid woman."

"That won't be for long," he retorted, taking her face into his hands and asking seriously, "Tell me, my Jeannette, in all the time that we were lost to each other did anyone fulfill your wish to look on the sea?"

"No, no one."

"Good," he said, with a sigh of relief. "I couldn't forgive you for playing me false by looking at the sea in any company other than mine."

CHAPTER 27

When she came back to the Rue du Mail, Jeanne's chest felt constricted as if by an iron band. How could she have got herself into this plight? Within a few hours her nostalgic longing for Vincent had turned into a crying need. But how could she say to Philibert "I'm going away"?

In Vincent's arms everything seemed possible, but away from them she realized the enormity of these three simple words. *My God, how Philibert needs me! How can I leave him?*

She bathed her eyes and went to the kitchen to make a cup of coffee. The smell and strong taste of the mocha did her good. She decided to spend Sunday with her friend Michel Adanson, in order to put off thinking about her problem. Philibert would not be back from Alfort until the following day, and this granted her a respite.

Jeanne was accustomed to going to Le Patouillet, where Adanson lived, whenever she spent a Sunday alone. His botanical knowledge and optimistic and fun-loving nature had won her over completely. She enjoyed romping through the countryside with him, as if they were brother and sister. Michel always welcomed her with open arms, pulled up a head of lettuce from his garden, added some cream to his vegetable stew, and prepared a pot of coffee. When they had dined he would borrow a creaking springless, mud-encrusted old carriage from the Abbey of Saint-Victor, hitched with four splendid dappled gray horses, and off they would go to visit the garden plots Adanson rented outside the city for experiments. They went to the villages of Ménilmontant and Clichy-la-Garenne, as far as Drancy and Arnouville, sometimes even to Roissy, on the road to Soissons. Sometimes, on the way back, they happened on a village ball, and stopped to dance. After this they drank wine and ate griddle cakes with the onlookers. These Sunday escapades with Michel gave Jeanne such happiness that, on this Sunday morning when she was so upset, she jumped, instinctively, into a cab and went to Le Patouillet.

Today Adanson was not alone. He was talking with Parmentier, the new assistant pharmacist of the Hotel Royal des Invalides. M. Parmentier was dedicated to improving the quality of a white vegetable root. He had discovered it while fighting the war against Hanover. Up to now only Adanson would take any interest in his project. The farmers refused to pay attention to this "pig-root." "Fit only," they said, "as feed for the pigs."

"Jeannette," said Adanson, "you've come at just the right moment. We're off to my land at La Pissotte to plant potatoes. If you work hard we'll make a detour on the way home by Ménilmontant and dance a jig."

"This is a good start to a Sunday," said Jeanne, unable to contain a smile. *How good it was to smile, even in the midst of a great sorrow.*

"Fortunately, you two have energy enough to both work and play," the pharmacist commented. "The fact is that most naturalists are in poor health. I was telling Aubriot the other morning that he can't shake off his cough because naturalists catch everything that's in the air, even the most exotic diseases. Has my chickweed wine built up his appetite?"

Philibert had told Jeanne nothing of this stimulant. All winter long he had coughed, but he always explained that his throat was sensitive to dust. Now she assumed a knowing air, in order to elicit more information.

"Monsieur Aubriot has always eaten lightly. But after a coughing fit he eats even less. All he wants then is milk, mixed with a decoction of periwinkle."

"Excellent for the lungs," said the pharmacist, "and if the milk is ass's milk, so much the better. But Aubriot knows all that. He's acquainted with all the medicaments beneficial to the chest. In fact, he's extremely erudite on the subject. He reminded me recently of an effective mixture of coltsfoot—*Tussilago vulgaris*—sulphur flowers and a scruple of amber, which gives great relief to persons suffering from consumption."

The word *consumption* made Jeanne shudder. She ceased to follow the conversation and tried to recall the sound of Philibert's cough. She saw him as a slim, muscular man, tireless in both love and work. An eternal student, he was ready to set forth on any adventure. *It's impossible. A consumptive is pale and tired, exhausted by the slightest effort and afraid of drafts. . . . Philibert has a weak throat, that's all. I'll bring home some poppy petals from the shop and make him a soothing tea.* Then suddenly: *Oh, my God! I won't be there to give him tea. Vincent has given me only until Thursday to stay with Philibert.*

When dusk fell and Parmentier had taken his leave, Adanson asked, "What's the matter, Jeannette? You seem to be far away, lost in your thoughts."

"I've nothing to tell. I was thinking of a novel I'm reading."

"What's it about?" asked Adanson craftily.

"Just the usual sort of thing . . . the torments of love. Tell me, Michel, what do you think of unfaithfulness?"

"I think . . . that a steady love is hard to keep going."

"No doubt that's the reason it's usually assigned to the weaker sex."

Heaven help us! She's found out that that rogue Aubriot is deceiving her. Aloud he said, "In the old days faithfulness was the exclusive property of virtuous women. Now women have little virtue, except those who go in for their own satisfaction, to revel in the sweet yearning for a distant lover."

"A distant lover is no lover at all."

"Oh, yes, he is! Novelists have benefited women by inventing a melancholy and chaste passion. Once upon a time a woman's unfaithfulness was physical. Now a woman can cuckold her husband with words written in love letters. The old-fashioned woman affected gaiety in order to compensate for her unfaithfulness. The modern woman is morose in order to punish her virtue."

"Michel, you make me laugh. Your reasoning is all in paradoxes."

"It was my purpose to make you laugh."

"But I don't think that the heroine of my novel will deceive her husband in the crude way which you've described. Her tempter is a sailor."

"The ideal lover. A sailor can offer an imaginative woman a maximum of romantic melancholy."

Jeanne sighed. "You don't believe in love, Michel, do you?"

He looked at her with a comic air. "Don't underestimate the advantages of hypocrisy, my dear Jeannette. Sometimes it provides the only way for a husband or wife to see the loved one without breaking up the marriage."

"But, Michel, isn't hypocrisy a rather compromising affair?"

"Jeannette, men have always cared for their own well-being. And the men of today are very busy. They must have a compromising sort of morality or no morality at all. Hypocrisy is a subtle form of morality. Because lying requires a keen mind and a good memory. No one makes such an effort if he isn't really in love."

"Do you really think so?" Jeanne looked at him uncertainly. Once more he told himself that she had learned of Aubriot's betrayal.

"Yes, I do," he answered firmly. "I think that most lies are inspired by tenderness. It's a rare thing to be in love body and soul. An unfaithful spouse's lies bear witness to a faithful heart. In fact, I think that love without lies is barbaric."

"Another one of your paradoxes!" said Jeanne, with a smile. "But one must know how to deceive. Besides it's plain that it takes two to make a successful lie."

Again Adanson misunderstood, and said what he thought would persuade her to close an eye to Aubriot's secret.

"We must help the one who loves us to lie. Why insist upon truth? Only perverts tell the truth, and that is because they are cruel. May God teach the heroine of your novel to lie. She'll be better off for it."

"Yes, yes," said Jeanne, with feverish anxiety, "I believe you are right."

* * * *

I'll take a spoonful of poppy syrup and get a good night's sleep. And we'll see what happens tomorrow.

In spite of her weariness, she climbed the steps two at a time, threw her hat down on the armchair in the entrance hall, and then detected a glimmer of light under the bedroom door. Philibert was already in bed, propped against a pile of pillows, with a book in hand.

"Oh!" Jeanne exclaimed. "How sorry I am that I wasn't here to get your supper. I thought you were staying at Alfort until tomorrow."

"I was, but I felt tired and came back early. Were you at Le Patouillet?" And he added, smiling, "Don't look so alarmed. It's nothing serious, just a spring cold that I'll throw off in three or four days."

"Have you taken . . . ?"

"I've taken everything the doctor ordered," he answered jokingly. "But if, before you go to bed, you'd make me a pot of periwinkle tea—three handfuls of dried leaves to a quart of boiling water—I'll drink it when I'm thirsty during the night."

Jeanne touched a small bottle she saw on the bedside table.

"Tincture of mistletoe, isn't it? Have you been bleeding from the nose or throat?"

"No, Madame Doctor. But because my throat is easily irritated I've been taking it as a precaution."

"Your eyes are too bright and your cheeks too red," said Jeanne. "Let's see . . ."

She seized both his hands, squeezed them, and gave a little cry. "They're burning!"

"Make my tea and go to bed. You're close to tears, and all for a bit of fever. It goes with the least touch of a cold, you know that."

"Swear to me that you feel no more ill than you say!"

"I swear it! Now go make my tea."

"What if I were to call Dr. Vacher?"

"Now you're a nuisance!"

"When you're the least bit ill I'm so afraid I want to call the best doctors in Paris."

"Don't do that. It would be the surest way to kill me. And you'd not do the doctors a good turn either, because it would be unethical to make me pay."

Jeanne hesitated a moment before saying, "Father Firmin has told me about a wonderful new healer on the Rue des Fossés Montmartre, a German, and not a bit dangerous. He simply runs his hands over the ailing spot, and that's the end of it. This last winter he cured five fathers of fever, in only one session."

"Jeannette!" he exclaimed, looking at her with amazement. "Don't ever bring me a healer! Even if I were dying I'd find the strength to get up and throw him out. I want to live or die in a modern manner. Make the tea, add to it fifteen drops of tincture of mistletoe, and go to bed."

"Yes, of course," she said hurriedly. "Forgive me for being so silly. I want you to be cured on the spot, by magic. I feel guilty about not being here when you arrived, ill. God help me! Why wasn't I here?"

She broke into sobs and wiped the tears off her face with the sheet.

"You're out of your mind, Jeanne," he said, half annoyed and half touched. "You're almost morbidly sensitive. I really ought to give you some soothing syrup. Dry your tears. My little attack isn't worth it. You're only raising my fever."

"Forgive me, forgive me!" she cried, getting up and running to the kitchen with her nose buried in her handkerchief.

She slept restlessly, a prey to nightmares and sudden awakenings, during which she listened or tiptoed barefoot to look at Philibert, who was sleeping or pretending to sleep. Toward midnight the moon emerged from the clouds and bathed the room in a silvery light which paled even the feverish red of his cheeks. She went back to bed, slightly reassured, and fell asleep, under a moonbeam.

Philibert's rapid, dry cough took several minutes to rouse her. She leaped out of bed and ran to him. He was sitting up, against the pillows, racked by the spasms of a cough that seemed to drive every breath of air from his lungs, bringing pink foam to his lips.

"Good God! You're spitting blood," cried Jeanne in terror. "I'll go for Dr. Vacher."

In spite of his exhaustion, he put out a hand to stay her, signaling her to wait until he could speak—which he did, at last. "I know exactly what's the matter. There's nothing Vacher can do about it. It's the moon. When I have a cough, the moon causes bleeding. But it's nothing serious. Give me some lemonade to rinse my mouth and then another fifteen drops of mistletoe tincture in some tea. After that, a few periwinkle leaves to chew on. Tomorrow you can take a prescription to Parmentier and ask him to drop by to see me."

Jeanne carried out his orders but said beseechingly, "Meanwhile, why not let me call Dr. Vacher, who is a good friend and right here, at the end of the hall? If you get worse surely you don't want me all alone at your bedside, sick with worry."

Slowly he sipped the potion and then, sighing with relief, let her bathe his face, neck, and hands in water with a few drops of vinegar and change the pillowcases before she propped him up again on straightened pillows.

Then, at last, he said, "Everything can be settled tomorrow, when I feel better, my Jeannot. For the moment the best treatment is rest and silence. Fetch me the poppy syrup from the cabinet. I'll take a couple of spoonfuls and give one to you. Go along, Jeannette, I promise I'll be better tomorrow."

But on the morrow he was worse. The fever had gone up to the point where he had fits of delirium, followed by extreme torpor, close to unconsciousness. Jeanne could not resist calling Dr. Vacher, who diagnosed acute inflammation of the lungs and a hemorrhaging ulcer. Because he was a professor of physiology rather than a physician he called in Dr. Bordeu, reputed for the treatment of respiratory diseases. Meanwhile, he sent for a surgeon to effect a bleeding. This, in spite of Jeanne's protests. Philibert, she knew, practiced bleeding only on heavy eaters or apoplectics. But now he was bled from the left foot.

Actually, the bleeding revived him, although he came to in a bad humor and gave Vacher cold thanks for his attentions. And it was with a keen as well as feverish eye that he saw the famous Bordeu—wearing a braided tan coat and a lace jabot—sit down beside his bed.

Bordeu discoursed for half an hour, dropping a few well-chosen Latin phrases on Philibert's ailment. His distinguished colleague, he said, was suffering from a tubercle of lymph, long lodged in the lungs and now, suddenly, in the process of disintegration. So much the better! The thing to do was to speed up its entry into the bloodstream by means of a purge, draw off the noxious part by another couple of bleedings, build up the weakened body with a soup made from turtle liver and young chicken, preceded, every morning, by a bowl of ass's milk and a big pill containing fifteen grains of powdered Briançon chalk, twenty grains of ground coral, eight grains of Poterius' fever reducer, and some syrup made from the leaves of creeping ivy.

Aubriot thanked him profusely for his learned analysis, assuring him that he would follow his orders to the letter and inform him of their beneficent result. But as soon as he and Vacher closed the door behind them, he tore the prescription into four pieces and called Jeanne to him.

She came slowly over to the bed and said in a weak voice, "The bleeding prescribed by Dr. Vacher did perk you up, you know."

"Sit down, Jeannette, and let's come to an understanding. You see, if medicine could cure the trouble in my throat, I'd have long since cured it. But today's medicine is in a sad state. It provides only a scenario in which doctors and patients, executioners and their victims, exchange words like characters in a comedy of Molière. This exchange serves only to calm patients' fears and feed doctors' vanity. But I'm a doctor myself. And recourse to Latin, which I know very well, doesn't impress me. So, please don't inflict their presence on me again. Is that understood? Do you promise?"

"But, Philibert, I'm the one that needs their help," she said, with tears in her eyes.

"Very good," he said, patting her cheek. "I won't deprive you of medical help. When you suffer too much from my ailments, call Tronchin."

"Do you believe in him?"

"Yes, I do. Because he thinks along the same lines as I do, that nature is the best healer and should be left alone to do the job. Come now, give us a smile. I'm not going to die, Jeannette. You want me to live forever so badly that I think you'll get God to make me immortal."

How could I think of leaving him? The distress of seeing Philibert spit blood and of hearing him rave in his delirium had made her anxiety over the prospect of losing Vincent seem quite unreal. Her anxiety kept her close to the sickbed and made her thrust out of her mind as sinful the slightest longing for the corsair. *Hadn't Philibert said that her love was keeping him alive?* Philibert couldn't die because she, Jeanne, couldn't imagine his dying. Although she was as lukewarm a believer as most of her contemporaries, she soon came to think that God or some supernatural power had struck down Philibert just in time to make her aware of her folly. Her desire for Vincent was only a spring night's dream, a physical aberration, as frail as a soap bubble.

On Tuesday she sent Banban to Madame de Boufflers' with a note for the chevalier telling him that Aubriot was seriously ill and she could not leave his side. If he were better the next day, she would go to the shop at five o'clock, for a short time, and be happy to see him. She wrote briefly and in conventional terms. Writing in the room adjacent to where Philibert lay, it was difficult to find the proper tone in which to address Vincent.

Vincent did not come to the shop the next day. When Jeanne arrived in the late afternoon she found only a letter delivered by Mario.

My faithless Jeanne, in so short a time I've lost you again. Obviously, one can't let you out of sight. Aubriot has the gods on his side. When you were fifteen I tried to abduct you. He lost his wife, and you stayed to console him. Now that you're nineteen I want to take you away.

He falls ill, and you must stay to take care of him. What can I do against the decrees of heaven? Neither passion nor wit can prevail over the contrary wind, which is intent upon doing you harm. I believe, Jeanne, that you're choosing the wrong course. But perhaps that's because I want your course to be mine.

I'm leaving Paris for Calais at five o'clock on Friday morning. I'll send Mario, on Thursday evening, to find you, wherever you may be, and pick up your last word. Come with me, Jeanne! Come, because I love you and you love me. If that's not enough, well, I'll marry you. But, I swear by my Cross, I'll never make you this proposal again.

Vincent

"Mademoiselle, what's the matter? Are you feeling faint?" cried out Lucette, hurrying to help her mistress to a chair.

"Give me some molasses," said Jeanne, suddenly pallid and short of breath.

"You're staying up too late, too long," said Lucette as she prepared the molasses water. "Let me take your place tonight with Monsieur Aubriot, so that you can get some rest. Or I'll run your errands, if there's something urgent," she added, casting a glance at the letter.

"Thank you, Lucette, but the only urgent thing I have to do is to look after Monsieur Aubriot."

To marry her! Vincent had proposed marriage! Was he quite mad? "If that's not enough, well, I'll marry you." That a Knight of Malta should write such words seemed to her so utterly impossible that she couldn't believe she'd actually read them. She pulled the letter out from between her breasts, unfolded and reread it without skipping a single syllable until she came, at the end, to the incredible sentence. She knew that Vincent was a member of the Order by special concession and that he had taken no vow. But it was easier for a knight-by-right to be relieved of his vow in order to make a suitable marriage than for a knight-by-special-concession to make an unsuitable one. A knight and a shepherdess joined together before God. What a dream. What an illusion! Incredulously Jeanne read, yet again, in black on white, the stupefying sentence. "If that's not enough, well, I'll marry you."

In spite of the ill man in the next room, in spite of her superstitious idea that his affliction was her fault because she was about to be unfaithful to him, she ran her finger over the magic words, smiled at them, kissed them, pressed them between her hands and then between her cheek and the pillow. Abandoning herself to an orgy of bliss, she went through a romantic wedding ceremony, a dozen times, and then found herself alone with her curly-headed knight in the green, red, and gold room of the little house at Vaugirard. As soon as Vincent's hands touched her—his bare hands on her bare skin—she quivered and stiffened, but was powerless to stem the flow of forbidden images that engulfed her. She fell asleep with her cheek pressed to the letter. Only when she began to dream real dreams did her face relax. Dreaming is no sin; one can't do anything to stop it.

The next day Jeanne handed Banban a letter.

"A letter for Chevalier Vincent?"

She shot a glance at the boy, then said directly, "His manservant will pick it up this evening, at the shop. Wait until he comes. I want you and no one else to put it in his hands."

"I understand, mademoiselle. It's an important letter."

The sheet of vellum had lain, since the evening before, on her dressing table, blank and as immaculately white as a shroud. There are no words for saying goodbye to the man you love when he has opened his arms to you. How could she say that last farewell—adieu, God be with you—when she didn't believe in it?

With a few strokes of the pen she wrote: "Chevalier, I shall love you forever, and I want only to die." This, at least, was true.

But that evening late, she received Vincent's reply:

> Jeanne, my incorrigibly indecisive Jeanne. Losing you for the second time is even more painful than the first. But, I swear by my Cross I'll never lose you again, for I'm giving you up forever.

Underneath the signature he had scribbled: "Your boy Banban and Mademoiselle Lacaille will transmit what I owe you. With my respectful regards."

While Jeanne was reading this second letter, Lucette brought out a wicker basket from the back of the shop. A servant from Mme. de Boufflers' and Banban had brought it the day before. In front of an excited Lucette and Magdeleine, Jeanne extracted the contents: the fine cashmere shawl that Vincent had thrown over her shoulders at Vaugirard; a sea-green silk summer dress, English style; a narrow-brimmed leghorn straw hat, with a green muslin ribbon, a pair of high-heeled green faille pumps, and a bamboo cane with a sawtooth-edged gold knob and a muslin bow. "Well, well, well!" Lucette exclaimed. "An outfit like that costs real money."

As for the promised parcel from the shop of Mlle. Lacaille, Jeanne waited for it without curiosity. Probably, she thought, Vincent was sending back her bonnet.

"Here's the bonnet," she said, when an apprentice of Mlle. Lacaille's turned up one day at the shop with a cardboard box.

"May I open the box?" asked Lucette.

"If you are so curious, but it's just a bonnet." And she buried her nose in the account book. Only when she heard Lucette's exclamations did she raise her head.

"This was worth waiting for, mademoiselle! I thought the box was too big for a bonnet."

And she held up, maliciously, a chemise in fine Cambrai cotton, with satin shoulder straps, bordered with Chantilly lace.

"Oh!" exclaimed Jeanne, unable to speak.

"It smells of the most delicate orange blossoms," said Lucette, sniffing with her little snubnose. "The bottom of the box is covered with sachets."

Jeanne stared at the dishonorable garment. "Lacaille's girl must have delivered it to the wrong address," she said coldly.

"Your name's on the box," said Lucette pitilessly. "And your bonnet is in it, too. Perhaps you gave the chevalier a chemise as well as a bonnet."

Jeanne flushed with shame. She strode feverishly toward Lucette, intending to snatch the chemise from her hands, but the girl was quicker than she and retreated behind the counter.

"Give it to me, Lucette!" Jeanne shouted. "I want to destroy this abominable thing with my own hands."

"Oh, no, mademoiselle! That would be too bad."

"Can't you see that it's an insult? How could the chevalier do such a thing? He must have a very low opinion of me."

This last idea so upset her that her anger turned to sorrow; she buried her face in her hands and wept.

Lucette carefully folded the chemise and put it back in the box, laid the bonnet on top, and closed it. Then she went over to her mistress and threw her arms around her.

"Come, mademoiselle, you must pull yourself together. It's nearly five o'clock, and the customers will be coming. I love you, and I don't want to see you upset for no good reason. The chevalier has nothing against you. I don't know why he chose to send you a chemise, but it's no insult. Just think of how much it cost! Believe me, mademoiselle, I know something about men. A man's way of treating you ill is to curse and beat you, to get you with child year after year if you're his wife and pay you practically nothing if you're not. Save your tears for treatment of this kind, but I trust you'll never have to endure it."

Jeanne blew her nose and wiped her eyes. "But to send me a chemise is impertinent. It's so improper that it would lead anyone to believe that he . . . that he and I . . . a chemise, Lucette, a chemise!"

"Don't you buy your garters from Au Signe de la Croix? The owner could tell you that Monsieur de Voltaire orders the most elaborate kinds of garters for his niece, Madame Denis. Is that any more 'proper'?"

"Well, everyone thinks that Monsieur de Voltaire goes to bed with his niece."

"But, mademoiselle, with all due respect, if people were to think that you and the chevalier . . . it would do no harm to your reputation, because a man like Chevalier Vincent is no sin. If God meant for women to always say 'No' he wouldn't have created such handsome men. Now I must take the box off the counter. Banban will take it to your house later on."

"Lucette . . . what if I were to send the chemise back to Mademoiselle Lacaille?"

"Try it on first," Lucille retorted.

Fingering the silky material, Jeanne agreed. Standing in front of the mirror over the mantelpiece she looked at her own face severely. The amber skin was taut and unwrinkled over the cheekbones, marked by freckles around the nose. *Sorrow has left no trace.* All her nineteen-year-old seriousness came forward as if she really feared that it had. Wetting her finger, she curled her eyelashes and let the light of a candle play on her moist, tawny eyes. She freed her hair, combed it with her fingers, and then spread it out over her shoulders, like a shawl. "No, Chevalier," she murmured to the reflection in the glass, "you can't do it. No, my love, you wouldn't have the heart to keep your vow never to see me again."

She saw herself as too desirable to be forgotten. Drawing back to the middle of the room, for a long-distance look in the mirror, she hesitated for a minute, then shed her undergarments and kicked them away. The reflection showed a slender, delicately modeled statue in tawny marble with the genitals covered by a golden fleece. Raising her arms above her head she swayed to and fro, with the grace of a young courtesan. Quite easily she imagined Vincent looking on at her dance of Salomé. She blushed, jumped to one side to be out of range of the mirror, then took the perfumed chemise from its box and slipped it on. The soft, fragile "spiderweb" cotton from Cambrai caressed her skin. She tied the ribbon shoulder straps, then ran back to the mirror to worship her own beauty. The scent of orange blossoms inebriated her with the memory of Vincent, and on her lips there was a triumphant smile. *Chevalier, you didn't send me a chemise like this, impregnated with your favorite scent, without thinking of the day you'd strip it off me!*

CHAPTER 28

t was good to come to life again in a free and easy abbey. Aubriot strolled in the flowering cherry orchard.

His ten days of pulmonary fever had been cured by the attention of all the wise men of the garden, plus the famous Dr. Tronchin. When Philibert got out of bed, pale and thin, Tronchin insisted at once on a convalescence in the country, where the air was clear and fragrant and the milk was pure and fresh.

He gladly accepted the invitation of the monks of Saint-Victor and a large room with a southern exposure in the main monastery building. Saint-Victor was as open as a windmill. Anticlerical wits said that it was a frivolous place whose monks were more intent on earthly pleasures than heavenly ones.

Aubriot looked on happily at Father Etienne, who supervised the planting of summer vegetables with the assurance of a man who knows he will be there for the harvest. He spoke, for a moment, with the good father, of radishes, lettuce, chervil, and marigolds, walked a little longer in the sunny alleys among the rows of cherry trees, and then went to the library to read until Jeanne stopped by to see him.

The immense library, with its splendid wood-paneled walls, was directed by Abbé Pierre and Abbé Armand, who allowed visitors to make free use of manuscripts and books. The library had thousands of books, not to mention those which the monks kept in their cells because they were not suitable for general reading. Sometimes a monk who had drunk too deeply of the Suresnes wine served at the monastery table dropped one of these choice books from his pocket and when Aubriot picked it up he found an unexpected stimulus to his reawakened desire for Jeanne. He found that his dreams were always of Jeanne, not of the marquise, and the idea that he was getting over his recent affair made for peace of mind.

He leaned out the window. The sky was blue, streaked with gold, eloquent of spring. Father Etienne's many-colored tulips danced in the breeze which scattered cherry blossoms over the garden. He saw Jeanne approaching, with long, graceful strides, from the far end of the mall. She was simply dressed, in the way he liked her best, in a green-and-white striped skirt, open at the ankles, a green jacket, a muslin scarf, and a modest bonnet perched on the hair piled on top of her head. A portfolio, containing papers, swung, like the pendulum of a clock, from her right arm. Her face wore the dreamy and somewhat sad expression which he had noticed since he'd been ill.

She's bored with me. He stared, with vague annoyance, at the portfolio. On this radiant day, filled with the song of birds, did she have to pull out her notes on the morning's lecture and discuss them with him? There are times when botany is a dry business. "My dear Brothers," he murmured, smiling, to the portraits hung around the library, "forgive us for abandoning you, but today we shall work in my room." There was no need to mince words. These rotund monks would know what was going to go on in the room above them. In their lifetimes, there was little they hadn't seen.

* * * *

Jeanne blushed and shut her eyes so as not to look into those of Philibert. For he had thrown her onto the bed and was deliberately undressing her, while gently covering her with kisses and caresses. He had taken off her jacket, skirt, petticoat, and stockings and was untying the ribbons of her chemise. It was clear, by now, that he had the resolute and indecent intention of making love to her inside the monastery walls, with the sun streaming in the open window, like an apéritif before dinner. All this gave Jeanne an entirely new feeling of licentiousness. She held her eyelids tightly shut and was trying to hold up her chemise when suddenly her breasts burst out of it.

"Oh, Philibert! The sun . . . the sun . . ."

"The sun? What about it? Since when have you feared the sun?"

His lips encircled the raspberry nipple closest to them.

"Oh, Philibert!" she murmured in a barely audible voice. "We're in a monastery."

"In this monastery austerity's not the rule," he said between two mouthfuls of raspberries. With a slow, skillful motion, he reversed her chemise and pulled it off as if he were skinning a rabbit.

The sun revealed the almost imperceptible blond hairs of her back and made her skin, still damp with pleasure, gleam. Playfully, Philibert gathered some strands of her blond locks together and tickled her with the ends. She quivered, and kissed his chest.

"Look at me," he said, winding a larger swatch of hair around one wrist.

She shook her head and said in a voice smothered by his chest, "I never want to look at you again! Oh, Philibert, just like that, in broad daylight! As if I were a courtesan!"

Philibert's laugh unnerved her still further and she burst into tears.

He pressed her head against his chest. Yes, she was as tempestuous as an April sky. You could no more check the flow of her tears than you could a shower of hail.

"Tell me, Jeannette, are you crying because I treated you like a courtesan or because, to your shame, you enjoyed it?"

Her tears flowed harder. She felt herself torn in two. This was the first time that Philibert had made love to her since the night at Vaugirard. During this period she had so languished for the lost kisses of Vincent and made him the center of so many impure dreams that she had wondered how she could ever again endure the caresses of Philibert. And now she discovered, with both shame and relief, that her anxiety had been in vain. Her body had remained responsive to his. She felt herself to be a monster, a woman with a divided heart, doubly unfaithful, essentially perverse. Here was more than enough reason for tears.

"Come, come, stop crying like an adolescent girl," said Philibert. "Otherwise I'll believe you groaned with pain rather than pleasure, and I'll have to try all over again, in the hope of doing better."

He grasped her hair and pulled her head up from his chest. She was angry, resentful of the power he had over her.

"Of course you can do anything," she said. "Why not? You can tumble me on a monastery cot, undress me, like a courtesan, in broad daylight and indulge your every whim. There is nothing I can say, and indeed, I say nothing. But it's not that I'm still your little girl, no, no! It's because I'm Messalina; yes, I've the soul of a Messalina, do you understand?"

He planted a kiss on her hair and said gaily, "We must celebrate your great discovery. Put on your chemise, Messalina, and we'll go dine on the Place Maubert. What would you say, Messalina, to a stuffed carp and some dry Mâcon wine?"

* * * *

The whole month that Philibert stayed at Saint-Victor was a sort of honeymoon. Jeanne got used to making love at noon in a monastery room. And afterward, as often as not, Philibert took her to dinner on the Rue des Fossés-Saint-Bernard, where he escaped the fatty fare and gossip of the monastery table.

Under Philibert's caressing black eyes Jeanne's cheeks turned pink with pleasure and she sighed with well-being as she sniffed the odor of garlic-flavored parsley butter, Burgundy style. With all its perplexities, life had its good moments.

When she arrived, late, at the shop, with a smile still flickering over her lips, Lucette's blue eyes shot her a mocking glance. "When you've a convalescent to look after, you must take time to cheer him up."

She added, "Monsieur Aubriot's stay with the jolly monks is just as good for you as it is for him. Last month, you were long-faced and silent, as if you'd no reason to go on living. Now you are happy again."

CHAPTER 29

eanne resumed the existence she had been leading before the tempestuous interlude with Vincent but with an increased passion for life, as if galloping through the day would hasten the coming of a perfect tomorrow.

When Lucette begged her to take five minutes off for rest she answered, "I dreamed too much when I was young. Now I've no more time to waste." Her chronic excitement benefited her health and enhanced her complexion. She was more charming than ever. Despite her renewed love and devotion to Philibert, she still thought in odd moments of the return of Vincent. She took care always to look her best; her dress was elegant down to the least detail.

Mlle. Sorel had told her that he had gone only to London to pick up another cargo of fashions. But Vincent did not come, and it was not until mid-June that she had news of him.

One afternoon, while she was arranging a display of sachets of fragrant herbs made up of pinecones and needles called *bain-des-forêts*, an Austrian came into the shop, with a young boy, turned-out and carefully groomed, with a curled and powdered wig. This elegant little fellow, who appeared to be about ten years old, was a musician with a cough. He played the harpsichord and the violin, Jeanne was told, and was on the way back from England. After taking one of the honey lozenges Jeanne offered, the boy seemed to stare at her. Suddenly he said a few words in German to his father, who stared at her in turn.

"Mademoiselle," he said. "You look extraordinarily like a portrait that we saw hanging in the captain's cabin of a French ship at Dover."

"Impossible, sir," said Jeanne. "No one's ever painted me."

"Well, it's an extraordinary resemblance."

"Isn't everyone supposed to have a double? You must have discovered mine. What was the ship's name?"

"*Belle Vincente*," said the Austrian.

Lucette dropped a sachet of *bain-des-forêts* and Jeanne blushed. She bit her lip and fought to regain her poise.

"*Belle Vincente*, as far as I know," she said, "is not a channel vessel. It's a freebooter. How did you happen to go aboard?"

"My son is a prodigy, mademoiselle," the Austrian said proudly. "The chevalier who owns this frigate heard him play in a great house in London. He ran into us at Dover, where we were about to embark for the Continent and asked if my son would play the harpsichord—a very fine instrument—which he has aboard his ship."

"Yes," said the boy, in slow but well-pronounced French, "he gave me a memento of the occasion and also a cross to protect me."

Jeanne leaned over to examine the objects which the smiling boy held out to her: a pocket watch with a flower design in tiny rubies, sapphires, and diamonds, and a silver-and-enamel Maltese Cross.

"Beautiful," she said, caressing his cheek. "As for the portrait," said Jeanne, "it was in the captain's cabin?"

"Yes, mademoiselle. A very fine oil. The model is painted as the goddess Pomona and in such bright colors that my son smiled at her as if she were real."

"Do you know the painter?"

"Monsieur Vanloo."

"Vanloo . . ." echoed Jeanne dreamily.

She remembered that at Mme. Favart's house the painter had looked at her a great deal and made a sketch in the notebook he always carried with him. Later, Mme. Favart had said he wanted to paint her as a garden divinity. Jeanne had eagerly assented, but, since then, the painter had died and she had heard no mention of a portrait by his hand. Yet this good man from Salzburg had seen, on Vincent's frigate, a Pomona by Vanloo which resembled her.

"And what's your name?" she asked the boy.

"Mozart," he said.

"Mozart . . ." said Jeanne, patting his cheek. "I'll remember this visit, and when they play your music at the Opéra I promise to go hear it."

Jeanne cautioned Lucette, as soon as the two were alone, "Don't let your imagination run wild."

"Mademoiselle, you can't censor my imagination. Even prisoners have freedom to dream."

"But I can hear your mind working."

"In that case you should smile. Because I'm thinking that the chevalier may be here for the summer solstice, for Saint John's Day."

"What makes you think so?"

"It's my little finger, telling me that the chevalier will come to buy a Saint Jeanne's bouquet at the corner flower shop."

"You're thinking nonsense," said Jeanne hopefully.

* * * *

Saint John was a favorite of the flower vendors. Many girls with the name of Jeanne could hope to receive flowers, and on the eve of a holiday people were ready to spend money. Fireworks would go off on the Place de Grève all night long on this the longest night of the year, and thousands of stars would fall into the Seine and be swallowed up by the water.

But she was disappointed on the eve of the solstice, when Vincent failed to turn up bearing a bouquet in his hand. Jeanne had already received several bouquets, from Philibert, her shop assistants, and various friends. However, a lackey wearing the livery of the House of Richelieu brought an unusually large basket, in the shape of a beribboned hat, filled with strawberries and cherries, laid out on a bed of green leaves. Jeanne stared at it with astonishment.

Months had gone by since she had seen the marshal or received any word from him. The Marquise de Mauconseil continued to talk about his charm, but Jeanne took this for the raving of a superannuated mistress. From the marquise she had learned that Richelieu had come back from Bordeaux to take his turn as first gentleman of the king's bedchamber and that he could not leave the side of his master, who was still mourning the death of the dauphin. Now the basket of fruit was an unwelcome intrusion.

An hour later, Mme. Favart burst into the shop, asking abruptly, "Jeanne, did you get the Duke de Richelieu's present?"

"Yes, here it is," said Jeanne, leading her to the rear.

"Well, how do you feel about it?"

"Annoyed, that's all. I'm not afraid of the duke."

"You're wrong there. He wants you, no matter what."

"Come, come! We're not living in the time of Louis XIV. No one abducts a shopkeeper."

"No, but she can be shut up. When she's tired of convent walls she'll pay any price for her freedom."

"Justine, you read too many old-fashioned novels. We've a chief of police, judges, and a king. No one can be shut up without a reason."

"Sartine, the police chief, can find a reason easily enough. Forgive me, but you're living with Monsieur Aubriot, and you're not married to him."

"I've no father or husband to lodge a complaint with Sartine," said Jeanne dryly.

"Neighbors will do. Offense to morals is a cause for scandal, and a punishable crime. Testimony can be bought for very little money. And the duke is a rich man."

"Surely the duke would do nothing like that."

"He would, he will, if you don't give in. He said as much to Madame de Mauconseil."

Jeanne stared at her with amazement.

"The duke is aware of your stubbornness and has talked about it to Madame de Mauconseil. He's dead set on having you, and hang the price."

"For a 'dead-set' suitor, he seems to me quite patient," said Jeanne ironically. "What you're telling me is sheer comedy. It's been months . . ."

". . . and he's wild with waiting. Yes, wild. He's had a skin ailment but as soon as he loses his last bandage he'll descend upon you. For months, the duke has been living with slices of veal on his cheeks and buttocks. Dr. Pomme prescribed the raw-meat cure. So he was in no state to go courting. All that was lacking was a sprig of parsley in his nose."

Jeanne laughed until tears came to her eyes. "I'm heartless, I admit," she said. "Tell me, is the poor man getting better?"

"He's very nearly cured. In a few days, I tell you, with a dab of powder on his cheeks, he'll be ready to go. He plans to invite you to the Opéra or to the Théâtre des Italiens, whichever you like. What shall you choose?"

"I choose to tell the duke, to his face, with all due regard, that I'm so foolish as to give him up."

"You'll get yourself into trouble, Jeanne, and Monsieur Aubriot with you."

"We'll see. Meanwhile, tell me, why doesn't Madame de Mauconseil herself convey the duke's threats and his passion?"

"Well," Justine replied, with embarrassment, "she wanted me to remind you that she spent considerable money on entertaining you and making you presents on the duke's behalf. If he should question you about them . . ."

"I see. Tell the marquise that I shall thank him for everything. I hope she didn't spend enough to justify his having a claim upon me. He hasn't offered me a townhouse, has he?"

"The duke doesn't make such large payments in advance," said Justine with a laugh.

"Then I feel better."

"Jeanne, I advise you not to be too outspoken. Play the game! I'm speaking from experience. You know, don't you, that I stood out against a marshal?"

"Yes. And what reason did they find to shut you up?"

"The one I predict they'll bring against you. I was accused of living in sin. Actually, I was legally married to Favart, but at Saint-Pierre-aux-Boeufs they could find no record."

"I'd never have given in," said Jeanne emphatically. "And I won't give in, ever."

"It's no joke to be shut up in a convent. Dignity and anger wear thin."

"But justice remains!"

Justine gave a bitter smile. "Soon after my . . . surrender, when I was installed at the Château de Chambord, I found the police file on my case. 'Mademoiselle Chantilly of the Théâtre des Italiens was taken today to the Ursuline Convent at Les Grands-Andelys, by order of the Prince Marshal de Saxe, whom she had refused to take for a lover.'

"The king, it seems, had a good laugh. He was fond of his cousin Saxe, and he's fond of his cousin Richelieu."

Jeanne looked hard at Justine, then embraced her. "That madman Mercier is right," she said. "We must have a revolution."

* * * *

The day after the feast of Saint John, Jeanne's well-organized life began to fall apart. As Banban passed in front of the shop of Mlle. Sorel, he saw men unloading cases from Calais. When Jeanne heard this she went straight to Mlle. Sorel, who told her that the boxes did, indeed, contain English goods, but that Chevalier Vincent had not come with them. A letter from London had announced their arrival and given instructions to pay his Paris banker.

Plainly, Vincent was not coming back soon. Had he lingered in London, gone off to Malta or to some place even farther away? Instead of returning to her own shop, Jeanne jumped into a cab and went to the Petits-Pères. If Vincent had consulted the maps in their library while he was in Paris, Father Joachim might know his destination.

But only further disappointment awaited her. Father Joachim told her that, by the king's orders, the maps had been transferred to Versailles, in order that recent coastal surveys be better protected from the eyes of foreign spies. He said, however, that the captain of a frigate commandeered by the Royal Navy could not leave a French port without notifying the Admiral of the Fleet of his destination. From the Duke de Penthièvre, he learned that the *Belle Vincente* had sailed to South America and would then go to the islands in the Indian Ocean and the Bay of Bengal.

Jeanne was totally downcast; her heart was like a stone. Her dream had taken sail and disappeared over the waves of an inaccessible ocean. She saw herself with white hair and wrinkles, full of the despair of a Penelope growing old without her Ulysses. Her sleep was one long nightmare, full of shipwrecks and cannibals from which the handsome corsair escaped only to fall into the arms of a sensual Creole or Spanish beauty.

* * * *

When the fair weather returned, it was Monsieur de Richelieu who returned to Paris and made his appearance on the Champs-Elysées. The duke was definitely cured of his oozing sores. After a long period of enforced rest he felt in fine fettle, with a skin as new as a baby's.

He waited for Jeanne to join him at the theater wearing a salmon-pink coat, embroidered with bouquets of flowers in a polychrome silk, a sword with a bejeweled hilt, and a diamond cross of the Holy Spirit.

He would have preferred to have Jeanne choose the Opéra rather than the Théâtre des Italiens. His enforced chastity, the fear of never getting well, of remaining an object of repulsion, of dying before he possessed her, had made his desire to recover more fanatical than ever. He would have liked to exhibit her in his Opéra box so as to demonstrate his health and virility after emerging from the slabs of veal. A hundred times more than before, the old duke was ready for any folly that would deliver Jeanne into his arms.

"Monseigneur, I did not come to see the performance, but to see you," said Jeanne with aplomb, after the duke had raised her from her graceful curtsy. "Let us step into the boudoir, where we can talk."

"My Nightingale, you're making me very happy," purred the duke. "Will you have a glass of Spanish wine? And let me see whether the sweetmeats I ordered for my pretty little girl have been delivered."

"Never mind, monseigneur," said Jeanne impatiently. "I've grown up a bit since we last met, and there is no need for blandishments. You wanted to see me. And here I am, ready to hear what you have to say."

She sat very straight and calm on the yellow sofa, with her hands folded on her lap. The duke looked disconcerted by her distant behavior. Although he was practiced in conventional gallantry he was not used to being in love. Finally, he picked up one of her hands and kissed it.

"Tell me, my Nightingale, during my absence have I made any progress in your heart?"

"Monseigneur, my heart is filled with filial affection."

"Is that all? Nothing more tender?"

Jeanne sighed deeply, then took a firm line. "Monseigneur, a heart can't be forced, you know that. I can't speak of love. Can't you be satisfied with affection and respect?"

"That depends," said the duke awkwardly. "I can be satisfied with your affection if you let me love you."

As if he had recovered the nimbleness of a young man he touched one knee to the floor and grasped both her hands in his.

"Be mine, Jeanne, and I'll make you the happiest of women. Only do what I ask. Love will come later. I give you my word that you can have anything you like, a townhouse, a place in the country, a carriage, the finest dresses, diamonds. . . . To satisfy your wishes will make me happy, that and just a bit of your time."

"Oh, if it's a matter of time, I'll give you that willingly. The question is what you'll do with it."

"Let me kiss you, just to give you an idea."

"No, monseigneur," she said, drawing back. "My kisses are not for sale, for horses, dresses, or diamonds. . . . Don't force me to lie, don't make me deceive you. Let me speak to you in all honesty."

He sat down beside her on the sofa, keeping one of her hands in his.

"I came to ask you to give me up, monseigneur. I appreciate the honor you do me in picking me out of all the pretty women eager to please you. But I care for you quite chastely, and you'll never persuade me to sink so low as to give myself to you out of self-interest."

"I'd never think such a thing," cried the duke. "Give yourself to me to save me from despair and, in return, allow me to surround you with beautiful things. It will be my delight to see you as the most beautiful, the best-dressed of women. The king's mistresses will be jealous, I promise you."

"That wouldn't take much," she retorted. "The king's mistresses are paid by the night, at the price of any courtesan."

The boldness of this remark caused her to bite her lip, but the marshal only laughed aloud. "I like the way you set yourself above such things," he said subtly.

And he breathed more easily. Jeanne, it seemed to him, had put things on solid ground. Every woman had her price. The fabulously rich Duke de Richelieu didn't need to bargain. No matter how much this girl asked, he'd glory in it, all the more because it would anger his hated son, Fronsac. He could imagine Fronsac's rage at seeing Jeanne with a hundred thousand francs' worth of pearls in her hair.

"My beauty, I beg you, ruin me with your whims," he said, kissing the fingers of her hand one by one, as if they were sweets from Olympus.

Jeanne could barely endure it and as soon as possible withdrew her hand. "Monseigneur, you must understand that I'm not trying to increase your bid," she said decisively. "I realize how risky it is to refuse you, but I know that you have a sense of honor, and wouldn't want a woman obtained by force."

"Do you want me to die?" said the duke, relapsing into a state of alarm. "Have the doctors saved me only to throw me upon your cruelty? Jeanne, my lovely one, my heart's desire, you can't say no, because I can't lose you. If I can't have you I'll die, and I refuse to die before holding you in my arms."

She leaned backward and he bent over her. Their satins rustled together, their muslins and laces mingled. Jeanne's fresh, golden face was almost mouth to mouth with the duke's heavily rouged cheeks. He enveloped her in his musk scent, fetid breath, and his aroused and burning desire. She felt as if she were being embraced by an old billy goat.

"Air!" she cried out. "I'm stifling; give me fresh air! I feel vapors coming on . . ."

He pulled himself up and took a bottle of vinegar from a drawer of the small dressing table. This he held out for her to inhale before he rubbed her temples and hands, murmuring endearments.

"You aren't reasonable, my love," he said, when she had recovered. "An excess of modesty is bad for the health. And when it's mingled with fear it positively offends me. You shut yourself up in your skirts and petticoats and leave me sizzling with expectation. By God, mademoiselle, I've been waiting for months. And I give you my soldier's word for it. Port Mahon, the invincible citadel, was not so hard to take as you are. Come, my lovely, give me just one kiss. That's all I ask for this evening. Look here, I'll give you this for it, and consider that the exchange is in my favor . . ."

Onto her lap he tossed the large ruby ring he wore on the little finger of his left hand, then leaned forward, greedily.

"No!" she cried out, holding him back with outstretched hands. She got up, abruptly, and the ring rolled onto the rug.

There was a long moment of silence. The young woman's frightened gesture clearly showed a physical disgust difficult for a lover to bear and insulting to a great lord accustomed to facile conquests.

"Madame de Mauconseil warned me of your stubborn virtue," he said dryly, "but not of your violence. I'll be patient a while longer, but I advise you to polish your strategy."

"For the love of God, monseigneur, get over your idea that I'm maneuvering!" she exclaimed angrily. "I'm simply trying to say, without giving you offense, that I'll never be your mistress. A refusal is no insult. Can't a woman dispose of her own body? Is virtue forbidden?"

And she talked on for several minutes, smiling, in the hope of touching his feelings. But her sentiments carried little weight in the world of the duke. In his world noblemen, lawyers, and bankers exchanged wives for a pleasantry, bid for dancing girls without bothering to consult them. Indeed, even a princess was known to serve as the stake in a game of dice. Judges entertained in a fashionable bordello before deporting aged prostitutes to the Americas. Respectable family men bought young girls from impoverished parents in return for a small life income and tossed a few coins into a servant girl's apron after they had unceremoniously taken her to bed.

Living in this amoral society, Richelieu had gone from dissipation to debauchery, and no means were too venal to satisfy his vices. His wife had died in childbirth, and with advancing age seduction had become a mania. The fact that, this time, he was "in love" with his prey did not affect his essential nature. He wanted to inject a bit of romance into the affair, but his primary aim was his own satisfaction. He didn't put much stock in smirks and smiles but relied, fundamentally, on his rank and money. When this stubborn little piece finally gave in he'd make her fortune, and she'd be content, like all her predecessors.

"My pretty one, that's enough talk of your virtue," he said brusquely. "You're quite capable of sinning when the fancy takes you. I'm urging you to change from one sin to another. And telling you you'll profit from the exchange."

"Forgive my frankness, monseigneur, but I love Monsieur Aubriot, and I don't love you."

"Your love is blind and causing you harm. You need some time to yourself, in which to think things over. I'll speak to Madame de Mauconseil about it. She can tell you of some quiet retreat, where . . ."

In her anger Jeanne dared to interrupt him. "Are you thinking of the Ursulines of the Grands-Andelys?"

"Do you prefer the Penitents of Angers? Their place is so dismal that it makes for a rapid conversion."

"Monseigneur, there are laws and courts of justice! Don't you see that philosophers and journalists might take up the cudgels for me?"

He raised his eyebrows in amusement. "Good Lord, girl, how you do go it! Hadn't *you* better stop to think who you are and what I am?"

This time the thrust hit home. General de Lally-Tollendal had been executed for losing a battle and the nineteen-year-old Chevalier de La Barre had been beheaded for religious disrespect. Both had the philosophers on their side.

Richelieu added, "Would you try to enlist the pen of Voltaire to protect you from his friend Richelieu?"

"Monseigneur, didn't your famous friend Voltaire say that conquest by brute force can't match conquest by persuasion? Didn't he give up a woman to another man whom she loved more and contented himself with being her friend?"

"Virtue, my dear, is tailored to necessity. Voltaire's said to be a bit of a . . . softie, in a place where I come on . . . hard!"

He was happy to see that his crude remark made her blush, and went on, blithely, "My beauty, my desire for you is that of a twenty-year-old. I can prove it on the spot, and whenever else you want to test it. So don't think your resistance can wear me down. I can maintain a long siege but, if I lose my patience, I can also mount an attack. In bed and under fire I've jumped the gun, and no one has held it against me because I'm a generous winner."

"So, outside the convent you give me a choice between rape and surrender. Is that it?"

"The only choice I give you is to be mine, for my happiness and your good fortune."

"Very good. I choose to surrender," Jeanne stated calmly.

With a quick gesture she restrained him. "That gives me the right, surely, to lay down my conditions."

"You can ask me for anything, my love, as I told you. But first, slip this trinket onto one of your pretty fingers."

He picked up the ring from the floor. Jeanne held out her hand and accepted the blood-red ruby without a word of thanks.

"Monseigneur," said Jeanne, "I'm afraid my morals are provincial. The idea of belonging to two men at the same time fills me with horror. I must leave Monsieur Aubriot before I can be yours."

"What I say, exactly. Leave him as soon as possible!"

"But you see, monseigneur, Monsieur Aubriot has been kind to me, and I can't leave him without some consolation."

"I understand. What will he want? Actually, I can imagine it. All scholars want the same thing. It will take time to get him a seat in the academy. Those impertinent gentlemen insist on having their say. But for the Cordon of Saint Michael, or . . ."

"I had another idea," she put in. "Better send Monsieur Aubriot away. And it so happens that . . ."

She suggested that Aubriot be attached as doctor and botanist to M. Poivre, the new superintendent of l'Ile de France, who was about to leave for this post.

Richelieu listened attentively, amazed at the precision of her demands. A salary of two thousand francs a year, a set of medical instruments, the traveling expenses and wages of a valet, lodgings on the island, and the engagement of two black servants . . . she must have figured it all out in advance.

The little deceiver! There I was on my knees and she was thinking of how to rid herself, with good grace, of her lover. She's thought out every detail, including the amount I have to get out of Louis for her doctor's new microscope. Why, I wonder, did she have to start out by saying no? There's nothing like the wile of a woman. They are all wily, not from necessity, but for sheer enjoyment.

"I'll send my secretary tomorrow to find out how things stand, and then I'll take the necessary steps. We need to speak to Choiseul. His cousin Praslin is the best intermediary. Fortunately Praslin wants to advance the career of a little actress at the Comédie Française and that, as you know, is in my domain. I see no reason why we shouldn't succeed. So, my lovely, is our agreement signed and sealed?"

He sought to take her in his arms, but she slipped behind the armchair.

"Yes," she said, "the treaty's signed and sealed, but the conditions still haven't been met. As soon as Monsieur Aubriot actually sets sail I'll fulfill my part."

"But now, Jeannette, a foretaste, a prepayment," he begged her.

Jeanne had gained courage in the course of their duel and now she played a daring card.

"Monseigneur, I'm disappointed in you. I resent being pursued, when I've given my promise."

Then, reading anger in his face, she added, with sudden dignity, "You wouldn't want the future favorite of the Duke de Richelieu to be treated like a little whore, would you?"

"By God, mademoiselle, I bow to your wit and presence of mind!" he said, matching the words with the gesture. "I have an idea, Jeannette, that I'm going to love you so much that I'll present you with a little bastard. Fronsac will be furious, and I shall be the happiest of young fathers."

"There are conditions for a bastard, too," said Jeanne, entering into the game. "You must promise me to make him a cardinal. In your family cardinals have won extraordinary success!"

CHAPTER 30

ince striking her bargain with the duke, Jeanne strode through her daily life with a singular concentration of purpose: to escape from an unsavory situation without soiling herself. She was reluctant to practice deceit, even on a petty tyrant who was forcing her to do so, but she couldn't indulge her pride by rotting away in a convent and engaging Philibert in a fatal struggle with one of the lords of the realm. Instead she chose to believe in the success of her plan. The plan had been a spontaneous reaction to imminent danger and at her leisure she had to admit that it was highly romantic. But this did not discourage her. Romanticism and realism had always balanced each other in her life. She was less worried than she was impatient to hear the result of Richelieu's maneuvers.

Richelieu would succeed, she was sure of that. He wanted her too much to fail. In her mind she began to prepare her departure. Whether she managed to flee with Philibert to l'Ile de France or had to take refuge from Richelieu at Charmont, when the time came to fulfill her part of the bargain, she would certainly have to go away from Paris. She would leave La Tisanière in the hands of Lucette, who with Banban and Magdeleine Thouin and their knowledge of herbs, would run the shop efficiently. La Tisanière would live on and prosper while the owner made another fortune on the islands.

This thought reawakened her blue-and-gold dream, the vision of a spice garden, fertile as paradise, suspended between sea and sun. A line of blacks, carrying sacks of pepper, muscat, and cloves, wound their way, singing, toward a harbor filled with white sails, dominated by the whitest of the white, those of her dreamboat, the *Belle Vincente*. In this hazy vision Philibert was in the new garden and Vincent in the harbor and she, Jeanne, showered her love upon both of them.

* * * *

"Well, mademoiselle," said Lucette one afternoon, "there must be lovely things dancing about in your head."

"I was thinking of a voyage," said Jeanne, coming down to earth, "one I've dreamed of for years and may actually undertake. If I were to be away for a while I wonder how you'd make out."

Lucette's blue eyes opened wide. "You'd leave me in charge of the shop?"

"If you feel equal to the task."

"Of course I do! With all due respect, I think I can make more money than you. There's a knack to it, and I have it."

"Then, who knows? I may decide to travel."

"Will you make a grand tour of Italy, like an artist or newly fledged lawyer?"

"Oh, I may take a look at the sea. I haven't really decided," said Jeanne, as casually as if she were planning a holiday.

"You've money enough, for sure, to indulge your fancy, mademoiselle."

This remark suggested a new element to Jeanne's mind.

"I may need a considerable amount of cash. Send Banban to collect the outstanding bills. I'd like to know what funds are available."

Lucette hesitated briefly, then went to the back of the shop, where she had her bed, and returned with an iron box whose key she took out of her petticoat pocket.

"Half of this is yours," she said, opening the box.

With amazement Jeanne counted three thousand eight hundred francs, a small fortune.

"Where in the world does this come from, Lucette?"

"From sales I make in the morning when—with all due respect— you are not around. I meant you to know one day, but I was waiting for the amount to be so big that you couldn't possibly be angry."

"Angry? Why should I be angry? . . . But what shameful thing have you been selling, at an exorbitant price, in *my* shop?"

"Nothing I call shameful. But, mademoiselle, when it comes to certain things you're somewhat of a prude."

"A prude?" exclaimed Jeanne angrily. "Show me, at once, what you've been selling!"

Lucette sighed, went again to the rear of the shop, and emerged carrying a big box.

"Here you are," she said, lifting the top. "And, before you explode, remember that they sell like hot cakes."

In the box there were small, fine sponges, each one with a narrow ribbon around it, and a couple of dozen little white pots filled with an agreeably pungent pink jelly. Jeanne gathered some on her thumb, smelled, then looked hard at Lucette.

"It's not for eating, mademoiselle," said Lucette, stifling a laugh.

"Then what *is* it for?"

"For not having a baby, to avoid having to submit three times a year to an abortion."

Jeanne continued to stare, and Lucette went on, as patient as a schoolmistress, "You grease the sponge with our magic jelly—that's the name I thought up—and insert it before receiving a gentleman visitor, if you see what I mean. When he's gone you pull the ribbon and out comes the sponge, together with what might have been a baby. . . . Come, mademoiselle, don't blush; it's all between us. And I fancy you know something about it. Your doctor wouldn't want you to worry about losing your slender waist."

Jeanne felt as if not only her face but her whole body had turned crimson. But this was caused less by Lucette's words than by the sudden thought that she might have Philibert's child. That had never occurred to her before, and it filled her with terror.

"You're talking nonsense, Lucette," she said angrily. "Of course Dr. Aubriot doesn't want a child, since we're not married. And I don't want one either."

Lucette laughed. "If you knew, mademoiselle, how many men beat up a wife when she says she's pregnant! And a woman's lucky if her man pays for an abortion rather than submitting her to a yearly childbirth. As for his making the effort to pull back and avoid a peck of trouble, well, you can't count on that, believe me. . . ."

"Lucette!"

"To get back to business, madame. Half the money we've made is due to Monsieur Michel."

"To Monsieur Adanson?"

"Yes. The sponges have been on the market for some time, but women dipped them into a sharp vinegar. I wanted to put out something better. And since Monsieur Michel gave us good formulas for antiflea and antimoth preparations, I asked him if he had something for babies. He and his friend Rouelle, the chemist, worked out a formula for this jelly which he calls a 'bug-eater.' It goes like wildfire, I tell you; I can never have enough in stock."

"How much do you charge?"

"It depends on, well . . . the way I size up the buyer. I ask more from Vaubertrand, whose attorney general gives her twenty-five francs a month, than from Fonatine, whose judge gives her only fifteen. And as for the girls from Brissaults' who deal with cabinet ministers and princes and those from Babet Desmaret's, who go in for high-ranking churchmen, I charge them as much as Countess de Boufflers and other ladies of the nobility. . . . I'm well organized now, and sell by weekly subscriptions. Banban delivers the goods so discreetly that respectable women are joining the ranks."

"Well, well, well, well," sighed Jeanne, finding no words for her astonishment.

When Lucette saw that her employer was properly stunned she brought out a tea box containing two thousand more francs.

"I may as well let you in on this, too. It's all for you. There's a silent partner, who provides the ingredients, but she's been paid in advance."

"So what's this money from?"

"From our 'Balm of Venus.' "

" 'Balm of Venus'?"

"Yes. Highly effective! It's made for me by the canniest midwife of the Temple."

"Effective in what sense, Lucette?"

"It's for perfuming a woman's intimate parts. And it has the further effect of recharging the man who comes in contact. . . . Now don't go telling me that it's wicked or harmful or anything of the kind. The maker sells it to the abbess of the Parc-aux-Cerfs, and if it were dangerous it wouldn't be given out to the girls that go to bed with the king. If it were poisonous Prince de Conti would be long since dead and so would the old priests at the Oratory. Mademoiselle, business and morality don't go together, and to make money you have to sell whatever's in demand."

Jeanne was too engrossed in counting the money to reply. She set aside the amount owed to Adanson, then turned over three hundred francs to Lucette.

"Here you are," she said. "You have a right to make something from your immorality, after all."

Lucette threw her arms around Jeanne's neck and danced with joy. Then she stopped short.

"So it's true, that you want to travel? We've been happy here together. This shop is a little bit of heaven. Look here, that sea you're always talking about, couldn't you wait till it rolls up to Paris? Men are like bees, you know; they always come back to the honey."

* * * *

The Duke de Choiseul rubbed his pudgy hands unctuously together, signifying that he was in a good humor. Thanks to his efforts, the dauphin's future marriage to the youngest daughter of Maria Theresa of Austria was assured. And the empress's ambassador, Count Mercy d'Argenteau, had expressed her gratitude. The alliance between France and Austria, needed to balance that between Prussia and Russia, would be magnificently consolidated. And when the ingenuous dauphin succeeded to the throne his wife, Marie-Antoinette, couldn't fail to support the minister who had made her Queen of France. Choiseul could hope to endure for long years, free of the secrecy of Louis XV and his confidantes.

On his great table, he unrolled the latest maps of the English coast. Chevalier Vincent had done a good job. Creeks, coves, beaches, and reefs were all recorded and described. When, oh when, the invasion? He pulled the cord of a bell and asked the answering lackey, "Hasn't Monsieur de Praslin arrived?"

"Not yet, monseigneur."

"As soon as he comes, show him in."

To talk with his cousin Praslin was always relaxing. Praslin was his favorite collaborator. Trustworthy, intelligent and, apart from the duchess, he was the person most convinced, in all the court, of the greatness of Choiseul. Every week, when they reviewed the affairs of the kingdom, Choiseul felt as if he truly ran the state—the king was a mere puppet and he pulled the strings.

There was a knock at the door, and the Duke de Praslin was shown in.

"Cousin, I'm in a good mood. Don't let's speak of the navy."

"Your navy's not so badly off," said Praslin. "It takes time to build ships and stock munitions, that's all. The navy will be renovated faster than the army, you'll see. The army's top-heavy with officers—nine hundred colonels for a hundred and sixty-three regiments."

"The country is ruined by its civil servants," countered Choiseul. "Every Frenchman wants to have a government job and none wants to pay taxes. How can one govern a people so illogical?"

"Well," said Praslin, smiling, "at least you can't complain about your philosophers. Rousseau is against you but Voltaire supports all your ideas. Epigrams are the rage, and he's a master."

"Maybe so, but a philosopher can't keep the Russian fleet in check. I don't trust them."

"Well, you know that Catherine's looking for an able French sailor in order to make an admiral out of him," observed Praslin.

"Sending her one might not be such a bad idea. At least we'd be able to keep an eye on her. Have you a candidate?"

"The same as yours, cousin," said Choiseul with a smile. "Chevalier Vincent would be the perfect man. He'd collect information in the best bedchambers. But that's just a dream. The chevalier wants to follow his own whims and win gold rather than glory. Besides, spying and betraying aren't practiced among the Knights of Malta. Anyhow, he's gone off to l'Ile de France. I've promised the governor and Poivre his help in fortifying Port Louis. If we resume war with England, it would make a good base for harassing English shipping in the Indian Ocean."

Praslin laughed. "Your face lights up at that idea, I see. You've a grudge to settle. But if I'm to conduct a successful colonial policy, you'll have to furnish me the means. I've come to ask for money for an eager adventurer who wants to inventory the natural riches of l'Ile de France and l'Ile de Bourbon, our newly acquired Mascarene Islands. The idea seems to me timely. We need to know what's there before we can exploit it."

"But does Poivre want to take your man along? Who is he?"

"Poivre has written to me about him. He's a friend, Dr. Aubriot. At present he's studying botany at the garden. Jussieu and Buffon both speak well of him. He's a doctor of medicine as well as a naturalist and botanist."

"Oh, Dr. Aubriot," said Choiseul ironically. "He's a highly recommended man. I seem to remember making him a royal censor, not long ago, as a favor to the Marquise de Couranges. And now I'm to ship him overseas, which won't please the lady. But, cousin, if everything points to him, go ahead. It's a modest project, isn't it, not too expensive? I'm glad to satisfy Poivre. He's a prickly fellow and has held out for two years against taking the post on l'Ile de France."

"There's something else I must tell you. If you send Aubriot, Poivre's not the only one who'll be happy."

"Who else, pray?"

Praslin paused in order to give his next words full effect "He's strongly recommended by Richelieu."

Choiseul drew himself up as if moved by a spring, struck the table with his fist, and then paced angrily up and down the room.

"Since when has that old troublemaker protected anyone other than an actress? How did such an illiterate get to know a man of science? Has Aubriot a remedy for the pox?"

Then, seeing Praslin's amusement he asked more calmly, "Tell me what the old battle-ax wants from Aubriot."

"Aubriot has a pretty mistress who has the makings of a merry widow."

"Ah! And does this little piece have anything in her favor?"

"She's said to be as pretty as they come. 'La Belle Tisanière,' she's called. She deals with my wife, and I can testify that she lives up to her reputation."

"The Temple beauty, eh?" said Choiseul, approvingly. "She supplies the duchess, too. I've seen her come and go. But she's a shopkeeper. Does a Richelieu now go to bed with a shopkeeper?"

"The duke proposes to install her in his house as his official mistress."

"My dear cousin, if the common people climb any higher we'll see a tart at Versailles! I have no desire to please Richelieu."

"But to keep the duke with his mistress on the Chaussée d'Antin might get him out of your way at court," Praslin suggested. "He'll neglect the royal bedchamber and the king will turn more and more to you."

"That's something to consider," admitted Choiseul. "Give the girl to Richelieu and let him sleep with her until he falls down dead on top of her. . . ."

"The Etoile des Mers is supposed to set sail for l'Ile de France in mid-September, and I was thinking . . ."

"That won't do," Choiseul interrupted. "Poivre won't leave before January."

"Aubriot would be glad to go earlier, and the commander of the Etoile des Mers would like to go by way of South America to collect herbs on the coast of Brazil and the bay of Montevideo. I'd like to grant him that."

"Grant away, cousin," said Choiseul lackadaisically. "I'm indifferent to dried herbs and empty seashells, but I know they're all the fashion. Just don't ask for too much money."

"Besides his modest stipend, Dr. Aubriot asks only for a valet. And I'll give him something better, the Bonpland boy, nephew of the Abbé de La Chapelle. Only eighteen, but already versed in botany. He's keen to travel and has offered to . . ."

"Agreed. You can see to the details," said Choiseul with a bored air. "Have you no other news?"

"Rousseau is coming back from Derbyshire. His hosts can't put up with him any longer."

"If he comes through France I'll put him up at the Bastille."

"You'll not have a chance. He'll go straight as an arrow to the Temple."

Choiseul paused before saying, between clenched teeth, "How can I make trouble for Conti?"

"Richelieu will do that for you," said Praslin, smiling. "The prince is proud of having the prettiest herb seller of Paris in his precincts. He won't like to lose her."

* * * *

"To the Observatory," Jeanne called out to the driver as she placed her white shoe on the running board of the cab.

Had Lalande been successful? He had an important role in her plan.

Ten days earlier Philibert had come back to the Rue du Mail with the certainty that he would soon receive the letter of appointment to a post on l'Ile de France. And forty-eight hours later he had the minister's letter in hand. He was to receive three thousand francs, a grant of twelve hundred more, and a stipend of two thousand a month. But Jeanne had blanched at the last line: "For the duration of the voyage you will have at your orders Augustin Bonpland, a student of botany who welcomes the honor of serving as your valet and secretary and whose salary will be paid by the King."—Praslin.

The unexpected intrusion of the name of Augustin Bonpland in the minister's letter had brought Jeanne close to tears. She had managed, however, to conceal them from Philibert. He must know nothing about her romantic plan until the moment of embarkation. So for help, Jeanne had run to Lalande.

As soon as the minister of the navy's reply had reached Aubriot the old marshal had tried to collect his due. But she would grant him nothing until she was installed on the Chaussée d'Antin, after she had actually seen Aubriot off on the *Etoile des Mers*.

Richelieu had arranged to send his "sleeping coach," drawn by six horses, which would bring her back, rested, in three days. Meanwhile he was redecorating a suite in his house. For the moment, Jeanne was free of his advances.

* * * *

A servant asked the visitor to wait for M. de Lalande in the "glass hut" where he would join her in a few minutes. Jeanne had always liked this glass enclosure, shot through with light, to which Lalande had brought her, by day and by night, to show her the heavens.

Today she looked down with a mixture of enjoyment and sorrow at the tender green elms of the Abbey of Port-Royal, the plots of red and blue cabbages in the vegetable garden and the flower beds where rivers of red geraniums flowed between borders of white verbena. Was this the last time she would see the landscape of ancient stones and greenery visible from the terrace of the Observatory?

How beautiful! In those far places where I long to go, shall I find any such harmony? Jeanne heard a door opening behind her but, seized by panic, she did not immediately turn around. Lalande approached without saying a word, leaving her another minute in which to drink in the loveliness of the day. As he started to speak she squeezed her hands tightly together.

"Jeannette," said the astronomer, "young Bonpland has given up l'Ile de France. Aubriot can take along a valet of his own choosing."

In her joy Jeanne threw her arms around his neck.

"And what do you say, Jeanne, to Aubriot's going away?"

"I say that he's lucky to have a chance to see another sky, new constellations, stars as big as . . . oranges. . . ."

"Yes, it's true that he'll find different stars. When my teacher, Abbé de Lacaille, went to the Cape of Good Hope he brought back ten thousand of them in his mind's-eye. But . . . what does Aubriot say to leaving you in Paris?"

Jeanne made a gesture of pique. "Monsieur Aubriot thinks that a woman who loves him is a permanent fixture. I'm no more likely to disappear during his absence than the house where we live on the Rue du Mail."

Lalande's black eyes flashed. "Go ahead," he urged her. "Speak ill of Aubriot; it will do you good."

"Monsieur Aubriot is a man, that's all," replied Jeanne. "There are times when men annoy, or even disgust, me."

"When a woman talks that way about men it usually means that she's ready to take on a new one in order to be cured of the others," Lalande told her. "Don't forget that I was the first to fall in love with you in Paris. I should have the first claim, especially as we're from the same part of the country."

"Mmmm," murmured Jeanne coquettishly. "I never imagined that the great man of the Observatory would stake a claim to me."

"Little liar! Tell me now, have you come across many intelligent men who didn't want to pay court to you?"

"Monsieur de Lalande, I care a great deal for you. You're a true friend," said Jeanne earnestly and in her most melodious voice.

"Call me Lalande, as I've so often asked you. Or make me happy by calling me Jérôme."

"Jérôme, I love you; you're a friend," Jeanne repeated.

Lalande rose and came closer. "By the way," he said, "aren't you the one, rather than Aubriot, that dreams of l'Ile de France?"

"Let's say that I gave a name to the dream that Philibert will make come true."

Out of his half-closed eyes Lalande observed her closely. Finally he held out his hands. She clasped them in hers and they stood there, in silent leave-taking, without breathing a word of farewell.

CHAPTER 31

wo days before leaving for L'orient, Jeanne could not refuse Richelieu's invitation to give him her opinion of the material for some hangings that he was planning to install in her suite. While she was there, the duke showed her a charming secretary, with a secret drawer, which he had just bought for her. As she was amusing herself by pulling out the drawer she had a sudden inspiration. Taking off his ruby ring, which she took pains to wear whenever she saw him, she threw it into the drawer.

"Let it wait for me here," she said. "I don't want it to travel."

He took from his little finger a flashing diamond and tossed it in alongside the ruby.

"It takes two to make three," he said, "and that's what I hope will happen."

Jeanne took on a wry air. "Monseigneur," she said, "you have such charming ways that it's hard to remember that you're a tyrant."

* * * *

All she had left to do was to entrust to Abbé Rollin her last letter from Paris to Mme. de Bouhey. She didn't want to run the risk of its falling into any other hands. One person, and one alone, must know the whys and hows of her mad project. Abbé Rollin had remained in Paris to keep an eye on Jean-François de Bouhey, who was finishing his military studies. Both of them came frequently to her shop to buy teas, potions, and toilet waters. She knew that, on Thursday evening, she could find them at Les Célestins, where they went to dine with their girlfriends.

The wooded garden of Les Célestins had been originally attached to a monastery. It was now a notorious summer meeting place, frequented by the king's Black Musketeers and, on their day off, by students of military schools. As soon as she set foot in the enclosure Jeanne picked out the red, gold-braided uniform of Jean-François' school. The exiles from Charmont exchanged embraces; the abbé introduced his Mariette and Jean-François his Antoinette.

"Monsieur l'Abbé, before I go with Dr. Aubriot to L'orient I've brought you a letter for Madame de Bouhey. Please ask her to read it when she's alone. It's important, and very private."

"Aha, mysteries!" Jean-François exclaimed. "Are you getting married? Is Monsieur Aubriot leading you to the altar before setting out on his voyage?"

"Don't say silly things," said Jeanne with annoyance.

"Oh, very well, I'll be quiet," said the young man. "There will be a wedding at the château. Jeannette, guess who?"

"Margot?"

"Yes, that's right. And who's the man?"

"Giulio, that handsome son of Pazevin, the shipbuilder."

"Well, well," said Jean-François. "Were you in on the secret?"

"It's no secret that Margot has been mad for Giulio ever since she was twelve or thirteen years old."

Abbé Rollin continued, "But what you may not know, Jeannette, is that, as soon as they're married, the young couple are going to make the same voyage as Dr. Aubriot, the one that you and I used to dream of in front of the globe. Giulio Pazevin wants to set up an office for slave trading at Port Louis."

"So Giulio and Margot, Monsieur Aubriot and Monsieur Poivre will all be together again on l'Ile de France."

She smiled, envisioning, over the heads of her companions, the blue and gold shores of her dream, miraculously peopled with familiar faces.

"Mademoiselle Robin will be there, too," put in Jean-François.

"What would she be doing on the islands?" Jeanne asked in surprise.

"She's marrying Monsieur Poivre."

"Well, well!" said Jeanne with amazement. "I'm happy to have all this news. When Dr. Aubriot arrives he won't feel too far from home."

* * * *

The *Etoile des Mers* was due to set sail on the fourteenth of September. Aubriot wanted ten days to explore the Brittany coast with Jeanne before she had to return, alone, to Paris. And so they traveled non-stop the whole way.

"Are you in such a hurry to arrive at the place where you'll leave me, Philibert?" Jeanne asked, in bitterness one particularly tiring day.

"To cover this distance in three days is an experience I was looking forward to. You'll catch sight of the sea sooner and enjoy it for longer. Aren't you happy about the ten days we have to explore?"

"I'm happy about the ten days, yes, but worried about the eleventh."

He put his arm around her shoulders and kissed her hair.

"Jeannot, I promise that if I stay on l'Ile de France longer than two years I'll send for you. At your age, two years means little."

She shook her head so hard that her long braid, tied with a black ribbon, brushed against his cheek.

"You don't know what it is to wait for you. But I know."

He took her hand in his. "I'll write often, Jeannot. No ship will sail for France without a letter for you. I'll tell you about absolutely everything."

"Even about the pretty Creoles?"

Aubriot gave one of his quick, short laughs. "Your jealousy is too great an honor. I'm going on forty, remember. I'm a middle-aged scientist. Young officers are the ones the girls go for."

"You'll find out that they go for an attractive scientist as well," said Jeanne sulkily.

There was a long silence while they sat back, rocked by the motion of the chaise. Heat came with the sun. In a village they bought some freshly picked, juicy purple plums. Back in the chaise Jeanne bit into one passionately, and Aubriot felt a wave of desire, imagining her biting his lips with the same eagerness.

"I truly wish I could take you along," he said abruptly.

She threw the plum stone out the window and looked at him with her tawny eyes.

"Monsieur Poissonnier, the Duke de Praslin's assistant, talked to me at length about the social life of the islands," he went on. "On l'Ile de France I'll represent the king, I'll be close to the governor and the superintendent. And Port Louis isn't Paris. Ideas are far behind those you hear at the Café de la Régence. It's a small town, where you live with doors and windows wide open, and everyone knows everything about you. A liaison like ours would not be tolerated."

"I never saw Arnould shut her doors and windows before going to bed," said Jeanne ironically. "Or du Breuille hesitate to wake up everyone in her house to get help against her lover Poinsinet. And I wonder if Frenchmen everywhere don't make love with doors and windows quite open. I, too, have been told about the islands. I've heard that men and women alike have lovers and that no one frowns on a colonist who goes to bed with his slave girl and adds little mulattoes to the population. I'm afraid that your Monsieur Poissonnier was setting forth a program of austerity meant for you alone."

Aubriot let a minute go by before answering, very gently, "Jeannette, I see that you're angry with me for leaving you behind, and unwilling to hear my reasons."

"I said what I think, Philibert, but I didn't reproach you."

"True. But now listen. There's a big difference, in the colonies, between a planter or businessman, a passing officer or sailor and an appointee of the king. I can't disregard my instructions and risk being shipped home. Don't you understand? This mission means a great deal to me, it's the answer to my dreams."

"Yes, yes, I know," she cut in wearily. "When you come back you'll be a great man, deserving the king's favor. You'll win honors and stipends and the admiration of your son. . . . But, meanwhile, won't you have another plum?"

She ate another herself, in order not to cry. The nearer they came to L'orient the less sure she was of being able to carry out her plan, and Philibert's last words made her think she would meet more opposition than she had expected. When she revealed it to him which of his two natures would prevail? That of the bourgeois scientist, unwilling to risk falling into disfavor with the king, or that of the man she had loved since childhood, who spoke his mind and cared not a fig for convention?

Her head, heavy with anxiety, came to rest on his shoulder and, again, he put his arm around her, as if he were consoling a child left out of a grownups' party. He spoke of her pretty shop and of all the distractions open to a fashionable purveyor of herb teas, then of the beaches of Brittany whose expanse extended almost to the horizon. She listened just for distraction.

He captured her attention only when he said, "You must admit that I accept your ideas whenever I can, even if they're not altogether reasonable. It was your idea that I should engage a valet at L'orient instead of Paris, where I'd have had more choice. I wonder, actually, whether I'll find anything better than a ragged fellow, invalided out of the navy and barely capable of carrying a small satchel."

Jeanne straightened herself up against the back of the seat. "I'll find you the right man; you can trust me," she said, her heart pounding. "By the way, since Monsieur Dussault, the harbor doctor, has offered you hospitality . . ."

"I can't accept it. You're with me, and we'll have to find an inn . . ."

"Nothing of the sort!" Jeanne exclaimed. "You can't refuse a colleague, and I need only stay dressed the way I am, like a boy. I want to have some fun, Philibert, to wait on you before you go away."

"Silly child!" said Aubriot, but he was smiling. "But at L'orient I'll be treated as a man on a king's mission, sailing with a captain who has quite a local reputation. I'll be entertained at dinner and supper. Can you see yourself acting like a valet, standing behind my chair and bringing me wine?"

"Indeed I can!" Jeanne said. "I see myself much happier there than wearing a skirt all alone in a room at the inn. You forget, Philibert, that valets belong to the luckier sex; they can go where they please.

Do you think that your mistress would be as well received by the society of L'orient?"

He was annoyed by being unable to find a reply.

"So you see," said Jeanne triumphantly, "at L'orient your Jeannette would be in the way, while your Jeannot will be able to enjoy everything. Let me tell you, sir, that if the wine is good, I'll drink all your dregs in order to console myself for not sitting at the table."

"Jeannette, I don't like to hear you talk so cynically. You've picked up Parisian ways, and in you I don't care for them."

"Forgive me. A woman must have a bit of wit to escape having more than a bit of sorrow. So, Philibert, you'll play the game, won't you, as a farewell present? Monsieur Philibert, at your service!"

CHAPTER 32

hey arrived at L'orient on the day that a ship came in from the Indies and their first impression was of the colorful crowd which almost submerged them. After covering some two hundred and fifty miles in three days in a rickety post chaise, the travelers finally got down in front of a row of elegant houses built of blue-gray granite, whose white specks shone in the sun. As Philibert knocked at the door of one with the brass knocker he said with satisfaction, "A fine, modern street!"

But Jeanne showed no interest in the architecture. Tugging at the driver's sleeve, she asked impatiently, "The sea! Where's the sea?"

"Just there," he said with his harsh accent, pointing to the sea wall.

"I'm just going to give a quick look," Jeanne threw over her shoulder to Philibert, but he caught her by the arm just as the front door of the house opened.

"Jeannot, wait a minute, please, and unload my bags," he said in a severe tone.

"Of course," she answered. And she added, to the driver, who was relaxing after the wild drive, "Give me a hand!"

The manservant, wearing a waistcoat and trousers cut in Breton style, did not understand French, but he made a sign to the effect that he was going for help. A minute later he came back with a big black woman whose round face was lit by gleaming white teeth.

"Can't be, I do declare, the doctor from Paris, and nobody home. Madam, Mamselle Amelie, Mamselle Anne, Grandmam Victorine, they all go buy goods from ship. Doctor at clinic or Hôpital de Bretagne. Like always they unload lot of sick folks. Here, m'sieur, you room next floor."

She chatted on interminably while leading them to a big upstairs room with flowered Indian cotton curtains at the windows and a parquet floor in wood from the islands. The pear-wood furniture, so highly polished that it sparkled even without a ray of sun, could have graced any house in Paris. But a pair of Chinese vases on the mantelpiece gave an aristocratic touch and reminded them that goods from the Orient passed constantly through the town. The black woman's eyes wandered from the bed draped with Polish-style curtains to Dr. Aubriot and from Dr. Aubriot to his young companion.

"Is you son, this pretty boy?"

"He's my secretary," said Aubriot, "but he can sleep in the room."

"Nice boy, and scrubbed so clean, of course he can. I'll put a cot in a corner or in the dressing room, where m'sieur says."

She busied herself around them for a few minutes, then said, "You eat something, yes? Long trip make empty stomach."

"We're not really hungry," said Aubriot, seeing Jeanne's impatience. "I'll go see if I can find your master. Perhaps I could make myself useful at the hospital . . ."

The black woman interrupted him without ceremony. Digging her fists into her broad hips she said, in a tone that brooked no reply, "Hospital always need doctor when ship come in. But you eat something. Or madame say Josephine have no good French manners and leave guests with empty stomach."

Since they had eaten nothing all day but prunes and biscuits, the pangs of hunger overtook them at the sight and smell of the tureen of fish soup. Around it there were dishes of shellfish: oysters, clams, cockles, and periwinkles. All these except the oysters were new to Jeanne, and she ate them so greedily that the black woman laughed with gusto as she buttered buckwheat crêpes and folded them twice before setting them down on the edge of the young man's plate.

Dr. Aubriot's valet was in a happy mood when the good woman

decided that the guests had had enough to eat and drink and could go
roam around the town.

* * * *

At last! At last Jeanne was breathing sea air! As soon as she was on
the street she opened her mouth to drink in the breeze and lick the
salt it left on her lips. The air of L'orient was charged with the smell of
the ocean; only to breathe it gave her a sense of adventure.

The sea was calm. Under a mass of white clouds with streaks of blue
sky, gray-green waves, barely crested by foam, lapped at the shore. But
this peace was rudely broken by the quivering, clamorous life of the
harbor. Three ships with furled sails lay in the roads of Penmarec;
others—in quarantine or about to depart—were anchored in the middle of the bay and one was scudding toward the distant horizon. Two
lines of porters were loading two store ships; a big freighter of the
Indies Company lay, turned over on its side, in drydock, where three
others were under construction. Everywhere launches threaded their
way. Carters, caulkers, and carpenters forced passage through the colorful crowd thronging the wharves. Ladies coming away from the
wharfside sales examined piles of goods, and the odor of spices mingled with that of the caulkers' tar.

This medley of noises, colors, and smells filled the foreground, but
the spectator's eye was drawn beyond them to the channel leading to
the open sea. The prospects, near and far, were such as to kindle an
inlander's imagination. Jeanne felt as if she were thousands of miles
from Paris, at the glittering gates of l'Ile de France, l'Ile de Bourbon,
Pondicherry, Chandernagore, Surat, Sumatra.

"It's dazzling," she murmured, leaning against Philibert's shoulder.
"There's a richness of life here such as I've never seen, even in Paris."

Then she fell silent. The sight of the sea raised an emotion too
great for expression. She felt a stabbing pain at the absence of Vincent.
Vincent, my love. . . . Somehow he was closer than ever. She longed
to touch the dancing green water on whose boundless expanse the
Belle Vincente was sailing. A seagull cried overhead. She lifted her
head to follow his flight as he soared aloft on flapping wings, then
floated along on an invisible current of air until he became a white
flake suspended in the blue. His strength and assurance were like
those of the corsair. Bird and man were both of a race that rode the
winds and had the sea for a home without ever submerging.

L'orient was, indeed, far, far from Paris. Sea trade brought in riches from all over the world. The money was spent on fine townhouses and on the châteaux and "follies" which sprouted like mushrooms in the surrounding countryside.

At all the festivities attended by Aubriot, Jeannot, a valet among valets, was free to indulge her curiosity. Never, in her native Dombes or in Paris, had she seen such colorful assemblies—gold-braided red and blue uniforms against a background of black servants, fearful and familiar at the same time, always ready to drop their domestic tasks and break into a native dance for the guests' entertainment. The presence of so many blacks, servile, and yet somehow threatening, gave the port city a fascinating exotic air. Jeanne was reminded, at every step, of Pauline de Vaux-Jailloux's stories of Creole life. And the ladies of Lorient, like Pauline, wore simply cut dresses of flowered India cotton or pastel muslin which gave them the look of island beauties.

The foreign atmosphere was also reflected in conversation. The make-believe Creoles, their husbands, lovers, children, servants, and even the local shopkeepers, constantly talked of sugar and spice islands, of China and the Indies, as if they were provinces adjacent to Brittany.

They said, "I'm just back from Pondicherry," "I'm leaving next week for l'Ile de Bourbon," or "We had good weather at the Cape of Good Hope," just as casually as if they had been talking of Rennes, Nantes, or the Bay of Biscay.

Soon Jeanne herself lost all sense of distance. Rio de Janeiro, where the *Etoile des Mers* was to make its first stop, seemed to her as close as Paris. Several times a day she ran to the harbor to gaze on "her" ship.

The *Etoile des Mers*, newly caulked, armed, scrubbed down, and partially loaded, lay in the middle of the bay. Although her design was simple and no sculpture decorated her prow, she was agreeable to look at, with her freshly painted red and yellow hull, black ribband, and shining brass. Like all armed store ships she had been relieved of most of her cannons in order to make room for freight shipped to the Mascarene Islands. At the moment, France was at peace and no meeting with an enemy ship was to be expected.

The captain, Viscount Vilmont de la Troesne, was a gentleman of Brittany, some fifty years old, short and stocky, with a faraway look in his gray-blue eyes. He was a direct, approachable man, keen on botany and astronomy, and deemed it a privilege to have for a passenger a naturalist from the King's Garden, acquainted with Buffon and Jussieu and an intimate friend of Lalande.

* * * *

One evening shortly before the sailing, Captain de la Troesne came by the Dussault house to tell Aubriot that the next day there was to be a supper, followed by a ball, at one of the prettiest of the nearby "follies." Dr. Aubriot had gone to transact some official business with the port commissioner, but Josephine told the visitor, "His little gentleman Jeannot says he be back soon. He know all about he master's affairs. He just there, in library, where madam give him room to pack he master's bags."

Sure enough, young Jeannot was engaged in carefully laying objects in a trunk. On a nearby table the captain saw hand mirrors, scissors, music boxes, alarm clocks, pistols, spyglasses, pillboxes, and cosmetics, wares from an assortment of shops.

"Aha!" he exclaimed. "I see here a private cargo to be sold on the islands."

"Exactly, sir," said Jeanne, with some embarrassment.

She might have known that, in spite of her prompting, Philibert hadn't asked the captain's permission to bring aboard some objects destined to trade.

"I hope, sir, that you don't seriously object to passengers bringing aboard a few items for private trade."

"If I did I'd be guilty of an excess of zeal," he said, laughing. And, after examining the articles on the table he added, "These are very well chosen. Monsieur Aubriot should get at least three times as much as he paid for them."

"To tell the truth, I made the selection," said Jeanne impulsively. "I conducted the search and struck the bargains."

The captain scrutinized her more carefully. This handsome young fellow, with refined manners and speech, had caught his attention from the start. As an old seadog he was used to certain goings-on among sailors and shut his eyes to them. He was not unduly shocked by the suspicion that Dr. Philibert Aubriot's valet was also his lover. What he failed to understand was Aubriot's declared intention of engaging another valet-secretary before embarkation. The situation was puzzling and he took advantage of this unexpected tête-à-tête to try to clarify it.

"Congratulations on your keen eye!" he said. "Your master is lucky to have you in his service. It's too bad he isn't taking you with him. The substitute that I've turned up and mean to present to him tomorrow is young and strong. He has good will, good manners, and some education, but he's not by any means your equal. I don't know, really, how the doctor will get along with him in close quarters. Tell me, why won't your family let you go? A sea voyage in time of peace presents no great danger, and it gives a young man an unusual opportunity to see the world."

Jeannot's fearful family was the excuse that Aubriot had given for engaging another boy to take his place. Now the captain's kindly attitude gave Jeanne the chance she had been hoping for.

"Monsieur," she said resolutely, "since you are so kind as to take an interest in me, I can tell you that your delayed sailing gave me time to write my aunt and beg her to change her mind. Just today I received her permission to go with Monsieur Aubriot if he still wants me. I haven't seen him alone for a single minute all day to show him my aunt's letter, and I'm afraid he may be tired of her many changes of mind ever since he first told her of his departure. And so, monsieur," she concluded, fixing her tawny eyes upon him, "I'm bold to ask you whether, if my master accepts my aunt's latest word, you would be willing to take me aboard instead of the other young man."

"Well," said the captain, obviously amused, "my orders are to take Dr. Aubriot to l'Ile de France, together with his valet. But the choice of a valet is up to him. For myself . . ."

He kept her waiting for a long minute, with a malicious twinkle in his eye, before finishing the sentence.

" . . . if the choice were up to me I'd take you. A pleasant, alert face, refined ways, devotion to your master—it's not easy to find all these qualities together."

Jeanne bowed her head, blushing at the compliment and also at the subtle mockery in the captain's voice. With a serious air he went on, "Shipboard space is limited and it's better to be served by someone you can tolerate having close by."

"In that case, monsieur, I'll do all I can to persuade Dr. Aubriot to take me. May I say that you're willing to have me aboard?"

"I'm sure that you'll bring him around," he said, laughing outright, "and that he'll inform me tomorrow. You're quite free to say that I welcome the idea, but I don't really think that you need my support. After all, you must know that your services are agreeable to him."

"True, monsieur. At least, I think so."

"If a valet is aware of his value, then the master doesn't have absolute rule over his own house. I'll be waiting for you, five days from now, on the *Etoile des Mers*, with just one trunk, mind you, of goods for trade."

* * * *

In the middle of the harbor the *Etoile des Mers* barely stirred on the glassy water.

Jeanne strained her eyes to stare at her. Out there, between the grays of sea and sky, her dream had taken on the reality of a wooden toy. In her excitement she felt like a baby bird, contemplating from the edge of her nest, with mingled eagerness and fear, the bottomless adventure before her. Suddenly, uncertain as to whether her weary eyes were deceiving her, she saw some sailors climb up a mast to test the new rigging. A smile broke out on her face: the toy was working.

A passing sailor stopped to look at the handsome, fair-haired young man, gazing ecstatically at the horizon.

"We'll be sailing together," said the sailor, raising his chin in the direction of the *Etoile des Mers*. "That's my ship."

"She's a beauty," Jeanne murmured.

"And a stout ship," said the sailor. "Rest assured, sir, she's a stout ship. She'll go the course, as far as you go."

BOOK TWO
*Love's
Progress*

PART

I

Etoile des Mers

CHAPTER 1

eanne's first days aboard the *Etoile des Mers* were spent curled up on her bunk in the wardroom. She had decided to keep a diary of the voyage by writing letters to Marie.

Marie, Marie! With my eyes wide open I've plunged headlong into my folly. How can I begin to describe the beauty and tranquility of this blue world I have entered?

As you must have guessed, it was not difficult to persuade dear Philibert to enlist my services as his valet. Oh, what joy to be so close to the one I love!

But the king's botanist was not as happy as I. For a week the poor man could not keep down his food. Green, gaunt, and hollow-eyed, slumped on his couch as limp as a rag doll, he cut such a frightful figure that the captain and the surgeon considered putting him ashore and sending him back home. And then one morning, a miracle! Whether from the saffron stomach plasters, glassfuls of seawater, whiskey, bags of salt on his head, or the tender mercies of the Almighty, one morning Philibert cheerfully devoured half a boiled chicken and kept it down.

Now that he has found his sea legs, he is certainly enjoying himself.

Captain Vilmont de la Troesne loves flowers and treats his king's botanist magnificently. Philibert dines at his table every day while his valet, "poor man," has had to content himself with the crew's mess. Fortunately, though, I've been granted the privilege of eating in Aubriot's cabin and even sharing it with him at night. While the sailors grumble over my special treatment, I know the captain means to avert an ugly incident down by the hammocks. After all, I am a handsome "fellow." Philibert would no doubt challenge half the seamen to a duel if he suspected that his morals were material for bawdy rumors up on deck. I have been dubbed the "doctor's pet." But the captain is indulgent toward his guests' private vices. And I'll never breathe a word of what others say about us.

Marie, Marie—now that I no longer worry about Philibert, I realize how wonderfully relaxed I feel at sea, floating like a seagull poised in the hollow of a wave. I've cast off from shore and left many cherished things behind. The immense blueness has become home to me sooner than I ever would have guessed.

But don't suppose for an instant, my dear, that the *Etoile des Mers* is a bed of roses! The odor of Paris is a highly civilized stench compared to what we have on board His Majesty's vessel—one hundred fifty-three ill-washed (if they wash at all!) two-legged creatures packed together, plus a four-legged contingent of every describable shape and color. To have provisioned the ship with salted or smoked meat would make life cleaner. But you can't expect sailors to go on eating bacon, biscuit, and dried peas forever. At least not the enlisted men.

M. Aubriot assures me that the fare is excellent at the captain's table, including leg of lamb, chicken, pigeon pie, and custard. To the rest of us mortals, that meat on the hoof means musty odors and vermin, so I keep my clothes well padded with lavender sachets. M. Pauly, the ship's surgeon, told me what to do about the foul air. You dab your nostrils with a bit of mint or sage crushed in one or two drops of oil; he always keeps some leaves in his sea chest and gives me a few.

Marie, I must tell you of the oddest thing—my first ball at sea. Imagine the incomparable setting, against a backdrop of ever-shifting blues of sky and sea, the vessel washed and polished, its brasswork gleaming. The captain on deck in formal dress, attended by his senior officers wearing red and blue sashes at the waist. The crew, all clean-shaven, spread out among the rigging like an invading flock of seabirds in possession of the sails. Trumpets and violins open the festivities. Sailors who want to dance hurtle down the masting—zip!—like trails of gunpowder.

The officers also entertain. Our captain plays the flute beautifully. His second-in-command, Trevenoux, performs sleight-of-hand tricks better than any juggler on the Pont Neuf. In short, everyone does his share to amuse the others. I danced a jig with such success that now I'm called on to repeat it whenever there's a party.

M. Aubriot is quite annoyed about these exploits. He lives in terror that one fine evening the band binding my chest will fall off, or my breeches will split open, or my hair will come loose from under my cap, or I'll make some girlish gesture and show myself to be even more feminine than I already look.

But it's quite clear to me that I'm not the only woman here masquerading as a man. One of our junior officers has the stubble-free, rosy cheeks of a virgin straight out of the convent. The same goes for Mignon, the little ship's boy. There's no telling whom to trust. I've set down a list of rules for my own survival: 1. Learn to look out for yourself. 2. Never approach the head without a bodyguard. 3. Walk sideways like a crab so you don't get your bottom pinched. 4. Practice keeping your chin up and a caustic tongue in your mouth. 5. Fall asleep only where it's safe.

It's a good thing I have the king's passenger looking out for me.

And so my life, Marie, is surrounded by water, peaceful and active by turns, cut off from the rest of the world. I often think how foolish it is to attach such importance to the minor upsets that happen on land.

There is some discomfort at sea to be sure, but it quickly becomes a shelter, leaving the mind and spirit marvelously free to roam. . . .

The master's whistle sounding up and down the ship, followed by the harsh bawling of the watch officer, drew Jeanne's attention. She left the wardroom to watch the lowering of sails.

Jeanne felt a tug at the seam of her jerkin and spun around with the ready defenses of a cornered cat about to strike. It was only Mignon.

"The cook's going to kill a pig for Sunday," the ship's boy whispered. "Have you got a sovereign? With a sovereign I could get us a nice chop and a sausage . . ."

"A sovereign!" Jeanne exclaimed in disbelief. "For a chop and a sausage? At that rate, how much would your cook charge for a pork dinner?"

"It's not so easy to peel off a portion of pig," the boy replied. "A pig's not as big as a cow."

"Two pounds," Jeanne said firmly. "Two pounds for a chop, a fine sausage and a hunk of blood pudding. That's a king's ransom for such a small feast."

Mignon shook his head. "Even if I could bring the cook down to my price, I won't get any blood pudding. Monsieur Toustain, the purser, would burst his valves for a dish of blood pudding. He knows to the inch how many portions are in a pig. They say that every captain he's ever sailed with wanted to toss him overboard. If he'd been privateering instead of serving the crown, it's certain he'd have gone under long ago."

"Mignon, you talk as if you've once sailed on a privateer."

"I have, twice," he replied proudly.

"At your age?"

"I may be the smallest boy aboard, but I'm not the youngest. I'm fourteen and I've already made two short runs with a corsair. If I hadn't been sick in bed when she left for the Indian Ocean, I'd still be working on the *Belle Vincente*. I signed on with Captain de la Troesne because he was bound for the Ile de France, where I might be able to catch up with Captain Vincent. Maybe he'll be delayed . . ."

"He will! He will!" Jeanne cried excitedly. "We'll catch up with him, you wait and see!" She felt like hugging Mignon.

"I was happy with Captain Vincent," the boy explained. "Serving the king and privateering are two different things. The king's officers are proud. They all act like royalty, even the lower ranks who come straight out of school and don't know how to use a compass!"

Vincent's princely profile floated before Jeanne's eyes. "The captain you miss, would he permit others to slap him on the back or laugh in his face?"

"I should say not! He wouldn't stand for disrespect—not that anyone would have shown it." Mignon paused, then added, "But he ate the same as everyone else. His food and ours came from the same pot. If he ate pork, we all received our share."

Deep in conversation, they rounded the deck and ran right into the surgeon. Pauly stared first at one, then at the other, with an inquisitive, amused expression, and hurried by.

When he passed her, Jeanne felt as if she'd just touched something slimy. "I don't think I like that man," she declared.

"Watch out for him," Mignon warned her. "The surgeon is really nasty. He spreads all kinds of stories."

"Is that so?" said Jeanne with seeming indifference.

"He started a rumor that you're a woman," Mignon replied, dropping his voice.

A chill ran up Jeanne's spine, and her mouth suddenly turned dry. "Monsieur Pauly has a twisted mind. I just hope that such an idiotic remark never reaches my master's ears, or he'll clobber whoever's responsible."

The bell rang for evening prayers. Jeanne was dying to make one last comment. But the boy knelt down and placed a finger on his lips. To be caught talking at prayers meant a threepenny fine.

* * * *

When the *Etoile des Mers* reached the Equator, pails of water christened everyone making his first crossing.

"Since our doctor surely will want to gather herbs along the coast of America, we can count on spending Christmas in Rio, which is fine with me. Great spot, I promise you! Handsome black women to lay and plenty to drink," commented Felibien, the boatswain's mate, a short, wizened chunk of a fellow.

"I've never been to Rio, only Montevideo," said the cook. "Do they have any geese?"

"When there's a holiday, and there's always a holiday, they roast succulent hams and a huge bird they call a *peru*, or turkey. All you can eat. Every kind of leafy vegetable, and fruits galore, sweet as honey. If you come to Rio with bleeding gums from scurvy, your mouth will feel better overnight. They also have a fruit called the jambo, which tastes like rose petals."

Nodding his head, the cook asked, "How about rum?"

Felibien shrugged his shoulders. "Like everywhere else. As long as you pay for it, you can drink all you want."

The sight of land lifted everyone's spirits. As the late afternoon closed in, a handful of the Saint-Malo sailor clan had gathered in one of the nooks at the foot of the foremast. Of the five who sat there talking, only Felibien and topman Belle-Isle had visited Rio.

Belle-Isle, a tall, blond, handsome young fellow was bragging about his experiences. "If you know your way around and shack up in some whorehouse with a woman who has keys to all the cupboards, you can have a roaring time in Rio," he assured them with a blissful grin. "And those little kegs of port or Madeira—God, that stuff never saw a vine, 'cause it's straight from heaven! Any crew that spends Christmas in Rio has got nothing to complain about!"

Crouching in the shadows thrown by some coils of rope, Mignon, the young Ternay Martin, Master Jouet's valet, and Jeanne listened avidly to the men's talk. Like everyone else on board, Jeanne was all excited at the prospect of reaching South America. But as long as Philibert was being entertained by the captain, she had to keep company with the "fillies."

"I guess you've put into Rio before, haven't you?" Jeanne asked Martin.

"Yes, twice," came the reply, loud and clear. "And both times I could have stayed on forever. Mulattos in Brazil are eager to find white husbands. But the Portuguese won't have them. Some of those colored women are very light-skinned, pretty and rich enough to win a Frenchman's heart. And in bed . . ."

The lad groped for words to express his ardor like a true sea dog.

". . . a colored woman positively sets your prick afire!" he declared proudly.

As his listeners eyed Martin enviously, Belle-Isle interrupted. "He's right, by God! I had a woman black as pitch—Maria Paula. I'll always remember her. She could never get enough of it. After the third go-round you went limp. What a treasure of an ass she had."

"You might run into her again," offered the cook hopefully. "And if she's too much for you to handle all alone . . ."

Jeanne stopped up her ears so as not to hear any more of this man-talk. Why did the sailors always end up talking about sex? Had they no dreams, no memories, no joys beyond their drunken binges, their savage brawls, and the lovemaking of whores in every port? Jeanne sighed as the men's banter reached its merriest pitch. She was about to say good night when the ship's carpenter approached.

Yves Cartier, from Saint-Malo, was admired by everyone as a master craftsman.

"Master Carpenter," young Ternay asked him, "the captain told the pilot that if you and Monsieur Pauly had wanted, you could have stayed in Rio and become gentlemen. Is it so? Did the beautiful colored women want to marry you too?"

The carpenter laughed. "I was never good looking enough to have anyone bid for my face. My luck's in my hands," he said. "But listen, lad, in any country where there's sickness, a surgeon can come from afar and make his fortune. A good carpenter can earn his living in a land of magnificent forests where the men are lazy."

"Master Carpenter, please tell us about the trees in Brazil," Jeanne said.

Cartier flashed a warm smile at the handsome, fair young man. "I can see that you're a timber-lover too," he said. "A carpenter works not with wood but with a tree—oak or ironwood, beech or ash, elm or walnut. And to fashion a ship according to my own way of thinking, I have to go into the forest and pick the trees out myself. I need the heavy as well as the tall ones, the straight, the curved and the twisted. God has planted them all. It's up to me to look and choose. You can tell when wood is blighted, but when it's possessed you can only sense it. You must never set a plank of possessed timber into a vessel."

"Possessed," Jeanne repeated, puzzled.

The carpenter took a puff on his pipe. "Sometimes a tree appears to be alive, handsome, and healthy, but it's dead. It's deadwood. There's no explaining why. It's demon spirits. You must never build a ship with deadwood."

Jeanne saw the three seamen cross themselves anxiously. "When my master goes ashore to explore the Brazilian coast," she said, "I'm certain he would value your company, Master Carpenter."

"As the good doctor wishes," the carpenter responded simply. "I'd be honored to accompany him. Rio de Janeiro is a paradise of trees. There's no way to describe the effect of such a splendid landscape. When that marvelous coastline rises before your eyes after two months at sea . . . you can only whisper a prayer."

CHAPTER 2

Jeanne's eyes filled with tears as the shores of Rio de Janeiro appeared before the *Etoile des Mers*. The carpenter was right. She could find no words to describe its breathtaking beauty to Marie. She wanted to touch Philibert's hand, but didn't dare.

Aubriot also felt his blood stirred by the splendid scenery, and kept silent. At last he sighed and managed to speak. "Thrice happy is the man whose eyes behold greenery."

The vision of Eden expanded now to fill the whole horizon. From the rocky, undulating coastline to the mountain ranges beyond, the land rose steadily, choking the sky with dense, gigantic vegetation. Glossy, leathery foliage glistened in the sunlight like a galaxy of tiny mirrors. Plant life flourished so abundantly that clusters of trees burst out of rocky crevices, their branches intertwined in wild embrace. Flowers hung in profusion from the topmost boughs, sending cascades of blooms onto the golden sands of pink, mauve, or lavender beaches.

A small fleet of fishing boats skirted the coast. Farther out, several more craft rode the waters off a large, rocky island dotted with palm trees bowing in the breeze, their fronds, like long dark tresses, bent to earth.

"Sugarloaf Mountain," announced the carpenter, pointing his pipe at the majestic granite cone rising out of the sea.

The *Etoile des Mers* entered the harbor channel. From the fort at Santa Cruz, guarding the entrance to the bay, came a hail. A Portuguese officer stepped aboard. In short order he left with the ensign, Monsieur de Chassiron, who was instructed to inform Count da Cunha, Brazil's viceroy, of the peaceful mission of King Louis XV's vessel. The French ship rocked gently in the bay, awaiting the return of its ambassador.

The immense, tranquil harbor, like a vast lake of sparkling azure waters, probably could have sheltered all the ships ever built. The water was so clear that Jeanne could see almost straight to the bottom. The sapphire waters, with their shifting iridescent light, and their luxuriant vegetation crowding the shore, combined to transport Jeanne's imagination back to primeval times. The majestic harmony of distant horizons lent a spiritual glow to this rich and varied tableau, and moved her deeply.

"We'll soon see whether the viceroy intends to let us enjoy ourselves on his turf," the chaplain commented. "He's a feisty soul and we *are* French."

"What of it?" Aubriot retorted in surprise. "France is not at war with Portugal."

"True," said the chaplain, "but white pennants and flags flying the royal lilies bring back bad memories to the Portuguese in Rio. Remember Duguay-Trouin, the corsair who was lured to this place . . .?"

"That's past history," Aubriot commented.

"The victors like to say so, while their victims can never forget the price they paid. The present governor had to pay a fabulous ransom. On top of that, the city and port were plundered and burned. Ships were sunk. In our eyes Duguay-Trouin was a first-class corsair. But here, he's nothing less than a ruthless pirate."

"Tell me, Father, is a corsair thought to offend God by his looting?" Jeanne asked suddenly.

"My word, no!" replied the chaplain in dead earnest. "Not when he's working for the King of France!"

The ensign, M. de Chassiron, returned shortly afterwards in a dugout escorted by a Portuguese guard boat carrying a lieutenant and eight soldiers. The boat came astern of the French ship and tied up under the baleful glances of the French command.

The ensign's face looked like a flag at half-mast. "A plague on our privateers!" he muttered as he stepped aboard.

Captain Vilmont de la Troesne gestured impatiently. "Tell me what happened. Will they give us safe passage ashore?"

"I've just had word of an incident, sir," said the ensign, "that we may have to suffer for. Late in September a French privateer flying the Maltese flag requested permission to anchor here in order to take on water and make some repairs. They were given four days, on condition that they store their powder and shot in the host magazine. They took on some water, then sailed to a small island north of here, where they put in. Nobody kept tabs on them since they had agreed to take six customs officials aboard. But on the third night, without a word or even the aid of a pilot, they slipped away and were outbound in the channel by daybreak. The garrison at Fort Santa Cruz spotted them and opened fire when their signals went unanswered, but the corsair evaded their volleys . . ."

By now the captain's patience had worn thin. "Come straight to the point, sir. Who is this corsair and what has he done to invoke the viceroy's wrath except to slip off unannounced?"

"He was a trader," replied the ensign, "the Chevalier Vincent."

"I know him," the captain interrupted. "Let's hear the rest of it."

"While pretending to be in need of repairs, he actually came here to take on cargo . . . small but precious items. There's talk of diamonds and rare-colored stones, guitars, hides, fine embroidery, as well as . . ."

The ensign chuckled and went on. " . . . combs and plumes for the hair, which are made here in the convents and are much prized by the Portuguese. Oh yes, and he took another product of the convents: fruit preserves from their kitchens. And parakeets. It's said that his loot will bring a fortune. And Count da Cunha blames it all on the French. Even worse, the customs inspectors, willingly or not, are still aboard the *Belle Vincente*."

Everyone crowded around the ship's officers to hear the news. Aubriot spoke up, perplexed. "Were these stolen goods?"

"No, no," M. de Chassiron assured him, "the corsair had been trading with the local people, but—"

For the third time the captain interrupted him. "The Portuguese, sir," he said, addressing Aubriot, "have never lost the arrogance they acquired when they had a commercial monopoly. While we French pay scant attention to their edicts, the Portuguese consider any foreign merchant a thief. In this port, Portuguese vessels enjoy exclusive trading rights."

"Anyway, the Brazilians who traded with the *Belle Vincente* have gone into hiding. Only two of them were found."

"Organizing a contraband operation with the aid of convents in a religious country is a stroke of genius," Trevenoux commented, smiling. "Chevalier Vincent has a talent for lining his pockets without firing a cannon."

"But what will happen to us?" muttered the shipmaster. "We must take on water. That we cannot avoid."

"And send ashore five sick men who are flat on their backs," added Dr. Pauly. "One's in bad shape."

"We all need some refreshment," said the purser. "I'm desperately short of sound planks for the carpenters."

"But," Aubriot began with growing apprehension as he realized the seriousness of the situation, "could the viceroy's ill temper really ruin our mission and prevent me from landing on the coast of Rio to collect specimens of flora and fauna?"

"It is indeed possible, sir," said the captain, "for our commission is signed by Louis XV, and Louis XV does not rule Portugal." He ordered the boatswain to step forward.

"Master Boatswain, nobody must leave the ship tonight. Double the watch, and you can pass out some drink to all hands." Without another word, the captain turned on his heel and left them.

With the captain gone, a heavy silence fell.

At last Aubriot spoke. "What will happen next? Are we prisoners on our own ship until further orders?"

Lieutenant Floch took up the question. "If you were a real seafarer, sir, you'd never feel a prisoner on any ship."

"That's true," Master Jouet approved. "But I wouldn't be so quick to despair." He paused, smiled at a fleeting thought, and continued.

"Countess da Cunha is an attractive and very bored lady. She loves to give amusing shore parties for visiting naval officers in her country house up the coast from Lisbon. Gentlemen, I promise you that very soon her tenderloin of beef with herbs, sausage, and tomatoes will leave an unforgettable taste in your mouth!"

* * * *

The next day Vilmont de la Troesne, with a well-scrubbed escort armed to the teeth, called upon the viceroy. As predicted, the viceroy returned the call. The shores resounded to the nineteen-cannon salute marking his departure from the ship.

The countess's invitation arrived that evening on the heels of a colonel in splendid regalia. They were to dine at the water's edge, in an arbor of orange blossom and jasmine. Dom Pedro's message, however, was not altogether hospitable.

The captain of the *Etoile des Mers* was authorized to remain in Rio for six days. Only long enough to take on food and water, provided they placed their gunpowder in safekeeping, did not attempt to anchor out of sight, took two customs inspectors aboard, and recalled the crew every day before sunset. The stretcher cases would be allowed ashore, and the royal naturalist could observe and collect plants in and around the city, as long as he didn't "borrow" anything from the public gardens.

"For God's sake, sir, send me ashore at once!" Aubriot demanded as soon as he heard this.

De la Troesne gazed at him, undecided. But Aubriot was determined to go.

"I'd risk prison, a duel, a bout of pneumonia, or a terrible fall to reach a flower I *had* to have," Aubriot persisted excitedly. "Send me ashore and relieve your mind of any responsibility. If I should die for the sake of a flower, my death at least would bear out my life."

The mariner smiled. "You seem to have the same trust in your earth as I have in my sea. Take a canoe and two blacks. Monsieur Toustain will represent you. They're less likely to cheat him. By the way, back in Lorient I noticed you had pistols in your gear. Do you know how to use them?"

"That's something you learn in medical school."

"And I'm a great shot," Jeanne announced with marked determination.

"Hmmm," the captain mused. "I'm still going to double your guard. I suggest that you choose a swordsman from among our young gentlemen."

Aubriot nodded and, in a voice choked with emotion, replied, "With your permission, Captain, I'll go ashore tomorrow at daybreak."

* * * *

Vilmont de la Troesne had a liking for botany which his legs could never sustain. A royal sailing ship measures barely 120 feet from prow to stern—not much of a training field for hikers.

The captain returned to the canoe before the botanists, with one or two of the blacks. He sent them off to fish and prepare a meal for the little expedition.

Jeanne insisted on walking back with him, knowing that he was exhausted, hobbling on one foot and sporting an eyelid inflamed from an insect bite. She nursed her limping companion, bathing his feet and applying a poultice of grated cassava root to the injured eyelid.

Now that he was sleeping, she took a moment to relax and enjoy the scenery. Nearby, a flood of tangled vines streamed from a crevice in the rock above. Clusters of giant morning glories cascaded onto the beach, their blossoms a ravishing shade of deep pink as rich and luminous as stained glass.

With arms outflung, she threw herself onto the warm sands, luxuriating in the radiant sunshine, her soul at peace, happy simply to exist. She opened her shirt collar, rolled up her sleeves, and took off her boots and hose. If only she dared to strip off that infernal band binding her breasts! Ever since she had arrived in this climate, the thick wad of cotton wrapped around her chest had irritated the skin and made her break out in painful blotches. Glancing toward the sleeping man, she shivered slightly as she thought she saw his eyelids flutter. Then she slipped the band down and off over her hips.

During these past four days the captain had had all the time in the world to observe her at close range. She was sure he had already guessed her secret. Glancing defiantly in his direction, she ran to the water's edge, waded in up to her ankles, and went on running until her breath gave out. She splashed herself wildly, dragging her toes lazily through the sand.

"How is the water?" challenged de la Troesne, stretching and yawning.

"Do you feel better?" Jeanne inquired, splashing her face one last time, and approaching the captain. "Let's see your eye."

"You're a fine doctor," he said teasingly, "and I'm a real handicap, right?"

"Oh, you're not a bad hiker. But you mustn't compare yourself with Monsieur Aubriot, who's a marathon runner."

"You seem in pretty good shape yourself."

"Chalk it up to my master," she retorted with a laugh.

Staring hard at her wet blouse, which revealed the curves of her breasts, the captain said, "Tell me, Jeannot, did Monsieur Aubriot think for one minute of sailing without you?"

Steadfastly returning his stare, she replied, "I imagine he thought of it but didn't believe I would allow it to happen."

He knows. There was no doubt of it. Jeanne assumed he would say nothing. He was too much a gentleman to embarrass so prestigious a passenger as the king's naturalist.

"The others will be along shortly."

"I hope so," Jeanne replied. "But Monsieur Aubriot is perfectly capable of forgetting the time when he's tracking down a discovery, and everything here is a discovery."

"Yes, it's like paradise, as our Indian guide says. We were lucky that the viceroy's temper cooled. Let's hope his goodwill lasts."

* * * *

Though they couldn't understand a word Aubriot said, the natives had been impressed and completely won over by the white gentleman. In his worn waistcoat and battered hat, he would weep ecstatically as he embraced the trunk of a nut tree, drop repeatedly to his knees to observe a plant, or stare for an hour through his magnifying glass at the corolla of a flower.

Now, as the afternoon drew to a close and the expedition headed back to its canoe, the natives ceremoniously bore on a cowhide platter the harvest of greenery that Philibert and Jeanne had collected. Although they had picked and chosen from the abundance all around them, Jeanne and Philibert felt like Adam and Eve banished empty-handed from the Garden of Eden. For, despite their labors, when the *Etoile des Mers* raised anchor, they would have to content themselves with only a pitiful little pile of wilted nature.

Vilmont de la Troesne understood their feelings. But Aubriot had told him that all you had to bring back to recreate the landscape were a few samples supplemented by copious scientific notes.

In Rio Bay the waters teemed with fish, thick as stars in the night sky. The tide, smelling of salt and iodine, fed Dr. Aubriot's expedition.

Jeanne licked her lips, thinking of the treat they were having for dessert today. At the end of the meal, Luiz or Joseph would run out to collect clusters of small oysters trapped among the tangled roots of mangrove trees exposed as the tide receded. They would set them before the fire to open lazily. Dessert was emerald green, edged with black, on a white shell plate, and topped off with a quarter of a banana.

Luiz and Joseph were butchering the giant crabs they had caught, and tossing the pieces into boiling water colored with pimiento.

Jeanne trembled each time a swift, sure stroke severed a crab's leg. But she reminded herself that the flavor of crab was, after all, exquisitely delicate. Small squashes stuffed with sweet cassava meal and smothered in hot coals sat waiting on a satiny green banana leaf that served as a tablecloth.

"The good life, the good life," Jeanne hummed to herself. Eyes shut, crouching on her heels, she rocked back and forth in time to her little tune.

* * * *

The good life continued for eleven days, although the viceroy's time limit for the *Etoile des Mers* had expired. But no one seemed to care, since Count da Cunha's sunny humor persisted.

In the streets of Rio, where the slightest excuse for celebration set off fireworks and native drums, the seamen spent their advance pay singing, dancing, stuffing themselves with good food, drinking themselves silly, making love, and then starting all over again.

Dugouts shuttled back and forth across the water, bringing local tradespeople of all colors to sell their wares aboard the French ship. Laughing young girls in white or striped cotton dresses, wearing big straw hats, earrings, and great looping necklaces of shiny black beetles flecked with gold, came to sell lobsters, giant fried crayfish, smoked wild pig, milk, toasted pistachios, hand-rolled cigars, pastries, fruit gathered from their owners' orchards, and brown wild honey, as well as parakeets and splendid macaws with crimson wings or brilliant blue-and-yellow plumage. The girls' bare feet marked them as slaves.

Indeed, everything was going smoothly in the best of all possible worlds.

Toward noon a large frigate entered the channel. The *Etoile des Mers* hailed the *Confidence*, which carried sixty cannon and was bound for the Indies. A leak below the waterline had forced her to put in at Rio for repairs.

Suddenly there were three hundred more French sailors and sixty more French cannon at the gates of Rio! The viceroy called it a "French invasion" and threw a tantrum.

Neither French shipmaster was received at the palace, and they were appalled by such shabby treatment. They both decided to quit this ungracious port as soon as the *Confidence* was seaworthy.

CHAPTER 3

he *Etoile des Mers* and the *Confidence* put to sea with no songs to mark the hoisting of sails. Nevertheless, it was a glorious morning. Flags of salute to the departing vessels snapped gaily in the sunshine, hung out by neighboring ships moored in the bay. A soft breeze drifting down from the peaks dispersed balmy fragrances over the coastal plain. The translucent bay lapped against the hull as gently as lake water.

* * * *

Jeanne sharpened her pen and continued her letter to Marie.

Basking in the sun along the shores of its great blue bay, Rio de Janeiro was lovely. Every church tucked into the crevices of its cheerful hills proclaimed the city a Christian refuge, and yet, Marie, there is something clearly pagan about it.

For some time I've had my eyes on one of those low-slung houses half-hidden by overgrown shrubbery. Aubriot let me use his telescope, and I could see it in great detail. The house must have a view of the whole bay. A man in a cotton nightshirt, open to his hairy chest, stood in the doorway smoking his first cigarette of the day and observing activities out on the water. Somewhere in the house behind him I could imagine the languid movements of sleepy, good-natured black slaves. Out in the garden, resting in a hammock under a canopy of jasmine, his wife in a lacy peignoir held an unread book in her hand as she daydreamed, rocking to and fro. With or without us, Rio will go on embracing the easy life.

The bleak coastal ridges of Brazil have vanished. Once again we are on the open sea. Blue-green below us, blue-white above us, and in between, time passes, each moment releasing a tiny stream of powdered eggshell into the ship's hourglass.

This morning we sailed alongside a school of flying fish, and right now we're surrounded by porpoises. The sailors treat anything that swims with the utmost cruelty. If a seabird happens to land on the deck, they won't harm a feather on it. But if they take a shark, they hack off the fins and toss it back into the sea just for the pleasure of watching it thrash about helplessly. The chaplain says it's because sharks devour sailors—and not in a single mouthful, either!

December 25, 1766. High Mass on Christmas Day under blue skies. We were dying of the heat. What a topsy-turvy world I'm living in! After Mass we had a very good dinner, each according to rank.

Several days ago we parted company with the *Confidence* and left her sailing for the Cape while we continued toward Montevideo. The pilot says that we'll be entering the Plata River soon. If all goes according to our captain's plan, we'll stay over at Montevideo for three months or more. The dead of winter in Europe, the height of summer here. Aubriot counts on finding a treasure-trove there for the King's Garden . . ."

Jeanne put down her pen and leaned over to pet Rufus, the ship's cat, who was rubbing against her legs, begging for attention. Bounding onto the table, he installed himself like a paperweight atop the written pages of Jeanne's diary, folded his paws under him, curled his tail neatly around his rump, and, with half-shut eyes, began to purr.

"Tell me, old salt, you who've already visited Montevideo—will I find what I came looking for? A pretty orchard with a river running past? Maria, the gypsy woman of La Courtille, said that this orchard would be in a flat region with low houses. In a land of black soil, its skies full of birds, its waters teeming with fish, and horses roaming the plains. She said that the men would wear broad white hats and the women white veils. Cat, does this sound like Montevideo?"

Wearily, Rufus opened a pair of green, intensely alert eyes.

"Will I find my knight on a patio at the tiny feet of a beautiful Spanish lady draped in a white mantilla?" She fixed her amber eyes on the green ones.

"Cat, you are a sage," declared Jeanne. "No sage takes it upon himself to announce bad news. It's too risky!"

* * * *

Shortly after noon on the next day, the watch sighted a sail on the port side. Not a singular event during the passage from Rio to Montevideo, but each time it seemed to cause a great commotion. No one really expected to have to dodge the volleys of a Dutch, Portuguese, Spanish, or English man-o'-war. France was at peace with all those powers, and pirate ships avoided this route. Simply put, it was a question of whether the newcomer would or would not salute the *Etoile des Mers*, since Vilmont de la Troesne never entertained the notion that his ship might advance the first salute.

In the captain's private code of proper maritime behavior, all other vessels had an obligation to hail the French king's flag. Unfortunately, however, propriety and civility on the high seas seemed to be a thing of the past. For while merchantmen raised flags of salute, an English or Dutch frigate would slip by on the port or starboard side with utter indifference and vanish without a hello or goodbye to the French, who would proceed to sulk over the insult. Still, the sighting of a strange sail always brought them on deck to hear the officers' comments and wagers.

"Frigate," announced Chevalier Trevenoux when the vessel at the tip of his spyglass became sufficiently enlarged. "Light frigate."

"Good sailer," declared the pilot appreciatively.

"Cautious, too," the captain added a moment later, meaning that the newcomer flew no flag.

"Good sailer," repeated the pilot, delighted by what he saw. "Sturdy little frigate, rigged out to the gills. She'd make a first-class privateer. I'll bet the Dutch at Brest had a hand in her."

"Yes, that boat comes from skilled craftsmen at Brest," the carpenter agreed. "Beautiful work."

"I count eight ports along each side, sixteen in all," observed de la Troesne.

"Cautious, all right," the carpenter again agreed. "Built at Brest for privateering, lightly armed, flag furled. Could be one of our corsairs."

"If it's one of ours, it's a bit late to say so," said the captain with a smile. "But if it's a ship from Saint-Malo, they'll never admit it and would rather pass for a foreigner than have to hail the flag of France. Those Saint-Malo salts salute with gunpowder only among themselves, and then they really pour it on!"

"Sir, I'll wager you that this one will salute," Trevenoux proposed.

"It looks as if you may win," Beaupreau said. "They're raising their colors."

"Maltese!" several voices gasped.

"Maltese!" Jeanne echoed with such fervor that it drew stares. Blushing and biting her lip, she walked over and stood close to Aubriot. "Would you lend me your spyglass, please," she whispered.

She peered at the scarlet flag with its white cross atop the mizzenmast, snapping in the breeze against the fair sky. Her heart pounded wildly. Moments later, as a second flag, white with the royal lilies of France, made its way up to the tip of the mainmast, Captain de la Troesne heaved a sigh of appeased vanity. "Let's see what happens next," he said.

Officers and deck staff waited anxiously, as if the ship's fate hung upon what the other captain did or didn't do. In the end he did what he was supposed to do. As he was about to cross the path of the *Etoile des Mers,* he hung out his topgallants and fired three cannon.

Beaming, de la Troesne declared, "It's a pleasure to know there are still a few gentlemen sailing the high seas. Return the salute, sir," he instructed his second.

When this was done, Trevenoux, who had been pondering the matter, suddenly announced, "It's the *Belle Vincente.* I'm certain of it. I recognize the figurehead. A fine piece of carving indeed. I remember seeing it in Calais. It's not the custom anymore to decorate prows with beautiful women. That's out of fashion, but the Chevalier Vincent insisted on it."

"An old love affair?" Beaupreau asked.

"A broken heart," Trevenoux corrected him. "Oddly enough, men always seem eager to carve a lost love on the prow of their destiny."

"Is it true that you know Chevalier Vincent well?" the captain addressed his second.

"I knew him as a greenhorn sailor aboard the *Eclair,* where I held the rank of lieutenant," Trevenoux explained. "Later on, when he was a lot wiser and bolder, we met again, fought fiercely, and afterward performed maneuvers together. Last spring I ran into Vincent at the Temple and, as you know, when a seaman meets a former crewman . . . Anyway, after spending a night talking and drinking, I got the urge to return with him to Calais and see his ship."

Jeanne's fingers on the telescope were quivering so that the carved and gilded profile of Vincent's "broken heart" began to dance crazily in the sunlight.

She never would have been able to describe it anyway, for the blood rushing to her head left her confused and only vaguely aware of Trevenoux's next words, which arrived like the surging tide in her ears.

". . . in short, gentlemen, she's a gorgeous frigate. I can understand why her captain is head over heels in love with her . . . for he is!"

"And the figurehead?" Beaupreau reminded him. "You forgot to tell us about that."

"Only because I don't know for sure," Trevenoux said. "I got the story from his valet. The boy is devoted to Vincent after years of service, but he's also from Provence, and in that part of the country they love to tell stories.

"In any event, the tale caught my fancy," Trevenoux continued. "I had noticed that the figure resembled a piece of sculpture more than a Greek goddess, which is rather unusual. I didn't want to question Vincent about it, so I put the matter to his servant Mario one evening when the chevalier had let him escort me to town. Mario informed me that the profile represented the knight's mother! I was amazed, to put it mildly, knowing that Vincent had never laid eyes on his parents, or even a portrait of them. Vincent was a foundling, taken in by the parish priest of Cotignac. When I got back to port I studied the figure more carefully and realized why it was so striking. Vincent had had it carved in his own likeness! It was my impression, and it still is, that the model for that lovely gilded figurehead is his imaginary mother."

The chaplain broke the silence to murmur, "What a touching tale!"

Jeanne struggled to hold back her tears. "A very sad story," she muttered as she handed back the telescope to Aubriot and turned to flee before the dam burst.

"My servant gets very emotional," Aubriot announced in response to a number of surprised stares. "He never knew his mother either."

Jeanne returned to the poop deck, where Beaupreau stood alone with the two ensigns. The *Belle Vincente* was like a great white seagull against the horizon. Only then did she realize that Vincent's route was precisely the reverse of theirs. Moments later, when she saw the Provençal, a southerner often ridiculed by his mates for his accent and exotic ways, sitting alone at the foot of the foremast, she felt the urge to talk to him.

"Provençal," she began, seating herself on a coil of rope, "do you know that ship we just crossed?"

"And how I know it!" the topman sighed. "I still can't get over the fact that it pulled out on me while I lay in a Breton prison."

"Provençal, why did you desert Captain Vincent?" Jeanne asked sternly.

"Because I'm a cockeyed fool! And because the girl—Amalia was her name—was so beautiful, so warm. I wanted her so much. I thought I wanted her forever. I was crazy! Did that ever happen to you? That you couldn't keep your hands off a girl?"

"Uh . . . no."

"You northerners!" The Provençal spat in disgust.

Jeanne laughed, questioning him further. "Do you know where the *Belle Vincente* was heading?"

"That's not my business anymore."

"When you signed on with him, though, weren't you told where he was going?"

"To the Indian Ocean, then up the Bay of Bengal into the China Sea to raid Chinese merchant ships. Only now, because of the damned truce everywhere, a privateer has to sail far and wide to land a good catch! China and all those places out there are crawling with infidels, especially Turks. To a Maltese, a Turk's a fine prize."

"I've heard that Maltese privateers have a weakness for piracy. But tell me something else. Why, if the *Belle Vincente* was heading for the China Sea, did it appear to be sailing toward the Equator?"

The Provençal puffed up his cheeks, expelled the air with a pop, and shook his head. "How would I know? Though perhaps . . ."

"Yes?"

". . . he planned to stop off at Santa Catarina Island. It wouldn't surprise me."

"Where's that?"

"Off the southern coast of Brazil. In Rio, you see, there was talk of a cargo too risky to smuggle in . . . it might be picked up at Santa Catarina later on, because it wasn't ready. Could have come from the mines, something of that sort. Anyway, since he couldn't stay in Rio and couldn't get too near the Portuguese, I suppose Captain Vincent found some quiet little nook to wait, like Tristan da Cunha Island, where he's always welcome."

"And where is that?"

"On the Cape route. Out in the middle of the Atlantic Ocean, the most isolated spot in the world."

"Are the people savages?"

"They're English. Shipwrecked sailors who stayed on because they liked it. They sent for their wives or girlfriends, built huts, planted gardens, raised children. They're happy there. About forty of them. Whenever Captain Vincent arrives, it's cause for celebration. He always brings them useful things. On Tristan, he's as safe as in his own home."

She paused, then decided to ask, "Home? Does Captain Vincent have . . . a house . . . or a woman on the island?"

The Provençal eyed Jeanne quizzically. "Why do you want to know? What are all these questions about my former captain?"

She thought quickly. "My master knows him well," she replied, and the Provençal's face lit up.

"Really? Well, then, if my ship lies in port, do you think your master would ask the captain for my pardon so I can go back to him? Your master's an important man, isn't he? Something like a missionary from the king?"

"When the time comes, I promise I'll ask him to help you," Jeanne interrupted.

"Oh, he'll take me back, I know he will!" declared the Provençal excitedly. "After all, I sailed with him for six years. He ought to have known how crazy I get sometimes. Sure, he'll take me back!"

"Provençal, I asked you a question," Jeanne declared in annoyance.

"What? Oh yes . . . a woman on the island? No, I don't know of any woman of his on that island. Can't imagine any that would suit him. So will you please ask your master . . . ?"

"Wait till the *Etoile des Mers* and the *Belle Vincente* meet in the same port," said Jeanne, smiling.

"It could happen, you know! If Captain Vincent put in to Tristan da Cunha, if he hasn't been to Montevideo yet, he'll come there. And if the *Etoile des Mers* stays over for three months as planned . . ."

Jeanne's heart was leaping. "Why are you so sure that Captain Vincent will come to Montevideo?"

"Because he has a good friend there. A Spaniard he likes to see," replied the Provençal. "The two of them run a smuggling business— the Plata region is good for that. The captain never passes that river without paying a call."

Jeanne wanted to question the topman further, but his head was somewhere else. Lost in thought, he hummed to himself dreamily, convinced that he would soon see the *Belle Vincente* again. His song was like a lover's complaint.

* * * *

The rising sun illuminated the mountains of Maldonado and the pilot announced that he would take them up the Plata River that evening.

CHAPTER 4

fter Maldonado's highlands, the region they were approaching seemed like a vast, endless coastal plain. They anchored in Montevideo Bay at daybreak. Thunder rumbled and rain began to fall, lashing the water far into the night. By morning, however, the sky had turned a deep blue, and the air was springlike. In good humor, the crew crowded onto deck to view the scenery and await the results of de Chassiron's trip ashore to discuss landing privileges.

Jeanne examined the landscape with keen eyes. It was not particularly majestic, but simply pleasant. The city rose in tiers, sloping upward gradually from the breakwater to a belltower atop a church. Jeanne noted a four-bastioned citadel, two chapel domes, a convent, a windmill, two rows of cannon pointing out to sea, and many small houses—simple, low dwellings without a single tree above roof level. *Did the citizens of Montevideo prefer unshaded gardens? If so, where in this city without greenery was she going to find the fruit-laden orchard that the gypsy woman of La Courtille had promised Vincent?*

"I wonder if the Plata region will be as delightful for botanizing as Rio was," Aubriot said echoing her own thoughts.

The jetty and docks were coming to life. Spanish soldiers and idle seafarers, barefoot fishermen dragging their nets down to a fleet of waiting boats, blacks and sun-scorched laborers stooping under heavy loads moved slowly about. Here and there a farmer led a mule harnessed to his vegetable cart. And there were riders everywhere, astride horses or mules.

Surely there must have been people of different social classes and occupations—planters and natives, masters, apprentices, craftsmen, judges, and soldiers. Yet white and colored dressed in an odd "uniform" consisting of a loose blanket with a slit where it passed over the head, and an immense white hat with upswept brim.

Jeanne realized with a tremor of excitement that what people were wearing—tentlike capes and outsized white hats—conformed exactly to what Maria the gypsy had foretold. Only the veiled women were absent.

"I don't see a single woman," Jeanne observed, passing the telescope to Aubriot.

"We're in a Spanish country where the women don't go out very much, I've heard, and probably not early in the morning."

"But I haven't even seen any servants or black women."

"They've adopted the habits of their owners. Or else we haven't been looking in the right place," suggested Aubriot, handing the spyglass back to her. "At this time of day, if you want to find women, you probably have to look outside the city. Start with the jetty and follow the shoreline to your left. The fountain of Montevideo ought to be somewhere in the vicinity."

Sure enough, a column of a dozen or more women was making its way to a verdant corner of the bay where there was a grove of trees. Children danced around them as they moved ahead at a leisurely pace, some with pitchers on their shoulders, others leading donkeys.

Jeanne shifted her spyglass back to the city, searching vainly for an orchard on a riverbank dotted with flowering shrubs.

"Our winter—or rather our summer—is getting off to a fine start," Aubriot reported to Jeanne on his return from lunch at the captain's table. "We should enjoy continued fair weather.

"The Spaniards are waiting to greet us with open arms," he continued happily. "Of course, our captain and some of his officers have social ties here, and friends they'll be visiting. De Chassiron returned from shore with the governor's own nephew, who stayed for lunch. Monsieur de la Troesne refuses to pay calls until after the siesta. Even so we have an invitation to dine with Don Joachim de Viana tomorrow evening."

"We?" Jeanne repeated, smiling wryly.

Aubriot peered at her out of the corner of his eye. "Jeannot, would you deny me a pleasure that you cannot share?"

"Sir, a valet expects no share of his master's pleasures, but he's always envious of people who are having fun!"

Aubriot burst out laughing and took her by the chin, gazing tenderly, longingly at her, the way he usually observed plants. Jeanne blushed under his intense gaze.

"Why do you stare at me with your laboratory stare?" she asked.

"I'm examining a moment of metamorphosis."

"Metamorphosis? Has the sea air changed me?"

"You are changing. And I'm forced to recognize that a young woman has crept up silently on a little girl and is asserting herself boldly."

"And . . . do you like the young woman less than the little girl?"

He paused, his eyes caressing her. "I'm the only man in the world for whom you will always remain a little girl," he said at last, desire overcoming him. He sought her lips, while his left hand reached out eagerly for a small round breast beneath Jeanne's shirt.

"Damn your armor plate!" he muttered as his groping fingers encountered only a cotton-wadded sheath.

"Your servant, sir!" she laughed, slipping out of his grasp and bowing low. "I gather you have your problems, too! Aside from *that* one, what can I do for you?"

"Air out my marbled gray silk suit."

"So that tomorrow the gentleman may look his best for the governor?"

"He can try! And they say that some pretty ladies will be there."

"Wrapped up in tents?"

"Not at all. It seems that in public the ladies of this country arrange their mantillas so as to show only one eye. Privately, they are very generous with their good looks. They even sing and dance. In fact, I've heard that they are most attentive to newly arrived travelers, and solicitous of departing ones."

As Jeanne eyed him with silent fury, he continued dryly, "I advise you to lay out your number-one change of clothes, as the seamen like to put it. For it's a known fact that serving maids imitate their mistresses, and since you're an attractive valet, you ought to pursue the young ladies."

Jeanne's amber eyes sparkled. "Do you mean you're taking me with you to the governor's palace?"

"Do you think for one moment that the chief naturalist who serves the King of France would step ashore into a strange city without a valet to look after him?"

Exultant, she threw her arms around him. "You're taking me with you! Oh, thank you, thank you! Sometimes I love you so very much, there's no room in my heart for anyone else!"

"Because dozens of others are jockeying for position?"

A violent blush turned her face crimson.

"The ruddy glow in your cheeks says you are guilty," he pursued mercilessly.

Holding her at arm's length, he stood gazing at her again. "Come now, out with it! Admit your little moments of weakness, your friend Lalande, and Michel Adanson, besides young Thouin, not to mention all the young men who flocked around the lovely shopkeeper at the Temple, eager to buy a cup of her lime-blossom tea. Come now, admit all those little flirtations that didn't include me!"

"Monsieur Philibert, there's only one missing link in your jealousy," Jeanne replied lightly, having recovered her composure. "You don't believe a word you are saying."

Aubriot burst out laughing as if to assure her she was right.

* * * *

Governor Joachim de Viana's dinner party was a splendid affair by local standards, and only a trifle less elegant than French custom prescribed. The table was set with a short white cloth and fringed napkins no bigger than handkerchiefs. On each silver service plate the valets placed a fresh white porcelain plate with a blue border to receive the next course.

After a first course consisting of shrimp paste, tuna fritters, and grilled fish, the meat course arrived, a succulent stew of mutton and green peppers steaming in its own spicy fragrance. Platters of beef cooked in a variety of ways were arranged around the mutton, together with a choice of boiled squash flavored with oil.

When the guests had eaten their fill of meat, the dishes were cleared along with the soiled tablecloth, which was replaced by a fresh, embroidered one and set with bowls of sweet preserves, colorful as a rainbow. Then the Spanish valets took away the silver drinking cups and decanters of Chilean wine and handed out bottles of Spanish dessert wine that the French valets poured into tall, stemmed glasses.

In setting down the wine goblet before her master, Jeannot, the handsomest of the French valets, bowed ceremoniously—low enough to whisper, "Don't forget to leave some for me! That Chilean stuff was dishwater!"

Smothering a smile, Aubriot drank half the glass and returned it to Jeanne, who tossed off the contents discreetly as she returned to her waiting place.

While the valets drank their masters' wine, the officers tried to solve their own problems of communication. Since half the company spoke French and half spoke Spanish, they had decided to speak Latin, which resolved the language problem rather elegantly. Peach preserves and jellied quinces were handed back and forth to the accompaniment of verses from Ovid celebrating the joys of good hospitality. Ladies, whose training in Latin was generally deficient, were not present.

Although it was not the custom in Montevideo to give dinner parties without women, Don Joachim did so when he had a large number of guests to entertain officially. The ladies sipped their maté and ate their jams with the governor's wife in her sitting room, joining the men later on in the reception room.

The reception room, a large rectangular hall with whitewashed walls and a tiled floor, was decorated with three bad paintings, and had a single glass window that was shut at night. Opposite the window stood a stage the size of a miniature theater, its floor covered with tiger skins.

On this stage, enthroned in an armchair of cranberry velvet, sat the governor's wife, encircled by six ladies sitting on stools. All were dressed alike in plain silk skirts fringed with silver or gold. Above the waist, all was hidden beneath a gauzy white mantilla with crisscrossed ends. Their glossy black hair hung down their backs in a heavy mass.

The Montevidean men dressed in the French fashion, while the ladies had invented their own lightweight, simple, and becoming style of dress. But Jeanne saw no need to study the eight women seated on the stage, for she couldn't see a single candidate worth Vincent's attention. Their complexions were swarthier than a prune's!

As the men entered the room, the dark-skinned women smiled vacantly, nodding graciously, acknowledging the men parading past the stage. But after making their bows, the men moved on to seat themselves of stiff, high-backed chairs of carved wood and tooled leather lined up along the wall. They sat smoking long, slender twists of tobacco leaves.

As the cigars were lit, the scene grew livelier. Two servants busied themselves at the maté table preparing the tealike beverage that was a great favorite with all. Two more servants passed around candies and glasses of cool water.

The women promptly took over the candy jars and began eating hungrily as they indulged in the strangest kind of game. With a flick of her fan, a lady beckoned to the gentleman of her choice, who would carry over a stool and sit so close to her that the two of them, whispering and giggling, were hidden behind the fan.

Jeanne watched, fascinated, and decided that this was how the "prunes," cloistered behind veils, managed to do a bit of courting.

The game went on until, at Don Carlos' request, the governor's wife, Doña Victoria, called for her harp. Along with the harp came a guitar player with lavender skirts, a mandolin player with blue skirts, a theorbo player in yellow skirts, and the concert got off to a fine start. Between string quartets, the lady in lavender with the guitar and the yellow-skirted young woman with the theorbo played a solo and sang a romance. The audience applauded wildly, demanding encores, which followed promptly.

Don Joachim then called for dancing and handed his wife down from her throne. With a great rustling of silks, the ladies stepped onto the floor. Don Carlos took charge of the abandoned mandolin, Don Domingo the guitar, while other guitars and mandolins appeared in the hands of the valets. To the sounds of muted chords the ladies opened the dance, scarcely moving, with a slow swaying of their skirts.

They danced with false modesty, eyes lowered, arms hanging limp below their mantillas, tapping the floor with tiny, rhythmic, toe-heel steps, scarcely moving their bodies. When a lively chord was strummed they undulated their hips, raised their arms, clapped their hands above their heads, and then returned to the slow, sensual movements that made onlookers long to join in. In the entrance hall, the black slaves had begun to shake and sway.

"Well, what do you think of the dancing?" asked a voice close to Jeanne's ear. It was Martin, Master Jouet's valet.

"I think there's a great deal going on here behind the masks of modesty!"

"You can find out for yourself," said Martin. "I've already tested the waters in Montevideo. I can assure you that the servant girls are attracted to nice-looking French boys. You can do anything you want with them in the Aguada grove, where the fountain stands. That girl in the yellow skirt," Martin continued, "with the braids halfway down her back. She's a beauty. And those glowing eyes promise a good time under her skirt."

"Men are all such dirty, lewd fellows," Jeanne blurted out. "They can't look at a woman without undressing her."

"And don't you do the same?" he shot back with a mocking glance. "Or maybe you happen to—"

"Happen to what?" Jeanne pressed him.

"Well . . . let's just say, on board they think your manners are a trifle too genteel for a man," Martin declared.

"That's because I'd rather behave like a gentleman than a roughneck," Jeanne replied crisply.

Martin sauntered off unsteadily, having had too much to drink. Suddenly the dancing in the main hall exploded wildly. There was shouting and stamping as the blacks began to clap out the throbbing beat of *la calenda*. A pretty young woman approached the handsome Jeannot and touched her on the arm.

"Hello, friend! Dance with Marieta. *Bailar.* Dance. Understand?"

"Of course I understand," Jeanne assured her, grabbing the girl by the waist. And the pair began to prance and wiggle their behinds as merrily as everyone else.

The dancing went on past two in the morning, uniting Frenchmen and Spaniards in spirit as nothing else ever could. Goodbyes and embraces took place in the garden, between men only. Aubriot nearly smothered in the hospitable arms of Dr. Jean-Baltasar Maziel, who couldn't bear to tear himself away from this distinguished colleague. Captain Vilmont de la Troesne and the governor hugged and complimented each other profusely.

"It was most kind of you, Excellency, to have invited all my old friends, " said the captain. "The only one I missed seeing was Don de Murcia, who held a tiger hunt in my honor the last time I visited your paradise. I'm still the envy of all my friends in Brittany. I imagine Don de Murcia was recalled to Madrid?"

"Don José? Not at all," replied the governor, "but no one can coax him away from his country house. He lives only two hours away on horseback, in his woodsy retreat. But he refuses to attend a dinner party in the city."

"How so?" asked de la Troesne in surprise. "Don José never struck me as a recluse."

"Love changes a man," Don Joachim explained. "Don José is in love."

"So he was when I first met him—several times over, I might say!" said de la Troesne.

"There's the difference," Don Joachim declared. "Two or more mistresses are hardly enough to keep any Spaniard off his horse. But a single one . . . and she is delightful. A French woman."

"French?" de la Troesne repeated in surprise.

"You know that we encourage desertion," Don Joachim said pleasantly. "Our city is so underpopulated that we feel it is the obligation of every passing ship to leave behind a crewman or two as a parting gift. But, mark me, we use charm, not force. We hold no one back. It is they who choose to stay.

"The girl's husband had come here to set up a pharmacy with Don José-Gabriel Piedracueva, whom he had met in Marseilles. If Montevideo still lacks a pharmacy, it's because Don José stole the pharmacist's wife before the shop could open. The pharmacist declared himself fed up with Spaniards and sailed off somewhere on an English frigate. We don't like to lose anyone, but it would have been far worse if we had lost the woman, for women bear children."

"I'm amazed that any pretty young French girl would be willing to shut herself up in the country just to populate your colony!" exclaimed de la Troesne.

The governor looked fondly at his guest. "My friend, any French-woman could feel very happy in the arms of a Spaniard. We Spaniards never tire of making love, a talent that pleases the ladies."

De la Troesne laughed and said, "I'm only sorry that I can't show Dr. Aubriot Don José's lovely orchard, but I suppose he doesn't receive visitors."

Hearing his name mentioned, Aubriot turned to the governor with a questioning glance. Jeanne, feeling hopelessly bored with the French valets, returned to Philibert's side in time to hear the governor explain, "Don José has a delightful grove of fruit trees, watered by a river with flowering banks and an abundance of fish."

The governor's words so surprised and unsettled Jeanne that she shivered. With pounding heart she strained to hear every word.

"Don José even raises vegetables. Recently Doña Emilia has added a patch of medicinal herbs."

"So the Spaniards in Montevideo are lovers of fine gardens," Aubriot noted with evident interest.

Dr. Maziel instantly crushed his hopes. "Don't believe it! This is grazing land. Most of my countrymen can't see any reason to grub roots or plant crops when they can buy a whole ox or a cow for a handful of coins. They prefer roast meat. Our friend Don José, with his flowering orchard, is attempting something new. Besides, he has two English gardeners who seem to be able to grow anything."

"Don't keep enticing Dr. Aubriot if you can't offer him a stroll under Don José's fig, peach, and guava trees," de la Troesne interrupted.

"Who says I can't?" Don Joachim retorted. "Just because he stays at home doesn't mean that Don José bolts his door. He gave a party for the Chevalier Vincent, whom you probably know. And he has promised to arrange a tiger hunt shortly, when the chevalier returns. Don José will surely invite you to his hunt, gentlemen. Meanwhile, he'd be only too happy to show his flowers and fruits to a botanist sent by the King of France. And Doña Emilia will be delighted to show you her medicine patch. She's very proud of it."

"Doña Emilia prides herself on her knowledge of botany as well as chemistry," said Dr. Maziel.

The group walked toward the garden gate, with Jeanne following at Aubriot's heels like a sleepwalker. She felt convinced now that the prediction of the gypsy of La Courtille would fulfill itself as a matter of course.

Having missed the start of the conversation about Don José, Jeanne had every reason to imagine the Spaniard playing the role of complacent husband in the French style, politely tending his peaches and guavas while his wife's lover Vincent sojourned in Montevideo. It made her so angry that her head began to throb. *Was Vincent simply toying with me that night in Vaugirard? Why would he care about my feelings for Philibert Aubriot if all the while he was carrying on a romance in La Plata? So he thought his secret lay safe beneath the Equator! What a rake! What lies! What an act he put on! What an innocent look he wore at Ramponeau's when the gypsy woman read his fortune and predicted the great love he would discover in some lovely faraway garden! He knew what color eyes the gypsy was seeing. He knew the scent of the lady's hair, the sounds of her passion, the curves of her body, the taste of her skin . . .*

"I detest him!" Jeanne hissed vehemently.

"What's the trouble, Juanito? Have you lost your voice?"

Jeanne returned to her senses and her role, realizing that she was a valet in the governor's garden. Marieta, the cute young girl she had danced with, was tugging at her sleeve and whispering a flood of Spanish words into her ear.

Marieta's shining black eyes gleamed in the moonlight like two jet-black marbles. "Tomorrow," she said. "Tomorrow, water. Understand? All right?"

As Jeanne couldn't think of a nice way to turn down Maria's offer to tumble her in the grass near the fountain, she replied, "Fine, Marieta, fine, good night, see you tomorrow!" and hastily grabbed Martin's arm as he passed.

Jeanne slept fitfully, awakening at daybreak. She dressed noiselessly so as not to disturb Philibert and climbed up to the forecastle, admiring Montevideo as the new day dawned.

The ship lay shrouded still in its nocturnal silence. When the chaplain emerged from his cabin, Jeanne went to greet the priest.

"Why aren't you asleep?" asked the chaplain. "Most young people sleep soundly."

"I danced too long," Jeanne replied. "Dancing doesn't help me sleep."

"Maybe it was because your partner was so pretty," he suggested with a wink.

"Not bad at all," Jeanne answered.

Slowly they made their way forward. The chaplain, whose overstuffed innards must still have been digesting mutton stew, leaned on her shoulder for support. On reaching the foremast, they paused and exchanged knowing looks. The Provençal was on watch, his plaintive, melancholy song drifting in the air.

> *"Dying for the sight of my captain*
> *The best that ever was,*
> *The best,*
> *Tra-la-la-la*
> *The best that ever was . . ."*

"That Provençal sings his heart out for his old ship," remarked the chaplain. "The human race never seems to stop making itself miserable. It rejects a prize at hand to follow a shadow. But once the shadow is within reach, the rejected prize becomes irresistible."

In his even, unruffled voice, the Provençal sang of his cherished captain. Jeanne was touched and her resentment toward Vincent melted.

> *"Oh, give me back my Vincent*
> *Or else I will die*
> *I will die*
> *Yes, I will surely die . . ."*

"Well, you old fool, when do you plan to desert next?" the chaplain called out sharply. "I warn you, though, the captain of this ship has it in for you. If he ever takes you back, he'll give you a taste of his rawhide and stick you in irons. And chances are your beloved Captain Vincent feels the same."

The Provençal's face broke into a blissful grin. "I'd light a candle for him in church if I had the money." He sighed and said, "I know Captain Vincent. He'll be furious but he'll forgive me."

The chaplain laughed and resumed his stroll.

Jeanne caught up with the Provençal before he went below to sleep. "Provençal, let me pay for your taper," she whispered, shoving some coins into his hand.

Surprised, he thanked her with a nod of his head. But instead of moving on, they stood looking at one another, each feeling that there was something more to say.

"Provençal, I'd like to ask you a question," Jeanne began. "Do you know this region well?"

"I know the port and the district around it. I've come here three times and we laid over twice for a good spell."

"Did you ever go into the countryside?"

"Countryside? Why would I go there? I hear it's full of horses and cattle. And wild dogs."

"Is it easy enough to explore, say a two-hour ride from the city?"

"Well, if you had a horse . . ."

"I suppose I could hire one, couldn't I?"

"Hire a horse here? You make me laugh. In this place, when you need a horse you go into the fields and rope one, or else pay an Indian to do it for you. Then, if you can afford a saddle and bridle, you're all set. When you've done what you want or arrive where you're going, you simply unbridle your horse and send him back out to pasture. That's the way it works here. With unbranded horses it's first come, first served. They're all gentle, as if nature herself had tamed them."

Jeanne's eyes opened wide in wonder. "Really? Then it's easy to go for a ride . . . say, over to the Spanish country villas?"

The Provençal shot her a piercing look. "None of my business, I know, but you're not planning to visit the grasslands alone, without your master, are you?"

"No . . . I don't expect so. Not the pampas. But today, since my master will be going off after lunch to see the herbarium of an old shoemaker, I thought I'd like to go out to the villas for a bit while he's away . . . just to look at the gardens."

The Provençal nodded. "None of my business again, but I wouldn't advise your going alone into the plains . . . sir. You need to know your way, or you need an escort."

"Is it dangerous? Because of the Indians?"

"From what I've heard, the Indians aren't the worst threat, though some are savages who band together by the hundreds and grab pretty much what they want. But the Maldonado bandits are worse than the braves. They're terrible, and always on the move."

"But aren't the Maldonado mountains far from the city?"

"Not for those bandits. They have a former Portuguese colonel to lead them. And all the fresh horses they need. Colonel Pinto's bandits patrol this whole region. They kill and steal right under the noses of the Spanish garrisons. With Indians, bandits, packs of wild dogs, and tigers, you couldn't pay me enough to get me out alone on the plains! That's a funny idea you took into your head . . . sir."

For the second time Jeanne noted the sarcastic "sir." Vexed, she turned to go. "Thanks for the information."

Annoyed at himself for having offended a passenger who had given him money, the Provençal tried to close the conversation on a cheerier note.

"Before I go below, do you want me to walk you up to the head to collect the things you had in yesterday's wash?"

"I'll get them myself. You go down and sleep. Between here and the head I won't meet any Indian braves or bandits or dogs or tigers," she declared in a mocking voice.

He opened his mouth to say something, then changed his mind. The topman turned on his heel to descend the ladder, but found his way blocked by the surgeon's two orderlies, who were bringing up heavy baskets of fresh linen. The three men encountered each other in silence, for the orderlies couldn't stand the Provençal's insolent manner. And he couldn't abide their cruel games.

About to set foot on the first rung, the Provençal glanced toward the ship's prow, where Dr. Aubriot's valet had already disappeared, then back at the orderlies' baskets. Without quite knowing why, instead of heading for his hammock, he curled up at the foot of the foremast.

Before risking a visit to the prow, Jeanne was in the habit of waiting to hear the ship's bell call the men to prayers. As soon as Father de Meslay began to intone the opening verses of *Veni Creator* on the forecastle, she knew it was safe to venture alone into the head. Nevertheless, she never went there without feeling the thrill of adventure.

The place itself, set low over the water and unseen from any part of the ship, encouraged such feelings. The men often called it the "cutthroat," for in addition to serving as a latrine and place to wash their clothes, it was an ideal spot for settling accounts secretly. More than one troublemaker had fallen overboard on his way to the head.

This morning, however, Jeanne strode briskly toward the head without waiting to hear the call to prayers. When the ship was riding at anchor, her prow lost its plunging movement. The head, draped with sailors' shirts and pants, was as unthreatening as a laundry. Jeanne went over to the handrail, removed two shirts, and gazed out at the frothy sea.

The vast blue expanse of the Plata River spread before her, dotted with sailing ships maneuvering cautiously between islands and sand bars. Clouds of swift-flying white gulls swept back and forth above the vessels, plunging after bits of refuse floating in the ships' wakes. Loons, snipes, teals, and fish-eating crows darted back and forth between shore and sea. Life below the surface revealed an incredibly distinct procession of gliding shadows. Far away on the shore, between two gleaming white beaches blanketed with gull feathers, a column of herons paraded lazily to the water's edge.

Jeanne had just decided to fetch Philibert's spyglass when she heard the patter of bare feet and spun around.

The surgeon's two obnoxious orderlies stopped dead in their tracks, leering at her. Once or twice in the past, they had managed "accidentally" to knock her off balance, running their grimy hands over her as they set her back on her feet. But she was agile and they never got very far. What luck now to find her all to themselves in a remote corner of the ship—with nobody else in sight!

Sensing instantly what this pair had in mind, Jeanne's impulse was to turn and flee. But pride overcame that impulse. Why should she run from such creatures, the scum of the ship, who would only exploit her fears in the days ahead? Resolutely she turned her back on them, as if to deny their very existence, and began collecting her dry laundry.

The bell on the forecastle rang for prayers. Seizing the moment, they attacked. The two orderlies dropped their baskets, grabbed a long, sturdy strip of bandage, and set upon their victim. Before she could cry out, Jeanne was gagged and her wrists bound behind her back. Then, while the one named John held her tightly from behind, his companion Yannick undid her jerkin and unbuttoned her shirt, disclosing the cotton sheath binding her breasts. Sneering triumphantly, he removed the pins and, with the nimble fingers of an apprentice surgeon, unwound the layers of cloth to lay bare the secret of the "doctor's pet."

Frantic with rage, Jeanne struggled desperately to free herself from John's iron grip, and unleashed a barrage of kicks that Yannick laughingly dodged.

"Say, if that isn't a pretty sight," Yannick observed as he slid his grubby fingers over his victim's chest. "Tell me, John, have you ever seen a pair of prettier titties? Have you? I've seen 'em bigger, but not so fair, and with their little noses pointed straight up in the air. Mustn't wriggle so hard, ducky, you'll bruise 'em. 'Twould be a pity to spoil such fine merchandise."

"If she's nice to us, we'll rub her pretty titties with our oil of lily to soothe those nasty bruises she's gotten herself," said John.

Jeanne's resistance was fading. Scarcely able to breathe under the gag that had worked its way up to her nostrils, she was losing her strength.

"So, dearie, now that we've seen the top, let's have a peek at the bottom. I've heard that what's female upstairs can be male downstairs, just like the sirens, half woman, half fish!"

John laughed huskily, while Yannick began to unfasten Jeanne's breeches.

As she felt him loosening her pants, Jeanne gathered all her remaining strength and let fly a vicious kick that struck Yannick below the belt. Cursing foully, he dropped his prize and doubled over, shielding his groin with both hands, his face contorted in pain. But Yannick was a tough customer, and when he managed to straighten up slightly, Jeanne became really terrified. Her other assailant tightened his grip, and she could read the hatred in Yannick's eyes.

"Bitch!" the injured man finally spluttered in a hoarse whisper. "We're having a little fun and you have to pull a dirty trick like this! You'll pay for it, you grubby little slut!"

"Take it easy, Yannick," John warned him, dragging his prisoner back a few steps. "We're not at sea and we can't feed the sharks, so don't be an ass. Come on, the joke's over. We'll help our friend pull herself together. She'll promise to keep her mouth shut about our little game, and we'll keep ours shut about her little secret."

"I tell you I won't let her get away with this. She'll shut up even faster when I get through with her!" Yannick snarled, still bent over in pain. "I tell you, no smutty little bitch is going to get the best of me . . ."

"Sons of bitches, let her go!" roared a voice suddenly. "Let her go this instant or I'll shout for help!"

The Provençal stood planted at the entrance to the head, eyes afire, fists clenched.

Maddened with pain and boiling with rage, the injured orderly drew his knife and hurled it wildly at the Provençal, who watched it sail into the water.

"Bastard!" hissed the topman. "I'll show you how to use a knife! And you, John, let her go. Or do I yell for my mates?"

John's only concern at this point was to vanish from the scene. "I was going to let her go," he insisted, maintaining his firm grip. "But it's in everyone's interests to shut up about this, right?" He glared at Jeanne, who nodded her head as the chanted words "*Domine, salvum fac regem*" reached their ears from the forecastle.

"C'mon there, Provençal, what did you think? We were just getting some information," declared John, trying to be friendly as he untied Jeanne's wrists. "We were just curious, that's all."

"Next time you stick your big nose into what isn't your business, remember that I don't miss twice!" Yannick hissed.

The Provençal laughed derisively. "You won't miss twice, you bastard, because next time you'll find my knife in your guts before you've had a chance to draw your own!"

"That's enough!" Jeanne's imperious voice rang out.

In a twinkling she had torn off her gag and fastened her clothes, and now she stood there tall and proud, with eyes flashing. She massaged her reddened wrists. Calm and self-possessed, she assumed authority.

"That will do. Nobody will draw his knife and everybody will keep his mouth shut. If so much as a whisper gets back to me, I'll go straight to the captain and tell him what went on here this morning. One more thing—don't think you can play your little game twice and get away with it. I shall never venture ashore or to the head without my pistols. And I know how to use them!"

The enraged Yannick coiled himself as if to spring, but his companion restrained him.

"It's just talk, Yannick. What do you care? Come on," John urged, "come soak your aching balls in some cool water."

"Thanks, Provençal," said Jeanne, when the two orderlies had disappeared. "You guessed that I was a woman, didn't you?"

"I've heard some say it. But after all, it's not so rare to find a woman aboard disguised as a man. Once I knew a sailor, a famous topman. Never found out he was a girl till the day I sewed her into her shroud after seventeen months at sea."

He paused eloquently, then continued in the same tone of voice, "You shouldn't have threatened them. They're dangerous."

"You threatened them too, Provençal. You said you'd slit their guts."

"I'm a man, y'know, and can handle a knife."

"I'm a good shot with a pistol."

Nodding thoughtfully, he said, "I knew they were out to get you. That's why I went to check up when I didn't see you come back."

"Thanks," she repeated. "I'll . . . my master will reward you by asking for your captain's pardon . . . when it's possible."

He nodded again, this time smiling. "In the meantime, be careful," he warned. "Are you going to tell your . . . master what happened?"

"No."

"Maybe it's best you don't."

Their eyes met in agreement.

CHAPTER 5

On the shores of a blue sea, under blue skies, in a warm, balmy climate, the indolence of the natives was hard to resist. The Frenchmen from the *Etoile des Mers* fell into step willingly with the easy-living Spaniards in Montevideo.

Each day at the captain's table there was fresh enthusiasm about the country's admirable hospitality. Raving about all the money he was saving, the purser recounted his bargains. He was feeding the whole ship sumptuously on less than five sous a day. Oh, what a colony the Spanish had!

All the sea captains using South American ports knew that to "create a deserter" was one of the few real occupations in Montevideo. For this reason, hanging on to sailors became the main concern of every petty officer on non-Spanish vessels in the bay.

The *Etoile des Mers* risked a catastrophic loss by planning to remain two or three months. To avoid this, Vilmont de la Troesne authorized shore leave by half-shifts only, in the company of two petty officers, whose reward—one sovereign per team returned—inspired them with doglike vigilance. But this system made the sailors grumble at losing one out of two days' shore leave.

Fortunately, volunteers were always needed for shore duties. Dr. Aubriot naïvely believed that a host of sailors wanted instruction in natural history. Whereas in Rio de Janeiro he had had to hire slaves to carry his specimens, in Montevideo he could simply choose his porters from among the crew.

Lieutenant Jeannot, who managed these men with so much competence and quiet authority, gained stature with the sailors. They began to regard him with more admiration than hostility.

Dr. Aubriot's valet made himself more enigmatic than ever by wearing his adopted country's dress: a peasant poncho of coarse striped wool and a white hat with a broad, upturned brim that hid his hair and brought out the golden highlights of a complexion far too smooth for any red-blooded male.

No matter, for even if Jeannot had doll-like cheeks, she had a boy's courage and a scholar's mind. Jeanne felt that the crew's respect would be her best protection against further aggression by the orderlies.

The presence of those two louts now made her feel so ill at ease that the sight of them sent shivers up her spine. In spite of her resolution to ignore Yannick, she found it hard to overlook the nasty, defiant glare he settled on her each morning when the botanizing team climbed into the rowboats to go ashore.

The orderlies were among the first volunteers accepted for the doctor's expeditions. Since Jeanne had kept silent about her misadventure, Philibert had no reason to mistrust the surgeon's assistants. On all their previous trips to Montevideo they had gathered ample supplies of herbs for the surgeon's use. Moreover, the crafty fellows had taken care to ingratiate themselves with their victim's master by telling him about the urinary property of *meona*, the perspiration-inducing effect of *payeo*, or the antivenereal virtues of *colaguala*. Willing or not, Jeanne had to put up with seeing Philibert treat the two pigs with some consideration. She kept as far away from them as possible and felt reassured by the company of the humming Provençal, who never let her out of his sight.

This morning she pulled on her poncho with a sense of satisfaction. She found the garment wonderfully comfortable. It protected her from the heat, the cool of evening, and the rain, and stood up against those sudden fierce gusts of wind so common in the plains.

She began to sing as she piled her hair into the little cap under her hat, casting a radiant smile at her own reflection in the mirror. After being a boy for such a long time, she was rediscovering the delights of being a girl. Being a boy was convenient and offered certain advantages, but all in all it was rather dull.

Aubriot opened the door and came in silently, stopping to observe the pleasant, self-indulgent scene. "So," he mocked, "you're flirting with yourself?"

She jumped. "I was thinking," she said, "that I would make a charming woman."

"Oh? Tired of being my servant?"

"Never," she replied, and curled her arms around his neck. "Where are we going this morning? Plants or shells?"

"We're going a long way, a two-hour ride on horseback. The governor has horses saddled and waiting for us. The captain just told me that Don Joachim has arranged an outing at Don José's villa. They've promised me, among other things, some wonderful lemon and orange groves. Jeannot, we're off to visit the Garden of the Hesperides! What do you say to that?"

"It's marvelous," she murmured softly. With a lump in her throat she turned away to examine her pistol.

"Ah yes, today you mustn't forget your pistol," Aubriot said, laughing.

He mocked her gently each time he saw her checking her weapon in a soldierly manner before placing it in her belt.

"Today," he continued, "we'll have to cross woods and rivers, and we may see tigers. And flocks of ostriches. We'll be a large party with choicer company than our gallant sailors. The entire Montevideo administration, three English officers, and the governor's wife are willing to give up one of their lazy mornings! Jeannot, I think we're going to have an exciting day."

"Yes," she agreed, "very exciting . . ."

* * * *

The ride out on horseback was an exhilarating adventure. The countryside was superbly wild. The plains sparkled with masses of blazing summer flowers. A rider surrounded by those endless plains could well believe that he possessed unlimited freedom in uncharted territory. There were no pathways, not even a trail. They galloped across fields and forded streams. They passed mammoth herds of cattle and horses, and flocks of horned sheep; reddish, humpbacked pigs like wild boar rooted in the tall grass. Sometimes there were flocks of plump quail. The French, smelling pâté, instantly took aim, bringing down a shower of game. A flight of eagles accompanied the cavalcade.

Dazzled, Aubriot couldn't shift his spyglass fast enough to focus on the images zooming by.

Jeanne would have liked to enter the enchanted wood, but the Spanish led them away to look for a ford in the river. This was the first time she had been on horseback since the day she bade a tearful farewell to Blanchette in the Charmont stables.

She dug her heels into her horse, and the spirited animal took off like the wind over the pampas until she reached the riverbeds. There she came to an abrupt halt, for the wide, fast-moving river was swollen from a storm in the mountains, submerging the ford. The governor explained that they would have to cross the river pampas-style.

Four Indians appeared as if by magic at the edge of the woods, carrying two canoes and followed by two dozen horses. Without a word, they slipped off their buckskins and, stark naked, harnessed two horses to the prow of each canoe. Then, clinging to the horses' manes, they forced the animals into the water. To show his visitors that crossing the water without a bridge was not at all perilous, Don Joachim handed his wife into the first canoe with Captain Vilmont de la Troesne and Sir James Harvey.

The two Indians tugged at the horses' manes and the hauling operation began. The reflection of Doña Victoria in her plum-colored riding habit danced on the foaming water. The lady smiled and chatted with the two officers as if she were seated on her own veranda.

Jeanne crossed the river in the second boat with Aubriot, enchanted by the adventure, glowing with pleasure under her broad-brimmed white hat.

Vilmont de la Troesne observed Jeanne with admiration. "The more I see of your servant, the more convinced I am that I would like to have him for myself. He really does everything so well, and so gracefully. If by chance—and God forbid it should happen—we were shipwrecked on some desert island, I would count it a blessing if you would give me half of your Jeannot in exchange for half of my Paimpol. We could divide their duties so that Paimpol did the heavy work and Jeannot the light."

Aubriot pinned the Breton captain with a penetrating gaze as he replied casually, "You're such a veteran seaman that I can't possibly imagine us running aground anywhere we didn't plan to go."

Don Joachim urged them to remount quickly. The swollen river had made them lose two hours. "Don José must be wondering if we've been attacked by Indians, Pinto's bandits, or even a hungry tiger. But I regret to announce that nothing more will happen between here and Don José's villa. Our friend, whose very rich father had the good sense to make him an only son, has civilized his estate with any number of private patrols."

Mounted once again, they set off at a canter, accompanied by a flock of ostriches.

* * * *

To a visitor from the plains, Don José's estate appeared at first sight like a fortified thicket. The villa and gardens were enclosed by a tall fence reinforced with strips of oxhide, with guard posts at the four corners. As one entered the gate, the house lay straight ahead, a simple, dazzling white box, with clumps of foliage fanning out behind. Solid black Andalusian grillework protected both ground-floor and upper-story windows and was the sole decoration. It was surprising to find such an unassuming house at the end of a courtyard with a thick carpet of grass mowed as carefully as an English lawn. As the riding party had been delayed considerably by the swollen river, they arrived just in time to eat, and sat down to lunch immediately.

After lunch, Don Joachim thanked his host for the cigarillo he had just been offered and asked, "Shall we have the pleasure of seeing Doña Emilia today?"

Don José smiled broadly. "Of course, my friend. I may be jealous, but I am pleased to show her off."

"Bring her to town with you. We'll have more occasions to compliment you on her behalf," Don Domingo said.

"No," said Don José, "Don Joachim would find some work for me to do, and the only occupation fit for a man in love is idleness. Not one of your French friends would dare contradict me on that score," he added, continuing to hand out the cigarillos.

"Nor would an Englishman. It peeves me to hear the French forever publicized as the world's greatest lovers. Don't forget that it was an Englishman who invented the most beautiful love story of all, *Romeo and Juliet.*"

Jeanne found it great fun to be eavesdropping on men instructing each other in the art of giving pleasure to a woman. She even sympathized with the well-meaning simpletons! But she felt impatient, morose, and distracted. Since her arrival at the villa, the expectation that something would happen had kept her uneasy.

Jeanne, alone in the hall, kept returning to the door, hoping to hear Don José propose a walk in his orchard.

The orchard.

She sensed its masses of greenery encircling her like a magic ring. In an hour, a minute, or a second, she would set foot in the orchard foretold by the gypsy of La Courtille. *Would this mysterious prediction come true? And what would it reveal? Oh, move, for heaven's sake, move! Don't sit around a second longer.* Again she went over to the door, separated two leather slats, and peered into the room.

This room didn't seem as exotic as the reception rooms she had seen in Montevideo. It was spacious, with a handsome black glazed-tile floor. The plain white walls were unspoiled by the dreadful tapestries or paintings that the Spaniards in La Plata seemed to favor. The sole ornament in the room was a bouquet of shiny leaves and sunflowers in an earthenware Indian jar on the floor.

Apart from this striking bouquet, the first of its kind Jeanne had seen, the room had only four small trolleys for serving maté, and many seats grouped around. In Don José's house there were the familiar uncomfortable wood and leather chairs with high, rigid backs, but there were also armchairs and Louis XV stools covered in green-and-white damask.

You couldn't call Don José handsome, but he exuded a warm and hardy masculine strength that was most attractive. The more Jeanne watched him, the nicer she found him. She thought he resembled a soldier of fortune more than a landowner. Undoubtedly, like many of the Spaniards of the pampas, he wasn't sure himself which was his real identity. He must have been between thirty and thirty-five, with a charming smile, brimming with good humor, that displayed a set of very white teeth against a face bronzed the color of gingerbread.

He spoke perfect French and was a naturally courteous host, much freer in speech and action than his compatriots. Nothing about Don José's manner would associate him with those stiff-backed chairs that seemed to encourage arrogance and self-importance. Yet he certainly knew how to impose his authority. His horses, slaves, and women unquestionably had a master, but one who carried a lump of sugar instead of a whip. Yes, Don José's people must have led a pleasant life, especially his women. His aura of good health and his simple, joyful attitude toward love left no doubt about it.

"It's really against my principles to philosophize on love. I don't believe love is any more a philosophy than it is an art. Love is an instinct, just like hunger. The best lover is most certainly the hungriest."

As several voices rose to protest that definition, Don José, still smiling, raised his hand to ask for the right to continue.

"As to whether we should learn to make love or whether we *can* learn it . . . can we learn how to arrange a bouquet or write a poem? If there are both bunglers and artists in love, I maintain that they were born that way. I've always believed that to try to make a woman happy, you have only to love her with all your power."

"That truth," put in Father Roch, laughing, "remains to be seen. But now that we've agreed Don José's idleness is commendable because it is instrumental to Doña Emilia's happiness, let's visit the orchard to please Dr. Aubriot."

"Who's talking about me, and what are they saying?" interrupted a lively new voice, which set Jeanne trembling from head to toe as she peered more closely between the leather slats.

A sky-blue patch had appeared in the doorway leading to the patio. Two ladies entered the room in a great rustle of silk. Jeanne clamped her hands over her mouth to stifle a cry. Her whole body trembled. *I'm dreaming. I've waited so long for something to happen that now I'm imagining things.*

Before Jeanne's astonished eyes, Mlle. Emilie, as nimble and relaxed as in her own green-and-white sitting room at Neuville, entered and sat down on a stool, graciously refusing the armchairs offered to her.

"I can stay only a moment. I shall return to enjoy your company. But right now I've come expressly to steal Dr. Aubriot from you, with his permission. Doña Victoria told me the purpose of your journey, sir. I know that you are curious to see Don José's plantation. I would be privileged to be the first to escort the king's botanist on a tour of the gardens."

"Madame, I could not imagine a more charming guide," he said, bowing to his hostess. "You will cast an aura of beauty over my first discoveries, and I hope to encounter some unknown flower that will deserve to bear your name."

"Sir, do not forget, I beg you, that I am as jealous as a Spaniard!" Don José said jokingly.

"Don José, don't be modest, you're as jealous as ten Spaniards," Emilie corrected him. "Thank God I'm as rebellious as ten French-women. Shall we go?" she added, turning to Aubriot.

She offered him her hand, as if to dance, and he held out his palm. He was relieved to get away from the idle, infantile chatter in the company of a pretty woman. Since his arrival in Montevideo he had seen enough dried faces with yellow smiles, and thick, unattractive waistlines to appreciate the value of this rare and deliciously lively woman, with her slender figure and milk-white complexion. As he followed her, he wondered what lay behind the mischievous look she gave him, suggesting some complicity between them. What secret could there be between him and this young Frenchwoman whom he did not remember having seen before? Maybe there was no more than high spirits in Doña Emilia's sea-green eyes, just as liveliness was in the bounce of her auburn curls.

As they were leaving the room, Aubriot looked around for his valet, whom he needed to carry his equipment.

Philibert's footsteps threw Jeanne into a panic. She barely had time to crouch down behind the only hiding place in the hall, a large table covered with a tapestry.

"All our people have disappeared," Aubriot said, letting the door close behind him. "The room's empty."

"They've gone to enjoy themselves with mine in the stables," Don José said. "They always do their partying in the stables."

"I'll send for your valet if he's still on his feet!" Emilie said. "Don José doesn't oversee his Chilean winemaking carefully enough."

"Iassi!" Emilie called from the patio doorway.

A young Indian girl appeared silently before her mistress.

"You must look for someone called Jeannot," Aubriot instructed.

From her hiding place, Jeanne guessed that the Indian had entered the room. She felt a pair of eyes riveted on the tapestry. Jeanne stood up, revealing herself, holding a finger to her lips. The girl stopped. Seeing that the valet was trying to tell her something through gestures, she approached and asked softly, "You Jeannot, yes? I understand French, a little. Mistress teach me."

"I want to talk to her," Jeanne whispered. "I need to talk to your mistress alone. Take me to a place where you can bring her that no one will see us. Quickly!"

The Indian girl didn't move.

Jeanne reached into her purse and took out a sovereign. "Here," she said, "a present for you, for a necklace."

The Indian gently pushed away her hand. "I go tell mistress."

Jeanne held her arm. "First take me to a hidden place," she implored in a hushed voice.

"Hidden?" the Indian repeated, suspiciously. "Why? You want hurt her?"

"Of course not!" Jeanne replied excitedly, trying to control her voice. "I love your mistress, I love her very, very much. I have come from France, her country, to tell her a secret. Do you understand?"

"A secret," the Indian repeated. "You woman!"

"Yes, it's true, I'm a woman," Jeanne murmured impatiently. "I've come all the way from France disguised as a man to tell your mistress a secret. Hide me and bring her to me or she'll be very angry with you. And she'll be very sad."

"Come!" said the Indian.

She took Jeanne into Emilie's bedroom. It was cool and dim behind closed blinds. Jeanne took a deep breath to calm her pounding heart. She was stunned, her mind blank except for three names: Emilie, Don José, and Denis. If Emilie was with Don José, what had happened to her childhood sweetheart, Denis Gaillon?

The sound of a door opening made her tremble violently. "Let's have a look at this mysterious messenger," said Emilie in an edgy voice. "Where is he?"

"Emilie . . ." Jeanne murmured feebly.

The newcomer's profile began to emerge.

"Iassi, let in some light."

The wooden slats of the blind rose.

"Emilie," Jeanne repeated softly, walking into the light.

"Jeannette!"

They fell into each other's arms, kissing, crying, and laughing. Emilie recovered first and drew back a step to look at Jeanne as she held her hands.

"My Jeannette! Here! I can't believe my eyes! And that outfit! Are you the servant Aubriot was looking for?"

"Yes, I'll tell you everything, but first, first, tell me about Denis."

Emilie's hands dropped.

"Denis is safe . . . far away. I'll tell you everything, Jeannette, but it will take time. I suppose that your companions are not aware of your disguise."

"No one but Monsieur Aubriot knows about it."

"We'll have to keep up our roles, then, for the walk in the orchard. But I'll find a way for us to see each other comfortably for as long as we want."

"Emilie, do you think Monsieur Aubriot recognized you?"

"He didn't appear to. I don't think so. I was still a little girl when he saw me for the last time. I had scarlet fever, which made me look awful."

"Will you talk to him?"

"About myself?" Emilie seemed very surprised.

"When I heard you invite him to go for a walk in the garden, I thought you planned to discuss your affairs with him."

There was a brief silence. Emilie's voice changed slightly. "I needed to walk for a while next to a man who knew Mistress Emilie of Neuville."

She shook her head and made the curls bounce. "Jeannette, I must go back to the guests. You . . ." She stopped short, her gray-green eyes sparkling. "I trust that the fact that you are wearing that outfit means Aubriot isn't simply your master?"

"No," said Jeanne, blushing.

"So he finally made up his mind. Good. Iassi!"

The Indian girl appeared silently from the shadows. Emilie told her something in Spanish and turned to her friend. "Join us in the orchard in a few moments, as though Iassi had just found you. For the rest, trust me."

They hugged each other in silence.

CHAPTER 6

ight had already fallen when Iassi led Jeanne back to her mistress's bedroom. Standing at the foot of her bed, Emilie held out her arms.

Speechless at first, they sat on the quilt quietly holding hands and gazing at each other. Emilie had changed to a white, lace-trimmed batiste negligée with a matching camisole. *How could Philibert not have recognized her when she still looked so much like the girl of fifteen who had run away from a Neuville convent?*

The slight, slender body had filled out a bit, or rather softened and become more feminine. But that irresistible, rosy little face—milk-white freckled complexion, lively curls, piercing sea-green eyes—the face still belonged to that mischievous, spirited, independent little girl. With tears in her eyes, Jeanne kissed Emilie's cheek.

"Three years," she said. "I wonder if after these three years I've changed as little as you have."

Emilie smiled, freed Jeanne's hair from its confining cap, and ran her fingers through it. She spread a heavy satin cloth over her friend's shoulders and brought her locks forward so that they lay like strands of ash-colored silk on the satin.

"It's beginning to feel like old times," she said, smiling. She picked out a lock and tickled the underside of Jeanne's nose. "Something's missing, though. You used to walk in a cloud of scented flowers. It was lily, wasn't it, your toilet water?"

"Blended with other flowers. But it wouldn't be natural for a servant to smell good. Not to smell bad is uncommon enough!"

Jeanne, who was examining the spacious white room, added, "Your surroundings were never so austere."

"Here, I got rid of furniture instead of collecting it. Spanish taste is insufferable. I don't know what it's like in Madrid, but here it gave me insomnia! I keep only what is absolutely necessary. Don José's bouquets are the only decorations I want. He's the one Spaniard in this region who knows how to make a bouquet *and* a cigarillo. Jeanne, you used to do such beautiful flowers for the parties at Charmont."

Emilie pointed to the living art placed around the room, a sumptuous assortment of multicolored zinnias, velvety blossoms in a cloisonné jar, sitting on a massive, dark lacquered bureau with turned-out feet. A single spray of giant long-stemmed mauve morning glories and golden daisies stood on the tiled floor in the corner of the room. There were two other loving touches: a tall branch of scarlet dog-roses with golden undersides on the dressing table, and a little bunch of delicate pinkish-white flowers with deep purple leaves atop the nightstand.

"Well, what do you think of Don José's arrangements?" Emilie asked.

"I believe they show he's very much in love with you," Jeanne replied softly.

Emilie lowered her eyes, then tossed her curls, saying, "Jeannette, we must talk seriously."

Jeanne smiled at her affectionately. "Three years, Emilie!" she exclaimed. "For three times three hundred and sixty-five days we've lived as best we could. We used to dream of our futures while nibbling sweets and sipping Mâcon wine at your house in Neuville. We were sure of ourselves then, sure of our hearts, of our desires and our strength of purpose. We were sure that perfect, lasting happiness was within our grasp if we managed to attract the man we wished. But we were only little girls, Emilie."

She took her friend in her arms, hugged her, pressed the auburn head against her shoulder, and murmured, "Emilie, little girls don't know that women are fragile. But I learned about my weakness at the same time that you did."

A muffled sob from Emilie made Jeanne hold her even tighter. But a few minutes together lightened both their hearts.

They smiled at each other as Jeanne said, "Where is Denis?" And Emilie said, "How is Marie?"

"Marie is very well," Jeanne answered. "At least she sent good news in her last letter, which I received before leaving Paris last September. She finally married her cousin Philippe and she has a baby daughter named Virginia. They live in Autumn in her Uncle Mormagne's house—he died."

"Paris?" Emilie interjected. "You were in Paris?"

"Ah, that's true. I'll have to start from the beginning," Jeanne said. Emilie offered her a comfortable armchair.

Jeanne glanced nervously at the door and the window. "Aren't you worried that someone will come by? This light, and the voices in your bedroom late at night . . ."

Emilie reassured her. "Forgive me, but I had to take Don José into our confidence. I couldn't risk his running a sword through you before I had time to explain the presence of a handsome young man in my bedroom. Spaniards are quick to act, especially in the colonies, where it is every gentleman's right to murder for passion. But Don José is a man of honor. He will never betray you. I can't promise, however, that he won't find some excuse to drop by."

A flicker of a smile accompanied her last words and she added hastily, with visible embarrassment, "By the way, how did Aubriot take the presence of Lady Emilie de la Pommeraie in the house of a Spaniard in La Plata?"

"I haven't said a word to Aubriot," Jeanne declared. "He has to share his bed with Father Roch. So he doesn't know that I'm with you or why."

Jeanne pushed her armchair close to the bed. A candle on the nightstand provided the only soft, glowing light. Elsewhere in the room there was shadow, except in front of the window, where two slits of moonlight stole through the blinds onto the dark glazed tiles.

She began her tale with Emilie's departure from Neuville. "For weeks everything was topsy-turvy there. The bishop camped out at the priory like a head of state. The local police were questioning everyone, including me . . ."

"I know about all the commotion after I left," Emilie interrupted. "Just tell me if my dear godmother wept for me. I left her a letter."

"I know," Jeanne said. "Lady Charlotte read it to me and Marie . . . just the two of us. Oh yes, she did cry. She loved you so much, Emilie. By the way," she added, blushing in anticipation of the name she was about to pronounce, "who told you what happened in Neuville after you ran off? The Chevalier Vincent?"

Emilie frowned, and Jeanne went on hastily, "He told no one about your affair. I thought he'd helped you get out of France, that's all. You came to Montevideo on the *Belle Vincente*, didn't you?"

"Yes. At my request the chevalier took us first to Malta, but we were not safe there from a royal summons. We knew we had to go farther. Our goal was South America, more precisely Montevideo, as Gaillon . . ." She paused for a second as though the name Gaillon had burned her tongue, and began her tale again in an impersonal manner.

"In Marseilles, Denis met a Spanish pharmacist—actually an adventurous barber—who hoped to make his fortune in Montevideo. Don Piedracueva spoke of La Plata as though it were El Dorado, a place where all Europeans passed for gentlemen, where a little bit of learning made you important, and running a shop paved the way to riches. Gaillon knew a good deal about chemistry and needed money and recognition urgently. So Piedracueva had no trouble convincing him to go into partnership. The idea of South America attracted me too. I felt that in South America Gaillon would become a distinguished chemist and justify my love for him. When the Seven Years' War ended and the Straits of Gibraltar were reopened, the chevalier set sail with us for Montevideo."

"In Malta, did you live in Vincent's little house?" Jeanne couldn't resist asking.

Emilie frowned again.

"I know he has a small house at La Valette, with a vegetable garden overlooking the sea," Jeanne added quickly, "and I thought . . ."

"Yes, we were there. Delightful place, Jeanne, delightful. I would have liked to stay on forever in Malta. The people live a gay life with plenty of style and spirit. Not so, alas, with a Maltese chevalier that I . . ."

Emilie broke off suddenly and continued in a different key, "But we're mixing everything up. It's you, Jeanne, who started to talk."

"You left in December 1763. Afterwards, life seemed to drag on until September of the following year. The days crawled by, colorless, lifeless, as they do when your sole interest is what tomorrow's weather will be. Philibert was traveling. I waited for him to return. When he finally came back and announced that he was going to live in Paris, he offered me a post. Call it a secretarial post, or head housekeeper, keeper of his heart, pet lady-in-waiting . . . I never really knew. Nor thought about it. It was enough for me to know that I was leaving for Paris with the man I loved."

And Jeanne briefly recounted her life in Paris, the success of her herb shop, and finally her desperate flight from the dangerous Duke de Richelieu.

"But," Jeanne concluded, "I often think it was my old dream of sailing to the Indian Ocean that spurred my escape from Paris, rather than fear of Richelieu."

"My desire to see you again is what brought you here," Emilie said softly.

Jeanne smiled. "Yes indeed, Emilie. Don José's orchard was in the cards. But now tell me about yourself. I see you are more beautiful than ever. How are you? Are you happy, Emilie?"

"Happy . . ." Emilie smiled with a serenity Jeanne had never seen before. "It's not the time to ask if I'm happy, my dear, because your being here tonight makes me perfectly happy. As far as I'm able, I'll tell you what's happened in my life rather than in my feelings. That way it will seem clearer.

"Jeanne, what do you think of Don José? Do you find him attractive? Could he have won your heart? Would you have taken him as a lover?"

Jeanne evaded the questions. "It is your love and your story I want to hear about."

There was a long silence. In the vast stillness of the night, an animal roared close to the house.

"That's a tiger," Emilie said. "I would have liked to stay in Malta. I would have liked to let Gaillon sail without me. I wish I could have changed my story. I would have loved a chevalier and lived happily forever with him on an island. Don't think I was afraid of the poverty awaiting me in South America. Actually, I dreaded the boredom I would bring with me. I know you loved Gaillon as a brother, but I was so bored with Gaillon that I felt I was leading a life of virtue rather than a life of sin. I didn't run away from the convent for that!"

Jeanne smiled and blushed at the same time. *So Vincent had attracted Emilie too.* Aloud she said, "What surprises me, Emilie, isn't that you were bored with Denis, but that you ever thought to amuse yourself with him." She looked at the pretty young woman, so slender and glowing, a duke's toy. "How did it happen that you ran away with Denis?"

"I had no one to love, and I wanted to love. Denis loved me and I confused that love with my own feelings. I was only fifteen, full of life, a young girl shut up with old ladies for six years. I thought—I still think—that a woman must have a good time before she's twenty."

Jeanne smiled. "I remember how disgusted I was when the Neuville order took you. I watched them tie a black and white ribbon in your hair, which the nuns called 'your husband.' You were married forever at the age of nine to a strip of cloth! Anyone would understand why you ran away. Nobody would have complained if you'd gone off with a young gentleman. But why on earth did you let the son of a steward carry you off?"

Emilie's green eyes sparkled. "My dear Jeannette, everyone knew I was poor. Young gentlemen these days are not very romantic. Their escapades are scarcely newsworthy. When one of them causes a scandal, it's by marrying a millionaire draper's daughter. But if their sister wants to rebel, she chooses her penniless poetry teacher. Our brothers and cousins like to marry above their means, and we below our class. It's called practicing equality."

"Now I recognize you," Jeanne laughed. "I expected a tragic tale and get comic relief instead."

"What can I do? My misadventure is either amusing or stupid. I'd rather make it fun. So there I was, bored with the handsome Gaillon—he *was* handsome, wasn't he! Allow me that excuse."

"Oh, he was handsome, all right, and intelligent, even knowledgeable and ambitious. He was sensitive. He was honest. He danced wonderfully. I can find you lots of excuses."

"Yes, he would have made a good husband," Emilie said, "but I only wanted him as a lover, and for that, wit serves better than brains, and a little imagination better than a lot of learning. I had a fling with a serious-minded man, and a fling without a touch of madness isn't worth the effort."

"Since you realized your mistake in Malta, why did you sail for Montevideo?"

"Because I'm proud. Only simpletons make little mistakes. I decided to carry my mistake with nobility, honor, and virtue. When I left Neuville I took my cross with me."

Tugging at the chain around her neck, she drew a large medal from inside her gown. Jeanne recognized the enameled cross edged in gold, decorated with fleur-de-lis and the inscription "Nobility, Honor, Virtue" beneath an image of Saint Catherine. The symbol of the cloister at Neuville.

"So you still wear it," Jeanne murmured.

"It wasn't just pride that made me follow Gaillon," Emilie continued. "Come and see . . ."

She jumped out of bed, snatched up the candle, and led Jeanne into a large room adjoining hers. Jeanne saw a black woman sleeping on a leather couch, who awoke suddenly in surprise.

Emilie motioned for her to go back to sleep and led Jeanne to a small bed where a beautiful, curly-haired child lay sleeping. "It's a boy," she said.

"My God!" Jeanne exclaimed, overcome with tenderness. "Oh, Emilie, he's so beautiful!"

Jeanne planted a kiss on the sleeping cherub's forehead and ran a finger over the curls, whose coppery strands glowed in the candlelight. "He's magnificent," she said quietly. "What color are his eyes?"

"They're just like mine, only bigger."

"How old is he?"

"Two."

"Two," Jeanne repeated after they had tiptoed from the room. "Two years already . . ."

"Yes," said Emilie. "Never take a twenty-year-old lover, Jeannette. He'll get you pregnant before you want to be. Aubriot hasn't made you pregnant, has he?"

Blushing, Jeanne shook her head. Anxious to change the subject, she asked, "What's his name?"

"Paul-Charles. Charles after Charlotte, and Paul after the twin brother I lost."

"So, Denis left you Paul-Charles. Where did he go?"

"To Glasgow. He met someone here named Watt, who was involved in perfecting navigational aids. Watt came from a Scottish family of mechanics, engineers, physicists, or something of the sort, and also was interested in chemistry. He and Gaillon became fast friends. Since I had decided to leave him, Gaillon didn't want to stay on in Montevideo. He preferred to return to Europe, the seat of science. Watt was planning to introduce him to learned circles in Glasgow. He waited for my delivery and then left for England ten days after Paul's birth. If he'd wanted to take his son, I would have sent him along gladly. I didn't much care for Gaillon's son."

"You didn't love your own child?"

"No, I thought he would weigh down my life as he'd weighed down my stomach. It didn't seem fair. By giving birth, I felt I'd done my share. I would have been glad for Gaillon to do the rest. But he didn't dare to ask. And I didn't dare to offer. It would have horrified a society that idolizes children."

"But you love your son now, don't you? How can you help but love him when he's so beautiful."

Emilie laughed lightly. "He's beautiful, therefore I love him. I'm a bad mother, no doubt about it. I didn't begin to love him till he grew beautiful, lively and gay. Iassi calls him *Toupen-verap*, Thunderbolt, because he's as quick as a little Indian and makes a lot of noise. Don José adores him. In fact, it was Don José who taught me to love him. Paul was born here, in this room."

"Here? So you were living here with Denis?"

"I left him before Paul was born. The heavier the baby grew, the less I could put up with the father. I must confess that I'd already met Don José. He knew how to love me without boring me. When I asked him to find me a place where I could be alone to give birth, he offered me his hospitality, which I accepted. So here I am. Now you know everything."

"Except the most important thing. Have you finally discovered happiness with Don José?"

"That varies from day to day. Memories of life in France are an obstacle to happiness anywhere else."

"But do you love Don José?"

"That depends. Love always tires of love. But apart from love, I've nothing else here. I live in a love nest surrounded on all sides by pampas."

"Why don't you go live in town? In Montevideo or Buenos Aires?"

"Sometimes we do. But in Buenos Aires, as in Montevideo, the greatest distraction for a woman is to entertain visiting officers from overseas. Don José is too jealous to allow me to do that. So I'm left to amuse myself by dressing wooden saints in churches. Go into the churches and look at the wardrobe of Saint Jacques or Saint Stanislaus. You'll understand just how bored the ladies are in Montevideo. There is no theater, no conversation, no fashion, no strolling on the boulevard, no novelists. The Spaniards of La Plata have invented nothing to amuse their ladies honestly. The women choose between devotion and infidelity, ripening like green figs by being handled!"

Jeanne smothered a laugh with both hands. Emilie's sea-green eyes sparkled playfully each time the candlelight caught them. The young exile seemed truly happy. Jeanne went on plying her friend with questions. But Emilie had little outside of her own love life to report.

"I've nothing to tell!" she insisted. "Not a single solid item of gossip. All they do here is ride, and centaurs only make dung."

"My dear, it's the riders who interest me," said Jeanne, laughing.

"The best riders, like Don José, are South Americans."

"Emilie, don't say such awful things! South Americans are black, dirty, mangy, and smelly. They live naked in the woods, and dress for parties or for war by painting themselves. They lend their wives to guests and kill them if they decide to sleep around without permission. South Americans are savages. Don José is not like that."

"Jeannette, you've just described most uninvitingly a native population which Don José and Iassi have taught me to respect . . . more or less. But these people will disappear. Many already have become slaves, decently dressed in ponchos. The unlucky ones are sold to Jesuit missions, the luckier ones to landowners. As for the remaining Indian braves, the Spanish kill them at the drop of a hat in the name of the king or in the name of the Lord. The time will come in La Plata when the people will either be landless slaves or Spaniards like Don José, calling themselves South Americans because they regard Spain as a foreign country."

"Is that the way Don José thinks of Spain?"

"He thinks very little of Spain. He was born in Montevideo, like Don Carlos, Don Armando, Don Marciso, and many others."

"They are merely rebelling against their fathers, which is also fashionable among young Europeans," Jeanne commented, smiling. "La Régence in Paris is full of such men."

"Jeannette, don't confuse your fashionable aristocrats with our gentlemen landowners. Before you cast off a noble father, you need to have one! Most of our landed gentry are social upstarts. In 1726, when the first Spanish settlers came here, Montevideo was a puny little fort lashed by the *pampero*. Tell me what well-born Spaniard would come to such a place? Those who risked it were beggars, illiterates, and pirates. They acquired the privilege of calling themselves 'Don' by courting adventure. Don José and Don Carlos are not turncoats. They are upstarts."

"Oh!" Jeanne exclaimed, shocked.

"But this is indeed the New World," Emilie consoled her. "Here, only the ignorant or impoverished sons of the original settlers hide their origins. The ones I call South Americans are happy and un-ashamed to be upstarts."

"That explains my attraction to Don José," Jeanne said. "He's sincere and shows it. But where did he learn the Old World manners he imitates so well?"

"Well enough," Emilie corrected her. "The adventurers who became rich sent their sons on a tour of Europe as part of their education. Don José spent six months in Spain, a year in Italy, and three years in France. After which he decided that the life of a rich young man in South America was the best. He returned to La Plata just in time to see his father die at the hands of the Indians."

"I heard that his father left him a rich man."

"Yes, old Eduardo de Murcia was a very talented brigand who saved his money. José de Murcia continues, steadily and purposefully, to build up his father's fortune."

"Emilie, do you expect me to believe that your Don José is a brigand?"

"This is 1767, not 1726. Nowadays no Spaniard of La Plata can afford to be a brigand. He's a smuggler. What else is there? You're not going to get rich on cattle at ten or twenty sous a head, even if you have fifty thousand head. Luckily, all commercial trade is more or less outlawed by Madrid. European goods cannot enter here en route to Chile and Peru. It's forbidden to do business with the Portuguese colony next door, or to sell leather and furs to foreign ships. There are so many restrictions that all the rowboats are making fortunes. In fact, Don José is the boss of the best team of smugglers in La Plata."

Jeanne laughed till her sides hurt. "You say that so cheerfully. I'm glad for you, but a bit surprised. It's hard to see you in love with the king of smugglers . . ."

"My dear, don't forget that I was the mistress of a mere pharmacist!"

"Emilie," Jeanne asked hesitantly, "does Don José think of marrying you?"

Emilie frowned. "Jeannette, I'm the one who doesn't think about it."

A lengthy silence followed. Jeanne finally asked, "Do you want to go back to France?"

"With my Thunderbolt? Never!" Emilie declared passionately. "I couldn't stand being the mother of a bastard. Here there are no bastards. When he grows up he'll be addressed as 'Don' like the others, and take his place in society. He can even share in his father's estate. All the gentlemen here publicly recognize their bastards, embrace them on the street and seat them next to their legitimate children in church."

"Really!" Jeanne exclaimed, wide-eyed.

"Yes, really. Here law and custom sanction illegitimacy."

"The New World is indeed a new world!" Jeanne said excitedly, her eyes shining. "It's wonderful, Emilie, a world that doesn't punish innocent children. I like it! Oh, Emilie, why don't you marry Don José, a citizen of such a tolerant country?"

"That's a long story, but let me tell you that Don José treats my little Paul like his own son. And I'd never take Paul away from him. Thank God I was able to save my son from ending up as the bastard of an ordinary French pharmacist!"

Jeanne reacted vehemently. "Emilie, you're far too arrogant about your past. Denis wasn't so . . ."

Two resounding knocks at the bedroom door ended Jeanne's outburst.

"May I come in?" Don José asked, poking his smiling face through the doorway.

"What if I say no?" Emilie replied with a toss of her curls.

"Don't be cheeky. I'm sure you've told all your secrets and are both dying of thirst."

He vanished and soon reappeared carrying a loaded tray. In the flickering light, Don José indeed appeared more like a South American smuggler than a European gentleman. He seemed to have nothing on under his thick white wool poncho. His Indian leggings matched the poncho, and he was barefoot. "There's quail pâté, jams, sweet brioche, wheat rolls, fresh curds, and champagne," he announced, setting the tray down on the bureau. "Tell me, ladies, is this snack to your liking?"

"Don José loves to play servant," Emilie explained, a bit uneasily.

"And whom would you suggest I rouse to feed you at this hour of the night?" he asked.

"You could have wakened a servant," Emilie said.

"Waken a servant? Good Lord, that would be harder than preparing a snack myself. And you're much better served by me, my love."

"Jeannette, Don José's slaves are so inert that from a distance you'd take them for cow dung lying in the sun," Emilie commented mockingly.

"Don't believe her, Jeannette. They lie in the shade." Don José burst into a deep, hearty laugh.

"Don José, you have a barbarous laugh," Emilie complained, covering her ears with both hands. "I'll never get used to it. You should save your laughter for the pampas, when the *pampero* is blowing."

"I always forget that French ladies have delicate senses," Don José said, winking at Jeanne. "Only their heads are as solid as hardwood."

Jeanne began to laugh too.

"Jeannette, would you like some champagne?" Don José asked. "We natives like a very full-bodied wine. But I serve contraband French wines to my honored guests. You've been told, haven't you, that I'm a very successful smuggler?"

"I told her that you were the best outlaw in the whole province, the worthy son of a gentleman brigand," Emilie confirmed.

"*Muchas gracias*, my darling," said Don José, kissing her hand. "Jeannette, have you seen my prize possession? Have you seen Thunderbolt?"

"Yes," Jeanne replied. "He's beautiful."

The Spaniard looked so radiantly happy that Jeanne couldn't resist making him even happier. She added, "Your son is truly beautiful."

Don José's eyelids fluttered against his dark skin, and he turned to Emilie. "Your friend is quite charming. I'd watch out if I were you."

"In France it's the women who choose," Emilie informed him.

"My sweetheart, you are the adorable proof that a beautiful Frenchwoman can make the mistake of choosing me," he replied.

Don José cleared some books off a small serving cart, which he then covered with a white cloth. He quickly set two places, and uncorked and served the champagne.

"I've put you two face to face like lovers," he said, stretching his hands to them. "Let's drink a toast to your reunion. To friendship."

The three clinked glasses and Don José tossed back his wine in one gulp. "This champagne has traveled remarkably well. It's a miracle!" exclaimed Jeanne.

"A miracle that never fails when my friend Vincent brings it," said

Don José. "Vincent already has brought me more than one treasure in perfect condition," he said, eyeing Emilie.

Don José's dark eyes glowed with tender passion. Jeanne saw Emilie respond instantly with genuine sweetness and warmth. Jeanne held out her empty glass to her host, reeling from the mention of Vincent's name. "I'd love some more champagne so I can make a wish," she said.

"Can we know what it is?" Emilie asked.

"No, you can't. But wish for it to come true."

"Jeannette, I drink to your wish," Emilie said.

Then the two women looked into each other's eyes and, overcome with emotion, burst into tears.

Don José looked at the weeping women, the empty glasses, the near-empty bottle, the two heads, blonde and auburn, and started to laugh very gently. He poured the rest of the wine into their glasses. Clinking his empty glass against theirs, he declared, "Tears that come from good wine cleanse the soul."

CHAPTER 7

Beauty, you are like a buttercup,
As precious, Beauty, as any treasure.

he song was the Provençal's newly adopted warning signal.

"I'm going to take a look at the weather," Jeanne called to Aubriot, and stepped out onto the deck.

The Provençal's face reflected his discontent. "I didn't draw a lucky straw today, so I won't be on your expedition," he explained. "Do you intend to camp ashore tomorrow night?"

"If possible," Jeanne replied. "Camping out every other night will save a lot of time. We'll be ready to go to work one morning out of two."

"I don't like it," the Provençal grumbled, "especially since it seems you're heading east."

"Yes, northeast."

"Walking or riding?"

"Riding, to go farther in. The orderlies say the flora nearer the Maldonado mountains are different. Those two pigs know the regional flora quite well, I must admit."

"I don't like it," the Provençal repeated. "I've never liked a good idea that came from that pair. I want to go with you. Can't you arrange it with the doctor?"

"I doubt it. The captain warned him not to favor anyone. It creates problems among the crew."

"You're going east and I don't like that. The route to Maldonado takes you into bandit territory."

"I've been hearing that the Pinto bandits are everywhere, yet we've never seen a single one. You know we have an armed escort of ten men with us at all times, plus a lookout and two officers who are excellent swordsmen. We're not at all in danger."

"There are six hundred of these Pinto bandits, all crack shots. When my captain ventures anywhere near their territory, he keeps his eyes peeled day and night, as if he were in rattlesnake country!"

"Does the Chevalier Vincent often come to Maldonado?" Jeanne asked quickly.

"Oh yes. In Montevideo, everything is forbidden. You can't load or unload so much as a straw without oiling the palm of the coast guard."

"I expect a lot of things are forbidden in Maldonado too."

"Yes. But the government is thirty leagues away. Look here, I still want to come with you. Tell the doctor that I'll do his cooking. I'm a good cook. Tell him I'll make him some soup! I'll fix him a *bouiabaisso* fit for a king!"

"Bouillabaisse, out on the plains? Beef bouillabaisse, then?" Jeanne said, laughing. "Well, I'll give it a try."

Aubriot resisted mildly, but in the end agreed to include the Provençal in his field trip. "And don't forget to bring your Provençal pipe," he advised. "I have yet to test your talents as a cook, but as a musician I know you're very good."

* * * *

On the heels of a rosy dawn and a warm morning, the *pampero* wind rose suddenly and drenched the party in a downpour.

Don Joachim had insisted Aubriot take an interpreter and two Indian guides selected from among the best warriors of his reserve. This precaution now proved to be particularly useful, since, without the encouragement of their Indians, who had seen far worse weather themselves, the Frenchmen would have thought their final hour had come. And it might well have, for they were nearly blown away by the tempest.

The guides took over, throwing them down behind a rocky rampart, covering their heads with cowhides, unsaddling the horses and forcing them, whinnying and protesting, to lie down behind the sheltering rocks. Then the Indians lay down among the animals, stretching their ponchos over their great old dirty hats and waiting motionless until the *pampero* subsided.

The deluge lasted two hours and stopped abruptly in a great burst of light that set the plains sparkling. The Indians got up silently and stared at the dazed Frenchmen, who were rising awkwardly from the muddy grass. Aubriot began to cough violently.

"This will help," said one of the guides, and handed him a jug of brandy. He motioned him to pass it around. Then he took off his poncho and hat and squeezed them out. Both Indians were stark naked.

"Señor, you should do the same. And the other señores too," the interpreter said to Aubriot, as he pointed to the two natives who were drying off in the sun.

"We better get started if we don't want to catch our deaths," Yannick declared, taking off his shirt. "Y'know, doctor, the *pampero* storm kills a lot of men in this country."

As Yannick spoke, he looked sideways at Jeanne. Aubriot noted the look and saw Jeanne laughing with the Provençal. She had followed the Indians' example and had already removed, squeezed out, and spread her poncho on a bush. She could undress no further, and Aubriot felt a sudden pang of fear.

From earliest childhood Jeanne had always been unfailingly healthy. This was the first time he had ever worried about her. He was shivering himself, and not just from the weather. Suddenly, in that slimy expression on the orderly's face, Aubriot was discovering how vulnerable Jeanne really was.

From his strong, devoted, inviolable little girl, she had metamorphosed into a very pretty young woman. Now, dressed as she was in a wet pair of breeches and a soggy shirt, exposed to the dangers of rough men and the wilderness, he loved her with boundless, childlike fervor, filled with tenderness and pain.

"Jeannot!" he called abruptly.

She ran to him, surprised by his tone of voice.

"Drink!" he ordered, taking the jug of brandy from Montaigu. While Jeanne drank, Aubriot looked at the scene around him with new eyes.

Beaupreau and Montaigu, naked to the waist, were rubbing themselves dry; several sailors with their breeches down stood around in hose that scarcely concealed their virility. They were beginning to joke and roar with laughter.

Aubriot exploded. "Get dressed at once, all of you!" he bellowed. "We're leaving. Machado told me there's an Indian hamlet nearby. We can relax there and fix ourselves a hot meal."

"But, señor, four horses ran away during the *pampero* storm," the interpreter protested. "Let's give the Indians time to recapture them or lasso four others."

"Machado," Aubriot addressed his interpreter, "tell the guides that four men will ride double. Once we reach camp, they'll have plenty of time to go out and rope horses."

* * * *

The village Indians killed and spitted two red piglets, then served a spicy mixture to their visitors while the roast cooked. As the brandy jug made its rounds and washed the meal down, the Frenchmen found themselves smiling benevolently at one another.

Jeanne stretched out on her stomach, folded her arms under her chin, and closed her eyes, dreaming of the parties Don José had promised to arrange so that she and Emilie could get together more often.

She had removed her jacket, boots, and hose to hasten the drying process. As the sun warmed her feet and back, she began to feel blissfully happy. She drifted off to sleep, floating with her handsome chevalier on a cloud of bright summer sunshine.

"Are you awake? The pork is cooked." Aubriot's hand shook her shoulder gently, and she sat up. An Indian was carving one of the roast pigs and passing out steaming hunks of savory, succulent meat.

The Indian hamlet had three large cabins. One, made of hides, was used for cooking and storage, while the other two were a mixture of dirt and grass over a framework of reeds. Two families lived there, about fifteen people in all—men, women, and children. They had invited the Frenchmen's guides to share their meal, a thick stew with a hot, spicy smell.

After wolfing down their food, which they ate straight out of the pot with a dried gourd shell, they proceeded to emit loud belches as a sign of their satisfaction, and to drink the jug of brandy Aubriot had sent them.

The eldest host got up and disappeared into the kitchen. He returned carrying something in his old military hat to present to his guests. The Frenchmen were astounded to see cigarros as long and good as those offered to them in the best drawing rooms of Montevideo.

"Can we buy some?" Montaigu asked the interpreter. "I would love to bring some back to serve my own guests."

Machado shook his head. "Forgive me, señor, but the Indians do not sell their tobacco. They believe one must not sell smoke. Smoke is heavenly," Machado explained.

"I agree," Montaigu sighed.

After finishing their cigarros, the two guides and the Indians left for the plains to catch the horses they needed. The two young officers went along to watch.

While they waited, John the orderly suggested a short excursion.

"Dr. Aubriot, if you want to see something special, you should cross the ford. On the far side the slope rises steeply. Up on the heights are stretches of yellow strawflowers that the Spanish medicine men call *vira-verda* and use to cure stomachaches. Monsieur Pauly used to boil them like tea, and it seemed to help the skipper, who often complains about his stomach."

"Up there," Yannick added, "we could also show you the reed used for making nets and fishing lines."

"Yes, I'm very eager to see those reeds," Aubriot said, addressing Jeanne. "That thread is practically as strong and beautiful as raw silk. I wonder if the weavers from Lyon could turn it into fine cloth? Let's go have a look."

Jeanne put her boots and her poncho back on. She glanced toward the river. The orderlies were already in the saddle and getting ready to cross, led by an Indian woman mounted on a frisky red pony. The river was quite wide and swift at that point, but Jeanne saw that even in the middle of the ford, the water reached only to her pony's belly. With a manly slap at the pistol in her belt, Jeanne turned around to call the Provençal, only to find him directly behind her.

"Look here, Dr. Aubriot," he addressed the botanist abruptly, "you don't intend to cross without an escort, do you?"

"Yes, we do!" Jeanne retorted gaily. "We are going up the hillside over there to pick some herbs for the captain's tea while we wait for our Indians to return. You are coming along. On your horse, Provençal! I'll race you to the top of the hill."

She jumped astride and broke into a gallop in the wake of the orderlies, who had reached the far shore.

"Stop!" the Provençal shouted. "Wait for me! Wait! Felibien! Felibien!"

"What is the matter?" responded the mate crossly.

"Felibien, don't let Dr. Aubriot cross the ford. Don't let him!" the Provençal bellowed as he leaped onto the bare back of a grazing pony.

Clinging to the animal's mane, he rode into the ford at full speed, making a huge splash. Jeanne glanced back, laughed at her pursuer, and spurred her mount. As soon as he came out of the water, her horse took off like the wind, and Jeanne reached the plateau even before the orderlies.

The plateau was bordered by woods on two sides, and covered with tall, waving green grass shining with dew and studded with thousands of small golden-yellow stars.

"It's so pretty," Jeanne exclaimed, entranced. "It's like a tapestry."

But she had no time to marvel. The Provençal was on top of her, bellowing, "Quick! Turn around! Let's go back!"

Leaping from his horse, he landed behind her saddle, snatched the bridle of her mount, and tugged at the bit.

"Are you mad?" cried Jeanne, struggling against the sudden command. Only then did she see the band of horsemen racing out of the wood in front of her.

The noose of a lasso choked her horse, which reared and sent the Provençal sprawling. Instinctively, Jeanne held on to the saddle with all her strength and shouted for help instead of drawing her gun.

Seconds later, still stunned, she found herself astride another horse with her arms trussed, clasped firmly by a bandit who was racing his mount ahead at full speed. Her kidnapper galloped to the music of thundering hooves. Tails flew before her eyes, manes floated in the eerie green glow of underbrush. She felt as if she were being abducted by a herd of horses that she had mounted all at once, as if in some fantastic nightmare.

Jeanne began to scream and could not stop. She screamed until her throat went dry. But the vise clutching her never loosened.

When at last she stopped screaming, she tried to think and assess her predicament. Looking around her as best she could, she saw galloping horses mounted by men in ponchos wearing large Spanish-style hats. She remembered hearing the report of a single gun just before her abduction. Her blood suddenly ran cold. She tried to shout the Provençal's name, but the cry emerging from her throat sounded strangely feeble.

The horses had slowed to a walk and were entering a thicket. The bandits had to cut through heavy underbrush to find the overgrown trail. Jeanne felt someone toss a cowhide over her, and she was plunged into darkness for some time. When the hide was finally removed, the sunlight almost blinded her. They set off once more at a gallop, more frantic than ever. Moments later, when she had recovered slightly, she called again in despair, "Provençal? Provençal? Where are you?"

"What?" the voice close to her neck asked, and she felt her captor urge his mount forward to overtake another horseman whom he called Julio.

Julio turned to the prisoner, beaming with satisfaction. "How can I help you, mam'selle?" he yelled out to her in flawless French.

Jeanne looked astonished. "Are you French?"

"At your service, mam'selle. There are people from all over in our village."

"What village? Where are you taking me?"

"To Colonel Pinto, a very gallant *caballero* with pretty ladies."

"Where is the man you captured with me?"

"He is behind you, mam'selle, tied up more securely."

She breathed a sigh of relief. At least she wasn't all alone among a band of outlaws.

Then, suddenly, her throat tightened once again. Julio had called her "mam'selle." "How do you know I'm a woman?" she asked.

He held up his hand. "We will talk later. For now, I suggest you look at the sights. Few ladies have such a beautiful ride to recount when they get back to France."

Under any other circumstances, Jeanne would have relished the scene. The band was tearing ahead through rugged country at the foot of a low line of hills with jagged crests, chasing a herd of about fifty wild horses. The horsemen had such an eye for picking their way through the vast prairie that they could cross the creeks without slowing down. They screamed like Indians and spun their lassos by the animals' ears to force the front runners to maintain their pace. It looked as if the horses of the Apocalypse were loose and taking their riders on a madcap chase.

Jeanne felt the horse under her slow and lose ground. *My God, he's going to collapse.* Then she realized they had come to the end of their journey.

Julio, the Frenchman, was the first to dismount. He untied the prisoner's hands and helped her get down with the same cheerful courtesy he would have shown a guest at a garden party.

She rushed toward the Provençal, tied up on a bandit's mount. One sleeve of his rough sailor's shirt had been torn off and was bandaging his forehead.

"Provençal! Are you hurt?"

"Hit with a butt-end," he said with a grimace, "because I shot a hole through one of these bandits' hats. God forgive me for missing his head."

"*Estupido!*" Julio exclaimed. "If you hadn't missed it, *your* head wouldn't be here to brag about it."

Jeanne swung around toward the Frenchman. "What do you intend to do with us?" she asked fiercely.

"With him, it will depend on his disposition," Julio said cheerfully. "If he wants to be one of us, we are willing to take new recruits. If he is too principled or too troublesome, he'll have his throat cut."

"You, filth!" the Provençal spat out, only to receive a swift punch in the ribs.

"Provençal, be quiet!" Jeanne ordered. "And what are your plans for me?" she asked the Frenchman contemptuously.

He bowed to her like a musketeer, with a great sweep of his hat. "Mam'selle, we hope your relative, or your lover, loves you dearly."

"You don't choose your hostages very wisely. I'm only a poor orphan, and my relative is not rich," Jeanne answered coldly.

"We shall soon see."

"Who advised you in this sorry business?"

Julio did not answer her, but stared instead at the far end of the plain from which they had just arrived. Two horses were cantering toward them, one holding two riders.

"Here come the two rascals who sold you, mam'selle," the Frenchman said. "These brutes sit on their horses like two bags of gourds. Look at that pair!"

A minute later Jeanne could make out the orderlies. One was hanging on to the bridle in order to stay in the saddle, and the other was bouncing around behind a bandit. They never dismounted, but simply dropped to the grass in two heaps. The bandits roared with laughter at the sight of Pinto's two newest recruits.

In response to the ridicule, the orderlies heaved themselves to their knees painfully, crawling on their hands.

"It's a gamble to try to teach pigs to ride. Pigs always walk on all fours," Jeanne commented scornfully.

Yannick had enough strength left to feel stung by the insult. His face contorted with hatred, he threw himself on Jeanne before anyone could stop him, and shoved her to the ground.

"You dirty little cow!" he roared. "I've got more than one thing to pay you back for!" He kicked her in the legs, but before he could bruise her again, he suddenly lurched backward, groping wildly for his neck with both hands, as a shout of rage choked in his throat.

A lasso dragged him back, helpless and choking, to sprawl at Julio's feet. Then Julio casually drew his pistol and sent a bullet into the man's head, as he declared, "*Amigo,* you must never touch the booty without permission. Around here it's unforgivable."

"You bastard! You dirty bastard!" John screamed, sobbing as he rushed to his partner's side.

"Are you all right? Nothing hurt?" Julio asked Jeanne as he helped her to her feet.

"Maybe a bruise or two," Jeanne replied in a broken voice. "Which were too dearly paid for. Is justice always this swift in Colonel Pinto's army?"

"Yes. You must never leave a culprit behind unpunished. It's bad for the general health. And failure to punish properly is ten times worse. You don't regret the death of the rascal who sold you to us, do you?"

"No," Jeanne said. "But that doesn't make me thankful to you for killing him."

"I am!" the Provençal said.

"*Amigo*, you and I might just hit it off," Julio declared, with a slap on the sailor's shoulder.

"Then why don't you untie me and give me a horse so I can finish the trip more comfortably?" proposed the Provençal. "What risk do you run? I'm no longer armed, and I'll follow you as long as you've got the lady."

"I believe you, *amigo*," Julio said. "Diego, untie him."

"Please, mam'selle, get mounted," he said, turning to his other prisoner. "Take that mare. She's pretty enough, and she'll give you a good ride."

Julio led Jeanne over to inspect a superb mare with a light bay coat. "You like her?"

Jeanne tilted her head slightly to cast him a sidelong glance. "So you trust me? You're not afraid I'll give you the slip?"

"Where would you go?" asked Julio, his grin widening.

Jeanne cast a longing look over the vast plain and its mysterious paths, sighed, and mounted the mare. In spite of her distress, Jeanne smiled at a herd of gazelles that leaped across the distant horizon and vanished like a dream.

Julio felt a twinge of admiration for his captive, who was holding out so bravely. "Sailor," he addressed the Provençal, "you can ride alongside the young lady, and I'll ride on the other side. That way she'll feel safe."

"Safe on one side only," the Provençal spat out.

Julio laughed heartily. "Let's go! *Arre, arre!*" he yelled, urging his horse forward and charging across the plains.

* * * *

They galloped for hours, changing mounts twice more with hardly a moment's rest. John, the surviving orderly, had been left behind with an Indian long before they finally stopped to camp, eat, and sleep.

"Mam'selle, I tip my hat to you. You are quite a rider!" Julio complimented her.

"I am nothing," murmured Jeanne, who was leaning against a tree, totally worn out. This endless ride, together with her anxiety, had exhausted her physical endurance. A remnant of dignity was all that kept her from collapsing in the grass. She saw the Provençal unbridling their horses and thought he didn't look much better. He carried Jeanne's saddle unsteadily, as if it were a full cask of wine.

"I don't think you will try to escape tonight," Julio remarked with a laugh. "Come into the inn, mam'selle. Our cheerful *amigo,* the priest of this parish, will be glad to put all his women at your service."

The spot was indeed charming, bathed in a romantic and peaceful country atmosphere, glowing in the sunset. Julio had led them to a reed-strewn hamlet nestled in a valley by the side of a brook. Two scampering dogs and some children romped in front of the church-cabin. They surrounded the newcomers, greeting them with shouts of joy. The women came out of their huts, smiling. Julio called to one of them, an Indian, and spoke to her briefly in Spanish.

"Yes, of course," the woman said gently as she came up to Jeanne and took her by the hand.

"Go with Luisa," Julio said. "She will give you a bath in water warmed by the sun. She does it every day for the priest."

Jeanne felt vaguely surprised that a country priest should be so fastidious as to bathe every day. But she was far too tired to think, and followed the Indian woman in silence. Only when the woman appeared to be walking toward the cabin bearing the cross did Jeanne react. "You bathe in the church? Luisa, do you . . . *bañarse en la iglesia?*" she repeated in Spanish, pointing to the cross.

"This is kitchen," the Indian replied.

There was a hammock hanging from two posts driven into the solid clay ground, and a heavy tub for bathing, mounted on rollers. After pointing it out to Jeanne, the Indian woman brought in two wooden buckets of water and emptied them in.

Jeanne glanced at the wide open doorway. The woman smiled, unrolled the leather curtain screening the doorway, came back for her empty pails, and went out. Jeanne undressed hurriedly, stepped over the edge of the tub, and plunged her throbbing buttocks into the water with a great, voluptuous sigh.

"Does it feel good, mam'selle?" Julio inquired from outside. "You can splash around to your heart's content in this cool spot. I'm sitting on the other side of the door."

"And I'm sitting next to the guard," came an echo from the Provençal.

"Thank you," said Jeanne.

The Indian woman came back and emptied more buckets over Jeanne's back.

"Mmmm," Jeanne cooed. "*Gracias,* Luisa," she said. "More! *Más!*"

Silent and smiling, Luisa came and went three more times until the tub was full. Over and over Jeanne pinched her nose and slid underwater. She could feel her hair, sticky with sweat and dirt, start to rise and float as the water cleansed it.

"*Bella*," said the Indian, smiling admiringly. She dried her off with a white cotton cloth, twisted her hair, and went to fetch a comb. Then she returned to untangle and smooth out the magnificent head of hair which, still wet, was clinging in long ribbons to Jeanne's back and breasts.

"*Gracias*, Luisa, you are very kind, *muy linda*," Jeanne said. "Brigand Julio, are you still sitting in front of my door?" she added, a little louder.

"Yes, mam'selle, at your service," came Julio's cheerful voice. "But just call me Julio for short. The Pinto family is not very formal."

"Thank you, but I won't," Jeanne retorted dryly. "You're an outlaw. But you might remember all the same that in France first names are meant to be used only by those who love us. Brigand Julio, I would like to ask you a few questions. Will you answer them?"

"It depends on the questions. I am not a very learned man."

"When and where will I see your Colonel Pinto?"

"Tomorrow night at his home."

"Is it far?"

"Another day's journey across the pampas."

She rubbed her aching buttocks, and continued, "Are you a chief, Brigand Julio?"

"I am one of the colonel's lieutenants. The colonel has an army of about five hundred men, with five lieutenants and twenty supply officers. That, plus some good Portuguese weapons and ammunition and as many horses as he chooses to rope in, makes him master of the countryside from the Brazilian border to the outskirts of Montevideo. So you see, Pinto is no petty local chieftain. Does that comfort you, mam'selle?"

Jeanne stepped out from behind the curtain and stood on the doorstep. "Maybe it does," she said. "I hope a first-class brigand has a solid head on his shoulders and handles his affairs intelligently, because at the moment I happen to be one of his affairs."

"You will be treated well," Julio declared. "You will not be imprisoned, starved, beaten, or raped. You will be sold back to your master for the highest price possible, that's all."

"That's all!"

"Come now, mam'selle, it's not so terrible. You won't be the one to pay. Besides, it's rather flattering. What woman does not wish to cost her lover a treasure in gold? And you're getting a fine sightseeing tour in the bargain."

"I'll remind myself to thank the colonel for the lovely outing," Jeanne said.

Julio's words had comforted her. As he seemed to wait patiently for more questions, she asked, "Could you have a letter delivered . . . to my relative, to let him know I am unharmed?"

Julio shook his head. "The colonel is the one to decide these matters. But don't worry, your relative's Spanish friends will have comforted him already. They know that the Pinto people do all they can to keep their trophies in good health."

"Well, in that case, be kind enough to have my supper served," Jeanne commanded haughtily. "I'm dying of hunger and thirst."

* * * *

The candlelight dinner took place in the largest reed hut, while the lieutenant's men drank their fill in the grass around the campfire. Padre Pastor had invited his youngest women, four rather pretty Indian sisters and one lively, chubby, very short Portuguese woman. After sipping maté, Padre Pastor invited the Indian women to dance for him. They danced to the strains of a black harpist and an Indian guitarist.

With a glass in one hand, he fondled his Portuguese woman with the other. He had polished off three heaping portions of a violently spiced tongue-and-pimiento stew, downed two flasks of Spanish wine, and now the rhythmic swaying of his women's rumps set his blood racing. Each time his bright eyes wandered from those fascinating behinds, they would come to rest on Jeanne with a languid, lecherous flick.

Finally she leaned over to Julio. "Isn't it time to go to sleep? I'm very tired, and our host is obviously anxious to go to bed."

But at that moment, Padre Pastor rose and clapped his hands, shouting, *"Ahora, la calenda!"*

Suddenly the communal hut filled with a crowd of frenzied women and children thumping their bellies and yelling happily. Jeanne found herself dancing face to face with Padre Pastor, dodging as best she could the rhythmic assaults of his bulging belly.

"Padre," she exclaimed, suddenly grabbing the priest by the arm, "Padre, save me! These bandits have kidnapped me! Send for the police, *la policia!* Oh, Padre! I'm their prisoner, *yo, prisionera!* Help me, Padre! *Socorro, Padre!* For the love of *Dios!*"

Padre Pastor took Jeanne's hands, tenderly held them in his own, but never said a word.

"Come now," said Julio's calm voice behind her, "come to sleep. Padre Pastor only pokes his nose into other people's affairs to give absolution. He wants to live forever."

* * * *

Jeanne awoke the next morning at dawn.

"I would have loved to sleep late," she said, appearing before the bandit lieutenant.

"It will have to wait till tomorrow," Julio said cheerfully. "Riding is wonderful in the cool of early morning."

Together they turned toward a cluster of pawing, stamping horses.

"Good morning," Jeanne greeted the Provençal, seizing the bridle he held out to her. "Did you sleep well?"

"Not quite as well as you did," the Provençal answered.

Julio burst into laughter which Jeanne did not understand as she hopped on her horse. The three of them rode around the hut to meet the others. There Jeanne saw a scene in front of the kitchen-church-cabin that left her speechless. All the children in the hamlet were sitting in a circle on a cowhide, each holding a clay dish while Padre Pastor, in his cassock, poured two ladlefuls of soup into every bowl from an enormous steaming caldron that two of his Indian women lugged behind him.

"Well, mam'selle, don't you find this family scene touching?" Julio inquired.

"I find it biblical," Jeanne replied. "Mass was said, I suppose?"

"Padre Pastor says Mass only on Sundays and holidays, when he thinks of it," Julio said. "But he says it wearing his poncho. He puts on his cassock only for burials."

"For burials?" Jeanne repeated, mystified.

"The padre attended a burial this morning," Julio told her.

"Who died?" she asked mechanically.

"John, the orderly," Julio said.

"Who?" She stared at him in bewilderment.

"John finally got here in the middle of the night and died almost immediately after," Julio announced evenly. "You see, he had not recovered from his friend's death."

"He died . . . of a broken heart?" Jeanne murmured.

"Yes, in a sense," Julio said. "He felt you were responsible for his grief and wanted to make you pay for it. We had to stop him from doing it."

Jeanne looked at Julio in horror. "So you've murdered again," she said in a hollow voice. "You like to kill. You are polite to me, but you would kill me outright if it furthered your ends. You are just a common bandit after all," she told him scornfully.

"I'm the one who killed the orderly," the Provençal admitted. "I slept in front of the women's hut. He had no business there."

"Oh!" she exclaimed after a pause, her voice changed. "And you, Provençal, you kill too, as the fancy hits you?" She looked at the sailor in dismay.

Julio shrugged his shoulders. "Don't be no naïve, mam'selle. Wouldn't you rather see the orderly dead than yourself? No one lives forever, you know. Each of us has to crush his own fleas in order to sleep at night."

"You're barbarians," she said. But even as she said it, a wave of relief and pleasure at being alive swept through her. For a moment she forgot her misfortunes.

"What gorgeous weather!" she exclaimed into the marvelous, rosy morning.

Julio noted the change in her voice and winked at her. "Things have improved since yesterday, eh, mam'selle? You see, one must never despair too much. God did a very wise thing when he made one day follow the next."

CHAPTER 8

into's village was large, consisting of some fifty dwellings crowded into a narrow valley between two hills.
Other cabins crept up the grassy slopes all the way
to the two hamlets perched atop the sharp summits that served as
watchtowers.

On approaching the village they discovered another settlement behind it, composed of a large barracks wedged against the cliff. The
bandit colonel's hideout was not really a town, but it deserved that
name in a province whose capital had a population of only two thousand.
A cluster of five huts was a village. Twelve hide dwellings and twenty-
two rusty cannon passed for a fort.

The cavalcade entered the village at a walk. They were immediately
surrounded by a swarm of motley humanity boldly flinging out their
greedy hands as they jumped up and down and yelled at the new
arrivals.

Terror-stricken, suffocating in the crowd, Jeanne almost lost her
senses. Nearly prostrate, she was vaguely aware that a horseman was
supporting her firmly with his hand on her left side. Another rider, on
her right, was leading her mount up a steep hill. At last they stopped.
Jeanne felt herself helped out of the saddle, set on her feet, and led
into a dark room. She allowed herself to be placed on a leather couch
with a pillow under her head, and heaved a sigh of relief.

"Drink a bit of this," a voice instructed her.

The pungent smell of alcohol burned her nostrils. She clenched her
teeth and pushed away the canteen with both hands. "No, no, I want
to sleep," she murmured, and rolled over.

"I'll get her some cold water," said the Provençal.

"Don't bother," said Julio. "She's fallen asleep."

After ten hours of rest, Jeanne awoke alone in a large white room.
There was a rough wardrobe and table, some leather stools, and two

beds. But there were some surprising luxuries. The window had glass in it, and the door was solid wood. Over the mud floor lay a rug woven Indian-style, with light gray and brown stripes. The cot on which she rested was a Portuguese *marquesa* made of supple oxhide stretched over a fine jacaranda wood frame. She noted that someone had covered her with a soft white woolen blanket, warm and light.

There was a second *marquesa* next to hers, on which lay, carefully folded, another white blanket just like hers. Jeanne wondered who had slept there so close to her, and who had undressed her. She was wearing only her shirt. Her clothes were nowhere to be seen. She got up noiselessly and stared at the tooled leather door, which looked as if it led to another room. She hesitated, then tiptoed to the window in her bare feet.

The house in which Jeanne found herself was built high on one of the two hills. She could see the bandits' village down below. Nearer, she was amazed to see a little garden planted with vegetables in front of the house. A vegetable garden! This luxury was even rarer in La Plata than a rug on the floor. *I'm in the house of a very rich bandit, maybe even Pinto's house.* The realization made her heart race. She decided, with bated breath, to ease open the door a crack . . .

The adjoining room was also white, and its door opened straight into the garden. Squatting on a mat in front of the door was an Indian woman embroidering a pair of leggings.

The Indian lifted her head instantly as the door squeaked open. She smiled at Jeanne, said good morning in Portuguese, set down her sewing, and left.

Jeanne went back to her room and sat on the bed. She slid her bare legs under the blanket and waited. What else could she do? Especially since she had nothing to wear but a shirt.

The Indian woman returned and Jeanne hurriedly washed herself and arranged her hair, then slipped the poncho over her bare and refreshed body.

She heard Julio's voice, pleasant as ever, from outside.

"May I come in, mam'selle? Wide awake, I see," he added as he entered. "Are you hungry?"

"What has Pinto decided about me?" she asked abruptly.

"He will tell you himself. But not before this evening. He has left on an expedition."

She flared up angrily. "Go and get him! I don't intend to stay here forever. I don't intend to wait forever at the pleasure of a bandit!"

"Whose prisoner you are, mam'selle," said Julio, beaming. "I had almost forgotten how much Frenchwomen dislike not being mistresses of their own fate. Please keep in mind, mam'selle, that you are in Spanish territory, where women do not make the laws."

"I am in barbarian territory," Jeanne corrected him.

"Barbarian? Of course not. Perhaps you are hungry? What would you like to eat? Curds, black-bean stew? Some slices of jerked beef?"

"I want my boots, a horse, a guide, and my freedom!" she raged.

And when he sighed comically, she added in a resigned tone, "Some milk or some curds. The rest is probably inedible. Where is my friend the sailor?"

"The Provençal is fine," said Julio. "He ate a whole roast swan. My black cook, a fine woman, likes him a lot.

"Pegassou . . ." he went on, turning to the Indian woman. He spoke a few words in Portuguese mixed with Indian to her.

"Pegassou? Is that her name?" asked Jeanne, when the young woman had left.

"Yes," replied Julio. "It means 'pretty little turtle dove.' "

"The name suits her perfectly," said Jeanne. "She is pretty and graceful."

"And very sweet," added Julio. "She's my wife. You are in my house."

Jeanne's amber eyes stared at the Frenchman a long time.

"You actually . . . married her?"

"Twice. Before her people and before Padre Pastor."

"Are there other Frenchmen here?"

"Three Bretons and a Basque. But don't look to them for protection. They are the most coarse and common of the bandits."

"And everyone else is Portuguese or Indian?"

"There are also Spaniards, Dutchmen, Englishmen, Germans, Negroes, mulattos—every color, every religion."

"But just one profession—banditry."

"Not so, dear young lady. We also have two bakers, a grocer, a butcher, lumberjacks, and prostitutes. You are in a civilized society."

"And how did all these people from the four corners of the earth wind up with Pinto?"

"Matter of chance, mam'selle. They all had to escape something—

the army, Spanish or Portuguese prisons, ships that anchored here, slavery, Jesuit missions. A hard life."

Jeanne frowned. "Escape a hard life and come here! You expect me to believe that Pinto makes life easy?"

Julio answered with an indulgent smile, "You don't seem to know anything about hardship, mam'selle. If you've never known anything but hardship, you don't dream of an easy life. A hard life, with a ray of hope in it, is enough."

"Hope?" said Jeanne, still caustically. "The hope of dangling by the neck at the end of a rope, or being perforated like a sieve and eaten by seagulls? What other hope can you have here?"

Julio continued to smile patiently. "I have already told you, mam'selle. The best thing is to hope that tomorrow will be another day. There are lots of people who never think that tomorrow will be another day. They are forced to live the same day over and over, forever, and that's bad. Here, at least, you never know what tomorrow will bring."

"Were you not in charge of my abduction?" Jeanne asked abruptly.

"I insisted on it."

She raised an eyebrow and waited for an explanation.

"I don't like Pinto to make money from kidnapping, but he wants to. A carefully chosen hostage can bring in a bundle," said Julio. "Ever since I demanded that the hostages be left in my care, they are returned in perfect condition."

"So you play the role of guardian angel in these raids?"

"Yes."

"The fact remains that this time you made a poor choice of hostages, as I already told you."

"Yes, and the Provençal agreed. It sounded like a better deal the way the orderlies proposed it to Pinto. They promised a princess traveling incognito on a mission for the king of France."

"What a yarn! And you believed it?"

"We've seen stranger things."

"Now that you know that I'm only a doctor's serving girl dressed as a valet for the trip, why not send me straight back to Montevideo?" said Jeanne hurriedly. She laid her hand on Julio's arm. "If you do it, I assure you my master will not press charges with the police. Or if he already has . . ."

Julio burst out laughing. "I thought I'd made it clear that Pinto is no petty chieftain. He controls the whole countryside, and the Spanish would never risk sending a column of troops this way. I'll speak to the colonel, but I know he won't give you back for nothing. He expects to turn a profit even from a bad haul. Surely the doctor will offer something to recover a valet like you."

* * * *

"If you were mine, senhora, I would give all my gold to get you back!" Pinto declared emphatically. "You are worth gold, senhora. Beauty is the rarest merchandise in the world. And rare merchandise is always worth a lot of money. To your health, senhora, to your beauty."

The colonel raised his glass and stood up to toast his prisoner. She looked ravishing in a loose-fitting dress of fine cotton, the height of fashion in Rio, which the wife of one of Pinto's lieutenants had lent her. The simple elegance of the chemise accented her slender figure. The pink candy-striped pattern lent color to her tea-and-cream complexion. She was like a tall, radiant summer flower. Each time the colonel looked at her, he puffed out his chest.

Pinto was still a good-looking man despite his fifty years and the jagged scar across his chin. He was a stocky mulatto, and rather imposing in his old Portuguese officer's uniform. It was a bit tight and slightly faded, but was enhanced by new gold braid. Furthermore, in putting on his uniform he also put on his good European manners. In spite of the circumstances, his guest felt quite at home. His smiles and affability made Jeanne almost forget that this was no real colonel across the table, but a bandit leader who killed not to benefit his king and country, but to line his own pockets.

Julio leaned toward her. "You know Dr. Aubriot's financial position better than anyone here. Name a reasonable figure and I will see that it is accepted."

Her vanity almost prompted her to say, *Ask for all the gold in the world from Dr. Aubriot. He'll get it to have me back.* But she said instead, "There is no reasonable price for what you already possess."

Julio repeated their exchange in Portuguese for the rest of the company, and gales of laughter followed. Glasses clinked a toast to Julio's idea, and Pinto turned to his guest of honor, beaming.

"Senhora, it will be as Julio has said. You set the price. You look in the mirror. You set the price on your head. I will certainly get a good deal. Guaranteed!" He winked at the circle and fired off a few words in Portuguese that set everyone laughing.

Julio translated.

"Pinto reminded them of a Portuguese proverb. He said that every wine wants to be worth the price of port."

Jeanne, however, refused to play the game.

Angered by what he called the "bad faith of the Frenchwoman," the colonel wound up banging the table with his fist in a manner that brooked no challenge. He would have his hostage appraised by a genuine connoisseur of women, his beloved nephew Paulino, who was expected "from one minute to the next."

Jeanne nearly burst into sobs when, the next morning, Julio told her that the connoisseur was at sea, returning from the Congo with a cargo of "ebony," which everyone understood to mean Negro slaves. It was true that Paulino was expected from one minute to the next— which meant in four or five weeks, if God and the winds did not delay him.

Frantic, Jeanne protested, "Does this bandit hope to keep me here the whole time?"

"He doesn't have to hope, he has decided to do it."

"I'll run away."

"You know you won't. The countryside is full of tigers and wandering Indians. If you escape the tigers, the Indians will take you and one of them will marry you. They are short of women. That might, after all, not be so bad. Among the Munuenes the men are tall and handsome."

"Oh, stop making fun of me!" cried Jeanne. "How do you expect me to live here for weeks on end?"

"Like anyone else—by eating, drinking, and sleeping. Singing too. Singing puts a spell on bad luck."

Seeing her tremble from trying to hold back her tears, he became more serious and gentle. "Mam'selle, if you behave yourself with Pegassou, the worst that will happen to you is that you will get bored. But I'll take you for walks from time to time. Come now, put on your boots and I'll show you our orchard. It will be a good month before the fruit is ripe, but the hedge around it is in bloom, and you'll find plenty of herbs and teas. It's a place any botanist's assistant should enjoy."

Jeanne heaved a sigh. "And this Paulino on whom my fate depends— what's he like?"

"Pinto raised him to be a gentleman. He gave him a Franciscan tutor, sent him to college in Lisbon and then on a tour of Europe. He's his son. Out of respect for his mother he calls him his nephew. A pure-blooded Portuguese was the boy's mother. Pinto still can't get over the fact that a white woman would willingly bear a child to a mulatto. He hopes that this miraculous boy will become an important man, a general, a governor, maybe a viceroy. He brought him up with these ideas in mind. You will be dealing with a young gentleman who already takes himself for the viceroy of La Plata."

"Good gracious! From the son of a bandit to provincial viceroy—what a rapid promotion!"

"Killing, stealing, and kidnapping," Julio said. "There are no other ways to settle in South America. The Spanish and Portuguese murder, pillage, and enslave in the name of king and country. The Jesuits do it in the name of Christ. As for us, we do it only to fill our pockets. And we do it so well that, when all is said and done, we are the least evil of the lot. The Indians flee the Jesuit God as they would flee the plague. But here, with Pinto, they become true believers."

"I can see it is futile to discuss mercy with you," sighed Jeanne. "Let's go see the orchard."

"You'll soon see the best orchard in the whole province, except for Don José's," Julio responded proudly. "He's a *hidalgo*, a landowner, in Montevideo."

Jeanne reacted instantly. "You know Don José's orchard? You know Don José?"

"Colonel Pinto deals with all the merchants of La Plata."

"You mean with all the smugglers," Jeanne corrected him.

"Smuggler, merchant, around here it's the same thing."

"Does Don José come as far as this village?" Jeanne asked, a trifle too casually.

Julio smiled his broad, indulgent smile. "Stop thinking of giving us the slip for free," he said.

Together they walked around the hill. The village orchard lay to the south, well sheltered from prairie winds, straddling a wide, fast-flowing river. It was bordered by a hedge covered with wildflowers, blue sloe, shining rose hips, and huge blackberries that were still green and pink.

At the entrance to the garden, Jeanne was amazed to see a long path of fig trees. From that perspective the bandits' orchard looked like Don José's, only a bit wilder, with large beds of white lilies and poppy sprays bordering the path. The babbling of the distant river grew louder as they advanced along the walk.

As they reached the end of the path, Jeanne spied the river below the fig trees, leaping over a bed of huge, smooth, round boulders. Two barefoot fishermen, perched motionless on slabs of rock, with pipes clenched in their teeth, were dipping their lines in the clear water. They glared at the newcomers.

"Fishermen like silence," Julio observed, responding to their mute greetings. "Let's walk under the trees."

"I never thought I'd see a bandit peace-loving enough to fish patiently for his dinner," Jeanne noted.

"You have lots of preconceptions about bandits," said Julio. "There are good ones and bad ones among us, gentle and violent ones, idiots and geniuses, drunkards and nondrinkers, big brutes and sensitive souls who write songs to their ladies. There are saints and sinners, sages and fools, high-livers and wet blankets. There is a bit of everything in an outlaw society, just as in any other. And if you stayed here long enough, I'm sure you would get to like some of the people. You can't hate everyone all the time, even in alien territory."

"Oh, yes I can!" exclaimed Jeanne.

But it wasn't true and she knew it. She did not hate this strange, wise, ambitious, and courteous Julio. She was fond of Pegassou and their cunning baby, the color of gingerbread. She surprised herself by playing house with them, winding up a ball of embroidery thread for Pegassou, laughing at the supper table, giving her advice on a seedbed in the vegetable garden. She even made puppets for little Francisco.

There was more than a glimmer of the world's splendor in her prison, and Jeanne was going to make the best of things from this moment on.

The Provençal seemed content, too. During the day he dogged Jeanne's steps. In the evening he came and sat, playing his pipe, in Julio's garden. Jeanne suspected that he slept rolled up in a blanket underneath her window, and she scolded him because it got very chilly at dawn. But the Provençal's songs reminded her of home, and she was lulled to sleep by his tunes. It sounded so good to hear his friendly voice serenading her in whispers from the garden:

> "Beauty, you are like a buttercup
> Beautiful as a treasure . . ."

Did Vincent know the same song? she wondered. The topman told her that every Provençal knew it. They all sang it beneath their girlfriends' windows on warm May nights when the rising sap made them think of love. Jeanne listened avidly as the Provençal named all the flowers of Vincent's Provence, and peace gradually overcame her.

On the ninth night, with her cheek on the white pillow embroidered by Pegassou, not sure whether or not she was dreaming, it seemed to her that the singer's voice had a different quality.

The song, hardly above a whisper, was not loud enough for her to tell whether the Provençal was singing, but her sensitive ear told her there was something unusual about the familiar serenade. Its simple melody suddenly seemed warmer, more colorful. When the voice began the third couplet dedicated to beauty, she was wide awake and holding her breath.

> "Beauty, you are like the open plains
> Where you've kept me running too long.
> I've run so long, and longer will run
> Till at last, Beauty, you'll be mine."

The voice repeated the last two verses, which she knew often occurred when the singer wanted to deliver a message.

> "I've run so long, and longer will run
> Tomorrow morning is when you'll be mine."

Jeanne noticed instantly the change in the last verse. She strained her ears to catch the rest, but the song stopped.

Either I'm dreaming or the Provençal has changed his voice to send me a warning. Her heart beat faster. She got up without a sound, tiptoed to the window, and glanced back at the doorway separating her from her sleeping hosts. She quietly slid the bolt.

The Provençal sat directly below the window, unfolding his blanket. Leaning over as far as she dared, Jeanne whispered, "Provençal, was that you singing?"

"Of course! Who else?"

The tone of voice seemed strange to her. She glanced toward the Barbary fig trees growing on the right side of the house. Nothing moved there or anywhere else in the warm stillness.

"I must have been dreaming," she murmured. "I couldn't seem to recognize your voice."

"Bah!" he said, then added, "Tomorrow morning I will come get you very early, very early."

"Ah, tomorrow morning," she repeated, imitating the Provençal dialect in the song. "Why so early?"

"I managed to make friends with the Dutchman at the barracks. He's lending us his fishing gear. We'll see the sunrise from the orchard river. And we'll catch us a good supper, a fine fish. By God, it will be a great party."

Jeanne sighed. "I'll come, Provençal. But you're too cheerful for a prisoner. Maybe we'll land a big one, but we'll eat it in a prison yard. I'm sad, Provençal. Each day I feel sadder."

Shyly, the sailor touched a long, silky lock of hair that hung over the wall and ran his finger over it caressingly, respectfully. "Don't feel bad," he said in a hushed voice. "Look up there, the sky is studded with so many stars that you can't see anything in between. A sky like that is no bearer of bad news. Tomorrow morning . . ."

He hesitated a fraction of a second, and then, like a lover promising delights, murmured, "Tomorrow morning we'll have weather to make larks sing and dragonflies glow blue!"

CHAPTER 9

A bright orange glow swept the countryside east of the hills.

The two sleepy guards, Portuguese mulattos, rode behind Jeanne and the Provençal with one eye open. Oh, this hostage was keeping them hopping! A fishing excursion was one thing, but why at dawn?

Normally, Basilio and Nando liked their job of guarding hostages. Each time one was brought back to the village, the hostage was placed in their care because they were excellent watchdogs—respectful, alert, calm, and ferocious. No prisoner ever complained about them unless he tried to escape. These guards viewed a hostage as good fortune, an excuse to stay peacefully in town rather than racing around the plains, facing death with every encounter.

This time, however, their prisoner was wearing them out, roaming here and there instead of moping in a hammock or playing cards with the guards, like any other decent hostage. This Frenchwoman didn't even observe the siesta.

Besides, the Frenchwoman was too beautiful. A girl who's too beautiful turns men into asses. Nando repeated at least ten times a day, "That one gives you something to think about." He would tilt his fat chin in her direction. He never said what it was that she gave him to think about, but surely it was the threat that a beautiful girl presents to a peaceful man.

"Isso da que pensar," he yawned, urging on his horse when Jeanne put hers into a slow trot.

The two French hostages and their keepers were the only horsemen stirring. Along the street in the lower village there were women and children up and about, and a few old folks sitting in front of their hide-tent kitchens, puffing on their first cigarros of the day.

"Only women, children, and the elders," Jeanne remarked. "You'd think we were passing through a village at war."

The Provençal raised his head. "That's right. Pinto and his lieutenants took nearly all the men with them. They left before dawn. A big haul, from what I heard. A wagon train of smuggled goods on its way up to Chile."

"Poor souls," murmured Jeanne, thinking of the traders.

"Yes," the Provençal agreed. "Especially since Pinto, who's known to hold grudges, means to avenge the men he lost to Maldonado's dragoons. From what I gather, that convoy reports to the government. There will be a Spanish escort, and our colonel plans to meet them and wipe them out, to the last man."

"How dreadful!" exclaimed Jeanne.

"Maybe," said the Provençal, "but at least they'll be gone for a good spell. They left behind only Lieutenant Julio and some forty lookouts up on the ridges. Once we're under the trees in the orchard, they can't see us, so we can consider ourselves free."

"But the sight of just one of their hats is enough to make me feel ill," sighed Jeanne, with a nod toward their guards.

They reached the orchard and rode down to the river. As soon as they dismounted, the Provençal said, "Now we'll have breakfast," and he approached the mule carrying the fishing gear and picnic basket.

"Already?" said Jeanne, astonished. "Thank you, but I'm not hungry yet."

The sailor spun around. "Yes, you are. You are hungry and we are going to eat right away," he declared, staring into her eyes. "Sit down on the boulder and you will eat."

She obeyed, mesmerized by the Provençal's voice. He brought over the basket, and the guards approached with interest, nearly drooling. The hostage had her faults, but she never bit into a choice morsel in front of them without offering them some.

The basket contained jerked beef, cold omelettes reddened with spices, goat cheese, bread, and three bottles of wine. The Provençal cut some bread, laid a piece of smoked beef on a slice, and put it in Jeanne's hand. "Eat!" he ordered. "And don't drink!" he added quickly as he leaned over to set down on a rock a pottery bowl into which he had poured a little wine.

Having given the delighted guards two spicy omelettes, he presented them next with the open bottle. "Here, boys, help yourselves," he said with a broad grin that spread halfway to his ears.

After each guard took a long swallow, they offered to return the bottle out of politeness. The Provençal refused them with one hand, waving the second bottle in the other. "No, friends, no. We have ours, you keep yours. To your health! Another omelette? They're hot enough to take your breath away. Drink up, now. Good wine never hurt anyone. Bottoms up!"

The guards munched away, laughing and toasting the pair, sharing the wine, then tearing it away from each other. A single bottle for two *pistoleiros* was so little, even at this early hour of the day when all good Portuguese were sipping maté with milk, that Nando and Basilio exploded with childlike glee when the Provençal tossed them another bottle. One bottle per man—what could be more natural? The guards divided the wine scrupulously, measuring each gulp. Just as Nando swallowed the last of his share, both bandits pitched over into the grass.

"Whew!" the Provençal whistled.

Jeanne sprang up, covering her mouth with both hands.

The Provençal kicked the guards to make sure they were out cold.

He turned to his companion, who stood mute and motionless, silenced by her own surprise.

He noted approvingly. "It's best not to shout. You never know. And keep your hands where they are. The surprises aren't over yet."

Hypnotized by the Provençal's movements, she watched him run off between the rows of young apple trees, bending double under their load of green fruit. He stopped at the foot of the orchard, where it met an unplanted field bordered by a thicket that blended into the forest beyond. Cupping his hands to his mouth, he sang out, a bit breathlessly, these joyful verses:

> "Who won the tilt?
> The one who loved the most!
> With Margo's fine wine
> Let's all drink a toast!"

Seconds later, Jeanne saw a white-clad horseman dash out of the copse, streak past the Provençal, who vaulted into the saddle behind him, and approach at a trot through the hanging boughs of the apple trees.

"Oh!" she cried, growing faint as she felt the ground rise up under her. Her back rubbed against the rough bark of a tree as she slid down it.

The rider in the white poncho leapt from his horse and snatched her up as she was about to faint at the foot of a guava tree. He held her up against the trunk to rub her cheeks, ever so gently.

"Now, now, Jeanne, this is no time to faint, sweetheart. We've got a long ride ahead of us!"

"Here, Captain," said the Provençal, handing him an open flask of whiskey, "this should bring her back to life."

"Vincent," murmured Jeanne, opening her eyes. "Vincent, my love . . ."

Her huge amber eyes, a well of honey, drank in the horseman's features. She opened her mouth obediently. The alcohol burned her tongue and throat and brought tears to her eyes. "Vincent!" she repeated ecstatically.

She stood there with lips parted, her head tilted back, clinging avidly to this exquisite moment.

He took off her big Spanish hat and rained kisses on her hair, forehead, eyes, lips, and neck. Then, as if emerging from a trance, he stopped suddenly and seized her with both hands.

"Jeanne, this isn't the time or place for games! Into the saddle, quickly!"

He put the hat back on her head, pushed her toward her horse, and saw the Provençal standing frozen in his tracks, wide-eyed with amazement at the love scene he had just witnessed. Vincent shook him roughly.

"Well, Amadou, are you going to fix up this garden, or do I have to kick you to get you moving? I'll send help. Will ten minutes be enough?"

"Yes, yes, Captain, ten minutes is fine." The Provençal spoke vigorously now. "Don't you want this flask?"

"Let's have it. We'll wait for you where I showed you yesterday. Start tidying up this place, and make it snappy. We're off!"

Vincent jumped into his saddle, cried, "Let's go!" and hit the rump of Jeanne's horse with his hat.

They cantered off through the apple orchard and the empty field. At the forest's edge two Indian horsemen waited. Vincent gave them a short command in Spanish. The Indians rode into the orchard at full tilt.

Jeanne held back her mount and leaned over to seize the bridle of Vincent's horse. "Vincent, how did you get here?"

He replied in the sarcastic voice she knew too well. "My dear, Senhor Paulino is a rotten sailor, it seems. He was going to risk making you wait for him . . ." His eyes swept over her with a lingering, glowing look tinged with roguishness. "And your friend, Lady Emilie, missed you terribly. I promised to bring you back to her."

"Oh!" said Jeanne, "so it was Emilie who told you?"

"I arrived at Don José's place just as he finished telling the story of your kidnapping at the Café Pulperia, the news center of this region. He was trying to figure out how to get you back from Pinto. The least I could do was volunteer to fly to the aid of a French lady in the hands of heathens. My dear, the Cross of Malta obliges. Let's go into these woods, but at a walk. The path is narrow."

Instead of obeying, she went on gazing adoringly at him and announced with great self-satisfaction, "Vincent, you came to get me because you love me. I know this because I love you."

Vincent's jaw tightened. He looked away from her, released the bridle of his horse, and snapped, "We have to go."

He rode ahead to clear a path for her. Fortunately there were no more than six hundred yards or so to go along the path. It had been freshly cleared with a machete, but they had to duck their heads continually to avoid low or thorny branches and liana vines that were already reclaiming the open space.

They came out into a vast clearing that the Indians had burned to plant corn. Some twenty horses, saddled and bridled, waited quietly, nibbling at tufts of grass at the edge of a grove of pomegranate trees. Their riders sat back against the trees. They got up slowly when the two horsemen appeared, except for one whom Jeanne saw rushing toward her with open arms and a beaming smile.

"How is our heroine? Did that dog Pinto treat her the way she deserved, like a princess?"

"Rest assured, Don José, I was treated like a gold nugget," said Jeanne, smiling. "But you're here too? With all these men? You must have raised an army."

"Didn't you notice that the countryside isn't safe?" exclaimed Don José. "Believe me, even with my twenty men armed to the teeth, we would have had trouble taking you by force. Luckily our friend Pinto is often away from home. The chevalier was dying to play the gallant hero by slipping into the citadel and sneaking around to your door. It's a pity, Lady Jeannette, that you didn't see him yesterday with his two-day-old beard, his tattered poncho, and his stinking old hat! He made a superb bandit!"

"Vincent, when did you get into the village?" asked Jeanne, remembering her strange serenade.

"Yesterday morning," Vincent replied. "And certainly without stinking as much as Don José claims. The Provençal recognized me the minute we met. I never saw a deserter throw himself so jubilantly into the arms of his captain! Don't you want to dismount for a bit?" he asked Jeanne, to change the subject. "You'll be in the saddle most of the day."

Don José stretched out his arms to her. "Forgive us for leaving you with the bandits an extra night while we camped nearby. But we needed time to get ready. Neither Dr. Aubriot nor Doña Emilia would have forgiven us for failing to rescue you."

"How is Dr. Aubriot? How did he take my kidnapping?" Jeanne asked quickly in a low voice, without looking at Vincent.

"He is taking it like a man awaiting the ransom note for a stolen treasure. Impatiently," said Don José, after some hesitation. "I kept him in the country under Emilia's watchful eye. Otherwise, he . . ." Don José changed his mind and finished the sentence in a different manner from the way he had intended. ". . . he probably feels better since we swore to bring you back. And you, Lady Jeannette, how have you survived your captivity?"

"Marvelously, since yesterday evening. I slept soundly last night, thanks to a serenade under my window telling me that someone was thinking of me," Jeanne replied, eyeing Vincent.

Don José's flashing black eyes shifted from Jeanne to Vincent. "Amigo, did you by any chance play the troubadour under the window of one of Pinto's lieutenants?"

When Vincent answered with a careless shrug, Don José continued forcefully, "Amigo, you are crazy! Pinto is a thoroughly vain man. Whoever dares to mock him draws his cruelty. If he happens on the miscreant after having a few drinks, he will hang him. Amigo, you are crazy!"

"Foolishness without tomfoolery isn't worth a sardine. You taught me that proverb yourself," said Vincent. "Listen . . ."

Don José lent an ear and shook his head. "No," he said, "not yet. Our men won't be here for another four or five minutes."

"I hope they tidied up thoroughly," said Vincent. "The later the alarm, the better."

"Rest assured," said Don José, "my Indians never leave a risky situation behind them. I suppose, mam'selle, that your hosts won't worry too soon?"

"Not before lunchtime," said Jeanne. "Knowing that the guards were on my heels, they let me do whatever I wanted."

"In that case, it's perfect," said Don José. "By noon we'll be far away. Keeping under cover of the woods, it will take a good hour to reach the plains. But once there, if we avoid the swamps, nothing can stop us from racing straight to the sea."

"Swamps?" said Jeanne. "I didn't see any swamps on the way here."

"We're not taking you directly to Montevideo," Don José explained. "Pinto and his men are in the way. We'll go the next best route, to

Maldonado. Vincent has sent his frigate there. He'll bring you to Montevideo by sea. It will be safer."

"Oh," murmured Jeanne.

She felt a tide of joy rising inside her, making her very scalp tingle. Her chevalier had arrived to rescue her from the bandits so he could carry her off aboard the *Belle Vincente*. Time performed an impossible miracle for her, a leap backward. She was fifteen years old at Charmont, and the chevalier had carried her off to sea.

She was surrounded by Vincent's arms, kissed by Vincent's lips, engulfed by Vincent's orange-grove smell . . . Leaning against her horse's flanks, with her eyes closed, she experienced a moment of utter bliss. When she opened her eyes again, Vincent was approaching to help her into the saddle.

She asked very softly, "Vincent, don't you remember doing this very thing another morning, in another forest, when you told me that you were going to take me out to sea, just as you will do today?"

She saw Vincent stiffen as he replied in a half-whisper, "My dear, your greatest shortcoming is to think of the past rather than the present. You are living out of your time. Only an actor could answer you properly, and I don't care to act with you any longer. Didn't you get my last letter before you left your herb shop?"

Tears welled up in her amber eyes.

"My God, don't cry!" he swore between his teeth. "I've always thought women's tears were intolerable blackmail. Come on, into the saddle. Do you really think you're back in the woods at Neuville? Here, there are tigers and cutthroats."

* * * *

It took them more than an hour, as Don José had predicted, to reach the plains. They rode through underbrush and over scarcely visible trails, advancing single-file at a walk behind two Indian guides from Don José's troop. They kept silent the whole time. On the plains they found the herd of relief horses under guard. Without even setting foot on the ground, they took off immediately at a gallop. They changed horses once again before Don José signaled a halt for a meal of jerked beef and wild cherries at the foot of a hill.

From the top of the hill a brook descended. Jeanne soaked Don José's handkerchief to mop her arms, face, and neck. The drops of icy water sent tiny shivers down her back and over her breasts and stomach. It felt delicious. She untied her hair, which was sticky with sweat, and made a halfhearted attempt to rinse it with handfuls of water. Every man's gaze focused on her long, flowing locks, sparkling in the midday sun. Once she became aware of this, Jeanne repeatedly fluffed out her hair in the sunlight, intent on trapping Vincent's gaze.

"We have to go," the knight announced abruptly. "This isn't a picnic."

Don José darted a look of surprise at his French friend. It was the first time Vincent had given a command in his presence. He saw the chevalier staring angrily at Jeannette's tantalizing motions. He raised one eyebrow and, being in love himself, understood that his friend was too. Unhappily, since Jeanne belonged to Aubriot.

"You are right, *amigo*, we must go," he said, getting up. "What magnificent hair, eh?" he added more softly, when he had drawn close to Vincent. "A ravishing creature, really. Her eyes are bright enough to ignite a cigar."

Vincent's only answer was a question: "How long do you think it will take us to reach the rendezvous?"

Don José was now certain that the chevalier was in love.

* * * *

The rendezvous was near a bend in the wood, some five hours from the coast. Vincent's sailors had arrived well in advance, the Provençal among them. To pass the time, they had hunted deer, which were now dripping fat over a large campfire. There would be fresh venison roast for everyone.

It was a muggy, windless night, and the surrounding boulders restored to the evening air the solar heat they had absorbed during the day. Jeanne felt uncomfortable. Her clothes stuck to her, rather painfully in places. She gazed longingly at the inviting river that flowed not far below the camp.

"Don José," she said, "if you would keep your men over here for a bit, I'd like to go for a swim."

"I can keep my men over here, but I can't hold off the tigers too. There are lots of them in this area."

"Bah!" retorted Jeanne. "There are too many deer and gazelles around that are far more appetizing than I am."

"But an inquisitive wild animal might wish to sample some French flesh," said Don José with a twinkle.

The Provençal stepped forward. "If you'd like, I'll stand guard."

"I'll go," said Vincent, putting on his pistols.

The pair walked down to the river without a word.

The river flowed gently between banks of rocks and rushes. It glowed in the moonlight, shallow and so clear that myriad white, yellow, and purple pebbles in its bed were visible. Jeanne took off her boots and hose and dipped one toe in the water. It didn't seem cold.

"I'll watch the woods. If you happen to meet a shark, shout," said Vincent.

He sat down in the hollow of a large block of lava with his back to the river.

Jeanne undressed hurriedly. The silvery night air clinging to her moist skin was like a balm. She untied her hair and jumped into the water, but couldn't restrain an "Ouch!" from the sudden chill. Vincent leaped to his feet, his hand on a pistol.

"It's nothing, Vincent. Only the chilly water," she shouted to him, smiling with pleasure as she splashed about.

She started to swim. Seeing the pale shadow stretching out sensuously in the water, Vincent shut his eyes quickly and returned to his lava perch.

Jeanne's voice rose from the river. "Did you know, Vincent, that even though I was their prisoner, the bandits offered me a warm bath at the end of my ride? They let me bathe before dinner and gave a dance in my honor afterward. And in between, fat roast partridges and Spanish wine. They served me unbelievable luxuries."

When he didn't answer, she persisted. "Vincent, can you hear me?"

"Of course," he said.

"Then why don't you answer me?"

"Because I want to listen to the night sounds," he replied sharply.

He's still angry. She swam for a few moments in silence and turned over to float on her back, her eyes on the stars. *How can he continue to be out of sorts under such a sky?*

She shivered and flipped back onto her stomach to move around. The exquisite coolness was becoming frigid. She swam toward the shore.

"Have you ever slept in the open?" Vincent asked suddenly.

"No."

"In that case, for your first night camping out you are lucky. It's warm and the stars are all out."

"Yes, I'm lucky." She felt like hugging the water and the pebbles and the fish and the moon above. Vincent had just spoken in his real voice. She slapped her chilled upper arms, reached out and grabbed a bunch of grass on the riverbank, and stepped ashore.

The warm night air blanketed her and began to lick the water off her skin. She wrung out her hair several times, happy and in no hurry to put on her shirt, which was stiff with dried sweat. Besides, it was terribly, deliciously exciting to stand there in the nude at Vincent's back when at any moment, anything might make him turn around.

Gradually she adopted the attitude of a timid doe, one hoof poised for flight, watching a handsome hunter, ready to flee, or perhaps to eat out of his hand. Trying to move silently, she took four steps toward Vincent.

"Are you dressed? Can I turn around?"

The doe halted, quaking. "No," she said.

She backed up a step and added nonchalantly, "The fresh air smells so good, but my shirt smells dreadful. And the material is so rough. Did you know that I borrowed this shirt from Julio the bandit?"

"A bandit gave you the shirt off his back? That's something I'd like to see!" said Vincent.

"It doesn't amount to much," said Jeanne.

"My dear, I would offer you my own, but this evening it's not worth more than yours."

Jeanne quivered with desire. "At least yours is soft," she said suddenly. "And I'm sure that it still smells of orange blossoms."

"No chance of that, I assure you. But if you think it's a good deal . . ." He got up, took off his shirt, and handed it over with his back to her still.

She approached on tiptoe, closer than necessary, snatched the shirt, and gulped in the body scents of the naked sailor. *If I touched him, what would he do?* Slowly her hand caressed the air above his shoulders and down his back, down to his waist and up again, then hesitated and moved away, definitely too shy to touch him.

"Won't you give me the bandit's togs in exchange for mine?"

In three strides she reached the bushes where she had thrown her clothes, rolled up the shirt, and sent it flying over Vincent's head.

"Phew! You're right, this cotton scratches like a hair shirt! Apparently banditry doesn't pay well enough to keep a man in muslin shirts."

"Yours is soft, Vincent."

"Yes."

"Would you help me find my boot? I lost a boot."

He turned around. She was in his shirt, bare-legged, with her wet hair gathered over one shoulder. And she wasn't looking for a lost boot at all. A lovely white form in the moonlight beneath the clinging muslin, she stood out against the shadowy bushes, motionless, with one foot poised for flight. He walked up to her quietly and leaned forward.

"Vincent," she murmured, holding him by the arm, "I know where my boot is. I just saw it."

He stepped away from her. "What else can I do for you?"

"I'm a little cold. Maybe if you rubbed my back . . . Ouch! Ouch! Ouch!"

"Am I rubbing too hard?" he asked innocently.

He had pulled up a handful of dried grass and was scrubbing vigorously at her back through her shirt.

"Ouch! You must think you're currying a horse!"

"A horse, no, but a mule, yes! Enough or more?"

"Enough, enough!"

"Now put on your poncho."

He helped her slip into the poncho and she found herself nearly in his arms.

"Vincent, kiss me."

"Are your lips cold too?"

"My heart is cold."

"It's your stomach. An empty stomach makes you cold. Come eat something."

"I hate you!" she cried as she grabbed her breeches off a bush.

He started to laugh, and stepped aside so she could finish dressing.

* * * *

As soon as the meal was over, Don José posted a guard. Everyone else rolled up in his poncho and began to snore. Vincent's sailors gave a blanket to Jeanne, and the Provençal came over to place a saddle under her head.

"All the comforts of home," he said. "Good night, lady."

"Good night, Provençal."

"Lady, why didn't you tell me that you knew the captain?"

Raising herself on one elbow, she looked at the sailor and racked her brains for a discreet reply.

"Forgive the question," the sailor said quickly. "Good night."

"Is everything all right?" It was Vincent, kneeling beside her.

"I'm not quite sure," she replied. "I think I might be a little bit afraid. Those tigers . . . ?"

"In this country the tigers are rarely hungry enough to go after human flesh. I'll lie down on your left, and Don José will be on your right. You can sleep like a baby."

She raised herself again and propped herself up against the saddle. "Vincent, do you remember Maria, the gypsy of La Courtille, and her prophecy?"

"That story is so old."

"I know you remember. For months I was jealous of that unknown woman who waited for you in a mysterious orchard somewhere in the New World. Maria called the woman 'the delight of your life,' and said that you would risk everything to carry her off aboard the *Belle Vincente*. And you know . . . I'm that woman."

"Any witch worth her salt who has a vision of your future is bound to turn it into a love story," said Vincent.

Jeanne ignored the cynical remark and continued in a low voice. "Last night, when somebody sang beneath my window, I knew instantly who it was. I didn't dare breathe your name, but my heart knew it. Yet I never would have imagined your singing that way, in sailor's slang."

"Why, you stuck-up little prig of a Parisian lady, the Provençal language is not some jargon used by sailors and farmers!" he scolded. "The Provençal tongue is also . . ."

He stopped and shook his head. "This matter is too close to my heart to chat about with a pretty little mule who is half asleep," he said gruffly. "Good night, my dear."

"Oh, please, talk to me in Provençal!" she begged as she put her hand on the corsair's arm to hold him back. "A little bit, just a little. If you want to."

He laughed. "When you were fifteen, you acted twelve. Now that you are nearly twenty, you act fifteen. What do you want me to say in Provençal 'slang' to lull you to sleep?"

"Sweet things. Things that will give me sweet dreams."

He made her wait a while, then murmured, *"Lou tems es tout clavela d'estello; es une niue de Dieu."*

" 'The sky is full of stars, it is one of the Good Lord's nights,' " she translated, delighted with the new game. "Yes?"

"Almost."

"Deman auren la mar blanco, douco coume d'oli."

" 'Tomorrow I'll have a—white?—sea, as sweet as . . . olive'? 'Like oil'? Yes?"

"It could be rephrased."

"More!"

This time he made her wait longer, for he found himself succumbing to the charms of the moment. This was a devilish trick she was playing, having herself rocked to sleep in the language of Vincent's childhood. He felt as if he were feeding her his own soul.

And how she listened! She seemed to listen with her entire being. The moonlight made her blond hair even paler, like silver. He decided that she had a talent for creating moments when it became very—no, too—difficult not to love her.

"More," she urged in a whisper. "Sing to me softly the song about the buttercup."

Vincent's eyes surveyed the camp littered with snoring bodies, and wrinkled his nose. "The landscape doesn't inspire me."

"But it's true, isn't it, that in the sun I glow like a buttercup? I mean, in your eyes. When you're not angry about trifles, when you love me a little, don't you find me as tempting as a buttercup?"

More than half defeated, he nearly ran his hand over her moonlit hair, restrained himself, and said as lightly as he could, *"Bouton d'or, sias bello coume un tresor, sias bello coumo une tarto d'ambricot! Vous prendiou ben per ma mestresso."*

" 'Buttercup, as beautiful as a treasure, you are beautiful as an apricot pie! I will make you my mistress.' I can understand Provençal marvelously," she murmured at last. "Do you like apricot pie very much?"

"I'm dying for some apricot pie!" he said, showing all his teeth. *"L'envejo me rousigo d'uno tarto d'ambricot!* Now, young lady, sleep! You know enough Provençal to dream of crickets!"

He fetched his saddle, rolled himself up in his blanket, and stretched out on Jeanne's left.

"Good night, Lady Jeannette, *buenas noches.* Dream a good dream of an escaped prisoner," said Don José as he lay down at her right. The Spaniard fell asleep instantly.

Jeanne turned toward Vincent and saw him staring silently at the star-studded sky.

CHAPTER 10

he weather changes quickly on the coast of La Plata. The clear night sky doesn't always keep its promise. When Vincent's little band arrived at Maldonado, a strong wind was blowing from the sea, sending a cluster of white clouds toward the grasslands.

The harbor was little more than an anchorage midway between the mainland and an islet that served as a prison—a dependable source of recruits for Pinto. Its suitability for smuggling operations made up for its total lack of comfort or charm.

The *Belle Vincente* rocked gracefully at anchor.

What a beauty! With a lean, raking bow and tall, slender masts, the small frigate was indeed beautiful. Her hull was a deep yellow with fine red markings and shiny black harpings. Her brasswork sparkled. Elegant gilding ornamented her poop as well as the prow, adorned by a figurehead with short curly hair.

"How lovely she is, Vincent!" Jeanne murmured, her eyes flooded with tears.

Vincent smiled proudly. "Wait till you see her under sail!"

"Mam'selle, hey! Hello, mam'selle!" shouted Mario, as he came limping toward her. Vincent's valet had sprained his ankle while breaking horses at Don José's villa, so his master had sent him back to the ship instead of taking him along to rescue Jeanne.

"Hello, Mario," said Jeanne warmly, glad to see the man who shared her memories of Vincent.

Vincent's officers waited nearby with great curiosity.

"Gentlemen," said Vincent, "allow me to postpone the introductions. The young lady would like first to rest a bit and freshen up. Mario, did you do what I asked?"

"Yes, sir. May I lead Mam'selle to her cabin?"

"I'll do it myself," Vincent replied.

Mario stepped aside, crestfallen, and the boatswain approached the captain, pushing the Provençal before him. "Forgive my delaying you, sir, but what do I do with him?"

Vincent looked stonily at the deserter. "Put him in irons. Three days."

Jeanne opened her mouth but shut it quickly.

"Come, mademoiselle," said Vincent, "you must be tired. Boatswain, put him in irons on deck."

"Aye, aye, sir," said the boatswain.

"You're not really going to put the Provençal in irons, are you?" she beseeched in whispers. "He was a great help to me. If he hadn't been there when the bandits took me . . ."

"Mam'selle, please don't try to give orders on board. The crew is not of a mind to take orders from a woman, even one in pants. Here is your room. It's mine, and I turn it over to you with pleasure."

"Oh!" she gasped, enchanted. She saw the painting and stopped in front of it.

The large canvas was a bust portrait of the goddess Pomona against an unfinished sky. She wore a flat little shepherdess's cap tilted over one eye, and a flowered calico dress. The dress was as revealing as muslin, since the artist had drawn aside the neckline to uncover one breast and half of the other. A long lock of rye-blond hair escaped from her upturned hairdo and spiraled down to tickle the pink nipple of her bare breast. The shepherdess Pomona had a wide-eyed look of innocence beneath perfect eyebrows, and skin the color of pale tea. She smiled sweetly as she held out a red and green apple in her right hand. The colors of the portrait glowed voluptuously, suggesting that the painter had taken great delight in modeling the features of such an exciting beauty, so lifelike and tempting that no man could refuse a bite of that apple! In the lower right-hand corner the canvas was signed with the initials *V.L.*

Jeanne contemplated the painting for the longest time. It must have seemed ages to Vincent before she turned around to say, "This canvas is signed 'V.L.' Did you get it from Carle Vanloo?"

"I bought it from his widow. After her husband's sudden death she needed money. I had wanted a Vanloo for a long time. I love his palette. It's so sensual, and I love a painting that delights the eye. Some old scolds complain that Vanloo flattered all his models, but who wants to hang an ugly woman up on a wall, or a beautiful woman who doesn't look as beautiful as she really is?"

Jeanne darted another glance at the portrait. "Do you think the sitter is an ugly woman made beautiful, or a beauty made even more beautiful?"

"Mademoiselle, I am more interested in hearing what *you* think."

"I think she resembles . . . me."

"Oh really? I didn't notice that. Now that you mention it, though . . . by God, yes, there's something to it! There certainly is something to it. And what do you think of the rest of my décor?"

"I think I shall have myself awakened every hour to admire it," she answered, pivoting around. "It would be a crime to sleep too long in such a lovely room."

The captain's cabin aboard the *Belle Vincente* was no bigger than any other cabin, but completely paneled with exquisite, finely carved woodwork painted pearl gray on a white background edged in gold. The coffered ceiling was a trompe-l'oeil affair done in gray, white, and gold. The bed, two armchairs, two stools, and a table were upholstered with a magnificent, emerald-green, raised-silk velvet. A bookcase and a small rolltop desk completed the furnishings. On the walls, in addition to the Vanloo painting there were two charming wash drawings by Boucher: a lady in a garden and a lady in town. A mirror framed in gilded rocaille hung between a wall clock and a barometer. One one side, concealed behind the woodwork, was a minuscule washstand, and on the other, a closet.

"You live in a floating palace," said Jeanne, overjoyed.

"I live as well as I can," said Vincent.

"You're only happy at sea, aren't you?"

"It's just that it's easier to be happy at sea than anywhere else. Haven't you noticed, Jeanne . . ."

She quivered because, at last, he had called her Jeanne, like the time he had found her in the orchard.

Seeing her start, he corrected himself. "Haven't you noticed, mademoiselle, that most every man has two incompatible desires in his heart. One is to settle in and put down roots and the other is to pull up roots and take to the road. At sea I can settle down and roam at the same time. I'm a wandering homebody."

"Thank you for lending me your handsome quarters," she said, adding in an afterthought, "By the way, where are you living now?"

"Next door, in the wardroom, which isn't bad. Now, wouldn't you like to freshen up and make yourself beautiful for dinner? I think my officers must be dying of impatience."

"Make myself beautiful?" exclaimed Jeanne. "With what?"

"You're on a privateer, mademoiselle, and on a privateer there is always some booty lying around. Look!"

He opened the closet and pointed to a chest on the floor. "It's full of dresses," he said. "You can even adopt the fashions of Rio de Janeiro, which are most becoming. And in this coffer . . ."

He took a small chest off the desk and placed it in her hands. "I shall have the key brought to you. Inside you will find a lot of duty-free gold and silver baubles. Ask Mario for some hot water and anything else you want. He's dying to leave my service and enter yours."

"Thank you," she said again with a loving smile. "I feel as if I'm living in a Christmas story."

She set the box down on the table and approached him as he stood at the door. "On Christmas Eve it should be Christmas for everyone. You're not going to let the Provençal sleep in chains on the deck, are you?"

Vincent shook his head. "A real little mule!" he declared. "Let's compromise once and for all. I'll have a blanket brought to him, but don't ask me to give him a bed."

As he opened the door, a pretty black cat jumped into the cabin with a single leap and pounced on the bed. "Allow me to introduce Licorice," said Vincent. "His mother belonged to Count Pazevin, the Marseilles shipowner. You know the count, I presume?"

"He's an old friend of Madame de Bouhey," said Jeanne as she stroked the cat.

"As long as I'm introducing my furry and feathered passengers . . ."

Vincent left the room for a moment and called out three times: "Chérimbané, Chérimbané, Chérimbané!" A dazzling bird appeared on his shoulder when he returned.

"Chérimbané is hunngrrry. What time is it?" screeched the parrot as soon as he settled down.

"How cleverly he speaks, and how beautiful he is!" cried Jeanne, amazed.

The macaw was truly a splendid bird. His upper back, wings, and tail were of the most vivid blue imaginable. The fine plumage around his neck and on his breast was pure gold. He looked as if he were dressed in a mantle of blue silk damask over cloth of gold.

"He's more a work of art than a bird," said Jeanne ecstatically.

"Chérimbané, say hello to Mademoiselle."

"Helllo," said the bird. "How are you?"

"I'm fine, thank you," Jeanne replied, smiling.

She held out her wrist, but the bird flew off to the Vanloo, and perched atop its frame.

"Are you the parrot's teacher?" asked Jeanne.

"Mario is," said Vincent curtly.

"He certainly seems to like your Pomona," Jeanne replied, smiling.

"Throw these creatures out when you want to," Vincent said as he took his leave, "I'm sending in Mario."

Left alone, she thoughtfully observed the bird with the royal plumage.

"Ha, ha! I see that my rascal has already found you!" said Mario gaily as he came in. "Here's the key to the little treasury, mam'selle. And here is a basin of nice hot water. I left a selection of the master's brushes, combs, and colognes on the washstand. Is there anything else you need?"

"Tell me, Mario," Jeanne asked, "did you teach the parrot to talk?"

"Oh no, mam'selle. The master forbids anyone else to do that. He wants his bird to speak impeccable French."

"He's called Chérimbané, isn't he?"

"Yes. That's a strange name, but it comes from his Indian owner. It means Thing-I-Love."

"Thing-He-Loves, I want you to be intoxicating," whispered Jeanne to her reflection in the mirror as Mario left.

Gleefully she set to work. Her Brazilian ensemble would give her the easy grace of a blond Oriental princess. She chose a flowing negligée of plain white muslin ornamented with cones of lace. The square neckline was just daring enough to make every man want to see what it hid. She opened the coffer and took out a tangle of those long gold and silver chains so typical of the sensual beauties of Rio de Janeiro. The chains were very slender and light. Jeanne put five of them around her neck, then a sixth, then a seventh, mixing gold and silver. She had seen some ribbons among the clothes in the chest, and so she tried to imitate the way Pegassou, the bandit's pretty Indian wife, wore her hair. She divided her own in half with a central part, made two heavy braids that she let fall over her breast, and slipped on a narrow gold headband. "Thing-He-Loves," she said to herself aloud, "you don't look too ugly this way. Now let's see which pair of slippers will fit you." She put on a pair in smooth and supple leather, dyed green and trimmed with silver.

"And some perfume to finish!" *Oh! Vincent's fragrance!* Slowly she laid trails of orange water on her braids, behind her ears, in the furrow between her breasts, and on her wrists. As she applied Vincent's cologne, every hair on her skin bristled with pleasure. When she was done she sniffed at her plaits and her wrists, hesitated, then lifted her skirt and slid the perfumed stopper over her stomach and on to the backs of her knees and her bare feet.

"Helllo, Chérimbané. Prrretty Chérimbané! Where are you, Ché-rimbané?" the beautiful macaw sang at the top of its lungs from its perch on the portrait.

"Here I am!" said Jeanne. "I have come, my friend. Are you so crazy that you court the copy when you have the original? You really are a parrot! I hope your master will prove a bit wiser."

* * * *

"What a pleasure to be invited to the captain's table," she said, taking her seat at Vincent's right. "So far I've been traveling on nothing but sailor's gruel!"

"Alas, mademoiselle, on my ship the captain's fare is awfully like the crew's," said Vincent.

"With something special added," the chaplain contributed, smiling. "Be assured, mam'selle, it is written in the ship's rules: 'The captain's fare will be that of the crew, but will include the best cuts in addition to something special.' Today's 'something special' is roast gazelle, which smelled quite good over the fire."

"Anyway, except in times of famine our gruel is more like a bouillabaisse—the fragrance of our native southland," said the surgeon.

Two ship's boys came in. One carried a huge, steaming tureen, the other a stack of bowls. They placed everything in front of the captain.

"Will you feel cheated if I give you only two ladles of soup?" asked Vincent.

"Not at all, sir," said the chaplain, and everyone smiled. They all knew about Dom Savié's gluttony.

The chaplain began to discuss the flavorful merits of bouillabaisse, which he considered a sovereign remedy for seasickness, indigestion, low spirits, and similar distresses. Jeanne listened with interest. Before dinner Vincent had told her briefly about the people she would be eating with, so she knew that this priest had left his Abbey of Saint Martin de Frigolet to join Vincent and see a bit of the world. If Dom Savié was a glutton, his gluttony had gone unpunished because after fifty years there was not an ounce of fat on his body.

The people at the captain's table formed a small group. Accustomed to the large officer staff aboard a king's ship, it was surprising to find so few officers here. There was the first mate, M. Aubanel, formerly of the East India Company; Baron de Quissac, a lieutenant from the royal fleet whose strong, attractive face was striped with welts that added to his virile looks; two very young ensigns, Daniel Gioberti, born in Malta of Genoese parents, and the Chevalier Brussanne, handsome and dashing, talkative and vain. Also at the table was the mandatory presence of the chaplain and Tourreau, the purser, who had the serious, melancholy mien of a life spent figuring sums. In addition, Vincent had invited his surgeon, M. Amable, a stocky, cheerful man in his forties from Marseilles, who enlivened every word with gestures and seemed as spirited and clever and talkative as any barber.

One chair remained empty, next to the surgeon's, and a bowl of soup sat waiting in front of it. As everyone began spooning up his soup after the blessing, the door of the wardroom opened and the boatswain appeared, in his Sunday best, excusing himself for being late.

"I had to look after something in the hold before washing up," he explained, standing in the doorway.

"Boatswain, come sit down," said Vincent. "We are happy to excuse anyone who looks after the safety of the ship. Mademoiselle, allow me to introduce Monsieur Gaspar, my boatswain."

Gaspar bowed, blushing like a girl, and, with his hat in hand, accepted Jeanne's gracious smile of greeting, lowered his eyes, and sat down quickly in front of his soup.

Jeanne forced herself to tear her eyes from Vincent and eat her soup. But Vincent's image remained in her mind.

The chevalier wore a suit of salmon-pink silk trimmed in the same color. Bewigged, powdered, and perfumed, and wearing a large blue sapphire ring on the little finger of his left hand, he looked more elegant and handsome than ever. His good looks improved with her mounting desire for him, and tonight that desire was at its zenith.

Why wasn't her passion strong enough to push all those irrelevant people back into the woodwork and leave her alone with Vincent, in Vincent's arms? She sighed to relieve the torment of waiting.

"Aren't you eating, mademoiselle?" asked Vincent.

"If your stomach troubles you, you should put something in it," advised the surgeon.

"It's not that, for my stomach has settled well," she said. "It's just that . . . that I've been admiring this room. The wardroom of the *Etoile des Mers* was nothing like this. It was simply the largest room on the ship. But this one . . ."

The walls were all inlaid with marquetry of precious woods from Brazil in shades of tan, brown, red, purple, and mahogany. The ceiling was deep brown, carved from fine-grained wood, and the rays of the setting sun piercing the tiny windows gave it a velvety glow. The room had a warm, appealing, elegant charm.

"Do you like this woodwork?" asked Vincent. "I admit that it would do honor to the best wood craftsmen in Paris. Well, mademoiselle, it was made by Negro carpenters in Rio de Janeiro. I show it to slavers so they may know what great artists could be rotting away, packed like beasts in their holds."

"I like your thoughts even better than your woodwork," said Jeanne as she laid her hand impulsively on her neighbor's sleeve.

Since everyone had eyes only for Jeanne, they were all quick to see the tender gesture, the exchange of loving looks.

Well, well! Business as usual! thought Dom Savié, knowing the privateer's successful record with the ladies. The handsome Brussanne grew upset and began to drum his fingers on the table. It was always the same story. Whenever a lady stepped aboard ship, she chose the ensign only if she couldn't hook the captain.

The tense silence made Jeanne realize her imprudence. She withdrew her hand hastily and searched for something to say. "Very few council chambers are so attractive, don't you agree?" she ventured.

"True, but some are magnificent," said Vincent. "As a matter of fact, instead of 'council chamber,' we call ours the music chamber."

"Really? Why?"

"Mostly because our captain hates meetings," said Dom Savié.

"Also because we have some excellent musicians on board," Vincent added. "We have drums and fifes, a pipe, mandolins, two good flutes, Brussanne's violin, and a harpsichord that our chaplain plays quite well."

Jeanne felt tempted to tell about her encounter with the young lad Mozart, who was said to be a virtuoso on this instrument. But instead she contented herself by gazing at the plain, small keyboard in its glistening mahogany case and listening to the small talk of the others.

A warm, convivial mood took hold, aided by the good Burgundy, and Jeanne began to feel relaxed. She found herself thinking, *I love him, he loves me,* as if it were a certainty. She ventured several caressing, wide-eyed gazes in his direction, imagining all the while that after this enchanting dinner an enchanting evening would have to follow.

"Praise God, mam'selle, you have caused a miracle," declared Father Savié. "Stay with us for a long time. Good food is a glimpse of the hereafter."

Her reply to the chaplain vibrated with loving confidence. "I think, Father, that I could stay on board such a ship forever. This is a privateer, and the word 'privateer' sets one dreaming."

"Especially women," Father Savié injected unctuously.

"That's because women are constantly deprived of adventures," said Jeanne. "And you can dream of adventure more readily on a privateer than on a merchantman. It seems to me that when you live on a privateer you always feel that you're bound for El Dorado."

"But you never get there!" exclaimed Vincent. "El Dorado doesn't exist for a sailor, because it's at the end of the world and sailors know the world is round."

"Well, so be it," she said, gazing at him intently. "El Dorado doesn't exist. But it might not be bad to live on the endless road that leads there."

"You can't argue with that, captain," said Father Savié. "Mam'selle's an even better philosopher than you. There's a Spanish saying: 'Don't worry about whether heaven exists, just follow the path that leads there, for it's the same as heaven itself.' "

The conversation shifted from heaven to heavenly things and places. As dusk fell and began to obscure the décor of the wardroom, the dinner party assumed the intimacy of a family gathering. At the same time the ship's rocking reminded Jeanne that she was back on a tiny island lost between sky and sea. The past already had the washed-out, unreal colors of a country buried under thousands of miles of water. Even her recent ordeal with the bandits was fading. The present, on the other hand, among all these attentive men, was most attractive. She felt protected and cushioned, like a precious Sèvres figurine.

Out on deck, the evening seemed to be progressing cheerfully despite a rolling sea. The songs and laughter of the crew filtered into the wardroom, along with the sound of hammering heels keeping time with the beat of tambourines and trembling mandolins.

"The men seem a bit noisier than usual," Vincent commented. "Are they celebrating anything in particular?"

"Yes, sir, your return," replied the boatswain. "They don't like the feeling that you're far away when they're under the gun."

Vincent smiled and said, "Anyway, if the men are celebrating my return, that means something. Boatswain, give them a drink."

Jeanne raised her honey-sweet voice. "Boatswain, do prisoners also get a drink from the captain?"

"Damned mule!" whispered Vincent, leaning toward Jeanne, as the boatswain, proud of being addressed by the lovely lady, answered gallantly, "Mam'selle, since you ask on their behalf, surely we could make an exception in your name, if our captain allows it."

"I ask it, boatswain," Jeanne urged, "and I beg your captain's favor."

"So be it," sighed Vincent. "What else can I do? We're even, boatswain. Don't you ever refuse me a favor. I'll remind you of this one!"

"A woman aboard is like the outbreak of chaos. In other words, a delightful excuse to experience an unforgettable moment," said Father Savié.

Night fell, windy and clear. The ocean rolled but showed no malice. The watch could sit down. Silence and obscurity reigned on board. A group of five remained on the quarterdeck, talking in low voices. Vincent chatted with his second-in-command. Jeanne had moved away with Father Savié, who kept her company. A motionless sailor held a lantern a few feet from the officers. Mario stayed near Jeanne, holding another lantern.

"I love this post-curfew silence," Jeanne said quietly to the priest, "when you don't hear people moving about. You hear the sounds of everything else, though . . . the ship's timbers, the shrouds, the sea."

"And God," Father Savié added.

Jeanne didn't answer. A shooting star appeared in one part of the sky and vanished before touching the water.

"A soul is entering heaven," said the chaplain. Then his voice took on a sarcastic edge. "But you're an educated woman, a botanist, so you don't believe in old proverbs, do you?"

"I believe in shooting stars . . . I've wished on one. As for other things, I don't know. God is as distant as the unknown, yet sacred rites impress me—the fragrance of incense in church, a little cemetery tucked away behind its chapel, an oath taken on a crucifix. In fact, everything impresses me, rational or not, the play of light and shadow in a forest glade as well as the dim beauty of a Gothic cathedral."

"You are of your time, my dear child—both skeptic and romantic, unbelieving and superstitious, standing in doubt before the host and blanching to see a holy medal shattered."

"It's true that at certain times I feel just about ready to believe . . . everything."

"Tonight, perhaps?"

The chaplain had adopted the whispering voice of the confessional, and she answered likewise. "Tonight, for instance."

The priest laughed and contemplated for a moment the beautiful, shadowy profile standing out against the paler darkness of the night, and then said lightly, "Dear child, nothing comes closer to loving God than loving a man."

He saw her tremble and wrap herself more tightly in the white wool shawl which Mario had slipped over her shoulders. "But, Father," she murmured finally, "what makes you think I'm in love?"

"Sometimes I, too, can hear what is inaudible," replied the priest.

* * * *

"As you see, mam'selle," Mario chattered when she and Vincent reached the cabin, "I've gotten rid of the tomcat and the chatterbox, and I've lit a lamp for you. But I should tell you about the lamp . . ."

"Mario," Vincent cut in, "Mademoiselle has traveled on ships for a long while. She knows what to do."

"I hear, I hear!" said Mario gaily. "But there is one procedure that Mam'selle doesn't know about. Since I bring you two fingers of orange port when you retire for the night, I thought that Mam'selle too might try this medicine because surely she has never tasted this Maltese delight. So I've brought the decanter here with two glasses and—"

Nettled, Vincent interrupted his valet once more. "Mario, everybody is not dying to try your homemade wine. Stop bothering the lady and make my bed."

"Sir, your bed was made long ago," said Mario, offended.

Jeanne smiled. "I'd like to try a little of this Maltese port, Mario. Would you pour me some?"

"Ah! Sniff it first, mam'selle!" said Mario, pacified, as he waved the decanter under her nose.

"Mmmmm," said Jeanne obligingly. "Mario, for the bouquet alone I *must* have the recipe!"

"Taste, mam'selle, taste!" Mario urged, beaming. "Let some of it rest in the hollow of your tongue."

"Good night, mademoiselle," said Vincent roughly, as he seized the lantern Mario had put down. "I'll listen to your opinion of this wine tomorrow." He turned and walked toward the door.

"Mario, not one word, please leave!" said Jeanne softly. And, aloud, she called out, "Captain, you've not taken your medicine. I don't want you to change your habits too much on my account. Do me the favor of drinking with me."

She saw Mario slip away without a sound and Vincent hesitate in the doorway. He assumed a stony look. She poured some orange port in the other glass and held it out with a bewitching smile. "Well, then, sir," she said in her beautiful, deep voice, "since you've decided not to love me anymore, it seems pointless that you have to be distant as well."

He stepped back into the room, closed the door, and took the glass. "So be it," he said. "Let's drink to our friendship."

"No."

"Why not?"

"Because one does not toast a sad thing."

"Well, to what shall we drink?"

"To my delight in this moment."

They took a sip and set their glasses on the table. They looked at each other. The silence between them vibrated like an overstretched string, and this went on until, very slowly, Jeanne closed her eyes.

She no longer knew what she hoped for or what she feared. Time lay suspended, and any clear thought had been driven from her head. Shreds of memories slid around her mind. It seemed to her that before this—long, long ago—she had worked out infallible strategies to bring this man to his knees in spite of himself, to make him love her with his arms, his voice, his lips. Now, at the hour of battle, all she could do was wait while her tremulous heart kept repeating, *I love you, I love you,* with the monotonous insistence of a prayer.

He looked at her steadily, without saying a word. She was resting her elbows on the narrow shelf atop his desk, almost directly under the Vanloo portrait, slightly to its left. He told himself that the artist, plainly a sensual man, had not really done justice to his model. Several essential details were missing from the Jeanne in the portrait. The buff flesh tone that gave a natural accent to her closed eyelids. Some tiny golden sparkles that the glow of lamplight gave the tips of her eyelashes. The quiver of her lips just as they were about to part. The white palpitations of muslin raised by a galloping heartbeat. The graceful, passionate curve of her body leaning on the mahogany desk.

"Untie your hair," Vincent said suddenly, his voice barely audible.

She opened her eyes.

"Take off your Indian-princess headband and undo your braids. Please."

Obediently she reached for the hair ribbon. Having loosened her hair, she tried to smooth it down with her fingers, made a sign to Vincent to wait a moment, and went to the washstand for a brush. After carefully arranging her hair, she returned to her place beneath Pomona, blushing and with lowered eyes.

A smile of great tenderness came over Vincent, which Jeanne did not see. "Here is my fairy with the blond hair," he murmured. "I like you better this way, Jeanne, with your hair the way it was at fifteen."

Inspired with hope, she raised her eyes. In three strides he was beside her, gathering up her hair and tossing it over her shoulders, except for one lock. Glancing up first at the Vanloo painting, he placed the shining curl on her breast.

Now that he was in a playful mood, she found her voice again. "I knew you had that painting," she said.

"Really? How could you know?"

"Mozart's father told me so. His son came to play in the hall of the Temple. I sold him a packet of cough drops. His father told me about the portrait, but the boy was the one who recognized me."

"This child Mozart has exquisite taste. God willing, he'll give us good music," said Vincent. "Did you pose very long for Vanloo?" he asked, looking once more at the painting.

"I never posed for him at all. Didn't his wife tell you? Her husband sketched me one Sunday at Belleville, Lady Favart's country house. He painted this from memory and the sketch. It shows, too, for it's not an exact resemblance."

"I also noticed some differences," said Vincent, his eyes darting from model to portrait and back. "The shadow on the eyelids, the exact shade of the eyebrows, the—"

"Oh, the face isn't too bad," Jeanne cut in boldly. "It's just that he didn't see everything . . ."

She stopped suddenly, blushing to the very roots of her hair.

"Oh?" said Vincent innocently, restraining a laugh. "Tell me," he urged, tilting her face upward with gentle hands.

"Well, it's . . . it's . . . There are just a few details that are . . . well, a painter paints what he likes, and there . . ."

She kept blinking, trying to evade the mocking brown eyes that seemed to take extreme delight in seeing her stammer. "Well, certain details are really a bit too crude and too pink," she said softly all at once.

"Is that so? Would you allow me to give my opinion?"

He slid his hands along Jeanne's back and began to undo her dress. She stood motionless. Slowly he unhooked her garment to the waist, then his hands glided back along her shoulders and he began to lower her bodice.

"Careful!" she spluttered, clinging to the dress.

"Careful? Why should I be careful? Does it bite?"

"I'm not wearing a chemise!"

When he laughed at that, she said hurriedly, "It's true, I have no chemise on. In your chest there were dresses, mantillas, negligées, ribbons, slippers, and even fans, but not a single petticoat, no stockings, and no chemise. So it's the truth. Be careful, I'm not wearing a chemise, I swear!"

"I understand, my dear. But why do you think I would be afraid of a woman without a chemise?"

"Oh!" she said, and stood gazing wide-eyed at him as the dress slid down her body like a quick white shiver. When it lay at her feet, she pressed her forehead against Vincent's shoulder. He gathered her hair in one hand to draw her head back gently, and placed a light kiss on her lips and then one on her neck. Slowly he covered her neck with kisses, then her shoulders and her breasts and, lowering himself to his knees, he kissed her stomach. He made sure that not a single inch of her skin was jealous of another, and felt his mouth becoming greedy and burning hot. With eyes closed, she quivered like a mimosa leaf stroked by gentle fingers. Finally she shook so hard that he heard her

* 415 *

teeth chatter. He got to his feet and held her tightly against him. "You're trembling so," he said in her hair. "Is it because you're cold?"

"Nnoo . . . no," her voice quavered.

"Is it from love?"

"Yesss . . ."

He swept her into his arms, kicked aside the white dress, and carried her over to the bed, where he laid her on the coverlet and gazed down at her beautiful, perfumed flesh glowing against the lustrous green velvet.

"My beautiful flower," he said softly, "my sweet flower. My passion flower."

CHAPTER 11

ucketfuls of water slapped resoundingly on the decks. Vincent threw back blanket and sheet, uncovering their two bodies lying skin to skin, brown and blond, in sweet-scented warmth. Gently he set out to untangle himself from the sleeping Jeanne. The hardest part was not to pull her hair.

"No!" she protested, and threw her arms and legs around him.

"Oh yes! I have to!" Vincent said, unclasping her arms. "Prayer is about to be rung."

"If you're fined three pennies for missing it, I'll pay you back," she declared, clinging to him again.

"Oh well," Vincent said, "you're worth three pennies, especially if you contribute them!" And with that he turned over and laid her beneath him, sweeping her matted hair off her face.

"I love you," she said. She plunged both her hands into the corsair's thick black shock of hair, ruffling it up adoringly. "I want a son with your curls, with all your curls, every single one!"

Vincent's mouth muffled a last moan on Jeanne's lips and he tore himself away from her, jumped into his shirt and breeches, slipped on hose and shoes, combed his fingers through his hair, and was out the door.

Jeanne made a feline purr of contentment into Vincent's pillow and nibbled at a corner of the ruffle impregnated with his orange-blossom scent.

"We beseech you to grant us a fair journey and good trading," Father Savié's voice droned on outside.

She lifted her arms, stretched, and smiled at the carved rosaces in the ceiling.

"I have a lover!" she said aloud, and sounded as if love was happening to her for the first time.

She jumped out of bed and ran to the mirror with the mad, joyful need to discover traces of Vincent's body on her own flesh.

What she saw in the mirror was a fair, amber-colored statue, tall, slender, graceful, strong, and flexible, a touch of burnished gold frothing on her lower belly, and her face, neck, shoulders, and breasts clothed in a tangle of silky locks. She grabbed her hair and pulled it back as Vincent had—then, bringing her hand forward to touch her reflection, she asked softly with a half-anxious, half-confident little smile, "Do I please you, my chevalier? Do I please you, my love?"

On the forecastle, Father Savié's voice swelled and declaimed, "Give us this grace through the mercies of Your Son. Amen." A whistle blew, and almost immediately there was a tap at the door.

"One moment!" Jeanne shouted, scrambling for some clothes.

She slipped on the first white cotton negligée she uncovered in the chestful of Brazilian clothes and opened the door, hiding behind it. "Oh, Mario! It's you! Come in."

"I thought you would surely need me," he said, full of expectancy, looking at her in such a way that she blushed. "The cook will soon have coffee ready for the gentlemen. But if you ask me for chocolate, I have—"

"No, no," she interrupted, "coffee suits me fine. Aren't we about to sail?"

"Alas, mam'selle, not yet. We have headwinds, plenty of headwinds, till you wonder which of us didn't pay his whore. Say, would you like me to do your hair for you till it's time to fetch the coffee?"

"Do my hair?" Jeanne said, taken aback. Mechanically, she ran one hand through her tangled hair.

"I'm a good hairdresser, mam'selle, you can ask the master. And I love to do ladies' hair. I can assure you they're always pleased with my work."

Jeanne frowned and asked smartly, "Do you often help ladies with their hair aboard this ship?"

Mario smiled sheepishly. "All right, did I blunder?"

"Yes," Jeanne replied. "And for your punishment you will have to answer my question: Do you often help a lady with her hair in the captain's room?"

Mario looked downcast. "Mam'selle, if I told you there's never been anyone before you, you wouldn't believe me, would you?"

"No."

"Then I might as well tell you the truth so you don't go breaking your heart over nothing. There have been ladies here, yes, but since you let us down one morning about five years ago, it's as if they didn't exist. Beautiful or not, they'd get cast ashore with the next tide, and we'd go back to moping and sighing over a hair ribbon or staring at your portrait."

"Is that true, Mario? Really true?"

"Cross my heart, if I lie, I hope to die! For five years now we've never shipped out without our broken heart, and we've dragged it along everywhere. It was not always good for me, either, since a master's bad moods always need a servant's back to fall on!"

"Poor Mario," Jeanne said with delight in her voice. "You're a fine valet. Will you do my hair?"

The dressing room was in a closet so narrow that the door had to stay open in order for her to sit at the mahogany table. Mario settled Jeanne in an armchair, seized the silver-handled hairbrush, poured a few drops of cologne on it, and began to brush her long hair with expert strokes.

"Mario, tell me about the chevalier. How old was he when you first sailed with him as a ship's boy?"

"He must have been eighteen, since I was eight and we are ten years apart. Now that I am twenty-five, I've been sailing with him for seventeen years." A note of resentment crept into his voice. "On land or sea, I'd never been away from him for a day till he left without me to rescue you from Pinto and his bandits."

"But that was because of your sprained foot, Mario. You could barely walk on it. He was afraid for you. Mario, look at me."

He raised his eyes and met Jeanne's in the round dressing-table mirror. She was smiling at him kindly. "Mario, you're not going to be jealous of me, are you?"

Vincent's handsome valet broke into a grin. "Ouch! Mam'selle, I'll have to get used to you, won't I?" he said laughingly.

"Mario, when the Chevalier Vincent was eighteen, did he already look the way he does now?"

"Are you asking me if he was handsome? Yes, for sure. Each time he paid a visit to the good parish priest in Cotignac, Father Puget, the abbot, had to confess half the village women and girls after he left. They all sinned just by thinking about him! I still remember the first morning I ever saw him."

"Tell me, Mario."

"I was six. I had sweeping duties at the parish schoolhouse. Father Puget came into the school with a tall, dark, handsome man, the most handsome man I'd ever laid eyes on. His smile was so gleaming white it made your heart burst. He wore his hair cut short like a convict's, but he still looked like a prince, a Moorish prince."

Jeanne felt a tug at her heartstrings as she listened to Mario talk about Vincent as a lover would. She could imagine the valet's every gesture as he waited on his master, the very ones Pauline de Vaux-Jailloux had described to her: Mario lovingly ironing Vincent's shirts, fluting his jabot and pleating his cuffs, spitting on his boots to shine them; Mario running the bath, lathering Vincent's body, toweling him, rubbing him down, spraying him with perfume, combing his hair, powdering him, slipping on his shirt and suit, handing him his sword.

Can a mistress ever possess a man as completely as his valet does? Seventeen years! Mario had lived so close to Vincent for seventeen years!

Filled with jealousy, she conjured up a vision of her own body, open and naked under Vincent's weight, so she could take away the master from his valet. With her eyes lowered, she reveled, deep inside, in the primacy of her female flesh.

Just then the door opened. "My dear, if you grant this boy the pleasure of brushing your hair, you will have to spend an hour each morning and night doing just that," Vincent said. "Mario, the lady looks perfect. Put down your comb and go get us some coffee. Coffee, cookies, and jams."

"There's some freshly baked bread," Mario said. "The cook made it with an eye to mam'selle's breakfast. Sir, will I shave you in the wardroom? It is muggy out in spite of the wind, so I put out a suit of light drugget and—"

"This morning I shall wear my uniform," Vincent cut in.

With a look of astonishment, Mario tried to speak, but his master anticipated him.

"Just for once, won't you stop asking questions. You will find out soon enough."

No sooner had the servant left than Jeanne threw herself upon Vincent's chest. "Do you still love me as much as before? If you love me a half-ounce less, I'll die on the spot!"

"Live, Jeannette, I'll give you good weight." He kissed her temple, near the roots of her hair, and held her back at arm's length. "In your fashion chest, can you find something to make you look as beautiful as last night, but a trifle more chaste?"

"If you don't care about my going around without a chemise . . ."

"It's your appearance that's important to me."

"Jealous?"

"No, careful. I have seventy men aboard. I'm asking you not to display your bosom."

"You will be pleased with me this morning. I want to dress like a boy and visit your ship from stem to stern."

"No."

"No? You don't want me to examine your frigate?"

"I don't want you to dress like a boy."

"Why not? Breeches look great on me."

"Yes, but Father Savié would not like to see me marry a pair of breeches. And personally, I prefer to be married to a skirt."

Jeanne gazed at him saucer-eyed. "I do not . . . you don't mean . . . what did you say?"

"I said make yourself beautiful because I want my bride to be very beautiful. A woman's beauty is a man's only excuse for his own folly."

She stood in front of Vincent looking frightened, no longer daring to touch him, and finally said in a weak, incredulous voice, "Are you telling me you're going to marry me? Marry me this morning? You're jesting, aren't you?"

He held her chin, searched her face. "Look me straight in the eye. Last night, Jeanne, was it a jest?"

"No, no, no!"

"Then I'm marrying you. This morning is marvelously appropriate. The winds hold us prisoners here, so we might as well do something."

She struggled to speak, but could make no sound. At last she whispered, "You know you cannot marry me. You are a chevalier and I am nothing. I am the daughter of a roofer from Burgundy and a peasant woman."

"And I'm the son of nobody and of an unknown woman," he said calmly. "Come in, Mario," he added, in response to a knock at the door.

Mario came in and bustled around the table, chattering away. "Coffee, milk, sugar, jams, fresh bread. Smell that bread! There was some custard pie left over, and I brought it for mam'selle. For you, sir, I thought a bit of ham and cheese from Rio—"

"Mario," Vincent cut in, "think silently, be quick, and go wait for me in the wardroom. I don't want to find a speck of dust on my uniform, and make my boots shine like mirrors. Go!"

Jeanne, beginning to collect her thoughts somewhat, said in a steadier voice, "Sir Vincent, I cannot allow you to commit this folly. I love you too much to let you do it. Besides, the grand master of your order . . ."

He grabbed her shoulders so roughly that she cried out and felt paralyzed by the imperious glint in his eyes. "Jeanne, you can no longer forbid me to do anything. It's too late," he growled. "I did not take you by force. But since you gave yourself to me, I will keep you by force, if not of your own free will. As God is my witness, after losing you twice, I had given you up. You and destiny have decided otherwise. Destiny sent me to your rescue and you flew into my arms. I took you because I'm not a saint, and I'll keep you because I'm not your puppet!"

Seeing the pallor of her lips and her shortness of breath, he sat her down roughly in an armchair and added in a tone of command, "Have a cup of coffee. It will give you strength. And get dressed. I have less patience with a capricious woman in the daytime than at night."

"Vincent . . ."

He waited in silence.

"Vincent," she stammered a second time, unable to go on.

He poured some coffee into a cup. "Do you like your coffee very sweet or not too sweet?"

"Vincent," she repeated a third time. She grasped one of his hands, pressed it to her cheek, and entreated him in a gentle voice, "Vincent, how can you doubt my love? You don't have that right, my beloved. But you also know that I'm not free to give myself away. Not today, in any case. Not before I have—"

Overcome with rage, Vincent tore his hand away, ripping her negligée and pinning her to the chair.

"Really, my dear, you make me laugh!" he rasped. "What is a woman free to give? Call up your memory, or else show less impudence. Listen to me, Jeanne, listen to me closely. I will not give you back to Aubriot! I have a corsair's soul, my sweet. I never returned booty fairly captured."

Her eyes flooded with tears. "Vincent, I love you, I belong to you, and I'll come back to you. Aren't you sure of it, deep inside you? How could I *not* come back to you now? But why demand that I be cruel or cowardly? Dear Vincent, be fair, allow me to go—"

"No!" he interrupted brutally.

She let out a sob, and he resumed more calmly, though no less bitterly, "Twice already I held you in my power, and twice I opened my hand and watched you go with the mad hope that you would come back to me on your own, your mind clearer, your heart soothed. Twice you did not come back and I called myself an imbecile. Today you have put yourself entirely in my hands, so I will close my fists because tomorrow I do not want to have to call myself a cuckold and a fool!"

"I beg you, Vincent, not to speak to me like that," she said, on the verge of tears. "Don't say such words to me, as if you only love me because you cannot hate me."

"My dear, sometimes I had to make an effort to hate you, since I could not forget you."

He bent down and drew her up to him by her elbows. "What the devil did you think my love for you was, Jeanne?" he asked, his face close to hers. "A sexless courtier's fancy? For years I have desired you, empty-handed. I yearned for you, I longed for you, I craved you, I wanted you with such a raging passion that I found myself dreaming the dreams of a schoolboy. I possessed you a hundred times while possessing blond mirages. A hundred times over I dreamed that I tore to pieces the dress and blouse of the giddy beauty who had locked herself up in my little house at Vaugirard to try on English fashions. A thousand times in my dreams I plucked a fragile flower, the delicious little girl in the woods at Neuville whom I had just kissed—her first kiss. And finally, last night I held you in my arms, warm and alive, and I was almost afraid to love you because I love you so. Jeanne, my golden fleece, I have won you at last, I will never again let you go, even if I have to lock you up in the hold to keep you!"

She was staring at him in ecstasy, as if he had poured a magic love potion in her ears. "My beloved, do what you want with me." she sighed in a passionate whisper of surrender.

"For now, all I ask you to do is get dressed and say yes in front of the chaplain," he said, letting her go.

She knelt in front of the clothes chest, only to look around again and ask in agony, "Vincent, what will happen when we reach Montevideo?"

He paused a moment, then said, "Dr. Aubriot is probably old enough and wise enough to understand that a little girl eventually grows up, leaves her convent, and says farewell to her schoolteachers and childhood infatuations."

"I'm not sure he will want to understand all this," she replied in a hushed voice, hoping also that Philibert would not agree to give her up that easily.

"Well," Vincent said, "if Aubriot wants this matter of love to become a matter of honor . . ."

She shouted, "No!" and Vincent raised his voice. "You will not interfere! When two men challenge each other's honor, a well-bred lady will lock herself in her room and pray."

Jeanne's rebellious spirit returned. "And how will God find his bearings when she prays to him to watch over both men?"

"My dear, I assume that God, like the good orthodox moralist he is, will side with the husband," Vincent said lightly. "I will soon be within my legitimate right. Be ready at noon."

The door slammed behind him.

Never, never, never! she seethed. Upset, aching, distressed by her own contradictions, Jeanne hammered her fists on the wooden clothes chest. *Never!*

She took out of the chest the most exquisite white chiffon dress she could find, with long, tight sleeves and a bodice made entirely of a delicate bobbin lace over a silk lining. She spread it on the bed, laid a mantilla of the same lace next to it, gazed fondly at their pearly sheen, opened the drawers of the mahogany dressing table, and began to dress for her wedding.

* * * *

". . . And I, by His authority, free you of any lien of excommunication and of any interdiction, within the reach of my power and of your need. I now absolve you of your sins in the name of the Father and of the Son and of the Holy Ghost. Amen."

Father Savié reached out with both hands to help her up. She patted her skirt, felt her mantilla, seemed to be seeking some ultimate paternal advice.

"You look quite lovely, my child," he said, smiling with approval at her graceful attire. "Do you feel ready?"

"Yes, Father," she said in a stifled voice, but she did not move, suddenly overcome by one of those small shivers common to natures as emotional as hers.

The chaplain rested his gaze on her. "My child, there is still time to reflect," he said. "Are you indeed marrying our captain of your own free will and in sound mind?"

"Sound mind!" she echoed almost plaintively. "Does sound-minded love really exist, then, Father?"

"Sacred love exists, which gives you joy, and which you never need to blush about, before God or man."

"But I'm of the sort that will blush in front of a ladybug," she said, with just the hint of a smile to apologize for her levity. "Father, don't ask me how I love. I love the way I love. When I love, I love without being able to stop loving. If I had to tear out my love for Sir Vincent, I would have to tear my heart away with it and fall dead."

"Save part of your heart for God, my child. He will never fail you. A mortal's love is mortal."

"Not his! Not his!"

The priest heaved a sigh, took her hand, and said with solemn friendliness, "By the Passion of Our Lord, by the virtues of his Mother, may all the good you accomplish for the love of your husband, may all your suffering for it, bring about the remission of your sins, the augmentation of holy grace within you, and a reward in eternal life. And now come, my child. They are waiting for us."

As she reached the forecastle, she was greeted by the bright, powdery light of noon. It lit her up, made her shimmer like a white, fairylike apparition against the blue of the sky. The wind was blowing her skirt and mantilla, but its breath was gentle and all it did was add a graceful billow to her light silk gown.

Jeanne was shocked by the silence now greeting her. It was so complete that she could hear the ship responding to the sea as it did at night. She took a few steps, stopped, and gazed at the mute spectre of the entire crew, standing at attention, looking at her in awe. Jeanne recognized the Provençal and gave him a beautiful smile, which she then shared slowly with the other men.

She heard a firm footstep behind her on her left, turned, and found herself facing Vincent. She felt weak with love. *I'm dreaming. Reality could not be this beautiful.*

Her lips parted to repeat in a whisper, "I'm dreaming."

The Knight of Malta looked magnificent in his red uniform with white trim and gold buttons, his light-colored breeches and waistcoat, the red scapular and white cross emblem of his order pinned to his chest, a goldsmith's sword at his side, and his black cocked hat tucked under one arm. He wore a wig and a look of cheerful determination.

He bowed to Jeanne. "Jeanne, pray forget the harsh words I spoke this morning, my violence and my tyranny," he said hurriedly in a low voice. "I demand nothing, I merely hope. Jeanne, will you agree to marry me?" Then he added, without any transition or change of tone, "That was to satisfy Father Savié. Your answer can only be yes."

She stifled a laugh, bit her lip, and whispered, "It couldn't work out better, for even if I wanted to say no, I'd still have to say yes!"

"Come!" he said.

He walked her to the chaplain, who was standing in the same spot where he led daily prayers. The officers stepped back to let the bride and groom take their places. A huge sigh rose from the silent crew.

"Sir, take your fiancée's hand," Father Savié told Vincent.

Vincent extended his long, dark, open hand and closed it over Jeanne's, which was trembling frantically like the heart of an ensnared bird.

Hidden behind a coil of tow rope, Mario burst into sobs.

CHAPTER 12

rom that mountain a nice little wind will come. It will come soon." Marius, the cargo master, paused and concluded solemnly, facing Vincent, "Tomorrow morning, Captain, you'll have stern wind!"

Like every cargo master, this one was regarded as an oracle.

"Let's hope so!" Vincent said, still speaking Provençal. "Can I trust you, Marius?"

"Believe me, Captain. It will come!"

Vincent thanked the cargo master solemnly.

Agenor, the black boy, fetched the brandy keg and Marius took a long swig.

Jeanne waited till the group had broken up to approach Vincent. "Do you really believe in the powers of your cargo master?" she asked.

Vincent smiled at her. "The bilge is steeped in the mystery of eternal night, and creatures that inhabit the night have always had a touch of magic—owls, bats—and cargo masters."

"You consider Marius a magician?"

"Oh yes!" Vincent said laughingly. "Every good cargo master is a magician. The proof is that he can fit a thing as big as oxen into space that would barely house a frog. As for the winds upon my word, Marius is wrong only every other time! I hope he guessed right today!"

She brushed Vincent's hand and asked softly, "Are you in such a hurry to get to Maldonado? If only I could stop time . . ."

"You'd not be as well off as you think," he said, pointing to the shore, which looked far too close.

She noted that it was busier than it had been during the morning, and borrowed Vincent's spyglass. "I see some of Pinto's men there!" she exclaimed after a brief observation. "I recognize three of them, old men, whom Pinto had left at the village. Does it mean they followed us?"

"You can count on it!" Vincent said. "I robbed them of their booty, and they're not very generous. There's just a handful of them, since others must have picked up Don José's trail or gone back to inform Pinto. Now that these fellows know where you are, thanks to the blabbing cowards at the fort, it won't be long till the rest of the troop hears of it. Tomorrow we'll have a pack of those savages on our back."

"No, tomorrow we'll have fair wind," said Jeanne.

"True, Jeannette, "*auren lou vent*—we'll have fair wind in the morning," Vincent declared. "God will never let me fight while my wife is aboard. He knows I don't like warfare, even when it's man to man."

Jeanne gazed at the corsair's virile profile. "Can it be that you genuinely hate war, Vincent?" she asked.

He nodded. "I do hate it, even if it takes the form of a thrilling naval battle. Wrecking ships and lives has always struck me as a senseless, cruel, and ruinous game."

"How can anyone feel that way and still be a corsair?"

Vincent laughed lightly. "My darling, I believe you have a few misconceptions about the corsair soul," he said. "It's the captains of the royal fleet who sail the seas seeking glory in the smoke of battle. As far as privateers are concerned, greed is what spurs them on."

"You're not greedy!" she protested.

"You dislike the word? But you don't dislike my few riches, do you? And I'm certain that you like the fine sheets on our bed, your luxurious Brazilian finery, the silver table service, the emerald ring I put on your finger. And I daresay you love to run your hand over my silk suit and rub your cheek against my exquisitely soft muslin shirts. Am I wrong? Well, my darling, all these things you love, or nearly all of them, I stole, captured, or smuggled with rapacious perseverance. I was born with nothing and I vowed I wouldn't die that way."

"Vincent, you're jesting," Jeanne said. "You're not a thief. You're not even a pirate. You share your booty with your Order."

"Between the two of us, Jeannette, what you're really saying is that every single item I plunder gets recorded in triplicate. And that's precisely what galls me so! You see, outwitting his accountant is a corsair's most trying task. No enemy hunts you down so mercilessly. Privateering has become an exercise in paperwork. Even when you belong to the Order of the Knights of Malta and devote yourself to preying on Turks, it is no longer possible to toss overboard the turbaned head you just cut off. For heads must fall on deck, where the clerk can record the number of turbans. He must even count the cannon shots to keep track of how much is being spent on cannonballs and powder—all this is written in the Rules."

Jeanne broke into laughter. "But come now," she said, "once the accounting is done, aren't you due a fair share of everything, including the smallest turban?"

"Would that were true!" Vincent exclaimed, adding under his breath, "I'd be luckier still if I managed to grab the turban's emerald before I'm obliged to share the proceeds of its sale with my shareholders!"

"Oh!" Jeanne said, glancing pensively at the magnificent jewel glittering on her ring finger.

"This one, I promise you, does not come from a headless Turk," said Vincent. "I acquired it in a gentler fashion."

"How does a corsair go about gently acquiring something that doesn't belong to him?"

Vincent darted one of his mocking little glances at her. "I thought I had already demonstrated that to you. Instead of assaulting one's prey like an ordinary, ill-bred pirate, one politely circles her until she is persuaded to lower her veils in surrender. Jeanne, I'm delighted to see that I can still make you blush."

"That's a pleasure you will often have," she said. "I do it so easily."

She looked up at Vincent, her eyes bright with excitement. "Where will you take me after Montevideo?"

Vincent gave a slight start, then took Jeanne's hand, turned it over, and kissed the palm. "Your question is a very pretty way of telling me that at last I have conquered you forever."

Only then did Jeanne realize that her question did in fact deny the existence of her past. A shiver of anxiety raced through her, yet she repeated boldly, "Where will you take me after Montevideo? Remember, you promised me a trip around the world."

"I won't break my promise. But I'll start with a visit to the coast of Chile."

"The coast of Chile?"

"You sound surprised."

"Yes. At the navigation office in Versailles, I heard that Captain Vincent's frigate was heading for the Gulf of Bengal."

Vincent peered at his wife under raised eyebrows. "So! Am I to infer that you inquired about my route at the Duke de Penthièvre's office?"

"Yes, you may believe it."

"And why?"

"So that as I walked my fingers across the map of the world, I could dream of finding you one day here or there in some blue, green, and gold tropical paradise."

Vincent's explosive laughter sounded so merry that the crewmen passing behind them paused to smile.

The sailors came and went busily behind the couple leaning on the handrail. The shipboard romance and Jeanne herself—her adventurous past and charming manners—captivated the men.

This frigate has become my home and these seamen my family. Jeanne caressed the woodwork fondly and fingered the tidy bundles of canvas and rigging whenever she thought no one was looking. She kept a nonchalant watch on the men's incessant and idle roaming.

Her new family was a motley group in pigmentation, origin, and tongue. They were a picturesque mixture of what Vincent called the "unclassified" because they were not on the registers of the French naval office. Like all corsair captains, Vincent recruited first the few registered sailors that the fleet hadn't claimed, then completed his crew with whatever was available: foreigners, prisoners he rented from neutral countries, Creoles and mestizos from the colonies, slaves enrolled by their masters as "navigation Negroes."

This small population seemed to coexist in relative harmony. To give some sort of cohesion to this mixed collection of recruits, Vincent had a second-in-command and a capable lieutenant, assisted by a top-notch group of petty officers. His officers were all Provençals, most of whom had served him for a long time and could hold their men in hand, firmly but justly.

In the closed world of sailoring, Captain Vincent's reputation was good. The Maltese had what it took in the eyes of adventurous seamen eager to reap the spoils of privateering. His skill and daring were matched by luck and good humor. And crowning all this, he was honest in a decent fashion, favoring his men over the accountant. During a looting he would close his eyes to the "small booties" they chose to keep for themselves. Furthermore, he was handsome and a good dancer and singer, seducing beautiful women in every port, which, to any crew, is a source of great pride.

In short, Vincent almost always found his count of men, with a minimum of freaks and sluggards. Life was cheerful aboard his ship.

Jeanne had been struck from the start by this cheerfulness. Once they were done furbishing the ship, the men would busy themselves with card games, dice, or knucklebones. They gambled only with chickpeas or their ration of wine, since it was forbidden to bet money. The head sailmaker, who at the moment refused to mend his sails for fear of sewing the present unfriendly wind into them, would tell fortunes with the tarot in exchange for some sweets his clients had stolen from the kitchen or begged from the surgeon, whose sea chest contained prunes and raisins for the sick. There were frequent songs and wild dancing.

"Your men are used to wedding festivities," Jeanne said gaily to Vincent. "They look ready to start yesterday's ball all over again."

"There's dancing and singing every evening aboard my ship," Vincent said. "The Irishman taught us a lovely hoisting song that will work magic when we set sail for Chile."

"By the way, why are we going to Chile?"

"I have a valuable cargo to deliver to Santiago for Don José. Sometimes it's less perilous to send merchandise around Cape Horn than by the inland route. It's chilly on the Cape, but I'll buy you chinchilla and sealskins in Chile to keep you warm. Wouldn't you like to have a long chinchilla coat and fur hat like the Russian nobility wear?"

"I'd love to have anything you gave me."

"My word, I'm incredibly lucky!" he said teasingly. "Most women want everything they can't have."

A mass of gold and azure plumage swooped down onto Vincent's shoulder, cutting short Jeanne's protest. "I'm hungrrry! What time is it?" Chérimbané screeched.

"It's almost time," Vincent told his parrot. Just then the lookout shouted at Vincent, "Captain, over there, on shore!"

Vincent trained his spyglass on the shore. About thirty horsemen were dismounting in front of the fishing harbor.

"Do you recognize those fellows?" he asked Jeanne, handing her the spyglass.

"Yes," she replied after a moment. "The man observing us with his spyglass is one of Pinto's lieutenants."

Lieutenant Quissac and several other officers were gathering around them. "Sir, do you believe they will dare attack us in their skiffs?" Quissac asked.

"I think they'll wait until more of them have arrived," Vincent said. "If the whole troop gathers before we get fair wind, we'll be in trouble. Pinto is clever. The first thing he'll do is send half of his men to the island so they can attack us from both sides at once."

"If their boats don't capsize on the way," said Quissac with a hungry smile. "It will be a great pleasure to send their boats to the bottom with two broadsides. Have no fear, madame, our gunners lay well," he added, turning to Jeanne.

"Lieutenant, I'm not afraid," Jeanne said, gazing at Vincent with boundless, trusting love. "Believe me, this won't spoil my appetite for supper. I'll get dressed for it this instant. I'd love to watch you give those bandits a bath. They don't wash often enough."

"I think we'll have time to dine before the party starts," Vincent said.

* * * *

At ten o'clock the bandits were still camping on the shore. The full moon and clear sky made them as visible as if it were high noon. They had lit a great bonfire, heavy with smoke and the aroma of roasting meat. Their distant laughter floated out to the *Belle Vincente,* along with singing and bawling and the voices of girls who had probably come down from the Maldonado cabins.

"They're already drunk, but double the watch anyway," ordered the boatswain. "The others might arrive, and this is a perfect night for a midnight attack."

Before midnight, a rapping at the bedroom door instantly drove Vincent out of bed.

"The bandits?" Jeanne mumbled, waking up with a start.

"Captain, the wind! The wind has shifted!"

The headwind had died abruptly, replaced by a light land breeze that was starting to blow down from the Maldonado heights. It was still merely the ghost of a squall, but the *Belle Vincente* could respond to the sky's slightest quivers. There was a bright moon, and Vincent decided to sail immediately.

"My lady love, I'm going to deny you the pleasure of sending your friend Pinto to his bath," he told Jeanne cheerfully.

The ship began to shake with the great bustle of departures. Jeanne retreated to an out-of-the-way nook from which she could observe the maneuvers.

There is such magic in setting sail! Three times now she had experienced that magic, but never as powerfully as on this moonlit night when the man she loved was guiding his frigate's flight. Tonight everything was the same, yet she perceived everything differently. The dream she had dreamt a hundred times was at last coming true. Vincent was taking her away . . .

The whole crew knelt down facing their captain to receive the chaplain's benediction. "Topmen, to your stations!"

The lower sails dropped with the slow plashing of sheets being hung out to dry, starting to flap gently and to moan on their brails.

"All hands to the windlass!" There was a sharp pattering of bare feet on the deck.

"Ready to come about!" The sound of clanking metal drowned out the loud traffic of bare feet, filling the moonlit night with confusion.

There were no songs, but a long, muffled, raucous, and rhythmical call: "Yo, heave, ho! Yo, heave, ho! Yo, heave, ho! Yo, heave, ho!"

"Straight up!" called Aubanel, the first mate, loudly to warn the captain in his singsong Marseilles accent.

"Hoist away the upper topsails!" Vincent's command rolled over the ship, reaching Jeanne like a deep caress.

"Ready to hoist!"

"Hoist away!"

As the topsails dropped off their yards, a song burst out, filling the warm, pale night with its lively rhythm.

> *"Hurrah! sailors, heave at the windlass,*
> *Goodbye, farewell,*
> *Goodbye, farewell,*
> *Farewell misery, hello novelty,*
> *Hurrah! ho! Santiago!*
> *Ho! ho! ho!*
> *And we will go to Valparaiso,*
> *Haul away, hey!*
> Oula tchalez!

Where others will leave their bones,
Hello, sailor,
Hey! ho! heave hey! ho!"

The captain's magnificent full voice dominated the chorus.

And then, as the majestic topsails ascended the masts, stretching out against the sky, smooth, superb, furrowed by the impatient squall sweeping down from the Maldonados, Vincent's voice rang out. "Ready to hoist the jib! Hoist!"

The delicate sail flew off over the figurehead, hailed by the great traditional cry that saluted a good sailing: "Hoist the jib, sailor, all is paid up!"

"Yo!" The roar of freedom must have reached and stirred the stars in their peaceful expanse. Jeanne felt herself listing limply to one hip as the frigate glided out to the open sea. It was as if she and the frigate were yielding, like two beautiful, submissive playthings, to Vincent's sovereign pleasure.

CHAPTER 13

What the devil are they scraping about?" Jeanne muttered sleepily, rolling over. Then she realized that the other half of the bed was empty. *Haven't we left the bay?* It was daybreak. Jeanne remembered falling asleep knowing that Vincent had gone up to join the helmsman. He would stay there until they were out to sea. Now, as the sun shown through the porthole, she stretched lazily like a cat in no hurry to leave its cozy nest. *Perhaps Vincent would return for a nap.*

A whistle shrilled, and Jeanne heard Lieutenant Quissac bellowing some unfamiliar orders. "Silence, sailors! To your posts, gunners! Topsailmen, aloft! Yardarm topmen, aloft! Any man not aloft, come down and take fighting stations! Put on arm guards! No talking! Ensign Gioberti, see to that! Ensign Brussanne . . ."

It's a drill! Jeanne told herself. *I want to see what's going on.*

She started to dress. Out on deck, the lieutenant's commands and the responses dovetailed in rhythmic succession. But Quissac's instructions made her pause.

"No cause for panic, boys! Think of it as a game of skittles. You're shooting for the front row. That's what will fall. Our gunners will give 'em what-for, and the wind always favors our captain! When you go to reload, stretch out flat on deck. Don't talk so you can hear orders. Let each man make his peace with God, show courage, and do his duty. I'm warning anyone who's never fought with me that I shoot spineless slackers on sight. Now, boys . . ."

Quissac is mad! How could Vincent tolerate such talk during drill practice? Or maybe the Pinto bandits . . .

In a sudden panic she pulled on her hose and boots, hastily tied her hair back in a ribbon, and was about to leave the cabin when a knock sounded. She opened the door and found Mario standing there.

"Ah, you are dressed, madame. I didn't think you'd be able to sleep through—"

"What's happening, Mario?"

"Don't be frightened, madame. It's really nothing. As usual, we'll polish them off in two winks."

"Mario, tell me what's going on, or else let me go see for myself," she beseeched, pushing him aside.

"Madame, it's an English privateer trailing us," he said, restraining her. "Same size as our ship. No, madame, you mustn't leave without me. I'm to escort you to the surgeon's cabin, below the mainmast."

"Why there?"

"It's the safest place on board. You won't have anything to worry about."

"Take me to your captain first."

"Forgive me, madame, but I can't do that. The captain would not want to see you up there. I must obey him, and so must you. You know, in time of crisis we must all obey and ask no questions. Everyone's safety depends on it. Allow me." He bent down to fasten the buckles on Jeanne's breeches, which she had forgotten to do.

On deck the lieutenant was bawling, "Attention, gunners! Silence! Master gunner, you're in charge!"

"Mario, what's all this about your English privateer? France is not at war with England, is she?"

"That ship is waging a private war on us. It's an old story that dates back to our expedition to the Indies. Without firing a shot, the captain used guile and the winds to trick them into surrendering a fine French prize they had just captured. For that, Captain Henley swore he would send Captain Vincent to the bottom. But don't let it upset you, madame. He's already tried four times. Today makes the fifth!"

"But the English have no right to do that in peacetime!" Jeanne protested.

Mario smiled and said, "Your husband will tell you that peace with the English is never certain on the seas. Now we must go."

As they left the cabin, Father Savié was solemnly intoning a prayer on the forecastle. "O Lord, thou who seest the justice of our cause, watch over us and protect us from the snares and wiles of our enemies . . ."

"We'll take the central ladder down," said Mario, offering his hand to help Jeanne through the cluttered guardroom.

They were obliged to pick their way gingerly among piles of storage as well as the barnyard menagerie, which had been relocated here to clear the decks.

Mario grabbed Licorice the cat by the scruff of its neck as it prowled after tail feathers, just as the pair reached the foot of the ladder leading up to the forecastle.

Jeanne touched Mario's arm to restrain him, and motioned upward with her eyes. She saw sailors with muskets in hand lined up behind the portside railing. She and Mario were shielded by a crimson bulwark. The openwork railings along the deck and around the various crow's nests were draped with long strips of stout red woolen cloth emblazoned with white crosses, making the ship look as if it were decked out for a jubilee instead of a battle. But the master gunner's orders, combined with Father Savié's blessing, left no doubt. They were about to see combat.

Mario began tugging at Jeanne's arm just as Vincent walked past the head of the ladder. Impulsively, Jeanne called to him, broke away from the valet, and scrambled up the ladder—only to find herself promptly returned to the foot of it! Her shoulders felt bruised by the grip of a very angry man who was shaking her and shouting, "Stay below! Are you questioning my orders? Get below!"

Crushed in body and spirit, Jeanne spluttered, "Forgive me!" adding childishly in her panic, "My love, do take off that scarlet uniform. You're a regular target."

It was the corsair's turn to pause in utter amazement. Then he pushed Jeanne toward Mario and sneered, "When I want advanced training as a frigate captain, I'll take it in peacetime. Go below!"

Mario dragged Jeanne off as fast as he could. The crew, after one last intoned response to the chaplain, fell silent. "Lord, have mercy on us, help us, lead us forward."

Orders from the master gunner rang out. "Unlock firearms. Put out the lights. Fall in line at the pulleys!"

Silence, followed by Lieutenant Quissac's booming voice. "Attention, gunners! Prepare to thrust cannon through gunports! Thrust!"

With Mario still tugging at the distressed Jeanne, the pair crept below into the shadows.

* * * *

M. Amable's cabin, elegantly candlelit, bore the delicious scent of burning eucalyptus. When expecting patients, the surgeon always simmered a few leaves in an open kettle to clear the air. He welcomed Jeanne with a warm smile. She shuddered to see the red-hot cauterizing irons, the saws and forceps for extracting musketballs, the hooks and spikes, and, lined up on a wooden plank, the vessels, plasters, ligatures, and threaded needles, both straight and curved.

"We have to be prepared according to regulations, but not everything gets used," said the surgeon, noting Jeanne's anxious expression.

"Yes, of course," she murmured. *My God, if Vincent were brought down here in a bloody heap, I'd die.*

"I'm well equipped, don't you think?" said Amable in an effort to cheer her up. "Since you know something about medicine, my orderlies will show you our greatest treasures: ointments, powdered disinfectants, astringents, honeyed compounds, essence of flowers, and cologne. I tell you, I'm the only naval surgeon—"

"Excuse me," Jeanne interrupted sharply, "does much fighting go on?"

"At sea?"

"I mean on board this ship. Do they fight very often?"

"No, privateers don't like to fight, and your husband least of any. Besides, France is at peace with everyone now. And first-class booty is hard to come by, so the privateers do more trading than preying. Bad piece of luck, that English ship."

A violent shock wrapped in a deafening roar shook the vessel and made Jeanne cry out. A chorus of joyous, savage shouts followed, feet pounded the deck, the guns creaked and groaned as they were being reloaded, and snatches of orders filtered through the bellowing of Quissac.

Suddenly, from the corridor outside, came the booming voice of a ship's carpenter calling for help, for medicine and bandages. The five people in the surgeon's cabin stood mute, listening intently. What must have been a few minutes stretched into an eternity for Jeanne. Suddenly a man burst into the infirmary, exhilarated almost to the point of laughter, carrying his bloody right arm in a sling.

"Hurry, Master Surgeon, hurry! Patch me up and send me back there! I don't want to miss a thing! Lord, did we take that Englishman down a peg with the first salvo!"

The question trembling on Jeanne's lips rang out first and loudest. "Tell us more! Is your captain safe?"

The injured man stared at her, as stunned to find her there as he was by her question. "What? Why wouldn't he be safe?" He spoke as if his captain's invulnerability were among the reliable certainties in his sailor's universe.

* * * *

On deck there was a great bustle of organized activity. The English frigate, slightly heavier than the *Belle Vincente*, teetered in the water off the starboard side. She was within musket range, her topsails lowered, her flag struck, her foremast and bowsprit shattered.

Jeanne picked out Vincent and the Chevalier Brussanne at once by their scarlet uniforms, but had sense enough to stay in the corner where Mario had pushed her. The command staff and the petty officers were arguing about something.

Mario went to listen in and came back to report that some, including the captain, were of the opinion that they should abandon the English ship, whose name was the *Lady Harriet*, without boarding her, since, for diplomatic reasons, the authorities would not condone her capture. Of course, the crew felt differently. They smelled booty. As the discussion dragged on, the men began to complain louder and louder, "Board her! Board her!"

A blast from the captain's whistle ended the chorus. Vincent turned to them, shouting, "*We'll* decide that, my lads!"

The muttering continued, more subdued now, until one loudmouthed sailor from Saint-Malo stepped forward to harangue his mates. "Hey, all you men from Provence, are you going to let them cheat you out of the booty you fought for? Big ship, big guns, and no loot. To hell with the captain and his crew! On any Breton ship they'd stick you all in the kitchen!"

In three strides Vincent was upon the man, and sent him sprawling with a clean smack on the jaw. "All right, you mush-headed Breton, who asked you to preach mutiny on my ship?"

The sailor dragged himself to his feet, livid with rage, and whipped out a knife that glinted in the sunlight. Before he could use it, the flat side of a sword disarmed him and his arms were pinned behind his back. "Lock up this son of a bitch in the hold until we decide what to do with him," the captain ordered.

The incident silenced all complaints. The officers resumed their discussion until the captain intervened.

"Gentlemen, you've given me your opinion and I thank you for it. Now the decision is mine. We will not board. At this time the capture of any English vessel would surely get us into trouble with the authorities. Besides, I hate to waste any more time. We need to put in briefly at Montevideo and then get away from this coast. We're the target of Portuguese munitions merchants who own the place. Now that we have the wind, I don't feel like being detained by a crew bent on drinking and looting and who won't work unless forced to. We will not board. I'll announce it to the men."

"May the Lord protect you, Captain!" growled the mate.

The crew sent up an angry howl when the captain announced his decision. Vincent took a deep breath and blared, "Silence, sailors! What happened this morning is fine, lads, as far as it went. We're rid of that dog of an Englishman who was out to sink us. Our only casualties are a couple of injured men. There's a long, fine trip ahead of us to the Gulf of Bengal and the China Sea. I'll repay you ten times over for the measly spoils you've given up today. The next capture we make, I'll close my eyes and let you go on a looting spree for a whole hour. I give you my word!"

A rousing "Hurrah!" assured the captain that he had regained the crew's goodwill.

Vincent raised his hand and announced, "Meanwhile, lads, double rations of wine and roast mutton tonight, and a ball afterward. And for dinner, Burgundy from my own private cellar!"

A joyful delirium ensued. The mate had to blast on his whistle to quiet them down. "Everyone stand still for a minute!" he ordered.

Turning to the captain, he said, "I suggest, sir, that before tidying up the ship we punish the sailor who drew his knife against you."

Hostile, cutthroat cries burst from the crew. Actually, they had forgotten about the Saint-Malo sailor, but once reminded of him they yelled for his blood with savage fury. In place of the forbidden booty, a comrade's tortured shrieks would have to do.

The captain's silvery whistle shrilled once again. "Quiet, all of you! On this ship, punishment is inflicted in silence. Let me warn the new hands that anyone who insults or strikes the offender will suffer the same punishment. Bring up the man. Drummer, fetch the whipcord."

Mario rushed to the corner where he had hidden Jeanne. "Hurry, madame, go below! What's about to happen is not for your eyes!"

"But I can't go below, Mario," she whispered frantically. "You can see that I'd have to pass in front of the captain, and he'd know that I came on deck without his permission."

In fact, Vincent and his officers barred her path to the ladder. On top of that, the crewmen had lined up on deck opposite their commanding officers as if for a spectacle. Jeanne was not about to run the gauntlet of all those eyes preparing for a kill.

"Hide me, Mario," she pleaded. "Stay in front of me."

"Yes, of course, and you must keep down out of sight."

But she couldn't block her ears when the lashes began to rain on the naked back of the sailor roped to the mainmast.

My God, make Vincent stop it before the fellow dies! Make him stop it. I beg you, Lord. She prayed mightily, her face hidden in her hands.

Finally, after an eternity of prayers, she heard Vincent shout, "Enough!"

"The bastard's got what's coming to him," Mario muttered.

She raised her eyes. A wild, piercing shriek rent the air, stifling her cry. Jeanne began to tremble like a leaf in the wind. "Did they . . . hang him?"

"No, nothing like that," Mario whispered. "They simply nailed his hand to the mast. That's the penalty for drawing a knife on board ship. Do you feel dizzy? God help us, please don't turn so pale! If you faint now and the captain sees it, he'll skin me alive for not keeping you below."

"It's all right, Mario, it's all right," she assured him, her teeth chattering.

Vincent passed close by and noticed only Mario, whom he ignored. Jeanne heard him tell his second, "Release the man and have him looked after. We'll put him ashore in Montevideo and forget about him. Until then, keep him locked up."

As soon as she could creep unseen up the ladder, Jeanne scurried back to her cabin and burst into tears.

* * * *

After giving her face a good splashing with cold water, she felt better. *I'm such a ninny, always on the verge of tears. Of course he has to discipline offenders if he's to remain the master on board.*

She washed, fixed herself up, and barely had time to slip into a pretty summer dress and comb her hair before Vincent walked in.

"Ah," he sighed, removing his pistols, "I'm glad that's over with."

She drew close to him and put her arms around his neck. "The last time we met, on the forecastle ladder, you were angry with me," she pouted.

"Because a corsair captain should never marry a woman tall enough to wander about the ship on her own," he replied with a straight face. "She should be small enough to keep in his pocket, and assume her natural height only in bed."

"I'm not sure I'll ever forgive you for that opinion," she said.

Cradling her chin in his hand, he kissed her. "How about now?"

"Now I forgive you, but I won't stop disobeying you. I'm not a saint, you know."

"Oh, I know, even better than you do. And I don't care. Saints don't appeal to me. I like exquisite human beings, with skin as soft as virtue itself."

"So you're only attracted by my skin?" she said teasingly. "You're not interested in the deeper side of me?"

He retorted mockingly, "Skin is often the deepest layer of a woman's being."

"Listen to that! Oh, you'll pay dearly for that remark!" she cried, pummeling him with her fists. "And stop laughing!"

"I'm laughing because I love you and love is fun."

"Yes, love is fun. Love with you is fun, my darling," she said as she wound her arms around his neck once again. Resting her head on his shoulder, she asked in a whisper, "When will we get to Montevideo?"

"Tomorrow evening, perhaps, or the day after, or never."

"Why never?"

"It depends on the sea, on the wind. Haven't you learned that we exist at their whims and fancies?"

"But you can command those whims." Hugging him tighter, she added, "Command them to shipwreck us in the middle of nowhere, under a coconut tree."

He lifted her chin and looked deep in her eyes. "Jeanne, dreaming in my arms is a waste of time. When you're in love, past and future are wasted time."

"But don't you understand that I dream of the future to forget the tomorrows? Don't you know that I'm scared of tomorrow because today is so marvelous?" she declared passionately. "I don't want today ever to end. I've dreamed of you, Vincent, for so long that even now, each time I see you again I feel I have to touch you to make sure it's really you and not a fantasy."

"At the moment, dearest, I feel as insubstantial as a fantasy!" he said, smothering a yawn in his wife's hair.

Outraged, she exclaimed, "What's this? I declare my love for you, and all you can do is yawn!" He burst out laughing, which made her laugh too.

"Forgive me, darling," he said at last. "It's only that I'm tired, believe me."

"Nonsense!" she pursued mercilessly. "If you had decided to board, you'd be collecting booty right now, never giving a thought to sleep. You might even be flirting with the ladies you'd find aboard the English ship."

"A job's a job, my dear, and relieving a lady of her jewels while giving her something pleasant to remember is all part of a corsair's trade."

"You mean to tell me that you steal women's jewels?" she exclaimed, horrified.

"It depends on how valuable they are."

"Indeed? And also on how pretty the owner is?"

"That's right. But I'm not to blame if a lady is prepared to lay down her beauty for her jewels or her wardrobe."

"Oh my!" said Jeanne, offended by the reply. Glaring at him, she said briskly, "You men always treat a smart woman like a plaything. I ask you, now, what can a poor female do who suddenly finds the ship she's traveling on invaded by hordes of yelping, rampaging corsairs? I suppose her only choice is to donate her possessions or be raped, and I think she does better to save herself and her belongings at the same time."

"I can't argue with you!" He gave her one of his lingering, mocking looks and continued, grinning, "At any rate, dear one, rest assured that I don't allow my men to assault women on a captured vessel. You've been reading too many second-rate sea stories. Under my command, rape is reserved for officers and is carried out with great courtesy, and always at the request of the vanquished ladies."

"Oh!" Jeanne exclaimed, glaring at him again. "Vanity of vanities! My dear knight, you can just forget that every woman who sees you would wish to be violated by you. It's a notion favored by all men in wartime."

"Every woman? Heavens, I'm not interested in the cooperation of all women. Just the pretty ones."

Jeanne strode over to Vincent and retorted with studied insolence, "Try as you will, you'll never convince me that you've taken any woman by force. It's not in your nature. I know what I'm saying. You didn't do it in the lodge in the woods at Neuville, or at your own little place in Vaugirard."

She looked up at him with her eyes so full of yearning that he couldn't resist teasing her a little longer. "Forgive me. I repent."

"Oh, don't apologize, you didn't mean anything wrong. You're simply not very astute in such matters," she told him with added boldness. "And to prove it, now that you've made me so furious that I don't even want to talk to you, you won't lift a finger against me and will march quietly off to bed."

He lifted her chin with one finger and replied in sugar-sweet tones, "No, dear heart, I won't disappoint you a third time." And with that he tore off his wig, kicked over the armchair she was standing behind, caught her up in his arms, and tossed her onto the bed like a pack of rags, then pulled up her skirts and fell upon her, showering her with kisses.

CHAPTER 14

or the special dinner promised to the crew, Jeanne had put on her white lace wedding gown and was waiting for the sleeping Vincent to awaken in the wardroom. She was reading a book of fables by La Fontaine, from the ship's library, as she absently petted Licorice.

The gentle rocking of the sea had slowed the rhythm of Jeanne's pulsing blood, and calmed her. Her anxieties slumbered. Soon enough, she'd have to deal with her guilty feelings about abandoning Philibert. She had been plagued for four days, until Vincent's loving caresses had assuaged all her conflicting emotions.

She ran her finger over a tiny bruise on her left breast, inflicted by Vincent's uniform button, and she sighed with love.

My God, I'm not very good at prayers, but please fill me with wonder whenever I'm near him. Make him desire me always as if for the first time.

Her book slipped onto the rug. She was infatuated with her chevalier to the point of wanting to live only for love, indolence, and folly.

"What a tremendous change I see, Licorice, in the girl who always dreamed of doing and thinking a thousand different things!" What would she do with this all-consuming passion when the time came for them to separate? She had just spoken to the Provençal, who implied that the crew felt her presence had deprived them of a looting spree. Vincent couldn't keep her on his ship forever. Sooner or later she would have to become a mariner's wife, and content with memories.

She shook her head impatiently. *Jeanne, nothing exists except the here and now.* Picking up her book, she returned to the transparent clarity of La Fontaine.

The sweet, compelling scent of orange blossoms invaded the room.

"Are you dressed, and may I come in?"

She answered with a smile, keeping her book open.

"You were reading? What were you reading?"

"Some fables I'm fond of."

"Let's hear the one I came in on."

She read in her slow, solemn voice, like a low-pitched violin:

> *"A man adored his pussycat*
> *He thought her cute and pretty and delicate,*
> *Her meow like sweet, soft chatter.*
> *He was madder than a hatter."*

"I've never heard you read before," said Vincent. "There are lots of things I've yet to discover about you. A thousand little acts that are new to me. One day I'll settle you into my house at La Valette, another day in my cottage at Vaugirard, and you will fill them all with Jeannettes. There will be a Jeannette in the parlor, a Jeannette in the garden, a Jeannette at the harpsichord, a Jeannette at her writing desk, a Jeannette arranging flowers. And I shall be most content. I believe that a husband should be his wife's guest. Women love to take charge of things, whereas a man would prefer not to be bothered!"

"It's true that I wouldn't mind running your affairs," she confessed so sincerely that it made him laugh in turn. "But don't put me in charge of the sails unless you want our romance to founder and sink!"

Vincent sat at his desk and began writing in his notebooks. Jeanne went on reading and stroking Licorice. From time to time their eyes met in a moment of tenderness. When at last Vincent had put aside his papers, Jeanne asked tenderly, "Vincent, tell me about yourself."

"About myself? Heavens, no! A husband has troubles enough without making confessions. Let him keep his secrets. You'll discover soon enough that yours has all the vices of a seaman and is the first to laugh at them and the last to want to change them."

"One day a customer at my herb shop told me that all sailors were superstitious, bigoted, lewd, and conservative."

"Conservative, yes, I'll concede that. I'm conservative."

"Pooh! That simply makes you a royalist like everyone else, except my friend Mercier, who likes to behave extravagantly."

"A conservative believes in something more than God and king."

"Such as?"

"Well, for instance, in spite of current social behavior, marital harmony, and the mistresses he chooses among the wives of others, he believes firmly that his own wife must be faithful to him, and he may go so far as to demand it," Vincent declared nonchalantly.

Jeanne snapped her book closed and stared at him warily with her luminous, impenetrable eyes. "Do you demand it?" she asked carelessly, a faint smile on her lips.

"Savagely!"

"I remember," Jeanne began, looking away, "I remember the buccaneer's marriage vow you taught me. I seem to recall that one had to swear fidelity on her husband's pistol, isn't that right? You forgot, my dear corsair, to make me swear it."

"Because you weren't yet married to a buccaneer," he replied. "But now that I've just pirated you . . . you still blush as charmingly as ever . . . now, by God . . ."

He came over to the table in front of her and sat on the corner of it where his pistols lay. Leaning over, he took her face in his hands and spoke seriously. "Jeanne, I wanted you, I took you. I never asked you about the past, but I hold you responsible for the future. And remember your vow," he added, his hand dropping to the pistol. "For if you fail me, Jeanne, I know this won't!"

The bantering tone had become so earnest that she paused thoughtfully before murmuring, "You make a very convincing buccaneer, but you can't get me to believe you would ever kill a woman, even your own woman."

"I hope not. That's why, if ever . . ." He stopped short, took her face in his hands again, and, with undisguised passion, went on, "If ever I should learn that you were unfaithful, I'd never see you again, I swear it, as much out of fear as bitterness. For if I ever saw you again I'd surely strangle you! Yes indeed, to relieve the hurt I would have no other recourse but to strangle you with my own hands as Othello did to Desdemona. Only those who love passionately can understand that madness. The final pleasure one can take from a faithless wife is to feel the tiny bones in her neck cracking between one's fingers!"

"Ouch!" cried Jeanne. "Can I really believe that you're filled with as much love and jealousy as the Moor? I recall that at Charmont you seemed to treat your loves rather casually."

"The fact is, my dear, bad blood is bound to reveal itself sooner or later. How do I know what flows in my veins? Judging from the color of my skin, it must be pretty dark. So, my Desdemona, behave yourself," he admonished her good-humoredly, with a pinch on the cheek.

She kept his hand in hers and asked in a husky voice, "Even if you were blind and deaf, could you doubt my love?"

"I don't doubt it, dearest. I only ask the blessing of being able always to rely on it, and I know that's an exorbitant demand, since even a mother's love doesn't last."

His undisguised confession moved Jeanne almost to tears. She rose, placed both hands on her husband's shoulders, and said softly, "Vincent, my beloved, I shall give your son the tenderness that you were deprived of."

"Yes, do, please," he replied. He pressed her hard against him, then shifted to a more jocular mood. "My dear, this is a very silly conversation. I think we're both used to more lively repartee. Luckily we'll be going to dinner soon, and it will be good roast mutton. I adore the chops. I asked to have them cooked with fennel, which our orderlies cut by the armload in the countryside while we were ashore."

Jeanne gazed at Vincent adoringly. He was heartbreakingly handsome in a plain black silk suit embroidered with tiny jade beads and a powdered wig with two side rolls, a broad black velvet bow at the nape of his neck. *If I had to barter my soul for this man's arms, I would do it without a murmur.*

"Hold me tight," she said, and flung herself into his open arms, hugged him, nipped at his ear, and tilted her head back for a better look. "You *are* handsome. I love you because you're handsome."

"No."

"No? You mean you're not handsome?"

"Yes, but that's not why you love me."

"I love you because you're so spirited."

"Fiddlesticks! Don't look for reasons for loving. Montaigne found the correct one long ago: because you're you and I'm me."

"I shan't say another word. Kiss me. You offer much, much more," she said dreamily, and gave him a long, lingering kiss. "You know, I can't say I'm too keen on making love in the buccaneer fashion. You oughtn't to leave me until tonight with such a rough remembrance."

He burst out laughing so heartily that it startled the cat, who began to howl for its dinner. "I must say," Vincent exclaimed with a broad grin, "I've never taken on a campaign so exhausting as the one I'm involved in! It's too bad you're not still selling herbs in the Temple,

for you could supply me with verbena from the Indies, which is reputed to give flagging lovers a fresh boost!"

* * * *

The dinner was a happy affair, the mutton fragrant. Father Savié,
priding himself on his culinary talents, had made a delectable crab
dish from a recipe he had picked up in the sugar islands. The blacks
there prepared the crabs with a bit of minced onion, parsley, herbs, a
dash of pepper, orange peel, egg yolks mixed with lemon juice, and a
pinch of nutmeg. Jeanne was about to congratulate him when a messenger from the boatswain's mate burst into the wardroom.

"Excuse me, gentlemen," he said, addressing Vincent. "Captain,
sails dead ahead!"

"I can well believe it," Vincent replied, raising one eyebrow. "The
Plata River is a popular waterway."

"Portuguese sails, sir!" the sailor specified. "And they seem to be
barring our path."

Putting down his napkin, Vincent excused himself from the company and followed the sailor on deck. Staring out across the water,
he was startled to see, bearing down on them, apparently from the
direction of Montevideo, the three-masted Portuguese man-o'-war to
which he had given the slip at Santa Catarina Island. It was close
enough for him to see through his spyglass the battle preparations on
the man-o'-war's deck.

Vincent was familiar with the *Vasco da Gama*. He knew she carried
seventy-four cannon and plenty of other artillery. She was heavily
armed but slow and difficult to maneuver. The Maltese corsair could
have challenged and probably bested the man-o'-war because of the
frigate's greater speed and agility. But Vincent was not one to risk
either his men or his ship for glory's sake. He made his decision
instantly.

"We run for it," he announced. "The Portuguese don't like us carrying off their parrots, and want them back."

"Hey, sir, they would probably have forgotten the loss of a few
macaws if you hadn't made off with some precious trinkets as well!"
commented Aubanel, the first mate.

"Still, it's surprising to find a Portuguese ship threatening an ally of
Spain in Spanish waters," Quissac noted. "The Spanish ought to
reinforce their fleet in these parts, for if the Portuguese feel so much at
home along the Plata River, they may move on inland. Really, now,

what a nerve they have carrying on the chase practically under the nose of Montevideo's governor!"

Vincent shook his head. "They'd never have entered the harbor. The *Vasco da Gama* must have found out from another vessel that we had returned to anchor at Maldonado. They've been waiting for us, expecting we'd head for Montevideo. The captain, Count d'Azurura, is aware that I trade with Don José de Murcia. Boatswain, please order the topsails up."

Moments later, the *Belle Vincente* wheeled about gracefully like a bird in flight, fell off, and headed back rapidly where she had come from with a fresh breeze behind her.

"I think we did well to turn tail, sir," said Quissac to the captain as he reappeared on the poop. "Look." He pointed toward the Portuguese man-o'-war.

A small brigantine previously invisible behind the three-master suddenly loomed on the starboard side of the *Vasco da Gama* and seemed ready to outrun her in pursuit of the Maltese ship.

"We're too far ahead and too fast for him," said Vincent. "Unless we're cut off in front," he added, fixing his telescope on the sails moving in from the ocean.

"Offhand, I don't see . . ." Lieutenant Quissac, who was also studying the mouth of the river through his glass, didn't finish his sentence.

At first glance the horizon appeared tenanted only by friends or neutrals. Apart from a variety of insignificant craft, closest by on the port side there was a clumsy-looking Dutch ship escorted by a brigantine, and behind it an armed corvette flying the flag of Spain—probably the watchdog of some overladen merchantman. Off the starboard side, in line with the merchantman but farther away, was a second Spanish ship.

Brussanne borrowed Quissac's telescope for a quick look. "My word, all those flags out there seem harmless enough," he said, returning the instrument.

"The flags, yes," Vincent commented. Addressing the lieutenant, he asked, "What do you make of that big merchantman?"

Quissac grinned slyly. "I'm of the same mind as you, Captain. Its innocuous look doesn't tell me a thing. Not a single gunport, for whatever that's worth. The bona fide merchant ships paint false ones on their sides. Anyway, whether it's an unarmed trader or a warship in disguise, I suppose we have to assume it's Spanish, don't we?"

"We should, yes," Vincent agreed, emphasizing *should*. "Likewise for the two corvette escorts. I have to believe they're Spanish, and I pray to God it's so!"

Turning around, he studied once again the enemy vessel they were fleeing. "That Portuguese brig glides along like a bird," he noted. "She's caught the wind as we have, and she's even lighter."

"We shouldn't have come snooping around these parts before getting rid of what those Portuguese are so determined to recover from us," grumbled the first mate.

Vincent patted him on the back. "First mate, you're closer to the truth than your captain," he told him good-humoredly. "Especially since the viceroy of Rio is a milksop and a birdbrain who doesn't know how to treat either his enemies or his friends. I promise you that once we're out to sea we'll head for Valparaiso and not return here until we're rid of all the hazardous cargo. By that time the viceroy will have simmered down and a gift of chinchillas will make him forget his quarrel with us. After all, my debt is not to him but to the king of Portugal, and it's astounding how large a debt I'll be able to run up just by making a small down payment to the viceroy."

Jeanne, who had come on deck close on Vincent's heels, trembled to hear him promising a change in their route. She had no time to think of it further because a warning shot fired by the nearest Spanish corvette on the port side so startled her that she inquired timidly, "Is that a greeting or a declaration of war?"

"Neither," Quissac replied with a smile. "They want to know who we are."

"And I'm not eager to tell them," said Vincent, scouring the surrounding waters through his spyglass. "If those Spaniards are really Portuguese and they hesitate more than a moment, with the wind full behind us now, we'll slip right past them."

He shouted to the boatswain, "Send men up into the rigging. When we're ready to engage the Spaniard broadside, I want all stunsails filled."

He returned to the forecastle railing, took a quick look around him, and saw that none of his officers was in uniform. "Spanish flag!" he ordered. "It will do as well as any other."

Flying a false flag was such a common device that no one batted an eyelash. Jeanne alone was surprised to see the Spanish colors sliding up the mainmast. Two minutes later, from the inquisitive corvette came three more warning shots.

"Now there's a suspicious lot! They're asking us to confirm our flag. How discourteous!" sneered the lieutenant.

"Let's wait," said Vincent.

"By waiting we may end up with the third warning volley across the bow," commented the first mate.

"Call up the master carpenter," replied Vincent.

Striding over to Jeanne's side, he told her, "My dearest, please go down to your room."

With a nod she turned and walked obediently to the ladder. Shortly afterward, a cannonball glanced off the frigate's bow.

Brussanne stared at the captain. "Do I haul down the Spanish flag?"

Surveying the scene from behind his spyglass, Vincent reassessed the situation. It was not rosy. The two ships were maneuvering to force the *Belle Vincente* to steer between them instead of letting her pass between the corvette and the sandbar as she seemed to be doing.

Never hesitating, Vincent spoke rapidly. "Gentlemen, since we can't turn back, the cards are dealt and we'll have to play the ones we've drawn. If these are Portuguese coming at us, sheer audacity is all that will keep us out of prison, assuming they are kind enough to cooperate. Ensign de Brussanne, confirm the Spanish colors!"

The ensign stood like a rock, unmoving. A deathly paralysis seemed to grip everyone on the poop. With time running out, Lieutenant Quissac, who had served his captain for many years and lived with him on a familiar footing, declared in his rough, matter-of-fact voice, "I wasn't aware, sir, that you wanted to wave farewell to the world with your feet. Getting hanged for piracy doesn't appeal to me, I confess, nor does the prospect of searching the seven seas for some safe haven from the law. So please," he added, touching Vincent's arm affectionately, "I beg you in the name of our friendship to countermand your order to Ensign de Brussanne."

Vincent's tense jaw relaxed. "Change it yourself, Quissac," he sighed. "Our bad luck today has got under my skin. And I fear we haven't seen the end of it."

Shortly after the Maltese flag went up, followed by a single cannon shot, the three vessels pressing down on him and about to cross his path lowered their Spanish colors and raised Portuguese flags. There were hoots from the rigging, and the boatswain began to holler foul insults at the Portuguese.

"I can't even say this surprises me," said Vincent. "But I ask you, gentlemen, what else could I have done to give them the slip without harm to this ship or crew?"

"Nothing," replied Quissac, and the others agreed. Only Brussanne objected. "We could have fought. We still can."

"Wedged in as we are? You have a lust for martyrdom, my young friend. You ought to be serving the king or that illustrious mariner Monsieur de Suffren, who leaves a trail of destruction wherever he goes."

"Remember that you're only twenty, Brussanne, and today's dungeons make tomorrow's memories, which can be very impressive to the ladies," added M. Amable, the surgeon. "When the captain and I were prisoners of the English . . ."

A flurry of oaths interrupted the garrulous barber's tale. In front of them the bogus merchantman had just unveiled her gunports along with a persuasive array of artillery on the main deck. Seconds later the Portuguese began signaling the Maltese frigate to heave to.

Vincent drew a deep breath of salt air. "Strike the colors and bring out the parrots," he instructed his lieutenant hoarsely.

* * * *

Dom Duarte d'Azurura was a fine gentleman. He had dined with Vincent several times in the Brazilian viceroy's house and had no reason not to treat his prisoner courteously, since his orders were to board the contraband vessel and bring her back to Rio without inspecting her hold. Count da Cunha must have wanted to examine the cargo personally before claiming it for his sovereign.

Having been assured of his safety by Vincent, Dom Duarte stepped aboard the *Belle Vincente*, sampled her French wine and sweetmeats, and then set forth the terms of surrender. On arrival in Rio, all hands would be freed except for the captain, the surgeon, and two witnesses to the capture chosen from among the seamen. The crew could reenlist if they chose. The command staff, petty officers, off-duty watch, and passengers would be sent home. The corsair was to remain a hostage in the governor's palace until ransomed by the grand master of his Order. As for the surgeon, he would be encouraged to join the viceroy's medical staff at a good salary. The cargo and the ship itself would be offered for sale, all proceeds to benefit the Portuguese crown.

The terms were justifiably harsh, and in any event the loser had no choice. Merely as a formality, Vincent consulted his officers, then returned to declare, "I accept everything," and handed over his sword, which Dom Duarte waved aside and refused to take.

"Sir, I have a young lady aboard," Vincent informed him. He paused a moment for effect. "She is traveling to Montevideo. May I ask you to escort her there?"

"Chevalier, I shall put my brig at her disposal," Dom Duarte offered instantly.

"Will you give her time to pack her things?"

"Of course."

Dom Duarte repeated his gallant offer when introduced to Jeanne. "Madame," he said, bowing very low, "you may take as much time as you need to prepare your baggage and bid farewell to the chevalier."

* * * *

She was trembling like a leaf in the wind and threw herself into Vincent's arms the moment the door to their room closed behind them.

Vincent shook her roughly. "No, Jeannette, no! In spite of Dom Duarte's polite behavior, we don't have much time. I want you to listen to me."

"But why must you send me away? I want to share your prison!"

"Never! That would spoil my escape."

"Oh!" She brightened, sniffling through her tears. "You plan to escape?"

"If I can. And one often can. I've done it already with the Turks and the English."

"Really?" Her eyes widened, the tears stopped. "But the Grand Master will pay your ransom promptly, won't he?"

"I'll surely have time to get away before that," Vincent replied wryly. "The great man always ends up paying to bring back his knights, but getting bled for gold is so painful to him that he parts with it drop by drop. Believe me, dearest, I'll come back."

"Tell me what I can do to help you," she said, drying her eyes.

"Think of me," he said, caressing her hair. "Right now I need to know that you love me if I'm going to see the sky through a prison window."

"I do love you," she murmured.

He kissed her lips, sat down in an armchair, and drew her into his lap. "Now listen to me. Nothing worse can happen to me than that I shall be well housed and fed in Count da Cunha's palace while he waits for the ransom money from Malta or for me to slip away. In the meantime, I want you to go to Don José's house and stay with your friend Emilie."

When she started to say something, he placed a finger over her lips. "I regret that I can't go to see Dr. Aubriot personally and settle our affairs. I have to leave that task to you. I'll give you a letter for him, and you can tell him that when I am free I'll talk to him wherever he is."

"But . . ." she began faintly.

"But what, Jeanne?" He set her on her feet and held her firmly before him. "What is it, Jeanne? Has your courage deserted you?"

"I guess," she whispered. "But I'll get it back. Anyway . . ." Holding back a flood of tears, she managed to say in a broken voice, "From the moment I leave you I'll need ever so much courage to live."

"I'll write the letter to Aubriot," he said. "Also a note to Don José. Call Mario and pack yourself some things in a trunk."

She called Mario and did her packing. Then she put on her valet's clothing and folded her wedding dress with the pained look of a young widow robbed of her happiness.

Vincent returned, tossed two sealed messages on top of a white mantilla, and slammed the trunk cover shut.

"Is it time?" she asked in a quavering voice, unable to convince herself that the moment would ever come when she had to tear herself away from Vincent.

"Listen to me once more," he said. Sitting her down on the trunk, he took her chin in his hand. "You won't leave alone. I'm sending the Provençal with you. At least it will keep him from deserting a second time. He'll serve you well because he's very fond of you. Just before you step into the longboat, ask Dom Duarte to let you take your parrot with you."

"You're giving me Chérimbané?"

"I'm entrusting the cage to you," he said slowly and deliberately. "Come have a look."

It was a wicker cage with an extra-thick floor, which Jeanne found surprisingly heavy.

"The diamonds and precious stones I bought from some smugglers on Santa Catarina Island are in there," said Vincent, patting the woven base. "The half that are mine I give you. The other half are Don José's. But your share alone will make you rich. So, my darling, let the bird go if he annoys you, but hang on to the cage!"

"Vincent, let me offer my share of this treasure to Dom Duarte for your freedom."

He smiled and shook his head. "Jeannette, Dom Duarte is a gentleman, and I am his sovereign's captive. He would take the diamonds and never let me go."

"But I can't bear to lose you! I can't, I won't! I won't!" she kept repeating frantically. "Please, Vincent, I implore you, take me with you to prison."

"Calm yourself," he said soothingly, as he rocked her in his arms. "Do you want the victors to see you in tears? Your eyes are too lovely when you weep. No conqueror deserves such a gift."

* * * *

The sky was as bright and the sea as frothy as if Jeanne were not about to lose Vincent.

Just as Dom Duarte prepared to inspect the passenger's baggage, a lookout sighted a royal vessel at the river's entrance. The long, graceful French frigate flew a white flag atop the mainmast, as well as the colors of Saint-Malo, a silver cross on an azure field with a red square in the upper right-hand corner.

Vincent reacted instantly, asking Dom Duarte to deliver his passenger to the French ship instead, where she would feel more at ease. The Portuguese had no reason to object. Following an exchange of salutes and signals, Brussanne was dispatched with a message to the French.

Brussanne returned from his mission accompanied by Chevalier Lamotte-Baracé de Bournand, offering sympathy and help to the Maltese. The French frigate bore the name of *Trieste Dame,* and was just starting a long voyage commissioned by King Louis XV. Her commander was M. de Bougainville and she carried a staff of five officers and the Prince of Orange and Nassau-Siegen, all of whom Vincent knew. Bournand, also a Knight of Malta, promised that as soon as he reached Montevideo he would write to the grand master of the Order to advise him of Vincent's fate.

Bowing to Jeanne, he said, "I will escort you aboard the *Trieste Dame.* If circumstances were different, your welcome would be a cause for celebration."

Jeanne cast an anguished look at Vincent. The corsair turned to Dom Duarte. "May we take the trunk down now?"

Dom Duarte nodded, then excused himself to go inspect the leather toiletries case that Jeanne had just handed to the Provençal. The Portuguese officer who was making the examination set out all the contents for Dom Duarte to see. The latter smiled wryly and, without a word, showed the open case to Vincent. Two handfuls of necklaces had been tossed in among the brushes, combs, and bottles of toilet water.

"As you see, sir, all this is just gold and silver stuff," Vincent answered evenly. "Of course you may seize it, but I could not reclaim it since it is a lover's modest gift."

Dom Duarte shut the toilet case, handed it to Jeanne, and said, "Madame, a lover's gift does not make a good prize." He was enchanted to see her blush.

The Provençal took the case out of Jeanne's hand and Grizzle, a Negro seaman, stepped over to the ladder carrying Chérimbané in his cage.

"Oh!" Jeanne exclaimed, as if she had just remembered something. "You have been so courteous," she said, turning to Dom Duarte, "I wonder if I have your permission to take with me the talking parrot which the chevalier has given me?"

"Naturally, dear lady," replied the Portuguese, admiring the handsome bird. "Let's find out what this feathered philosopher has to tell me before he leaves."

"Chérimbané, say hello," Vincent told the bird nervously, anxious to get the performance over with.

"Boom!" declared the parrot, giving a fair vocal imitation of a cannon firing.

"What does he say?" asked Dom Duarte.

"Boom!" repeated the parrot.

Vincent hurriedly came between the Portuguese and the bird. "You'll have to forgive his limited conversation today. He was on the forward deck when the ball from your escort corvette hit my prow, and he hasn't yet recovered from the shock of it."

"Boom!" the parrot agreed.

"I trust, dear lady, that your bird will regain his talent for speech and court you on behalf of this knight," Dom Duarte offered gallantly.

He had barely finished his sentence when the slave carrying the macaw rushed to the ladder to hand the cage to the Provençal.

"Madame, your hat, if you please." Jeanne glanced up in surprise at the search officer, but held out her hat, which proved to be empty.

"Now, if you please, your boots."

"Just a minute!" Dom Duarte had stepped forward. He addressed Vincent. "Chevalier, have I your word that the lady carries nothing precious on her person?"

"You have my word, sir," Vincent replied.

"Then you may go," said Dom Duarte, saluting Jeanne.

Bournand approached.

"It's time now," Vincent told her softly. Their eyes met in one last, lingering caress.

"Take my arm, if you will," said Bournand to Jeanne, and together they descended into the longboat.

CHAPTER 15

At Don José's villa, Philibert was slowly recovering from a lung infection. Aubriot had come down with pneumonia the day after his "valet" was kidnapped. He had been so ill that one evening a priest had been summoned to perform the last rites.

Ten days after Jeanne's return, he still was not strong enough to be up for more than a short time each afternoon, writing or walking in the orchard at a snail's pace, magnifier in hand. Unable to sleep at night, he would doze off at dawn and not wake until late morning, so Jeanne fell into the habit of eating breakfast with Emilie.

The spacious white room with bright bouquets in which her friend lived became Jeanne's refuge. Redheaded Emilie, so lively and cheerful, brought back the days of girlish excitement over broken hearts and tearful love stories. In cozy intimacy with her friend behind half-shut blinds, she almost managed to forget the burning desire in her flesh and her bruised heart.

"Emilie, I don't know what would have become of me if you hadn't been here. I probably would have planted myself at Philibert's bedside and drowned in my own tears."

"You know that isn't true. You would have nursed him and saved his life through sheer determination, just as you actually did. There's more courage than appears in those melting eyes of yours."

Jeanne paused a moment, then said in a muffled voice, "I may have courage, but I haven't the strength to forgive myself."

Emilie glanced at her in surprise. "I hope you don't think it's your fault that Aubriot caught pneumonia in the pampas? You need strong lungs to ride the plains in all sorts of weather, and Aubriot is not too strong. He's coughed blood before, you know—he told me that. So stop blaming yourself for his illness. He got it from the storm you rode through, not from grieving over your abduction."

To escape Emilie's concern, Jeanne fussed with a bulging bouquet of fuchsias on the desk. "These flowers are really elegant," she observed. "I never saw more than one fuchsia bush in the King's Garden, in a hothouse tended by my friend Thouin, but its blooms were much paler and more slender than yours. Where do the fuchsias in your garden come from?"

"They've been here longer than I," Emilie replied. "I was told by one of the gardeners that the rootstock came from Valparaiso. It seems that there are lots of wild fuchsias in southern Chile."

"Valparaiso," Jeanne murmured as she gulped back a sob rising in her throat.

Emilie flew to her friend's side and spun her around. "Dearest Jeannette, what heartache are you hiding? Aubriot is getting better, yet you seem to grow sadder every day. What secret are you keeping, Jeannette, so painful that my fuchsias make you weep?"

Jeanne broke down. "It's that they come from Valparaiso, where I won't be going," she murmured in a hushed voice.

"Come sit down," said Emilie after a pause, then added, "I thought l'Ile de France was where you always dreamed of going."

"Yes."

"Valparaiso isn't on the way."

"No."

"So why do you miss a port you didn't plan to visit?"

When Jeanne didn't answer, Emilie waited a moment before resuming. "I seem to recall hearing from Don José that before the Chevalier Vincent was captured, he had planned to deliver some of his cargo to Valparaiso."

"Yes," Jeanne sighed, avoiding Emilie's gaze.

"And he probably asked you to go with him. Were you sorely tempted?"

Jeanne looked at her friend, her eyes moist with tears. "I swore I wasn't going to tell you, Emilie, but I'm so miserable I could die. My conscience torments me so. Oh, Emilie, I feel as if I'm being punished far worse than I deserve! But of course that isn't true. I'm relieved to go on living a lie for just a little longer, if only to spare a sick man a cruel blow."

Emilie gazed at her friend with a mixture of tenderness and scorn, totally unshaken by this emotional outburst. "You've hardly changed at all since you were fifteen," she said at last. "You still tend to dwell on your heartaches until they make you ill. Come now, Jeannette, Aubriot isn't asking for a confession. As for your feeling guilty, why not turn your remorse against the chevalier instead of yourself? He is the hunter and you the doe. Not every doe escapes the hunter. But it would be odd indeed if, added to the pangs of surrender, the doe also felt a sense of shame!"

An expression of disbelief spread over Jeanne's face. "Really, Emilie, to speak so frivolously you can't have grasped what has happened to me," she said in a trembling voice.

"Oh, yes I can! I see the handsome Vincent in a white poncho rushing up on his charger to save you from the bandits, then carrying you off to his pirate ship. Why, a woman as sensitive as you would faint with far less provocation! Come, Jeannette, smile! And stop thinking of Vincent as a sin when he's more of an alibi."

"Emilie, when will you stop this banter?" Jeanne scolded her angrily. "Don't you understand that I'm in anguish? I love two men, both of them in danger. I don't know for which of the two I should be tearing out my heart! I don't even know if I have the right to pray for them both," she murmured.

"Prayer is everyone's right," Emilie replied. She noted Jeanne's hands clutched tensely in her lap. Finally she rose from her armchair, pulled up a stool opposite her friend, and took Jeanne's hands in hers.

"So, my dear, the handsome chevalier was not just a passing fancy. You really love him?"

"Emilie, I adore him!" came the reply, so vibrant with passion that it made Emilie tremble.

"And you don't love Aubriot anymore?"

"Oh, I do!" Jeanne nearly shouted. "I'd be a monster if I didn't love him still. How, or why, should I stop loving him? From the time I was ten I loved him, and I'm nearly twenty now. It would be like wrenching out half my life."

Emilie carried the thought to its logical conclusion. "If that is true, my dear, you're left with two lovers on your hands."

The crudeness of the remark provoked such a look of horror on Jeanne's face that Emilie went on impatiently, "Come now, Jeannette, don't reach for your hair shirt! Some ladies take on more than two lovers without losing any sleep, or weight, or their church pews."

Emilie changed her tone. "Forgive my harshness. I learned at a very tender age, from the Marquise de la Pommeraie, that it wasn't necessary to leave one man before taking up with another. And isn't a mother always right?"

Jeanne reached out and squeezed her hand. A mute bond of affection held them close for a long moment.

Once again it was Emilie who broke the silence. "Well, Jeannette," she began with a faint smirk, "didn't I tell you that every woman ought to have sampled the delights and aches of love before turning twenty? You'll be twenty this coming spring, while I've two years to go, and here we are already with a collection of happy and unhappy memories. I think we ought to rejoice rather than despair. At least we are assured of not growing old without ever having loved and been loved."

"You speak in the past, like some ancient dowager whose loves and griefs lie buried in the mists of time. But then your conscience never troubled you, because you had the strength to make a choice."

"The strength or the cruelty," Emilie corrected her. "Jeannette, the right to choose is not reserved to men only. They take us, deceive us, abandon us, return to us, or forget us. They think nothing of asking us to switch from love to friendship, from passion to indulgence. I don't say we should adopt their ways and take up habits that suit their convenience; rather, I say that we, too, if necessary, can choose our happiness at their expense."

Jeanne sighed and said sadly, "Emilie, you didn't love Denis, and it took so very little cruelty to choose Don José. But in my case . . ."

"Jeannette, you must stop feeling sorry for yourself," Emilie began firmly. "Aubriot is getting better, the chevalier will escape from wherever they put him, and that should be enough to lift your spirits. Let's talk about the rest of your affair. I know your heart. You love freely. I can't imagine how you could feel the same kind of love for Philibert and Vincent. A threesome like yourselves is not uncommon in urban society. For me, Aubriot represents an older spouse you go on feeling very fond of while you are mistress to a handsome corsair who seduced you. Why make a tragedy of it?"

"Emilie, I'm not the corsair's mistress. I'm his wife."

"What?" Emilie stood up in shock, then sat down again more calmly and asked, looking hard at Jeanne, "Are you telling me that the chevalier married you?"

"Yes."

Stunned, Emilie sat stonelike for a few moments, then finally said, "It's true that he was granted knighthood. And he has no family."

"Yes," said Jeanne in a burst of annoyance, "he could have married practically anybody."

Emilie ignored the remark. Slowly a smile formed on her lips, then there came a happy peal of laughter as she leaned over to kiss the bride on both cheeks. "I'm so glad he married you, Jeannette. You have such a loyal heart and a fountain of tears behind your eyes. You were born to wed a seagoing man."

Her voice suddenly filled with joy. "So why the devil are you moaning? From the minute he made you his wife, you belonged to him, and that's that! God and the law require you to prefer him."

Jeanne hung her head. "You saw Aubriot's condition. He was so happy to have me back. My being here has done him so much good. He's beginning to plan all sorts of projects that include me. His confidence makes me feel terrible, Emilie, terrible. I bear it like a cross. At the same time, I love knowing how precious I am to him. I have deceived him. My silence continues to deceive him, and I couldn't bear it if he ever stopped loving me. To remain in his heart is no less a need of mine today than it was yesterday."

"I can understand," said Emilie. "After all, you want a man in your bed. No more than one at a time. And you'd prefer him not to be the first to turn his back on you."

"His scorn would kill me," said Jeanne.

Emilie heaved an impatient sigh. "But why the devil must you talk of scorn? A practical woman is not wholly responsible for the effects of her every heartbeat. You found yourself in a romantic situation . . ."

"No," Jeanne interrupted softly, "I didn't just happen to give myself to the chevalier. I had known for ages that I loved him. There's a lot I could tell you about the two of us. For instance, the night in Paris when I almost fell into his arms after a wild drinking party. That was the onset of my betrayal of Philibert."

Emilie arched her eyebrows in surprise. "Don't exaggerate, Jeannette. In matters of the heart, a missed opportunity to betray is not an act of betrayal," she declared.

"Oh, yes it is! You've always managed to dismiss your conscience— along with everyone else's too," said Jeanne rather sourly.

"And you, Jeanne, have always shown a talent for loving in such a way that you end up with the pain but never the pleasure."

"The pleasure of loving!" Jeanne repeated contemptuously. "You see me floundering about from one betrayal to another, and you talk of—"

"This is ridiculous," cried Emilie. "I won't have you beating your breast and taking sole responsibility for your error. Call it betrayal if you must, but remember, my dear, that Aubriot had your love. He could have married you first. The Aubriots of Châtillon are a fine family, to be sure, but you received an aristocrat's education, Jeanne. The distance between you and him was never insurmountable."

Jeanne didn't answer at first. Then she murmured low, as if in a confessional, "I believe that even if Philibert had married me . . . when I was with the chevalier it wouldn't have made any difference."

"That may well be. But by marrying you, Aubriot would have spared himself the grief of losing you the day you deceived him. And at the same time he would have spared you from feeling guilty. A cuckold loses neither his status nor his privileges, and his wife ordinarily takes pleasure in deceiving him."

Jeanne got up suddenly. "I have to go now," she announced. "Don José arranged for an escort to accompany me to Tiger Point."

Emilie restrained her. "You're not really in such a hurry. I'm afraid I hurt your feelings. Forget what I said, and stay a bit."

"It was a mistake to open my heart to you. I know by now that you only argue or joke about love."

Emilie's eyes wandered over the white walls, lingered on each of Don José's splendid flower arrangements, and returned to fasten on her friend. Finally she spoke with unwonted seriousness. "It's true, Jeannette, that when you make love it's as if you cast yourself upon a bed and melt into running water. It used to exasperate me. It still makes me angry. Even so, I envy your ability to surrender totally to love. In that melting submission there must be some kind of pleasure I've never experienced." She fell silent for a moment, then resumed, "If a woman is like a fruit to her man, then you must taste like the flesh and I like the pit!"

Jeanne couldn't help laughing.

"Hurrah!" exclaimed Emilie. "At last I've made you laugh. Tell me, Jeannette, how can I help you?"

"I don't know."

"When will you speak to Aubriot?"

"I don't know."

"But you *will* speak to him, won't you?"

Jeanne hesitated before answering, then murmured, "I hope so." She spun around to face Emilie and said bitterly, "I don't want to choose! I don't want to be asked to choose! A minute ago you were talking about our right to imitate men. Well, do men always choose between lovers? Emilie, if you were in my shoes, what would you do?"

"My dear, sweet friend, I'm not you. I'm a defrocked canoness. For the rest of my days I know that when life becomes too difficult to navigate, there will always be the restful peace of the cloister. I will probably return to Neuville and babble about my doubts and fears to the good nuns over a cup of chocolate. Dame Charlotte would serve it with cinnamon, because at Neuville they think Ceylon cinnamon drives away low spirits."

After a deep sigh, Jeanne said, "I know you left Neuville in order to live. But have you lived, Emilie?"

"I often ask myself that. As a little child I made the choice of seeing the world only in meditation. Perhaps it dulled my senses. To a little girl who is cooped up and who thinks rather than feels, the world soon becomes as flat and smooth as a picture album. When she steps out of her glass cage at the age of fifteen, perhaps it's too late for her to start perceiving things in three dimensions."

"No," said Jeanne intently. "When I saw you again, I had to get to know you little by little. But from the start I was sure you had changed."

"Really?"

In her friend's voice Jeanne noted more hope than disbelief. "Yes, I know you've changed. Oh, you still play your favorite role of the pretty porcelain countess, brittle and shiny and very witty. But I think your heart has softened the porcelain, and it's becoming tender."

"Jeanne, do you believe that I love Don José? You who feel so sure of your love, how can you tell whether a lover isn't simply one's flag of defiance, a plaything or an excuse to talk about love? I've lived with so much unreality, provocation, rebellion, and haste since I fled Neuville. I'm no longer certain whether to believe myself when I think I'm in love."

Jeanne answered with a smile, "You must know that better than I."

"The day I met Don José, everything became so simple. I was trying to live out my disenchantment proudly when he appeared. I discovered my sadness and, soon afterward, my desire to be consoled. When I think back, I realize that he took me in tow the moment we met, and I was happy to lean on him. It all happened in the governor's reception hall. I was pregnant and feeling nauseous from the cigar smoke. Gaillon was talking chemistry with Don Piedracueva. I hated him for neglecting me, though not to the point of wanting to leave. Leaving would have meant returning to the boredom of our life together.

"Suddenly Don José came up to me, held out his arm, and whispered, 'You don't look very well this evening, Doña Emilia. You're expecting a child, aren't you? I think a walk in the garden would make you feel better.' "

"Oh!" said Jeanne. "He spoke of your baby just like that?"

"Indeed he did! I took him instantly for the unceremonious man he is. And in fact the lack of ceremony was so welcome that in short order I became a part of it. Do you know how I parted from Gaillon? I said, 'I'm leaving. Don José will fill in the details.' "

"Oh!" said Jeanne once again.

"Jeannette, if your courage is failing you, wait for your chevalier to return. Pray that he hasn't made you pregnant. Invent migraines, depressions, or whatever will keep you out of Aubriot's bed when he recovers, and wait for your chevalier. He'll straighten things out with Aubriot. A duel settles matters more permanently than a love affair."

"It would be such an admission of frailty," murmured Jeanne, tempted.

"Frailty becomes a woman—at least that's what men think. Find me a single man who prefers a strong woman to a frail one! The chevalier will be thrilled to rescue you a second time, even from yourself."

There was a moment's silence. They were both curled up in a cavernous green velvet armchair, red curls next to blond tresses, in their white wrappers, holding hands. Iassi suddenly appeared silently before them. The Indian girl stared at Jeanne. "Don José is looking for you," she said. "You are to go walking."

"Yes," Jeanne yawned, scarcely budging. "Tell him I'll be along soon."

Iassi contemplated the two young women, drowsy-eyed from their long conversation. She lifted the cover from the empty coffeepot and asked, "More?"

"No, thank you, Iassi," Emilie answered.

"But I would like a cup if you'll offer it to me," came Don José's cheerful voice from the doorway.

Iassi grabbed the empty pot and disappeared silently.

"Don't stir!" Don José went on, seeing the two women about to get up. "You make such a pretty picture, the pair of you. I must be disturbing you. Shall I vanish?"

"No, no!" The reply was a duet, so spontaneous that Don José reacted with feigned surprise. "Then I shall stay?"

"Absolutely," Emilie said with a smile.

Don José pulled up a stool, sat down, winked at them fondly, and leaned over to ask, "Can I be of help?"

"Simply by being here," said Emilie jokingly. "We were just commenting on the pleasant usefulness of men. It's a good thing you came along to remind us that we do indeed like to see one now and then."

Don José's piercing eyes eagerly explored the face of his mistress.

How he loves her! Aloud Jeanne said, "Don José, I'm sure you will excuse my being late now that you know I used the time to hear good things about you."

"Heavens!" protested the Spaniard. "Are you certain, ladies, that you don't need my help?"

Jeanne sighed. "Not help, alas, but a miracle. We need the impossible."

"I see nothing extraordinary about that," Don José replied. "A woman will try to pluck pears from an elm tree. And when there are two women . . ."

The three of them laughed and Don José continued, "Before performing any miracles for you, Jeanne, I gave your mail to a rider who will deliver it to a French corvette in Montevideo harbor that is on its way back to Bordeaux. What a bundle! Did you write to everyone in France? You must have dozens of French admirers." He paused for a moment and became more serious. "Something else, *amiga mia*. Did Aubriot tell you he intends to resume his voyage as soon as possible in order to finish up his work?"

Jeanne was too astonished to speak, and Emilie put in hastily, "Where did you hear that? Wasn't it agreed that Aubriot and Jeanne would spend the whole summer in La Plata, gathering herbs for Monsieur de Buffon?"

"That was the original plan, but it seems that Aubriot changed his mind," said Don José. "I heard it from Captain Vilmont de la Troesne. Maybe the doctor took a dislike to this area after the nasty experience that befell his "valet." After all, collecting plants and shells along these shores is only one stop among many. His major assignment awaits in l'Ile de France, and he has advised de la Troesne that he is anxious now to get started on it."

He smiled at Jeanne, who was staring intently at him, and concluded, "Whims of this sort do occur after recovery from a serious illness."

Jeanne's pleading look once again spurred Emilie to ask questions for her. "When does Aubriot want to leave for Port Louis? Did he give the captain a date?"

"No," replied Don José. "He doesn't care a rap for the advice of his doctors, but de la Troesne would have him looking more fit before they sail."

"Oh, he'll recover fast," Jeanne murmured. "He has tremendous vitality, and such a passion for exploring strange flora . . ."

There was silence while Emilie and Don José exchanged glances, after which the Spaniard asked bluntly, "Jeannette, will you be accompanying Aubriot to Port Louis?"

Jeanne gave a start, and blushed violently. "Why shouldn't I?"

The savory aroma of coffee preceded Iassi's entrance. Don José took the pot from her and dismissed her. He poured three cups, and as he handed one to Jeanne, he declared briskly, "*Amiga mia*, let's not beat around the bush. I don't like to play games. In my desk drawer is the letter you gave me from the Chevalier Vincent. So I know that it will break your heart to have to leave here, since Montevideo is nearer to Rio than is Port Louis."

Jeanne's eyes filled with burning tears, and she hid her face in her hands. Emilie stroked her hair, her eyes pleading for help from her lover.

Don José sat down on his stool again, removed Jeanne's hands from her face, and held them. "Jeannette, I have ways to send mail to Rio, even into the viceroy's prison. Wherever you go, Vincent will know about it. He will also know that you remain under my protection, because if you wish to go to Port Louis, I will go with you."

Rather pleased with the effect of his little speech, the Spaniard displayed his broadest grin to the astounded pair and went on teasingly, "I really must not fail my friend Vincent when he has asked me to look after someone who is very precious to him. I would expect the same if I entrusted Emilie to him. Also, it occurred to me"—he darted a meaningful glance at his mistress—"that Dame Emilie de la Pommeraie, after spending more than two years among the boorish centaurs of La Plata, would not be averse to visiting a French settlement where she could laugh and dance in the French manner—that is, with the wit and polish we lack here."

The two women stared at each other, then at Don José, unable to believe their ears.

"Are you serious?" Emilie finally asked. "Do you really intend to give up your horse and take me for a civilizing cure to l'Ile de France?"

"I intend to keep an eye on our friend Jeannette," Don José corrected her. "Can you ever forget, dear heart, the debt I owe the Chevalier Vincent? He brought you up the Plata River to me."

"Don José, I can't thank you enough," said Jeanne, once she had found her voice.

"Well, then, it's all set and you need say nothing more," he answered, kissing both her hands. "And you, my dear one, have you nothing to say?" he added, turning to Emilie. "I give my horse a carrot when I'm pleased with him."

"Here, this is for you," she said, fishing out a chunk of pineapple from the jam pot.

"My dearest, the elm tree is doing its best to produce pears for you," he said with a wink.

CHAPTER 16

ubriot had to spend another month or so in the country. Impatient as he was to sail for l'Ile de France, he never complained. Little by little his strength returned, and with it his boundless enthusiasm for whatever he saw or touched—a plant, a bird, a fish, a shell, or a pebble.

Jeanne went along, of course, on these frenzied explorations. Besides bringing her pleasure and opening her mind to a host of strange new natural beauties, it was good medicine. And as a further distraction from her increasingly awkward situation, neighbors by the droves rushed to call on her at the de Murcia villa, proud to be able to visit someone who had come back alive from the bandit camp. By having to repeat her tale over and over for every curious visitor, Jeanne kept reliving the start of her adventure, forgetting to feel guilty about the end of it.

The populace of La Plata had christened their heroine "La Bougainvillée" because they had gathered at the riverbank to welcome her to Montevideo on the arm of Colonel de Bougainville, captain of the *Trieste Dame.*

Jeanne had looked lovely in a white muslin frock with a lacy mantilla over her shoulders.

Arriving with the recovered hostage, Colonel de Bougainville had made an even bigger splash than if he had appeared merely as Louis XV's ambassador.

He had taken Jeanne to see Captain Vilmont de la Troesne, announcing with a smile, "It appears, sir, that you lost a valet passenger who was reported to be a handsome youth. Look what I've brought you in his place."

In Buenos Aires and Montevideo there was an endless series of balls, concerts, dinners, and picnics. Don José and Doña Emilia, Dr. Aubriot and "La Bougainvillée" were invited to all the events. Though they never ventured as far as Buenos Aires, "the end of the earth," Don José took Emilie to Montevideo often, and Jeanne went along. As for Aubriot, he would always excuse himself on grounds of poor health, and kept on working at his country retreat. To tell the truth, the scholar shied away from having to recite over and over again how, in Lorient, he had engaged a young, good-looking valet whose feminine gender was not disclosed until they crossed the Equator, when Jeannot refused to remove her shirt to have a shoulder treated after a fall. This fable, which he and Captain de la Troesne had invented to preserve the honor of the king's naturalist, had only one blemish—nobody believed a word of it!

Jeanne, on the other hand, didn't mind acting out the touching role of an orphan seeking her fortune in the household of a kind master the only way she could—as a boy. And when she answered questions about her stay in Pinto's camp, it gave her endless opportunities to pronounce Vincent's name, to roll in on her tongue, to savor its succulence. In bed at night she kept on whispering it, breathing it over her arms and making the flesh prickle with desire, desire that crept along, invading her spine and progressing down her middle, descending her long, lonely thighs. She ventured a butterfly kiss on her warm, satiny skin, then another. She cajoled herself with endearing names, touched her breasts until she could feel Vincent's greedy hands upon them, and raged with frustrated passion as she hugged her pillow and battered the sheets.

Yet, when she rejoined Aubriot the next morning, she felt the same loving affection for him, and less guilt at having betrayed him through her silence. Strange as it seemed, her remorse faded as her love for Vincent surged. When she wrote to Marie, the sins she described seemed to take on a delicious glow.

"Emilie," said Jeanne one morning during breakfast, "I hate myself. My guilt is disappearing."

"That's because guilty love is unnatural," replied Emilie. "Ask our priests to tell you how difficult it is to pry out!"

"It's also because I have your contagious example before me," said Jeanne, pouring herself a cup of coffee.

Emilie winced. "I gather you think I'm quite immoral."

"It's not your fault. You were born to do whatever you please. But in my case," Jeanne sighed, "I'm deluding myself."

Emilie held out the plate of buttered toast to Jeanne and concluded gently, "I'm certain that God does not punish love that is all-embracing. No one rejects his own invention."

"You take strange liberties with God's thought processes," said Jeanne with a smile.

* * * *

They were returning to Montevideo, along with the cream of local society, to witness the departure the next day of Captain de Bougainville's *Trieste Dame* and her Spanish escort vessels for the Malvinas. Don José had loaded two carts with a miniature forest of potted saplings that his gardeners had prepared for Bougainville to present to the Breton settlers. To the cuttings Jeanne added three cases of plants and two of seashells which Aubriot wanted to contribute to Commerson, the naturalist on Bougainville's expedition, whenever they managed to catch up with him. He had left the port of Rochefort aboard a supply ship in the Trieste Dame escort, and had not yet arrived on the Plata River.

"I thought my colleague would be glad not to have missed out on the flora and fauna of La Plata, even if he arrives here too late to go ashore," said Aubriot.

Bougainville received the gift with due reverence, though he was not especially interested in botany. In place of dried greenery, Bougainville undoubtedly would have preferred La Bougainvillée herself, alive, fresh, and appetizing.

Jeanne was busy giving last-minute advice to the handsome Prince of Nassau-Siegen, who had promised to keep an eye on the sailors responsible for the care of the seedlings. But his eyes, too, devoured the teacher.

Bougainville interrupted them, "I doubt that the prince will remember anything but your face and your voice, mademoiselle. Hadn't you better accompany your own plants to the Malvinas?"

The invitation made her blush with pleasure. "If I didn't have to be in l'Ile de France with Monsieur Aubriot . . ."

"But in time and with God's help, my ship will also reach l'Ile de France," Bougainville assured her. "Port Louis is one of my scheduled stops."

"Is it really?" said Jeanne. "But if I'm to believe what I hear, you will be taking a roundabout route. Is it true that you will be sailing around the world?"

Bougainville and Nassau-Siegen burst out laughing, and the former asked her, "If I persuade you to believe it, will you give up your expedition to join mine?"

"In my thoughts, yes," Jeanne replied, smiling. "I shall trace all the unknown seas on the map and guide you in my prayers. But for now, gentlemen, with your permission . . ." she said, holding out her hands to receive a necklace of flowers from a waiting slave, which, with a warm smile, she placed around Bougainville's neck.

Emilie and the señoras decorated the rest of the ship's officers, who were enchanted by this gesture of farewell and the splendid chain of deep purple blossoms tinged with mauve and carmine.

"What do you call this flower?" Bougainville asked.

Aubriot answered, "Most of the plants I've given you for Monsieur Commerson are new to me. This one has yet to be named."

"I will ask Commerson on your behalf to find a name for it, if, please God, I have the good fortune to meet up with him and my supply ship," said Bougainville.

"Tell him that you like the flower and he'll surely name it after you," said Jeanne. *"Bougainvillea* sounds lovely. *Bougainvillea platasiana grandibracta."*

"My word, you botanists saddle poor flowers with such barbaric names!" exclaimed Bougainville. "But I accept it joyfully because ordinary folk will surely pronounce it Bougainvillée, and that name will remind me of the lovely prize I took from a corsair in the Plata River."

* * * *

Capetown's verdant shores began to melt into the shimmering water. Soon the tip of the African continent all but vanished from sight. High above the *Etoile des Mers,* the black-and-white petrel wheeled persistently.

"Next stop, Port Louis," Emilie announced.

It was a gorgeous day, with so little swell that she ventured on deck with Jeanne and Don José despite a queasy stomach. The three of them smiled each time they exchanged looks, as if they shared some perpetually renewed secret.

"Now you realize, *amiga mia,* that the seagoing world is so round that no sailor ever gets lost unless the sea claims him," Don José concluded to Jeanne.

"Yes," Jeanne murmured, pressing one hand to her heart as if to make sure that Vincent's note was still wedged between her breasts.

* * * *

On his last day ashore, the Provençal had run into a black crewman from the *Belle Vincente* who, released by the Portuguese in Rio, had, after a series of misadventures, found himself marooned in Capetown. He had, however, managed to hold on to a letter from Vincent which he happily turned over to the Provençal. The letter contained two messages, one for Don José and one for Jeanne. Jeanne's message overflowed with loving tenderness, while Don José's recited all the news.

After one week in a tiny, stinking little cell, the corsair had been spared further misery by the viceroy's wife, Countess da Cunha, who impressed him into service as a dinner guest. His fine muslin shirts, his orange-blossom toilet water, and his valet, Mario, were all restored to him. He was installed quite comfortably in the countess's apartments when her sister, Countess da Silveira, offered to house the prisoner. The viceroy gave his consent, if only to antagonize his wife on behalf of Senhora Maria-Luiza, his mistress.

Vincent's new jailer provided him at last with pen, ink, and paper, and his officers were permitted to visit, something that Count da Cunha had expressly prohibited in order to discourage any escape plots.

Meanwhile, the *Belle Vincente* had been sent under escort to Cobra Island, there to be disarmed, her powder and cannon deposited in the island's arsenal. With the cargo under seal, the *Belle Vincente* was scheduled to sail for Lisbon to be auctioned off, lock, stock, and barrel, to the highest bidder. The proceeds would fatten the Portuguese treasury. Half of the crew had already signed aboard other vessels, but the others—Maltese, Negroes, the men from Provence—were within hailing distance of the ship, wandering along the quays and dockyards of the arsenal. The chief officer, the lieutenant, the chaplain, and the boatswain and his mate had all refused repatriation and were living in town, waiting.

* * * *

"Do you really think they'll recapture the *Belle Vincente?*" Jeanne asked for the tenth time.

"I do," replied Don José once again. "Your chevalier is not planning to wind up his prison sentence on foot," he declared confidently. "I've known him for quite a while and I'm sure he has a trick or two up his sleeve. He was very young when the Turks captured and sold him into slavery, but three months later Vincent was back in Malta aboard a Turkish galley he had stolen right out of the harbor at Tripoli. Dear Jeannette, I don't expect to see your chevalier return from Rio without his frigate. He loves that ship of his madly. He won't turn her over to the Portuguese, even if he has to go all the way to Lisbon disguised as a caulker to get her back again."

Jeanne heaved a deep sigh as two tears crept down to the tips of her eyelashes and hung there in the sunlight, glistening like two golden pearls. "That could take a long while," she murmured. Then she added, with unconcealed anguish, "And to get me back after I disobeyed him by not staying at your villa, do you think he'll come all the way to Port Louis? Do you think he has received your messages and my letter?"

"I gave them to a trusted carrier with entrée to the Brazilian viceroy," replied Don José. "And I sent two other messages by different routes. As to the rest of your question"—he took her hand and clasped it warmly—"I do believe he will come to you. To appease its torment, love's passion will swim the seven seas."

Emilie took little Paul below for a nap while Jeanne and Don José remained talking. The African coastline had vanished from sight.

"Thank God the sky makes such beautiful patterns in mid-ocean, for how else would we pass the time?" Don José commented abruptly.

"The voyage bores you, does it?"

"No, because Emilie finds it amusing."

Jeanne turned around and leaned against a railing so as to face him, then asked suddenly, "Don José, am I a monster?"

His eyebrows flew up as he parried, "What else, since you're a woman!"

"No, seriously. I want to know if a man . . . Don José, can you understand my behavior?"

"Yes, *amiga*. But that's because I'm not Vincent."

"And if you were?"

"I would grab you by the hair, drag you to a convent, and lock you up. After that I would probably kill Monsieur Aubriot."

"Oh!" said Jeanne.

"*Amiga*, love is a simple matter for a Spaniard. We waver between two poles, passion and revenge."

Jeanne heaved a sigh of relief. "I'm afraid the chevalier must have Spanish blood!"

"Mediterranean temperaments are much alike. Jeannette, once Aubriot arrives safely at his destination, what will you do?"

She replied instantly, "I will buy a plantation and farm it."

"What?" Don José looked thunderstruck. His eyes popped, his mouth hung open. "I must have misunderstood you. You plan to . . . what?"

"Buy a plantation and farm it. You sold my diamonds to that Dutch diamond cutter for an excellent price. I hope to acquire a lot of land and enough slaves to work it properly. I'll put in herbs and spices and send off shiploads to my shop in the Temple. I left it in charge of a woman with a good head for business. If I supply her with rare and exotic items, I know she'll reap me a fortune without neglecting herself. Later on, maybe I can branch out to serve clients in Lyons and Marseilles by shipping to Delafaye and Count Pazevin. I think I'll enjoy carrying on an overseas business."

She looked calmly at Don José, who was gazing at her in rapt amazement. "Well, what do you say to my plans? Go ahead and laugh! I see you're dying to laugh!"

"Only because I can't believe my own ears! You have such strange ideas, *amiga,* fit for a man!"

"No, I assure you," she replied calmly. "I'm not going to lug cases of herbs to the harbor. I know I'm just a weak woman."

Don José eyed her for a moment, perplexed, then asked, "And where does the chevalier fit into all this? Do you expect to turn him into a planter?"

"No, and I shan't try. But I also hope he won't try to mold me into a corsair—at least not too often. When he leaves me ashore, I don't want to spend my time waiting for him to return. Don't you see, Don José, I need to be occupied. Having a plantation would make me happy. You'll see. It will be the best run place on the whole island."

"Could you be happy with it even if Vincent is not? If he tells you—as I myself would tell you—that a woman's place is not running a plantation or a business, but loving a man? If he tells you that, what would you say?"

"That he's right. But unfortunately he's not a Spaniard in La Plata who allows his wife to love him and never leaves her alone."

Don José nodded. "Too bad I'm already spoken for, isn't it?" he joked. "By rushing about in search of this and that, a busy man lets his soup grow chilled at home. But take a Spaniard from La Plata and he will always have time to make love, because his busiest workday is always tomorrow! *Mañana!*"

The joke made her laugh. He continued, "Really, Jeannette, we are so truly lazy that vacant land in La Plata will cost you far less than in l'Ile de France. So if you really want to become a planter, *amiga,* do your planting near my villa."

Jeanne shook her head. "Don José, Port Louis will be nearer than Montevideo to Vincent's routes. I know that the government wanted to make Port Louis the main French base for shipping to the Indian Ocean, both to provide a port for merchantmen dealing with our markets in the Indies and in case war with England should break out again. Vincent is bound to make his fortune as a trader and privateer. He will surely come roaming around l'Ile de France. In any case, his present plans call for him to return home via the Gulf of Bengal. He will go there if he succeeds in getting his ship back, and Port Louis will be on his route."

Don José digested all this for a minute, then nodded his approval. "You must be right. There isn't much left in these waters to attract a corsair. But, *Dios!* How logical the French are! A Spanish woman waits for you where you left her, sipping maté."

"So why do you all choose a Frenchwoman over a Spanish one when there's a choice?"

"Because the devil has his foot in our love affairs," sighed Don José.

* * * *

Time passed rhythmically, monotonously, like the sea lapping against the hull. Then, one evening, came the cry they were all so eagerly waiting for.

"Tropi birdie! Tropi birdie!" The slave Dodo's piercing cries broke the after-dinner stillness. Everyone climbed onto the decks, eager to see the satin-white bird that welcomed sailors just off shore to their island paradise.

The bird of good tidings obligingly wheeled above, encouraged by the shouting crew, then flew off into the sun. Expecting to see land at any moment, the passengers lingered on the poop deck, braving the wind, their eyes scouring the horizon. Next morning, a whole flock of tropic birds circled the rigging for hours. They dove after crumbs of hardtack tossed out onto the main deck, boldly skimming the sailors' caps. Land appeared at nine o'clock on the morning of May 9, 1767.

With her heart in her throat and her teeth clenched, Jeanne gripped Emilie's hand.

"Well, Jeannette, at last you've reached the shores you told me about so often when we were children in Dombes. Do you think it will turn out to be the magic place you imagined?"

After a silence filled with memories of childhood conversations, Jeanne replied softly, "The magic, Emilie, is that it really does exist."

PART

II

Allspice

CHAPTER 17

o a new arrival in the "Indies island"—a romantic
vision cherished by many Frenchmen eager to flee
their native soil for a tropical sugar wonderland—the
first sight of Port Louis proved to be a great disappointment. From the
sea it resembled a hollow surmounted by balding mountain ridges atop
sun-scorched hills, and jagged crests from which two rivers descended
boldly, only to dissolve farther down into a pair of muddy trickles.

The town consisted of about five hundred small frame houses built
on wheels, reflecting general indecision as to whether to leave or
settle permanently on this harsh, stony soil. The dwellings had no
glass or curtains at their windows, not a single rosebush in their fenced
gardens.

The port itself was falling into decay. Storm-wrecked vessels by the
dozen littered the harbor, their timbers rotting, their guns rusting and
encrusted with barnacles, causing mud bars to form that eventually
would make it impossible for ships to anchor at all at Port Louis.

On arrival, the passengers aboard the *Etoile des Mers* were under no
illusion that they had reached the Promised Land.

This poor impression improved very little as they entered town.
The streets were neither paved nor shaded by trees; the rutted, rock-
strewn ground was murderous on the ankles and incredibly muddy
besides, since no one looked after the state of public roads. The town
was in fact divided in half by a swampy ravine that one had to wade
across. Behind, extending all the way to the foothills, lay the vast
gardening experiment installed by Mahé de la Bourdonnais, a former
governor, and abandoned when he left the island. Decidedly, Port
Louis bore no resemblance to the claims of Louis XV, who touted it as
France's jewel of the Southern Hemisphere.

Surrounding the rectangular plaza or parade ground stood Government House, the Intendancy, the naval and war offices, the guard-

house beneath its clocktower, and the Hall of Justice. Although the masonry work and the flat roofs were pleasant enough to look at, the names of the buildings were far more ostentatious than were the edifices themselves.

It was here in Government House that M. Desforges-Boucher, the last governor the French East India Company was ever to appoint, had lodged Dr. Aubriot and his party on their arrival.

The house, an attractive three-story building with two wings attached at right angles, bulged at the seams with people and things. Before long, Don José and his household had to be shifted over to the Intendancy. Aubriot and Jeanne stayed on in the mansion, sharing two sparsely furnished bedrooms and a closet.

Aubriot had eyed these lodgings morosely from the start, though Desforges-Boucher kept assuring him that the discomfort was only temporary. In short order it became apparent that anything better probably didn't exist, at least not close to the center of town.

The island as a whole was nearly deserted, yet the settlement of Port Louis remained overcrowded. Out of a population of some twenty thousand, eighteen thousand were slaves living in huts on plantations. A few hundred free African and Indian laborers were crammed into waterfront shacks next to taverns packed with drunkards, deserters, thieves, and prostitutes. The white residents, numbering less than two thousand, a good one-third of whom lived in town, were all more or less poor and shared the frame dwellings. In short, hired lodgings were practically nonexistent in Port Louis.

Don José, self-appointed supply officer for the Aubriot unit, had scoured the town and port for housing spacious enough to accommodate them all. The newcomers had set their hearts on savoring the magic of the tropics, which Port Louis could not offer. The elusive bliss of the Indies lay somewhere in the untamed countryside.

Aubriot and Jeanne went in search of it right away. Not far outside the disappointing town, the sea broke endlessly against the coral barrier reef. There you could swim in a warm sheltered cove, plant footprints in the damp, white, velvety sands, dry off under a palm tree swaying in the salty breeze, and, on awakening, gather a meal of oysters from among the tangled, uplifted mangrove roots, or mussels and purple sea urchins hidden among the stony coral.

They wandered about in the solitude of vine-laden forests and alongside a mountain stream rushing over rocks, and reveled in a botanist's paradise of cinnamon, olivewood, milkwood, ebony, gum benzoin, sandalwood, and nutmeg. Yes, the saga of Robinson Crusoe could still be lived in l'Ile de France, simply by turning one's back on the harbor.

Glutted with marvelous new finds, Aubriot could hardly eat or sleep. As for Jeanne, she cast herself eagerly into this breathtaking profusion of nature, and prepared to explore it with every nerve in her body. It was a good way to numb her yearning for Vincent and her guilt over Philibert.

Despite Emilie's constant prodding, Jeanne still had not talked to Aubriot. Each day she promised herself . . . tomorrow. Then tomorrow became today, and there was Philibert calling out to her, "Up you go, my Jeannot! We have a world to harvest!" So off she went, trotting beside him once again on a new adventure.

Because she was resolved to enjoy the happiness before her, she went on bearing her secret shame in silence, the way a schoolgirl hides a mistake from a teacher she adores, imagining that if she ever disclosed it he would reject her forever. Her fear of Philibert's rejection continually vanquished the urge to confess, and often made her appear to be craving a caress from the lover she was avoiding, a caress that, when forthcoming, she promptly eluded with a silly, affected laugh. At such times Aubriot would observe her closely behind his penetrating eyes.

It wasn't difficult to see that she was behaving oddly toward him.

Ever since she had returned from captivity among the bandits, dear little Jeanne, who had always been so open and frank with him, had forced him to question himself.

While recovering from pneumonia at Don José's villa, Aubriot had sensed that Jeanne was strangely distant. First it had occurred to him that she might have been raped by the bandits. She swore that wasn't so, yet a woman thus abused might wish to keep her dishonor a secret. But his doubts had grown as time passed and his child mistress continued to refuse his caresses. He began to long for the loving Jeanne had so freely given.

Sexual abstinence always put Aubriot in bad humor, and this time it made him bitter. If someone had hurt her, why shouldn't she confide in him, the only doctor who could help her? The sullen lover, he was old enough to assume the role of an affectionate father and so he controlled his urge to pressure his capricious companion.

Thus Jeanne deluded herself into thinking now and then that the impossible miracle had happened—she was a child once again and the apple of Philibert's eye.

But at times the fire in Philibert's veins blazed out of hand. The sun beating down peppered his flesh with desire. Sometimes, during their midday siesta on a deserted beach, he found himself struggling frantically against his body's urgent demands. Fortunately for her oath of fidelity to Vincent, Aubriot did not feel inclined to reconquer his lost love in their present cramped and unprivate quarters.

Life under that roof was a nonstop public social event. Desforges-Boucher kept open house at dinner every evening, followed by games and conversation that continued well past midnight. How could the governor's newest guests get to bed early? Everyone was curious to meet this novel foursome composed of the king's naturalist, an important landowner from La Plata, and two lovely ladies.

Emilie blossomed with all this attention. Her astringent wit had never sparkled more gaily as she thrust and parried her way through a host of compliments and flirtations. Jeanne rather welcomed these frivolous, amusing evenings. But Don José raged with jealousy, and Aubriot, after a month of this sort of thing, refused to waste any more time entertaining Port Louis society. So, when the invitation for them all to leave town arrived, he was overjoyed to become a guest of the Creole mistress of Mongoust.

* * * *

Mongoust was the name of a plantation belonging to Judge François Etienne de Segrais, who had died the year before. An avid amateur botanist, Segrais had laid out an extraordinary garden, planting trees, fruits, and flowers gathered from all over the world. Visitors to this universal orchard could sample the flavors of Bengal or China, Batavia or the African Cape, Brazil or Malta, Touraine or Provence. And while grapes from France obstinately refused to ripen and grow sweet, a visitor sampling *pamplemousse*, a tart citrus fruit with the fragrance of a rosebush from Cadiz or a jasmine plant from Rio, had to admit that it tasted miraculously good.

The governor never failed to send travelers he wanted to please on a tour of Mongoust, for he knew it also pleased Mme. Manon, who was an old flame of his.

The Creole housekeeper of the late judge, politely known as his widow, grew exceedingly bored at Mongoust once she found herself alone with only the slaves and their overseer. For a while she kept hoping that Desforges-Boucher would ask her to come live with him at Government House, but seven years had passed since the governor had set eyes on the Creole, and seven years can change a man if he lolls in a hammock and eats too much.

Resigned, Mme. Manon went on entertaining Desforges-Boucher's guests with her natural grace and charm, hoping that someday one of them would acquire the plantation and its housekeeper along with it. In welcoming Aubriot and his friends, her hopes surged. The local gossips reported that Don José needed to rent or buy a house, and was loaded with money. As she poured tea, Mme. Manon once again touted the peaceful, healthful quiet of the Pamplemousses district.

"On the island we can grow anything we want, even two crops a year," she bragged, handing Don José a fresh cup of tea. "Our Chinese rosebushes don't know what winter is, our orchards are always in fruit and flowers."

Jeanne darted a glance at Don José, who said quickly, "Yes, living here must be very pleasant, but Mongoust isn't for sale . . . or is it?"

"I'm not quite sure at the moment," Mme. Manon confessed. "But what does it matter? I supposed that you were interested in renting comfortable accommodations rather than buying a place."

Another glance from Jeanne prompted Don José to pursue the subject. "This will surprise you, but I am indeed looking for a place to buy. It's far more difficult than I thought. I want to buy it in the name of my wife, who is French," he announced, turning to Emilie.

Mme. Manon flashed a smile of understanding. "In that case," she said, "your wife should obtain a land grant. Buying land from a settler is not to your advantage. But if you obtain a land grant from the government you can pay over a long period, particularly now that the island is owned by the king. You can always owe the king money, for the king is a nobody!"

After everyone stopped laughing, Jeanne observed, "You speak of a grant, but I believe no more official business can be transacted until the new administration arrives. Every evening I hear the governor complaining that he no longer has the right to sell a single acre."

"He has to say so aloud, for there must be two hundred applications in his files," said Mme. Manon.

"Two hundred!" Jeanne repeated in amazement. "Are there that many would-be planters on the island? All I seem to see are officers, seamen, accountants, and tradespeople."

"They are the very ones who want grants," Mme. Manon answered. "Not for planting but for resale. Reselling what you never paid a penny for is an opportunity not to be missed."

And with a sly glance at Emilie, she added, "I don't imagine that the lady plans to till the land, either, after she buys it."

"Oh, yes she does!" Jeanne exclaimed, a trifle hastily.

The Creole looked dumbfounded. "You must be joking!" she murmured.

"Not at all," Emilie insisted gaily, entering into the spirit of the game. "I can already see myself as a lady farmer. After all, I was raised in the country. I'll look after the house, my friend Jeanne will take care of the gardens, Don José will see to the pasture and the grazing animals, while Dr. Aubriot will cultivate the finest, rarest spices and make us all richer than the Dutch in the Spice Islands."

Mme. Manon, still convinced this was a joke, questioned Jeanne further. "Are you seriously thinking of making money from the land?"

"Yes, seriously," Jeanne replied. "We believe the earth is the best source of wealth."

Mme. Manon looked extremely doubtful as she listened to Jeanne. She made a face and said, "Now there's a philosophy that may do on the continent, but never here. The only things farmers cultivate on this island are debts. They end up living on undeveloped land because they get tired of tilling soil that bears nothing."

"The right to become wealthy is the basic and best right men have!" Don José declared fervently.

"It must be a pleasant right for women too," said Jeanne. Turning to the Creole, she added, "I promise you that if I become a farmer I shall cultivate cash."

Once again Mme. Manon pouted in disbelief. "Whatever you produce, your customers will be poor. The islanders are poor. Only the ships bring in money. Coffee grown in l'Ile de France is excellent, but the planters get only seven sous a pound for it. At Lorient it would fetch thirty-six."

"Then we'll sell our coffee in Lorient," Jeanne declared.

Emilie shot her a mischievous look. "That's right. We'll find a captain with a spice merchant's heart and arrange to ship our products to the best markets."

Mme. Manon lounged languidly in her rattan armchair, listening to Jeanne and Emilie chattering on about cultivation and commerce. Sunk in a listless torpor brought on by the scent of yellow roses in the air, the Creole listened carefully to every word of their conversation, making mental notes of whatever related to money. Mme. Manon would have felt cheated if she couldn't collect a commission from any deal made on the island.

Jeanne was talking seriously about maritime trade, as if she could well afford to purchase a vessel.

Mme. Manon rejoined the conversation. "You can make just as much money importing as exporting," she declared. "Select your imports carefully, rely on me to find you good solvent customers here on the island. You'll reap five times the cost of your cargo."

"Ah, now there's a profit margin to attract a man's interest," exclaimed Don José. "And what must you sell on this island to make that kind of money?"

"Fresh meat," replied Mme. Manon. "We are terribly short of cattle and slaves. Didn't you realize that?"

Don José nodded energetically. "You may be sure that the scarcity of livestock is the first thing I noticed. To me, the scarcity of cattle and horses is simply outrageous. Not to mention the *luxury* of traveling on horseback. And traveling by litter requires four slaves in harness. I haven't seen even one potential member of such a team. I believe a slave trader could make a fortune by bringing blacks to your island. But I have no desire to grow rich on 'ebony.' Since slaves are a necessity, I'm willing to go after them once in a while, but only for my own province. I would never supply slaves to the French. Your countrymen, dear ladies, are terribly hardworking. Such constant activity would wear any slave out."

The women's laughter was interrupted by pounding hoofbeats coming up the road.

Mme. Manon stirred from her torpor, listened hard, and announced hopefully, "I wonder if that isn't Monsieur de Messin? Monsieur de Messin and the judge were old friends," explained Mme. Manon. "He lives far from Mongoust, but he always drops by when he comes to Port Louis. I know he's been in town for three days. If our visitor is indeed he, you'll enjoy meeting him. He's a stock breeder as well as a planter. You'll have all sorts of questions to ask him."

M. de Messin arrived with his nephew, M. de Chavanne, who had come over from France a few months earlier. He was introduced as a very inquisitive young man on his way around the world. As soon as they had brushed off their clothes and refreshed themselves, the two travelers joined Mme. Manon and her guests on the veranda. With its handsome woven latticework, its light rush and rattan furniture, its planters filled with dwarf China orange trees, its pots of carnations and the pervasive fragrance of jasmine vines climbing up the pillars, this lovely, sprawling porch was a most pleasant spot.

Jeanne sat back in her chair, her elbows nestled on the armrests, and let her eyes wander over the delightful scene, listening distractedly, saying little. In her mind's eye she was conjuring up a vague, wonderful dream of another flowering veranda where she would be waiting in the soft perfumed air for Vincent to come home to dinner. She breathed a lingering sigh, more like a soft moan filled with the longing of impatient flesh. She realized instantly that her neighbor had heard her.

Rousing herself from her reverie, she smiled at Chavanne and said to him in a hushed voice, "I think I was dreaming."

"Dreaming is most becoming to you," Chavanne replied quietly.

She had changed clothes, and in place of her hiker's pants and jacket she now wore a simple white frock. As the fine India cotton ruffled in the breeze, she thought that she must look rather pretty in her fluttering skirts.

Once more she sighed. She missed Vincent's arms so desperately.

"You really must take these ladies and Don José for a visit to Rivière Noire. They ought to see what a prosperous and well-run plantation on the island is like," Mme. Manon said to M. de Messin.

"The soil in Rivière Noire is good," said M. de Messin with feigned modesty. "The grain grows thick, and the grass stays green and tender all year round in the pastures."

"So the best place to look for a plantation would be in the Rivière Noire district, is that right?" Jeanne asked, suddenly interested once more in the conversation.

"Don José wants to locate a plantation for these ladies, who intend to grow spices," Mme. Manon inserted.

Young Chavanne burst out, "What good news! My word, Uncle, if your adopted land begins to attract such delightful persons, maybe I'll have to wind up my trip around the world right here. I beg you to help Don José find some property right next door to yours."

"Rivière Noire is rather isolated, you know. Far from the governor's balls and the distractions of town life," M. de Messin hastened to tell them. Like any other farmer, he was in no hurry to acquire competitors as neighbors. "Young ladies surely would have a better time in Moka," he continued.

"But isn't land in the Moka district much fought over already?" Jeanne asked.

"All the good property on this island is fought over because half the land is still jungle and underbrush, while the rest is planted to crops or grazing land."

"The lady can afford to pay cash," Don José remarked casually. The eyes of the two islanders lit up. "But no one seems to have much land to sell."

"Lots of small landowners instead of a few large ones, that's the current policy, and apparently the new regime won't change it," said M. de Messin. "The small ones are poor, hardworking farmers. The large ones are marquesses, colonels, and bankers who return to France and wait for their property to appreciate. Right now you can't own more than six hundred and twenty-four acres, and there's talk of reducing that even further."

"And here we were thinking that we'd come to a new French settlement where everything was still for the taking!" exclaimed Emilie, darting a glance at Jeanne, who was biting her lip. "Thank heavens, when the king's people arrive, things will be run a bit differently. There'll be room for accommodation."

"I don't doubt it," M. de Messin agreed with a smile. "The governor has just received from Count de Maudauve, our representative at Versailles, a purchase order for ten thousand acres in the name of Count de Polignac, who certainly has no intention of coming here to plant them. Desforges-Boucher has put the order aside. He intends to dump it in his successor's lap. But he's willing to bet that the count will get what he wants. Messieurs Dumas and Poivre will have their favorites as well as those of the king, just as Desforges-Boucher has had his as well as those of the East India Company. Will there ever be a government without favorites?"

"Monsieur Poivre will be a just intendant," Jeanne declared. "I know him well and can guarantee it."

M. de Messin sniffed. "I'm sorry to hear it. Things are going so badly for everyone here that instead of a fair intendant, we need an unfair one who takes our side. Pray that you have misjudged Monsieur Poivre."

"One very small and select injustice doesn't make a man unjust," Jeanne asserted as if she believed it, and everyone laughed.

M. de Messin turned toward the Spaniard. "Are we merely thinking aloud, or am I to believe, sir, that you are looking for property for these ladies?"

"He is indeed serious," Emilie replied eagerly.

M. de Messin observed a lengthy silence. His eyes narrowed and seemed to focus on a distant image. When at last he spoke, it was to Mme. Manon, who, he could tell, was hanging on his every word. "I was thinking about Allspice."

"If I had thought Allspice could be sold to an individual, I'd have mentioned it long before you arrived!" Mme. Manon exclaimed, already sick at the thought of having to give up half her commission, even though she felt sure the deal was unworkable.

"Allspice?" Jeanne repeated with fresh interest. "Allspice. I love the name. Why Allspice? Where is it? What is it like?"

"Good heavens! Such enthusiasm!" said the Creole, smiling. "Allspice is in the Moka district, and I must say that if the whole island is a garden, Moka is the garden to end all gardens. Allspice is located in one of its loveliest sectors. It's a rather large plantation, with buildings and grounds. But unfortunately it's all overgrown now. In our part of the world it doesn't take long for nature to reclaim the land."

"But why the name Allspice?" Jeanne insisted.

"Our slaves invent many of the names on this island. They like picturesque ones that tell a story," Mme. Manon explained. "At Allspice they had planted a great many fennel flowers to produce allspice."

"Really?" Jeanne exclaimed, growing more and more excited. "Which spices had they put in? What happened to them?"

"The land was reclaimed some fifteen years ago, when Monsieur Poivre was trying to introduce spice culture to the island," said Mme. Manon. "Apart from fennel flower, which grows like a weed, the Saint Méry family put in pepper and vanilla plants, cinnamon trees and a few precious nutmegs or cloves—I can't recall which—that Monsieur Poivre had given them."

"What became of the Saint Mérys?" Don José asked.

"They went back to France for good after the great cyclone of 1760. That cyclone disheartened a great many planters. It was devastating.

It wiped out years of toil, pulverized houses, and killed a host of livestock and slaves, not to mention men, women, and children. It ruined a lot of settlers and scared them to death. The ones who suffered most didn't have the courage to start afresh. To get an idea of the force of those hurricane winds, you need only look at the harbor. The litter of smashed hulls is all that remains of the splendid royal naval squadron that was anchored at Port Louis in 1760. A whole squadron tossed up on the shore! Trees were flying. Roofs were flying. Cows and sheep were flying. So you can imagine what happened to the spice bushes!"

Another long silence. Finally, Jeanne murmured, "The breeze this evening is so soft and pleasant. It's hard to believe it could suddenly turn ugly and destructive."

"Our island is a trollop," said M. de Messin. "A friend of mine used to call her 'the adorable trollop.' She left him a beggar. She is beautiful, fragrant, bewitching, exciting, soothing, and suddenly treacherous to the man who slumbers confidently in her arms. A trollop."

"So all that remains of Allspice is a name attached to fallow land?" Jeanne sighed, feeling utterly crushed.

"Not at all. The main house survived, protected by the slope behind it," said M. de Messin. "It used to be one of the handsomest houses on the island."

"They say it looks more like a stable now," Mme. Manon interjected.

"It's true," M. de Messin agreed. "The son still lives there, or rather camps with half a dozen slaves who stayed on. Whites and blacks live under the same roof and share the same food, the same idle existence, the same drunkenness, the same females. Two mulatto women make the rules, and a brood of pickaninnies of every shade of brown are sent off to steal chickens from the neighbors. I tell you this island can ruin a man and turn the scion of an ancient French family into a savage. Humbert de Saint Méry isn't the only example of a civilized man's return to nature."

"I find it odd that a man who's become an animal should still be concerned enough about money to want to sell his home," declared Don José. "The bear clings ferociously to his den."

"It's the Negresses who are after money," said M. de Messin. "I mean, they have hopes. Only . . ."

Mme. Manon finished the sentence with relish. "Only Allspice is riddled with debts to the East India Company, debts up to three times its value."

"Buying from the heir or from his creditors doesn't make a great difference. The price alone counts," observed Don José.

"Things are never quite so simple in the tropics. Nothing was clearly spelled out at the start," said M. de Messin. "Since you'd like to stay here, let me tell you how things are today. It's been impossible to get the settlers to pay their debts."

"Humbert de Saint Méry was born on the island. A Creole doesn't recognize his debts to people he thinks of as foreigners. He feels that if they don't like it they don't have to stay here," Mme. Manon concluded with a laugh.

"My word," said Don José, "as a Spaniard born in La Plata, that's exactly what I would say to any Spaniard from Madrid who complained to me that I was lazy or wanted to dun me for taxes. So then, ladies, let's forget about Allspice," he urged, looking at Emilie and Jeanne. "It's devilishly hard to negotiate a purchase when you've no seller to deal with!"

M. de Messin assumed a cunning air. "Don't you believe it. On our island, at the moment, the harder it is to trace the ownership of a property through masses of official records, the better your chances are of pulling off a good deal. The intendant is on his way here, but hasn't yet arrived. If there's a dispute among several parties, it's to their interest to settle it and hand over the property to you, rather than await royal arbitration. Didn't you tell me, sir, that you're prepared to pay cash?"

"That's right," Mme. Manon blurted out, before Don José could open his mouth to confirm it.

"That's right, sir. I will pay in piasters."

M. de Messin and the Creole exchanged eloquent glances, "With piasters you can buy anything here, even what isn't for sale."

"Don José, we really must look at Allspice without delay!" exclaimed Jeanne, pink-cheeked with excitement, her amber eyes sparkling.

"Yes indeed, Don José, we ought to go," Emilie insisted. "I hope Monsieur de Saint Méry hasn't become such a bear that he gobbles up his visitors!"

"His mulatto women will be very proud to receive two lovely ladies.

They rule the roost at Allspice," said M. de Messin. "I'll take you there if you wish."

"I'll go too," sighed Mme. Manon. She paused, and her voice grew hazy with memories. "Allspice is a place for pleasure. I have some wonderful recollections of it. Madame de Saint Méry gave delightful parties there. I recall a summer picnic to celebrate their first peach harvest. There were more than two hundred guests sitting on the lawn, eating off white tablecloths! Edmée de Saint Méry had borrowed linens, dishes and silver from all her friends. There were three men-o'-war in port at the time. All the officers . . ."

Mme. Manon interrupted her reminiscences to call out crossly to a little black girl of about twelve who had suddenly rushed into the room. "What is it, Sophie? Is dinner ready?"

The little slave girl rolled her big eyes and replied, "Momma want to talk to you. Need you."

"Now what?" Mme. Manon exclaimed impatiently. "What have you dreamed up to spoil my evening?"

"It's Adele. She's mad, spitting fire. Can't swallow no more. Momma yell at her but Adele don't care. Momma say M'am come give Adele kick in behind." Sophie yelped out her message in a shrill little voice without pausing for breath.

"Good Lord!" Mme. Manon sighed. "Please excuse me. I'll have to go or else we won't eat till midnight," she told her guests. "I chose one of my prettiest black Creoles to wait on table, and the ninny simply refuses to get along with Sophie's mother, who's in charge of the kitchen."

"Pretty girl don't mean quality girl," the little slave declared sententiously, no doubt quoting her mother.

Despite the crisis in the kitchen, the dinner turned into a very pleasant affair. Just before sitting down they were joined by the three Mestralet brothers, eldest sons of a rich Bordeaux merchant, who had come out to the islands seeking their fortune. They were working hard to develop their property, situated between Mongoust and Monplaisir, the handsome country house of l'Ile de France's governor.

Mme. Manon always sent them an invitation each time she had company. Young and full of vigor, Honoré, Maurice, and Justin Mestralet were neither ugly nor stupid, and usually were quite willing to enter-tain their Creole hostess when she was alone. But tonight they neglected her shamelessly for the sparkling-eyed blond and the acid-tongued redhead with the milky complexion.

Mme. Manon consoled herself by seating Dr. Aubriot at her right. Since the table was small and the places quite close together, she could feel his breath on her.

At the age of thirty-five, the Creole of Mongoust was still attractive. She had put on some weight, of course, but the added upholstery was well distributed. Her face had remained fresh and smooth, her skin wrinkle-free and fair. She wore a striped dress of pale chintz cut very low in front, as was the local fashion, currently favored by discerning European men.

The seven male guests of Mongoust's hostess were in for a treat that evening. The two black serving women displayed themselves wantonly in even lower-cut bodices than that of their mistress. They were pleasant to look at, especially Adele, a tall, handsome, well-proportioned girl with a dancer's sinuous body and a belly that seemed to rotate tirelessly as she walked. With her well-shaped breasts and sparkling teeth, she could have fetched top price in the slave market at Port Louis.

She set down the steaming soup tureen in front of M. de Messin, who pinched her waist. "At your service, Mam'selle Adele," he said playfully, reaching for the silver soup ladle. "So you've already had a spat with Mama Lucinda and made her cry, you bad girl!"

"Mama Lucinda no cry, she screech," replied Adele. "Is no woman, is she-donkey!"

"That will do, Adele," Mme. Manon scolded amid the laughter. "I forbid you to talk against Mama Lucinda. Either you do what she says or I'll sell you to a planter who'll put you out to work in the fields."

"My dear lady, you know very well he'd put her into his bed, and there's nothing she'd like better," whispered M. de Messin.

Adele overheard and observed, "White man no punish pretty girl. For pretty girl, white man has big eyes—big eyes in big ass!"

"Really, that's the limit! Be quiet, you shameless girl!" Mme. Manon shouted at her, at once angry and embarrassed, while laughter exploded.

When the insolent waitress was sent off to the kitchen for more bread, M. de Messin proposed straightaway to his hostess, "If you really want to get rid of Adele, sell her to me."

"I was just about to ask the same thing," said Don José. "These ladies need someone to look after them. Please help me get our little household started."

"Indeed, sir, maybe we can work something out," chirped Mme. Manon, delighted at the prospect of a deal.

"Shall I serve you?" M. de Messin inquired, about to plunge his ladle again into the fragrant shellfish broth spiced with pimiento.

"Yes, tonight I'll have a little," said Mme. Manon, and went on to explain, "I really adore this shellfish soup. But for some time now, whenever I eat it at dinner I get dizzy spells during the night."

She was about to attack her plateful of soup greedily when Aubriot, whom she had twice pressed accidentally with her knee, leaned over to whisper, "Don't deprive yourself of a feast. There's a very pleasant remedy for nighttime vapors."

This irresistible proposal so enchanted the "widow" that she nearly choked on her first mouthful. She began to cough violently, with the result that her heaving breasts flew straight out of her bodice!

M. de Messin promptly wiped off the soup ladle on a corner of the tablecloth and proceeded benevolently to use it to gather up one by one the pair of charming stragglers and restore them to their cottony nest. Following which the imperturbable gentleman went on ladling out soup for the male guests. The incident, which Mme. Manon found uproarious, set the tone of uninhibited gaiety for the rest of the meal.

Jeanne, rosy-cheeked, felt proud to watch Philibert display his intellectual gifts. She hadn't seen him so animated for a long time.

He was eloquent, caustic, amusing, and very attractive in his iron-gray suit, guiding the conversation at his own pace and injecting it with wit. Admittedly, she was a little surprised to see the learned Dr. Aubriot exerting himself to impress and entertain so modest a gathering. But, she decided, Philibert's active, probing mind needed to explode from time to time. All to the good for the lucky ones present!

In fact, Aubriot's activity that evening was less cerebral than Jeanne supposed. Mama Lucinda's deliciously spiced food, the off-color chatter, the free-flowing Entre-deux-Mers wine, the radiant faces of Jeanne and Emilie, the provocative behinds of the handsome black slave women with their shrill laughter, and the amber-and-musk fragrance of his neighbor, Mme. Manon, conspired to make Aubriot ready for bed.

There are nights when desire reaches out hungrily and blindly, driven by inner need. The doctor took advantage of a round of laughter to lean toward his hostess and murmur, "May I count on your having one of your shellfish spells tonight?"

"Decidedly, sir. I expect one the moment I lie down," she sighed, her parted lips as soft as mango flesh.

Almost simultaneously, on the heels of a pun from Honoré Mestralet, Jeanne's wholesome laughter rang out. Her laugh sent a queasy shiver through his stomach as he contemplated the lumpy Creole pastry he had just ordered for his midnight snack.

CHAPTER 18

 eanne discovered that the reality of life on a plantation did not discourage her. She and Aubriot had decided to visit Rivière Noire for a week.

M. de Messin had managed to prosper as a gentleman farmer from fat livestock pastured on rich grasslands, black pigs that made savory eating when roasted on a spit, and an assortment of wildfowl and poultry. The main house looked something like a Norman farm surrounded by banana and citrus trees, everlasting flowers of the Cape, and banks of creamy-white tuberoses, which delighted Jeanne's eyes and nose.

Nearly three hundred slaves worked at Rivière Noire, which took its name from the river flowing through it. The overseer led the slaves off to the fields at daybreak, snapping his whip behind the stragglers. Aubriot and Jeanne, also early risers, often passed the long column of blacks before turning off into the woods. They would smile and wave at the slaves, who suddenly came alive, responding cheerfully. When the botanists returned at dusk from their excursion, they would find the slaves sprawled on the grass outside their huts, eating from a steaming pot of corn mush or mumbling a chorus of prayers to the Good Lord for their master's prosperity. Often, as Philibert and Jeanne were organizing the day's harvest of plants, they could hear snatches of song, the roll of drums, and distant laughter.

"I like to hear them happy," said Jeanne one evening, always anxious about what was happening to the slaves. "Monsieur de Messin must be a good master."

"I'm not sure you can call them happy," said Aubriot. "More likely they're trying to forget their misery."

"Do you think so?" said Jeanne. "Do you think all of them are unhappy? Even the ones who are well treated?"

Aubriot thought a minute, frowned, and finally answered, "I really can't say, Jeannette. My skin isn't black."

"Suppose that a kind master or mistress treats them decently, doesn't punish them cruelly, gives them bananas and meat every Sunday and a shirt on New Year's Day, cares for them if they're sick, doesn't separate husbands and wives or a child from its mother, don't you think they could be happy?" she pressed him anxiously.

Setting down his magnifying lens, Aubriot stared at Jeanne. "Are you by any chance thinking of becoming a planter . . . a planter with a conscience?"

She trembled and turned her face away from the candlelight so as to blush in the shadows. Aubriot seized her by the shoulders and whirled her around to face him. "Well?"

"I don't see why you . . . it's Emilie's idea," she said, lowering her eyes.

"Emilie? Now there's an idea that suits her about as neatly as wooden shoes on a duchess. What does Don José have to say? I must admit that I can't see our Spanish friend spending the rest of his life on an island where the only means of transportation is one's own two feet."

"He's already bought three horses. Anyway, investing money in colonial land doesn't mean you have to live there. It can be managed. Madame de Vaux-Jailloux lives very comfortably in Dombes on her income from a plantation in Santo Domingo."

"And I suppose Emilie wants you as her manager here?"

"Isn't that a good way to keep from being cheated?"

Aubriot's hands slid down Jeanne's shoulders to her wrists. He perched on a corner of the table and drew her close. "So you're toying with the idea of settling here? And once my work is finished, are you going to let me return to France all by myself?"

Tears washed away the candlelight reflected in Jeanne's eyes. "Why must you think about leaving already?" she asked unhappily. "You've just arrived and you know that your mission is a long one. You still have to visit Bourbon, Rodriguez, and Madagascar. Besides, Monsieur Poivre will never let you go home. He needs you here. You know—"

"I know that I left a son in France whom I intend to see again before I die," Aubriot interrupted.

Taken aback, Jeanne recovered quickly and said, "Look, you can send for Michel. Little boys adore adventure. There's nothing more for you to do in France. You already have identified every blade of grass that grows there."

"Don't talk such nonsense. It's true, though, that I rarely encounter anything new at home," he admitted sincerely.

"There, you see! And how many times have I heard you dreaming aloud of exploring botanical wonderlands in the Indian Ocean? You won't do it in a single day."

"You have a good memory for my longings," he said. Then, smiling wryly, he altered the sentence slightly. "You have a good memory for *certain* longings of mine."

Jeanne paid no attention to the reference. "Since you will have to stay here quite a while, wouldn't you be more comfortable living in a pleasant house than in the cramped quarters offered by the government? What's more, you'll help us make a fortune in the spice trade. We plan to raise spices. I need good India herbs to add an exotic touch to my shop in the Temple. I'll have a patch of tea, coffee, and cocoa for our own use. I need . . ."

He listened as she rambled on about her plans. Then he released her wrists and stood up. "I see you've been keeping all this from me for some time."

"Are you angry?"

"No," he replied sharply.

"I think you are."

"No, I tell you." He added sarcastically, "Dame Emilie de la Pommeraie is under no obligation to tell me about her secret plans for the future. And you seem to have taken a leaf from her book, haven't you?" So saying, he turned his back on her.

Jeanne approached him from behind and tugged timidly at his sleeve—a gesture that went back to her childhood. "Don't be vexed," she pleaded. "I want so to tell you about Allspice."

"Allspice?"

"It's a plantation I know to be for sale. Monsieur de Messin . . . ah, but we don't have time to go into that before you have to dress for dinner."

She slipped between him and the table in order to look him in the face, and went on in her most beguiling voice, "Philibert, you know I have trouble talking about myself. To you more than anyone else, though you're the one person in the world whose understanding I need and . . . and . . ."

And whose forgiveness I crave, she thought desperately to herself.

"I need your understanding," she repeated in a hushed voice.

He drew up a chair and sat down, waiting to hear more, riveting his attention on her.

Jeanne felt trapped. Her hands gripped the edge of the table as she leaned against it. "I've so much to tell you," her voice quavered. "There are a thousand things that I want to say to you, but . . ." A half-drowned sob choked her. The rest of her sentence wavered tremulously.

"I seem to recall . . . when I was a little girl . . . that you were aware of everything . . . everything. I was so little, and you were a famous scientist who understood everything without needing to hear it put into words."

He didn't seem anxious to talk, and went on gazing intently at her. Jeanne roused herself and said, with an affected little laugh, "After all, a doctor has only to take one look at a patient to know everything there is to know!"

A cold sweat broke out on Aubriot's forehead. *Is it true, then? That brute Pinto or one of his bullies abused and soiled her . . . or made her feel utterly soiled. Why didn't I guess it after she kept refusing my advances?* He had felt relieved as the weeks passed and she hadn't become pregnant with some bandit's bastard.

He got up suddenly, composed himself when she appeared startled, and reached out routinely to take her pulse. "Jeanne, I'll worry later about all the ideas you're toying with. Right now I want you to tell me what's ailing you physically. Out with it!"

Astonishment tied her tongue.

He pressed her. "Talk to me, Jeannette. Tell me what's on your mind. I'm not a judge. I'm a doctor . . . you just reminded me of that fact. Where do you hurt, dear Jeannot? What are you worried about?"

"But . . . really, I don't know why you suddenly think I'm ill," she said with growing bewilderment. "There's nothing the matter with me, really. I feel fine, as always."

"You're sure of it? You're not lying to me?"

"Why should I lie?"

"Perhaps to avoid hurting me." He observed the flush that crept into her cheeks and her fluttering eyelids.

"If I had to tell you something that would hurt you, I might very possibly choose to lie," she murmured, then added quickly, "but as for what you ask, I can only say truthfully that I feel fine."

"Do you swear it?"

"Yes, of course," she said, utterly mystified.

"Well, then, swear. Swear on my head."

Stunned, she stared at him for a long time before saying, in a faltering voice, "Swear on your head? Must I? All right. It can't harm your head, I daresay. I swear, Dr. Aubriot, on your head, that I feel as healthy now as I always have—as solid as the Pont Neuf!"

"That's good," he responded, letting her go.

He took out his handkerchief and dabbed his forehead, no longer afraid for her. "Since you're all right, please stop playing these childish games with me," he said irritably. "Let's finish putting things in order. It's nearly dinnertime."

Mute, discouraged, or simply unrelieved by her cowardice, she hastily tidied up Philibert's room and went upstairs to her own in the attic. She changed her clothes and came down again just as Philibert was arranging his wig.

"Shall I powder you?" she asked.

"Don't bother. We're in the country," he replied primly.

The strained silence dragged on. The botanist made notes of his day's observations. Sensing that he was deliberately ignoring her, Jeanne burst out resentfully, "You're so distant this evening that I feel as sad as a poor Negress."

"You'll get over it. When I went to the kitchen for some water, I saw them preparing a fruit salad of bananas and pineapple with lemon juice."

"So you think a fruit salad is all it takes to make me happy?" she exploded.

"Well, yes, for the moment."

"Monsieur de Buffon once told me that three quarters of mankind dies of grief," Jeanne declared.

"Grief over a missed decoration for one's lapel or a missed academic appointment," said Aubriot. "You're a woman, so you'll die for less foolish reasons."

"I might die for want of love."

He eyed her grimly.

She bit her lip in panic, fearing that her secret had become transparent. Then she busied herself by rearranging the folds of her dress and inquired lightly, "By the way, where are we going tomorrow? Farther inland or along the shore? Monsieur de Chavanne is waiting impatiently to join our shell-gathering expedition."

"We still have work to do in the woods," said Aubriot. "Besides, I'm not too anxious to have Monsieur de Chavanne around. He talks too much for an ignorant young man. Aren't you as happy as I am, tramping the forests in unspoiled silence?"

"Yes," she agreed. She began to put away the pencils and paintbrushes Aubriot had left out on his work table.

At the close of each expedition, the botanist returned to his room and spread out the day's finest specimens. He would make a record of them with detailed sketches. This evening he had drawn some mushrooms gathered from an ancient tree growing along the bank of a stream, spectacular mushrooms with rippled bands of faintly streaked colors.

Polydor, the slave that M. de Messin had lent them for their excursions, appeared suddenly at the door. The Malagasy was decked out in his Sunday best, a bold red and white loincloth. His heavily oiled, glistening hair was done up in an impressive arrangement of braids. He waited for Aubriot to speak, then came forward and pointed to the watercolors.

"Moussié Docta is artist," he said, and brought out a broad wooden comb decorated with carved monkeys. "Polydor artist too."

"It's lovely, Polydor," said Aubriot with genuine admiration.

"Very lovely, Polydor," Jeanne echoed in her honeyed voice.

The slave gazed at her for a moment without smiling, his eyes filled with some secret message. Finally he handed the comb to her. "You want?"

"No, no!" Jeanne exclaimed hastily. "I do thank you, Polydor, but I wouldn't think of taking one of your treasures away from you."

The slave's arm dropped, and he looked so dejected that Aubriot intervened, "Polydor, would you like to sell us your comb? What shall I give you for it?"

The slave put the comb down on the table. "Polydor give this to Mam'zelle. Can give money to Moussié Messin, that pay Polydor."

Seeing that Aubriot didn't appear to understand, the slave tried again. "Pay for Polydor, Polydor belong to you."

Aubriot's eyebrows flew up. "You want me to buy you? Take you with me?"

The Malagasy grinned from ear to ear, nodding his head frantically.

"Polydor, I can't take you with me," Aubriot told him as gently as he could. "Your master probably wants to keep you. Anyway, wouldn't it make you sad to leave your hut and your family? You're married, aren't you?"

"Not," came the reply. "Me loved by ugly old woman."

"And why the devil do you take up with an ugly old woman?" asked Aubriot, laughing. "You're young, handsome, and healthy. You could have a pretty young woman."

"Not," Polydor replied. "You find pretty woman, master take her from you."

"But why?" Jeanne asked in astonishment.

"For put in his bed," Polydor replied, then paused and added, with philosophical gravity, "Is no way poor boy get to keep pretty woman in his house."

"My friend, that happens to white men also," said Aubriot, clapping the slave on the shoulder sympathetically. "Go now, Polydor, and take your comb with you, since I can't buy it. I'll see you tomorrow."

The Malagasy darted a mute appeal at Jeanne, who turned her eyes away.

The next evening he was back with the same request, bearing more gifts wrapped in two tattered loincloths. Dumbfounded, Aubriot unwrapped twenty-seven tiny samples of wood, each sectioned so as to best display its own individual grain and beauty. It made a handsome collection for any naturalist. Jeanne set it out on the table.

"Can you name all of these?"

"Me can," Polydor began, pointing to the first piece. He proceeded to reel off the names of the trees down to the very last sample, a cube of lemon-colored citron.

"Polydor," said Aubriot, "I'm very pleased to have all these, really I am." Knowing in advance what the response would be, he ventured nevertheless, "How much would you like for your wood? Shall I give you a shirt? A mirror? Some smell-good? Would you like to have two piasters?"

"Buy Polydor, Polydor happy," came the predictable reply.

Seeing Aubriot about to indicate his refusal, the slave spoke up, repeating firmly, "Polydor happy and Good Lawd happy too. Good Lawd happy when poor nigga happy, priest say dat."

* * * *

M. de Messin could scarcely refuse to sell a slave to the King of France's naturalist, who was on loan to the island's governor.

"I want to pay the fair price . . ." Aubriot began.

M. de Messin's hand flew up. "Let's not talk of money," he protested. "Let's just say you'll give me back another strong young man when you go to buy yourself servants."

"Then tell me, when will the slave market take place?"

"If you buy at the market in Port Louis, you'll end up with third-rate, toothless baggage," said M. de Messin. "You have to buy smuggled goods. The best stuff never reaches port."

"Why is that?" Aubriot asked.

"Because the governor has to make a profit for the East India Company. The Company pays for transporting the slaves. The ship captains prefer to handle the cargo on their own, especially if it's valuable. A slaver captain likes to charge the costs to his shipowner and pocket the profits."

"I can well imagine," said Aubriot. "But don't they get caught? Sailors have big mouths."

"Every hand aboard a slaver gets a share of the sale," said M. de Messin. "What's more, in this part of the world, anybody who can catch a black will sell him. A first-rate Malagasy will fetch over five hundred pounds, though I can assure you he's not worth it!"

"Why?" Jeanne challenged him. "Polydor is from Madagascar and strikes me as a fine fellow."

M. de Messin flashed an indulgent smile at her. "Before you say that, you ought to wait until he has been with you awhile. Even the best of your blacks end up rubbing you the wrong way. Malice and cunning run in their blood. You can be a fair and generous master, but they're sure to play some foul trick on you. Yesterday I had to order a female slave whipped because she aborted her baby. And she'll do it again."

Jeanne grew pale and put down her spoon. "Maybe your Negresses don't care to people the world with more slaves," she said in a husky voice.

"Don't credit these poor devils with philosophical pretensions, mademoiselle," said M. de Messin. "Believe me, these women do it out of malice, to offend the white man's God and to give their owner a hard time. They care only about dressing up, arranging their hair, dancing, singing, making love, and eating stolen pigs. The minute one of them considers himself mistreated, he escapes into the woods, or hangs himself in order to ruin his owner, or stirs up the others to join together and drown themselves at sea."

"What?" exclaimed Aubriot in amazement. "You mean they feel desperate enough to commit mass suicide?"

"Not really. They set out for Madagascar, the cradle of their idleness," said M. de Messin. "They steal a dugout, but without food or compass. They usually end up feeding the sharks."

"How horrible!" murmured Jeanne, on the verge of tears.

A deep sigh from Jeanne inspired Chavanne to try to lift her spirits. "Eat," he urged her. "I see you're going through the same thing I went through when I first got here. It takes time to cast off one's European sensibilities. It made me sick to see them hunting humans like wild animals. But how else can you recapture runaway slaves? Veteran runaways actually become savage beasts, terribly cruel and terribly dangerous. They come out in hordes at night, like wolfpacks, to steal food and crops and women. The maroons are devils of the worst sort and have to be hunted down. But we try to take them alive, as my uncle can tell you."

"That's true," M. de Messin confirmed, "even though a recaptured slave isn't worth much. Still, the government has set a reward of a hundred pounds for a fugitive brought back alive, and only fifty for a dead one. That makes the soldiers think twice before firing their muskets."

"Such precautions would seem to inject a note of humanity into slave-hunting," Aubriot commented sarcastically.

* * * *

As Jeanne poured six drops of essence of cypress onto Philibert's pillow to keep him from coughing during the night, a Creole song rose from under the window. A slave on his way to the recreation shed was singing in a mournful voice:

Love's Progress

"Me live in tiny hut
Must bend down to enter;
Me head go through roof
When me feet touches ground.
Poor nigga no need light
When he want sleep at night,
Moonlight shine, thank de lawd,
Through big hole in roof!"

Jeanne lingered by the window, her forehead pressed against the pane, listening to the song as it grew fainter.

"Well, aren't you going up?" Philibert asked. "What are you thinking about?"

"I was thinking . . . when Monsieur de Buffon told me that three quarters of mankind dies of grief, he must have been counting only the French."

CHAPTER 19

With Polydor as their guide, Aubriot and Jeanne set out once again for Port Louis, taking an inland route. For two long days they trudged, up and down rocky goat trails, across wild streams, through junglelike vegetation choked with giant ferns and twisting vines. Tugging on these vines, the explorers brought down clusters of breathtaking new orchid species. From time to time they picnicked under a tree, listening to noisy congregations of chattering green parakeets. Overhead, where the foliage parted, a fleeing red monkey, at once curious and timid, vanished from sight. Off in the distance, the breaking surf piled wreaths of foam along the coral ridge surrounding the island. Beyond that rampart stretched the placid blue sea, like some great deserted lagoon.

"How gorgeous it is!" Jeanne once cried out in blissful contentment, and even Philibert forgot momentarily to rattle off the names of every tree in the landscape.

They shared the last of their roast pigeon and bananas in a peaceful valley in the Plaines Wilhelms district, a prosperous settlement. After finishing their meal, they wandered down toward the town.

At the entrance to the slave camp on the edge of the settlement, a pile of refuse gave off a sickening odor. Holding their noses as they skirted it, Jeanne and Aubriot were horrified to see a grizzled black man bent over the body of a dead horse, cutting off strips of flesh.

"Good Lord, Philibert, stop him!" cried Jeanne, her stomach in knots. "He'll poison himself!"

"Come, let's be off," said Aubriot, grabbing her arm. "We have nothing better to offer him. Hunger makes anything edible."

"Polydor give him something," said their slave, and walked over to give the old man a banana he had kept hidden in his pack. He returned with a big grin on his face, saying, "Poor nigga happy. When poor nigga happy, Good Lawd happy too."

Pausing to study the expression on the slave's face, Aubriot said, "I see, Polydor, that you are very anxious to please the Good Lord. Do you really love the white man's Lord?"

"White man's Good Lawd is black man's too," he said reproachfully.

"Yes, of course, He looks after everybody," Aubriot agreed hastily.

* * * *

When the threesome arrived at Port Louis, there were two more vessels anchored in the harbor. The *Jan Adriaensz*, a Dutch merchantman, and the *Shuttle*, a cargo vessel belonging to the French East India Company which made several trips a year to Madagascar, bringing back beef and slaves.

Though the *Shuttle* always returned with beef—sometimes in the form of smoked meat—it rarely brought slaves, at least not to Port Louis. Captain Charcot from Saint-Malo was the boldest, most notorious slave smuggler in the whole Indian Ocean.

That day, as Jeanne and Aubriot entered the town late in the afternoon, there was a great ruckus outside Government House. This time Charcot had really outdone himself. It was rumored that the two hundred blacks the captain had set ashore the previous night at Cave Point, presumably to offer at auction, had been delivered instead to two rich planters in the Moka district.

Outraged farmers were demanding Desforges-Boucher's head, accusing him of taking bribes. The moderate voices called for a military march on Moka to seize the contraband slaves and distribute them among honest needy folk. Slaves, poor whites, and mixed-bloods stood elbow to elbow in the plaza, eager to fight or to carry on the celebration already begun in taverns along the steaming waterfront.

"We'll be lucky to get home by midnight!" Aubriot grumbled.

"White man make trouble, make trouble for black, not very pretty. White man no should do, white man not savage," Polydor observed airily.

"Our Polydor has a sharp eye, a good tongue, and common sense to boot," Aubriot whispered to Jeanne.

Jeanne's exclamation cut him short. "Well, look who's coming!"

Don José appeared, riding out of the courtyard of the Intendancy. The sole horseman on the scene, he guided his mount slowly and deliberately through the dense throng. Aubriot waved his hat to attract the Spaniard's attention.

"Where are you headed at this late hour?" he asked Don José as he rode up.

"Nearby," he replied, jerking his chin in the direction of the traders' warehouse, on the far side of a muddy crater. "The slaves from the *Shuttle* will go on sale there at six o'clock. The farmers are so busy complaining about what they missed out on that they pay no attention to what they can still get."

"I'm going with you," said Jeanne, holding out her hand for Don José to lift her into the saddle behind him.

"Polydor, pick up the baggage," Aubriot ordered. "*We're* going back to the house."

* * * *

Five men in business dress were already in the sale room when Don José and Jeanne arrived. They recognized a very fat gentleman stepping out of a litter. He was a frequent dinner guest at the governor's table.

"I was curious to see what was left of the cargo," said the fat gentleman.

What was left didn't look very promising. There were eight puny males, four boys, and three girls, young but ugly even by lanternlight. They all had olive-gray skin and the frightened look of cornered animals. They clung to each other, shivering. Customers circled the forlorn little group, testing arm and leg muscles, inspecting teeth, hands, and feet, screwing up their noses in disgust.

"We'd be doing that robber Charcot a favor by buying one of these wrecks," sneered a customer.

M. de Bouffault, another gentleman known to Jeanne and Aubriot, marched into the room like a drum major and proceeded to survey the merchandise. Then he turned and, with a face like a thundercloud, strode over to a ship's officer in a far corner of the room.

"Listen to me carefully, Monsieur Machard," he began roughly, "I'm not going to complain to the governor or stir up trouble in Moka. My quarrel is not with your lucky customers, but with your captain. You tell that scoundrel I demand my share of his next shipment. If I don't get it, I'll write to the naval minister."

The mariner turned on his heel and went off to help another potential client, a pudgy fellow with flushed cheeks, who was busy inspecting the lot of slaves, touching, sniffing, poking. He checked everything thoroughly, calmly, and dispassionately, as if he were studying the display at a meat market. He wound up selecting two women, a man, and a boy. He examined and poked them again, finally he ran the tip of his tongue under the arm of each, spitting and wiping his lips after tasting each skin.

"There's nothing like the taste of sweat to tell you how healthy a body is," he declared excitedly.

"Don José, let's go, please, I beg you," came Jeanne's tremulous plea from behind the Spaniard's back.

Don José appeared not to have heard her. He approached the ship's officer. "Officer Machard, I don't want to stay for the bidding. Buy me the smallest boy and send him to me at the Intendancy, where I'm staying," he said in a low voice. "I want to give him to my son."

"Good," replied Machard. "I'm glad you're buying him. Once he's deloused and stops crying for his mother, he'll make a fine playmate. He's a pretty child, and clever."

"Are you really buying that black boy for Paul?" Jeanne asked.

"Of course," replied Don José. "Iassi has to scold him every day before she can get him to go out for a walk. He's ashamed to be seen without a black boy trotting at his heels. In La Plata, no boy of good family goes anywhere, even to school, without a slave escort."

"Yes, I noticed that," said Jeanne. "By the way, you seemed to be acquainted with the boatswain from the *Shuttle*."

"There's a private code of understanding among smugglers," Don José replied, laughing. "The best goods from Captain Charcot's next shipment will be for us. That is, if you haven't changed your mind in the meantime."

"Changed my mind? About what?"

"Come now, Jeannette, about whether you still want to buy a plantation and the slaves that go with it."

"Of course I do! I'm no will-o'-the-wisp, Don José!"

"No?" he said, rolling his eyes in mock surprise.

Jeanne blushed with annoyance. "Don José, don't judge me by one event in my life which you never witnessed. I am not capricious, believe me," she declared firmly. Vexed at having to defend herself, she added, "Certain . . . moods, which some people interpret as flightiness, simply prove the heart faithful to its many feelings."

Don José said nothing, but merely frowned. Finally, with just a hint of a smile, he said humbly, "I trust your reasoning. It takes a woman to feel perfectly at home in matters of the heart. So if you're still firmly committed to your plan, I'll take you to Allspice tomorrow."

Hearing a little gasp behind him, he twisted his head around and winked at her. "Lost your tongue? Happy? Not a bad spot, you'll see."

"Who took you there?" she asked, breathless with excitement.

"An old, fake baroness whom I courted for one whole evening because she knows that district inside out. The ladies here all jump at the chance to make some money on the side. They'll do anything to be of service."

"Allspice," Jeanne murmured, her head already in the clouds.

CHAPTER 20

Jeanne knew instantly that Allspice was the place she wanted to live.

Her dreamland exhaled the scent of aloe. Over this whole section of the Moka district floated the syrupy, bitter-honey fragrance of treelike aloeswood. The plants grew as tall as a man and sent out clusters of thick, spiny leaves. From the heart of each cluster sprang a stiff, flowering stalk bearing a host of yellow and dark red spikes interlaced with hundreds of giant cereus plants whose green-and-white snakelike leaves were armed with poisonous spikes. Drawing their only nourishment from the rocky soil, these rugged shoots of aloe and cereus formed a primitive, heavy-scented jungle standing in a sun-scorched silence. Beyond this rampart of foliage lay the rough-timbered double gate to Allspice.

On the other side of it, a long, straight path sloped upward. It had once been a broad and majestic entranceway. The double rows of towering tamarinds and thick, acacia-like foliage arched overhead to form a vault. The air beneath it had a greenish glow and was delightfully cool, in contrast to the field of aloes. This front portion of the property, sheltered from winds by the surrounding hills, was wildly overgrown.

It took a keen eye to pick out, amid the new growth of vine-draped hedges, the outlines of a former pomegranate grove or a stand of fig trees. Thickets of wild banana plants and raspberry bushes filled what must have once been a square field. Now the tangled growth had been cut into quarters by machete, providing access to the neglected crops. Here too, overgrown rosebushes of Chinese origin wandered up tree trunks and crept across branches, producing an occasional striking blossom with deep lavender petals. Thus, somewhere behind the stifling beauty of its tropical luxuriance, Allspice still possessed the remains of imported plantings and the attractions of a once-cared-for country place.

Jeanne's nostrils quivered as she imagined the perfumed yesterdays of Edmée de Saint Méry.

"Well?" came the voice of Don José nearby, interrupting her thoughts.

"Well," she echoed, pausing for a long time before she spoke again. "I know this place has seen some terrible times. Yet it seems to hold the promise of better days ahead. I think there is happiness here, just waiting to return."

"Maybe it's been waiting for you."

"Maybe so."

"I should have read your fortune in the tarot cards last night. We'd have seen whether you and Allspice were destined to grow old together."

She shook her head. "I trust my heart more than your tarot. My heart tells me that I come here as a friend, not as a stranger."

"Indeed," exclaimed Don José, "it's not hard to feel at home in a deserted place."

There was no sign of human life. They might as well have been approaching Sleeping Beauty's castle. "I tried to whet our doctor's appetite this morning with the promise of some extraordinary feathers, but he couldn't be persuaded to come with us. I think, Jeannette, that he is decidedly annoyed at your plan to settle on the island."

"Rather than a plan, he considers it just a passing fancy," said Jeanne.

"That's because he doesn't realize that you're rich enough to act upon it," replied Don José.

He reached out for the bridle of Jeanne's mount and reined in both horses. "Really, though, Jeannette," he said, sweeping his arm across the landscape, "aren't you the least bit discouraged by the prospect of so much heavy spadework before you can even think of planting a clove tree?"

"Don José, I've noticed it doesn't take much time to get used to the idea of doing something impossible."

"Ha!" laughed the Spaniard. "I declare, *amiga*, it's easier for me to accept the idea of not doing what it is possible to do!"

"How you do brag about your laziness! Yet you scoured the island in search of my fancy, as if you believed in it."

"Bah! I just got on my horse and went," said Don José with a shrug.

They rode on slowly and passed a stand of pomegranate trees. Just beyond lay the house.

It seemed very large to Jeanne. Despite the profusion of frangipani trees screening the façade, she could make out quite clearly the main lines of a two-story structure, simple and graceful, in the style of the colonial houses pictured in engravings of Santo Domingo. The ceilings must have been rather low. Sheltered by an overhanging roof, the balcony was enclosed by woven pandanus trelliswork in need of repair. The veranda below was supported by eight pillars.

"Heavens! It's a miniature château," she exclaimed.

"A château that has known war, looting, and occupation," Don José added, wincing. "The balcony is held together with string, the roof . . ."

"Please, Don José, don't list all the details, not yet," she pleaded. "For the moment I don't want information, I want enchantment."

"Hmmmm!" said Don José, reining in his horse.

Just as Jeanne was about to express her delight, a noisy swarm of black children and dogs burst from the house and advanced on the riders, crowding around them, laughing and barking.

"Clearly we are not unwelcome," observed Don José as he urged the horses forward with his clicking tongue.

They hadn't gone more than a few steps when Humbert de Saint Méry appeared in the doorway with a mulatto woman on either side of him. The marquis ambled across the shaded veranda into the sunlight. The women both had on red skirts and men's shirts, with the sleeves cut off at the elbows and shabby, frayed open collars.

The homestead's owner, bare-chested and bare-legged, wore a pair of striped cotton knee-length shorts, a slave's Sunday outfit. His head was well covered with a long mane of faded blond hair, and his cheeks were bristling with a week-old beard.

"I've brought my friend Mademoiselle Beauchamps to see you," Don José said to him as he slid out of the saddle in front of the trio.

Saint Méry bowed slightly and gestured toward the shady veranda.

The two visitors found themselves seated on rough wicker chairs. The pair of colored women had vanished into the house on a sign from Saint Méry, who looked at Jeanne and spoke for the first time.

"Pardon my outfit, mademoiselle. I wasn't expecting company. If you'll excuse me a moment, I'll go put on a shirt. The ladies of Allspice insist that I mind my manners." He walked to the door and turned, saying, "I won't be long."

Jeanne leaned over to Don José. "I was afraid we'd find him drunk," she whispered. "Thank God he isn't. We did well to arrive before midday."

"Saint Méry may prove a worthier man than his reputation. The French settlers here can't stomach his way of life and probably criticize him far more than he deserves. I know for a fact that he gets hopelessly drunk only on Saturday nights. He told me so the first time we met, so I'd be sure not to bring you then."

"I can't believe a drunkard can get drunk only once a week," Jeanne whispered.

"*Amiga*, how much do you know about heavy drinkers? You've never hung around the Café Pulperia. No two behave alike," observed Don José. "Shhh, now! Never speak of rope in the house of a man who's been hanged."

They studied their surroundings in silence. Finally Jeanne said, "This veranda is far lovelier than the one at Mongoust."

Don José screwed up his nose at the untidy clutter piled here and there—the dirty wall, the spiderwebs drifting down from the beams. "I think you must be seeing yesterday's reality," he commented dryly.

"No, tomorrow's," she replied.

Their conversation was interrupted by the reappearance of the two mulattos.

The colored women had changed into clean, faded flower-print dresses and had wound madras turbans around their heads. The younger one brought a tray with three porcelain teacups and three small silver spoons. The older woman carried a ceramic teapot whose ugliness she did her best to cover with her big hands.

"Is tea," announced the older woman. "If you no want, you like sun juice?"

"Sun juice is our orange syrup mixed with mountain water," Saint Méry explained as he came out of the doorway. "Tea, sun juice, or homemade arrack. That's all I can offer you."

Jeanne studied the face of her host. He had tied back his hair at the neck, and shaved, nicking one cheek in the process. His beardless face made him look younger but also revealed a weak chin and puffiness around the eyes.

"Some tea will do nicely," Jeanne said, smiling at the old mulatto.

"Go put some on, Nanny, then fix us a lunch," Saint Méry ordered.

"Our picnic follows us by mule," Don José interrupted. "Of course, my borrowed slave is fooling around somewhere along the way."

"Yes, the moment you let them loose, slaves find ways to enjoy themselves," said Saint Méry. "They know how to waste time. And what makes life more enjoyable than wasting time?"

They drank their tea and chatted.

Eventually, Saint Méry roused himself, thrusting out his sunken chest. "Would you like to see the house first, or the property?" he asked.

They entered the house.

* * * *

On the spacious ground floor there were four large rooms, an entrance hall, and three other rooms. Saint Méry presented the two largest as the company room and the dining room. Both seemed very dark and gloomy because the windows had been boarded. The dining room, with its carpet of rush matting, must have served as sleeping quarters for the slaves, because a heavy odor hung in the clammy air and an assortment of personal belongings littered every corner.

By comparison, the company room seemed quite civilized. Its fabric-covered paneling was still intact here and there. A handsome re-minder of stylish yesterdays, an English crystal chandelier with six empty candle sockets hung from the ceiling. A couch and chairs, with their stuffing streaming out, were piled one on top of the other in a corner of the room, under a silken gray tent of spiderwebs. Cling-ing to the wall in a circle of sunlight, a stunning green and azure lizard lay motionless.

"The kitchens are this way," said Saint Méry, guiding them to a door that led to the back of the house.

Two small, square outbuildings with attics and pandanus-thatched roofs stood facing each other at opposite ends of the house, one a working kitchen, the other a storage room for broken furniture, gar-den tools, and assorted homeless objects.

"There's a bit of everything in there," Saint Méry sighed.

"Lots good stuff!" Nanny declared impudently.

"Good stuff cost money," said the younger mulatto supportively. Saint Méry called her Zoe.

"Go on, you two, leave us alone. Off to the kitchen with you and make us some lunch!" ordered Saint Méry.

The women didn't budge. "Mamzelle, now you must go see," said Zoe, pointing upstairs.

"Enough! I told you two to clear out!" Saint Méry snapped. The sudden fit of temper must have been so unfamiliar that it frightened Nanny, who lumbered off moaning to herself.

"Must take Mamzelle up," Zoe repeated, staring boldly at her master.

"Zoe, get out of here before I really get angry!" Saint Méry warned her, this time in a hushed, controlled voice that Zoe must have known pretty well, as it made her retreat.

Saint Méry turned back to Jeanne. "If you're not too tired, would you like a tour of the grounds? After lunch it will be too warm." Jeanne had the impression that he was not too eager to show her the upstairs.

"You take the horses," advised Don José. "I made the tour the other day. I'll wait for you on the veranda, sipping sun juice."

* * * *

After riding lazily along winding trails for a good half hour, Saint Méry brought them to the edge of a pond and dismounted. "How about stopping here?"

Jeanne slid out of the saddle without waiting for help. "What a picturesque spot this is," she said. "I love it."

"It's the best place I can show you, because it seems to withstand every hurricane and hasn't suffered too much from neglect. But the rest of the property . . ."

"You've told me all about it."

He smiled. It was always the same ready, gentle, slightly ironic smile that spread to his eyes. "Yes," he said. "Though I sometimes lose my memory, I'm the best witness to better days at Allspice. To resurrect them, you'll have to buy me along with the house!"

The warm air of midday buzzed and danced and shimmered with insects. Jeanne had never seen so many dragonflies. Along the pond at Allspice the dragonflies were superb. Their elongated purple bodies and jewellike heads, red as rubies, glittered in the sunlight. Jeanne was ecstatic.

"I've never seen such glorious dragonflies!"

At that moment one of them pounced on a ravishing black butterfly with pale blue markings, seized it, crushed it, and dragged it off. "Oh dear!" cried Jeanne. "That butterfly was so lovely too."

"Another will come along," Saint Méry promised her. "Allspice is an endless source of bounty. No matter what you kill here, there's always another butterfly, another deer, hare, or fish for tomorrow's dinner."

She tried to read something more in Saint Méry's eyes, but found only a vapid blue haze. "Monsieur de Saint Méry," she addressed him softly, "why do you want to sell Allspice?"

This time the blue eyes focused on Jeanne. "It's you who wish to buy the place."

"Does that mean you're willing to sell?"

"Yes, if you can get the East India Company to agree. What I mean is, if you can arrange to pay me personally what you ought to be paying the Company, without the Company claiming the property or my money."

Jeanne softened her voice even more. "You've explained to me quite clearly how I should go about buying Allspice. What you haven't explained is why you're willing to sell it."

"It's not every day I meet someone like you, who is clever enough to make me rich illegally yet safely."

"And you want to be rich?"

"Not in the least. But I want even less to see myself driven out of my own house one day. You never know. I was familiar with the East India Company, but I've no idea what kind of a landlord the king will be."

"I understand," said Jeanne. "But if Allspice is sold, where will you go?"

Saint Méry's right hand motioned vaguely, like a leaf in the wind. "I'll have money. Money can provide lodging."

"Will you go back to France?"

He seemed surprised. "France? Why there? I was born here. Not at Allspice, but on the island. Didn't you know that?"

"Yes, but I supposed . . ."

Saint Méry shook his head. "My parents died. My sisters . . . I had five little sisters. The youngest is over there." He tilted his chin to indicate the islet in the middle of the pond. After a silence, he went on. "The cyclone took a terrible toll."

"What happened to your other sisters?"

"The eldest died in childbirth. The prettiest decided to enjoy life, despite her poverty. The other two lead quiet lives tucked away in the Touraine countryside, housed by a well-meaning aunt. They are still waiting for me to provide their dowries—when I've revived the plantation!"

"I understand," said Jeanne a second time.

This peek into Saint Méry's private life reassured her. He needed the money to marry off his sisters. Jeanne felt almost absolved of the sin of coveting Allspice.

"Have you no wish to see France, to visit Paris?" she asked.

"I know Paris already. I was sent to school in France when I was eleven. At that time my family was well off. All prosperous settlers sent their sons to France as soon as they were old enough to appreciate the Negresses here."

With a wry smile he concluded, "Luckily, when the sons returned from abroad, the lovely Negresses were still lovely."

"And in Paris, were you bored to death?"

"Paris is beautiful and lively. But a city without black faces . . . I can't see how anyone can live in a city without blacks, a country without blacks, a house without blacks. Half of myself was missing."

Seeing the look of wonder on Jeanne's face, Saint Méry tried to explain. "We Creoles must have suckled the need for a black presence along with our nurses' milk."

"What will you do with Nanny and Zoe? Would you let me have them?"

"I don't think they'd leave me." He fell silent and seemed to be thinking. "I'm not even certain that the men would go. Like all Malagasies, they dream of their big island, and mine have been dreaming for years. You see, even the slaves who hate us don't hate us absolutely, and to complicate our lives, some of them are even fond of us."

"If I ever owned slaves, I'd like so much for them to be fond of me," said Jeanne eagerly.

"You stand a good chance," said Saint Méry. "There's an endearing note in your voice."

She blushed, and it seemed to intimidate him. There was a long silence. A caterpillar dropped out of a eucalpytus into Jeanne's hair, and Saint Méry got up to remove it. Instead of sitting down again, he reached out both hands to her. "Suppose I show you the upstairs now?" he offered.

* * * *

Don José felt he should let them go up alone.

Six doors, evenly spaced, opened on the long, deserted corridor. Saint Méry opened the first. "My bedroom," he said.

"Oh, please don't trouble yourself," Jeanne protested, backing away. "I'll be happy to see the others."

Saint Méry opened the second, third, and fourth doors. "My sisters' rooms. Please go in."

Though each room was silent and empty, Jeanne felt a strong sense of the past. Only the faded, moth-eaten cotton paneling with its bluebird motif remained.

"Each room has its own water closet," said Saint Méry.

Jeanne glanced rapidly into one water closet and went on to the next two rooms.

In his mother's room, where the silk-covered panels patterned with crimson peonies hung in shreds on the walls, stood a handsome lemonwood wardrobe, the work of a local artisan. Saint Méry opened it to display the fine arrangement of shelves and drawers as Jeanne stood transfixed, imagining neatly folded piles of linens and laces, the intimate secrets of Allspice's vanished mistress.

"I seem to have a talent for invoking ghosts from my mother's wardrobe, like a magician producing rabbits out of his hat!" said Saint Méry with a smile.

"Just about," she agreed, smiling in turn. "Your house rings of the past. It begs to be held close to the ear like a seashell."

"I hope you have time to do that one day," he said after a marked pause. Shutting the wardrobe doors, he leaned back against them, facing his guest, and said something that astounded her. "I hope you succeed in taking Allspice from me."

Her eyes misted over.

"A man can't turn a house into a home," Saint Méry went on. "With a man in charge, a house soon comes to look like a dockside café."

CHAPTER 21

t had rained earlier, but now the moon shone brightly. A nocturnal, fairylike rainbow had formed that must have spanned the entire harbor of Port Louis. Jeanne gazed thoughtfully at the segment perched over the garden. "I'll never tire of the night skies in this country," she sighed.

"Too bad," Don José sighed in return.

Leaning on the Spaniard's arm, Jeanne said, "Don José, don't side with Monsieur Aubriot against me. I really want to settle on this island. Allspice is such a beautiful place. You can sit on a hilltop there and look out to sea. Don José, I'll never live anywhere that doesn't have a view of the sea."

With ill-concealed impatience, Don José replied firmly, "Oh yes, I can see it all, Jeanne climbing the hills morning and night, scanning the horizon with her telescope until one day the long-awaited sail appears. What happens next, though, is a mystery to me. You'll have to prepare Aubriot for the shock of meeting your husband when he suddenly surges up out of the waves! And please don't ask me to stick around for their meeting. I'll be far away, nursing my shame at having failed to protect you from yourself. If my friend Vincent asks me why I participated in this fraud, I shall simply bare my chest to his dagger and die the death I truly deserve. Without grace."

"Don José, I . . ."

"Jeannette, I feel terrible," he interrupted her. "I love Vincent, I respect Aubriot, I am very fond of you, and I have betrayed you all."

"Don José, let me try to explain."

"Explain?" he burst out. "Can an unfaithful woman ever explain her infidelity? A man does his best to hide it."

"That's because an unfaithful man is truly unfaithful," Jeanne replied.

Don José stared at her, uncomprehending. "I would be curious to hear you elaborate on that," he said.

Jeanne sighed and murmured, "It's difficult." After a moment's pause, she said, "A man hardly changes at all from one mistress to the next. But Philibert's Jeanne is not Vincent's Jeanne. That's what I mean. Do you understand?"

"I'm trying," he answered. "Really, I'm trying, Jeannette, but try as I may, your behavior shocks me."

She gave a little shrug of discouragement. "I might have expected it," she said sadly. "I'm probably the only person who can understand that I'm deceiving neither the botanist nor the chevalier."

"You are indeed! And I fear you'll not be able to make either of them understand it!"

On the moonlit beach he stopped and took both her hands in his. "Jeannette," he said eloquently. "Little sister mine, so pretty, so gentle and tender, so honest and sincere, is it possible that you, who were meant for great happiness, have willingly chosen to live between two lies?"

He kissed her gently on the forehead and sighed. "What a predicament!"

Then his manly good sense overcame his emotion and he asked, "All the same, if you don't call it a lie, what do you call the extreme care you've taken to keep Aubriot ignorant of your life with Vincent?"

She replied flatly, "I call it modesty."

"Modesty," Don José repeated. "*Por qué no?* I guess I prefer that word too. But it doesn't solve a thing. Sooner or later you're going to have to figure a way out."

As they strolled past the French doors of the governor's reception rooms, they noticed Aubriot among the guests. The doctor was talking animatedly with two Creoles, Messrs. de Cossigny and de Céré, avid botanists whom he had already befriended. Jeanne smiled to see Philibert's elegant dress suit of ribbed black velvet. She herself had picked out that fine-ribbed cloth.

"Don't you think Aubriot looks very handsome in his new suit?" she asked Don José excitedly. "He has never looked so well. The black velvet makes him look dignified, but not too stern. And, of course, I like to wear light-colored evening gowns, white or rose or peach, and when I'm standing next to that soft black texture, it does wonders for me."

Darting a sly glance at her, Don José commented airily, "I don't doubt it. This evening Aubriot blends in admirably with your dress. You were wise to bring him along to the dinner."

"Oh, come now!" she said, offended.

He glanced at her once more, deliberately, and asked, "Jeannette, do you still love that man?"

" 'That man.' What a way to put it! You talk as if Aubriot were just an ordinary man I fell in love with yesterday."

"So you *still* love him," said Don José after a pause. "Emilie claims that you love him as much as ever. And that you love your corsair no less. Emilie feels that you'd be perfectly happy with both, if you could keep them from killing each other!"

"Please don't think I'm fickle," she pleaded gently.

"Certainly not!" he exclaimed. "When a fish set down between two cats dreams that things can go on that way, it's not fickleness, it's sheer innocence!"

"Well said, Don José, that's exactly it. I am innocent of what happens to me," she declared gravely.

"So be it, Jeannette. For the moment, I declare you innocent. And in the future, may God have mercy on you!" He heaved a sigh of resignation. "With a woman around, who needs a mule?" he muttered to himself.

She pressed his arm. "Please listen to me. A sailor's wife evokes either a pleasant yearning in his heart or instant forgetfulness. I learned that at sea. I want to be the object of Vincent's yearning. And I want to beckon to him from a house perfumed with frangipani, surrounded by eternal summer and ever-blooming flowers and fruits."

She paused and frowned as the fond memory of Pauline de Vaux-Jailloux's cheerful country house came back to her. Tossing her head to rid herself of the thought, she said, "I want to be an object of yearning that is powerful enough to destroy all others before it."

"That doesn't astonish me," said Don José. "A woman in love is convinced that love entitles her to every privilege, even the cruelest. All right, *amiga*, I surrender. Have your Allspice and make it a paradise for your chevalier." Then he added sourly, "I hope Emilie won't like it too much."

"Why do you say that?"

"Because I love my villa. I love the pampas with their herds of horses ten sous a head. I love roast ribs of beef. I love to hear Spanish spoken. I love the Café Pulperia, sunsets along the Rio de La Plata, maté, good cigars, bad Chilean wine, guitars, dancing . . ."

"And you also love Emilie, who doesn't come with all the rest," Jeanne cut in. "So don't complain about the contradictions in me when you've got your own."

"Yes, I do, after all." Laughing at himself, he asked, "Do you know what we say about such things?"

"A proverb, surely," said Jeanne.

"Woman is God's way of arranging a beautiful disaster to befall each man."

* * * *

Before rejoining the other guests, Jeanne took off her shawl and tossed it over the shoulders of Adele, who already was wearing Emilie's.

Don José had managed to inveigle the Creole mistress of Mongoust into selling her best-looking slave woman, Adele, for a mammoth price. The beautiful Adele made a very decorative attendant for Emilie and Jeanne. She stuck to them like a glove, keeping her eye on their shawls and makeup boxes.

Jeanne smiled to see Adele shoulder the shawl without even turning around. She stood in the doorway to the reception hall, her arms and feet motionless, her rump wiggling, her lips parted in a happy grin as she took in the spectacle of M. Desforges-Boucher's distinguished guests.

Unconsciously, Jeanne followed Adele's gaze to a corner of the room where she saw Dr. Aubriot flirting with Mme. Manon, who looked as tempting as a plump praline in her pink gown. The judge's merry widow had mastered the art of laughing so as to make her bosom heave.

That's the limit! He's ready to flirt with the first petticoat that comes along. Her jealousy reached such a pitch that it infected Adele, who turned to look at what was bothering Jeanne, and chuckled.

"Eyes of Mamzelle not like pins, like scorpions! M'am Manon win a sick man. Is good! She need Massa Dotta."

"Stupid girl!" Jeanne hissed, furious at having her mind read. "Do you imagine that the doctor pays any attention to your old mistress's flattery?"

"Age no count," Adele said with a grin, only too happy to pour oil on the fire. "May say you can make good soup in old pot."

* * * *

Saint Méry wanted sixty thousand pounds for Allspice. It was little enough. Land values had risen astronomically, and Allspice covered three thousand seven hundred acres. Humbert de Saint Méry was visibly taken by the prospective buyer. By trying to sell her what he didn't own, he, in all honesty, intended merely to cheat his creditors. But to accomplish the purchase, the trio had to put their heads together and come up with a plan of action.

The conspirators wisely decided not to negotiate the affair before the arrival of Intendant Pierre Poivre, whom Jeanne believed she could influence. But summer turned to fall and fall to winter, and by mid-July, M. Poivre still had not appeared. The fate of Poivre's ship, the *Dauphin*, was beginning to prey on everyone's mind when, on July 14, 1767, the governor appointed by Louis XV landed at Port Louis and reported that the good ship *Dauphin* was not far behind.

The islanders thought it rather odd that the new governor and his intendant had chosen to travel separately, since they were supposed to govern jointly. No one could possibly have guessed that from the moment they met at Lorient, the pair couldn't stand each other and had agreed to meet as little as possible.

And therefore the governor set foot on his new turf in excellent humor because his intendant was nowhere in sight. The welcome celebration would be for him alone!

The crowds gathered, curious, noisy, and cheering. There was a twenty-one-gun salute, flags on every ship in the harbor, drums beating, and the garrison, polished and gleaming, turned out in double ranks, marching from the dock straight up to the church, where a *Te Deum* was sung.

On the following day the island's new master presided over a parade of civilian and military personnel. They came to present their respects, and seemed delighted by the dinner and ball given that evening by M. Desforges-Boucher. Grinning from ear to ear, he acknowledged the bows and smiles of the island's most distinguished citizens and their ladies. He lent an ear to reports of future business deals requiring the benevolent and practiced eye of a well-informed governor. Everyone hoped that he would be more concerned with the colony's "real" interests than M. Desforges-Boucher had been.

The governor was much decorated. A military man to the core. He was honorable, courageous, and devoted to his king. He was respectful of authority, and therefore intolerant of any opinion that went against his own. He had a passion for bureaucratic order and documents in triplicate, and clung tenaciously to his private notions of right and wrong. He stood as straight as a ramrod, had a jaw like the prow of a ship, always carried a whip, and possessed a harsh tongue.

All the complaints about my easygoing rule will sound like compliments now that a real tyrant is among us, thought Desforges-Boucher. He told his secretary to pack up, feeling a sudden urge to return to his estate on l'Isle de Bourbon where he planned to retire.

He stopped by to see Dr. Aubriot and advised him to stay at Mongoust rather than be treated discourteously by the new tenant.

Aubriot stiffened. "Sir, I am the king's naturalist and responsible to the intendant of these islands!"

Desforges-Boucher waved aside the remark with a careless flick of the wrist. "Sir, the intendant hasn't arrived yet. My successor, for all his medals, isn't likely to care a fig about plant collecting. Madame Manon has offered many times to put you up. She is like a meringue, and known to be feathery light. But such a reputation is not unbecoming to a Creole, and . . ."

In the adjoining room where she sat inscribing plant names, Jeanne didn't wait to hear more. She set down her pen and left the room quietly to seek out the terrible M. Dumas.

She had trouble getting to see him. But once she was inside his office it was even harder to get out again! For the charming Mlle. Beauchamps inspired the governor with an urgent, unsuspected appreciation of botany. Jeanne left his office smiling. Dr. Aubriot would not have to move in with Mme. Manon.

"Bravo," Aubriot retorted coldly on being so informed.

Jeanne observed him, hunched over his magnifying glass, examining a splendid butterfly, *Vanessa radama.*

In her most beguiling voice she said, "Monsieur Dumas seemed quite aware of the importance of your work and admires you very much."

The scholar raised his head. "Please, I beg you," he began, eyeing her more severely than usual, "don't add charity to your activities as courtesan."

"Courtesan, oh no!" she exclaimed, cruelly offended.

"I always try to use the correct word, you know," he said, returning to his butterfly. "What else can I call a lady courtier who goes off to curtsy and roll her eyes at the king in hopes of obtaining favors?"

"You know very well, sir, that a female courtier is not the same as a courtesan," she retorted vehemently.

Aubriot smiled wanly. "Courtesans have a certain charm," he said. "Speaking of charm, don't use all yours up on the governor. Keep some for his intendant, who's the one I must rely on."

* * * *

The *Dauphin* was sighted at daybreak a month later. The whole town turned out to celebrate. Governor Dumas promptly put a damper on the festivities, which he considered an excessive display for a subordinate. But he couldn't stop the crowds from gathering at the dock. It was one of their favorite pastimes. All the poor whites from town, the soldiers, the Negresses in flowered skirts and colorful madras turbans, congregated on the wharf.

M. Poivre came ashore in a flurry of public celebration.

Clutching and unclutching her hands, Emilie drew closer to Jeanne. "I'm going in," she murmured. "I shouldn't have come. I don't like gaping crowds."

Jeanne looked at her in surprise. "It's an official reception," she said. "Everybody is here. Aren't you anxious to—"

"No!" Emilie interrupted nervously. "I'll attend mass, but I'm not going to greet Poivre. He's never laid eyes on me. The idea of finding myself face to face again with Françoise Robin—with Madame Poivre—is more than I can bear. The Robin girls used to attend mass in Neuville."

Jeanne took her friend by the arm. "Don't run away, Emilie. Why should you? You can't avoid Madame Poivre forever. The governor is a bachelor, so Françoise will be the island's first lady."

"I know that," Emilie replied. "But I prefer not to have to answer to her astonished looks. You visit her first, Jeannette. Tell her . . . tell her whatever you like. Just make sure she understands that my name here is Doña Emilia, no more, no less."

"I remember Françoise Robin as a shy, sweet, reserved young girl," said Jeanne. "Why should she go out of her way to betray or humiliate you?"

"I don't think she would," said Emilie. "I just don't feel like seeing her. She belongs to my . . . past. I don't want to hear her talk about Neuville, but I'm not sure I can tell her that."

Her last sentence ended in a whisper. Feeling Jeanne's hand on her arm, she took a deep breath and murmured rapidly but resolutely—as if the noise of the crowd allowed her to make a shameful, barely audible confession—"Jeannette, it's no easier for me to be both Dame Emilie and Doña Emilia than it is for you to love two men at the same time."

There was a movement in the crowd as an officer called for attention. Emilie disengaged her arm from Jeanne's.

"I shall ask Don José to escort me to the Intendancy. I'll wait for you there."

* * * *

The mail was unloaded and distributed late that afternoon.

Seated side by side on rattan chairs, they gazed silently at the sheets of writing paper spread out before them on the table. There were three handwritings, Mme. de Bouhey's, Marie's, and Dame Charlotte's.

"I can't help feeling a bit happy, even if it isn't nice. Marie, dear sweet Marie. Marie," Jeanne said, smiling faintly through her tears.

"I still can't believe it," Emilie said, picking up Marie's letter.

"I found you in the backwoods of La Plata and here you are with me in l'Ile de France. That's unbelievable too!" said Jeanne. "No more unbelievable than if Marie comes to join us. In my girlhood dreams of the Indies, could there have been strength enough to propel all three of us here together?"

Emilie put Marie's letter back on the table, resting her hand on it like a paperweight. "I need to actually touch the words to believe them. Otherwise, I'm afraid it will all go up in smoke."

Marie was coming to Port Louis with her brother, John, and her daughter, Virginia!

Lieutenant Philippe Chabaud de Jasseron was dead. In Metz, where he was garrisoned, Marie's husband had dueled with another lieutenant for the love of a flower seller. Having drunk more than his opponent that evening, Jasseron never stood a chance. That had taken place in October of the previous year, after Jeanne sailed away on her great adventure. The grieving, humiliated widow had packed up her daughter and herself, left Autun, and gone to her mother's at Rupert. After a time the Chabaud de Jasserons grew impatient to see their daughter-in-law and their son's only child. They threatened to take the matter to court, demanding guardianship of Virginia and control over her mother's property. At that point Mme. de Rupert began to marshal her allies in high places. To do so, from a country house in Dombes, was not easy. Marie was very troubled by her situation. The idea of escaping the country was suggested by her Aunt Saint-Girod.

In Lyons, Countess Saint-Girod had heard Pierre Poivre talk enthusiastically about his appointment to l'Ile de France and the neighboring island of Bourbon. He planned to put his little empire on the map. The central problem facing any administrator of those islands was how to increase the population. So Poivre had begun at once to advertise the charms of these golden tropical isles in the salons of Lyons. He hoped to attract recruits and some good company for himself. Geneviève de Saint-Girod had carried his enthusiasm back to Rupert.

To Marie, desperate to get away from her in-laws, Pierre Poivre's words were music to her ears. At first Mme. de Rupert thought her daughter's idea was quite insane. But she yielded when her son John, an infantry lieutenant, assured her that his colonel could arrange to have him transferred to the garrison at Port Louis. Marie could travel under her brother's protection.

Half the young woman's modest fortune had already gone to pay her husband's debts, and here was M. Poivre promising a pot of gold to prospective settlers in the isles of bliss. One thing at least was certain—Marie's in-laws would not be able to pressure her to remain in France, if she, a Frenchwoman of good birth and character, agreed formally to settle in the colony destined to become the jewel of France's "highway" across the Indian Ocean.

Marie's dream began to materialize when the *Dauphin* finally left Lorient. Marie would be sailing from that very port on April 14 with her daughter, a maidservant, and her brother's regiment. The good ship *Espérance* was scheduled to arrive at Port Louis in mid-August, God and the winds willing.

"Marie will be here for the Saint Louis Ball," said Emilie. "Pinch me, Jeannette! How good it will be to hear Marie's laugh! How old is Virginia?"

"Let's see now." Jeanne began counting on her fingers. "She must be almost two years old. If she looks like her mother, she'll be awfully cute."

"I hope Paul will fall in love with her and behave like a big brother," said Emilie. "It will be better for him than teasing his slave boy."

Jeanne studied her friend's face. "Do you think Don José will be willing to stay here long enough for Paul to become fond of a little sister?"

Emilie quivered. "I don't intend to leave right away for La Plata," she declared coldly.

Jeanne repeated her question. "But will Don José be willing?"

"I shall insist on it," she replied.

Suddenly, Emilie grew very animated and the words tumbled out of her mouth. "I'm accountable to no man, only to God! I've done nothing wrong. My only sins are in the eyes of God. I left Gaillon, but I'm not to blame if his conversation put me to sleep. I don't want to go back and shut myself up in Don José's villa. It's not my fault if Spanish society bores me to tears. Would you, Jeanne, be willing to live like a recluse behind closed blinds in a land where women have nothing to do and no power? Where men believe that the ideal couple consists of a man and his horse?"

Jeanne burst out laughing.

"Don't laugh. You *must* take me seriously," said Emilie. "The ladies of La Plata are so spineless, they allow their husbands and lovers to do without them most of the time. They seem willing to lead useless, humble lives, unaware that humility is a woman's last resort, not her chosen position. Living like that makes you overweight and dull-minded."

"But you do care for Don José, though you deny it," Jeanne said, smiling.

"That's because I'm still trying to Frenchify him just a little. Don't you think that at certain times Don José deserves to be French?"

"So you've decided that for his own good Don José should settle part-time in l'Ile de France?" Jeanne concluded in a mocking voice.

"Yes," Emilie replied. Putting her arms around Jeanne's neck, she laid her red curls on her friend's shoulder. "Don't tell me you thought I would agree to go back into exile when I've just discovered a breath of France . . . and you . . . and now Marie!"

"No, I didn't imagine you would," said Jeanne. "But I'm very fond of Don José and I wish you loved him."

"Ah!" Emilie sighed. "Sometimes I wish I knew how to be more loving. Anyway, Adele, that little minx, told me that the island's climate is good for love."

They chuckled together over Adele's comment. Then Emilie glanced at the table. "Let's reread the letters," she said with relish. "First the one from Dame Charlotte."

Tears filled both their eyes as they read . . .

> Who knows, Jeannette, in your travels you may just happen to run into my Emilie. She must be somewhere! In this wide world of ours, it seems that ships meet more often than landsmen imagine. And now that I know you're on the seas, I pray that your paths will cross. I pray so loud in the ears of God that surely, to have peace, He will answer my prayers!

The former canoness clutched the letter from her godmother in both hands. "Neuville," she murmured with unwonted affection in her voice, "Neuville. When I look back on it, after my rustic affair with Gaillon, after two long years on the pampas with a gentleman smuggler, Neuville seems like a beautiful fairy tale!"

Emilie fell to weeping on Jeanne's shoulder.

"Dear heart, you really need something to keep your mind occupied," said Jeanne, rocking her gently. "I hope Monsieur Poivre will get down to business quickly."

CHAPTER 22

ierre Poivre was sick and shivering with fever when he landed, but he set to work immediately. That was the way he operated. Since the intendant began to govern in one fashion while the governor had already begun in another, the result was civil war.

How foolish of the Ministry of Naval and Colonial Affairs to imagine that two such independent and imposing personalities could rule jointly.

To Governor Dumas, who was vain, authoritarian, intransigent, stubborn, rough, loquacious, hot-tempered, and abrasive, the ministry had assigned a deputy who was altogether agreeable, open-minded, precise, thoughtful, and conciliatory. Moreover, the two men had different goals. Dumas, a militarist, meant to turn l'Ile de France into a fortress, a naval base for his country in time of war. To the governor, the archipelago was simply an armed outpost against England's Indian empire. Haunted by fears of an English invasion, all Dumas could think of was drilling his black and white regiments on the parade ground.

Poivre, on the other hand, an avowed lover of nature, partial to shared community labor, envisioned l'Ile de France as a great spice garden. He had a dream that one day Port Louis would become the rival of Batavia on the Dutch island of Java. He intended to make the island a great agricultural preserve and a prosperous shipping center, winning over its black and white inhabitants to the tranquil joys of farming.

What made the prospect of cooperation between the two men even more unlikely were their divergent attitudes toward slavery.

Poivre opposed slavery in principle, sanctioning it only as a temporary means of developing an underpopulated area. He was determined that, under his rule, the slaves would be treated humanely.

Dumas considered himself an expert on slavery, having been second-in-command during the upheavals in Santo Domingo. To him, slaves were the dregs of humanity, fit only to be dominated, whipped, and strung up.

* * * *

Indeed, things moved forward at a merry clip. Planters and farmers alike wanted solid confirmation of their land titles. A land board was quickly constituted, its primary function to preserve the claims of owners who had fallen into debt to overseas investors through no fault of their own.

On August 11 the property known as Allspice, with ill-defined boundaries, was officially attributed to the Marquis Humbert de Saint Méry under conditions acknowledging his past record of inept management. He was to receive a hundred thousand livres cash and was given a month to resell the property to a French buyer pledged to reside there and raise spices. The buyer had to be approved by the intendant and was required to furnish proof of financial means adequate to undertake such an agreement.

Since only one individual happened to be in a position to fulfill those terms, on August 13, 1767, at eleven o'clock in the morning, the property known as Allspice passed from the hands of Saint Méry to Mademoiselle Jeanne Marie Antonine Beauchamps, aged twenty, Catholic, a native of Saint-Jean-de-Losne in the province of Burgundy.

The buyer, an orphan, declared under oath and before witnesses that she was in sole possession of her fortune and free to act in her own behalf.

"Free? Hmm, I wonder," Don José couldn't resist muttering to himself, discreetly as ever.

As they left the notary's office, Jeanne, radiantly happy, managed to whisper in Don José's ear, "I'll never believe that marriage is a prison. That notion was invented by a man." Then she fell back in step with Poivre, who had acted as her chief witness.

Aubriot had refused to come. He was in a vile mood for several reasons. First and foremost, Jeanne's growing independence of mind was becoming unbearable to him, though she had tried patiently to elicit some sign of his approval before she acted. On top of that, convinced as he was by Jeanne that Don José had put up the money for a dummy French buyer, he could not understand why the Spaniard had chosen to confide in Mademoiselle Beauchamps instead of himself. As the son of a notary, Aubriot was well aware that Allspice, under

Poivre's benevolent eye, represented a golden opportunity for financial gain in which he could share by lending his own name to the transaction. Annoyed and frustrated, he decided suddenly to classify the gardens at Monplaisir in the Pamplemousses district.

Jeanne felt crushed. "Now you want to set out in the opposite direction from Moka, where I have to travel to make my arrangements with Monsieur de Saint Méry."

"I'm not asking you to go with me," Aubriot cut in sharply. "I'll manage quite well with Polydor."

"Couldn't you wait a few days?"

"No. I want to make an inventory of Monplaisir while it's still untenanted. Dumas and Poivre are arguing over whose summer residence it's to be. I don't know which one will win, but I shouldn't care to have Dumas on my back."

"But—"

"No, Jeanne. I don't know what's bothering you. I'm old enough to travel alone. I did it before you were born. I will stay at Mongoust." Then he added cuttingly, "You know I'm always welcome there."

Jeanne barely managed to hold back her tears. "I'll join you for dinner at the Intendancy," she said, standing up. "First I'm going to see Emilie."

When Aubriot said nothing, she added to annoy him, "We have to discuss our gowns for the Saint Louis Ball. We want to look our best. And I want to shine because I'll be the mistress of Allspice."

"I wonder when you will learn that you don't have to capitalize the first letter of every Latin word," Aubriot snapped. "*Commelyna Benghalensis* has two capitals, that's correct, but really, now, for *Heliotropium hybridum,* one is quite sufficient, thank you!"

With a snort of anger she flounced out of the room and headed for the front door. There, on the threshold of Government House, the Provençal dashed up to her.

The young topman, who, after Vincent's capture by the Portuguese, had been assigned to accompany Jeanne back to Montevideo, had elected to stay on the island rather than return to France aboard the *Etoile des Mers.* Ever since their shared adventures, he had taken to following her about like a faithful watchdog, convinced that his chances of rejoining his captain improved greatly if he stayed close to the captain's wife. For her part, Jeanne was glad to have him around. One day or another on the waterfront, he was bound to hear something about the *Belle Vincente*. Whenever Jeanne saw him coming, her heart would leap with hope.

"Provençal!" she greeted him.

"Ah, Mam'selle Jeanne, we meet again," he said happily. "I was looking for you. I have a good piece of news!"

Her head reeled and she had to lean against a column on the veranda.

"What's wrong, mam'selle? You look so pale. It's not the news you're hoping for, but it's good news all the same. I met a rider from the north who told me he'd seen a small three-master rounding Mirror Cove at midmorning. It could be the ship *Espérance* you've been waiting for, with your friend Madame Marie."

"Marie," Jeanne murmured, and she rushed off to tell Emilie.

* * * *

Jeanne and Emilie, neither of whom had slept a wink during the night, turned up at the dock as soon as the sun rose. Out beyond the channel still, the ship rode astride bouncing swells.

"Good Lord!" Emilie kept muttering. "I hope Marie doesn't get seasick."

Around ten o'clock, Iassi brought Paul down to watch the passengers land. But at midday the island winds were still blowing so fiercely that Emilie sent her son home to lunch with Iassi. She and Jeanne stayed on and ate the fruit that Don José had brought them, refusing to take their eyes off the ship.

Finally, at two in the afternoon, Jeanne glimpsed the figure of Marie through her spyglass. "I think I can see her!" she exclaimed in a voice choked with emotion.

Emilie took a look in turn and confirmed that it was indeed Marie. "She's wearing black—of course. It's hard to recognize Marie in black. She always wore light colors. Mercy! Just watching her rise and fall with the waves sets my stomach afloat! The poor dear!"

"Quick! Let's see!" Jeanne urged, tugging at Emilie's sleeve.

"Wait . . ." Emilie said, then exclaimed, "Well, imagine that!"

"Imagine what?" Jeanne demanded. "Come on now, hand it over!"

"There, on Marie's left," said Emilie, still peering into the telescope. "Either I'm dreaming or it's Madame de Vaux-Jailloux!"

"You're dreaming!" Jeanne declared, snatching the telescope. Then she gasped.

"You see her too, don't you? I'm not imagining things?" Emilie

* 530 *

insisted excitedly. "It's really the mistress of Vaux, isn't it? Hand me the glass."

"Pauline? But why?" Jeanne repeated. She began to doubt that she had ever seen her.

"Perhaps Marie was afraid to make the trip alone," Emilie suggested. "And since Madame de Vaux-Jailloux is a close friend of her mother's . . ."

"But that's ridiculous, since her brother John is supposed to be on board," Jeanne protested.

They exchanged worried looks. Don José's voice startled them.

"From what I hear, ladies, the *Espérance* is delivering more company than you expected. Vaux-Jailloux—the name rings a distant bell. Is it by chance that Creole lady from Santo Domingo whom the Chevalier Vinc—" He stopped abruptly, furious at his blunder.

Jeanne spoke first, however, her words dripping with sarcasm. "Indeed, Don José, it's the very same lady Vincent must often have spoken of."

"Ay!" he moaned, and laughed awkwardly, "Well, then, let's wait. There's no use asking ourselves why and how. We'll simply have to wait."

"Indeed we will!" Emilie echoed mockingly.

* * * *

Less than three hours later, three little girls from Dombes, now grown women, were weeping and kissing each other's cheeks. They stood alone amid the hubbub of the noisy, bustling port. Their friends waited patiently, trying to keep from being jostled by the crowds.

At last Don José stepped forward and took Emilie and Jeanne by the arm, separating them from the new arrival. "I think that any more tears should wait for tonight," he suggested kindly. "Dame Marie must be tired."

"Marie," said Emilie, "this is Don José."

"Don José?" Marie repeated, her blue eyes focusing on the Spaniard.

"Don José de Murcia," said Emilie, completing the introduction.

"Dame Marie, we'll tell you all about us tonight or tomorrow morning. Right now you ought to rest . . . and your little girl too. Allow me to look after you."

"Oh yes," said Marie, suddenly reminded of her weariness. "Thank you, Don José."

Pauline and Jeanne found themselves face to face, staring mutely into each other's eyes. Pauline was smiling. And she answered Jeanne's unspoken question.

"I did everything I could to encourage Marie's departure. By marrying, she lost a good part of her fortune. I know that being one of the early settlers on a tropical island can mean prosperity. I want her to plant sugar cane. I'll stay as long as it takes to get the project going."

Pauline's voice, which Jeanne hadn't heard since the day she left Charmont, moved her nearly to tears. The Creole spoke in hushed tones, for Jeanne's ears alone. Her sensual drawl suddenly brought back memories of cozy afternoons by the fire in the salon at Vaux.

In a burst of warm feeling, Jeanne stretched out both hands to Pauline. "I'm happy that you've come," she said, her voice choked with emotion.

"Really?" said Pauline, cocking her head a bit to one side.

Don José took command of the little group. "You, Iassi, take the child. Her nurse looks exhausted. Provençal, you take the toilet cases."

"Mama," Paul burst out, tugging at Emilie's sleeve, "is that Virginia?"

"Yes," Emilie replied, and added in response to Marie's tender, puzzled look, "Yes, that's my son."

"What a charming boy!" said Marie, moved to tears as she walked toward the boy. "What is his name?"

"Dame Marie, long stories are for later on," Don José repeated, taking her arm. "Lean on me. We haven't far to go. I found you a little house in town, with just two rooms, but . . ."

"My name is Paul," shouted the boy. "Is that Virginia?" he asked once more, pointing incredulously to the large white bundle nestled in Iassi's arms. After one last fit of sobbing in the launch, the baby had fallen sound asleep, unperturbed by the commotion around her.

"Yes, I've already told you it's Virginia," Emilie scolded. "Now hang onto Iassi's skirts so you don't get lost."

"But she's so little. She's only a baby. Much too little to play with me."

As she was about to follow Don José, Marie turned to Jeanne and said, "My brother will come looking for me . . ."

"Set your mind at ease, Dame Marie, we're not on the docks of Marseilles. Nobody ever gets lost in Port Louis," the Provençal reassured her. "When the regiment comes ashore, your brother will have plenty of guides to show him where you are staying."

Pauline walked off with her arm linked in Jeanne's. Despite the weariness etched on her face, she seemed to enjoy the bustling tropical waterfront.

"I can almost imagine I am back in Santo Domingo," she said contentedly. Just then they skirted a reeking sewer and she added, laughing, "Even the smells remind me of it!"

Emilie left Marie for a moment and approached Pauline, saying nervously, "It's hard to know where to turn to hear all the news at once! But I must admit," she said to Pauline, "you are the biggest surprise of the day!"

"I wouldn't say that," Pauline countered, darting a look at Paul, who trotted after Don José with his little slave boy at his heels.

Emilie looked stunned. "I'll leave it up to my friend Jeanne to explain all the surprises to you. Right now I only want to listen." And she hurried back to Marie's side.

"I'll tell you all about it tomorrow," Jeanne promised Pauline. "Emilie is right. For now, the news from France takes priority. Did you bring me a letter from my dear baroness? How is she?"

"I have a whole packet for you," said Pauline. "Madame de Bouhey is fine, in between fits of gout and bad temper."

Jeanne laughed. "I think gout and bad temper keep her in good health."

"She is as high-spirited as ever," Pauline confirmed. "She was delighted to see Marie and me leave for l'Ile de France. She'd probably send half the population of Dombes out here to provide you with company, even if it worked against her own interests. But I think you'll have all the company you want."

"What do you mean? Will there be more people coming to Port Louis?" Jeanne asked eagerly.

"Oh, aside from Giulio Pazevin, who'll be arriving soon with his young wife, Margot Delafaye—you must have heard about them already—I can't add much," Pauline replied. "Aboard the *Espérance*, though, at the captain's table there was talk about the Duke de Praslin's wanting to make Port Louis a popular spot. It seems"—Pauline paused a moment and drew a deep breath—"that the naval minister has asked several of our most successful privateers, who don't know what to do with themselves in peacetime, to base themselves here. It's said that the war with England may spread to the Gulf of Bengal and that the privateers will be in the front ranks."

At last, Jeanne had learned the truth. *Pauline didn't come just to help Marie plant sugar cane. She came hoping to see Vincent sooner than if she waited for him at Vaux.*

Pauline had every right to think that Jeanne had forgotten about Vincent, since Pauline had seen her go off to Paris, radiantly happy, with Philibert.

"It's a fact that the French in these parts still feel threatened by England, as if there had never been a peace treaty. There's nothing they'd like better than to have a few of our corsairs around," said Jeanne. "But since I've been on the island, I'm sorry to say I haven't seen the ghost of a privateer in Port Louis."

"Really? Not one?"

"Not a single one," said Jeanne.

They fell silent. Emilie rushed up again before they could continue the conversation.

"Now what are you two talking about?" she asked. "Thank heavens we're here at last and I can have both of you to myself!"

"Yes, thank heavens we've arrived," said Jeanne, annoyed by her friend's nervous activity. "The house is very small but clean, and we've put in new rugs and furniture. We'd only planned on Marie and her daughter, but there's room to bring in another bed . . ."

"Oh, don't trouble yourselves," Pauline interrupted. "A straw mat would do fine for the moment." Heaving a deep sigh, she leaned harder on Jeanne's arm and walked more slowly. "I didn't realize that I'd be so worn out."

Jeanne gazed at her and her eyes softened with pity. Pauline's face powder had coagulated, leaving a thin layer of tiny white beads on her cheeks and forehead. She looked rather pathetic, like a beautiful woman advancing in age, like a fragile flower sensitive to drafts. A flood of sympathy overtook Jeanne, the sympathy of a young rival in the prime of life.

Placing a firm grip on Pauline's arm, she whispered in her ear, "I haven't seen a single corsair in Port Louis, but at sea I met one who should be heading this way."

A little gasp from Pauline prompted her to add quickly, "He's stuck in Rio de Janeiro at the moment, in the viceroy's prison."

CHAPTER 23

he morning of the Saint Louis celebration began with a dawn dressed for a ball—a shimmering crêpe-de-Chine pink. In the town a noisy bustle arose, punctured by artillery fire and offshore salutes.

After high mass at nine o'clock, delegates in formal dress crossed the plaza bound for Government House to pay their respects to the king in the person of his governor.

The parade went on throughout the morning as more and more people arrived from all over the island. The island's jubilance was palpable. In Government House, His Excellency Governor Dumas was living out a divine moment. His cult of the Me was brought to a climax around midday when Intendant Poivre made a deep bow before him. With a charming smile the governor asked his intendant to entreat Mme. Poivre to act as his hostess at the dinner for the Knights of Saint Louis.

The Saint Louis Ball was the ball of balls for the year. Each of the governor's female guests aspired to enter history as queen for the evening, superbly bedecked.

Having disembarked just three days before the ball, the officers of the *Espérance* found themselves besieged. In a mad scramble, they sold everything stylish they owned for solid gold. The ladies of the island had all but leaped into their arms, adding their favors to their gold so as to diminish the buying power of their rivals.

The ball was to begin at five in the afternoon, and at four o'clock errand boys were still trotting after an ensign or a lieutenant from whom some last windfall was expected. Chinese and Malay porters ran around town offering a trinket, a fan, a ribbon, a shawl, or a necklace that they had slyly kept hidden until the last minute, hoping to get an astronomical price for satisfying an urgent desire.

For the last two days, rouge from Paris was fetching the fabulous price of ten crowns a jar!

"Françoise told me that her husband was outraged at the money wasted all over the island on this ball," said Emilie. "Since coins are scarce, he forbids their use on the domestic market, especially to pay for nonessentials. He is furious. He couldn't persuade the women that silk, pearls, and rouge are not essential items."

"How virtuous Monsieur Poivre has become," said Jeanne, not believing a word of it. "In Lyons, when he was making a speech before an audience filled with ladies, he never looked at the poorly dressed ones."

"Clothes make the man," said Emilie, "even though the intendant is obliged to preach economy. The Chinese are spreading stories all over town that not a single lady will spend less than twelve hundred pounds for her toilette."

"What! Twelve hundred pounds!" Jeanne repeated, alarmed. "They may put on a better appearance than we do! Let me have another look . . ."

Emilie grudgingly moved aside from the tiny mirror.

Jeanne looked at herself from all sides with the help of Iassi, who was holding a hand mirror. She was wearing her Brazilian-style wedding dress of white muslin trimmed with bobbin lace. "It's certainly very graceful, but next to a fine French gown, I'll look like a pauper. When I think what I left in Paris!"

"You're wearing a pound of gold around your neck!" commented Don José, who had just entered the room.

"I like these Indian slave chains," said Jeanne thoughtlessly. She blushed when she saw Iassi's face in the mirror.

Iassi corrected her gently, "Indian princess."

"It's vewy pwitty," said little Paul peremptorily.

"Very pretty," Don José repeated. "You're as pretty as a picture. Are you ready now? It's five o'clock. Monsieur Aubriot must be waiting for us at Government House."

Jeanne had come to dress at her friend's, where Iassi could attend her. The slave girl Adele had been lent to Marie and Pauline.

Emilie, wearing sea green, her favorite color, went to the window. "What a crowd outside!" she exclaimed. "Did you imagine there was so much society on the island? That parade of palanquins is every bit as impressive as the file of carriages in front of the Tuileries on Opera Ball night!"

Many of the litters had been painted and decorated. The porters wore culottes, loinclothes, and superb headdresses. Their skin shone as if waxed with boot polish. After alighting from their boxes, the silk-clad ladies and gentlemen strutted around in the sunshine before entering Government House. On their way through the crowds, the prettiest ladies drew compliments, some of which were very bold.

Jeanne was fascinated by the spectacle. Emilie had opened the window, filling the room with the festive clamor from all over town.

"When you come right down to it, this ugly town is beautiful. It's not a great town for houses, but it is for people. After all, a people town is certainly as good as a house town. I love living in a port in the Orient. Now, shall we go?"

* * * *

Humbert de Saint Méry bowed to Jeanne as if he had been waiting for her. The Robinson Crusoe of Allspice was a marquis, and lazy or drunk as he might be, a marquis has his place at a king's ball.

"Mademoiselle, if you are not in too great a hurry to dance, I would like to have a word or two with you."

Saint Méry guided her away from the flood of new arrivals to the end of the gallery. He wore a suit of faded beige silk drugget that fit him too snugly. But the lace cuffs and jabot were impeccable, and his wig was fashionably combed and powdered.

"You have made me so rich that I was able to afford a shirt, stockings, a wig, and even fine shoes," he said to her candidly, flashing the little smile she liked. "But I didn't have the courage to get myself a new suit."

"Oh! The one you have still looks nice on you," said Jeanne kindly.

"Only ladies who don't love me are indulgent," sighed Saint Méry. "Nanny and Zoe have treated me like an old scarecrow. But I didn't detain you to talk about fashion. I wanted to tell you that I took the liberty of buying you a slave."

"You did?" she said with a questioning look.

Saint Méry went on, "I bought him for you. But if my gesture or the man displeases you, you have only to tell me and I'll manage to get out of it."

"And why the devil would I refuse a black from you, when I need to find two hundred blacks as soon as I can?"

"He's a maroon. He's already run away twice."

Jeanne remained silent, waiting for an explanation.

"I didn't have the heart to let him be ruined. He's a superb speci-men of a man, a Senegambian. He must be about twenty-five. He's not a Creole, but he was brought to the island when he was very little. He belonged to my—to your—nearest neighbors, the La Barrées from Eaux Bonnes. Last year the La Barrée's son borrowed the black's virgin fiancée from him."

Saint Méry shrugged his shoulders. "*Droit de seigneur,* you know. Ulysses took it very badly. To make matters worse, the La Barrées sold the fiancée to get her away from their son. Rivière Noire is far from Moka. Ulysses ran away to see his Rosa. They caught him and cut off his right ear. So naturally he ran away again."

"And they caught him again?"

"Yes. He had taken Rosa away from Rivière Noire. She was seven months pregnant and ill. They got caught when they came to ask for help at the black camp of Plaisance. For Ulysses, that would have meant a lame leg to drag behind him for the rest of his life. I thought it would be a pity to hamstring such a fine fellow."

"I'm pleased that you saved him," said Jeanne. "Where is he?"

"At my . . . at your place. I mean . . . at Allspice. I had a hard time getting him, even for a thousand pounds. I understand the La Barrées. Not punishing runaways sets a very bad example. I let them whip him all they wanted. His skin will grow back."

He smiled dryly and added, "Nanny is putting herbs and oil on it. That's better than ashes and vinegar."

"And Rosa?" asked Jeanne.

"What?" said Saint Méry.

"What happened to Rosa? The fiancée?"

Saint Méry made a little gesture that caused his cuff to quiver. "Her? There's no need to worry about her anymore. She died in childbirth right after she was recaptured."

"Poor things," Jeanne murmured. "I'll take Ulysses," she decided, her voice changed. "I owe you a thousand pounds."

"I paid too much for him," Saint Méry apologized, "but I couldn't have got him at a lower price."

"A strong young Senegambian is worth more than a thousand pounds," said Jeanne. "Not a maroon, of course. But under the circumstances, indeed, monsieur, you'll have to teach me how to get along with a maroon."

"I advise you to make him your overseer," said Saint Méry immediately.

Jeanne stared at him in amazement. "Are you serious? Make a former runaway my overseer?"

"Giving a slave a whip is a very good way to change his ideas about slavery. The younger and more handsome an African is, the more he dreams that he would have been king in his own country. Make his brothers march in rows, crack the whip at their heels and shout down at them, pass out the manioc and bananas and protect the pretty girls in the camp—that's a job for a king."

"No doubt you're right," said Jeanne, after a pause. "I had thought of taking on a mulatto. I had heard that for an overseer one had to choose a mulatto, but—"

"Don't do it. You have a kind heart," Saint Méry interjected. "A mulatto takes out on blacks the scorn he gets from whites."

She hesitated before speaking, and suddenly changed the subject. "Monsieur, you're not going to leave Allspice tomorrow, are you?"

"That, too, is something I wanted to talk to you about," he said. "I'm to have the little Guiscard house in town. It's been promised to me. But they won't be able to move until the beginning of October. Would it put you out very much to keep me till then? I'll shut myself up in my room, and as for my slaves . . ."

Jeanne interrupted him, placing her hand on the beige silk sleeve. "Here's a better suggestion, if I dare make it," she said blushing.

He waited patiently, his hazy blue eyes meeting Jeanne's blankly. She swallowed several times as she groped for words. "You see, monsieur, I'm wanting in experience. I don't know your land. I'll need a man . . . I mean an intendant, a . . . a kind of adviser who . . ."

She was stammering so hard that Saint Méry came to her rescue. "Are you offering me a position as your manager, mademoiselle?"

She turned scarlet. But as he was smiling at her, she smiled back. "I know that my offer is impertinent, Marquis. But I also know that you have no plans. And I'd really like to keep you at Allspice."

"As a good luck charm?"

"Perhaps."

He took several steps along the gallery, shaking his head, and came back to face Jeanne.

"Do you think it is reasonable to want a bankrupt landowner for your manager? Someone who is also a drunk, a debauchee? One who has lost his reputation?"

"No," she replied. "On the other hand, I act as often out of instinct as out of reason. And it usually works."

They looked at each other for a moment in silence.

Then Saint Méry declared, "You've never seen me on a Saturday night, mademoiselle."

Disconcerted, she searched her head for something to reply, but he didn't leave her enough time.

"Let's continue this conversation tomorrow evening, do you mind? Today is a holiday and it's hard for me to talk seriously about everyday matters."

He gave her his arm. "You were so kind as to think that my suit was satisfactory. Is it good enough for me to escort you in to the ball?"

Together they joined the great crowd, a friendly throng of good company, leisurely traversing the salons, their silks rustling. It was not yet dark outside, but the crystal chandeliers were all aglow, dazzling lights whose golden sparkle above the powdered heads set the mood for pleasure.

Snatches of music came from the great assembly hall where the dancing had begun.

"It's beautiful," Jeanne murmured. "All the uniforms . . ."

The blues, reds, whites, greens, grays, and yellows of the island regiments and the French, English, Spanish, and Dutch staff officers of the vessels at anchor, their magnificent silver and gold epaulettes, their gold and silver buttons, their gold braid and gold aiguillettes, their garters with gold buckles, their gold and enamel crosses—all these melded together, swaying and quivering, glistening in the flickering light of the candles, forming a symphony of colors that intoxicated the eyes. Next to the stiffly cut and brilliantly toned military uniforms floated gossamer India muslins, airy and supremely graceful gowns.

Jeanne began to move about as best she could, distributing smiles to her left and right.

"We'll have trouble finding our friends again," said Saint Méry.

But they immediately came upon Pauline and Marie.

Radiant and blooming in a Creole-inspired gown of pink taffeta, her black hair unpowdered, set with pearls and jasmine blossoms, Pauline was chatting in home territory. She had been enthusiastically greeted by the Maillards from Bel Etang and the Plessis-Dufours from Sans Souci. These two families had emigrated from Santo Domingo, where they had not prospered.

Marie, very pale in a white gown that Jeanne had lent her, was standing apart from the group, silent and sad. Jeanne slipped over to her and put her arm sweetly around her waist.

"You see, I came," murmured Marie, "but I feel ashamed."

"My dear Marie, one comes to the islands to make a new life," said Jeanne.

A cry escaped from Marie. "But how does one forget?" Then she went on, a little more vivaciously, "I'm not here in a white gown, about to join the dancing. I'm in a black dress, sitting in a corner with a book in my hand."

"Marie, I forbid you to be morbid," Jeanne scolded her. "You are a widow, Marie. You're not dead."

"Isn't it the same thing?" sighed Marie.

"Don't be stupid!" said Jeanne impatiently. "L'Ile de France has a tremendous need for women. Look around you. We are drowning in a sea of men. You should consider yourself under orders. No lady here has the right to hide in a barrel. Especially if she's pretty."

Marie laughed weakly. "Would you claim also that a widow should start flirting the moment she arrives?"

"I only know that she won't last a month as a widow!" Jeanne burst out thoughtlessly. Too late, she bit her lip. "Smile!" she commanded. "Everyone is looking at us!"

They were soon surrounded by officers from the *Espérance* and joined by M. de Messin, M. de Chavanne, and two other young gentlemen.

"Ladies, I have just seen your friend Don José, and he's looking for you," said M. de Messin. "So is Dr. Aubriot."

"Oh!" put in Saint Méry. "Everybody is looking for somebody, and will be until dawn. That's the great Saint Louis game. It's practically all we do."

"Which reminds me," interjected M. de Chavanne, addressing Jeanne, "have you seen that English lieutenant who seemed so anxious to join you? He was asking everyone for a *Miss* Beauchamps."

"A lieutenant from the *Rockingham*? What could he want with me?"

"Some trifle about a bonnet or a snuffbox from London," suggested a midshipman from the *Espérance*.

"How curious," said Jeanne. "Monsieur de Chavanne, could you find this officer for me?"

"Let's try," said Chavanne.

They found the Englishman in the ballroom. "Your Lordship, I have brought you Mademoiselle Beauchamps," Chavanne said to him, and discreetly vanished.

The Englishman bowed to Jeanne. "Lord Achray," he introduced himself.

"I am Mademoiselle Beauchamps, but are you sure I'm the one you are looking for?"

"I don't doubt it for a moment, mademoiselle."

"Why not?"

"Because you are very beautiful. You are sufficiently beautiful to receive a message from the captain of the frigate whom I dined with two months ago at the viceroy's in Brazil."

He had pulled an envelope out of his pocket. Jeanne took it, trembling. "I . . ." she began, then stopped, unable to say another word. She was shaking from head to foot.

Lord Achray offered her his arm. "Is your heart palpitating, mademoiselle? Shall I take you to a chair?"

"If you please, milord."

They found two chairs along the wall. Jeanne fanned herself nervously. He waited for her to speak.

"That's much better," she said. "My! The heat in this room caught me by surprise."

"Oh, surely it's the heat," said Lord Achray gravely.

"Well . . ." She didn't know where to begin her questions. "You were still in Rio two months ago? You had fair winds?"

The Englishman nodded. "The *Rockingham* is a good sailer."

Jeanne took a deep breath and said, "And so you dined at the viceroy's?"

"Yes," said Lord Achray, "and I had the pleasure of meeting his French prisoner."

Her feigned disinterest suddenly collapsed. "How is he?" she asked with a burst of passion.

The Englishman politely turned his eyes from Jeanne's face. "He was extremely well," he replied. "It seemed to me that Count da Cunha was treating him wonderfully. I believe he is very fond of the Frenchman's company."

She heaved a sigh. "That's what bothers me. A jailer's attachment to his prisoner is not a good thing!"

"Permit a sailor who has been a prisoner to contradict you, mademoiselle. One is in much better lodgings in a palace than on a ship's bridge. Bed and board are better, and time passes the same."

"Tell me about your evening there, milord," she begged him fervently. "Tell me everything."

He looked at her sympathetically. "Alas, mademoiselle, I was at the palace in Rio only for dinner. I can tell you that the food was good, the port wine excellent, the conversation animated, and we had music."

"Music," repeated Jeanne. "There were ladies there, naturally?"

"There were some ladies . . ." He glanced at her, then added, "From society."

An interval of silence was punctuated by the hammering bass note of the chaconne.

"You must have seen the Chevalier Vincent for a moment alone, since . . ."

The Englishman shook his head. "No. A lady, a relative of the viceroy, I believe, was the one who gave me the message from the chevalier the day after the dinner."

"Countess Silveira?"

"Yes."

"I know her," Jeanne lied. "Is she still as pretty as ever?"

Her question sent a faint smile flickering across Lord Achray's lips. "If I were you, Miss Beauchamps, I wouldn't worry about the beauty of other ladies," he said.

The response made her blush. She folded the letter from Vincent which was still in her hand, and put it in her petticoat, then asked, "Did you see the chevalier's frigate in the bay at Rio?"

"Yes. It's in the basin at the Arsenal. Disarmed, closely guarded. It is rumored that she will be sent to Lisbon as soon as they can recruit a Portuguese crew to take her there."

Jeanne rose. "Your Lordship . . ."

He stood up immediately.

"I would like you to help me find a secluded corner," she said. "I can't wait another minute to read my letter."

CHAPTER 24

eanne drew the letter from her petticoat pocket and broke the seal.

My fair-haired Jeanne, my flower. Jeanne, my sweet flesh. I miss you to the very marrow of my bones. If only I had had the wits to steal a vial of that perfume you use on your hair, I could go to bed each night with a few drops of Jeanne sprinkled on my pillow. Alas, like a fool I let you leave intact. Now all I have is a vivid memory of you that keeps me awake all night.

Jeanne, my blond little flower, my pigeon. I shall behave like a starved man when I see you again. I'll wear you out with kisses until you cry for mercy. After that I shall surely beat you to punish you for having disobeyed me by leaving La Plata.

I note that M. Aubriot has forgiven you for marrying me. Yet he insists on dragging you behind him to take care of his bags, his plants, and his colds. Must I cross swords with him and let fate decide, if you will not?

Jeanne, my wild one, believe me, get rid of your valet outfit now, or I will kill your master. If I do that, I shall really be angry, for I have always sought to avoid making war.

I am furious at Don José and would never forgive him, but for the knowledge of your siren's voice and golden glances which bewitch him. When a woman doesn't have a good argument, she uses her beauty. If she has a face like yours, no man is quick-witted enough to avoid committing a folly.

How is the bird Chérimbané? I want you to ask Don

José to sell my merchandise to a Dutchman. You can buy or build a fine place to live in the mountains of Port Louis, where it's cool. Understand me, my dear, I'm not interested in sheltering your old master and his cumbersome passions. I forbid that. He can be lodged at the crown's expense. I'm the one who will need a residence for several years in l'Ile de France.

I beg you therefore to choose one for us. Furnish and decorate it and wait for me like a good girl with my friend Don José and your friend Emilie. If they are willing to keep you company until my return. This desire for a pied-à-terre in l'Ile de France is not new. I had it in mind when I left France for the Indian Ocean. I cannot at this time trust my reasons to a letter. But what difference do they make? You would merely seize upon them to justify your disobedience. You will say that you went to Port Louis with the desire to help me, so I ought to praise you for following your own instincts instead of mine! Well, so be it, my sweet. I'll control my anger. I'll beat you only a little bit. Perhaps hardly at all, if I like the hideaway that you are going to prepare for me on the island.

I don't think I shall be able to leave Rio de Janeiro before the beginning of next year. They are waiting for a Portuguese crew, who won't arrive for another five or six months, before sending my frigate to Lisbon. Until then my beauty remains moored in Rio, binding me to her as surely as if I were tied to her mainmast. I could escape my prison without too much effort. But, as I've told you, sailors are great homebodies and, like the hermit crab, don't wish to leave their shell behind. The viceroy is so sure of this that he allows me to go about as I please, as long as he keeps my ship.

I wander all over town while Father Savié comes by to play chess every evening. M. Amable has settled in as my surgeon and keeps an eye on me day and night, although I couldn't be healthier. A daily staff meeting is held in my chamber. Baron Quissac and my boatswain Gaspar bring me plan after plan for fleeing Rio under the very noses of the

Portuguese. All of them are fantastic. Alas, they are not stupid, as we like to think. So we must be patient.

Besides, Rio is a lively place. The town sings, dances, laughs, drinks, dines, plays, and fornicates to its heart's content. Some of the ladies here are pretty, and all are agreeably wanton. I would like to have a fling, since debauchery is the antidote to lovesickness. Why must it be that my sickness tastes sweeter than the remedy?

Adieu my dear, adieu my dream. Adieu my pain, adieu my joy of yesterday and tomorrow. Adieu my blond love. I pray that this letter will cross the sea safely and drown only in your tears.

Jeanne sat paralyzed in her chair, eyes shut. Vincent's letter was clutched in her hands and pressed to her lips in an endless kiss.

Marie surprised her thus, kissing Vincent's words of love. Her face was glowing as if she had just experienced a miracle.

"Do you realize that we've been looking for you for an hour?" cried Marie. "And if it hadn't been for that lieutenant from the *Rockingham* who finally told me, I never would have found you! What are you doing here, all alone in a room full of filing cabinets? Are you an English spy, searching through the governor's files?"

"Read this," said Jeanne simply, handing her the letter.

Intrigued, Marie took the letter and began to read. "God!" she said suddenly, and looked up at Jeanne.

"Read it," Jeanne repeated.

Marie returned to her reading and finished it without another word. Slowly she refolded the pages and put them on Jeanne's lap. Her eyes were misty. "I'm happy for you, my dear," she murmured. "It's so good to receive news from the one you love."

"Yes, so good," repeated Jeanne. "Absence is such a cruelty." She felt Marie squeeze her arm so hard that it made her grimace, and she turned an astonished face to her friend.

"You don't know what absence is, Jeannette. Thank God you don't know what it is," said Marie bitterly. "The man who wrote you those words is far away from you, nothing more. Someday he will return. Death is quite another kind of absence. Oh, Jeannette, Jeannette, I would so like to receive a letter from Philippe!"

Jeanne took Marie in her arms and rocked her. Marie wiped away her tears. With her head still nestled on Jeanne's shoulder, she touched the letter.

"Don't you find it marvelous that the chevalier is asking you to do what you have already done, buy a house above Port Louis? There's no doubt that your souls speak to each other across space."

"I like to think so," said Jeanne dreamily. "It's true that Vincent is not entirely absent from me. It's strange. When I was with him, he bedazzled me. Now that I need to imagine him, to reconstruct the way he looks, I almost succeed in bringing him closer to me."

She raised her head, and her voice became animated. "I wonder, were he to reappear before me in flesh and blood, if he would fascinate me as much as ever. Would he numb half my mind and all my willpower?"

Releasing Marie, she took Vincent's letter in both hands and went on with mounting vehemence. "He orders me! Did you notice that he orders me around and uses me as if I were one of his crewmen? He wills, decides, commands, and lays down the law. He thinks that after God he is master of our love boat. Do you think he knows that Louis XIV is dead and we now live in an era when women are allowed to speak and act for themselves?"

She was aroused, but not really angry. Marie laughed and said, "It won't do you much good to pretend to get excited. I can't take your revolt too seriously. I think you don't really resent being ordered around when it's your chevalier who's doing the ordering. I gather that it didn't take you long to let yourself be forced into marriage."

A sudden sadness replaced her smiling expression, and Jeanne said in an altered voice, "Don't remind me of that, Marie. Thank God the chevalier writes more like a lover than a husband. You see, I would have liked to remain his mistress. I would have preferred to keep him, and for him to keep me, solely through the charms of love. I didn't want to see us chained to each other by the bonds of marriage."

"But, Jeannette," murmured Marie disconcertedly, "it was surely to show his respect for you that the chevalier married you."

"Assuredly," sighed Jeanne, "for the male makes life difficult as much through his respect as through his egoism." Marie stood gaping in amazement at her friend's remark. Jeanne concluded, "I fear, Marie, that Vincent wanted less to marry me than to lock me up. A corsair's jealousy is a fleeting pleasure. A corsair's mistress is obliged to learn to tear herself free between embraces. To live free or fade away in impatience—those two modes of existence are often her only choice. I am the wife of a dream, Marie. I am married to an absent lover who will return only for brief visits. I really must gain the courage to bear my destiny. I love a man imprisoned by the viceroy of Brazil for the crime of smuggling and diamond theft. Why should this man object to my getting rich while I wait for him? I told you, Marie, I want to live every minute of my life, including the times when Vincent is only someone I'm waiting for. I want to do a thousand things so I don't spend all that time in tears. When my chevalier comes ashore, he'll find a living woman and not a packet of wet handkerchiefs!"

"How excited you are!" said Marie. "I've never heard such impassioned talk from you."

"It's because I'm so happy I could shout!" said Jeanne, enclosing Vincent's message once again between her folded hands.

"I'm happy, Marie. I am touching words that Vincent has touched. Can you understand? Oh! I have to let my happiness out or I'll burst! Come! Let's go and dance!"

* * * *

She had seen little of Aubriot since the beginning of the reception, and none at all during the previous two days. He had gone off to make further observations at Monplaisir with M. de Céré, and she had not wanted to leave Marie and Pauline the day after their arrival.

Surrounded by Poivre and some other avid botanists, Aubriot was holding court under the ancient fig tree. The way he described it, the *Ficus carica* became a living character. The delicious fruit had been wildly praised in Greek and Latin by gourmet poets since the remotest Mediterranean ages.

"Monsieur, you give me a yen for sweets," the Marquis d'Albergati whined comically. "And doubly so because your remarks remind me of a dainty that sweetened my childhood. Are you familiar, monsieur, with the variety of fig which, in my home, near Aubagne, is called drop-of-gold?"

Aubriot responded instantly, "I see a fat, light-colored fig, which, when ripe, splits to reveal beads of beautiful amber juice of great sweetness."

"Ah, monsieur, when you say that the juice is sweet, you do it scant justice!" cried the Marquis d'Albergati. "It is a thread of honey, monsieur. Honey of the most exquisite quality, which flows from the eye of the drop-of-gold. And now just imagine two or three of these fruits at their supreme bursting point, spread on a slice of country wheat bread and sprinkled with freshly ground pepper to remove the blandness . . ."

The regimental captain closed his eyes, clasped his hands together, and savored his bread and figs in utter ecstasy.

"Gentlemen," he said, opening his eyes, "I have just given you the recipe for ambrosia. I have never doubted that the food of the Olympians was prepared from perfectly ripened drops-of-gold."

"The marquis is passionately fond of sweets," said Father Duval, laughing. "But I'm forced to absolve him of the sin of gluttony because it so happens that I consider it venial!"

At that moment the men were surprised by the pretty laughter of a woman descending upon them.

"Gentlemen!" said Jeanne, taking the arms of both Poivre and Aubriot. "I feel like dancing with witty men who will fill my ears with something other than platitudes. Monsieur Intendant, I ask your hand for a short minuet, and monsieur," she added, turning toward Aubriot, "I reserve yours for a little chaconne."

"What nonsense!" exclaimed Aubriot, taken aback by this sudden burst of audacity that Jeanne had never showed him. "Am I really to believe, Jeanne, that you've drunk enough wine at supper to think we are still of an age to enter the dance?"

"Speak for yourself, my dear fellow!" Poivre protested jovially. "It's the Saint Louis Ball, and when a beauty invites me, I feel as young as she. Come, Jeannette, I promise to court you like a true *caballero.*"

A few minutes later it was Aubriot's turn. He resisted for honor's sake. "You're mad, Jeanne. You've had too much to drink. You're insane!"

"The chaconne is a very stately dance," she said, dragging him onto the floor.

"You're mad," he repeated, tapping out the first of the chaconne's three tempos with his foot. Actually, he felt like laughing.

She seemed genuinely delighted to be dancing with him, and glided along on a carpet of rose petals. She kept her eyes lowered. Though he knew her face by heart, he marveled with fresh emotion at those long, delicately tapered eyelids fringed with bronze lashes. He drank in her beauty, letting his eyes wander appreciatively over each feature of this familiar golden flower.

Tonight she looked radiant with the seductive glow of a potential new conquest. *My little girl has grown up.* Bittersweet memories of their love flooded his mind, the love she had lately chosen to withdraw. A hundred times before he had asked himself why. Suddenly it occurred to him that Jeanne might simply have abandoned Jeannot as a butterfly abandons its chrysalis—the cocoon of infancy. And if this were so, why be surprised or vexed at a butterfly that's simply heeding the laws of nature? Better to feel sorry for oneself for not behaving more sensibly.

Sensible was the last thing in the world Aubriot wanted to be. He chided himself for his flight of romantic fancy, trying to make Jeanne and Jeannot converge into the person he knew, a pleasing enlargement of the admiring little girl at the Château de Charmont.

"My word, but you smell good!" she said unexpectedly, her nose twitching as she raised her eyes. "I thought I was imagining things. But sure enough, you must have used toilet water for the ball. That *is* something new! And which courtesan provided this perfume, may I ask?"

"No, no, the lady at Mongoust has nothing to do with it," he said with a laugh. "Madame de Céré makes it herself. I was looking at her frangipanis and telling her that their common name derives from the sweet-cream scent once used by Italian glovemakers to perfume their hides. My hostess held out her hand and assured me that her skin always smelled of frangipani. Would you believe it? I was so taken by that delightful scent that she gave me some of her cologne for my shirts. I must have used too much. Do I smell awful?"

"You perfume the air. And I love it! You know what a greedy nose I have! Mmmmmm!"

She leaned over and buried her face in Aubriot's lace collar, inhaling the frangipani with nostrils aquiver. "If there weren't such a mob of people around us, I'd fall upon your shirt in rapture!"

"You're a peacock butterfly," he said.

"A what?"

"A peacock butterfly, the female of the species. To attract a mate, the male emits an odor so striking that she rushes over. All he has to do is give her a second whiff to make her fall swooning between his wings."

"Is that so?" she said, tilting her head and casting one of her irresistible glances at him. "Flutter your arms a bit, will you?"

She was enticing him so brazenly that once again he thought, *She's had too much to drink.* Yet he hoped it wasn't true. A wave of happiness swept over him. He felt mildly ridiculous dancing at his age. But he didn't dare stop for fear of breaking the bubble of desire that was reviving again between them.

"You dance marvelously," said Jeanne. "I knew you were a good dancer. I saw you dancing once at Charmont when I was a little girl." Her voice trembled as she added, "But you never danced with me till now."

He looked at her. Her big amber eyes shone with happiness. "Well, I was wrong till now," he said softly. "And the loss is all mine."

After a pause she murmured, "That's a lovely thought, Monsieur Philibert."

The music stopped. There was a great rustle of silks as voices broke out.

"Let's find ourselves a dish of sherbet," Aubriot proposed.

"Oh, no! Champagne, please! I want to go on flirting with you, and I'm afraid that sherbet will cool me off."

He laughed, amused and flattered by the remark. "Frankly," he said, "I really wonder if you need any more champagne."

CHAPTER 25

hilibert's hands awakened her late in the morning.

She loved having him wake her with his hands, tenderly stroking her face. This morning he spent a long time at it. She drifted out of sleep into the real world, her eyelids fluttering as she clung stubbornly to her drowsy bliss.

But at last Philibert seized her by the shoulders and shook her. "It's noon," he said.

"Noon!" she exclaimed, sitting up like a bolt. Realizing that she was stark naked, she pulled the sheet up around her neck and blushed.

"Why hasn't Don José come by to see if I was ready?" she asked, draping the sheet around her and sliding out of bed. "We're supposed to go out to Allspice to meet the masons and carpenters on loan from the king."

"You may be sure Don José isn't ready either! No Spaniard gets up early after going to bed at dawn. Polydor has brought you some coffee."

As she drank, the doctor had a violent fit of coughing that left his cheeks beet red.

"I'll wager you forgot to take your cough medicine while you were at Monplaisir," Jeanne cried in alarm.

"I need to find some black radishes," he said. "They make a much better syrup than maidenhair fern."

"There must be some radishes at Monsieur de Messin's place in Rivière Noire," she said. "We'll get some." She fed him a teaspoonful of syrup. "Bring me your handkerchief so I can sprinkle a few drops of essence of cypress on it."

"I will," he replied. "But first get dressed. Don't worry. I've always had a touchy throat and have managed to get along with it. All this pollen in the air doesn't do me any good. With the never-ending sun and wind on this island, there's pollen all year round."

She went into the dressing room and he heard water cascading into the wash basin as Jeanne hummed an old Parisian melody. She emerged briefly from the toilet, blew him a kiss, and returned to the wash basin.

Draping herself in the sheet again, she stuck her head back in the doorway. "I'm so happy," she announced with a smile. "I'm twenty years old and have found the place I want to live. A corner of paradise called Moka, where it is always sunny, cool, and green. Where life will be as fragrant and sweet as ripe figs. Why shouldn't I be happy? I've reached my promised land."

" 'Promised land, land of wheat and barley, of grapes and figs and pomegranates, of oil and honey,' " Aubriot recited. "Before your Allspice can resemble anything like that, my dear will-o'-the-wisp, it will take a lot of time and money, and the sweat of black men."

"And knowledge," she added with a cajoling smile. "You've forgotten knowledge. But I'm not worried about that, for we've that in good supply."

He shot her a somber glance. "I trust you are not counting on me to acclimatize your spice plants?"

"Who better than you, Sir Royal Botanist?"

"Jeanne, don't count on me," he said roughly. "Do not count on me. I don't want to get involved in this affair. My work keeps me busy enough and absorbs me completely. Not one of you three asked my advice before embarking on this adventure, so you can just work it out yourselves. You were always a good pupil, so things ought to turn out all right." Then his voice took on a sullen edge as he added, "I'll try to teach Polydor to take your place so that you'll be free to play around with your spice raising."

With the sheet draped like a toga around her, she walked up to him. "I don't think you'll have the heart to refuse me your help. Even if I managed singlehanded to make my little paradise grow, I would still need you to admire it. No one will ever convince me that a beautiful garden is really beautiful if you're not part of it. No one. Not even you!"

Her voice was so intense, almost sorrowful, that Aubriot was moved and kept silent.

At last he patted her cheek. "I must say you're not yourself today. Do go get dressed, my mimosa. And don't look for ways to make yourself sad. I have neither the time nor the inclination to become a planter. But I never said I wouldn't come look at your plantation."

* * * *

A breeze rustled the foliage of the great old fig tree out on the islet. The huge leaves rose and fell, flapping languidly like green elephant ears. In the slanting light of late afternoon the wooded slopes melted into a single dark mass, while shadows rose from the ground and began to fill the copse nearby. The soothing murmur of a mountain stream added to the profound romantic stillness, broken here and there by the screech of a monkey or a parakeet.

Jeanne threw herself down on the grass. Above her, the light, graceful leaves of the eucalyptus swayed. This handsome tree was the only one left standing on the near shore.

I'll put a bench under it, she thought. A wave of happiness swept over her. A dove landed close to her and began to stroll about, cooing.

Yes indeed, my fine feathered friend. There are times when life makes you want to sing. Moments when, no matter what you do, you're not ashamed of yourself. A thousand and one nights of guilt are better than making Philibert suffer a single hour.

Her thoughts rolled on, tinged with hypocrisy. Had she made love with Philibert purely out of charity? *I was so happy to receive that letter from Vincent . . . and when I'm happy, I have the greatest urge to keep on being happy . . .*

* * * *

Jeanne went to find Saint Méry in the garden. They walked toward the site of the black camp, where there were sounds of hammering.

"When are your blacks supposed to leave Allspice?" Jeanne asked.

"Yesterday!" replied Saint Méry. "Immediately. I found a ferry bound for the big island that would take them for a thousand pounds apiece. For two days they talked of nothing else. Then they came to me and asked if I would keep the money and dole it out to them as they needed it. They're convinced that they'll lose it if they take it all at once, or that someone will rob them."

"But if they want to return home . . ." Jeanne began.

"Home, unfortunately for them, is with me!" said Saint Méry. And with a weary sigh of resignation, he went on to explain. "They'd be overjoyed to sail for their big island if I were coming with them. But without me they'll go no farther than the port. They'll wind up in some grubby shack in the slums and then come whining to me about their troubles, beg a pound or two off me with the same bunch of lies they'd tell me if the money didn't belong to them. And that will go on until they die or I do."

"Suppose you asked permission to free them?"

"Would that change anything? To free a slave, either the slave must be very young or the master very cruel. To impose freedom on someone who looks on it with terror is no gift. There's a saying in Bourbon. Instead of 'happy as a fish in water,' they say 'happy as a slave working for the nobles at court.' The poor whites invented that, and the blacks repeat it."

"It's possible . . ." Jeanne mused. "I hope that one day in l'Ile de France they'll say 'happy as a slave at Allspice.' "

When they arrived at the work site they found the three black carpenters nearly finished with the first two huts. The men set down their tools and grinned proudly as they waited for mam'selle to appear.

Farther away, at the foot of a hill, three black masons had begun lazily to lay the foundations of a third dwelling, which appeared to be roomier than the previous two.

"They're waiting to receive your compliments," Saint Méry prompted.

Jeanne entered one of the huts. "It's very nice. I'm quite satisfied, and I think your work is excellent," she said.

The carpenters exchanged happy grins.

"Really, it's very nice," Jeanne repeated sincerely. Then she glanced up. "Did Don José order the next one built up there above the wind? Is it for the overseer?"

"The overseer must live in the camp," said Saint Méry. "Up there, if you don't mind, is where I'll be living."

Jeanne was so taken aback that she stood gaping. "You offered me the job of manager," Saint Méry continued. "If you're still willing, I'd like to build my house there. Two rooms will do, with a veranda and a large hut for Nanny and Zoe—and the children, the ones who belong to Zoe," he concluded hastily, not wishing to admit openly that he had fathered Zoe's five coffee-colored boys.

"Well, this is news!" she exclaimed. "So you're going to stay?"

"Your amazement worries me," said Saint Méry. "If you've changed your mind . . ."

"Certainly not!" said Jeanne, recovering her composure. "I was overcome with pleasure."

"As to pleasure, mademoiselle, wait and see," said Saint Méry, an ironic smile on his lips. "I have no idea how it will work out, since there's little hope of my reforming. Let's give it a try. You can always change your mind and throw me out."

"It will work out," said Jeanne, extending both hands to him.

He squeezed her hands, and Jeanne's amber eyes met his blue ones squarely.

"I know I shouldn't have accepted your offer," he said. "I know I shouldn't, but . . . it was easier."

"You love this place, and you'll be the best manager it could possibly have," said Jeanne. "I'll help you."

"What a stroke of luck it is to be nobly born!" he said scoffingly. "A marquis's title makes up for a bad record. Instead of winding up in the poorhouse, I'm offered shelter by a beautiful lady."

"Let's have a look at the manager's house," said Jeanne.

They walked to the foot of the slope where the masons were working. The overseer was sitting on the trunk of a fallen pomegranate tree. He cracked his whip and shouted orders as he saw the whites approaching.

Ulysses was there too. The magnificent Senegambian, whom Saint Méry had bought from the La Barrées, kept his distance from his "noble" brother, the king's overseer. Alert but silent, Ulysses' whip rested on his knees. A red and white turban was wound about his head, concealing the scar where once had been an ear. It was undoubtedly the remains of a loincloth that Zoe had given him. He watched Jeanne's movements and rushed over to place himself between her and the king's overseer, whom she was about to address.

"Work go fine, mamzelle," he told her solemnly. "That bunch can work good."

"Then maybe you can put aside your whip," she said with a smile.

Ulysses looked horrified, and Saint Méry drew Jeanne aside. "Mademoiselle, I've never seen an overseer put aside his whip. He lives, eats, sleeps, and dies hanging on to it, like a rat to his tail. And don't think that these men hate the sound of a cracking whip . . . as long as it doesn't land on their backs. When I feel like pleasing my own slaves, I wake them in the morning by cracking my whip in the air three times."

"I daresay you have a lot to teach me," said Jeanne.

CHAPTER 26

Port Louis was becoming more and more like a comfortable inn where distinguished travelers from all over the world dropped by and stayed on. At the Intendancy, Mme. Poivre was obliged to lead a far more active social life than she desired. No doubt about it, her provincial origins and her shy and pious upbringing had ill prepared this young woman to become first lady of a colony.

Timid Françoise felt terrified of not succeeding in her social role, and of disappointing her brilliant husband. She clung to Emilie, who took charge of her salon with great style and gusto. Emilie obviously enjoyed the job, and it suited her perfectly. Soon she was asking Don José to build her a house on Government Row.

Don José resisted. He had no intention of lingering forever on this island. He grew sadder as Emilie enjoyed herself more and more.

"Jeanne," he asked one day, "when your house is finished, do you think there'd be room for us? I hope Emilie would be willing to live there. Maybe it would take her mind off building a place of her own in town."

"I'll see if I can't get the second floor finished soon," Jeanne replied.

"Thank you," said Don José, taking her two hands and pressing his lips to them in his gallant fashion. "I must say that I'm not at all keen on building anything in Port Louis."

His statement was accompanied by a sheepish look, and Jeanne said affectionately, "I love your indulgence of Emilie's whims. You treat that capricious lady very sweetly."

"Oh," he said, "it's so easy to be indulgent when you know you're not loved. You try to please for reasons other than yourself."

"Don José, she does love you!" Jeanne exclaimed with tears in her eyes.

He looked at her, eager with hope. "Yes? But how is it, then, that I don't know it? Am I the original village idiot?"

"Don José, even she doesn't know it yet. Patience!"

He nodded resignedly, and Jeanne continued in a different tone, "Count on me to have the second floor furnished and livable by the end of November."

As it turned out, Marie, not Emilie, was the first to move into Allspice, with her baby daughter, Virginia. This made Paul very angry, because his plaything had been taken from him. So when his mother got tired of scolding the boy, she packed him off with Iassi to join Virginia. Pauline also moved out to the Moka district.

Jeanne watched her house grow lively, her land come under the plow, and her "front garden" begin to take shape. She was excited. She was putting down roots, deeper and deeper every day, in the soil of her plantation.

Aubriot's bedroom and study had been finished first—pleasant, spacious rooms on the main floor, with French windows opening onto the veranda. You could still breathe the fragrance of the rustic sandalwood furniture Jeanne had ordered in Port Louis from a Breton cabinetmaker.

Each day she would visit Monsieur Philibert's rooms to see that they were dusted and tidy, and she would leave a vase of fresh flowers on the corner of the desk before she went out again with a sigh.

Aubriot clung petulantly to his uncomfortable lodgings at Government House. He sulked. He simply could not believe Jeanne had implemented a plan that he was not consulted on. He had hoped, after she had slept with him the night of the Saint Louis Ball, that he could persuade her to give up her idea. But all of his talk had no effect. Jeanne remained up to her neck in her folly. Aubriot's vexation was soon coupled with anxiety, since she wouldn't disclose how much money she had, or where it came from. She had led him to believe that Don José was the source.

To the son of a cautious notary, the idea of owing money was enough to make him physically ill. Resentfully, he disclaimed any responsibility for Jeanne's debts. He lay awake at night plagued by insomnia, staring into the dark, fretting and worrying, condemning her ingratitude and duplicity, complaining bitterly to himself of "that child on whom I lavished so much love and tender concern," and who was now rewarding him so foully. He swore he would never set foot at Allspice.

Jeanne waited patiently, changing the flowers in his study each day. There was so much work to be done that her patience never felt tried. Saint Méry helped her all he could, forcing himself to be active and sober—six days out of seven.

And Pauline was teaching her to be a planter. The Creole had rediscovered her former role of mistress of the manor. Born on a plantation in Santo Domingo, she felt at home with the blacks, and could order them about, thwarting their little tricks, gaining their respect, and laughing with them. On her advice, Jeanne had let the Mozambicans retain their African names. Pauline encouraged Jeanne to reunite lovers, and to give priority to the construction of a large shed to serve as a recreation hall for the black camp.

Every Saturday night the vibrating strains of drums, tambourines, and harps rose from the shed. Sitting on the still somewhat dilapidated veranda of her house, Jeanne listened contentedly to the exuberant voices.

"I love the sounds of Saturday night festivities," she said one evening to Pauline. "I wonder if it means they're happy."

Pauline smiled. "They're having fun, at least."

As an explosion of shrieks burst from the direction of the shed, she continued teasingly, "You see now, Jeanne, that on a well-run plantation the slaves don't sit around weeping. When I told you that in Dombes, you refused to believe me."

Jeanne blushed, causing Pauline to laugh softly.

On Saturdays, the mistress of Allspice served dinner later than usual, at ten o'clock. This was to mark the end of the work week and to take advantage of the festive atmosphere provided by the distant rhythms of African harps and tambourines. It was also to give Aubriot, Emilie, and Don José, in Port Louis, time to reach Moka if they wished.

As a rule, however, Emilie kept Don José in town for one reception or another, and as for Aubriot . . .

"Another Saturday that won't bring us our forgetful friends in Port Louis," said Pauline as she unfolded her napkin. "It appears that we have to go to them if we want to see them at all. Will you be attending mass tomorrow?"

She had eyed Jeanne and Marie in turn, and Marie replied, "Probably," while Jeanne answered, "Yes, certainly."

"If I don't sleep too late, I'll go to mass too," Saint Méry said.

The three women stared at him in disbelief. It was the first time they had ever heard him express any religious inclination.

"I want to be in on the scandal. I've heard that Don José shocks the parishioners every Sunday by filing in with his entire household and allowing his slaves to sit in the pew alongside himself and Madame Emilie," said Saint Méry.

"Yes, that's a Spanish custom," said Jeanne.

"Holy of holies!" exclaimed Saint Méry, laughing. "I must go have a look at that. Not the Spanish custom, but the French faces staring at them. Here all the God-fearing settlers are willing to convert their slaves on condition that they stand at the back of the church. A place to sit down, that's for later on . . . in heaven. I wonder how they put up with . . ."

"They are *not* putting up with it," Marie interrupted. "I heard that the governor has received a number of complaints and has directed the intendant to reprimand Don José. But so far Monsieur Poivre has merely shrugged off the note and filed it away."

"Just wait, the issue will end up in court!" said Saint Méry, with a wry smile. "Sooner or later the king will have to decide where Adele and Aiam must stand or sit to hear mass in the church at Port Louis."

As if on cue, the black children of the household burst into the room all at once, without a word, each holding a glazed porringer.

"You're too early," Pauline told them. "We're not ready for dessert yet. On Saturdays you always arrive too soon."

The children lined up along the wall and waited quietly for the right moment to hold out their bowls for the treasured sweets.

CHAPTER 27

O n Sunday morning Pauline was up first, and left in a buggy for Port Louis.

Jeanne watched as the black stableman saddled the three horses she had ordered. "Wait for me, will you?" she said to Marie. "Saint Méry is late. I'll go see how far along he is with his dressing."

She passed through the slave camp where now there were two rows of solidly built huts, some thirty in all. On this particular morning the place seemed tenanted only by children, dogs, hens, and pigs. Everyone was sound asleep under thatched palm roofs.

She rode up the hill to Saint Méry's house. An uneasy silence seemed to surround the house. Jeanne felt inclined to peek through the window, but, restraining herself, she walked up to the door instead and banged on it with her riding crop. When there was no answer she banged louder.

A bearlike growl, followed by Saint Méry's hoarse, peevish voice came out. "Whoever you are, go to the devil and leave me alone! It's Sunday, for God's sake!"

Jeanne rapped on the door once again with her whip.

"It's time for mass," she announced coolly.

"Time for . . . what?" came the voice, yawning lazily.

The door opened slightly, just enough to admit Zoe's slender body. She wore a gauzy underskirt and nothing more, keeping her arms folded over her breasts. No sooner had she stepped out the door than she began to roll her eyes and plead with her mistress in hushed tones.

"Mamzelle no come in, Moussié Maquis not go to mass, not possible. Mamzelle not come in. Not good Mamzelle see Moussié Maquis like dat. Mamzelle go 'way from here, for Good Lawd's sake!"

Jeanne heard out Zoe's speech, then retorted, "All right."

She was about to turn on her heel when the door was flung open and a disheveled, bare-legged Saint Méry appeared on the doorstep. He was hastily stuffing an immaculate white shirt into a pair of flowered knee-shorts.

Greeting Jeanne with exaggerated politeness, he braced himself against the door frame and invited her in. "Mademoiselle, if you'll do me the honor . . ."

Jeanne hesitated, returned his mocking smile, and went in.

"Take a seat," he said, grabbing his white linen everyday suit off the rattan armchair.

Saint Méry fascinated her. The half-sober drunkard was more appealing than the sober man she knew. Maybe it was because he didn't seem so remote. Alcohol seemed to have dispelled his hazy isolation. His blue eyes shone dully, resisting Jeanne's scrutiny.

"You want to talk to me?" she asked, for lack of anything else to say.

"Me?" he scoffed. "You've got things mixed up, mademoiselle. You're the one who came looking for me."

She felt herself blushing. He noticed this, and a hint of tender concern crept into his mocking gaze.

"I had planned on talking to you, mademoiselle. But since you're here, I can only say that you are beautiful and it's a pleasure, fresh from sleep, to set eyes on you. Just a moment, please," he added, with a gesture intended to prevent Jeanne from leaving. "Just one moment . . ."

He disappeared into the next room. She heard him rummaging in a wardrobe, swearing to himself.

She looked around the room she was in. Though not very tidy, it was clean and comfortable, with a table, an armchair, and a cabinet filled with books. A rope hammock stretched across one corner.

Saint Méry returned with a basket containing two plates and glasses, utensils, two bottles, ham, and bread, which he set out on the table. "Beer or arrack?" he asked, pointing to the bottles.

"Thanks, but I'm not thirsty. Or hungry," she added, seeing his knife poised over the ham. "What are you up to, Marquis? A moment ago I was about to leave without seeing you. Then you appeared and asked me in, and now you're having me to lunch. What's it all about?"

"You came to see the bear in his lair, so I'm showing him to you," he replied with a touch of insolence. "You've missed seeing him at his savage worst by several hours. Let's hope he doesn't disappoint you too much. On Sunday mornings the bear drinks liquor instead of coffee.

Any serious drinker will tell you that arrack is much better than coffee for a hangover."

He was about to pour himself a second glass, but she restrained his arm. "Marquis, why are you destroying yourself? Why do you drink?"

He shook his head. "No, mademoiselle, when I want to make a confession, I won't come to you. You don't listen the way a priest does. While you're mumbling, he's thinking of his dinner, or about the cucumber seeds he has to plant. Your way of listening is altogether non-Catholic, mademoiselle. You sit there so tensely, with your inscrutable golden eyes that sear—"

"I don't listen with my eyes," she said, smiling for the first time.

"Oh, yes you do. And with your brows too. They're so long, so beautifully arched, and they accentuate your eyes so perfectly that it's as if you had two sets of eyes, bright and shining as the sun. It's—"

He reached out and grabbed the arrack before she could stop him, and took a long swig from the bottle. "And you ought to be going right now, mademoiselle," he said hoarsely. "You'd better leave before I tell you with my hands that you're beautiful. You realize, mademoiselle, that a drunkard is no different from any other man, only less of a gentleman. And you're divinely beautiful!"

To reach the door she walked unhurriedly past Saint Méry, who seemed to have positioned himself so she would have to brush against him. The marquis's rasping breath grazed her neck and made her shiver. She stopped in front of him and offered her hand. He took it, pressing it to his lips fervently, like a devoted lover.

* * * *

Dr. Aubriot did not show up for mass. After church, Jeanne went looking for him at Government House. He wasn't there, and nobody could tell her where he had gone. He was being very petulant indeed.

Nevertheless, Sunday dinner turned out to be a lively, pleasant affair. Work on the house and grounds still had to be done before Jeanne could entertain "society," but she invited her friends regularly. Emilie and Don José always came, and the Poivres visited every other Sunday with Françoise's sister, Minette. Marie's brother, John, a lieutenant, came whenever he was not on duty, and this time he brought a friend along. Lieutenant Robert de Boussuge was a tall, distinguished-looking young man who played the violin marvelously and sang love songs as he gazed at Marie.

After dinner Jeanne had the rattan chairs brought out and everyone sat and chatted under the umbrellalike canopy of a tropical almond tree, the only one at Allspice to have survived the hurricane of 1760.

"Unfortunately, this tree is fragile," Poivre said. "You're lucky to have it still, Jeanne. It makes a pleasant greenhouse and reminds me of Monsieur de Villeneuve, the great amateur gardener and commander of the East India Company's fleet, who brought it from India and planted it here with his own hands."

"I love my trees to have a history," said Jeanne.

"That's all well and good, but don't neglect botany for poetry," said Poivre, smiling. "A poet on a plantation is happiest in nature gone wild."

"Monsieur Aubriot will never let me be that poetic," said Jeanne.

"But he never comes here," Poivre commented, leaning toward her and dropping his voice. He saw by the nervous twitching of her hands that the remark had touched her to the quick. She promptly changed the subject.

"Clearing of the land is progressing slowly. I'm eager to get on with the planting, but I don't have enough workers. Have you any word of the slave-hunting expedition you sent to Foulepointe?"

"Mercy!" sighed Poivre. "Must we talk of slavery when I've just dined on the most exquisite fish stew? Slave trading at Foulepoint is getting worse and worse, Jeanne. At least that's what I'm told. You'll know before I do how many miserable creatures the *Garonne* is transporting from the big island."

Jeanne and Pauline exchanged glances as Pauline, with a flick of her toe, sent Paul's ball bouncing back to him. "Jeanne," she said, "the slaves from the *Garonne* may be a long time in arriving, but those at Belle Herbe are close at hand. They are just down the hill from us, and haven't had much to do since the Moreau de Bonnevals gave up raising sugar cane. Perhaps they'll be willing to turn them over to you?"

Poivre arched his brow. "The Belle Herbe slaves are for sale along with the property."

"We could find an accommodating buyer for the Bonnevals," said Jeanne, "who would transfer about twenty slaves to me or else let them work for me by the day."

Poivre's shrewd eyes shifted back and forth several times between the two women before he exclaimed in mock terror, "Oh no! Don't tell me you want the three thousand acres at Belle Herbe for Madame Marie, the whole thing on credit?"

"Marie might be able to find some solvent associates," suggested Pauline.

Poivre's eyes followed Pauline's to the other guests who stood laughing in the roadway.

"You and Jeanne both know that I would like to please you by pleasing your friend. But what associates are you talking about? The only solvent person I see out there is a Spaniard who can't wait to return to his home soil."

"But Dame Emilie likes it here," said Pauline.

"And she also likes the house at Belle Herbe," Jeanne added.

"You're not serious?" said Poivre. I thought she wanted a house in town, which Don José isn't at all interested in."

Jeanne motioned for Emilie to join them.

"Well?" asked Emilie, still flushed from the game and from laughing. "Are we hatching some kind of plot?"

"Yes, against me," said Poivre.

"We're talking about Belle Herbe," said Pauline.

"Oh, Belle Herbe!" Emilie exclaimed, interested at once. "Charming house, a little on the small side, but charming. The old fake Baroness de Damville took me there the other day and I couldn't bear to leave. You'd think you were back in the Burgundy countryside among rich farmers."

"The Moreau de Bonnevals come from Vonnas," said Poivre. "The house they built is like the one they had in France."

"Yes, they told me that," said Emilie, "and also that they'd like to go back to France to claim an unexpected inheritance. What will become of their lovely farm? I wish I had it, in place of the townhouse that Don José doesn't want to build. That's it! Belle Herbe must be mine or I'll die for want of it!"

"Come now, Dame Emilie, what kind of talk is this?" Poivre chided her gently. "You can't be serious . . ."

He got no further. Emilie's eyes implored his support with the mixture of pride, mischief, and mock helplessness that men found so irresistible.

Poivre questioned her in a businesslike way. "Dame Emilie, tell me exactly what you have in mind."

"Nothing that should displease you," she replied hastily. "I would like to live someplace on the island where Don José would not feel deprived of his grasslands. There are pastures at Belle Herbe, cattle, dairy cows, and horses. Aren't you glad, sir, that I am trying to keep Don José on this island?"

"Yes," Poivre admitted. "I'm tired of people who come and go. You can't build a French outpost in the Indies with passersby and slaves. I'm not averse to the idea of keeping both of you here. But I think it's a bit risky to discuss the matter right now. I'd prefer for Don José to come speak to me first."

"He doesn't know yet that this is what he wants," said Emilie, with her usual frankness. "But I'll open his eyes. Belle Herbe will enchant him."

"Monsieur," Jeanne interrupted, "if Belle Herbe is to go to my friends, can't I arrange in advance, without affecting the king's credit, to buy a group of slaves and some mules from the Bonnevals?"

"My dear young friend, the deal is not done and you can't pin me down," said Poivre. "By the way, do the Bonnevals have mules?"

"Twenty-eight," Jeanne replied instantly.

"You seem well informed of their resources!" Poivre observed sarcastically. "I ought to take you on as my secretary. Two weeks ago I asked for an inventory of the property at Belle Herbe, and I haven't received it yet."

Pauline drew a folded sheet of paper from her petticoat pocket and casually dangled it before Poivre's eyes. "Here it is, sir, in full. I'll have it copied for you in the morning."

Poivre remained mute for an instant, a faint smile on his lips. "I repeat that we ought to have women for secretaries. It could only improve the way our affairs are run." He added mischievously, "I'll bet that a woman secretary wouldn't allow me to play favorites, and would see to it that I never indulged a pretty face."

"The profits of injustice would simply benefit a different sex! Your signature would favor handsome officers," Pauline said.

They all laughed so heartily that Françoise and her sister walked over to find out what they had missed.

"Your lady friends are driving me wild," said Poivre.

"We were just speaking of Belle Herbe," Emilie explained.

"Oh! Belle Herbe!" Françoise and Minette exclaimed at the same time.

"Can it be worked out, dear?" Françoise asked as she placed her hand on her husband's.

Poivre looked from his wife to his sister-in-law to Marie and then burst out laughing again. "Well, I see that everybody's in on the secret except for the intendant in charge of the affair, and the other poor fellow over there who's totally ignorant of the plans in store for him."

The sound of galloping hooves interrupted the conversation and turned every eye to the roadway.

At last! Jeanne was overcome with joy.

"A pleasant Turkish scene!" exclaimed Aubriot as he jumped to the ground. "In town they say we have an intendant who works himself to the bone from six in the morning till nine at night. But now I see that on Sundays he plays the sultan to his pretty little harem!"

* * * *

"Well, Jeannette," said Aubriot as soon as the Poivres had gone, "will you show me around the property?"

She replied with a radiant smile, "Let me change into my breeches first. The paths at Allspice are not as well manicured as the Tuileries Gardens!"

"I'll go ahead," said Aubriot.

He set off along the path leading to the former spice farm. Jeanne saw Aubriot wandering off into a patch of woods not far from where she stood. She went to join him, climbing over clumps of bushes.

Hearing the crackle of Jeanne's steps, the doctor shouted to her without turning around, "Have you taken a look at this place?"

"Not yet. I was waiting for them to clear it out a bit."

"Maybe that's a bad idea. Come look." The botanist was standing in front of a pretty little tree that looked like a laurel. The rounded top shone green. Amid the spear-shaped leaves hung clusters of tiny yellow buds and several round, yellow fruits the size of peaches.

With a trembling hand Jeanne touched the cracked skin from which a honeylike sap was oozing. "It isn't . . . ? It can't be . . . ?"

"My word, it *is*," said Aubriot. "And it seems to be a healthy one too. A bit stunted, perhaps, from not getting enough sun, but you'd have to know its age."

"But . . . but then . . ." Jeanne's voice quavered as she stared in fascination at the fruit nearest her. "Then it must be . . . it has to be . . . a nutmeg tree?"

"If the nutmeg hasn't altered its destiny in moving from the Moluccas to l'Ile de France, then it is indeed a nutmeg. And since the fruit is yellow, it must be ripe."

"Ripe?" Jeanne repeated incredulously. "But what about all the flowers?"

"This is the first adult nutmeg I've actually seen. But from what I know, the nutmeg produces flowers and fruits the year round," said Aubriot. "You surprise me, Jeannette. How can you hope to be a spice planter without reading up on the subject?"

"I've read a lot, but reading and seeing are two different things," Jeanne exclaimed joyfully. "Oh, Philibert, do you realize that you're standing in front of the first nutmeg tree at Allspice? My first nutmeg tree! It's mine, Philibert, all mine! It's bearing fruit and I shall have a nutmeg harvest. My first harvest! It's like a dream, Monsieur Philibert!"

"A harvest!" said Philibert mockingly. "I counted six nuts. There might be another two or three hidden in the foliage, but that's about it. Your tree is still pretty stingy. I don't think you could pick enough from it to repay your loan from Don José."

Ignoring the barb, Jeanne questioned him eagerly. "Philibert, are you sure? You couldn't be mistaken, could you? These are real nutmegs? I mean aromatic ones. They couldn't have degenerated, could they? Become shells . . . without nuts? Or a kind of wild thing, hard and—"

He cut her off impatiently. "Of course not. Shall we pick one?"

Taking a deep breath, she said, "I'll pick it." She was not quite tall enough to reach the nearest fruit, so she boosted herself up by climbing onto the lowest branch of a neighboring custard apple tree, seized the fruit, and tore it from its stalk.

The nut nestled in the palm of her hand, round, solid, golden. She presented it to Philibert like an offering. A golden nut plucked from the garden of the Hesperides.

"It's heavy," he said, taking it from her. "Very heavy. It must be the female. Shall we open the shell? It's very ripe, ready to open," said Aubriot. And it did open easily, into two valves of white flesh, one of which held a bright scarlet egg-shaped nut.

"I think this is the middle husk of the berry, what's known as mace," said Aubriot.

He detached the little stone from its valve, sniffed it, and handed it to Jeanne. "It has a faint smell," she said.

"Wait . . ."

The lovely red mace was a waxy, fibrous husk that seemed to bleed under Aubriot's scalpel and peel off, revealing a second cover that was smooth, hard, and brown. They both held it up to their noses and sniffed it greedily.

"The nutmeg is just underneath," said Aubriot. He had a hard time peeling off the last layer, but finally it lay naked in his hand. The kernel was almost round, grayish, thick and hard, oily, full of broad branching veins, and intensely aromatic. Aubriot set the nutmeg in the palm of Jeanne's hand and said, "Here's the start of your fortune."

She inhaled its fragrance voluptuously. With eyelids closed, nostrils dilated, a soulful smile on her lips, she looked like a female Buddha in a trance.

"Don't overdo it," Aubriot joked. "Large doses of nutmeg have a stupefying effect."

"Oh!" Jeanne sighed, her eyes still closed. "I'm already in a divine stupor!"

Amused and even touched, he let her have her fill of the spicy aroma before smelling the nutmeg himself. "You have good quality here," he said, then bit into the pit and cried, "Ouch! It's not soft like a hazelnut. Shall we look for others?"

She stared at him in delight. "Is there any chance of finding others?"

"Let's have a look. A miracle in the vegetable kingdom is a rare event."

They searched for an hour and found only one other survivor not far from the first, but it was puny, with malformed flowers and not a single fruit.

"Never mind," said Jeanne, sitting down next to Aubriot on a rock bench. "It doesn't matter. The only nutmeg trees on the island were planted at Monplaisir and here. The ones at Monplaisir have died. That makes me the first landowner on l'Ile de France to have harvested her own spice for seasoning."

With a choking sob, she fell weeping on Aubriot's chest.

"I was just thinking," the doctor said softly as he stroked her hair, "when you don't weep at least a bucketful of tears, it's not a solemn occasion. There now, blow your nose. And let me clean you up a bit . . ." He began to pick off bits of vines and weeds clinging to her hair and clothes.

"You do think, don't you, Monsieur Philibert, that we are living a great moment?" she asked, her face still buried in Aubriot's neck. "You do believe it, don't you?" she pressed him, tugging on the lapels of his jacket.

"Yes."

"Seriously?"

"Seriously."

"When Monsieur Poivre finds out, he'll be ecstatic."

"That's certain! Not the king, however."

"I want Monsieur Poivre to come and pick my nutmegs. He lost an arm in his quest for spices, so the one he has left ought to reap the harvest of his passion."

She took the nutmeg out of her pocket and held it under her nose. "Mmmmmm! Delicious! And it's true that it goes to the head like champagne! Monsieur Philibert, I'm so happy! Ready to burst! Embrace me!"

He laughed and took the nutmeg. "Apparently there's a good reason for using this spice to produce essence of Italy."

"What is essence of Italy?"

"An aphrodisiac liqueur I made by the barrel to earn pocket money when I was a medical student at Montpellier. The city was full of rich old men who had taken young wives the second time round."

She raised her head to look at him out of her liquid amber eyes. "And do you still remember how to make that liqueur? Perhaps it would inspire you to kiss me."

"Impudent mademoiselle! For some time now you've been awfully free with your tongue! Tell me now, are you bent on making love in the woods?"

"The air of this island corrupts," she declared. "Everyone says so. Corrupted women are simply victims of the air."

* * * *

Polydor had finally arrived with his master's baggage by the time Jeanne and Aubriot returned to the house. He had dawdled away three or four hours en route.

"I had the bed made up in the doctor's room," Pauline whispered to Jeanne, smiling with an air of complicity.

"Thank you," said Jeanne, embarrassed. Her relations with Pauline were strained, whether she spoke of Vincent or of Aubriot. In spite of constant rebukes from Marie and Emilie, Jeanne still had not informed Pauline, much less Aubriot, of her marriage. Naturally, the Creole woman imagined that things were still the way they had been when Jeanne left Charmont on the arm of her beloved scholar. And as time passed it became almost impossible for Jeanne to tell either Pauline or Aubriot about the duplicity of her love life.

She was absorbed by the everyday realities of life at Allspice. Vincent's prolonged absence lent a dreamlike innocence to her passion for him. On this pleasant Sunday evening, Jeanne hated Pauline's complicit smile as the older woman realized that Aubriot would at last be staying the night at Allspice.

"I've ordered a good supper," she added. "Good supper, comfortable bed, and all the rest. There's never been a better way to trap a fickle lover."

"Thanks, Pauline," Jeanne repeated hastily, then went off to see what Nanny and Lalitté were cooking.

As she was strolling in the yard behind the house, she saw Saint Méry arriving.

The marquis wore a freshly ironed white linen suit and carried a fat bouquet of India roses, the lemon-yellow flowers that Aubriot called African marigolds. As soon as his house at Allspice was finished, he had planted his India roses in the garden. Jeanne had never seen him cut any before this.

She felt touched when he offered her the handsome bouquet. "They don't have a nice smell, but I know you like their shape and color."

"I'm delighted with them," she said, holding out her hand.

This time Saint Méry kissed it more discreetly than he had earlier that morning. Making a determined effort to withstand her scrutiny, he said nothing for the longest time. Then, when she remained silent, he finally ventured, "I hope you'll forget the way I treated you this morning. Just tell me when I have to go, and I won't hang around. I'll take Zoe and her boys, but I'll not ask Nanny to come, so you won't lose her. She's crazy about baby Virginia."

"Marquis, what are you talking about?" Jeanne cut him short. "Have I ever asked you to move out?"

"No, but—"

"But what?"

"Frankly, mademoiselle, it depends. I'm not sure I want to stay."

"No? Why is that?"

"I can't stand sermons."

"Have I threatened to deliver any?" The hazy blue in Saint Méry's eyes seemed to condense into a solid color before Jeanne's gaze.

"We'll see," he said. "Sometimes it is the unspoken sermons that are the most intolerable."

She mocked him gently. "Marquis, please stay. I love you as you are. So much the worse for you!"

He gave a little pout, half incredulous, half admiring. "If you can keep your promise, mademoiselle, you'll be a most extraordinary white woman. Usually, only a black woman will love you for what you are."

CHAPTER 28

The nutmeg harvest at Allspice was a solemn celebration that drew crowds.

The mistress of Allspice plucked the most perfect fruit and presented it to the governor, requesting that he forward it to His Majesty Louis XV as proof that a rare spice had taken root in his colony of l'Ile de France.

The governor received the nutmeg and passed it to his intendant, who in turn gave it to the captain of the port with instructions to deliver it to the commander of the first vessel sailing for France.

What a great day it was! A passion for botany floated in the warm summer air. The nutmeg tree at Allspice had revealed itself to be miraculously fruitful. The moneylenders foretold a golden age for l'Ile de France, and envisioned acres and acres ploughed and planted with colorful exotics.

"My dear Jeannette, I forbid you to use your nutmegs to flavor stew. You must plant every one of them," said Poivre as he was leaving after the ceremony. "Set an example, Jeannette, and you will do me a great favor."

Leaning on Poivre's arm as she accompanied him to his carriage, Jeanne said, "I'll set all the examples you wish. I'll put in hundreds of trees. I'll raise healthy spice plants, grain for the table, and bananas by the shipload. At Allspice we won't chop down the wooded banks of rivers. We'll plant vegetables and raise chickens and pigs. We'll stock the streams and the pond with fish. We'll protect the birds and make war on monkeys and rats. To put it in a nutmeg shell, I shall make Allspice the model plantation of your colony—if you'll help me. If you'll let me buy some slaves from my future neighbors at Belle Herbe. For without them, and in spite of my good will, I haven't the man-power to do what you ask."

Poivre laughed and thought to himself that the shy little Jeannette he had known in Lyons had acquired an iron will! "Well, I can see that I must force Don José to obey his women. But tell me honestly, just between the two of us, do you think he wants any part of Belle Herbe?"

* * * *

Don José bought Belle Herbe, without enthusiasm but with a good-natured smile. He had never seen Emilie so happy—deeply, genuinely happy. And finding her thus, he even wound up seeing certain advantages in it.

For Don José had found an excuse for him to return to his homeland. He also had another ulterior motive that he didn't advertise. He counted on using the two ships to bring in something less space-consuming and more valuable than meat. Piasters.

A silver piaster was worth four pounds sixpence in Montevideo, and between fifteen and eighteen livres in Port Louis—a very profitable exchange rate indeed. And while he waited, he could enjoy his mistress's good temper.

Bubbling over with happiness, Emilie rushed up to throw her arms around Jeanne and Marie. "I'm moving into Belle Herbe, can you imagine! What a pleasant life we shall all have! You'll come to dinner and we'll talk in a green and white salon. It will be just like old times—the three of us, relaxed, greedy, and naughty, chatting for hours over a feast of shellfish. At last, thank God, my life is about to begin again the way I want it to!"

Marie and Jeanne glanced at each other, then at Don José. Emilie babbled on excitedly about future dinner parties for little girls, and elaborate teas over which she would preside.

"Really," she concluded, "I love everything I've planned for Belle Herbe. Only one thing bothers me, and that's Don José's trip to La

Plata. Supposing he doesn't want to leave his wild grasslands? I would be perfectly happy if that one thought didn't spoil the picture."

Emilie's penetrating voice carried, and Don José overheard her last remark.

He turned to his mistress and said softly, "*Amor mio,* don't worry, I promise that I'll never take you back to La Plata by force." After a pause, he went on with a note of sadness in his voice, "I won't promise not to return there now and then. But you'll have friends to pass the time with while I'm away. My absence will seem much shorter to you than to me."

"Now and then?" Emilie repeated hastily. "Is there some new arrangement, then? I thought you were only committed to a single trip."

"That's true," Don José replied, "but—"

"But you've taken it into your head to volunteer for the trips that follow, at least 'now and then,' " Emilie interjected nervously. "Fancy that! You know I'm happy with Belle Herbe, and now you want to spoil it all by announcing that you'll be running off. Don José, I'll allow you one trip and that's all! Do it as soon as possible, leave tomorrow, come back the next day, and then sit quietly on your veranda and smoke a cigar. *Claro, hombre?*"

Don José had no time to reply as Emilie rattled on. "If you want to please me, leave tomorrow, come back the next day, and don't make me fret with all this talk of traveling. It bothers me to have to do without you. I'd rather have the bother behind me than in front of me."

"*Claro,*" murmured Don José, bewildered, incredulous, pondering what his mistress had just said and feeling his heartbeat quicken. Was he reading too much into her words? Had she indeed confessed her fondness for him?

Jeanne glanced over at Marie, who watched the two lovers. What had passed between Emilie and Don José appeared to have affected Marie so personally that Jeanne wondered if her friend hadn't fallen in love with the Spaniard.

* * * *

Don José took over Belle Herbe four days after the *Colbert* sailed. From then on, the work at Jeanne's place progressed twice as fast. The slaves at Belle Herbe went regularly to lend a hand at Allspice. Don

José didn't complain, since he had no intention of running a working plantation.

Belle Herbe was the country house Emilie had always wanted, a villa like José's own in La Plata. All they planted was a showy garden surrounding the house, and enough banana trees and grain to feed the slaves. The fields of sugar cane were returned to grassland, except for a six-hundred-acre parcel that went to Marie under the name of Sugarland. At this time Aubriot moved permanently to Allspice.

Strong winds had gusted at the beginning of the summer, posing the threat of a cyclone. But the scare had passed, and now the summer weather in Moka was delightful—cool nights perfumed with jasmine and frangipani. There was planting at Allspice, hoeing at Sugarland, gardening at Belle Herbe.

Work and worry were minimal at the start. Life seemed endlessly rewarded by hibiscus bursting into bloom, the recovery of a sickly litchi tree, the overnight appearance of a row of tiny tea shrubs, the fresh charm of a room paneled with figured cotton cloth acquired at a waterfront auction.

Every day produced a new first which brought everyone running to peer and admire, then celebrate over a glass of French or Cape wine. They were savoring the joys of a lifetime.

Even Don José was too busy laying out the garden at Belle Herbe to remind himself that Emilie had imprisoned him in her fancy lair. Rarely were they seen in town, and then only to buy something or dine with the Poivres.

Françoise Poivre was a sensitive soul who wept copiously. She felt as if she were living between two warring wolfpacks, and she was. The hostility between the governor and his intendant grew worse, nearly coming to blows. Crises erupted in the council chamber, sending the combatants racing for their pens. The minister for the colonies, far across the ocean, wondered what was happening to his model project as a flood of complaints swept over his desk. Island society was now clearly divided into two hostile camps, each out to have the opposing leader's head. Since any decision of this nature rested with the king, the adversaries carried on their battles with banana peels, plots, and slander, each trying to wear the other down.

The slavery issue was one apple of discord between the governor and his intendant. Poivre made no secret of his opposition to slavery, whereas Dumas found all sorts of godly wisdom in the fact that certain creatures had black skins, primitive manners, and no religion at all, which automatically fitted them to serve the white race.

On l'Ile de France, under Dumas, the slave laws were severely enforced. If a runaway was caught, he was tied to a ladder and flogged, an ear would be cut off, and he would be sent back to work wearing a triangular iron collar. If he ran off a second time, he was flogged, crippled in one leg by hamstringing, and put in chains. For the third offense he was flogged and hanged. Official justice was so merciless that slave owners, either out of mercy or their own self-interest, avoided denouncing runaways and thieves, preferring to inflict their own punishments.

The self-serving protection of their owners didn't always save the blacks from the king's justice. One morning a fugitive slave who had escaped from prison was found collapsed in a field at Belle Herbe, shivering with fever.

The fugitive was a Creole woman of twenty years who belonged to M. de Chazal. They nursed her at Belle Herbe for three days. Word of this reached the governor and he dispatched a sergeant and four blacks from the civil guard. They appeared at Don José's door and politely claimed the escaped slave. Don José decided that it would serve no purpose to surrender the fugitive, so he simply refused, offering to pay the prescribed reward and to repay the owner. After giving the guards a drink and sending them on their way, he went back to seeding his flower beds.

The next day Aubriot and Jeanne were lunching with their friends at Belle Herbe on a veranda ablaze with nasturtiums when they were surprised to see the governor ride up with his adjutant.

"Now here's a visitor who's certainly not dropping in just to be neighborly," Don José muttered before rising to greet the caller with a flashing smile.

Colonel Dumas accepted a demitasse and a cigar, and even exchanged a few trifling remarks before stating the purpose of his visit. The order that he, the governor, was attempting to establish in l'Ile de France had been thwarted by an "irresponsible" act on Don José's part. A runaway who went unpunished was an intolerable indication of disorder.

"Sir," Aubriot interjected, "Leibnitz would disagree with you, for he holds that the overall order of things presupposes minor disorders."

The governor swept aside Leibnitz with an impatient gesture and retorted dryly, "Doctor, Leibnitz was undoubtedly speaking for his fellow Germans. I am speaking for the French, among whom disorder has a way of expanding rapidly. And so . . ."

And so he returned his attention to Don José and ended his little speech militantly, urging him to turn Lolotte over to the guard he had "courteously" stationed at the plantation's entrance.

Don José's smile broadened to stunning proportions. "Governor, may I offer you a special liqueur distilled by the missionaries of Saint Lazare. Father Duval gave it to me. It's divine. The heavenly bouquet will make you weep. Perhaps you've already tasted it?"

Nonplussed, Dumas muttered a vague acquiescence. They drank the liqueur. Unfortunately the governor was not one of those happy individuals whom alcohol mollifies. Having emptied his glass, he called for Lolotte, this time standing straight as a ramrod, with his chin flung out.

Stifling a sigh, Don José rose in turn. "Governor," he said calmly, still smiling, "you have spoken of French order. Forgive me for being Spanish. A Spaniard does not surrender anyone who asks him for refuge, nobleman or beggar, white, black, or yellow. I will pay whatever fine is due. Charge me what you wish for the reward and for the price of the slave."

Dumas' jaw hardened. He had to restrain himself from striking his fist on the table. "Spanish gentleman, you are the guest of a French province," he said cuttingly. "I shall not interfere with the customs of La Plata and I will not permit you to challenge ours. I don't intend to let happen here what happened on Santo Domingo, where the runaways invariably defected to the Spanish sector and thumbed their noses at the French."

"Mercy, Governor! I haven't the slightest idea what's going on in Santo Domingo, or why the slaves are deserting the French for the Spaniards. I suppose they lean toward the idle life! Since idleness is not a virtue in your eyes, I can't see any reason to feel slighted," said Don José with unconcealed irony.

"Kindly cease trying to appear so innocent and distracting our discussion, señor," said Dumas, boiling under his collar. "As long as I govern this island in the name of my king, the authority of his deputy will not be thwarted! And believe me, if I'd been in charge in Santo Domingo instead of second-in-command, the Spaniards would not have encouraged our runaways to defy us. At the first opportunity I would have thrown them all into the sea and occupied the whole country!"

"Yes, just the way you drove the English out of Canada," said Don José evenly.

"Gentlemen!" exclaimed both Aubriot and the adjutant, anxious to cool the argument. The adjutant added, glancing toward the hostess and her friend, "In front of the ladies . . ."

But it was too late. Nothing could console Dumas for the loss of Canada. For he was a good soldier, loyal and brave and not responsible for his royal master's miscalculations. Reminding him of the French defeat in Canada was like applying a red-hot iron to an open wound. He turned pale as a ghost and his eyes flashed. "I believe, señor, that you have just insulted me," he declared icily. "I don't suppose you have any objection to giving me satisfaction for it?"

Aubriot took a step forward. At that moment Don José replied, "Mercy, no, sir, if you feel insulted by the truth."

"Don José!" Aubriot warned. "Please, gentlemen . . ."

Dumas ignored the interruption. "My second is present," he said, designating his adjutant. "Kindly choose your own, señor."

Momentarily stunned by all this, the two young women recovered their wits and Emilie exclaimed, "I must be dreaming! Don José, you're not going to . . ."

"Go in the house!" Aubriot ordered.

"Jeanne, take your friend in along with the children. Now! Dame Emilie, if you please . . ."

Jeanne dragged Emilie inside, with Paul and the slave boy Fanfan clutching their skirts.

* * * *

"I can't believe it! I simply can't believe it!" Emilie kept repeating as she paced the floor. "Don't tell me, Jeanne, that Don José and the governor are dueling over Lolotte! Over a slave!"

"Marie's husband dueled to the death for a flower seller, and Vincent fought with Lauraguais over a dancer. I dare you to find a man who duels for a worthy cause!" said Jeanne angrily. She, like Emilie, was pacing the floor and twisting her handkerchief. "But they won't come to blows. Monsieur Philibert will stop them."

"He will, won't he?" said Emilie in a tiny, plaintive voice that Jeanne had never heard.

"Yes," said Jeanne. But her hopes were dim. She knew that Philibert had also dueled for trivial causes. Once for the pretty baker's wife in Châtillon, and again and again with who knew how many cuckolds in Montpellier in his student days. Every good swordsman was quick to draw.

As if to echo her thought, Emilie murmured, "Don José is a good swordsman, thank God. In La Plata the men used to fight at the drop of a hat. I never knew about it till later, from gossip. But now . . ."

After a moment's silence her voice took on a nervous edge. "This suspense is unbearable! I have to do something, I must do something! Jeanne, excuse me a minute. Stay with Paul and don't let him follow me."

Jeanne knew instantly that Emilie had gone off to pray. Through prayer, would Emilie at last find out that she loved him?

* * * *

The duelists emerged from their ordeal beaming at each other. Blood brothers. Don José with a slash on his right wrist, and Dumas with a gash on his left hip, overjoyed by their wounds. They celebrated the event in festive spirits with the host's best Spanish wine and coconut biscuits, while the doctor rolled bandages on the veranda. Not a word was said about Lolotte or Canada. The conversation focused on famous Parisian fencing masters. Their feints and their nimble defenses, their lunges, their parries in tierce and quarte, and finally that stab in the back which neatly ran the opponent through— standard practice among the best practitioners of the art.

Emilie leaned over to Jeanne. "You can see they're sorry they didn't poke bigger holes in each other," she murmured sarcastically. "And to think that a moment ago I was almost trembling for a man who was merely playing games!"

"You *were* trembling," Jeanne corrected her, smiling.

"Well, don't tell anyone," Emilie shot back airily.

Jeanne thought that she would pass on the good news of Emilie's anxiety to Don José.

She headed back toward Allspice, so full of happiness that on reaching her property, instead of riding to the stable, she galloped up a hill.

She rode up the clearest part of the slope, inhaling the overpowering fragrance of aloes in the summer heat. The hilltop was shaded with listless palms that looked out to the horizon. Ahead lay the shimmering green sea and lacy white clouds in a silken blue sky. As

Blanchette pawed the ground, her hooves sent up faint herbal scents. In this pagan paradise, Jeanne imagined herself down there barefoot in the sand. A starfish in the sand.

Bird, a beautiful view on a beautiful day is near perfect happiness. Bird, go fetch me Vincent to make it perfect! She begged wordlessly to a swan-white tropic bird swooping and gliding toward the harbor. Sitting down on a lava rock, she gazed rapturously at the landscape. A sail no bigger than a seagull was creeping along the horizon from the direction of l'Ile de Bourbon. Jeanne's heart raced. One of these days the approaching sail would belong to the *Belle Vincente.*

From her pocket she drew the corsair's last letter. A Maltese frigate traveling via Rio had brought it to her just the day before.

December 8, 1767
My fair-haired love, my songbird, my little fig, my lambkin,

I am fiercely jealous of the bearer of this letter, as he will see you shortly. I long for you more today than yesterday and less today than tomorrow, the proof being that I write platitudes.

Don't despise me for it, my licorice drop. For as I write, I imagine you preparing for bed with myself as your valet, and I am off on a delightful adventure that dulls my wits. Yet I need them, and all the cleverness I can muster. The ship's captain sent from Lisbon has just arrived in Rio to take my frigate to Portugal. He seems like a pretty sharp fellow. But sailors don't keep secrets from each other, and that's what makes the sport of naval battles so interesting.

Enough! I'll find a way to be on my ship the day she leaves, even if I have to go as a stinking caulker or a rat in the hold! They've stolen my two mistresses from me. I'll have to recover one if I'm to go off in search of the other. It's likely that I'll succeed, for no streak of bad luck goes on forever. That's one of the first lessons you learn at sea. And there's a song we Provençals like to sing:

> Mistress mine, love draws me to you
> And soon, without my telling you so
> You will know it from the window
> Where you hope to see me appear.

Though I haven't translated the lines too well, they mean
that love is as swift as the wind in reaching out to one's
love. My beauty, my buttercup, I . . .

Pebbles rolled into a basalt ditch along the hill. Jeanne quickly
folded Vincent's letter and turned around.

"Ah! it's you," she greeted the Provençal, smiling. "Were you looking for me?

"Provençal," Jeanne said kindly, "the day before yesterday the master of the Maltese frigate came to bring me a letter from your captain.
He's in good health."

The topman crouched on his heels, lowering himself to Jeanne's
level. "I thought you'd had a letter from the *Saint Michel*," he said. "I
was almost positive. It hurt that you didn't tell me so. Because the two
of us, after the adventure we went through together, you know, well,
you and I, with all respect, Mam'selle Jeanne, we're almost like old
sailing mates . . ."

"We're sailors," Jeanne corrected him gravely.

A smile spread over the Provençal's gingerbread complexion. "So
the captain's all right?" he asked.

"He's fine. I think his prison is comfortable—even pleasant."

"Oh!" said the topman. "A handsome captain like ours will never
end up on a prison ship. He manages to make friends even among his
enemies. I say the Devil himself would open his door to our captain!"

"I don't doubt it," said Jeanne.

"And I don't suppose the captain told you when he hopes to sail?"

"No, he didn't. Provençal . . ."

The topman riveted his eyes on her, awaiting her question.

"Provençal, do you really believe that the captain will be able to get
the *Belle Vincente* back from the Portuguese and escape aboard her?"

"Lady, if you asked me to swear while standing on a bed of hot coals
that I believe it, I'd say yes," replied the Provençal.

Their eyes met, and Jeanne felt herself blushing. The immense
devotion she read in the sailor's eyes embarrassed her. She lifted up
her loose hair to cool the back of her neck, then began to braid it.
Blanchette suddenly tossed her head and pawed the ground, impatient
to return to greener pastures below. The Provençal got to his feet,
contemplating the ash-blond tresses streaked with gold that Jeanne
was plaiting.

Jeanne leaned back against the burning trunk of a tatamaca and closed her eyes. Inside her head she could hear Vincent's resonant voice singing beneath the window of the little house belonging to Pinto's lieutenant. The sailor's song left a taste of sun-scorched tears in her mouth.

> *"Beauty, you are like a fair buttercup,*
> *Lovely as a treasure.*
> *Like a gentle treasure*
> *I would take you for my mistress.*
> *Beauty, you are like the violet*
> *That grows all alone in my heart."*

CHAPTER 29

he delicate state of grace in which Jeanne had managed to maintain herself ever since she opted for duplicity fractured unexpectedly one evening in mid-May.

The *Belle Vincente* had left Rio Bay the previous February. Surely the corsair was aboard, for he had flown his princely prison. News of this was brought by the *Reina Isabel*, a Spanish corvette bound for Manila. A leak had forced the captain, Don Vallejo, to put into Rio for four days.

It appeared that the prisoner of whom his excellency had become so fond, a Maltese he had wined and dined on port and plump turkeys, had flown the coop. Cleared out just like that. As if the friendship of a Brazilian viceroy meant no more than a pile of sawdust.

Don Vallejo stayed with Don José while he was in Port Louis. He responded to a barrage of questions with the following account of what had happened in Rio.

Shortly before entering the bay, he had crossed the frigate *Belle Vincente*, which was bound for Europe. Curiously enough, the Spanish and Portuguese captains greeted rather than ignored each other because Don Vallejo and Don Ribeiro were acquainted. They had even saluted each other with speaking trumpets. Don Vallejo felt certain that all was well with the Portuguese captain conducting the captive vessel to Lisbon.

The following day he heard about the escaped prisoner. The viceroy's fury set the town talking. To relieve his frayed nerves, the little tyrant had swept everybody on the streets into prison, and executed three convicts accused of dubious crimes. In addition, although he did not expect results, he had dispatched his guards to search the surrounding countryside, and sent a frigate in pursuit of the *Belle Vincente.*

Unfortunately, that was the extent of Don Vallejo's knowledge of the affair. Jeanne kept imagining the *Belle Vincente* sailing from Rio harbor, but beyond that she could only dream. She climbed to her hilltop balcony and watched for Vincent's sail, only to return sighing, disappointed.

When she looked at Philibert she tightened her lips. Her friends peered at her, Marie sympathetically, Emilie critically. Jeanne's gaze told them, *I'm thinking only of him.*

She was exhausting herself in nightmares and silent inner struggles when one evening after dinner, alone with Emilie, she announced suddenly, "I've decided to explain everything to Philibert after the anniversary party for Allspice. I don't want to spoil the celebration. That's when I'll also talk to Pauline."

Emilie stared at her silently as Jeanne added, "You've already told me what you think of my cowardice and my delays. Don't say anything more. Wait till the party is over and you'll see. This time I'll keep my word. I have to, for my back's against the wall."

Emilie nodded. "Jeanne, this is your business. But it makes me so angry to see you treat Aubriot's bed as if you've taken a religious vow. You make more fuss about leaving it than I did when I left the church."

"Emilie, you were never happy there. You always forget that slight difference between us, my dear. I like to be happy now. Once I used to like to make myself sad . . . but not anymore. I'm obliged to find the strength to forget what's troubling me. I pray that I can forget it just a bit longer, until the anniversary of Allspice."

"You've six days to go," Emilie replied. "Six times *mañana!* Don José would call it eternity!"

* * * *

The anniversary party given by the mistress of Allspice was set for the first Sunday in July.

Since the king had taken over the island, prosperous settlers had returned to the practice of holding get-togethers in the country as they had done before the great cyclone of 1760. Winter was not the best season for garden parties, but Jeanne was dying to show off *her* Allspice.

The vast estate had not been completely cleared of its rampant overgrowth, yet one could easily imagine what it would look like in a couple of years. As one approached the house, off to the right where it was flat, the land had been divided into fields of sugar cane, corn, and manioc. On the left, where the hills rose gently, they were still restoring a stand of pomegranates. The pepper plantation had been reseeded in front of the few cinnamon trees that had survived the terrible hurricane. Next to the pepper plants was where Jeanne's future fortune would soon lie, in the nutmeg and clove trees that the *Vigilant's* captain had stolen from the Dutch in the Moluccas. Beyond the cinnamon trees lay the hills, the forest slopes, and the horizon. Double rows of tamarind trees towered majestically along the entranceway.

The house had regained its simple charm. It had been repainted lemon yellow with white doors and windows, accented by a dull red shingled roof. Invading vines had been torn out and replaced with cuttings of a tropical ever-blooming creeper that sent out multitudes of pink cups filled with blackcurrant liqueur. Jeanne called them her "bougainvilleas" in memory of the ones she had looped about Captain de Bougainville's neck. Opulently colored zinnias and nasturtiums bordering the walkway paid tribute to the never-ending tropical summer.

On Don José's advice, Jeanne had had blinds made for the French windows, which kept the ground floor pleasantly cool. Except for Aubriot's study and bedchamber, the house still resembled a collection of rustic rooms freshly tiled and painted. Jeanne had furnished them with simple wood and rattan pieces, the whitewashed walls awaiting wallpaper from the East that a Dutch ship captain had promised to deliver. Upstairs, the decoration had progressed farther, each bedroom now having been paneled in printed fabrics with flower or bird motifs.

Jeanne's room had blue carnations, and her dressing room was painted the same shade of turquoise blue. The bed had a smooth golden hull and tall, white, gauzy sails of mosquito netting that rose and fell with each breath of air. It looked like a ship. A lovely bed, indeed, to be rocked in the arms of a corsair!

* * * *

"Certainly mamzelle light candle to Good Lawd for fair weather," said Suzon gaily as she laid out her mistress's clothes on the coverlet.

Jeanne smiled fondly at the finery she would wear as hostess. With both hands she scooped up the white muslin gown lined with pale lemon faille. It shimmered with pink and gold iridescence. Jeanne held it and gazed at herself in the mirror. The faille crackled and swished, bringing the rustle of the ballroom to her ears.

Mme. de Bouhey had sent her the measure of faille in her favorite color. It had arrived early enough to have a new dress made by Dorothy, the best seamstress in Port Louis.

Jeanne's gift from her beloved baroness arrived aboard the *Countess Margot,* hand-delivered by Pazevin's son, Giulio, who had come to seek his fortune as a trader in Port Louis with his young wife Margot.

The ladies of Allspice and Belle Herbe greeted the youngest of the Delafaye girls with open arms. There was kissing and hugging and chattering all day and night. The Pazevins stayed with Emilie. They were building their new townhouse not far from Government House. It was to be a handsome, spacious stone mansion in a park, and was to be large enough to combine their private lives with the business office of the island's first important mercantile tradesman.

"Do you think Margot will wear the latest Lyon silk dress made by Delafaye?" Jeanne asked as Marie entered the room.

"I think Margot will deck herself out so as to make all your guests eager to spend money imitating her," said Marie. "Her family makes these silks, her husband sells them, and she wears the costliest fashions!"

"Now there's a good husband for you," exclaimed Jeanne. "Do you hear, Suzon? Monsieur Pazevin wants his wife to spend lots of money to make herself beautiful!"

"Suzon mama always say, 'Chile, nice words ain't no sentiment. Every man wants same thing. When you see his money you know is real love.' "

"Fine piece of advice that is, Suzon! Aren't you ashamed to measure love by money?" came the stern voice of Aubriot.

Framed in the doorway, he wore an expression of mock indignation. "Father Duval's catechism doesn't do much to improve their outlook," he added after Suzon had gone out. "You two ladies have chosen as chambermaids the shrewdest of the black Creoles that Madame Manon sold to Jeanne."

"We chose the prettiest, the youngest, the healthiest, the liveliest and gayest, and the most flirtatious. We chose our maids the way a man chooses his," said Jeanne matter-of-factly.

The doctor darted a meaningful look at Jeanne, which she caught and returned.

"I'm going now. I have to get dressed," said Marie. Standing in the doorway, she turned to Jeanne. "I only came to ask you . . . do you think I should wear pink?"

"But, my dear, I've begged you for months to do it! You look your best in pink."

"Yes, but still . . . pink, in my situation?" Marie murmured, still undecided.

"It's a funny thing," said Jeanne, smiling. "Because the church forbade its nuns to wear pink outside the cloister, you took to thinking that a pink dress is sinful. Even Emilie is frightened by the color pink."

"Madame Marie, I agree that you should wear pink. Pink is so becoming to a blue-eyed blond with a milky complexion," Aubriot declared graciously.

With a look of surprise, Jeanne shot back, "Marie, dear, I'm glad you asked that question. It's taught me that Monsieur Philibert has a passing interest in female apparel and believes he knows something about it. I wonder, monsieur, if you would care to comment on the appropriateness of my dress?"

Marie burst out laughing.

"I prescribe pink for your friend the way I prescribe remedies," said Aubriot. "It's well known, my jealous one, that a pink dress is an excellent cure for widow's depression. Certain colors have medicinal effects."

"Go right ahead, cure my jealous spirit by complimenting me on the color of my dress," Jeanne persisted.

"Whatever color your dress is, you'll be the belle of the ball, as usual," said Aubriot, leaning out the window to examine the "bougainvilleas" climbing up the façade.

"I give up!" Jeanne sighed, disappointed. "Since the medical practice offers mere common courtesy, I shall flirt with the naval units! So there!"

"I'm sure you will!" said Aubriot, turning around. "Over here, the women seek consolation for just about everything with the fleet. And today there'll be more seamen than you bargained for."

"Really?"

"A corvette from the royal fleet bound for India arrived yesterday evening, just in time for the officers to dine with me at the Intendancy. I've invited them all to your lawn party since I knew you'd be happy to have news of your rescuer in La Plata. It seems that in mid-ocean, en route for the Cape, the royal vessel was followed by a frigate that saluted and hoisted the French flag. The frigate was at quite some distance, but the corvette's commander, the Chevalier Morlière, swore that he recognized the *Belle Vincente*. And since it wasn't sailing anywhere in the direction of Portugal, one can only infer that . . . Jeanne, are you listening or are you smoothing your dress? Aren't you at all interested in the fate of the gentleman who was captured as a result of rescuing you from the bandits?"

"Yes," she said, trying desperately to control her mounting agitation. Her dress trembled in her hands. She stood dazed and speechless, staring fixedly into Philibert's inquisitive eyes.

"What's got into you?" he asked suddenly, surprised and impatient.

Busying herself at the table, Jeanne regained her composure. "You didn't finish your story of what Morlière told you," she said without looking up.

"There's not much to tell. It seems that the Chevalier Vincent's frigate was sighted somewhere in the Atlantic en route for the Cape. More than that I can't tell you. Captain Morlière knew nothing about the chevalier's imprisonment by the Portuguese, but he was almost certain the frigate had followed his own route to the Cape. He was sure it didn't have a Portuguese captain because, out of cannon range, a Portuguese ship would never salute a vessel flying the colors of France."

"Well, that's open to speculation," said Jeanne, after a pause.

"Yes," Aubriot agreed. "It seems incredible to me that the Chevalier Vincent could have recovered his property from his jailers, but the seamen I dined with seemed less surprised than I. Morlière—actually he's a Knight of Malta—reminded me that the sea is a different universe from the one we landlubbers know."

For a second Jeanne shut her eyes, then she murmured, "There are three types of beings: the living, the dead, and the sailors."

Aubriot nodded. "A nice concept," he observed appreciatively. "Where does it come from?"

"Oh," she said, walking into her dressing room so as to blush in peace, "I heard it from a seaman with whom I once danced a gavotte at Charmont."

Suzon handed her a white cotton peignoir, seated her in front of the mirror, and began to remove the curling papers from her hair.

Aubriot leaned against the door frame. "I see you're wearing English-style curls. I wish that wigs were out for women too."

"Monsieur Philibert, you're a man who's managed to keep his hair. But since most everyone else has only a bald pate to show, I'll wager they won't support your fashion and go bareheaded to advertise their licentiousness."

Aubriot gave a short laugh and said, "Do you believe that licentiousness and baldness go hand in hand?"

"Isn't that what they say?"

"It is. To get my degree I had to debate that very question before the medical faculty at Montpellier, but I took the negative view." He walked up to her and whispered in her ear, "I was spending a fortune on the ladies, and hated the idea of going bald as a result!"

For a moment Jeanne felt immensely relieved and broke into a laugh.

"Philibert, I love it when we laugh together," said Jeanne, as she turned to him.

"Let Suzon fix your hair. It's almost nine o'clock," said Aubriot. "I have to finish dressing too."

As he was leaving, he did something he had never done before. Seizing one of Jeanne's curls, he removed the curling paper and pulled it down gently, then let it rebound like a spring, grabbed it again, and twirled it around his finger. "A woman's silk is the finest there is. The silkworm cannot compete," he said. "I'll see you later."

Pale and trembling, Jeanne touched the curl that Philibert had just fingered. *Would it be possible? Could he just possibly love me a little more because I vexed him?*

The curl he had fondled, dangling like an African amulet from her head, seemed like a pledge of boundless, all-forgiving affection.

CHAPTER 30

he party was in full swing. As the afternoon drew to a close, guests who lived far from Allspice began leaving. About fifty lingered on, unwilling to end a beautiful day. Several courting couples meandered under the majestic tamarinds. The intendant held court on the veranda while, beneath the tropical almond, the governor held his own.

Along the path lined with banana trees which led to the slave huts there was constant traffic as the house servants took turns watching the African dancers.

Pauline and Jeanne relaxed on the veranda, enjoying the spectacle below. With a sigh of contentment, Pauline got up from her rattan chair and linked her arm in Jeanne's. "Shall we walk a bit? The breeze is like a velvety hand on the skin. Shall we go?"

Jeanne hesitated. Several times now, ever since she had heard Morlière's own account of the encounter with the *Belle Vincente*, Pauline had tried to take her young friend aside. Jeanne knew she wanted to talk about Vincent.

"Toward the pond?" Pauline proposed. "Everyone's strolling the other way."

Yielding to inevitability, Jeanne followed along.

Behind the house the landscape was much the same as when Jeanne had moved in. The fruit trees, wildly overgrown with tangled vines and brambles, reached out to join the woods beyond.

The scents of the orchard, confined by the surrounding hills, wafted along the path. The air smelled so very sweet when orange and pomegranate blossoms stirred in the breeze.

Pauline pressed on Jeanne's arm to get her to slow down. "Mercy, Jeannette! Learn to walk like a Creole! The best way to enjoy life is at a leisurely pace, I can assure you."

"Forgive me," said Jeanne, slowing her steps. "Monsieur Aubriot has taught me to walk like a hiker."

"Monsieur Aubriot has done a pretty thorough job of teaching you to please him in all respects," said Pauline.

Jeanne frowned. "Are you suggesting that he's turned me into his slave?"

"What a harsh word!" exclaimed Pauline. "That's not what I'd call a woman who voluntarily bows to the wishes and needs of a man—I'd say you were a woman in love."

"A woman in love," Jeanne repeated dreamily. "Emilie calls me that too."

"It's not an insult!" said Pauline with a laugh.

"I wonder. Would you describe a grown man in that way?" She hesitated a moment, feeling the color rush to her cheeks, then pursued her thought. "Would you say that Monsieur Aubriot is in love with me?"

Pauline noted her embarrassment and smiled. "My word, Jeannette, one would think you were asking yourself the question for the first time!"

"Maybe I am," said Jeanne. "At least it's the first time I've asked anyone else, and I feel quite ridiculous."

"Ridiculous?"

"Childish, if you prefer."

With an understanding look, Pauline said gently, "Jeanne, I'm sure that Aubriot is fonder of you than he thinks. A scholar his age doesn't think of love, but if he makes it, that's a good sign."

There was a silence, after which Pauline went on playfully, "For men to make love the way we would like them to, they'd have to be women. But then we'd have all sorts of other complaints. And so, all told, it's best that things stay the way they are. For all the rest—the delicacy of feeling, the word or two softly spoken, the thoughtful attentions—for all the rest, let us each love one another!"

With a frivolous laugh that she delivered on purpose, she added, "Seriously, Jeanne, one should make pleasure with men and love with women!"

"Oh!" said Jeanne, taken aback.

"You see," Pauline continued, "ever since I chose to live at Vaux, I've never missed Santo Domingo. But when I return to Vaux I will probably miss l'Ile de France because I'll miss Allspice. Belle Herbe is so close that we could call the whole area 'Four Ladies.' Pauline, Jeanne, Marie, and Emilie. Our little woman's world is dear to me. I think that we make love very well!"

Jeanne acknowledged the joke with a smile. A phrase of Vincent's, which she had never remembered before, popped into her mind. *Pauline and I have promised each other nothing but friendship and pleasure.*

"Pauline . . ." She hesitated, then finally said, "Since we seem to be discussing love and pleasure . . . is it true, do you think, that a man's pleasure is enough to satisfy a woman?"

"As long as *she* believes it . . ." said Pauline after a pause that suggested she no longer believed it.

At Pauline's words, the ghost of Vincent, hovering near them both, seemed to come alive, and their conversation drifted naturally to him.

"Do you think Morlière knew what he was seeing?" Pauline asked. "A good many frigates look alike, if I'm not mistaken."

"That's a landlubber's notion," said Jeanne. "I've lived close to a crew and was always surprised that they could identify most vessels they met, as if the sea were a little village peopled with familiar faces."

"But if Vincent really recaptured his frigate," said Pauline, "and if it was his ship that passed the *Resolve* en route to the Cape, why didn't Morlière hear about it on the Cape? And if the *Belle Vincente* rounded the Cape without stopping, why haven't we seen him here? Isn't Port Louis the favorite port of call for French ships bound for the Bay of Bengal?"

"I think we'll have to stop beating our heads against the wall," said Jeanne, who continued to do just that. "The chevalier is a fugitive captain. Maybe he had to throw pursuers off his trail. Maybe he hid out on some secret island. Maybe . . ."

"*Anything* could have happened," Pauline interrupted in a leaden voice.

"No," said Jeanne.

"The sea . . ." Pauline began, then stopped, her throat in knots.

"No!" Jeanne repeated louder.

Pauline smiled wanly. "Jeanne, you have the confidence of youth and have yet to learn that life is fragile, especially the life of someone you love."

My chevalier is alive because I feel he is. Jeanne gazed at Pauline with mild condescension.

A worried look clouded the Creole's lovely features, stripping away her easy, offhand manner. At that moment Pauline looked older, resembling an overripe beauty. Anxious concern etched fine lines beneath her face powder. *The heartaches of love don't bring out the best in Pauline,* Jeanne thought.

"Do you know what probably happened?" she said aloud. "I think he is still somewhere in the Atlantic, on an out-of-the-way island like Tristan da Cunha. I think he needed to repair a leak, or seek shelter for a spell, or hide his cargo."

"I never heard him mention that island," said Pauline, a trifle jealously.

"The Provençal knows all about it."

"Wherever he is, I hope it's not some blissful isle where he'll linger on," murmured Pauline. "I haven't a great many years left . . . for him."

Jeanne trembled so visibly that Pauline eyed her strangely.

"Let's rest for just a minute," Pauline pleaded, spying the bench that stood beneath the eucalyptus on the edge of the pond. They sat down.

"In l'Ile de France, just as in Santo Domingo, the climate encourages love. Maybe I came just for that . . . for a climate where love is made easy."

"I always suspected that you didn't come just to help Marie plant sugar cane," said Jeanne.

Pauline ignored the jibe and continued, "Don't you see, Jeannette, when I realized that Vincent would be away from France for a long time . . . when I found out that he wanted to make Port Louis his base of operations for the smuggling trade . . . I couldn't stay behind and wait while my hair turned gray."

She drew closer to Jeanne, shivering a bit, and slipped an arm through hers. "Look, I know well enough that a young lover is bound to leave you sooner or later. But why sooner if you can make it later by simply going on a voyage? The ocean crossing was pleasant enough, and my complexion has improved from the moist, balmy climate of Moka. Isn't that so?"

Now, right now . . . I ought to tell her!

"Your complexion is fine," said Jeanne, with some effort.

Pauline gave a little laugh and shook her head. "You really want to tell me that at my age it's sheer folly to be roaming the seas in pursuit of a lover. So tell me it's crazy, Jeannette. At least I'll have the satisfaction of including myself in the ranks of lovestruck fools."

She leaned over and picked a few sprigs of wild basil from a sun-soaked patch, crumpled the leaves between her palms, and held them out for Jeanne to smell. "Aphrodisiac," she said. "Pluck, crush, inhale, and nature will intoxicate you, adding your follies to her own."

Lost in her own thoughts of love, she was unaware of her companion's persistent silence.

At last Jeanne could stand it no more.

"Pauline, you've done enough talking about your chevalier. Now it's my turn to talk about mine . . ."

* * * *

Silent now, but moving along as close to each other as they had on the way out, they returned from the pond as if from the ends of the earth.

"You go on ahead," Pauline said suddenly. "I want to fix my face up. I'll go in by the back way."

Jeanne kissed her hand lightly. "Forgive me, Pauline, I didn't want to hurt you. I shouldn't have done it today, with everyone looking at us. But today, finally, I had the courage to speak out. I couldn't bring myself to lie any longer."

"Oh!" said Pauline. "It was kind of you to lie. The only trouble with a lie is that you can't stick with it forever. Hurry, Jeanne. You're the hostess, you've been away from your guests too long already."

Just as Jeanne was leaving, she saw two men coming round a bend in the path and heard Don José's exultant shout, "There they are!"

"At last we've found you, ladies," said Lieutenant de Boussuge when they met. "Your friends were anxious and sent us off to fish you out of the pond."

"Is anyone hungry?" Pauline asked, forcing herself to sound lighthearted.

"They have plenty to drink, and that seems to satisfy their wants," said Don José. "Saint Méry has had a bit too much," he whispered to Jeanne.

"Good Lord!" she murmured.

"Don't worry. It has simply rid him of his sullen humor," said Don José, "while all around him are in such happy spirits."

The governor had had to leave without saying goodbye to Jeanne. His courtiers had followed soon after, but the rest of the company seemed loath to end their fun. The violins went on playing for the open-air dancing, livelier now that the house servants had joined in.

Jeanne rejoined Emilie, whom she spied sitting apart from the dancers, half hidden from sight. "Emilie, what the devil are you doing in this corner? It's the first time I've ever seen you pass up a chance to dance!"

"That's because I don't feel very well," said Emilie in a peevish tone. "When I'm pregnant, I get bouts of nausea all day long!"

"Emilie!" exclaimed Jeanne, astonished. "Emilie, are you serious?"

"Yes, unfortunately. Please, now, let's not have any compliments! My condition is available to any foolish ninny. Confound those Franciscan friars in Montevideo! They distilled me a vinegar I've run out of, and wouldn't tell me how to make my own. They make a fortune supplying customers in La Plata with a vinegar that restores a woman's honor. It's worth every penny of the price, but they guard the recipe with the zeal of alchemists. Oh, I'm so furious at those people!"

Jeanne heard this outburst and smiled. "I'll wager Don José isn't furious at them!"

"Good Lord! He doesn't know a thing about it."

"He doesn't? You haven't told him? But why?"

"Because it would make him happy!" Emilie thundered. "And I want to put off making him happy for as long as possible. It's my revenge!"

"You're wrong," said Jeanne. "If you told him about it, you would be carrying *his* joy instead of *your* burden. You might even feel better."

Emilie's hostile stare riveted on Jeanne, then softened, and her sea-green eyes recovered their lively sparkle.

"I'll see," she said, her lip curling. "In any event, I won't be able to travel by sea for a while. Seven more months to go before my confinement. Then a tiny baby . . . so I shall be fastened to Belle Herbe for some time."

"That's not such a bad thing," said Jeanne, smiling. "And now you'll surely agree to marry Don José, won't you?"

"Jeannette, you always forget this," she said, drawing from her bodice the enamel-and-gold cross of the Neuville order.

Jeanne waved it aside impatiently. "When you were given that cross, Emilie, you were only a child. For God's sake, don't act like one now. Do you honestly believe that your sins are diminished more by your having lovers and bastards than they would be if you took a husband?"

"My dear, the lovers and the illegitimate children of a canoness are not mortal sins," Emilie replied dryly. "To marry, however, she must be released from her vows. Let me assure you, Mademoiselle Beauchamps, that Dame Emilie de la Pommeraie knows a great deal more about the subject than you do."

"I don't doubt it, Countess," Jeanne replied, smirking. "But promise me that you'll have bastards only by Spaniards in La Plata, who treat them very well."

The laugh she expected from Emilie never arrived. Instead, with affected carelessness, Emilie retorted, "Yes, I promise. And I'll also give them Spanish names, which I find very colorful. If I have a girl I'll call her Juana, Juanita for short. Would you like to become godmother to a bastard child, Jeanne? I'll try to produce a pretty one without freckles, with the tiny feet and big dark eyes of Spanish ladies. Don José has a portrait of his mother, not too well painted, but the eyes are wonderful. That portrait would be a good model to imitate."

She is dying to talk about the baby. Suddenly Jeanne had an idea. "Do you happen to know Señora de Murcia's first name?"

"Maria Juana," Emilie replied.

Jeanne smiled inwardly. "I suppose she was called Juanita?"

"Perhaps," Emilie replied primly. "Or perhaps Marietta." With a fresh burst of belligerence, she added, "Don't imagine that's what made me . . ."

"I'm not imagining a thing, my dear," Jeanne interrupted, kissing her friend's forehead. "I've simply noticed that you don't always succeed in being as nasty as you'd like."

* * * *

"You'll have to find some leftover ham to share with us for supper," said Poivre gaily as soon as Jeanne returned. "Françoise and her sister refuse to stop dancing. They seem to have forgotten that this poor intendant gets up at six every morning to further the welfare of his community."

"We'll find something to go with the ham," Marie promised. "Meanwhile, I'll have some blackberry syrup brought to you."

"I shan't refuse it," said Poivre. "Listening to a bunch of chattering imbeciles always makes me crave a sweet reward. Ugh! I've been besieged for a whole hour by my own people. The minute a chief sits down in company for a moment's relaxation, it seems to be the signal for every imbecile on his staff to try to show off. I don't know why they can't do it during working hours!"

Jeanne laughed wildly as Aubriot joined them. "My dear friend," said Aubriot, "remember that you need only know how to debate in Latin to enter the medical profession. Tell me if you don't consider that custom the most dangerous one of all!"

He turned to greet Pauline, who now approached, smiling warmly.

"Are you hungry yet? The Marquis d'Albergati wishes to do the honors of his vegetable casserole. He has taught Nanny to make it. He swears that his ratatouille will perfume the air and gladden our stomachs . . ."

Jeanne watched her guests stream toward the house. *What a good face she puts on! Or is she really as composed as she looks?*

Pauline was moving among the guests, laughing, joking, flirting, as if Jeanne had never taken Vincent from her. She had been so afraid to say a word, thinking it would devastate the Creole.

Jeanne looked over at Philibert and tried to project what *afterward* would be like for him. He discussed the future education of l'Ile de France with Baron Grant and a group of cultivated listeners. Maybe her words would glide right off him, too, without leaving a trace. That would be all right. All right yet unbearable. Feeling a desperate need to cry, she bit her lip until it bled, and then she returned to the veranda.

Dusk had fallen and the stars were out, studding the sky with their usual brilliance. *The sky is infinitely indifferent to human sadness.*

Moving out of the light shining through the French windows in the salon, Jeanne walked the length of the veranda and melted into the shadows. There she nearly tripped over Saint Méry, who was balanced on the two rear legs of a rattan chair.

"Pardon me!" he said, and pulled in his legs. When he started to get up, she motioned for him to remain seated and sat down beside him.

The picnic was ending, and the hum of it reached them along with the fragrances of Allspice, which nightfall never failed to revive. Two carriages and their teams moved along the path from the stable, climbed the split-log steps, and waited on the walkway in front of the house.

"The loveliest of Sundays is ending," Jeanne murmured.

There was no sound from Saint Méry for the longest time. Finally he said, "If you stay here, you'll miss the last bits of it."

"So will you."

"I don't know how to get rid of my thirst, so I get rid of wine."

Something about the tone of Saint Méry's remark told Jeanne that the marquis was in one of his rare moods when one could really speak frankly with him.

"I must have interrupted your daydream," she said. "What were you dreaming about?"

"The Burgundy was good. I wasn't dreaming, thank God, I was dozing off."

"Well, continue, Marquis. I don't feel like talking, and my sitting near you might scare off any others who do."

He laughed softly. "You need a good watchdog, mademoiselle. For tonight, I'll fill the bill. 'Marquis' . . . that's a good name for a dog. Very dignified."

She tapped him gently on the arm. "I forbid you to be so self-deprecating."

"What comes after the tap?" he said. "If I behave myself, do I get a lump of sugar? A nice mistress always follows up a tap with a lump of sugar."

The cry of a parakeet came from the direction of the pond. Without warning, Saint Méry suddenly asked, "Are you worried about something, mademoiselle?"

Jeanne trembled. "What makes you think so, Marquis?"

"A tickling in my ears. I just told you that this evening I feel as clever as a watchdog."

She was sitting very close to him. When he turned his head to speak to her, she caught a mild scent of wine on his breath, just enough to reassure her. He had the indulgent manner of a wine tippler.

"Does it feel good to be swimming in wine, Marquis?"

He nodded. "It does indeed. What wretchedness do you feel like drowning in wine, mademoiselle? One lover too many? Or one too few?"

Jeanne stiffened. "Why do you think I am wretched, Marquis?"

"I look at you often, mademoiselle." With his head bent, he seemed deep in thought, struggling hard to assemble an intelligible sentence from a hazy web of thoughts.

Finally he said, "It shows when a woman looks around her as if searching for something . . . I assume it can't be the man she's with. And when she climbs hills to gaze out to sea . . ."

"Monsieur Aubriot doesn't know anything about that," Jeanne said hastily.

"Monsieur Aubriot is a sober-minded man," said Saint Méry. "When I was a student in Paris and was curious about all sorts of things, I happened on a passage dealing with ancient Teutonic customs. It was written that those wise barbarians made it a practice to consider a question twice, once sober and once drunk, in order to have a double view of it. Monsieur Aubriot doesn't have double vision. He is consistently sober."

Jeanne burst out laughing. "Marquis, all of a sudden you display such arrogance! It's arrogance, not pride, to hold up one's sins as virtues. No matter, I'm pleased with you tonight, pleased to discuss love."

"Are we discussing love?"

"I thought we were."

"Oh? Well, if that's the case, let's get on with it. The subject suits me. Your turn, mademoiselle."

She shot him a piercing look. "Tell me, could you love a faithless woman?"

"Depends on the woman."

"A pretty one."

"Well, I'll tell you, mademoiselle, if she looked like you, I'd sooner put up with her infidelity than her indifference."

A wave of feminine cruelty swept over Jeanne. She leaned closer to Saint Méry so that her perfumed hair tickled his nose, and asked in a hushed, coquettish voice, "Marquis, are you in love with me?"

"Distressfully so," came the reply.

"Oh!" she said, taken aback by his outspoken avowal.

"Does that make you feel better?" he asked without a trace of bitterness.

"Let's walk a bit," she suggested, getting up.

She put her arm in his, which surprised him into silence.

"Our alley of tamarinds—your alley—has grown back handsomely. It's one of the prettiest entrances on the island, don't you think?"

"I think it's the prettiest," said Jeanne.

He coughed and cleared his throat. "Mademoiselle . . ."

"Yes, Marquis?"

"Is he a sailor?"

"Yes, he's a sailor."

"Who'll be coming to Port Louis?"

"Yes."

Saint Méry heaved a deep sigh. "Next time you have a party with lots of wine, we'll have to speak of love again, mademoiselle."

She couldn't resist one last flirtatious remark. "So, Marquis, you would really love me if I were unfaithful, and never hold it against me?"

"Would you like to try?"

The marquis's eyes bore down on her so directly that they made her cheeks burn.

"Let's go back," she said. "The last of the guests must be leaving."

"It's been a fine Sunday," said Saint Méry.

* * * *

"Well, Jeanne, are you satisfied with your first party?" Pauline asked. "I think it was a success, don't you?"

"Yes," said Pauline, dropping onto the couch. She sighed, stretched her arms, and said, "It's a Sunday I won't forget."

"Pauline . . ." Jeanne's voice became choked, and she sat down on the couch.

Pauline put her hand on Jeanne's. "Let's not get sentimental, Jeannette. We're not on an equal footing when it comes to tears. It takes me too many beauty masks to repair my face. The harbor captain told me that the *Minerva* will sail in two weeks, which gives me plenty of time to pack. So if Monsieur Logeart is willing to take me, I'll return to France aboard his ship."

"Return to France?" Jeanne exclaimed. "You want to leave? But . . . what about Marie? You were supposed to . . ."

"Jeannette, let's be serious," Pauline cut in. "I needed Marie to need me until the chevalier arrived. Now . . ." She forced herself to smile. "One woman per port. Surely that makes life easier for a seaman once he comes ashore."

Jeanne blew her nose and mumbled into her handkerchief, "I know what you're going through, but I don't know what to tell you. I didn't do it on purpose, Pauline—fall in love with Vincent."

Pauline uttered a shrill little laugh. "My dear child, you certainly should have. The black Creoles in my Antilles have a proverb that strikes me as the best philosophy of life. 'If Good Lawd throw you banana, don't close yo' eyes, open yo' mouf.' "

She got up and tugged at Jeanne's hand. "Let's go to bed. It's late. Tomorrow we'll invent a good lie to explain my leaving on the *Minerva*."

"I'm not sleepy and neither are you," said Jeanne, forcing Pauline to sit down again.

"And you feel like talking about Vincent now as much as you once did when you came to Vaux?"

"Maybe," Jeanne admitted, leaning her head against Pauline's silken shoulder.

"I'm not sure that I'm game for this sort of thing anymore. I no longer hold the upper hand."

Jeanne sat up again and fixed her eyes on Pauline. "I need to know. I want to know. You never really loved Vincent, did you?" She blushed and added, "He mentioned one day that your friendship was based solely on pleasure."

"Oh?" said Pauline, turning pale. "He told you that?"

"Isn't it true?"

Saying "yes" barely above a whisper, Pauline went on in a faraway, drawling voice, "We agreed that our relationship would be free and easy. It suited his sailor's existence and my reluctance to mope on the sidelines like a wallflower. But I'm vexed, I must confess, that he remembered it so clearly."

With a smile that turned into a grimace, she added, "In the long run, one always resents a man who keeps his word about such things."

Jeanne gave her a searching look, in response to which Pauline observed carelessly, "Hah! That's feminine vanity for you! Wanting to get more than was bargained for, that's all."

"That's all?"

"Yes, that's all," Pauline replied immediately. "What would you like me to say, Jeanne? That it won't kill me to give up Vincent? All right, then, I promise that it won't kill me. I have some pride, and at my age I'm not about to have my heart broken. Though it seems"— her voice sharpened with irony—"it seems that heartaches can arrive when you're least prepared for them. At fifteen, when nobody takes you seriously, or at forty, when everyone laughs at you."

"I suffered terribly at fifteen," Jeanne sighed.

Pauline smiled. "At fifteen, heartache is ecstasy. The suffering is sheer torment, but there's always hope."

Jeanne was leaning her head once again on Pauline's shoulder. There was a long silence, which Jeanne finally broke. "Pauline, don't

leave. I'm afraid. Ever since I've known that the chevalier was somewhere on the Cape, I've felt afraid."

"And do I reassure you?"

"Maybe you do."

Pauline was trying to understand her friend's meaning when Jeanne
murmured against her neck, "I confessed everything to you, and you
don't hate me. Do you think Monsieur Aubriot will be understanding
too?"

So that's it! "No, I don't. But he'll accept what you tell him. He,
too, has reached the age when one bows out gracefully. He'll have to
be content with your affection."

"The chevalier will always feel affection for you, too," said Jeanne,
hesitating just a little.

"Affection . . ." A sudden flood of tears blinded Pauline. She shut
her eyes and breathed deeply to staunch the tears, which were so new
to her that their briny taste seared her throat. *No! No!* The tears
stopped, replaced by a pain in her chest. She sighed. *Affection. The
farewell gift left behind by a thoughtful lover as he disappears out the door.
Affection from a distance, or by mail, or at arm's length over a cup of tea.*

Jeanne's muffled voice made Pauline open her eyes. "Why don't you
say something?"

"I was just thinking," said Pauline. "And I thought I saw a shooting star."

"Make a wish, Pauline."

"A wish? I wish that I shall become a pretty little old lady."

"What an idea!" exclaimed Jeanne. "What's the use of being pretty
when you're old?"

"It's useful, because when I grow old I don't want my former lovers
to feel ashamed of themselves when they look at me."

Staring at Pauline, Jeanne became pensive, biting her lip. Finally,
in a burst of defiance, she shot back, "You must think you know how
to love him better than I do."

"Yes," said Pauline. "But since you believe your love is ten times
better than mine, we're even. And the advantage is all on your side.
You *can't* teach me your fair-haired beauty or your youth, whereas I
can show you how to make the cherries jubilee and the Antillean
punch he's so fond of."

"Pauline, I ought to hate you, but I don't. And you love me, don't
you?"

Pauline reached out to stroke Jeanne's satiny amber cheek, then her neck. "My dear child, you have the adorable fragrance of young flesh," she said as she caressed Jeanne with her eyes as well as her fingertips.

Like a cat, Jeanne stretched out on the couch with her head in Pauline's lap and lay there motionless while a pair of gentle hands stroked her golden hair. The smoky stub of a dying candle finally aroused them both from their cozy posture as it sputtered and went out. Jeanne lit two fresh candles and handed one holder to Pauline.

"The first anniversary of Allspice is definitely over," she declared with a tiny shiver.

* * * *

At the breakfast table the next morning, Aubriot announced straightway that he had arranged the previous evening to make a grand tour of the island with his botanist friends de Cossigny and de Céré.

"We've agreed that we'll wander along like snails. Ever since I came here I've been dreaming of such a leisurely excursion, and they welcome the chance to teach me about their native land. I think both of them are rather disappointed not to have been offered my job here. If I collaborate with them in the classification work, it will make up somewhat for the injustice they feel. Jeannette, will you come with us?"

Jeanne felt Pauline's and Marie's eyes glued to her.

"The trouble is," she began hesitantly, "I'm really needed here. Monsieur Poivre is having half the tea plants delivered to me from Abbot Gallois, who has gathered samples in China. I really must be here to put them in the soil."

Aubriot nodded in agreement. "Anyway," he said, "this expedition might not be too much fun for you. We're going into deep woods where we'll probably have to camp out like savages."

"What if maroons come after you with their dogs?" Pauline volunteered.

"We'll carry guns," Aubriot replied. "The captain of the regiment will be in our party."

"How long will the trip take you?" Jeanne asked.

"About two weeks," said Aubriot. "I want to do more than take just a quick look at the things that interest me."

"When will you leave?"

"Right away, as soon as I can get ready," said Aubriot. "We're meeting at Palma, the de Cossigny place, and Monsieur de Messin, who's spending the night at Belle Herbe, suggested that I go up there by dugout. He wants to come back in the afternoon."

* * * *

"It's not my fault!" Jeanne burst out belligerently after Aubriot had gone into his study to prepare for his trip. When Pauline and Marie said nothing, she went on contentiously, "I would have spoken to him, yes, this very day. Now he's going away. Am I to blame? Do you expect me to ruin his pleasure right at the start? Anyway, he's in a rush to leave. You heard him say so yourselves."

Silence still. In a final effort to ease her guilty conscience, she added, "It was ordained that I defer once more the harm I have to do. Is that my fault?"

"Don't go repeating that to Emilie," Marie said at last. "She'll tell you just what she thinks of the way you make heaven responsible for your own cowardly actions!"

Gentle Marie so rarely rebuked her that Jeanne felt stung by it and hastened to join Aubriot in his study.

"Do you need some help packing your knapsack?" she offered.

"I never refuse it," he said gaily.

"You seem happy as a bird to be leaving us."

"I must admit that I'm eager to go romping through the woods. I like to grow moss on my old jacket and put a few more creases in my battered old hat."

As he walked by her, he gave her curls a tug, saying, "I'll miss having my Jeannette trotting along behind me this time. But I understand your having to be here for the tea plants."

She kept him from reaching into his book cabinet by twining her arms around his neck. "Will you really miss me?"

He raised one eyebrow. "Why do you doubt it?"

"Maybe because I don't deserve to be so indispensable to a very learned botanist."

"Sometimes you're very silly," he said, trying to move away.

She linked her arms even tighter about his neck. "Monsieur Philibert . . ."

"Oh, now comes the important message?"

"Monsieur Philibert, what do I mean to you? Do you like me a little? A lot? Tenderly? In a special way?"

He looked at her in surprise, and saw that she was blushing scarlet. "Jeannette, do you really think it's the right time to bring up this subject? You know Monsieur de Messin is waiting for me at Belle Herbe."

"I know, and it's not the right time," she said, snuggling up against his shoulder. "But before I let you go away for a long time, I wanted . . . I needed to know what I mean to you. You've never told me."

"For the moment you are my giddy little girl who's feeling playful and is making me late," he said with a trace of impatience, forcibly unwinding her arms and returning to his packing.

But when he heard her deep sigh of disappointment, he looked up at once. "Let's be done with this childishness, Jeannette," he scolded her gently. "What do you need to be reassured about before I leave? Tell me honestly."

"No," she retorted spitefully. "Why should I beg you for treats? I won't get them. It's hopeless ever to expect you to feel sentimental!"

He laughed cheerfully, which sent two tears creeping down Jeanne's eyelashes. She sniffled angrily. "I'd never be able to explain my feelings to you because as soon as I'd try you'd get bored or make fun of me. I'd end up saying nothing. And it would be all your fault!"

He laughed again and sat down on the edge of the desk. "Come over here," he told her.

She approached sullenly and stood beyond his reach. He got up and took her hand. "Come here," he repeated, drawing her toward him. "Now, what is it you want to tell me?"

She shook her head. "Nothing, I've forgotten what it was."

"Well, then, I'll tell you something," he announced good-naturedly. "I like you a little, lots, tenderly, in a special way. Is that enough for you? No?"

Deeply affected by her great man's unexpected words, she devoured him with wonderstruck eyes.

"I see that I'll have to add an ounce of cure," he said lightly. With his thumb and forefinger, he pinched her affectionately on the cheek. "Jeannette, *ti voglio bene*," he declared.

Jeanne trembled. Her eyelashes quivered.

"So, life seems to be flowing back into the statue," Aubriot observed. "Now I can return to my packing."

Aubriot checked his pistols as Jeanne absently gathered up colored pencils and replaced them in their leather holder. Her head seemed a million miles away from her hands, which moved remarkably slowly.

"*Ti voglio bene*," she murmured suddenly, as if thinking aloud, and pouted. " 'I wish you well.' The Italians must be even more casual than the French in matters of the heart, having found words to avoid saying 'I love you.' "

"Do you think so? I rather imagine they found an impersonal way to say 'I love you.' "

Jeanne's heart leaped, then galloped. Clutching the pencil holder in both hands, she asked very quickly and in a hushed voice, "Monsieur Philibert . . . did you mean to say 'I love you'?"

He didn't hear her question. Or pretended not to, as he shuffled papers around on his work table. "Where the devil did I stick that other marvelous lens the English captain gave me?"

"I borrowed the lens," she informed him with a sigh. "It's in my room. I'll go get it for you."

* * * *

They watched Aubriot disappear down the grassy passageway leading to Belle Herbe. Polydor, loping along behind his master, was swallowed up in turn as he rounded the bend.

"The chevalier may arrive here before Monsieur Aubriot," said Pauline.

"Yes," said Jeanne, so haughtily that it discouraged further conversation.

Pauline turned and went back inside the house. Jeanne walked down to the stable, had Blanchette saddled, and rode up to sit for a spell on her hilltop balcony.

CHAPTER 31

milie," said Jeanne, "why not admit honestly that at last the love of Don José has won your heart? That's what we'd really like to hear."

"Oh, yes! We'd all be so happy! Don José would be wild with joy!" Marie cried as she flung her arms about Emilie's neck, then suddenly burst into tears and fled.

"You just reminded her that she's a widow," said Pauline. "She cried when she learned that you were going to have a second baby."

"She is sensitive to whatever connects me to Don José," Emilie said. "She's in love with him. Haven't you noticed?"

"Yes," said Jeanne. "But we didn't think that you . . ."

"I've got two good eyes," said Emilie. "And I'm not grieving, either. It will fade. Marie is a patient sweetheart. She's fonder of her dreams than of real life, especially if they make her weep a bit. Marie has taken a fancy to the love Don José offers me, rather than the love of Lieutenant de Boussuge. She avoids sleeping with him and makes her own heart bleed a bit."

"Mercy! I'd like to believe what you say," said Pauline, smiling.

"Believe it," said Emilie. "But I didn't come here to gossip. I have something important to tell Jeannette."

Pauline withdrew discreetly.

Emilie spoke up at once. "Jeanne, your husband is in Capetown and in good health, it seems. He should be arriving shortly in Port Louis."

The color had drained from Jeanne's face. For an instant she clutched a pillar on the veranda for support, and shut her eyes. "Emilie, where did you hear that?"

"A Spanish frigate anchored here this morning. Captain Rafael Machado is an old friend of Don José's, a fellow smuggler whom the Chevalier Vincent also knows. In fact the two frigates, the Spanish one and Vincent's, sailed to Capetown together after meeting off Tristan da Cunha Island."

"Why only as far as Capetown?" Jeanne asked. "Why did Vincent stay there?"

"Don Rafael told us that the *Belle Vincente* was damaged somewhat when she was rescued from the Portuguese. There are excellent Dutch ship's carpenters at Capetown. The repairs will only take two or three weeks. So the *San Isidro* has only a two-week lead over the *Belle Vincente*."

The two stared at each other in silence. At last Jeanne murmured, "I was right. Vincent hid out for a while on Tristan da Cunha. Did Don Rafael tell you why he finally left there?"

"Yes," said Emilie. "He has nothing more to fear from the Portuguese. Before his escape from Rio he had learned that the irascible viceroy was soon to be replaced by a more gentlemanly sort, Dom Antonio Rolim da Moura Tavares."

Jeanne sank into a chair. She remained pale, pressing both hands against her heart to still its wild beating. Emilie surveyed her discomfiture without the slightest sign of sympathy.

"My dear," she began in an eminently mordant key, "you've now reached the point where you've been heading all along—a tangled mess more knotty today than yesterday. You've had plenty of time to untangle it."

"Emilie, please . . ." Jeanne entreated her.

Emilie shrugged and fell silent, while her fingers drummed impatiently on her skirt.

Raising her head, Jeanne asked, "Don't you have a letter for me from Vincent?"

"I was expecting that question," Emilie said. "I'm surprised it took so long. The answer is no. Don Rafael brought no letter for you."

"But why? Isn't that strange?"

Emilie nodded. "Don José was surprised, and I am too. But after all, Vincent knew he was only a few days behind the *San Isidro*, and that you would already have had word of him."

"Still, it's very odd," Jeanne repeated after a long pause. "He has written to me in far more dangerous circumstances. Why not send me a note with the *San Isidro*? Does he think so little of my concern for him? Can he so easily put off for two or three weeks his need to communicate with me? And if—"

"Jeanne," Emilie cut in sharply, "do you really think Vincent's faults ought to alarm you just now?"

* * * *

The next day was Sunday. Pierre Poivre arrived for lunch at Allspice with a note from Aubriot, which he handed to Jeanne. "Our dear doctor will return tomorrow and would like you to bring his horse to the landing."

"The landing?"

"Read it. A rider delivered it to me this morning."

While herb-gathering along the coast of Grand Bay, the three botanists had encountered Father Rochon. He had been correcting the error-riddled maps of the Ministry of Naval Affairs. The botanists volunteered to do a little astronomy with the priest. They embarked with him on his brig, the *Shepherd's Hour*, understanding that it would deliver them to Port Louis after a spell at sea.

"I'll go," said Jeanne, folding up the note.

Surely this was the final reprieve.

Later that afternoon, when all her guests had left, she went for a swim at Grande Rivière, her favorite "bathtub." It was a splendid day. The green ripples licking the sand turned to bright blue tinged with mauve and indigo farther out. The edge of the sea and the rim of the sky melted into a shimmering gold horizon. *I'll never tire of this magical landscape.*

Jeanne plunged into the sea and continued out as far as the coral reef. She floated facedown, staring into the water. Fifteen translucent feet below, a lobster family wandered among the branches of coral. The sight of this magnificent submarine world below compensated for the stinging salt in her eyes. The cold, silent landscape penetrated and cleansed her soul.

Peering into the water gave her a false sense of peacefulness. But her peaceful moments were numbered.

* * * *

The launch from the *Shepherd's Hour* delivered its passengers ashore just before dusk.

They all ate at the Intendancy. Though the conversation centered on botany and astronomy, Aubriot excused himself early. He felt tired, and coughed from time to time.

Outside, in the plaza, the sky was clear and starry.

"A fine night for a romantic gallop from Port Louis to Moka, don't you think?" said Aubriot, mounting his horse Bruna.

They set out at a canter, inhaling the moist plant odors that drifted on the island breezes. The horses' hoofbeats caused a panic among bands of thieving monkeys that were helping themselves in the cornfields. They scurried off, leaving trails of half-eaten ears behind them. In the distance, shrouded in mysterious silence, the woods they were skirting creaked, trembled, and shivered. They strained their ears to recognize sounds of nocturnal life. Without having spoken a word to each other, they entered the bittersweet aloeswood forest screening the entrance to Allspice.

Jeanne and Aubriot reined in their horses. They both loved to inhale the aromatic aloeswood. By moonlight the tall, splendid trees looked more dramatic than ever. The silent, sleeping house rose before them, pale against the darkness. Its ribbons of false bougainvillea had climbed to the second story and branched out along the balcony.

Aubriot took a deep breath of voluptuous pleasure before announcing abruptly, "I shouldn't get too used to coming back here as if it were my home. Sooner or later I'll have to start thinking of returning to France."

"Don't try to scare me," said Jeanne. "Monsieur Poivre has told me about his plans for you, and they're all long-range."

Philibert adopted a tone of complacent resignation. "Poivre's projects are fascinating, I'll admit. I don't know if I'll have the courage to pass them up. If I accept, I'll be dragging along a burden of guilt. I know that a son needs his father, and I've left a son behind in France, Jeannette."

She replied carelessly, "You left him with a loving uncle."

"Yes, I don't doubt that I'll find my boy well versed in his catechism," said Philibert caustically. "When I left, Michel was too small to take around the countryside, naming the plants, insects, and pebbles on our way. Poor boy, I never even had time to show him my vineyard."

Jeanne rode up close to Aubriot's horse. "I was just a little girl, Monsieur Philibert, when you did all that for me," she said in a hushed voice.

Until then, Philibert had never made her understand quite so clearly, that she, far more than his son, Michel, was the patient creation of the learned Dr. Aubriot. She was his child, claiming his affection, his paternal ear, his indulgence. His forgiveness. Now was the time to tell all! Now, in the softness of the night that disarms the armor-clad persona in all of us.

They dismounted. Polydor unloaded their knapsacks and led the horses off to the stable.

"I'm not the least bit sleepy," Jeanne announced as she entered the house. "Couldn't we sit in your study and talk for a bit? Words seem to flow much more freely at night."

Philibert smiled a weary smile. "I'd rather put off our little chat till the morning," he said. "You know I'm not the best sailor. I'm tired."

"Are you feeling sick?" she asked in alarm.

"I said I was tired, that's all."

He glanced at the assortment of cold meats and fruits Pauline had set out on the table before she went to bed. "I'd rather have a cup of herbal tea than any of that," he said, with a vague gesture of distaste. "Sage tea would be nice."

"Why don't you get ready for bed while I make your tea. You've been swimming in the ocean too much. You know it isn't good for you, whatever you say."

From his cage in the entry where he was kept at night, the parrot Chérimbané heard Jeanne's voice and opened his eyes. "I love you, Jeanne!" the bird screeched lustily in a Creole dialect as he stretched his sumptuous wings.

"I don't know who taught him that, but it seems to be his favorite phrase. He repeats it everywhere," Jeanne observed.

"Your marquis taught it to him," said Aubriot.

Jeanne turned around. "What did you say?"

"I said your manager, Saint Méry, taught the parrot that sentence."

"Well, now!"

Aubriot gave a little mocking smile. "That doesn't astonish you, I presume?"

She blushed and darted a glance at him. "A number of discerning men find me attractive, I must admit."

Nodding, he walked toward his bedroom. She followed him to the doorway and fired away.

"You know, being attractive isn't always a pleasure. It can overwhelm you like . . . a fatal destiny against which a woman is defenseless."

"Oh, I do believe it!" Aubriot scoffed. "I am prepared to believe that a pretty woman spends most of her waking moments like a doe pursued by hounds. Be patient, though. It won't last forever."

She hesitated to reply in a way that would facilitate her confession, then bit her lip and finally gave up. "I'll go make your tea."

"Jeanne, I love you!" Chérimbané shrilled again as she went by.

* * * *

The night dragged on, drop by drop, second by second, to the perpetual rhythm of her sleeplessness.

I'll say to him, You must forgive me, Monsieur Philibert, or else condemn me to die from your scorn. I have behaved odiously, yet I hope that you can find it within your heart to forgive me. Don't you see, I've not acted like a grownup, really . . .

She got up and took a sip of sugar water, then went back to bed and snuffed out the candle.

There's no doubt about it, I haven't grown up yet. . . . Two magical things have happened to me. I believed them both, just like a child. A famous scientist appeared when I was ten. Then a handsome corsair when I was fifteen. I loved them both with all my heart. Two loves mingling . . . at Charmont, in Paris, on the sea, and now here in l'Ile de France.

She relit the candle and puffed up her pillows, battering them vigorously with her fists.

What can I do, dear Lord? What can I do about these two loves that have struck me like the sun's rays? Each time I try to tidy up my heart a bit, I fail miserably because my heart is in no way troubled by this abundance.

Exhausted, she finally fell into a restless sleep just as the servants in the kitchen below were beginning to stir.

CHAPTER 32

eanne was awakened by Nanny's frantically shaking her.

"Is it so late?" she mumbled sleepily, sitting up in bed.

Nanny shook her head. "Ma'm Pauline an' M'am Marie sleepin' still. Is Moussié Dotta who sick. Want herb tea. I tell him need Papa Coffi."

Jeanne jumped out of bed and ran halfway down the stairs in her nightdress, with Nanny at her heels shouting after her and holding out a shawl.

Bundled up in his dressing gown, Philibert was about to leave his room when Jeanne burst in.

"Why aren't you still sleeping?" he asked with a rasp in his throat. "Well, it's a lucky thing. I've caught a fever. I was going to help Nanny make an antifebrile tea. Now you can do it for me. I'm going back to bed."

"Yes, do go back to bed," said Jeanne. "I'll make you some dog's-tooth."

"If you make dog's-tooth, put some orange peel in the pot. Otherwise it tastes so horrid . . ." He had to force himself to speak above a whisper.

When Jeanne returned with the tea she found him shivering, his forehead on fire.

Philibert's dark eyes glowed eerily, and two scarlet patches colored his cheeks. He was having difficulty breathing, and his voice sounded peculiarly flat.

In her petticoat skirt, with her turban all awry, Zoe came to join Nanny in Aubriot's bedchamber. With her arms dangling helplessly at her side and her kind black face the image of despair, Nanny watched the sick man trying to swallow his tea, pausing between sips to draw breath.

"Poo' Moussié Dotta get sick. Need Papa Coffi," she whispered to Jeanne as she went by.

Papa Coffi, a former African slave freed by the La Barrées of Eaux Bonnes, was medicine man to all the blacks of Moka.

Dr. Aubriot frequently had found him squatting next to the sleeping mat of a sick slave at Allspice. More often than not, while waiting for the white doctor to arrive, the medicine man had produced good results. Nevertheless, Jeanne was not inclined to call him to treat a great scientist.

"Go back to your kitchen, Nanny," she said, "the doctor will manage to cure himself."

The moment Poivre learned of Aubriot's illness, he came to see him. He was alarmed and sent for Dr. Deltheil to help treat him.

The two physicians had carried on a rather lengthy conversation alone, one consulting the other. Now, as he stood in the entry, about to leave, Dr. Deltheil felt Jeanne's eyes upon him.

"I can't give you any prognosis for forty-eight hours," he said at last. "Monsieur Aubriot was good enough to agree with me," he added smugly.

Dr. Deltheil was a former ship's doctor, a barber who was not averse to disputing on equal footing with a noted colleague and graduate of the prestigious medical school of Montpellier University. He considered himself a good doctor. But he acted on his own and quickly.

"It's unfortunate that my illustrious colleague won't hear of being bled," he continued a bit pompously. "He has a high fever and there's an obstruction in the lung that ought to be relieved. Try to talk him into it. I'll come back this evening and bring what I'll need to prepare the vesication. I would prefer to bleed him first, though. Meanwhile, keep him perspiring with lots of tea and plenty of blankets, and don't give him anything to eat."

He took his hat and riding crop off the table. Jeanne saw him out to the veranda.

Feeling desperately in need of reassurance, she said, "You know, Dr. Aubriot has already had several pulmonary attacks, but he always recovers easily and doesn't seem to suffer aftereffects."

Dr. Deltheil merely nodded.

Aubriot consented to be bled that evening. His fever dropped slightly, but rose again during the night.

His colleague had applied a painful compound to his chest composed of flour, vinegar, and a finely ground Indian herb that served as an effective substitute for the costlier Spanish fly. The ordinary procedure was to apply the poultice for about ten hours, remove it, pierce the blisters that had formed on the patient's skin, and gently expel the serous fluid. The doctor would then cover the area with oil of almond and a dressing.

On the following afternoon the sick man said that he felt better. Propped up against a mound of pillows, he appeared stronger. He still had fits of coughing from time to time, and there were bloodstains on his handkerchief, but the stitch in his side had disappeared. He was breathing freely, his temperature was down, and he even began to fret about the seedlings he had brought back for Allspice.

"So I'm on the mend again without having lost too much time in bed," he said to Jeanne with a weak smile. "My lung is the strongest weak lung I know. A family inheritance. The Aubriots tend to die of pneumonia, but not before the age of seventy!"

For three days his condition remained stable. He had to be restrained from reading or writing too long, despite the waning fever. They had moved him upstairs to a room with a better view of the countryside. He drank every drop of chicken broth they brought him and began to complain about all the powders and potions his colleague had brought. He quietly replaced them with his own prescriptions. In short, he was improving.

Poivre was allowed to visit, and presented him with the first raspberry bush to reach l'Ile de France from the Moluccas. It was the gift of a Dutch sea captain. The raspberry plant had been so well potted and cared for during its voyage that it looked fresh and vigorous.

"Now you see that you must be up and about as soon as possible," said Poivre cheerfully. "And to inspire you, I've brought our latest adopted infant. Look after it, for it's the only one I've been able to get. The Dutch are not exactly generous, and I'd like to see it multiply. I tasted these raspberries in the Moluccas when I was there. I can promise you they're even more succulent than our own Oriental variety. They make a better liqueur, too."

Aubriot gazed delightedly at the tiny shrub that the intendant held up for him. But he motioned for Jeanne to take it. "Your raspberry bush is too tempting for me to hold in my sick hands," he said. "Jeanne's cool ones will be better for it."

Jeanne went off to plant the raspberry bush in the acclimatization bed she always kept ready. When she returned to Aubriot's room, he was asleep and Poivre had left.

She hesitated to go back downstairs. A sudden pang of anguish gripped her when she saw the way Philibert had fallen asleep.

Indeed, his illness had changed him in a very short time. His hair, sticky with sweat and tied back in a ribbon behind his neck, accentuated his haggard features. His face had taken on a yellowed ivory glaze with two dabs of rouge on the cheeks. She had to restrain herself from calling his name to make him open his eyes and restore a semblance of life to the enamellike mask.

Instead, she opened a book and sat by the closed window. Outside, life was glowing, buzzing, burgeoning, flowering, exhaling its fragrances. She saw Iassi chase after Paul, catch him, and drag him off to sit under the almond tree. An elderly black woman came by, carrying a basket of small shellfish—snails, mussels, and clams. Life went on pleasantly at a leisurely pace.

Allspice is solidly established now, with its own daily routine. It looks as if it could weather wind and tide, hardship and grief. She gave a little sigh, glanced over at Philibert, who had not moved, and returned to her reading.

A rustle of bedclothes made her look up from the page. Philibert was awake. "Are you thirsty?" she asked, approaching the bed.

"I have to get up, I have a lesson to give Michel," said Aubriot hoarsely as he tried feebly to push back the covers.

She stared at him in dismay. "What are you saying?"

With a start, she realized he was delirious.

A second copious bleeding returned him to his senses. He asked

✳ *613* ✳

immediately if it was the day when Father Duval would come to see him.

"Since you've been ill, he comes every evening," Jeanne replied with a smile. "Don't you remember?"

"My notion of time is confused," he murmured.

After Dr. Deltheil had gone, the two of them were alone in the room and Philibert called to her, "Jeannette . . . Jeannette, come sit on the edge of my bed."

Rather than flatten the straw mattress, she drew up a chair and sat down, placing the sick man's burning hand against her cheek.

He tried to smile, a weary smile. "Our collections," he said, "all our collections . . . are for the King's Garden, all of them . . . but before sending . . . I'm relying on you to put them in order . . . or if you can't . . . ask your friend Adanson to do it. Let him . . . classify them . . . so nobody can say that Aubriot has done . . . a sloppy job of botanizing . . . for the Garden. O God, all the work, all the research that needs to be done . . . I haven't . . . achieved a thing."

He spoke in whispers, catching his breath between words. His voice was so changed that Jeanne would not have recognized it. She scolded him gently to silence him. "Really now. Is this the time to be thinking about your herb collections and your studies? Now maybe you'd even like to go shell-gathering. I'm working regularly on the things in your study. Whatever isn't ready to give to the *Indienne* when she sails, we'll give to the next ship bound for Lorient. I doubt that Monsieur Buffon is ready to wind up his *Natural History*. Drink your medicine and sleep a while."

He drank it, returned the glass and beckoned to her. She propped him up against his pillows. Twice he inhaled deeply, as if to store up enough breath to get through what he had to say.

Jeanne winced as she heard the rattle in his throat. His congested lungs were struggling to pump air.

"For the grasshoppers . . ." he began. "To manage the grasshopper problem, I forgot . . . to tell Poivre . . ." He got no further, for he was already winded. Breathing deeply also made him dizzy and he lost his train of thought. "Later," he murmured, closing his eyes.

She lingered awhile at his bedside, bathed his temples, and placed fresh camphor-water compresses about his wrists. He opened his eyes.

"Thank you, Jeannot," he said, and took her hand in his. "I haven't had time . . . to find a flower for you."

Jeanne trembled. *Was he delirious again? No, he was trying to smile.*

He pressed her hand, saying, "I meant . . . to name a flower after you. There's already the springtime Jeannette . . . our French daffodil. It's hard . . . to find something . . ."

Jeanne's eyes flooded with tears and she couldn't see. She dropped to her knees at his bedside, wiped her eyes on the sheet, and kissed Philibert's hand, which burned her lips.

"I love you so very much," she said, swallowing the rest of her tears. "I'm happy to know that you're looking for a flower for me. And for once I won't help you try to find it! Please, if you can, I'd like you to discover it yourself!"

"I will try . . ." he murmured, before closing his eyes again.

She got up and went over to the window, pressing her forehead against the glass pane. She imagined strange new flowers bordering the lawns at Allspice, honey-colored and long-stemmed. *How the devil would he manage to translate "Jeanne Beauchamps" into botanical Latin?*

There was a knock at the door. She opened it for Father Duval.

* * * *

She dropped into a rattan chair on the deserted veranda, and fell asleep instantly.

Saint Méry ambled by, stopped, and gazed at her as he leaned up against a pillar.

Nanny appeared in the doorway and rushed out to Saint Méry. She had been waiting for the chance to pour out her troubles to a friendly ear.

"Aiee!" she moaned, casting a pitiful look at her mistress. "Poo' Mamzelle get sick at heart, need Good Lawd help her . . ."

Suddenly she whispered in a tone of command, "Moussié Maquis go get Papa Coffi! Mamzelle waste time, poo' Moussié Dotta need Papa Coffi, is no get bettah, Moussié Maquis do somep'n!"

"Shhhh!" Saint Méry hissed, seeing Jeanne stir. "Go back to your kitchen, Nanny," he said a moment later. "Let Mamzelle Jeanne sleep a while. I promise to come back soon and talk to her about Papa Coffi."

"You lose time!" Nanny scolded him before she disappeared.

Saint Méry lingered on, admiring the sleeping beauty, and thus Pauline found him.

The Creole stopped short when she saw him. She was very pale and her hands were clamped together. Her dark eyes met Saint Méry's hazy ones long enough to tell him what she had to say. Saint Méry blinked and looked over at Jeanne.

"I'll have to wake her," Pauline murmured. She approached Jeanne silently and touched her shoulder. "My dear, Father Duval is asking to see you—upstairs."

"No!" Jeanne screamed, loud enough to be heard by the children under the almond tree. Marie put down her embroidery, gathered up her skirts, and ran toward the house.

CHAPTER 33

anny heaved an enormous sigh. "Not eat, not sleep, not talk even. Not good at all. Stay on island in pond. Weep over grave or stay shut up in room. Aiee! Ma'm Pauline, not good. Mamzelle wanna get sick, wanna die. Soul in the wind already."

"No, no," Pauline murmured, as if to reassure herself. "It will pass, in the end it will pass. She's too young to die of heartache."

"Oh!" Marie said suddenly. "Look who's coming! Just like our old Sundays . . ."

Pierre Poivre was trotting up the entranceway to Allspice with a soldier escort.

The two women left the shade and walked out to welcome the intendant.

"I came to find out how Jeanne is getting along," he said. "I saw Don José yesterday and he talked at some length about her. It alarmed me."

"She can't accept it," said Marie. Also . . ." The young widow paused, as if comparing her own memories. "Jeanne's grief is like a child's," she said at last. "You know yourself that"—she paused again, searching for the right words—"that her love for Monsieur Aubriot was something she acquired as a little girl. She took it for granted that he, like the air, would always be there."

"I know that. But I also know . . ." He stared at each of them in turn, then said simply, "I know all there is to know. Don José told me everything."

"Everything?" Pauline repeated.

"He told me about Jeanne and the Chevalier Vincent."

Marie turned her head away in embarrassment.

Pauline remained icily calm. "I don't suppose Jeanne asked Don José to speak for her, do you? Why the sudden indiscretion?"

"He did the right thing," said Poivre. "I'm a friend."

Uncrossing his legs, he leaned toward his hostesses as if to emphasize the climate of friendly confidence. "I'm very fond of Jeanne, now she is mourning another friend who was very close and very dear to me. I would like to help restore her spirits. The fact that she's married to a corsair whom I need desperately at Port Louis simply fuels my desire to pry her out of her shell. Does she speak of the Chevalier Vincent?"

"Lord, no! Certainly not!" Pauline and Marie exclaimed in concert, then Pauline went on, "Vincent's name is like a scorching flame. I mentioned it once or twice to her, purposely, and I could see that it seared her heart."

"She hates herself for having loved the knight," said Marie. "She believes that God has punished her duplicity by taking Dr. Aubriot from her."

"I'll go see her," Poivre decided. "Where is she now?"

"Alone in her room, as always when she isn't at Aubriot's grave," Pauline replied.

"I'm going up," said Poivre.

"Do be careful," Pauline pleaded. "No matter how gently you treat her sorrow, you may end up wounding her more."

"I've no intention of consoling her with words," said Poivre. "I want to send her on a mission. I want her to go to Capetown for me and bring back the corsair whom I need here," he explained.

Pauline recovered first and said, "That's a piece of news that needs more explanation."

"I'm in urgent need of sound ships and trustworthy captains to carry out delicate expeditions. The Duke de Praslin promised me those ships, but they haven't come. In any event, the minister will never send me his best frigates or his top seamen. I need two or three fast ships captained by two or three honest privateers. Don't ask me why . . ."

Pauline interrupted with a shrill laugh. "It's not much of a secret! You are eager to steal the spice trade from the Dutch, to harass English shipping in the Indian Ocean. And you wouldn't be averse now and then to relieving Chinese pirates of luxury goods from Canton. It's quite clear why you need corsairs. But I was thinking that your plans sound as if they would fit right into the Chevalier Vincent's scheme of things. He'd be glad to come back to Port Louis."

"As a matter of fact, I was expecting him," said Poivre, scrutinizing Pauline's expression, wondering what she knew about Vincent's plans. Like everyone else in Lyon society, Poivre had heard about Vincent's affair with the beautiful Creole from Vaux. "Yes, I expected Vincent to be here long before I left France. The Duke de Praslin had arranged it. He was to have made Port Louis his base of operations. As you're aware, the Portuguese delayed him. But he's been delayed again. This time without good reason. What I mean is that his reason may be one I disapprove of strongly."

"Really?" said Pauline, tense with expectation. "What reason?"

"Do you know the Count de Maudave?" he asked.

"I met him twice after his return from France and before he left for Madagascar," said Pauline.

"He dined here one evening," Marie added. "He had all kinds of ideas for civilizing the Big Island and turning it into a prosperous colony."

"Yes," said Poivre, with more than a touch of irony. "Maudave would like to be the sultan of an ideal Madagascar. He brought with him from France what he considered the essential elements of his rule—secretaries, valets, actors, dancers, and cooks, plus all twenty-eight volumes of the *Encyclopédie*. Now he's camping out at Fort Dauphin with his retinue and his library. He realized almost immediately that he needed a few engineers to prop up his decaying capital and some ships and crewmen to turn it into a commercial port. I would not like to see one of our best corsairs lured by the temptations of Fort Dauphin."

"But why should the Chevalier Vincent be lured?" said Pauline in surprise.

Poivre smiled knowingly. "Impulsiveness goes hand in hand with boldness. Corsairs fall prey to temptation. They prefer to be their own masters. Right now Fort Dauphin seems to be a port where piracy is tolerated. At Port Louis I want only honest corsairs, working for the king. I know that Count de Maudave offers more liberal and therefore more attractive conditions."

"But have you found out something specific?" Pauline pressed him. "You must have known, as we did, through Captain Rafael, that the Chevalier Vincent was headed for Port Louis some three weeks behind the *San Isidro.*"

"That was ten weeks ago," observed Poivre.

"I know," murmured Pauline, clutching her skirt nervously.

"No, the sea has nothing to do with it," said Poivre, noting her gesture. "The *Belle Vincente* was indeed three weeks behind the *San Isidro,* but she put into Port Dauphin. She stayed there about a month, then left for Capetown to pick up supplies for Maudave's settlers. Doesn't this at least prove the chevalier's penchant for free enterprise?"

Pauline and Marie looked at each other, stunned. "You must be misinformed," Marie said firmly at last. "Jeanne read me her chevalier's letters, and I can't believe he would have come so near without stopping off to see her."

"We get pretty accurate information about what goes on at Port Dauphin," said Poivre. "Nobody misinformed me."

He didn't mention that he and Dumas—in accord for once—were spying on Maudave.

"Nobody misinformed me," Poivre repeated. "That's why I must act. I'm not going to let a first-class corsair, whom I need here, work for Fort Dauphin. My first thought was to send Don José, who's a friend of his . . ."

"Don José will never leave Belle Herbe before Emilie's baby arrives," Marie interjected.

"He told me so," said Poivre. "He doesn't want to go to Capetown, but he is also mystified by Vincent's activities."

Marie shook her head. "Send Jeanne. But all she can do at the moment is weep."

"Here that is the case," said Poivre. "But perhaps her tears would drown in the ocean. I recall that the chevalier is a most attractive man."

"Do you really believe she would be willing to run off in search of consolation?" Marie exclaimed, scandalized.

"No," replied Poivre, "but I would not be foolish enough to propose a pleasure cruise. I plan to offer her nothing less than an official mission on behalf of the government of l'Ile de France."

* * * *

Jeanne gazed absently at her hands entwined and resting limply on her black skirt. She sat in silence. Her chin trembled. "Your proposal comes as quite a surprise," she said. "In fact it overwhelms me." She eyed Poivre suspiciously. "Why charge *me* with such a mission? Me, a woman?"

"You once pointed out to me that the king did not take enough women into his service. By calling on you to serve the intendant of one of his colonies, I am calling on you to serve the king."

Not altogether convinced, she continued to eye him distrustfully as he added, "The role of ambassador strikes me as quite suitable for a woman, since it calls for persuasion."

"You may say 'persuasion,' but you really mean she must please," Jeanne corrected him quickly.

"Persuade or please, it's all the same for a man or a woman ambassador. Do you think ideas have ever convinced an adversary?"

"You're teasing me."

"Not at all. Meaningful diplomacy is a game of cat-and-mouse. If the cat is female, that's a distinct advantage. A woman observes a man's actions more keenly than does another man. To compensate for her physical frailty, she has secret weapons that can outguess, outmaneuver, and ultimately vanquish him."

She smiled sorrowfully. "You see the matter one-sidedly. Such a woman has to be ultraconfident of her power over men."

With a sigh, she asked, "Won't you admit frankly why you chose to send me, at a time when I'm not myself, to parley with the Chevalier Vincent?"

"My dear, I've just told you that I'm trying to recruit an intelligent, spirited woman deeply committed to the welfare of l'Ile de France."

Jeanne continued to stare incredulously at the intendant, whose countenance remained unruffled.

"It's true that I'm surrounded by men eager to serve me. You know as well as I do that there aren't more than half a dozen settlers on this island for whom profit isn't their main concern. I've always thought that the mistress of Allspice would become a native of l'Ile de France. Who better than a patriot could vaunt the delights of her own country to a vacillating confederate?"

"My own country . . ." Jeanne murmured, and her eyes filled with tears. "I have no country anymore. There is no haven anywhere for me, anywhere . . ."

Poivre was moved by the note of desperation in her voice. He sat down at her side, took her hand, and pressed it to his breast, trying to inject some warmth into her bleak despair.

In her plain black skirt and caraco jacket, she looked pitifully thin. Her amber coloring seemed pale. The rings under her eyes made them look bigger and brighter than usual, like two golden ponds set between hollow cheeks. Her beautiful hair was gathered at the nape of the neck in a black satin pouch. Poivre felt her tremble slightly when he touched her.

"Jeannette . . ." he began softly.

She cut him off abruptly. "No, please. I'm grateful to you for coming here and talking to me about something other than . . ." She made a vague gesture. "But I don't want to be comforted. My enjoyment of life is ended. In one day it happened. Suddenly, with a sigh, it was gone. There's nothing anyone can do about it."

"Time, Jeannette. It's the most banal thing I can tell you. But it's true."

"Please!" she begged, squeezing the hand holding hers.

"I don't want other people who loved him to tell me about the healing nature of time, as if they were encouraging me to forget him. Not every sorrow can be eased by time."

"A painful absence can't be forgotten, but it can cease to bleed. The wound forms a scar," said Poivre, looking at his own empty sleeve. "It becomes a sleeping presence, always faithful, which we carry about for the rest of our lives, in our work, even in our joy."

"No, no!" she cried vehemently, freeing her hand. "That would be too easy. After I have watched Philibert die, you want me to take up my daily routine as if nothing had happened? You want me to enjoy the springtime, the blue sky, the trees, the birdsongs, the beauty of flowers and seashells, enjoy all the things he adored, while he has nothing?"

Unable to bear it any longer, she broke down and wept. As the tears trickled down her cheeks, Poivre felt the power of her despair. "Nothing . . . he has nothing. Nothing . . . but darkness. Oh no! I can't stand it!"

"Jeanne, God exists!" he told her firmly.

"No!" she cried fiercely. "There is no more God! The God who created the splendors of the world would not have allowed Philibert's eyes to close, leaving him nothing but darkness."

Poivre recited in a soothing voice, " 'O Dawn, which is naught but the start of the day for our planet, but which glows with the light of midday on the celestial shores, receive him in the bosom of Light . . .' "

She wiped her eyes. "The seminary taught you an answer for everything," she complained bitterly. "I, for one, don't believe death is a beginning. Forgive me. I didn't mean to hurt you. Your friendship means a great deal to me."

"Then let my friendship help you, Jeannette. Listen when it counsels you not to lock yourself up in your room."

"Whenever I look at a flower, I see it as much with his words as with my eyes. My eyes are not mine alone. He taught me to recognize the forms and colors of nature. I see the most common blue bellflower through two sets of eyes, and hear Philibert's voice telling me that it loves dry, chalky soil."

With a firm hand, Poivre turned her around to face him. "Jeanne, my dear friend, haven't you just proved to yourself beyond a doubt that whenever you gaze at a flower, Aubriot will always be there too?"

She broke into sobs and wept on the intendant's shoulder. He sat her down again and waited for her tears to subside.

"I'm very glad you came," she said when she had regained her composure. "Thank you."

"Really? In that case I'll come back often. We'll continue our discussion later on. Now, about your mission to Capetown . . ."

"Oh," she said, "that's something else. I don't think I want to budge from here."

"You'll feel like going after I've told you that the Duke de Richelieu is sending an envoy for you."

"What!" she cried in alarm. "What did you say?"

Poivre gazed at her, smiling. "I said that a messenger from the Duke de Richelieu will be arriving shortly to find out how you are."

"That's all I need!" she hissed angrily. "So the duke still remembers me, does he?"

"Jeanne, you are part of a dreamworld that's not easily forgotten," said Poivre.

Suddenly Jeanne realized the implication behind the intendant's remark. "So you know about the duke?" she questioned him. "May I ask who told you about that silly remnant of my life in Paris?"

"The mail aboard the *Argonaut*. Among other things, it informed us that we were to receive and house envoys from His Eminence the Duke de Richelieu, aiding them in their search for a certain Mademoiselle Jeanne Beauchamps, an employee who deserted the duke and was believed to have run off to l'Ile de France."

"An employee of the duke's!" Jeanne shouted, outraged.

"Calm yourself," said Poivre. "Dumas and I don't believe a word of it. Some handwritten notes that always accompany official communications told the true story."

"In that case, don't tell me the governor would willingly hand me over to the duke's people so they can escort me to the duke's palace and his bed?"

"The laws of France apply here, and would certainly not uphold the duke's purpose. But I don't know who these people are that he is sending. They may try to make things unpleasant for you publicly. According to the *Argonaut*, the next ship from Lorient should arrive in about three weeks. I suggest that you be on the water then to avoid a distasteful scene. It will make it easier for us to persuade the visitors that you've left l'Ile de France."

There was a long silence. Finally, Jeanne spoke in a hushed voice. "The idea of leaving Allspice, even for a short time, frightens me. I feel as if I ought never to go away from here. Here, the *before* survives. Here, I'm able to believe that Philibert's life is not ended."

She hesitated to continue. It wasn't easy to express her grief. Then she murmured haltingly, "The last words he said to me were, 'I will try.' He was talking about a new flower he wanted to discover . . . and to name after me. He said, 'I will try,' and that's all I heard. Since then I repeat the words over and over to myself and they haunt me. Can such words truly mark the close of a lifetime?"

"Jeanne," said Poivre, "every soul departs an unfinished life." He kissed her gently on the forehead. "I'll be back soon," he said. "Think about my offer."

CHAPTER 34

Jeanne began to conjure up memories of her chevalier. Tender moments, anxieties as well as heartaches, bubbled to the surface—thoughts in which Philibert had no part. *Why had Don Rafael not brought her a letter from Vincent? Why had Vincent gone to Fort Dauphin without stopping at Port Louis to see her? Why had he set off again for Capetown without sending her a message?*

Over and over again she asked herself these questions, and they left a bitter taste in her mouth. She could find no plausible explanation other than the unpredictability of a corsair caught up in some enticing venture. Time after time he'd extolled the sea's power to make one forget everything but the present. Hadn't he said that the sea removes the past and the future, yesterday and tomorrow? To be sure, it was hard to make herself believe that she, Jeanne, could so easily become part of Vincent's past, just another happening in his life. But the facts were there. And the facts kindled an anger that burned hotter each day and reduced somewhat the pain of her loss.

Vincent's absence became a desertion, his silence an indifference. He should have been there to hold her hand and ease her sorrow. Instead, he was enjoying himself in Capetown, working out plans for some bold adventure with Count de Maudave.

Vincent's bright, disarming laughter haunted her. She imagined him, at the close of the day, dining at the governor's country seat and strolling afterward with a pink-and-white porcelein Dutch girl on his arm under the sweet-smelling scarlet blossoms of pomegranate trees.

"Actually, he's a Moor at heart," she declared out of the blue one morning to Pauline, who was supervising the servants' ironing. "Like a Moor, he's insensitive to the things women care about. It's well known that Moors consider women mere decorations whose function it is to sprawl on cushions and await patiently their lord and master's pleasure.

* 624 *

What the master does is none of their business. They're not supposed to ask about it. He's a Moor!"

Pauline, who had not been privy to the secret thoughts of her friend, was surprised, and gave her a questioning look. It was the first time in weeks that Jeanne had mentioned any subject other than Philibert Aubriot, the first time she had opened her mouth to say more than three words.

Pauline smiled and said, "You're speaking of Vincent, I suppose?"

"Who else?" Jeanne replied curtly.

Pauline folded the last camisole placing it in the laundry basket, shook out the flounce on a petticoat, and sat down next to Jeanne. "Are you going to Capetown?" she asked point-blank.

"Of course not! Did you think I would?"

"Why shouldn't you go? Poivre's idea sounds like a good one. You love the sea. A stretch on the water might work wonders for you."

"I could also sail with Father Rochon, who's returning to the Seychelles and will travel as far north as Ceylon."

Inevitably, what she had just said made her think of the last happy days she had spent with Philibert and the astronomer abbot when they anchored off the coast of Clam Island.

With an effort, Jeanne pulled herself back to the present.

"I don't think it would do you any good at all to leave with Father Rochon right now," Pauline said to her.

"Don't worry," said Jeanne, "I was only thinking aloud. I've no more wish to go to Ceylon than to the Cape. And I wish people would stop suggesting how I might amuse myself!"

"My dear, it's a mission, not an entertainment, that Poivre came to offer," Pauline reminded her gently.

"Well, it doesn't appeal to me. Nor do I care to go looking for Vincent. The chevalier is not devoid of pride. It would humiliate me if, on arriving at Capetown, he were to think I had come there to win him back."

Pauline smiled sadly. "You know," she said, "winning back a sea-farer is something that has to be done periodically."

The remark came as an uncomfortable reminder to Jeanne that Pauline had a few more years' experience with Vincent than she did. In a surge of jealousy against the mistress of Vaux, she lashed out spitefully, "That's one habit I shall certainly not acquire. I don't happen to have the affable temperament of a brothel keeper."

Then, angry at herself for such a cruel jibe, she ended the conversation abruptly. "Excuse me, but I must prepare the crates of shells and plants I want to send aboard the *Argonaut*."

About to leave the room, she turned and said, "Pauline, please don't ever mention that Capetown mission again."

* * * *

Vincent's letter, which arrived the next day, finally persuaded Jeanne to make the trip, in a fit of anger. She was working in Aubriot's study when the Provençal brought it to her.

"It comes from Fort Dauphin via the *Shuttle*," he told her. "I'm not quite sure why it came that way." The topman was not aware of the latest movements of the *Belle Vincente* and thought she was still under repair at Capetown. As he backed out of the study he said, "I'll be outside on the veranda—in case there's anything you want to tell me when you've read it."

Jeanne broke the seal. The blood rushed to her cheeks as she read the opening lines. With that burning sensation inside her head, she read it through to the end. The words danced before her eyes. Finally she went to the desk, spread out the letter, and began to read it over, very slowly this time, savoring every spiteful word. She sat biting her lip until the blood ran, both hands clamped on the paper.

Someone scratched at the door and opened it slightly. "Jeannette, it's Marie," came a voice. "The Provençal just told me that—"

"Come in, Marie," Jeanne invited without turning around. "You've arrived just in time to hear a very witty letter. Here, read this." She pushed the letter away from her. Marie picked it up and began reading.

> I was not planning to send word to you, madame. As I've told you, I shall never play the role of complacent cuckold, even by letter. I was preparing thus to forget you when it occurred to me that in spite of the excellent price Don José must have obtained for your valuable diamonds, you might soon be running short of funds.
>
> In Capetown, I was told by a gentleman from l'Ile de France that you were admirably installed in a rustic little kingdom, treating your lodger friends extravagantly. Now, we know that thrift is not among your vices—that makes one less—and wouldn't befit the wife of a corsair. Whatever is come by dishonestly ought to be shared willingly. Never-

theless, I should not like to learn that my wife was squandering the funds of Don José or, worse still, those of her lover. I prefer that her lover sponge off me. Don't be surprised by an attitude that deviates so notably, I'm told, from current practice in Port Louis. It derives from my lack of humility, the legacy of a bastard childhood supported by undivulged sources of charity. I pray you, therefore, madame, dip generously into my purse in order to maintain your style of life. Just send a sealed message to the Chevalier of the Rose at Saint Denis on l'Ile de Bourbon, and he will provide you with money.

Since rumors fly like gunfire in the Indian Ocean, perhaps you may have heard that I am planning to make Fort Dauphin my base of operations. The rumor is not untrue, but Saint Denis seemed to me a more civilized spot to open your bank account. Your messenger can get there in two days. I don't expect you will do this too often.

Luckily for me, your tastes attract you to bookish persons, who are infinitely cheaper than dandies. A man with the inner resources to amuse himself constitutes the cheapest lover that any husband can hope to find. What's more, by supporting him, the husband acquires a reputation for supporting Science, a reputation altogether honorable and admirable these days. I have you to thank for this.

Farewell, madame. I wish you good health for many years to come, something you could never look forward to if I had committed the folly of seeing you again. What would I have done? I would have run my blade through M. Aubriot, a useful man to botany and to his patients. I would have choked you to some degree, and, worse still, I might have been faint-hearted enough to bring you back to life upon his grave just long enough to make love to you, not out of spite, though with distaste undoubtedly, once it was over.

All this smacks a bit of antiquity. A relic of earlier times when a woman's word and deeds could be relied on. And while I've always prided myself on dressing and behaving in the height of fashion, I'm afraid today's woman passes for a whore. Enjoy then, madame, whatever enters your flesh or your spirit. Enjoy it tranquilly and without remorse, knowing that you have left me the invaluable gift of never being able to wed the current object of my fancy. Safe behind this shield you have given me, I'll seduce all the women in all the ports! For every woman is beautiful, my dear, if you don't stick with her too long!

Once and forever, I kiss your fingertips, if your incestuous papa will allow me this ultimate familiarity.

Vincent.

Marie's hand, with the letter in it, dropped limply to her side as she stared at Jeanne.

"Well?" said Jeanne, her voice trembling with fury. "What do you think of my long-awaited message?"

"I think," said Marie after a thoughtful pause, "that it was written by a jealous husband. If I were you, I'd take it for a love letter."

"Well, that just makes you one of those women who love to be beaten!" Jeanne burst out angrily. "I'm not that way. I don't appreciate being called a whore! I'll never forgive him for these two pages of insults. Never! Don't you realize how odious, how perfectly disgusting, now that . . ." A sob escaped her. She blew her nose with an angry snort.

"Jeannette," said Marie gently, "when the chevalier wrote that letter, he didn't know. He still doesn't know." She approached her friend, who was sitting back stiffly in her chair, intent on preventing her anger from melting into tears. "Jeannette, Aubriot's death doesn't alter the fact that you have wronged the chevalier. Admit it."

"I hate him!" Jeanne hissed. "How can you defend him?"

"I'm certain Emilie would interpret the letter as I have," Marie insisted. "Let's go down to Belle Herbe and show it to her."

"We'll do nothing of the kind! Our childhood days are over, Marie. I don't need Emilie's opinion to understand how a man is treating me. What do you mean by saying I've wronged the chevalier? Any wrongs I've done him are more than eclipsed by his outrageous remarks. He's nothing but a Moor, a Moorish pirate! A woman, to him, is a quick round of pleasure in the local bordello. Or else a piece of goods that's tossed into his bedchamber and told to keep quiet until the day Mario, his valet, kicks her out to make room for another. Not for one moment has he ever bothered his head about a woman's refined sensibilities.

Why should he? All he wants is to possess her, to hold her the way a dog clamps on to a bone!"

Her anger had boiled up as she spoke. Marie, who had never seen her so inflamed, listened tongue-tied.

When Jeanne finally stopped to catch her breath, Marie slipped in a timid rejoinder. "All the same, Jeannette, if the chevalier was informed by someone he met at Capetown, God knows what kind of a tale he heard. Aubriot lived here in your house on a familiar footing that could lead anyone to think . . . Tongues waggle, you know, without stopping to separate fact from fantasy."

"Did I grab my pen, Marie, to vent my spleen when I heard that the chevalier was spending his prison sentence under Countess da Silveira's wing, well housed, well fed, and all the rest? I would have been wasting my breath to complain of such willing infidelity. Has he the right to punish me for mine as if it were just a casual pastime, a sporting adventure, when he, with all his perfumed Don Juan trappings and his lady-killer instincts, was the one who caused me to deceive Philibert?" With a snort, she concluded icily, "I wouldn't think of apologizing to Vincent for any wrong I shall have to account for eternally to Philibert."

A silence fell between them. Jeanne persisted in staring straight ahead of her.

Slowly a smile began to form on Marie's lips. In her mind's eye she saw the stylish Knight of Malta, a bit showy, yes, but how charming! She saw his sparkling eyes the color of burnt coffee, heard his gay laughter and charming speech. He took her hand to dance with her. He was a marvelous dancer. He smelled of orange blossoms and made her wish right from the start that he would woo her just a bit.

Marie's smile broadened and she couldn't help saying with just a trace of mockery, "You know, Jeannette, from what you've told me and what I remember about the chevalier, I can't quite see him driving you into his bed by force."

Jeanne started. "Were you there?" she demanded with renewed anger as she lashed out at her friend.

Marie silently handed her the letter. Jeanne took it, crumpled it in a ball and flung it into a wastepaper basket. In the next instant she plucked it out again, put it on the desk, and began smoothing it out with both hands.

"No!" she mumbled. "No, it would make the break too painless for him if I kept silent. He would have had the last word, and I don't want him to have it! I shall have that satisfaction myself!"

Waving the letter under Marie's nose, she went on, "One day in the Temple I told him what I thought of him for some trifling thing he wrote which can't compare to this. In those days he used dots for the word 'whore'—I should have known it wouldn't last! I'll make him swallow his own ink! I'll make him chew up this filthy rag! I can't do much with a sword, but I can shoot a pistol well enough to kill a man."

"Jeannette!" cried Marie, aghast.

But Jeanne went on undaunted, in a cold rage. "Marie, please have Blanchette saddled for me while I put on a pair of breeches. I want to ride down to the harbor and find out if the *Argonaut*'s captain can take me aboard. He's leaving the day after tomorrow."

Totally confused, Marie headed obediently for the door. Once there, she turned and said, "So you're serious about it? You're accepting Monsieur Poivre's mission and will go to Capetown in search of Vincent?"

"I'm going to the Cape to have my revenge on Vincent," Jeanne corrected her. "I don't know how yet, but I'll find a way!"

CHAPTER 35

he morning of November 8, 1768, dawned radiant. The breeze drifting down from the heights of Moka onto the bay, where trails of nighttime mist still rose, carried the powerful scent of cut sugar cane warming in sunlit fields. A light froth covered the blue-green water, and flags flying from vessels at anchor waved farewell to the departing *Argonaut*.

There were crowds on the quay despite the early hour. Encouraged by the heat of summer the women came out in their lightest, palest, lowest-cut frocks. Together with the men in loose white nankeens, they formed a fresco of pastel figures dotting the splendid shoreline against a backdrop of gently rocking sails.

Poivre and Don José met at the waterfront and contemplated the lively scene from a distance.

"It's going to take a lot of work, I'm afraid," Poivre remarked, "to make Port Louis into a prominent military and commercial outpost, with such a lazy population."

"Indeed!" Don José agreed. "In a warm country the wise man has no desire to live by his labor. He smokes his cigar in the daytime and makes love at night."

They walked toward the circle of skirts surrounding Jeanne. All they could see of her at this point was the brim of her cocked hat. From near and far, friends had turned out to see her off on the *Argonaut*. Even Mme. Manon had staggered out of bed at three in the morning to come in from Pamplemousses. For the women, it was a great and memorable event to be dispatching a member of their own sex to represent the island's interests.

"Have a good trip, Jeanne," said Poivre, when he finally got close to her, "and be sure to bring us back the frigate we so desperately need here. Come back safe and sound aboard the *Belle Vincente*, and I promise you a heroine's welcome."

He led a round of solemn official applause. The dignity of the occasion was shattered by a yelp from Adele protesting the amorous pinches of a sergeant of the guard.

Emilie ran up to hug Jeanne one last time. "Jeannette, don't forget my advice and your resolve. Don't apologize for anything and don't ask forgiveness. A husband is not a confessor who can award you a corner of paradise in exchange for your penitence."

The last voice on shore that Jeanne could identify as the longboat took them away was that of Paul, screaming at the top of his small lungs, "Tante Jeanne, don't forget to bring back Moussié Corsair!"

He had mastered the *r* sound at last, but at the cost, it seemed, of acquiring an African drawl.

* * * *

"Well, that's it," sighed Don José, moments later.

The *Argonaut* was gathering speed. A white scarf still seemed to be waving on the poop. "*Vaya con Dios, amiga,*" the Spaniard murmured, raising his hand for the last time.

"Yes, that's it," Poivre repeated abruptly. He was still amazed at how quickly Jeanne had come around to accept his proposal. He gazed thoughtfully at his Françoise, who was conversing with some friends. She, too, was young and pretty, and had a husband much older than she.

"Well, it's time for me to get back to work, and I'd like to have some lunch first," he announced loudly enough for his wife to hear.

"My dear, have you noticed the incoming ship that's about to cross the *Argonaut?*" asked Françoise, pointing out to sea on her right.

Several people were commenting with great interest on the latest surprise the sea was bearing them.

A naval officer standing near Poivre informed the intendant, "It must be the *Trieste Dame*. We heard she ran aground on a sand bank last night near Gravesend Bay at about three o'clock. Luckily they were able to cast off seaward. Gunner's Quoin had sent them a pilot, but the blockhead probably steered them wrong."

"The *Trieste Dame*," Poivre repeated, a smile spreading over his face. "Isn't that Monsieur de Bougainville's frigate?"

"I really don't know the captain's name," said the officer.

"Zounds!" Poivre cried out excitedly. "If that is Monsieur de Bougainville's *Trieste Dame*, she may be on her way back from a trip around the world! Bougainville left France shortly before I did. There were rumors that he had set out to circumnavigate the globe."

"In La Plata it was more than a rumor," Don José said with a smile. "Diplomatic secrets and bed pillows exert a magnetic attraction on each other. In Buenos Aires, we have Spanish pillows that specialize in collecting naval gossip."

Poivre turned to look out over the ocean once more, shading his eyes with one hand. For a while he stood watching silently as the *Argonaut's* rigging dwindled and the newcomer's ballooned. Soon puffs of white smoke burst between the two ships.

"There goes Monsieur de Bougainville, hailing his Bougainvillea!" exclaimed Emilie gaily. "Let's get ready to welcome him."

* * * *

Long, blue, monotonous days, for rocking. Starry nights, for dreaming. Frigate birds flying high in the sunlight, dazzling white. Greedy, silver-bellied fish playing in the waves. Sailors dancing and singing after the evening meal. Sunsets. Pageants in crimson, flame red, scarlet. Broad bands of deep rose fringed with green and gold. Blood-red veins in a vast mauve cloud streaked with every shade of lilac. This evening the *Argonaut's* passenger found the display remarkably impressive—a full range of pastel tints, vivid violet, pearl gray, and turquoise combined with a delicate pale blue that glowed in the vanishing sunlight.

The splendors of the earth. She put her hand to her heart and her heartbeat told her yes, it still suffered from the knowledge that Philibert no longer could perceive the splendors of the earth. That was good. She wanted always to carry deep inside her a heart ever conscious of her loss. A heart so bruised that it winced in pain at the slightest pleasure. Knowing that her heart suffered gave Jeanne the right to delight in the pleasure of a sunset.

She untied the ribbon at the back of her neck, shook loose her hair, closed her eyes, and held up her face to the salt air, greedily welcoming the first cooling breezes of evening. Suddenly aware that sailors were staring at her loose blond tresses, she quickly retied her ribbon, returned to her room, and fell to musing over a book.

But her mind kept wandering to images out of the past, neither logical nor sequential, simply bittersweet. By lolling in the arms of sea and sky, she had regained a measure of serenity. She would never recover from the loss of Philibert, yet she still loved life. Her own life. At times she felt an unfamiliar zest. A desperate delight. A delight at once sensitive and vulnerable. The delight of a survivor.

The sound of bare feet galloping over the deck made her prick up her ears and look toward the door. "Come in," she said, as a knock sounded.

The Provençal burst in excitedly. "Mam'selle Jeanne, we've sighted the first albatross of the Cape!"

* * * *

Land appeared the next morning, just before prayers.

Birds danced across a sky dappled with clouds. A ballet in black and white. Frigate birds, petrels, sea swallows, black-backed gulls, and gannets, as well as flocks of albatross, welcome messengers of the Cape. The immense wings cast dark shadows on the faces gazing up at them.

The wind drove the ship shoreward. The mountains along the African coast came into view on the horizon. Captain Lejeune asked to see his passenger.

"If the wind doesn't drop, we'll reach the entrance to the bay in three hours," he told Jeanne. "I think you know that I don't plan to anchor at Capetown. I'm due in Senegal as soon as possible. To save time, I'd prefer not to moor too close to shore, but I wonder if you'll be able to stomach a fairly extensive ride in a longboat?"

"Captain, please suit your own convenience," said Jeanne. "My business is not on shore but on Captain Vincent's frigate. So if the *Belle Vincente* is in the harbor and as visible as Monsieur Poivre assured me it would be, the boat can simply take me there."

The captain nodded his approval. "When we are in position to look over the vessels at anchor, I'll send your faithful Provençal to the crow's nest."

* * * *

Between Robben Island and Hangman's Point the bay opened out, serene and inviting. Puffs of mist like snowballs hid the crest of Table Mountain. From afar, the whitewashed town at its feet resembled an array of sugar-cube castles.

Perched in the crow's nest, the Provençal called out a running count of the ships he could see as the wind and the rising tide propelled the *Argonaut* shoreward. "Nine . . . ten . . . eleven . . . twelve . . ."

Suddenly a jubilant whoop reached Jeanne's ears. "I see her, Mam'selle Jeanne, I see her! I see my ship! They're moored near the town! *Hoi, hoi, hoi zou!*" The topman flourished his cap wildly in the air and shouted greetings at the top of his lungs.

Captain Lejeune handed Jeanne his spyglass and was astonished, moments later, to see it shaking in her hands.

"I think it's time to prepare your baggage, mademoiselle," he said. "The wind serves us admirably. We're skimming along like a seagull."

The crew looked on mournfully as Jeanne prepared to enter the longboat. Such a pretty blond girl—good sailor too—a pity they couldn't keep her aboard for a mascot, like a ship's cat.

The Provençal also gazed at her, surprised to see how handsome Jeanne could look, dressed as a young man. She wore her well-tailored traveling suit of black silk and a white muslin shirt with a lacy frill at the neck. Her cocked hat was immensely becoming. Even better, the Provençal thought to himself, was the delicious perfume she had on.

He drew close to her, whispering, "The captain is going to be so surprised! Holy Flower! A cake fit for a king! Golden batter, like butter!"

The Provençal's unbridled enthusiasm persuaded Jeanne that she had better prepare him for a cool, none-too-cordial reception.

On the spur of the moment she came up with this explanation: "Provençal, don't expect a warm welcome. In his last letter the captain ordered me not to leave Port Louis."

"Holy God! Then what are we doing here?" the Provençal cried out.

"Shhh!" Jeanne hissed.

As the longboat was lowered into the water, the Provençal stared at her in wide-eyed wonder, scratching his head. "Mam'selle, I'm not too happy about what you just told me," he said. "This letter you got, did it say anything about me? Was I supposed to wait at Port Louis? Because with the captain, you know, an order's an order. Give him an argument and he gets tough! And how!"

Jeanne laughed defiantly. "If you get scared, Provençal, you can hide behind me! The captain's bound to be as tough as leather, but I've got good teeth!"

"Well, I don't know about that . . ." muttered the topman, unconvinced.

CHAPTER 36

incent dropped his arm, his fingers clamped tightly around his spyglass. Anger made his jaw twitch. On his right, he could feel Quissac's stare after they both had observed the approaching boat. Without turning to look at or speak to his lieutenant, Vincent left the deck and went to his cabin.

He paced back and forth in the cramped, low-ceilinged room, composing himself somewhat. Still, he managed to bang one shin painfully against a chest of silverwork. He kicked it and cursed, which made him feel better. A knock and Quissac's voice at the door sent him into a rage.

"Go to the devil!" he shouted with unwonted rudeness. "I'm tired. I want to sleep."

The door opened. Quissac stood in the doorway and said, "If you're going to sleep, sir, shall I take charge, since the first mate is ashore?"

When the only response was a snort of exasperation, the lieutenant proceeded to repeat what he had said before opening the door. "Sir, I'm asking permission to bring aboard the two persons in a longboat sent by the captain of the *Argonaut.*"

"I don't want anything to do with those people! Send them back to the *Argonaut.*"

"Sir, the wind has risen. There's a swell."

Vincent shrugged. "The boat's obliged to go back there, isn't it? Or let it take the passengers ashore, which isn't very far."

Quissac hesitated, unsure what to do or say. Vincent planted himself squarely in front of him and addressed him imperiously. "Lieutenant, I am master of this ship, and I will not have those two people aboard. Don't wait for a counterorder. There won't be any."

The lieutenant nodded sourly and left. But five minutes later he was back in the doorway. "Captain . . ."

This time he found Vincent seated at his desk, his hands resting on the ship's log. His expression was the characteristic mask of utter indifference he wore in time of crisis, to retain his composure. Since it indicated neither benevolence nor malevolence, Quissac relaxed a bit.

"What is it now?" Vincent asked curtly.

"Sir, the lady who's asking to board is apparently not just an ordinary individual, but the ambassador for the government of His Majesty in l'Ile de France. Here is her commission."

Vincent reached out and took the sealed document. He frowned. A mocking smile began to play on his lips as he glanced at the brief note signed by Intendant Poivre and countersigned by Governor Dumas.

"No matter how much you've learned about women, you can never figure them out completely. There's always one who manages to teach you a new trick by coming up with some untried, underhanded strategy."

Quissac waited silently.

"Quissac," said Vincent, "I don't like having to rescind an order, but I can't refuse to see the governor's envoy. Have them bring . . ." He stopped short, unsure how to refer to Jeanne. He glanced at the note from l'Ile de France which he had tossed on the desk, and said contemptuously, "Have Madame Ambassador shown aboard. You can put her in the wardroom and then we'll see what she wants from us. The letter doesn't mention that."

Seeing Quissac about to object, he added, "Take our purser with you. That way the lady may be sure she has a trustworthy witness to what she has to say."

Quissac decided not to argue, but just before leaving he turned to ask, "What shall I do with our foresail topman, who's accompanying the lady? Shall I return him to the crew?"

"Absolutely not! When she's accomplished what she came for, the lady undoubtedly won't care to leave without her escort."

Vincent was annoyed to hear the crew cheering Jeanne's arrival on board. They loved her, those cabbage heads! From the moment the longboat had pulled up alongside the frigate, there was nonstop singing and horseplay on the foredeck, and talk of special treats to come that evening.

Vincent shrugged and, finding it hard to sit still, went over to his bookshelves. Nothing seemed to tempt him this evening. He opened one book after another, read a sentence or two, and put it back in place, sighing in disgust. With mounting resentment he tried to block out the voices now coming from the next room.

One voice in particular grated on his nerves, inordinately low and soft, like the ribbon of melody unfolding from the strings of a violoncello. Suddenly he grabbed a book of poems and began to read aloud, fast and furiously.

The door behind him opened. "Yes?" he said, without turning around.

"Sir," said Quissac, "the lady from l'Ile de France feels she must deliver her message to you personally."

Vincent slammed his book shut. "I was afraid of that," he said. "Let's get it over with, Quissac."

A faint smile hovered on Quissac's lips. "The *Argonaut*'s boat has left," he said. "The orders were for her to deliver two passengers, but not to pick them up again."

"Is that so? Well, never mind, we have an excellent longboat of our own. And now, Quissac," Vincent went on with studied indifference, "bring in our visitor so I can get through with this in a hurry. The ship is starting to dance a bit, and I think we might do better to spend the night ashore. What say we pay a call on the Dutch girls?"

"Say now . . ." Quissac's eyes lit up. "First, I'll fetch you the lady," he said.

"If you please," Vincent retorted.

Instead of leaving, however, Quissac approached him. "Sir," he said, touching him on the arm, "we've gone through thick and thin together for so long that we've become like kinsmen. Let me offer you a kinsman's advice—"

Vincent cut him short. "No!"

"I'll say it anyway, like a good friend. Afterward, if you feel I've overstepped myself, you've only to punish me for it. Sir . . ." Quissac pressed Vincent's arm affectionately. "Ever since the evening that bag of wind in uniform from Port Louis nearly dented our ears with all the island gossip, you've seemed depressed. And—"

"Really, Quissac! Since when have you turned romantic? My dear fellow, it doesn't suit you at all, not with that scar on your face! And if you think I'm sad, your eyes are deceiving you. I've got all sorts of cheerful and financially rewarding projects on my mind."

"They're not making you very happy, it seems. And all this after listening to a lot of unpleasant rumors. Now I ask you, should you believe a rumor? Is a rumor from the salons any more reliable than a piece of shipboard gossip from the head? They each need to be whittled down to size if you want the truth."

"Quissac, you amuse me," Vincent sneered. "I've never known you to defend a woman. You usually enjoy watching Mario get rid of one. I was convinced that you considered a woman on a ship dead weight, or, let's say, unsaleable goods."

"In this instance I consider her an object of art," Quissac ventured boldly.

"Lieutenant, be my guest. Help yourself," Vincent retorted icily. "Your captain is no longer involved. The lady likes to take up with seamen for recreational purposes when she's done with her botanical chores."

The look that Quissac flashed him nearly made Vincent blush with shame. "Well," he snapped, "are you going to fetch your favorite or not? What are you afraid of? Do you see me about to greet her with a whip in my hand? I shall simply send her to the devil—very politely, I promise you."

The door banged shut after Quissac. Dozing peacefully on his master's bed, Licorice the cat gave a start and twitched his tail angrily against the green velvet coverlet.

Jeanne's timid scratch at the door was so faint that it would have passed unnoticed if Vincent had not been listening for it.

"Come in!" he shouted.

"Good day, Chevalier," she said almost in a whisper. She looked as pale as her tea-colored complexion would allow. She hadn't changed, alas, and still radiated the same false promise of tender beauty offered. Her whole being seemed to quiver like a leaf. Infinitely touching, she might have inspired a stranger to fold her in his arms to steady her.

He pulled a chair out from under the table and offered it to her. "Madame, please sit down."

Vincent's voice, unfriendly as it was, brought a lump to Jeanne's throat and tears to her eyes. *You are handsome and I love you. You are my life and I love you.*

"Please sit down."

She moved forward like a sleepwalker and reached out to touch him.

"Vincent."

He recoiled so abruptly that he smacked his left shin a second time against the chest of silver.

"Madame, if you please, kindly save us time by stating your business. I'm expected at a little party in town." He took Poivre's letter off his desk. "This merely announces your arrival. Tell me the rest."

Jeanne sat down in the chair he offered her, took a deep breath and began. She told him of Poivre's request, listing all the reasons he had given her for wanting a corsair vessel based at Port Louis. She was amazed to be able to deliver her message clearly and audibly. While she went on thinking, *I love you! I love you!* she devoured the eyes in that long-absent face.

Patient as a prowling tiger, he was watching her too. Though outwardly calm, he could barely control a murderous impulse. Summoning all his mute energy, he stared at her ominously, hoping that she would do something foolish enough to justify his crushing her with his own two hands. He had a frantic need to feel her flesh between his hands, crushed beyond repair . . .

"I shall confer with my staff about my reply to Monsieur Poivre, and will deliver it to you tomorrow morning," he announced. "Have you made plans to spend the night ashore? My lieutenant can discuss such details with you." He walked toward the door, attempting thus to end the interview.

Jeanne rushed to the door and planted herself in front of it with her arms crossed.

"No!" she cried. "I haven't planned to spend the night ashore. The *Argonaut* probably has left by now for Senegal. I haven't planned anything beyond seeing you." She saw Vincent's jaw and fists tighten. "I see that you don't care to remember that I am your wife. But I'm aware of it and I don't intend to let you forget it. I am asking for shelter on your ship."

This time the expression she read on Vincent's face in response to her boldness frightened her so badly that she threw her hands up in front of her face, crying, "No!" as if to ward off a blow.

There was a long silence, punctuated by their heavy, rapid breathing, before Vincent said sadly, "You did well to cry out, madame, for it kept me from doing something utterly vulgar. All during my youth, you know, I had to struggle against the violence inside me. I still have trouble controlling it. I did not appreciate your ordering me to remember something you so easily forgot the minute my back was turned. Besides, I think you're being unfair. I believe on the whole that I've acted fairly by seeing to your financial needs through a brother Knight of Malta on l'Ile de Bourbon. I'm surprised you didn't receive my letter. I sent it aboard the *Shuttle*."

The mere reminder of her husband's insulting remarks sent the blood rushing to Jeanne's cheeks. "Alas for you, Chevalier, I did receive your letter. Worse still, I read it," she said, struggling desperately to speak calmly. "For a while afterward I thought I could never forgive you. I thought that if I read it often enough it would destroy all my feelings for you. I accepted Monsieur Poivre's embassy for the sole purpose of coming here to repay your insults, though I had no idea how to do it. Since then, the sea has been at work on your words. The sea, as you know . . . after all, it was you who taught me that it washes everything clean. Before we left the Mozambique Channel behind us, I had torn up your odious letter and tossed it over the side. Even then, even as we rowed here from the *Argonaut*, I was still imagining how I would make you pay for it, and I felt very hostile to you. But when I saw you again I knew that I had come here only to love you . . . and to have you love me . . ."

"Is Aubriot on a journey somewhere?"

Vincent's reply cut her like a whiplash. He had stood there listening to her without moving a muscle or batting an eyelash. This unexpected sarcasm brought tears to her eyes.

"Let's not have any of that, please," he said coldly, proffering a handkerchief that dangled from limp fingertips. "At your age a woman ought to know that men detest tears that they have no desire to comfort."

She buried her misery in the scent of orange blossoms, blew her nose, and dabbed her eyes as she blubbered, "I'm not crying because you mock me, monsieur, though you are far more cruel than you could know . . ." Raising her misty eyes to him, she murmured, "Monsieur Aubriot is dead."

Jeanne broke down again, weeping as much from grief as from her frustration at not being able to hold back her tears for Philibert in front of Vincent.

"Oh?" was the chevalier's response as he looked on impassively while Jeanne sobbed. Finally he took a carafe from his dressing table and poured her a glass of water. "Drink this."

"Thank you," she said, reaching for his hand, which he promptly withdrew.

A glimmer of a smile hovered on his lips as she sipped the water slowly. It was not a friendly smile. When she set down the empty glass on the table, he picked it up and replaced it on his dressing table, saying with affected sympathy, "So Aubriot is dead. Well, I'm sorry for science and for his mistress, both of whom seemed to think the world of him."

"No, please! I can't bear such cruelty!" she pleaded.

"Oh?" he said in the same offensive tone of polite indifference. "Rest assured, madame, that I have no wish to insult the memory of a departed soul who is now in God's hands. But I really don't see how I can help you make good your loss. I don't suppose he left this task to me in his will, did he? As I'm neither a relative nor a friend of his, I make no claim to his property."

Jeanne sat up stiffly, then had to support herself with both hands on the table because her head was reeling. "Go away, Chevalier," she said weakly, in a muffled voice. "Go quickly. Let's end this conversation before we wind up slinging names at each other."

"Let's end it indeed, madame. There's nothing I'd like better! I didn't ask to meet with you. And let me remind you that this is my home. You may stay, however, and I will leave. I'll send Mario in. He can remove my things and bring in yours, along with some supper. You'll be more comfortable here than in the wardroom while you wait for my reply to your embassy."

She had driven him away, but could not bear to see him go. "Vincent!" she called to him in spite of herself.

About to step out the door, he turned around, looking exasperated.

"No . . . nothing," she said.

No sooner had he gone than she fell sobbing onto the bed and wept her heart out. As the tears poured down her cheeks, she stroked Licorice and hugged him, but the cat soon protested against the tumultuous fondling and insisted on being released.

"You don't love me either," she complained childishly. Rolling over onto her stomach, she hid her teary face in her folded arms and steeped herself in despair until she heard footsteps on the floor.

"Hello, Mario," she said, raising her head just enough to speak. "Before you do anything else, I wish you'd bring me a pitcher of fresh cool water."

"I am not Mario," came the singsong voice of Father Savié, almost directly above her.

Jeanne got up, wiping her cheeks with her shirt cuff. "Father! Oh, Father, I feel so miserable!" she said earnestly. "The chevalier has been unbearable. He hasn't said a single kind word or made a single gesture . . ."

"Did you deserve them?"

She settled herself on the edge of the bed and looked hard at the chaplain. "What do you know, Father, about his rage against me?"

The priest frowned. "Do you expect me to repeat what was told me in confidence?" Seeing her head droop, he softened his voice. "I can tell you, however, that I was with your husband and Baron Quissac at a party in Capetown when someone began reporting social gossip from l'Ile de France. And since you had just settled there in rather comfortable surroundings, the talk naturally came round to you, and continued at some length because the chevalier asked all sorts of questions."

"And what did the rumormonger you were listening to know about my living habits?" Jeanne demanded, her temper flaring. "What did he know, beyond appearances?"

Father Savié looked Jeanne in the eye for a long time, until she blushed. "A husband who loves his wife needs only the outward appearance of betrayal to have a fit of jealousy," the chaplain told her, "if he is so inclined to begin with . . . and remembers certain things."

"Certain things?" Jeanne echoed excitedly.

She might have said something rash if the priest had not taken her hands in his as he said, "Remember, my daughter, that I was the one who heard your confession before you took a vow of fidelity to your chevalier."

She got up quickly and went to the desk, then came back to kneel on the rug at Father Savié's feet. "Father, I love him," she said, exerting all her self-control. "I love him with every ounce of my being. I can't imagine not loving him. If he refuses to love me, I shall die! But before that I want to live, I want to try my best to replant myself in his heart, to live! Help me, Father! I beg you to help me!"

Once again he took her hands in his. "Only because I want to help do I say that I can't think of a better idea than yours. Love him. Love him all you can, with the utmost patience, until you melt the armor he wears."

"With the utmost patience," she repeated in a long-suffering tone. "Oh, but Father, I long for him to touch me, ever so lightly. Even a caressing look or a word would do. I could take heart if only he had said something to me that . . . if he had called me Jeanne just once, rather than 'madame.' For my part, Father, I couldn't stop myself from saying 'Vincent.' "

"Now you've told me that even before the first day was over, your poor patience was demanding a pledge from him." Father Savié sighed. "I know your husband well. It will take him a while to relax. Like every shipmaster, he is a solitary man who deliberates in private and makes his decisions alone, refusing to be swayed by the arguments of his officers . . . or his chaplain."

"He was merciless to me. He never let up for a second. And what if"—Jeanne's voice broke off—"and what if his heartlessness is not a suit of armor? What if his love for me is gone . . . forever?"

"I can't believe that!"

"But if he still loves me, why does he appear to hate me?"

There was a faraway look in her eyes. "Someone once told me that Italians never say, 'I love you.' They say, 'I wish you well.' "

"I'm not certain that all Italians put their words into practice," Father Savié said with a smile. "I've heard that in Italy many people die for love."

"If that's true, it must be the women who are dying," Jeanne sighed. "A man's love is so inflexible . . ."

"That's because a man transfers to each new love a fresh image of chaste innocence and infallibility that he has clung to over the centuries. The image of unblemished purity."

She got up off the rug and drew another chair close to the priest's. She scooped up the cat and set him in her lap. As she stroked Licorice's soft fur coat with both hands, she found herself staring at a large rectangular area on the paneling above the desk, pearly gray in stark contrast to the faded gray wall around it. "The chevalier must have discovered some distasteful blemishes on his lovely portrait of Pomona," she said sadly. "Did he throw it overboard?"

"The idea may have struck him in one of his bad moods. I put it in my own room when he took it off his wall."

A smile hovered on Jeanne's lips, the first since she had set foot aboard the *Belle Vincente*. "Did Saint Pomona appear chaste enough to enter the chaplain's quarters?"

"A good painting makes one think of God, to thank him for creating it," said the priest, returning her smile.

Jeanne put her hand on the chaplain's sleeve. "Father, will you pray each day that he returns to me?" she begged.

"I would have done so on my own. How can I fail to pray that a love I have blessed will triumph in the end over all misfortunes?"

She pressed him. "You do believe it will triumph, don't you?"

"I believe that love, if it deserves that name, possesses the prodigious power to remove whatever stands in its way." He rose from his chair and changed his tone of voice. "I've kept Mario from looking after you. It's time that I sent him in. And by the way," he added after a pause, "only once before did our captain give up his room to camp out in the wardroom. That was at Maldonado, to store a rich prize he had taken from the bandits of La Plata."

This time she really smiled, one of those tender smiles that made her eyes sparkle. "If by any chance he should question you, Father, tell him that I adore him. I adore him!"

CHAPTER 37

eanne finally fell asleep just before daybreak, only to be wakened shortly afterward by the familiar sloshing sound of water smacking the deck. Still hazy with sleep, she yawned, stretched, turned over on her stomach, and buried her nose in the scent of Vincent's orange-blossom cologne. She hugged the pillows as if to embrace him . . .

Mario found her up and about an hour later, when he brought in a pitcher of water and some coffee. Undecided what to wear, she was fingering the three dresses she had brought to Capetown, wondering which would be most becoming.

"If I were you, I'd wear this one," Mario volunteered, pointing to a gauzy white frock spread out on the coverlet.

It was the white muslin dress with bobbin lace that she had chosen the first time Vincent had welcomed her aboard his ship.

It did look quite nice on me, I'll admit.

"And I would loop gold and silver chains around my neck . . . if you happened to bring them with you," Mario proposed.

The handsome valet held the snowy white gown up and gazed at himself rapturously in the dressing table mirror.

As she wound the chains around his neck, Jeanne teased him. "For the next masquerade ball on board"—she hesitated, then decided to risk it—"I'll dress you up as a beautiful Creole lady. You'll look perfect."

Mario returned the dress and jewelry with a sigh. "The captain forbids me to dress as a girl," he said with a pout.

Jeanne smirked and poured herself a cup of coffee. She wolfed down the buttered bread spread with honey that Mario had brought, not having realized how hungry she was. The battle wasn't won, but at least she'd made it past the barricades. It's a well-known fact that the stomach always claims its share of the victor's spoils. "Mario, would you butter me another slice of bread?"

"Right away!" he replied cheerfully. "And afterward you'll let me do your hair, won't you? I hope you remember what a good hairdresser I am!"

When she was dressed, she helped him arrange her hair, parting it down the middle with two long braids, and using a gold chain for a headband. Thus she made herself into the blond Indian princess whom the knight had been unable to resist back on the Plata River.

Not daring to set foot outside the room, she opened a book and waited.

* * * *

Jeanne waited two hours, despairing that Vincent was in the process of penning a polite, carefully worded refusal to Poivre, which his lieutenant or the chaplain would soon bring her. She was so overcome with joy when he appeared that she leaped to her feet, sending the book tumbling to the floor.

He paused in the doorway, as if struck by the sight of the blond Indian princess, but recovered instantly, saying as he entered the room, "I have come, madame, to discuss your proposal."

His tone of voice that morning was coldly polite. She imitated it as best she could, replying, "Chevalier, I am prepared to listen."

Before sitting down, he bent over to pick the book up off the floor, glancing at its title and smiling wryly. Jeanne had chosen to read the *Dialogues of the Courtesans*. He put the book down on the table and began talking as soon as they had taken seats opposite each other.

"Madame, I cannot tell you that I would be delighted to drop all my plans and rush off to serve Monsieur Poivre. But I promised the Duke de Praslin I would always make myself available to the government of l'Ile de France. Having been greatly delayed myself, I was under the impression that the ships the duke had promised were already there. But since that isn't true, I shall keep my promise. I shall go to Port Louis, if only to explain my position to the representatives of the crown." Almost as an afterthought he added, "And to escort back their ambassador. We shall sail as soon as I finish taking on a cargo for Count Maudave which I intend to drop off at Fort Dauphin on the way. If, in the meantime, you care to go ashore, I'll have you taken there. You have only to say the word."

After a moment's silence he pressed her for a reply. "Well, madame?"

Jeanne sat rooted to her chair, her mouth open, devouring him ecstatically with her eyes. "You're coming?" she murmured. "You're actually coming?"

"Isn't that what you were sent here to get me to do?"

An unspoken "yes" formed on her lips.

"Maybe you'd rather I refused?"

"No! Oh no!" Suddenly her joy burst through her astonishment. "I'm so happy, so very happy that you're coming!"

"Madame, you should be happy merely to have completed your assignment satisfactorily," he observed curtly.

Uncrossing his legs, he got up, went over to his rolltop desk, and leaned his elbow on the upper shelf. "Now that our official business is settled," he said, "would you care to discuss our personal affairs?"

"Our personal affairs?" she repeated, blushing.

"Believe me, I'd prefer to ignore them, but that's impossible, now that we're going to Port Louis together. You are my wife, and I would appreciate your conducting yourself as such while I am in l'Ile de France. I don't want to hear snickers behind my back. Once I arrange things so that I'll never have to see you again, you are free, as I've already told you, to take all the lovers you like and send me the bill. Meanwhile, when you feel so inclined, take a cold bath and remind yourself what a dangerous diversion you've become to any man unlucky enough to tumble into your bed."

He approached Jeanne, who sat motionless and entranced, and said, "Remind yourself, too, that your pretty little swan's neck is very slender . . ."

He watched as her two hands flew up instinctively to protect her neck. He continued to smile. "But as long as you behave yourself in your own house and just look after your flowers and your herbs, I won't touch a hair on your head or refuse you a penny. I'll even take you to the governor's balls. You are a very decorative wife, and will make me the object of every man's envy. Bastards are proud fellows. I like people to envy me."

He paused momentarily as if half expecting a reply, but Jeanne merely stared at him, her breath coming short and fast, so he continued in the same tone of cold cynicism, "I am not asking you to swear you will do what I have decided. I know that you don't keep your word. I shall see to it personally that you do what I ask."

She got up slowly and went over to the mirror where she deliberately took her time smoothing out her dress. Finally she turned to face

Vincent. "It appears to me, Chevalier, that we have not completely settled matters." She spoke in a steady voice. "You mentioned that I could have all the money I wanted and go to balls. Does that mean that I may expect to share all the pleasures of marriage except your bed?"

"I'm not quite certain, madame, what other pleasures you have in mind."

"Your company, for instance?"

"My word! Of course we will dine together from time to time, especially in other people's homes. And if the cooking at Allspice is good, I promise not to stay away. And if you want me to join in a game of checkers . . ."

"In short, I'm to have everything I could want in exchange for sleeping like a nun?"

"I think you are beginning to understand."

"Not altogether. May I ask, Chevalier, if you intend to behave yourself in your bedchamber while I'm behaving myself in mine?"

Vincent burst into forced laughter. "How you do go on, madame! Would you put that question to a sailor on shore leave? I've always had a yen for the ladies, and I don't intend to deprive myself of that pleasure for having married one whose flesh disgusts me!"

The cruel remark struck Jeanne like a dagger. She blanched, and her knees melted. She clutched frantically at the back of the chair she was leaning against and closed her eyes.

Remaining thus for several moments, she struggled to pull herself together. When she was able to breathe again she looked up at Vincent, who had not stirred a muscle. Still very pale, she waited until she found the strength to speak. "You are indeed a Moor," she managed to say at last. "You want a woman shut up in a harem while you're off playing somewhere else, is that it?"

Cynically, he nodded.

She went on, as her temper flared, "You're even more unpleasant than a Moor. For a Moor, from what I've heard, enters his harem from time to time to make love to his captive."

There was another long silence. Then Jeanne suddenly decided to play the cynic too. "If you mean seriously to set up your harem at Allspice, you'll have a number of women at your mercy. My friend Marie lives there, whose husband so thoughtlessly left her a widow, as well as Madame de Vaux-Jailloux, who came with her to Port Louis."

"I was aware of that," said Vincent smoothly. "The Indian Ocean is a fountain of information."

"In that case, maybe Pauline's presence in this part of the world is not unrelated to your rapid decision to accept Monsieur Poivre's proposal. The minute you land at Port Louis, you'll fall right back into old habits. Your darling will be there waiting."

Vincent took on an amused expression. "You are mistaken, madame, if you think that, when it comes to love, a Moor is content to fall into old habits. If that's what's bothering you, forget it. I promise not to limit myself to Pauline. Thank God, she's one of those women who make love superbly without taking it too seriously. Such women are well-meaning liars who make no attempt to be sincere. They are delightfully useful."

Jeanne dropped her eyes, pretending to smooth a fold in her skirt. Her cheeks were burning.

Vincent observed her discomfiture with amusement. "But I can see that the kind of life I'm suggesting doesn't appeal to you. On second thought, perhaps you'd prefer the option offered in my last letter, free of any attachment to me, our sole contact through a banker? You may still choose that. I can try to find a Dutch shipmaster willing to become an honest pirate in the service of Monsieur Poivre in my place. I'll turn you over to him so that you won't have to return empty-handed to Port Louis—without a privateer or a husband."

When she didn't say a word or look at him, he persisted, "Madame, you may still choose the easiest future, the one in which I shall not appear."

Now she turned to him, her eyes filled with tears and unabashed love. "No," she said, adding resolutely, "Vincent, I want you and I will have you. I ask no pledge from you for the future, because I have faith in the past love we shared."

The chevalier winced slightly, indicating that she had touched him. In the silence that followed, he fingered the book on the desk, flipping the pages, and finally said grudgingly, "There's a concert and dinner tonight in the gardens of Nieuland . . ."

"I will go too," said Jeanne. "I'll go to decorate your arm. Though in matters of dress, you're more likely to need something removed than added!"

"And you're just the opposite. You're always missing something," said Vincent, annoyed by her remark. "Add one or two scarves, if you please. I believe I once asked you not to parade your bosom in front of my crew."

She took a chance and replied boldly, "I wonder, Chevalier, if you are not already breaking our agreement. It was my understanding that in matters of the flesh you deny me your touch, but not the small pleasure of having other eyes caress me."

Vincent's hand grabbed her arm so hard that it nearly bruised her. "Another thing I ask you is not to provoke me," he hissed. "You are a shameless flirt, but by God I'll make you stay faithful—willingly or not—and for your sake I hope it's willingly!"

He released her arm as brutally as he had seized it, and slammed the door on his way out.

Standing before the dressing table mirror, a smile on her lips, Jeanne gently rubbed her sore arm with a soft muslin sleeve.

"Well, Jeanne, you're not doing too badly," she said to her reflection. "He's going to find it hard never to touch you."

CHAPTER 38

he coast of Madagascar, the Big Island, faded away like a bad dream. Jeanne sighed. Father Savié looked at her and sighed in turn. "The chevalier can be a handful when he's dancing with the devil," he said.

At first Jeanne didn't reply. Why talk about those four dreadful days of their stopover at Fort Dauphin? Vincent had entertained himself royally with a pretty actress, part of the cargo that Count Maudave had destined for his settlers on l'Ile de Bourbon.

Jeanne said wearily, "He is trying the patience you recommended to me."

"Call it hope. It's the same thing. It sounds more cheerful."

"I'll try. But I can see that even when I've won his heart back, there will be stormy days ahead. I'll probably worry a lot."

"I hope you do," said the priest. "Love without worry disintegrates into friendship, and I know that you don't want to live on friendship."

"No," she admitted. Yet . . . she would have welcomed a glimmer of certainty in his love.

Solitude. She had never realized what it might be like. In making her agreement with Vincent, she had considered only the pain of her frustrated desire. Chastity was merely the active side of the punishment her husband was inflicting, the steady humiliation, the source of her sleepless nights, and the burning in her flesh whenever she glanced at Vincent. Yes, chastity had a flesh-and-blood life of its own. But loneliness was even worse. It was the direct result of Vincent's polite indifference. Gray, bleak, frigid gloom.

Sometimes an immense longing for Philibert gripped her, the desperate longing of a sorrowful child. But that was over now. Never again would anyone love the little girl in her.

As time passed, suspended between sea and sky, grief left her pale and thin. Strangely enough, Vincent's flagrant behavior during the whole time they had been in Fort Dauphin had made her smile, an imperturbable smile of proud defiance which she wore from dawn to dusk. From dusk to dawn the smile dissolved into an orgy of tears, rage, and imprecations. Once they had resumed their voyage, she tried to forget about it and to live with the dull ache of sadness. Active suffering, she had discovered, really wasn't any better than mute despair.

Now she turned her back to the horizon and her face to the sun.

"We're homeward bound," said Father Savié.

"Yes," she said, smiling at the thought of it. "Summer is beautiful at Allspice. You'll see. The scent of aloes is stronger than at any other season. Father, will you come and stay at Allspice while you're ashore?"

"Would it help you?"

"Yes."

"Then I'll come."

"Oh, hurry! hurry!" she said, opening her arms to the breeze. "Hurry! I long so for my house. I think that in my own house I will feel more in control of my life. Actually, a wife is quite helpless beyond her own doorstep. She becomes just like any other woman. Father, pray to God for a wind that will speed us homeward like seagulls!"

God did more than that. He sent a roaring tempest.

The ship nearly went down.

January is not the time of year to go sailing in this part of the world. The winds are treacherous, often violent. The brunt of the storm hit at midnight. The sea pitched wildly. The carpenters nailed wooden crossbars over all the window shutters.

With a thunderous explosion the ship reeled backward, catapulting Jeanne out of bed. A wave crashed against two of the wardroom windows and knocked them out. After groping for a candle, she looked around in panic at a scene out of some nightmare.

Without thinking, she dashed from her room into a watery cloud outside. Through an icy mist she could see a crowd of ghostly figures and lanterns dancing about wildly. Beyond them, a stream of water burst through the open door of the wardroom. With a cry of alarm, she rushed into the room and found Vincent well in control, shouting out orders.

"Oh God, your harpsichord!" she lamented, like a good housewife intent on rescuing the family furniture once she's sure the family is safe.

The untimely remark escaped Vincent's notice, but not the sight of Jeanne. With an oath, he grabbed her by the wrist and dragged her unceremoniously to her room, pushed her inside, and ordered her to stay there.

After one hour of being blindly tossed about by the hurricane, she couldn't stand the suspense any longer. Slipping outside, clinging to the door, peering around her in the darkness, half blinded by the pelting rain and the spray from waves crashing on deck, she glimpsed just enough of the ocean in the ghostly glare of lightning bolts to feel scared to death.

The frigate bobbed like a cork on mountainous seas. At the zenith, each mountain peak, like some monstrous whale, spouted its jet into an inky sky that thundered and roared. It was the first storm at sea that Jeanne had ever weathered. The frightful din made it impossible to hear what the phantom shapes roaming the deck were saying to each other as they clutched at the ropes to haul themselves forward.

With eyes stinging from the salt spray, she searched for Vincent, shouting his name frantically into the shrieking wind. Finally she saw him, with Quissac and Ensign Brussac, firing his pistol at a roving sea chest.

The chest, worth a fortune, had broken loose from its brace and was tumbling about the deck, threatening to crush everything in its path.

The pistol shots had blown open the locks. The top flipped open. In a matter of seconds it ruptured and the bottles inside spilled onto the deck and shattered, leaving the sea to lap champagne. Two carpenters grabbed the remains of the chest and flung them overboard.

Jeanne shouted even louder to Vincent. A crewman staggering by with a lantern heard her cries and told the captain.

Vincent pounced on her. "You must be mad! Do I have to strap you down to keep you in one place? Go back inside!"

"Don't leave me alone! I'm so scared!" she moaned, her shame dissolved into panic.

"We're all afraid, madame. It's time to pray. Look at this one!" he shouted, aiming a kick at the rear end of a kneeling crewman. "Pray to the undertaker, my lad! The lady will take care of all the saints! Now, madame, in you go!"

"No, I beg you, don't make me go in there!" she entreated in a quavering voice as she clung to him. "I don't want to drown out of sight of you! I'm so frightened!"

He sneered. "I give you my word that when the game is up I'll come for you and anchor us both together so we feed the same shark. Now let me go! I have things to do! My crew wouldn't share your rapture at drowning with the captain! Let me go!"

"No! I won't stay here alone!" she cried excitedly, hanging on to him for dear life. "I'm the wife of a seaman, and if we are to perish, then let me be manning the ropes like everyone else when the sea comes to claim us!"

"So be it," he said, eyeing her for a second. "But before you can help sail the ship, you'll need to stand upright!"

He took her by the arm and brought her over to the giant of a black sailor whose name was Grizzle.

Jeanne found herself next to this hulk of a man who was trying with lacerated fingers to repair a burst cable. The ship was running under its foresail, the rest of the canvas having been hauled in. From the rear of the forecastle, where she stood fastened for dear life to the black sailor, she watched in horror as the front deck plunged over a watery precipice. She felt the sea closing over them. She clenched her teeth so as not to cry out. Under showers of foam and a sky that was exploding all around the masts, lighting them up with an eerie glow, the nightmare continued. Worn out along with everyone else by terror and fatigue, Jeanne prayed for dawn to come soon, so that she might not die in the darkness.

A twinge of happiness relieved her suffering when Vincent's hand landed on her shoulder and his strained voice asked, "How's it going, sailor?" before passing on to the next man.

She shouted back, "It's all right, Captain!" and tugged with renewed vigor on her length of rope, which shredded the flesh on her palms.

At daybreak the ship still danced on mammoth waves. The west was leaden gray, the east fiery red. Above them the sky held a mixture of fleecy white and coppery-brown clouds, with patches of blue in between. The feathery crests of the waves, ballooned by the wind, began to shimmer with color.

The ship had emerged from the darkness of hell. After one parting whirlwind that tore up the foresail before it could be hauled in, the storm abated. Officers and crew dropped to their knees in prayer, led by a worn and haggard chaplain minus the wig he had lost during the night. After the final amen, the cook brought out a keg of spirits.

Jeanne knew that if she lived to be a hundred, she would never forget the joy of that swig of rum following the hurricane.

It was a tradition aboard the Belle Vincente that in the aftermath of some great peril the captain would take the first swig of rum and pass the measure to a sailor whose courage he had observed. This time, after downing his rum, Vincent raised the empty measure above his head, shouting, "Thanks to all of you, my boys, and cheers for the novice!" Whereupon he tossed the measure to Jeanne. It was refilled and she drank.

The raw alcohol burned the very pit of her stomach and brought tears to her eyes. Exhausted by her ordeal, dizzied by Vincent's flattering gesture, overpowered by the rum, she fell asleep sitting up, her cheek nestled on her left shoulder, her injured palms lying faceup on her breeches.

Vincent pointed them out to the surgeon. "Monsieur Amable, you'll need to put on bandages right away. The novice isn't tough enough yet to handle the rigging."

Grizzle carried Jeanne to her bed. She awoke while the surgeon was treating her hands, but kept her eyes shut. Vincent came in just then to see how she was, and assumed she was sleeping. The surgeon vanished discreetly.

Half opening her eyes, she reached out to Vincent with a hand smelling of embalming oils and stuttered, "Licorice—he isn't here. Do you think he drowned?"

"Rest now," he said, taking careful hold of the bandaged hand and setting it back on the sheet. "When he's over his fright, the cat will come out of hiding."

As he left the room he ran into the Provençal, who was carrying the terrified animal in his arms. "Mam'selle Jeanne must be worried about the cat. I'll take him to her."

"Give him to me," said Vincent, and grabbed Licorice by the nape of the neck.

Jeanne was asleep now with her fists clenched. He deposited Licorice on the coverlet, sat down nearby, and gazed at the sleeping figure. Bitterness welled up inside him. *Why, Jeanne, why? How, with such a face, can you be so falsehearted?*

Matted and sticky with salt water, her hair spilled onto the pillow in a golden tangle. Vincent's hand was dying to stroke her hair—but he stroked the cat instead.

CHAPTER 39

incent settled down at Allspice quite willingly, and much to Jeanne's surprise. But then, he was used to making himself right at home wherever he landed. Moka was the nicest part of the island, and his wife's residence pleased him so well that he began to settle in.

Jeanne had planned for the two rooms next to her own blue-flowered bedroom to be Vincent's. One was arranged as a study, and the other was a bedroom with a commode. She used brilliant, silver-crested birds on yellow Chinese silk for a wall covering. The furniture was made of island woods and bamboo.

Nanny's spicy cooking was acceptable to Vincent, with the result that Jeanne found him seated at her table frequently. Yet, more often than not, he took his meals at the Intendancy or at Government House.

The corsair had decided to make Port Louis his base, consulting with Poivre about plans to raid the Dutch Moluccas, preparing for voyages to the Gulf of Bengal and the Sea of Oman to spy on English trade and to defend the French outposts in India. Meanwhile, the rehabilitation of the Ile de France port and coastal batteries was a full-time occupation.

Jeanne realized that Allspice would doubtless serve Vincent for years as a home base to which he would keep returning to drop anchor. Behind her smiles, Jeanne was furious, edgy, and inclined to explode in Marie's ear.

"But at least you see him, my dear, and to see your lover whenever you wish is the important thing," Marie consoled her, believing that her friend was exaggerating when she complained about a rich and polished husband who only failed her in bed. It was really a trifle, since sleeping with a man could be such a bother.

Exasperated, Jeanne made no response to the girlish Marie and merely went back to thinking disparaging thoughts about her friend's departed husband, Philippe. Gossiping about men with Pauline would have made her feel better, but this she denied herself. Vincent was spending a great deal of time at Belle Herbe, enough to make her feel cool toward Pauline.

The trip to La Plata that Don José was to make in April was most interesting to the corsair. He welcomed the idea of becoming partners with the Spaniard in setting up a regular piaster-smuggling operation between Montevideo and Port Louis, using the trade in meat and hides as their cover.

Dinner or supper hour would arrive while they were discussing their future plans. Emilie would have to call them to the table so often that Jeanne jealously thought Pauline should have stayed at Allspice so as to see her former lover less often! One thing, nevertheless, reassured her. He scorned the flesh of his former mistress as utterly as his young wife's.

But Vincent had not completely lost his appetite. He had taken up with the Dassonville woman. Mme. de Dassonville was not a woman of the streets but of society. The blooming widow of a viscount, captain of the guards, she was surviving as best she could. Her source of piasters and pleasures were so well chosen, and treated so discreetly, that not even the island's cleverest gossips could fault her. But unfortunately, the Dassonville woman's tenant proved less discreet than his hostess. All of Port Louis knew of her latest affair, even as far as Moka.

Equally well known was the fact that the Chevalier Vincent was also working off his excess energies in partnership with Mlle. Dorothy, the superb and talented mulatto woman who dressed the flower of island society in Creole style. Mlle. Dorothy never spurned a distinguished seafarer who could supply her with cloth at a good price.

"Patience," Father Savié kept telling Jeanne. He was, she thought, a trifle too indulgent toward masculine failings. But who in all the colony would have been ridiculous enough to judge the Chevalier Vincent harshly? He made the mistress of Allspice an ideal Louis XV–style husband, most amiable, well-mannered, good-humored, elegant, and charming. He had character, class, and the good taste to be a liberal and a free-thinker. He paid his gambling debts down to the last penny. His only failing was the prudishness of his wife, who curtly dismissed importunate dancers and punished any boldness with a flick of her fan. The chevalier was pitied as much for his wife's virtue as he would have been for a false note in his attire.

Underneath the good behavior imposed on her, Jeanne seethed with rancor. Eager to provoke Vincent, she found an opportunity she couldn't resist one evening at a Government House ball. She began to flirt openly with the Chevalier Brussanne. She lured him into the garden, where her game ended almost before it started!

The two of them were strolling arm in arm in the moonlight. He was whispering words of desire. She was listening with sighs and encouraging titters when suddenly Vincent rose before them. Deadly calm, he asked his ensign to go immediately and see if all was well aboard ship. Pale with humiliation, the young officer was about to rebel when he felt his captain's hand on his shoulder. "No, my brother, not that," said Vincent. "Go."

"What's got into you, Chevalier?" Jeanne demanded as soon as Brussanne had left. "Aren't you aware that one of the duties of a good ensign is to amuse his captain's wife? Should I be the one to remind you of naval tradition?"

"Let's return to the dance," Vincent said, ignoring the provocation, and he offered her his arm.

"What?" exclaimed Jeanne in mock astonishment. "You're not stran-gling me? Why not?"

"You don't deserve it."

"What a pity! And I only fooled around with that Brussanne boy so that I could feel your hands around my neck afterward!"

He turned to face her, and seized her arm above the elbow. "You're a little trollop, Jeanne! You're the worst kind, because you don't look like one. But I'll make you behave yourself whether you choose to or not. I'm warning you." He left her and strode back into the salon.

"He called me Jeanne!" she sang to the stars, her head thrown back.

But at dawn, when he took his wife back to Allspice, Vincent showed neither annoyance nor love. Their bittersweet hide-and-seek life continued without further outbursts until the first Sunday in April.

* * * *

It was no ordinary Sunday. Marie had announced her engagement to Lieutenant Boussuge. Widowhood has to end at some point, and Boussuge was a good excuse to end it. Emilie had convinced her that the slender, bashful, and pale young poet would suit her perfectly. He probably would be no great burden on a woman. In addition, he was of good birth and not too poor, and he idolized Marie and adored Virginia.

That day they would celebrate the engagement, Don José's depar-ture for La Plata, and Jeanne's twenty-second birthday.

Jeanne, in a green and white striped silk gown, was chatting on the veranda with the first arrivals. The Poivres had brought along Dr. Commerson and his Rosie from their lodgings at the Intendancy.

M. de Bougainville had left Port Louis after a brief stay, to complete his trip around the world. He had left Commerson, his expedition's naturalist, behind to continue the task left unfinished by Dr. Aubriot. Commerson was living with his housekeeper, a plump, solid little redhead, full of life and botany. Since the girl followed him everywhere, Jeanne always invited her too. She was very fond of Rosie and appreciated Commerson's vast learning.

She was ready to make him her friend because he had officially given the name "bougainvillea" to her climbing vine with the magnifi-cent purple flowers. Yet it was an effort for Jeanne to botanize with Commerson and Rosie and to invite them to her home, so much did the couple remind her of herself and Philibert.

On this beautiful April day, as she listened as they raved about a giant vermiform crustacean they had just discovered at Sands Point, her partially healed wound reopened and bled. The pain cast her back into that bottomless pit of despair.

Marie served the punch and Jeanne took it as an opportunity to go back into the house to see why Vincent had not yet come downstairs. She ran into him on the landing as he was leaving his room. He wore his plain cream-colored drugget suit with cloth-covered buttons and no braid.

"I'm late," he announced when he saw her, "because I was already dressed in gray when I remembered that you preferred me in this suit for your weekend parties."

"Thank you for changing," she said. "You look very handsome." She stepped nearer and repeated beguilingly, "Chevalier, you are very handsome."

"I'm not ugly. But neither are you. We make a rather good pair . . . for dancing. If I am back by the twenty-fifth of August, we'll have a good time at the Saint Louis Ball."

"*If* you are back?" she questioned him sharply.

"The month of April marks the return of good sailing weather in the Indian Ocean. My frigate is fixed up like new. I'm counting on shipping out in about a week, after seeing Don José off to La Plata. But it will only be a short voyage to the Maldives and Ceylon, where I'm taking Father Rochon for his coastal observations. I'll try to be here for Saint Louis."

She froze, saying nothing, and he added, less distantly, "Does my leaving upset you? I'm a sailor. You'll often see me depart."

"I know," she said softly.

Jeanne and Vincent made a handsome pair, like a couple in love for the first time. Emilie, in her peach-blossom gown, wittily held court, while Pauline captivated her dinner companions with her soft voice. Vincent complacently narrated his amusing experiences in various prisons. At dessert, in full voice, he led the singing, and after coffee was served, he dutifully courted all the ladies. Except his own. Games and conversational groups were formed under the almond tree or in the perfumed shade of the frangipanis.

Saint Méry, sitting alone dreamily at the very end of the veranda, was enjoying his usual mild intoxication.

Toward the end of the afternoon, the master of the house, along with a handful of men, decided on a walk to the far side of the pond.

Vincent returned with a gash in his forehead. At the edge of the hillside orchard they had surprised a marauding runaway slave who threw stones at them as he tried to flee.

Vincent and Giulio Pazevin dragged the frantic slave between them and delivered him to Saint Méry. There was no sense in punishing the poor wretch, who was a frightful, scabby, starving bag of bones. For the moment they could only feed and care for him, and Saint Méry had Zoe take him to the slave quarters.

Jeanne followed Vincent upstairs to wash his wound. The cut had bled a fair amount, but was superficial. When at last it dried, she dabbed it with marigold oil.

"I don't want to put on a dressing. It will heal faster in the air. Instead of smelling sweetly of orange blossoms, you'll reek of *Calendula*! You'll find that my remedy is excellent for closing the skin without leaving a mark. Tomorrow it will look better."

"Scars go with a pirate's face," Vincent said good-humoredly.

"But not with my chevalier's face," said Jeanne. Since she had removed his wig to dress his wound, she took the opportunity to run a fine brush and a comb through his flattened black ringlets. She took her time, her heart beating wildly, her fingers tingling with pleasure. She marveled at his passivity, letting her have her way with it.

Father Savié appeared in the doorway. "I've been sent to see if the damage is repaired," he said. "I see that it is."

"It's hardly worth mentioning anymore," Vincent said, and he jerked his head out of Jeanne's reach.

* * * *

After supper, when only a few intimates remained, Vincent accompanied his friends from Belle Herbe back to their house. Emilie went directly to Juanito's room, then to prepare for bed. Don José settled down on the veranda to enjoy the last cigar of a good day.

Pauline and Vincent remained alone in the silence of a small drawing room lit by chandeliers and sconces, idly chatting about trifles.

"Don't let your hair get into your cut," Pauline said suddenly, extending a hand toward Vincent's forehead. He was perched casually on the arm of a chair, and he leaned over so that she could push back the straggling lock and run it among the others. This gesture, carrying echoes of their sensuous past, disturbed the peace of the moment.

Pauline trembled. "Before you go back to Allspice," she said as she rose, "I'd like your opinion of a fan the Chinaman has for me. I haven't said yes or no yet." As she opened the drawer of a small desk, her bare, dark creamy shoulders stood within reach of Vincent's mouth. He bit gently into the cream, then licked his lips, hot with greed.

Pauline was leaning on the desk with her hands, her neck bent forward. She straightened up, feeling panic in her flesh at Vincent's caprice, her heart plaintive.

"Vincent, why?" she whispered. "Why make Jeanne weep?"

"My dear, you don't do yourself justice. You suffice unto yourself," he retorted with a laugh. He tried to take her in his arms, but she repulsed him.

"No, Chevalier, I won't help you to hurt Jeanne."

"Oh, to hell with it!" he grumbled. "What kind of inhospitable shore is this, where your mistress refuses to receive what you don't choose to give your wife, out of consideration for her rather than out of love for you? Am I in l'Ile de France, or is this Lesbos?"

"The Dassonville woman will be happy to receive your caresses," said Pauline, as coldly as she could.

"Madame, since I remember that you have always been of good counsel to me, I believe I shall follow that advice," he declared, thanking her with a nod of his head. "There's nothing like a woman who doesn't love you to help you get over two women who do."

Thinking that he was stepping forward to take his leave, she held out her hand and found herself in his arms. Their lips pressed firmly together, and she yielded.

Passionately she returned the cruel kiss. It was a joke on his part, but she drank it in greedily, telling herself that it was no doubt love's final offering from the lover who would be her last. When Vincent's lips left hers, she would have accepted anything he willed. And he knew it.

Feeling satisfied, Vincent bowed to her and said with a smile, "Good night, Pauline. Sleep well."

When he had gone she lowered herself into a large armchair, threw back her head, and pressed one hand to her wildly beating heart. After a while she sat up, then rose and walked over to the mirror. She brushed her fingertips lightly over her face, where drops of perspiration had caked the powder. *If I don't sleep I'll look a hundred years old tomorrow.* She went up to her bedroom to repair the ravages in her face. *It would never do for Vincent to ask himself tomorrow how he ever happened to bestow a kiss on such a wreck.*

CHAPTER 40

he chevalier hasn't returned yet from Port Louis," Jeanne said mournfully. "At least I suppose he's in town. Late last evening, after he came back from Belle Herbe, I heard him leave again on horseback."

Pauline examined her more closely. "Bathe your eyes," she said. "They are more beautiful than usual."

"He'll end up ruining them for me," sighed Jeanne. "Or else he'll make me as dried up as an old harpy!"

"No," Pauline said. "Don't give him time to do it. That's what I came to tell you. Jeanne, you've wept and waited long enough for his good pleasure. From now on, lie to him."

There was a pause before Jeanne said, "I don't understand."

"Jeanne, there is a time for honeymoons. That time doesn't revolve around us like the moon in the sky revolves around the earth. It moves straight away from us. Don't let him waste his nights and yours anymore at the Dassonville woman's or at gambling. He doesn't really want that."

"He wants me even less!"

"That's true. He wants the Jeanne of his dreams. Give her back to him. Tell him a lie."

"But . . ." Jeanne began and stopped, at a loss for words, literally speechless.

Pauline's eyes flashed a smile tinged with irony. "As far as I know, the chevalier did not forbid you to continue loving Aubriot like a father."

It took a long time for Jeanne to grasp the full meaning of this suggestion. Finally Pauline saw her blush. With eyes averted, Jeanne whispered, "He won't believe me."

"He wants you, therefore he *will* believe you in order to get you back without losing face." Suddenly a thought struck her, and Pauline added, "Unless you've been silly enough to tell him everything."

"Heavens! How could I!" cried Jeanne, blushing deeper than ever and crossing her arms in great embarrassment. Her head drooped. "But he heard enough stories from that officer to know that—"

"Stories can be denied," Pauline said.

Jeanne grew more stubborn. "To deny all that so suddenly . . . he won't believe me," she said. "He'll insist on an oath."

"Well, do you love him too little to risk your soul so you can have him back?"

"I don't believe in the devil," Jeanne answered. "But to lie to him . . . to lie to him while I deny Philibert . . ."

Her golden countenance blanched, and then shone. "Pauline, I'm a sincere person, however it may appear. The only thing I've ever done is to be faithful to my heart. It's true that I lived a lie for a while. But why refuse me the right to love sincerely? Could such sincerity be a sin?"

"It's a dagger, my sweet! Plunge it into your breast as often as you please, but don't plunge it into others and expect them to thank you for it!"

Jeanne began to shake her head gently. "Even if I could find the right words to lie to him, they would stick in my throat. It would be so unworthy! It would be unworthy of my love for Philibert. I can't deny yesterday's love, Pauline. It's eternal."

Like an unhappy child, she buried her face in her friend's perfumed neck. "Why won't Vincent understand me? You're advising me to use odious words. Do you really believe that he will never, never be able to understand what I have done?"

Pauline began to run her fingers through the unruly hair escaping from the pretty nightcap. "Don't try to be understood anymore. That's for little girls. Be content to be desired. You'll understand later that that's not so bad."

Gently she pushed Jeanne away, chucking her under the chin. "Get dressed. Put on pink. Green is no good when you've slept poorly. Make yourself beautiful. You can lie better when you feel beautiful."

"Oh!" Jeanne cried frantically. "You don't think I will have to do it so soon? I have to reflect. I . . . ."

"Jeanne," Pauline cut in, "if you have to tell a lie sooner or later, do it before the next nightfall. You can't imagine it at your age, but at mine, when you add it all up, one night more or less really does count."

Jeanne dared to ask the question that was burning her. "Pauline, why are you so anxious for me to win Vincent back? With things going the way they are, you yourself might have tried instead."

The Creole smiled enigmatically. "I'm lazy," she said.

"No," said Jeanne, "you love me," and she gave her a kiss.

Pauline returned the kiss threefold, on Jeanne's temple, ear, and neck. That skin which Vincent loved had always seemed sweet to her lips. Soon it would smell of his orange-blossom cologne and, better still, console her, the forgotten one, as she caressed and kissed the pussy still warm from the caresses and kisses of the one who forgot her.

* * * *

Dressed in a white muslin peignoir lined with pink taffeta, Jeanne was finishing lunch when he entered the dining room.

"My goodness! I've come just at the right time!" he exclaimed, sniffing the air. "May I have some of your coffee?"

"Chevalier, you are in your own home."

Zoe served him.

"You may go, Zoe," said Jeanne, as soon as the slave had finished serving. "I know that Nanny needs you."

She changed chairs and sat down next to Vincent, then buttered him a slice of golden-brown toast. "Would you like some honey on it? Or jam?"

"Some Chinese raspberry jam, please." He chewed a mouthful of savory roast, nodded approvingly, ate the whole slice of toast, and deigned to admit that it was not unpleasant to come home after a rough night on the town.

"It was so boring!" he added, deliberately cynical. "Lord! How depressing Port Louis pleasures are! The best part is staying up all night to listen to everyone telling what they miss about Paris. And even that's hard to do, because most of the island society has memories only of the provinces."

Artfully she imitated his bantering tone. "Spend some of your insomnia on me, monsieur. I can tell some good stories about the Temple, the theater, the philosophers at the La Régence, and even the eccentrics from the King's Garden."

"So I've noticed," he said graciously, and continued in his mocking tone, "I admit that I'm unlucky to have taken an aversion to the most amusing lady on the island."

Irately she slapped down on his plate the second piece of meat she had just chosen for him, and got up to arrange some flowers that had no need of arranging.

Tears pearled her lashes. *Well, too bad. You asked for it!* She spun around, leaned against the sideboard, and looked on coolly as he crushed raspberries nonchalantly over his meat.

Her heart was pounding so hard that she could barely hear herself attack him, and it helped her.

"Chevalier," she began, "does the idea ever occur to you that your attitude toward me is odious because it might be unjust?"

"Unjust?" he repeated, raising an eyebrow. "We must not have the same view of justice. Aboard ship, punishment always follows offense, and that is called justice."

"But if you apply punishment to an offense by hearsay, an offense that was never committed, doesn't that bother you a little?"

"I never do what you are saying."

"Are you sure?"

He put down the second piece of meat, which he had scarcely touched, and faced her. "Madame, I didn't get much sleep last night. Kindly explain what you mean."

Pauline's words came to her ready-made and issued hoarsely from her lips as they suddenly went dry. "As far as I know, you didn't forbid me to continue loving Monsieur Aubriot like a father."

Silence fell between them. It vibrated like the air during a storm. To try to stop her trembling, Jeanne turned again to her bouquet of flowers and rearranged three zinnias. Vincent's gaze pierced her back, and she sensed his approach. Nervously she broke off the stem of a marigold.

Directly behind her, Vincent's calm voice announced, "You are rather late, madame, in bringing up this subject. Why?"

"I do have some pride! You hurt me terribly by doubting me on the strength of a piece of gossip. I wanted you to apologize without having to defend myself."

"And you have suddenly changed your mind? Why?"

"Let's say that I have more love than pride, and I can't hide it from you any longer."

"It appears to me that this love has taken its time to overcome your pride. Was it so feeble?"

The sarcasm of Vincent's last words did not sit well with her. She could not bear it that her lie was not instantly repaid with a return of confidence.

She clenched her fists and turned around to him, revolt on her lips. "And *your* love, Chevalier, how long would it have taken to gain the upper hand over *your* pride? Pride is a man's precious possession, which must be maintained, come hell or high water, and never, never be humbled before love! Whereas I have only a woman's honor, and everyone knows that a woman's honor is to serve her lover humbly, regardless of what it may cost her. The more her husband deceives her, far away or under her very nose, with his jailer, her seamstress, or the local siren, the longer she can go around town with her head held high, provided she limits her revenge to weeping and praying. But *he*, on the contrary, feels mortally offended and insists on the right to treat her like a whore and a prisoner when he learns that she has been faithful to her dearest childhood affection. Well, take heart, Chevalier. Continue to keep our marriage going Turkish-fashion, but don't be surprised if you end up making me dislike you as much as you dislike me, so that the only good your pasha's revenge will do you is to deprive me of displeasure!"

Having finished her tirade, she stopped breathlessly. Her breast heaved, her cheeks were aflame, her eyes bored point-blank into Vincent's without batting an eyelash.

He watched her without any show of feeling. Finally he said slowly, still watching her, "What you implied to me before you let yourself get carried away—would you swear to it before God?"

"Whenever you like!" With a rapid gesture she laid her right hand on the Cross of Malta that gleamed in the chevalier's boutonnière. "Do you want me to?"

In a flash of cruel defiance he retorted insolently, "When I feel an urge for you," and removed her hand from his jacket. "Right now there isn't time for it. I've got to change. I have business at Government House."

Calmly, he turned back to the table, picked up the slice of bread he had put down, and drank the last of his coffee.

Jeanne had a moment to recover her equanimity and managed to ask almost naturally, "Will you be back for dinner?"

"If I'm not held up by something in town," he said, bowing to her, and out he went.

* * * *

What if she was lying today? He changed his suit and linen, reviewing his suspicions one by one, recalling the tales of the officer who, after drinking vast amounts of Constantia wine, had recited the saga of amorous adventures taking place in Port Louis.

And while the officer's voice called up unbearable images, Vincent searched his jealous memory for any gesture of Jeanne's that might clearly confirm the affirmations of that braggart. But all he could recollect were the gestures, looks, and words of a woman who denied nothing and wore a touching expression of virtue, having chosen to defend herself with the dignity of silence and the benign lure of her proffered love.

Now, suddenly, her overworked silence had broken. Vincent found it hard to believe her words and was afraid to lower his guard before a liar. Only God knew to what extremes his violent temper might drive him if her ruptured silence turned out to be merely a change of tactics.

His blood boiled once again as he pictured the Jeanne he had once possessed in the arms of another man. He shook his head to clear it of his burning jealousy. Mario grumbled as he pulled down on the wig he was just then fitting.

If only he could believe her! At least he had his memories of her. Slowly he undressed Jeanne's amber, fluid body, aroused it with his kisses, laid it passive and trembling beneath him, submissive to his desires with the blissful patience of a slave wavering between timidity and ardent passion.

Mario was complaining. "Let's get back to sea!" he urged. "I'm not having any fun in this port, sir. I always reflect your humor, but here I am doing your hair, fancying you up as best I can, and you haven't made me laugh once. It's like that too often nowadays. I wept buckets at your wedding, sir, and you teased me for it. But I knew better than you that life would be drearier once the marriage took place."

"Shut up, you idiot!" Vincent scolded. "Finish dressing me without another word, or I'll pack you off for good."

Thanks to this imbecile, he had lost the thread of his voluptuous dream.

* * * *

Jeanne collapsed against the door as it closed behind her. When she was sure Vincent could no longer hear her, she exploded, hammering the door with her fists as she pressed her head hard against it. Shame and fury took possession of her. She had degraded herself with a sinful lie. It was as if she had denounced Philibert. Taking her continued goodwill for granted, Vincent had cast her aside as a sultan might capriciously reject one of his girls, removing her hand from his person and going on his way!

The day dragged by as she followed Saint Méry on his rounds. He had set the slaves to clearing the big orchard that climbed the hillside. Watching them work made time crawl less slowly than in the house. As the old plantings emerged, they discovered things that Jeanne forced herself to rave about excitedly.

Saint Méry pretended to believe she was really elated, but he sensed that something was amiss and stayed by her side, as mute and adoring as a puppy.

After a while she grew tired of the noise and the singing and went off to the islet in the pond, where she sat by Aubriot's grave.

"Forgive me," she murmured, touching the sun-warmed basalt. "And please don't think that I'm trying to get over your absence."

Once again the image of Poivre's empty sleeve flashed through her mind. *We cannot be cured when a part of us suddenly vanishes. Perhaps we cannot ever be cured and must be content simply to welcome a few joys alongside our griefs.*

She curled up against the standing cross in the way that had become habitual with her, pressing her ear against it, listening for the heartbeat that was no more, but that, by wishing hard enough, she always managed to hear. Sometimes the slow, pulsing rhythm of that heart even put her to sleep as it once used to. This late afternoon it did so.

A monkey's screech roused her with a sense of urgency. She saw daylight fading and leaped to her feet.

* * * *

When Jeanne emerged from her herb-scented bath, Suzon covered her with a fine cotton towel and began to rub her down. After she was dry, Jeanne stretched out on her bed.

"Suzon, get every jar of fragrance and pomade that you can find on my vanity table and rub all the perfumes of Araby into my body!"

Treating herself like a courtesan gave her a sense of bitter, ironic pleasure. Since one had to be deceptive, let the deception at least be artful. Eve against Adam. The eternal duel. Long ago, with his artist's instinct, hadn't Carle Vanloo placed the apple in Jeanne's hand?

Beneath the oiled fingers of the slave girl massaging her back, she relaxed. "Don't forget my thighs."

"Tee hee hee!" Suzon tittered, pounding away at her thighs and buttocks. "Tee hee! Mamzelle gwine have good time tonight, me think! Tee hee!"

"Do you think so, you witch? Do you think it's a good night for that?"

"Every night's good fo' dat, mamzelle. Wind o' no wind, rain o' no rain, you no care!"

"Do my feet. Put some on my feet."

Soon she was kneeling before a silken heap pulled out of her wardrobe. Along with all the lightweight fancy gowns, she had also taken out her Paris gowns, the ones she had received on the *Fulgurant* just before Philibert's death. Her shop manager, Lucette, had packed them well and they had arrived in perfect condition.

"I really do feel like getting all dressed up," she said, "with hoopskirts. It will be the first time in ages. What do you say, Suzon, to this silk with the red flowers?"

"Dat nice red fo' de ball, not so good fo' Mamzelle's idea. Betta Mamzelle put on dat one," Suzon said, picking up a ravishing Creole-style dress of white muslin lined with iridescent pink faille, which Jeanne had worn on the last Saint Louis.

"Mo' easy take off!" she added, poking her mistress with her elbow.

"My gracious, you may be right," said Jeanne. "You'd make a cleverer courtesan than I do."

The Negress dressed her in the gown she was holding, hooked it up, and went to the dressing table for the curling iron.

"No! Stop!" cried Jeanne. "Leave my hair down. Just tie it back with one of my gold chains."

Her task done, the slave stepped back to contemplate her work, and clapped her hands. "Dat good work, mamzelle! Tee hee! Moussié Chevalier take Mamzelle into bed so fast even de skeeter net come down!"

Jeanne stared attentively at her reflection and, in spite of what she saw, murmured, "Do you think so, you witch?"

"Dat easy to see, mamzelle. Dat sho', jes lak two 'n' two make fo'. No man in dis poo' world gwine be able to say no. Tee hee hee!"

Hurry now, my chevalier! Hurry, before my dignity returns! She trembled as she heard the horse gallop up the alley of tamarinds and then fade on the grassy path to the stable. The minutes went by heavily and dropped into the pit of her stomach one after another. At last the sound of a boot echoed on the tile floor of the entry hall. Two doors opened. Directly below Jeanne, in the dining room, she heard Vincent speaking with Zoe.

Jeanne looked over at her little table set with a white cloth and a cold supper of meats and fruit. She imagined Zoe telling her master that Madame Marie had no appetite this evening and Mamzelle had had supper served in her room.

Then the stairs creaked. She heard Vincent enter his room, joined by Mario. The seconds seemed like hours. While Jeanne waited, she refreshed her feverish brow against a windowpane cooled by the night breeze.

From beyond the door came the sounds of water and clinking bottles, the valet's chatter and brief orders from his master. But she heard it all over the pounding of her heart.

Although she had imagined it ten times before it happened, Vincent's tap on her door sent an icy rush up her spine.

He looked dazzling in the pale salmon satin suit she had seen him wear once before, aboard his ship, the evening she had sat at the captain's table for the first time.

Wild with desire, she felt her bones melt. She was nothing but limp, mindless, desperate desire. To complete his conquest, he wore his sweetest smile. What did she care now if he couldn't understand her troubled heart?

His eyes were shining, caressing her bare flesh while she imagined his magical mouth and velvet hands. Her body paralyzed with fascination, Jeanne was on the verge of crying out, *Come to me! I love you!*

Instead she said graciously, but with a tremor, "I'm delighted that you have chosen to be here with me tonight."

She picked up the candlestick from her bedside to light the candles on the table.

In three strides he was next to her, snatching away the candlestick and laying her hand on his Cross of Malta.

"Swear to me!" he said.

FINI